UNHOLY TRINITY

THE COMPLETE SERIES

USA TODAY BESTSELLING AUTHOR

CRYSTAL ASH

UNHOLY TRINITY

THE COMPLETE SERIES

CRYSTAL ASH

To every beautiful, unholy person out there. Don't let anyone suppress your magic.

UNHOLY TRINITY PLAYLIST

Click here to listen on Spotify!

Oh Lord - In This Moment
Wicked Ones - Dorothy
Closer - Nine Inch Nails
Angels Fall - Breaking Benjamin
Bittersweet - Apocalyptica
Black Wedding - In This Moment feat. Rob Halford
I Am The Fire - Halestrom
I Put A Spell On You - Annie Lennox
Woman King - Iron & Wine
So Human of You - Shireen
Inside of You - Hoobastank
Not Strong Enough - Apocalyptica feat. Doug Robb
Missile - Dorothy
The Sacrament - HIM

AUTHOR'S NOTE

This story takes inspiration from various mythological and historical events and figures, which have been liberally adapted to fit this fictional tale. These adaptations do not reflect the author's personal beliefs, nor should they influence your own.

Christianity in particular is not looked upon favorably in this story. If you find this offensive, this may not be the book for you.

WITCH'S DAWN
UNHOLY TRINITY BOOK 1

PROLOGUE
DEJA

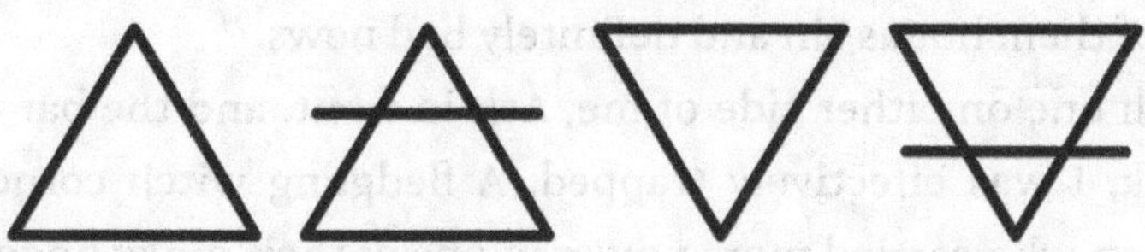

"So you've finally found the place."

Raum, the one with the shoulder-length dark hair and a raven tattoo on his forearm spoke first. His eyes, dark and deep as a midnight lake, gleamed mischievously. He was the troublemaker, the one I really had to watch out for.

"I take it you've learned some things," he added as he slid his lithe, powerful body into the barstool next to mine, much like a lion would sneak up on its prey.

"I only found out last night," I said.

Yeah, the reality of learning my supernatural status was slowly sinking in. The tension in the air when I first saw these three men suddenly made sense. They were like me, or at least something similar. That was obvious enough by the four of us sitting in this bar, disguised by magic to look like a dilapidated building on the outside to any unsuspecting humans.

Sal, the one with stunning green eyes and auburn hair took the seat on the other side of me. His power was the most volatile, ready to strike at any moment. The aura surrounding him crackled with energy that felt like a mixture of simmering rage warning me to stay away, and fiery passion daring me to come closer.

Only Ash remained standing, the quiet, aloof leader of the bunch. He regarded me with icy-blue eyes that burned with curiosity and seemed to take in every detail of me. A hand stroked his short blond beard thoughtfully. The motion made him look like some wise Viking scholar who also happened to be tall and broad enough to go into battle.

All of them hot as sin and definitely bad news.

With one on either side of me, Ash in front, and the bar against my back, I was effectively trapped. A fledgling witch cornered by three men who carried more power in one of their pinky fingers. And I still had no idea what they wanted from me, or why I saw them in my dreams. But either from naivete or something else unknown, I didn't feel like I was in danger.

Instead, I felt the opposite. Protected.

"So I take this to mean you three are witches, too?" I asked, swiveling in my bar stool to make eye contact with all of them. "Or warlocks or wizards? Whatever the male titles are."

A collective chuckle of amusement rose from all of them and I wondered what was so funny.

The answer came from Sal, his mouth intimately close to my ear.

"Not exactly."

1

DEJA

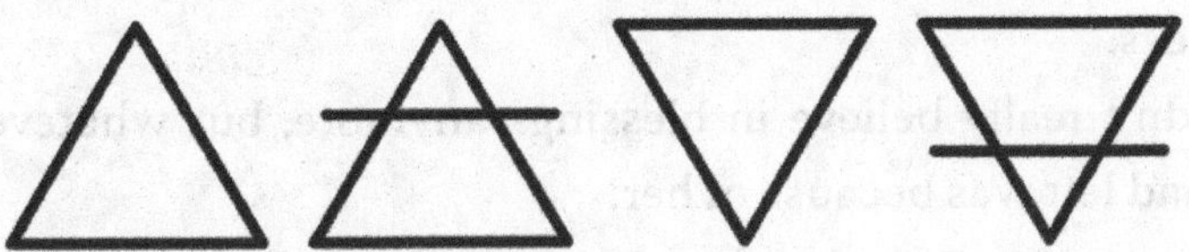

The chilly air bit at my skin like an invisible entity with sharp teeth.

I pulled my scarf over my mouth and nose and released a harsh, open-mouthed breath to warm my nose and hands.

At the same time, my butt and thigh muscles burned from the effort of walking uphill on concrete. Soon enough, I'd be in a warm room with my ass in a chair and a drink in my hand.

At least that's what I kept telling myself.

"What's that Mark Twain quote?" I grumbled to Nona, who kept a steady pace next to me on our uphill trek. "The coldest winter I ever experienced was a summer in San Francisco or something like that."

Technically, it wasn't even summer yet but even rare sunny days in my new hometown came with a chilly, Pacific breeze. And that was only if the fog hadn't rolled in and made it feel like winter again, as it did several times a day in my neighborhood.

Clearly, as a southern California native, I had no idea what *real* weather was like.

"He never actually said that," Nona piped cheerfully. "That quote is commonly mis-attributed to him."

She, a San Francisco native, did not seem nearly as distressed by the chilly air or the uphill climb.

"Little Miss Smarty Pants strikes again," I teased, cracking a smile.

Honestly, I was beyond grateful for Nona being not only a wealth of information, but a hard worker and the most genuine, kind-hearted person I ever met. As the only employee at my tiny, hole-in-the-wall tea shop, *Witch's Brew*, she was worth at least five mediocre employees.

I didn't really believe in blessings anymore, but whatever little faith I had left was because of her.

I came to San Francisco last year to get away from my oppressive, religious upbringing down south. When I stepped off that Greyhound bus with nothing but a duffel bag and the clothes on my back, someone tried to pickpocket me within seconds. Nona just happened to be riding by on her bicycle and yelled loud enough to get a cop's attention. She'd been a guardian angel to me ever since.

Until I opened my shop and started networking with other small business owners in my neighborhood, she had also been my only friend.

And in a large city filled with people, politics, and attitudes that gave me a hefty dose of culture shock, I couldn't ask for anyone better to huff and puff up a hill beside me.

We finally crested the hill and came to a row of businesses and commercial buildings, almost all of them closed. Not even in San Francisco would an accountant be open at nearly eleven at night. But on the next corner, we approached one shop with a warm glow from the inside and the muffled sound of punk rock playing from speakers. People in leather and denim jackets already pressed against the windows from the inside.

"Damn, she really decked the place out," Nona mused as we paused to look at the outside facade.

I nodded my agreement. The large window facing the street read

Trailblazers, Inc. in flowing gold and black vinyl paint. Just underneath the shop name was an illustration of a laughing skeleton riding a motorcycle and kicking up a cloud of dust.

I stepped back slightly and smiled at the window, feeling a sense of pride swelling for my fellow local business owner.

"Shall we?" I cocked an eyebrow at Nona.

"After you, madame." She pulled the front door open with a flourish and swept her arm back as she lowered into a curtsy.

I chuckled as I stepped through the open door. Nona's quirks never ceased to amuse me.

Right away the noise of fast, upbeat punk music hit me like a slap to the chest. The heat of many bodies pressed into a small space soaked into my pores.

Yellow glassy eyes with odd, rectangular pupils were the first to meet my gaze from across the room.

"Holy shit," I breathed. "That thing is huge."

The goat's head mounted to the wall was gigantic, easily three feet tall by my estimate. It was entirely black and its horns curled back in perfect, majestic symmetry.

It looked like some kind of pagan deity overlooking a heathen gathering of drunkenness and debauchery. My parents would have gasped at the sight, clutched their cross jewelry, and run home immediately to say their prayers.

"Deja, you made it!"

An arm carrying a drink that looked dangerously close to spilling, wrapped around my neck while a pair of lips kissed my cheek at the same time. Myranda, the shop owner, pulled away and beamed at me.

"I'm so glad you came," she gushed. Her cheeks were flushed and her raven black hair was tossed carelessly into a messy bun, but her dark burgundy lipstick and winged eyeliner remained on point.

"Congrats on your grand opening!" I yelled into her ear. "The place looks great!"

She grinned with all the giddiness and excitement that could only come from working your ass off to open a business and finally being able to kick back and enjoy the labor of your blood, sweat, and tears.

"Thanks, babe! I can't believe there are so many people here!" she shrieked with joy and swirled the ice in her cup. "I used your peppermint tea to make mint juleps and they are the bomb! Come have a drink!"

"In a minute," I promised her. "I want to check out your shop first."

"For sure! Take anything that catches your eye, babe. Just keep bringing me that bomb-ass tea." She winked and went off to mingle before I could protest. Her wares were far more expensive than my meager dozen bags of tea.

"She's a generous drunk," Nona observed.

"She's really sweet," I said almost as if trying to convince myself.

Not that it wasn't true, but San Francisco definitely shook my deep-seated perceptions of people who did not look like me or my family growing up. Myranda was covered from her feet to her neck in tattoos and I never saw her wear any color other than black. Many of the people in here had similar looks. Until I left home, it never even occurred to me that nice, caring people could also smoke, drink, wear dark lipstick and have sex before marriage.

"Oooh, look at these!" Nona's coos pulled me out of my thoughts.

She pulled me over to a display shelf of crystals in every color imaginable. Some were polished to a high shine, others further cut into shapes like skulls and dragons, while others appeared to be in their rough, natural form.

"This is what you need." She wiggled her eyebrows as she picked up a smooth orange stone and placed it in my palm. "Orange calcite for awakening sexual energy."

"Sure. I'll get right on that," I scoffed.

Owning a business and growing up in California's version of the

Bible belt was not a combination for an active sex life. The last time I slept with a guy was in college, which felt like ages ago.

While Nona poured over the rocks and crystals, I slowly turned around in a circle to see more of the shop.

Like Myranda herself, her shop couldn't be placed neatly into one category. *Trailblazers, Inc.* carried everything from skulls and taxidermy animals to vintage clothing, jewelry, patches, and pins. It was part punk rock attire, part curiosity shop with a dash of woo-woo.

And somehow she made it all work.

"Oooh Deja, look!" Nona sounded like a child filled with wonder at Disneyland as she pointed excitedly.

Tucked off in a corner past the wall with the giant goat's head was a sign that read FREE TAROT READINGS (tips appreciated!).

"Let's get our cards read!" Nona exclaimed. "I've always wanted to!"

"Oh, you go ahead. I'm good," I told her.

Yes, tarot was just another check mark on the long list of things that made a recovering Christian uneasy. But that wasn't the reason for my hesitation.

Just underneath the massive goat head appeared to be a tattoo station. A sign on a table read FLASH TATTOOS $40. The artist was hard at work, sitting in a swivel chair while inking something onto a man's forearm. Two other men stood nearby, drinking and laughing with their friend getting tattooed.

All three of them looked absolutely gorgeous.

And dangerous.

They were dressed from head to toe in black. Distressed black leather jackets on top, slim-fitted black denim and leather boots down below.

I would have to walk past them to get to the tarot reader and didn't dare come an inch closer.

Attractive men always made me nervous but never like this. Their presence seemed to fill up the whole shop. Aside from the tattoo artist, everyone else seemed to give them extremely wide berth. Even at a good ten feet away, I could feel them as if I was standing right next to them.

I went from being comfortably warm to overbearingly hot. My face felt like it was on fire. Every instinct in my body warned me not to get any closer to them. Only Nona seemed completely oblivious.

"Come on, Deja. It won't be any fun without you!"

With surprising strength, she took my arm and pulled me toward the tarot sign. Toward them.

All three of them stopped conversing and stared right at me.

The whole store seemed to slow down and go quiet as I locked in on three pairs of shining, hungry eyes. Icy blue, emerald green, and brown, almost black. They stared me down, and I felt like I was walking through jello.

A hot, sensitive pulsing started between my legs and spread throughout my body. My face grew even hotter as I realized how my body responded to being physically closer to these three men.

The one with dark eyes, sitting and getting tattooed, lifted one corner of his mouth in a knowing smirk. The green-eyed one standing next to him echoed the same wicked smile. Only the blue-eyed one kept his face neutral, regarding me coolly as I seemed to walk by in slow motion.

We rounded the corner, and it felt like a spell was broken.

I blinked, now looking at a woman sitting at a small table in a small, private corner of the store. She smiled at us warmly, surrounded by candles, crystals, and card decks on her table.

"Welcome, lovelies!" she greeted. "Come for a tarot reading?"

"Yes, for both of us," Nona said, shooting me a pointed look. I stared back at her blankly. Did she really not feel the same overwhelming power and lust that I just did?

"Have a seat," the tarot reader offered as she picked up a deck of cards and began to shuffle.

"You go first," I said to Nona robotically, my mind still haunted by those three pairs of eyes just on the other side of the wall.

Their effect on me was paralyzing and somehow also fiercely magnetic. It shook me. It was more than just noticing three hot guys, it was like something came over me physically. Something that wasn't normal attraction. It was completely overwhelming and even just a little scary.

Once we got this tarot reading over with, I could only hope they'd no longer be there.

2
DEJA

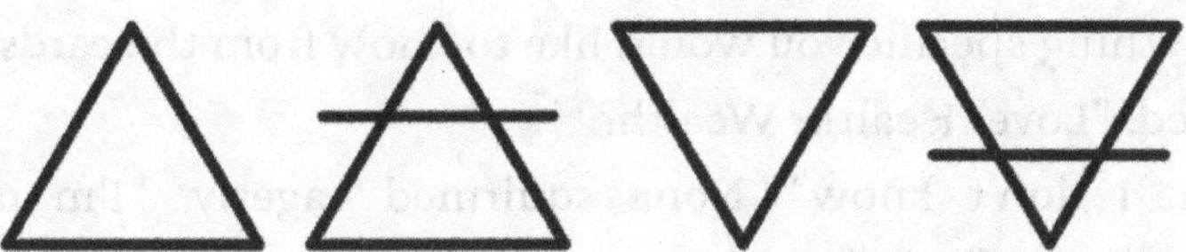

"Do you know anyone named Diana?"

It took me a moment to realize the tarot reader was speaking to me.

"Huh?" I blinked.

Nona sat eagerly in the chair in front of the table, awaiting her fortune to be told from pieces of cardstock. The woman continued shuffling her deck with fast, experienced hands. Her smile was directed at Nona but her eyes trained sharply on me.

"Diana," she repeated. "Does the name ring a bell?"

It did.

Once the fog lifted from whatever the three pretty-eyed men did to me, my mind felt clear again and that name struck a chord.

However, I couldn't think of a face to match it.

Diana. Yes, that name meant something to me. I knew someone named Diana but couldn't begin to remember who or how I knew her.

But even weirder, how did this woman know to ask me that?

She continued shuffling while watching my face carefully. Nona still waited patiently for her to lay out the cards.

I lifted one shoulder in a lazy shrug, feigning nonchalance.

"Nope, can't say it does."

The woman's lips pulled into a tight smile as if she knew I was bullshitting but decided to humor me all the same.

"Well, when you see her, tell her Minerva said hello."

Ohhh-kay, lady. I'll do just that.

She finally turned her attention to Nona as she cut her deck into three piles.

"Anything specific you would like to know from the cards, dear?" she asked. "Love? Health? Wealth?"

"Oh, I don't know." Nona squirmed eagerly. "I'm open to anything they tell me."

"Very good!" The woman rubbed her hands together. "Pick whichever pile calls to you, dear."

Nona chose the left pile and Minerva—I assumed—brought all three piles back together into a single deck with Nona's selection on top. She drew from the top and laid 3 cards out on the table.

From what I could see, the cards depicted people in various scenes and interacting with coins engraved with five-pointed stars.

"Ah, the suit of pentacles," Minerva cooed over the cards. "This is very good news! Much earthly abundance will be coming into your life within six months, dear. You'll be sowing the fruits of your labor soon and come into more money than you ever thought possible."

"Really?" Nona's eyes widened.

"Oh yes! But you will also come into more challenges and responsibility," Minerva said, pointing to one card. "I sense a shifting tide coming your way, one that carries you upward to a very comfortable financial position but it is unlike anything you've ever done before."

Nona glanced at me. "Sounds like I'm due for a promotion, boss," she smirked.

"That or you'll end up leaving me for something better," I retorted, trying to keep the edge out of my voice but it was truly one of my worst fears. I paid her the most I could afford and she still deserved more. Eventually, the time would come where she'd find her dream job and I'd be left trying to find someone to live up to the Nona-shaped void in my life.

"You know that'll never happen," she answered solemnly. "I love working for you."

"These things never happen in the way we expect," said Minerva as she swept up the cards and shuffled them back into the deck.

"Oh. Is that it?" Nona asked, looking slightly disappointed.

"For free readings, yes dear," Minerva answered with a syrupy smile. She gestured me toward the chair. "Now you."

"No, that's okay," I protested as Nona got up and fumbled for a few dollars to throw in the tip jar.

"Sit," Minerva said more insistently.

I narrowed my eyes at her. Who the fuck do you think you are, woman?

"Come on, Deja," Nona pleaded, seemingly oblivious to the tension in the air. "Maybe you'll win the lottery and split it with me!"

"A likely story," I mumbled as I reluctantly sat in the chair.

Minerva's eyes closed halfway as she shuffled her cards again. Through her heavy eyelashes, I could only see the whites of her eyes as if they had rolled back in her head. She took deep, heavy breaths in and out of her nose as she shuffled.

I cast a skeptical sideways glance over at Nona. Already this reading was going in a completely different direction than hers.

"There is so much conflicting energy surrounding you," Minerva announced, her eyes returning to focus on me. "My guides are weeping for you. They tell me your truth has been hidden away like a shameful secret. The time is approaching for your truth to be revealed to the world."

Oh. Kay...

"Cool," I said, forcing a smile. Whatever it took for this weird little puppet show to be over with.

Minerva did not look amused as she laid out my cards. Three of them face down. She didn't cut the deck and tell me to pick one like Nona. Her bejeweled hands hovered over my three cards for a moment before she finally flipped them over.

Something came over me the moment my eyes registered those little pictures. My heart skipped a beat and my scalp felt like it was buzzing.

The images depicted were far more dramatic than Nona's and didn't have the same little coin symbols. Each card had a word written on the bottom below its image.

The Tower. The Devil. The Lovers.

I scratched my head absently but the buzzing sensation only seemed to grow stronger.

"This is your truth, my dear," Minerva said, tapping The Tower with a long, acrylic fingernail. "When you discover it, it will shake you to your very foundation. Your entire world will be turned on its head and you'll question everything you ever knew to be true."

"That's comforting," I muttered.

In the picture, a bolt of lightning struck the top of the tower with two figures falling toward the ground. It looked ominous and dark, but the picture I couldn't tear my eyes away from was The Devil.

He had long, curling horns exactly like the giant goat's head just on the other side of the wall. His head looked somewhat goat-like as well, with the torso of a man but his legs had fur and claws like an animal. Standing in front of him were two naked figures with chains around their necks.

"What does The Devil card make you think of?" Minerva asked carefully. "How does it make you feel?"

I opened my mouth, but no words came out. My whole body buzzed now with a strange energy coursing through me. My skin was hot and that dull ache pulsed again between my legs. I clamped my thighs shut for some relief and I couldn't stop thinking of those three men just on the other side of the wall.

"Um, it represents sin? And lust, I guess." I crossed my legs, trying my best to look bored.

Minerva made that smile again, the one that said she knew I was bullshitting but would play along anyway.

"Yes, from a Judeo-Christian view it represents those things," she said, picking up the card and holding it up. "But he also speaks of enslavement to a certain mindset, an addiction if you will. And the ability to choose a different way. You always have free will, Deja."

The way she said my name echoed in my mind. It sounded familiar like she knew me from before I could remember her.

"However," she said, picking up the final card, The Lovers, which depicted a nude couple embracing. "I feel strongly that The Devil and The Lovers are linked for you. Perhaps you will fall in love with a devilishly handsome man and he will free you from the mental prison that you still carry inside you."

She set the card down on the table. "Or," she said with a wide, knowing grin. "You may even fall in love with The Devil himself."

3
ASHTAROTH

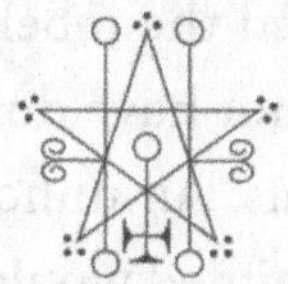

We all knew the moment we saw her. Each of our connections with her was slightly different, but we all definitely felt it. Mine felt like a cooling salve applied to a burn, then a gentle whisper against my skin.

"That was her." Sal was the first to voice it. His green eyes were wide and wild. "Fuck me. She's really back."

"Are you sure?" Raum, always joking, looked up from his tattoo. "I don't know, that warm breeze through my feathers could have been anything else."

"I have zero doubt," Sal said excitedly, nearly giddy as a child. He rolled his eyes up to the massive goat head mounted on the wall we leaned on. "Thank you, Lord, for leading us here."

The goat did not reply, but the three of us in unison felt a heating in our skin. Hidden beneath our clothing, our tattoos of Lucifer's sigil glowed like a hot iron and would burn the flesh off any human who dared to touch it. But for us, it emitted a pleasant warmth with the approval of our Lord.

He had been just as sorrowful as we were. The ruler of Hell kept extremely busy, but he mourned her loss with us for centuries. Before he and I fell, he was preoccupied with his rebellion and paid no attention to her while she was on earth.

No, it was me that she captured the first day I saw her.

I rebelled for her, a human woman. I didn't fall from heaven, I flew down when the earth split open and took her with me.

It was in the early days of Hell that her charms and beauty won Lucifer over. Sometimes I sensed jealousy from him like he wished he had her first. He may have led the rebellion and earned the right to rule over Hell, but he could not have done it without Beelzebub and I. The three of us were equals. An unholy trinity. He knew she was mine, and anyone else she claimed would be her choice.

But because I stole one of God's creations, I had to pay a terrible price. We all did.

She was stolen not only from us, but from humanity that adored, cherished, and listened to her. We stopped her from being killed but after nearly a thousand years without her, it felt remarkably like she was back from the dead. The pieces of her, fleeting glimpses we saw in women throughout history, barely held a candle to her original wit and beauty.

And because of Lucifer's affection for her, he vowed to lead us straight to her when she became whole again. Raum saw it in his visions, and I could hardly believe that she was finally here.

"Something's wrong, though," I said, ever the serious one. "I saw her aura and felt our bond but did everything else seem stunted to you two?"

"She is stunted," Raum said calmly as he handed a wad of cash to the tattoo artist. "Her powers have been blocked. She may not even realize she has them."

"Blocked by what?" Sal snarled.

"Really, Sal?" Raum chided. "What do you think?"

"So what's our next move?" I asked, folding my arms. This was a delicate matter we couldn't rush. We could not afford to fuck this up and live another thousand years of painful, lonely misery.

"Oh, she's getting some valuable insight right now," Raum grinned. "The gears upstairs will definitely be turning. And she will have some clarity very soon. But," he paused. "It will be up to us to do the rest."

"So we wait," I stated, raising my drink to my lips. "We get close slowly to make absolutely sure. And most importantly, we pretend like we're meeting her for the first time."

4
DEJA

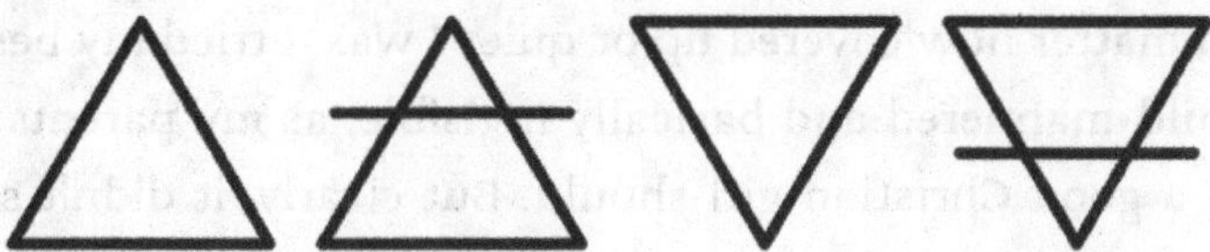

"**W**ell that was insightful," I muttered as I left the tiny tarot alcove to rejoin the party. "I'll never get those five minutes of my life back."

I had thanked the woman for her time, gave her a tip and walked out of there as fast as I could with Nona on my heels. It was high time for a drink.

I ordered a mint julep from the bar and fought the overwhelming urge to turn around.

Those three guys were still there, hanging out underneath the goat's head. I didn't allow myself to look at them but I could feel their presence as if all three were breathing down the back of my neck.

It was unmistakable. And eerie how much it affected me. I couldn't ignore that I felt the same sensitive heat when I saw that Devil card. Why did they pop into my mind the moment I saw that imagery?

Whatever, it didn't matter. Tarot was a load of bunk, anyway.

"Looks like you have some admirers," Nona observed. "They keep talking among themselves and looking at you."

"Great, so now they're being painfully obvious about it."

I sucked my drink noisily through the skinny black straw. It felt like a switch flipped in my brain and I was suddenly in a crappy mood. That tarot reading seemed to get under my skin more than I anticipated.

I also detested being the object of someone's attention. Growing up, I would always get in trouble when a guy tried to talk to me or tell me I was pretty. My parents always made it seem like it was my fault, no matter how covered up or quiet I was. I tried my best to be quiet, mild-mannered and basically invisible, as my parents taught me that a good Christian girl should. But clearly, it didn't seem to work.

"Are they still looking?" I asked Nona.

"Yup, checking out your ass shamelessly." She ran her tongue across her teeth. "They look like bad news, which makes them even hotter. Maybe one of them is the Devil you'll fall in love with."

"Not if I have anything to do with it."

I sucked down the remainder of my drink and whipped around. Two of the men smiled as I returned their gaze. Only the blond-haired one with blue eyes kept a cool, neutral expression as he leaned against the wall. The black goat's beard just barely brushed the top of his head.

All three of them stared me down hungrily like a juicy steak waiting to be carved up.

My body heated and pulsed under their smoldering gaze but the rational part of me was sick of it. Sick and tired of being the object of male lust when all I wanted to do was relax after a long day.

Before I could second-guess myself, I started toward them, hoping my walk passed off as confident and not the hot, swirling mess of nerves that I was inside.

"Hey," I greeted.

And flashed a smile as I put a hand on my hip because my mind went completely blank.

"Hey," returned the one with dark eyes and dark brown hair that fell in a shaggy, sexy mane to his collar. His *hey* sounded like rolling thunder. He had been the one getting a tattoo and a bandage now wrapped around his forearm.

His full lips, surrounded by a five-o'clock shadow, lifted into a smirk as his chocolate eyes roamed shamelessly over me.

"Why don't you take a picture?" I snapped, finally remembering what I was going to say. "It'll last longer."

To my utter embarrassment, he and the guy standing next to him with short auburn hair, a clean-shaven face with a sharp jaw, and green eyes, burst into laughter.

My confidence, as fake as it was, deflated like a balloon.

"I'd be glad to, beautiful," said Green Eyes, retrieving a phone from his jacket pocket. "How about a pretty smile first? Or even better, a little flash of someth--"

"I apologize for these two."

The quiet, serious-faced one with blue eyes suddenly stepped between me and his friends. They shrank back ever so slightly, almost unnoticeably but I somehow caught it. Whoever these guys were, Blue Eyes was in charge.

Every cell in my body practically hummed in vibration as he stood inches away from me. He was broad and tall like a viking, with a fuller beard than Brown Eyes but still trimmed short and neatly. I nearly gasped when I got a closer look at his eyes, they looked almost like contact lenses. Such a pale, icy blue like an Arctic landscape.

"These two are like animals," he said in a lighthearted but commanding tone. "I'll make sure they control themselves and don't ogle you."

I narrowed my eyes, unconvinced.

"You were ogling just as much. Don't pretend to be innocent."

"Oh," his mouth lifted into a wry smile for the first time. "I wouldn't dream of pretending such a thing. At least I," he brought a hand to his sculpted chest. "Am a gentleman about it."

That was the moment I should have walked away. This man was far too charming. Raw masculinity came off him in waves. It did from all three of them but the strongest from him.

There was something else too. Some kind of power or energy that I couldn't place. At first, it seemed to keep everyone away from them at this party but now that I stood within inches, it drew me in like a magnet.

"Whatever," I said, trying to shake off this hold they had on me. "Keep your eyes to yourself."

"I'll make no such promises," he said with a wicked gleam in his icy eyes. "So how was your tarot reading?"

"About what you'd expect. A great change will befall me and I'm going to fall in love with the devil. Oh, and my truth which had been suppressed will soon be revealed. Seriously, I should be a tarot reader because I bet I actually can make this stuff up."

"I'd love to hear what you'd come up with," laughed Dark Eyes. "That tongue of yours cuts straight to the point."

The alcohol must have hit me right at that moment because I suddenly realized I was actually having a conversation with these men. They formed a semicircle around me, regarding me with more curiosity now than hunger. Maybe it was just my lowered inhibitions, but I didn't feel threatened or objectified anymore. Instead, it felt nice talking to new people who weren't customers in my shop.

"What are your names? I keep thinking of you in terms of eye colors," I blurted.

"Our name is legion, for we are many," said Green Eyes in a low, eerie tone.

I blinked. "What?"

"Nevermind him," grinned Dark Eyes. "I'm Raum."

"Sal," said Green Eyes with a wink.

"I'm Ash," said Blue Eyes, raising his drink slightly. "And you are?"

"Deja," I answered. "So how do you guys know Myranda?"

"Who?" asked Sal.

I couldn't tell if he was serious or joking.

"Myranda, the owner of this shop?" I said teasingly. "The host of this party? Come on, Sal. Something tells me you're smarter than that."

"We may or may not be crashing this party." Ash's face was serious but his eyes were mischievous.

"Oh. Well, whatever. It's open to the public anyway," I said.

"Although we did come here for a very specific reason." Raum watched me carefully as he spoke, a grin spreading across his face.

"Yeah, what's that?" I asked. "To check out girls' asses without an ounce of tact?"

"Actually no, not this time," Sal chuckled. "We came to pay respect to our Lord and Savior."

"And who might that be?" I cocked an eyebrow.

All three of them pointed upward. My gaze followed their fingers up to the black goat's head mounted on the wall, whose glassy eyes seemed to be looking down at me with the same mischief as the three men standing below.

What. The. Fuck.

"Okay then." I forced a smile. "Nice talking to you all."

I quickly turned on my heel and sped away as fast as my feet could carry me.

5
DEJA

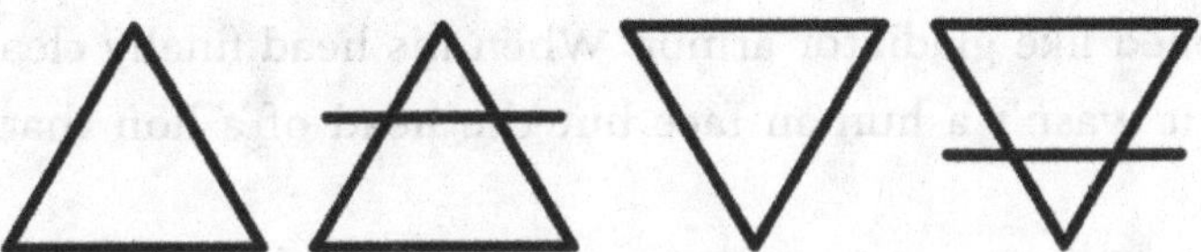

"Hello? Earth to Deja!"

A pair of fingers suddenly snapped in my face and jolted me out of my daydream.

"Hm?"

Nona gave me a look of concern mixed with a hint of annoyance.

"I said we're low on the Earl Grey loose leaf. Can you get some from the back while I take care of the line?"

A pang of guilt hit me as I saw how many people stretched from the cash register to the front door. Nona had been essentially working by herself while I dozed off in la-la land.

Or should I say Devil Land.

"Yeah totally, Nona," I said, springing from my seat. "I'm so sorry. Be right back."

I hustled to the storage area in the back of my tea shop as quickly as I could, but my eyelids were heavy and my limbs felt like lead.

I barely slept at all last night. After scurrying away from those guys at the party I felt like a damn fool. My stupid Christian instincts kicked in again after picking up the insinuation that they were devil worshippers. By the time I realized they were most likely joking, I was too embarrassed to talk to them again. As such was my luck with men.

But when I got home and fell into bed, my dreams were plagued by visions and creatures I'd never seen or heard of before. They were as vivid as my own hand in front of my face and yet so surreal.

In my dream, I saw the ruins of an ancient city still burning. Through the smoke, I saw a figure walking toward me. As he got closer I could make out breastplate armor, gauntlets, and a shield that looked like gladiator armor. When his head finally cleared the smoke, it wasn't a human face but the head of a lion that roared at me.

Suddenly, I was in a dark forest and heard a raven cawing. The large black bird jumped from branch to branch on a tree in front of me, cawing and flapping its wings as if taunting me. A shiny diamond ring gleamed in its beak. I blinked and instead of a raven, there stood Raum holding the ring out to me.

And the most disturbing vision of all which kept me from going back to sleep, I saw Ash naked. Oh, I wouldn't deny the human parts of him looked *exquisite*. His physique looked carved from marble and his head carried a heavy jeweled crown. He would have looked normal and delicious if it weren't for the massive, black feathered wings on his back and the biggest snake I'd ever seen coiled around his arm and shoulders.

But what absolutely terrified me was the thing he rode on.

It looked like a bat with one of those really ugly faces, only it walked on all fours like a dog. But it still had large, leathery wings and a long scaly tail like the snake wrapped around his shoulders.

I woke up in a cold sweat at three in the morning. I'd only been asleep for two hours and didn't dare close my eyes again.

Now during the lunch rush the next day, the lack of sleep was catching up to me.

I wonder if I need a therapist or something, I thought as I rummaged through the cooler for the bag of Earl Grey. Surely a stupid tarot reading and three guys joking about the devil wouldn't affect a normal person this much.

By the time my bleary eyes found the tea and my feet stumbled me back to the front counter, Nona had already rang up everyone in line.

Saving my ass again. I knew she was superhuman.

"Thanks for being on top of everything," I groaned, leaning my elbows on the counter and rubbing my eyes. "I don't know why I'm so out of it."

"You can't be that hungover from one drink," Nona proclaimed as she wiped down teacups.

"I'm not," I insisted. "I just couldn't sleep."

She flicked a dish rag over her shoulder and gave me a curious look.

"So what did those guys say that made you high-tail it out of there?"

"Something stupid that I totally overreacted to." I dipped a clean tablespoon into a canister of Irish Breakfast, eager for more caffeine.

"Like what, did they suggest a crazy, drunk orgy? Because you should have sent me their way if they did."

"What? Jesus, no!"

"See, that's your issue. Too much Jesus in your life," she teased, poking me in the ribs.

"I'm already aware," I muttered.

"Speak of the devil," she said under her breath.

"You know, I'm getting a little tired of the D-word," I snapped more crabbily than I intended.

"And what word is that?"

I looked up to the source of the deep, throaty voice and nearly dropped the canister of tea I was holding.

A pair of warm brown eyes twinkled back. Raum leaned on my counter, smirking as casually as if he came here regularly. His sexy mane of hair was tousled carelessly like he— or some woman— just ran their fingers through it.

This morning he ditched the black leather jacket for a snug, gunmetal gray T-shirt that hugged his chest and biceps.

"Deja can't be the D-word you're so tired of," he mused. "It's a beautiful name, possibly my new favorite D-word. Although I can think of a few runner-ups."

His teasing grin spread slowly across his face, daring me to ask what those other words were.

I steeled myself, suddenly wide awake, and did my best to ignore the heat growing in my cheeks and core again.

"Can I help you?" I asked pointedly.

His smile diminished and his brow furrowed slightly with concern.

"I wanted to stop by and apologize," he said in a low voice, softening his gaze. "We didn't mean to offend or frighten you last night."

My eyebrows lifted, taken aback. I got the sense that this guy didn't make apologies very often.

"I'm kind of a jokester and sometimes I take it too far," he continued, his eyes resembling that of a sad puppy's now. "I hope we didn't ruin your night."

My chest and stomach fluttered as I tried to keep my face aloof. I had to admit it was flattering to have a man put aside his pride and grovel before me. Maybe that was an exaggeration but my ego thoroughly enjoyed this.

"That's alright, I suppose," I said as coolly as I could muster. "How did you find my shop?"

"I have my ways," he answered evasively, the wily smile returning. "How about a truce over a cuppa?"

I shrugged my acceptance, figuring he asked Myranda or someone else at the party who'd been a customer of mine.

"I think we can manage that." I pulled out a clean ceramic cup and a fresh tea bag. "Any preference?"

"Surprise me," he winked.

I let my eyes rest on him for a moment, drinking in his features. The rough stubble, the olive skin over high cheekbones and the slight crows feet at the corners of his eyes. I wondered how old he was.

"You don't strike me as a fruity tea kind of guy," I mused. "I'm thinking something more earthy, with a hint of spice."

"Yes, girl. Keep talking tea to me," he teased, leaning further over the counter toward me.

I had to chuckle at that.

"I'll give you some of what I'm having. Irish Breakfast with a bit of ginger and cinnamon blend for a bit of spice and to kickstart the immune system."

"Sounds perfect, and something I never would have thought of myself." He watched me curiously as I heated the kettle and prepared the tea. "How did you come to startup this place?"

"Long story short, I've always loved growing varieties of herbs and mixing up flavors," I said, trying to keep my cool as I worked, despite my insides somersaulting. "I've made my own tea blends for as long as I can remember. I make my own spice blends for cooking too. Back home, I was never really encouraged to be creative or entrepreneurial. So I took a chance and left. This was as far as my bus ticket would go, so here's where I ended up."

"Where's back home?"

He picked up the teacup I set in front of him and gently pursed his lips to blow on the hot liquid, his eyes never leaving me.

"Bakersfield," I answered, trying not to stare at his lips too much.

"Ah," he said after taking a sip. "I can see why you left."

"Yeah," I sighed. "I never really left home before coming here. San Francisco has been a pretty big culture shock."

"Really?" He sounded amused as he took another gulp of tea. "How so?"

I wrung my hands behind the counter, unsure of how much I

wanted to tell him about the life I ran away from. At the same time, some part of my brain shot off fireworks with excitement that this guy seemed so interested in me.

"I was just sheltered growing up, I guess," I said with a shrug. "My parents never really exposed me to cultures and lifestyles outside of our own."

His charming grin reached its widest point yet.

"You really have no idea what you are, do you?"

I looked at him, bewildered.

"What do you mean by that?"

But he just set his teacup down, slapped a few dollars on the counter, and gave me a wink.

"Thanks for the tea. See you around, Deja."

As he turned away to leave, only then did I notice the mark on his arm— a raven holding a jeweled crucifix necklace in its beak. My mind spun as I realized it was the tattoo he received at the party last night.

And somehow it already looked fully healed.

6
ASHTAROTH

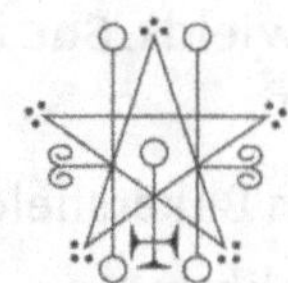

I sensed Raum's return before I ever saw him.

Within moments I heard the telltale fluttering of wings and annoying, "Caw! Caw!" at my windowsill.

"I agree. You are quite the birdbrain," I said, not looking up from my book of the day. This time it was *The Turn of the Screw*, an old favorite.

"Caw! Caw!"

I shot him a death stare, knowing he was cawing things he wouldn't dare say to my face in human form.

"No pretty trinkets in your beak this time," I observed. "Any reason for that?"

He shifted into human form and shot me a sheepish grin as he leaned against the window.

"Maybe I'm getting soft in my old age but I just couldn't bring myself to steal from her. And anyway I had no reason to. She gave me a gift."

"Oh?" I said in a bored tone, returning to my book. "And what was that?"

"She made me tea."

He was trying to get a rise out of me, to make me jealous. And honestly, it worked. Even demons in the first hierarchy weren't above petty human emotions. How else did we know how to manipulate them so well?

But after watching humanity pass by over the last several thousand years, I learned to keep my face neutral.

"So was my hypothesis correct?" I asked, keeping my bored tone.

"It was." Raum lowered his head in a respectful nod to me. "She has no idea of the power she wields. She is definitely blocked."

"And the reason for that?"

"A sheltered upbringing in Bakersfield."

As a devout Christian, most likely.

The thought left a foul taste in my mouth and I snapped my book shut. If she truly was the one we'd been waiting for all these centuries, being reborn as a Christ-worshipper seemed like a particularly cruel joke. Salt in the proverbial wounds.

With one glance at Raum, I knew he wasn't telling me everything. I knew him better than anyone. He'd been my disciple since the dawn of Christ himself and enjoyed being tricky and keeping secrets, possibly too much. Lucifer had little patience for him but I saw his potential as an ally. It took a keen eye to draw the necessary information from him but I had two thousand years of practice.

"Spill it," I urged. "What else have you seen?"

"She'll find out the truth soon," he said, eyes glazing over slightly. "She'll be receiving a visitor who will teach her who she is."

"In regards to us?"

"No. In regards to herself."

"Well, one step at a time then," I sighed, leaning back in my chair and resting my feet on the worn, overcrowded bookshelf.

Raum's eyes remained glassy for a few moments, indicating he was somewhere else. The past or the future, he could see it all.

His eyes refocused, and he blinked while looking around the room.

"Where's Sal?"

"Who knows? Probably burning down cities or infecting terrorists with anthrax. You know how he gets when he's frustrated."

Salmac was easily the hot-headed one of the three of us. Raum and I had to physically restrain him from going after Deja when she essentially ran away at the party. He was about to tell her everything right then, ruining our careful plan and make the poor girl likely run to the police. She'd never believe she was anything but a normal human woman after that. Albeit a crazy one.

We had to do this extremely carefully, and Sal was an emotional, impulsive fucker. Not even I could reel him in when his temper ran hot. Only Raum seemed to keep him on an even-keel.

"You know," Raum said, his trickster grin returning. "I could just make this a hundred times easier for all four of us."

"Don't. That's an order," I snapped. "She will come to us of her own free will, or not at all. When she realizes the full extent of who she is, it should happen naturally. It will happen, as it was meant to."

"Of course. That was a bad joke on my part." Raum lowered his eyes.

"Not everything is about trickery and manipulation, Raum," I growled. "We bring more humans to our side through simply revealing the truth."

"You're right," he agreed. "She will see through any attempt at deception, anyway."

I stood and looked out the window where Deja's tea shop and apartment just above it sat in plain view. I wondered who her supposed visitor would be and what kind of influence that person had over her.

"Let's certainly hope so," I said.

7
DEJA

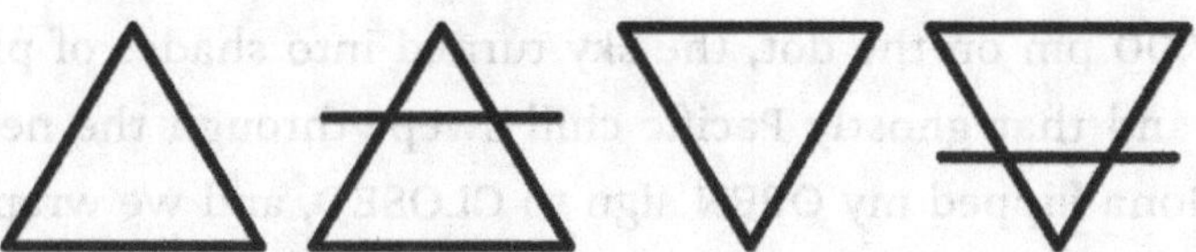

My energy level kicked into high gear after seeing Raum that morning. I couldn't begin to explain why, other than the expected giddiness at having a smoking hot guy talk to me.

"You keep smiling," Nona teased as we prepared tea orders side by side. "Did you get a date? Or at least his number?"

"No." I let out a sigh that was somewhere between happy and frustrated. "He said he'd see me around and other stuff that was vague. So who knows, he's probably just a flirt."

But at least someone flirted with *me*.

I should have felt uneasy about his tattoo, which matched what I saw in my dream almost perfectly. Scratch that, I should have been downright freaked the fuck out. But for some reason, the coincidences didn't bother me.

Life was just easier when I wasn't trying to make sense of everything. When I was younger, I wondered if odd coincidences were signs of God trying to tell me something. It would legitimately stress me out to the point of anxiety. But the simple mental act of letting go gave me the courage to step on a bus and leave the home I'd known forever. It allowed me to make the decisions that turned me into a successful business owner.

Sometimes things didn't happen for a reason and that was okay. Realizing that was the most free I'd ever felt in my life.

Maybe the tattoo meant something. Maybe I caught a glimpse of it at the party and it was in my subconscious. Whatever the reason or lack of, it was beyond my control and it wouldn't do me any good to fret about it.

At 7:00 pm on the dot, the sky turned into shades of pink and orange and that ghostly Pacific chill swept through the neighborhood. Nona flipped my OPEN sign to CLOSED, and we wrapped up another good day at the shop with a high-five and blasted P!nk's latest album as we quickly cleaned up for the day.

A half-hour later she hopped on her bicycle to head home and I carefully walked up the creaky stairs to my apartment above the shop.

The whole building was an older Victorian style but kept up well and charming. The wood floors were original and polished to a high shine but what I loved the most were the huge, beautiful windows that let in breathtaking natural light.

I began my evening after-work ritual of pouring myself a glass of wine and watching the sunset over the herb garden in my front living room window. As far as I was concerned, sunrises and sunsets were the only testaments to the existence of God or anything else unexplainable. Of course, anyone could look up the science-based, atmospheric reasons for all the gorgeous colors in the sky but why take away the beauty and wonder? While I didn't consider myself Christian or even religious anymore, not everything had to be explained scientifically either. The world could still be magical in its own way.

The sky shifted from orange-pink to a cool, dusty purple before the sun finally slipped below the horizon. I shivered as the temperature dropped even lower and shut my window against the chill.

Wine glass now empty, I hopped off the window seat and returned to my small, humble kitchen to pour another and contemplate dinner.

I didn't even open the fridge before an insistent knock came to my door.

Narrowing my eyes into a glare and muttering curses, I stormed over, ready to give my meddling neighbor a piece of my mind. *For the third time Janice, I am* not *the one smoking weed out my window!*

I yanked the door open, ready to hurl some creative words at her but stopped dead in my tracks.

Instead of my uppity hipster neighbor, an elegant, willowy woman with long white hair and bright, amber eyes full of wisdom stood in my doorway.

She appeared elderly, maybe in her seventies, but not incapacitated in any way. She had clearly aged well and stood with the posture and confidence of someone half her age.

Diana.

The name popped into my head as if someone whispered it, and my pulse quickened. I'd never met this woman in my life and somehow I knew this was the Diana the tarot reader had been alluding to.

"Hello Deja," the woman said with the barest hint of a smile. "Do you know who I am?"

"Diana," I breathed the name barely above a whisper. Saying it out loud seemed to cement it into reality, which only confused me even more.

"Yes, that's my name," the woman chuckled. "But you never used to call me that."

Diana's smile faded at my blank, confused expression. Her brow furrowed as her lips pressed into a thin, tight line. Her eyes even seemed to well up with tears.

"My gods," she whispered, her voice full of emotion. "You really don't remember me, do you?"

"I'm sorry but no," I said, feeling a stab of pity for her. "What did I used to call you? Maybe it can jog my memory."

She stepped closer to me and took one of my hands. Immediately a sense of warm, comforting nostalgia filled me. Memories I hadn't recalled in years filled my head and brought a lazy smile to my face. Sunshine and laughter. Cool earth between my fingers and toes. The smell of fresh-cut lavender, thyme, and oregano.

Diana watched my face carefully. She was doing... something to me, something to make me recall these images, scents, and feelings with a simple touch of her hand. I couldn't explain it and wanted to demand, *what the fuck is this!* But it felt so good and nice, like reuniting with someone I loved that I hadn't seen in years.

All the feelings and sensations slowly faded away. Her smile returned when my eyes refocused on her.

"You used to call me Grandma," she said softly.

8

DEJA

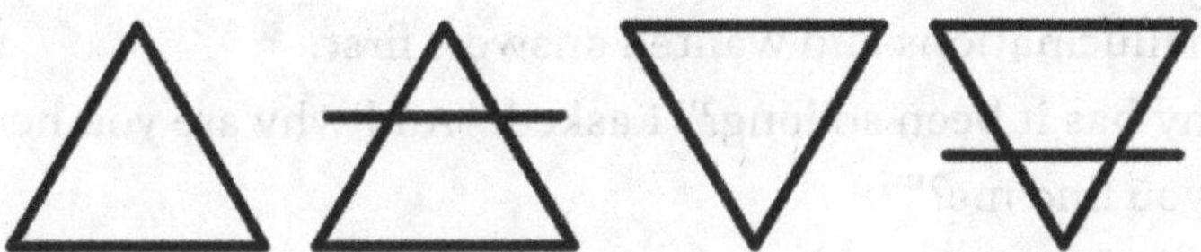

"Would you mind if I come in, Deja?" Diana asked. "It seems we have a lot to talk about."

In a daze, I stepped aside to invite her into my apartment. My mind reeled as it sought to make sense of what she just told me.

"Would you like um, something to drink?" I said as I closed the door behind her, my frayed brain cells somehow still remembering to be hospitable. "Tea? Water?"

A playful gleam twinkled in her eyes.

"Do you intend on sharing that bottle of wine?"

I grabbed the bottle and two glasses while Diana settled herself down on my couch. I poured in silence, watching the burgundy liquid splash like blood.

The image of the Tower card flashed through my mind and I wondered if this was that pivotal moment Minerva was referring to. I could ignore some coincidences but this was all proving to be too much to ignore.

Clutching my wine glass in my palms, I sat next to Diana on the couch with still a few feet of space between us. She didn't seem harmful but this whole situation made me extremely uneasy. I didn't fully trust her yet but was still eager to know what she had to say.

"So you're my grandmother," I began.

"I am," she said with a smile. "You were just a chubby little toddler when I last saw you. I've thought of you every day and missed you terribly, Deja."

She reached out to touch me again and I drew my hand back in response. I had no idea if she was truly filling my head with memories or hallucinations and wanted answers first.

"Why has it been so long?" I asked. "And why are you here now? How'd you find me?"

Diana chuckled as she took a hearty sip of wine.

"So much information to cover in such little time." She arched an elegant white eyebrow at me. "Your parents never told you the truth?"

"I don't even know what that means anymore," I cried with an exasperated sigh. "You're the third person in two days who's said the truth will be revealed or whatever and I still don't fucking get it."

Diana looked sympathetic to my frustration but otherwise unfazed.

"Poor dear," she said, reaching for my hand again and this time I let her. No memories or feelings came over me, thankfully.

"We'll start at the very beginning, then." She set down her wine glass and turned to face me squarely. "Deja, you were adopted as an infant."

"I... what? Adopted?"

The information hit me like a shock, and yet I wasn't completely unsurprised. My parents and I were never close. There was always a disconnect between us that I couldn't place. I figured it was natural rebelling against their religious teaching at first, but I never grew out of it. I never felt completely comfortable in their world and that was essentially why I ended up leaving.

"I'm your biological grandmother," Diana continued, her voice shaking slightly. "Your adoptive parents allowed me to be in your life for a short time. Until they stopped me from seeing you, that is."

A flash of anger surged through me.

"Why did my birth parents give me up?"

"They didn't. Well, at least not your mother." Diana's eyes welled with tears. "Your birth mother, my beautiful Deirdre, died shortly after you were born."

I closed my eyes and remembered a dream I used to have when I was younger. It had been so many years, it was barely a memory at all at this point. But when I was around six or seven I saw flashes of a woman's smile in my dreams, and possibly amber eyes like mine and Diana's.

My own throat tightened with emotion now as I fought hard to recall anything about my birth mother at all.

"How?" I choked.

"I've never been able to prove it," Diana said in a low, threatening growl. "But I'm convinced that your birth father killed her."

"What?!"

The room spun around me in dizzying circles. All of this information was too much. Too heavy.

"He was a young man of the local Christian church," she continued in a scathing tone. "He came to our front door one day and Deidre answered. She enjoyed debating religion with the Christians and especially enjoyed flirting with him. She thought she was bringing him away from the church and maybe he thought he could convert her, I don't know. But they became involved, and she got pregnant."

Diana gripped my hand so hard I nearly yelped from pain. Her eyes carried a far-away look as she continued her story.

"Deidre saw the good in everyone. She wanted them to raise you and be a family. But he didn't care about you or her. His reputation would be tarnished forever if he had a child out of wedlock and with a filthy heathen? Well, that was just icing on the cake. He was desperate for her to end the pregnancy but she wouldn't. He tried bribes, threats, promises, but she wouldn't budge. As her belly got bigger, he got even worse."

Diana's eyes returned to focus on me and she pressed a hand to my cheek.

"Aside from the stress he gave her, her pregnancy with you was extremely healthy and easy. Nothing at all was wrong until she reached thirty-three weeks. Then she got incredibly sick. She started losing weight. One day she passed out and was rushed to the hospital."

Two tears rolled down Diana's cheeks but she smiled joyously at me.

"You were born seven weeks premature but by all accounts, you looked full-term. The doctors had never seen such a strong, healthy preemie before. Deidre was so worried about you but you were the last pure source of happiness in her life."

Grief filled my chest as I listened to my grandmother speak, watching the scene play out like a movie in my mind. How utterly unfair to have my mother taken away so cruelly. I felt heartbroken for a woman whose blood flowed in my veins, but who I barely knew.

"She passed a week later from an infection that went septic but not before that God-fearing sperm donor showed up," Diana spat. "He made a convincing show of being the doting father, actually holding you and he even signed the birth certificate. But the moment Deidre died, he turned around and adopted you out to a couple from the church."

Diana shook her head as she reached for the bottle of wine. "It was like he *knew* she would die. I don't know what he did but that coward didn't care what would happen. As long as he remained in good standing with *them*. Pathetic."

"He wouldn't let you adopt me?" I asked, still bewildered by everything I just heard. "I mean, don't they try to place kids with family first?"

"He was legally your father so the decision was up to him," Diana said sadly as she filled both of our cups. "I'm sure the adoption agency suggested it but he told all kinds of lies about how I was unfit to raise you. They already knew what we were so that put me on shaky ground from the start. I fought tooth and nail just to be able to visit you. To be honest, I'm surprised they allowed that for as long as they did."

"Di— grandma," I said, wrapping my hands around my drink as I tried to prepare for the information that was still to come.

"Yes, love?" she beamed at me.

"What do you mean by what we were?" I asked. "Why did he call my mom a filthy heathen? Just because she wasn't Christian?"

Her face fell as she blinked at me.

"My gods, Deja. Do you really not know?" She cupped my chin in her hand as she stared deeply into my eyes as if searching for something.

"Know what?"

The left side of her mouth ticked up into a smirk.

"That we're witches."

9
DEJA

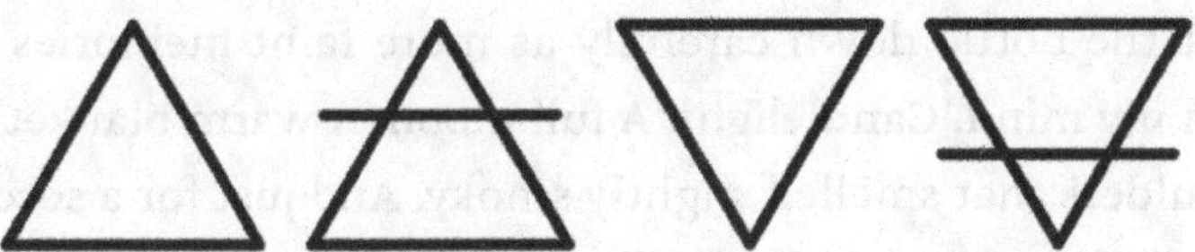

"Come again?"

Diana's smirk spread into a full-on grin.

"We are witches, Deja."

She might as well have turned into an eight-foot-tall man with a long, dark beard and said, *"Yer a wizard, Harry."*

"What... do you mean?"

I must have been misunderstanding her. She couldn't have possibly meant that in the traditional sense of the word.

"This is what I mean."

Diana brought her hand in front of her face and rotated her wrist. Nothing happened at first. Then a flash of movement caught my eye, and I nearly jumped out of my skin when the wine bottle levitated into mid-air.

"What the hell!"

Diana flicked her wrist in a downward motion and the bottle tipped over, pouring more wine into my glass first and then hers. With another wrist flick, the bottle returned upward and gently settled on the coffee table.

My heart pounded like a war drum in my chest, my ears, everywhere. *How could this be possible?*

I snatched the bottle off the table, looking for a fishing line or something at the top or bottom that would explain what the ever-living *fuck* I just saw.

"Magic is real, Deja," Diana said calmly. "I think deep down you've always known that, despite your adoptive parents trying all they could to suppress your abilities."

I set the bottle down carefully as more faint memories flashed through my mind. Candlelight. A full moon. A warm blanket around my shoulders that smelled slightly smoky. And just for a second, red tendrils curling through the air like miniature fireworks.

"You showed me witch... stuff when I was little," I said. "You tried to teach me."

"You can say witchcraft dear," Diana chuckled. "But yes, I showed you basic spells and rituals in the precious little time I had with you. It was difficult, however. They never left me alone with you. But I couldn't let them erase your history. This is your birthright, these are your gifts." She looked at me sadly. "After they moved and kept me away from you, I see they tried as hard as they could to do just that."

I slumped back against the couch, utterly speechless and overwhelmed.

"So... that. What you just did." I waved my hand around, imitating how she picked up the wine bottle and poured without touching it. "You're telling me I can do that?"

"Oh yes. And much more, with training and practice." Diana said warmly.

"Did you use magic to find me?"

"In a sense," she said. "Witches related by blood or marriage can feel each other's power across great distances. It's a magical signature, of sorts. Yours was always unusually strong. Deidre and I felt yours when you were still in her womb. I imagine that's how you were so healthy even when she was terribly sick. But after your adopted parents prevented me from seeing you, it became harder to sense you."

Diana let out a shuddering sigh and placed a hand over her heart.

"It absolutely broke my heart. They were shoving their oppressive religion down your throat to try to erase the magical part of you. And there was nothing I could do. But as long as I sensed your magical signature, however weak it was, I held out hope that I would see you again."

Her eyes brightened as she looked at me.

"And last year, it grew stronger than ever before! I saw you in my mind as a grown, beautiful, independent woman."

"That was when I left," I said quietly. "That was when I realized I could never believe the things that they wanted me to."

In some wild, completely illogical way, it all made sense to me.

"Those feelings and images I got when you first touched my hand," I said. "That was your magical signature."

"Yes! You're catching on quickly, my dear." Diana beamed proudly at me. "If I'm not nearby and you picture my face in your mind, you'll feel those sensations again. How strongly you feel them depends on how near or far away I am."

I nodded slowly. Questions would have been flying from my mouth and racing across my mind if I hadn't been so dumbfounded.

Diana patted my hand affectionately.

"Thank you for the wine, dear. I know this news has been overwhelming, so I'll leave you for now to digest it all."

I held onto her hand as she stood, feeling internally like a four-year-old child again. Now that the only true parental figure in my life had returned, I wasn't ready to say goodbye yet.

"Do you have somewhere to stay?" I asked.

"Oh yes, dear. My old bones can still look after myself," she said with a wink. "I'm staying with my old friend, Minerva."

"Minerva? The tarot reader?" I blinked. "She's a witch, too?"

"That old bitty knew you were my baby girl the moment she saw you," Diana laughed. "She's quite clever, using her magic in such a way that makes regular humans *ooh* and *ahh* but doesn't raise any alarms."

I walked Diana reluctantly to the door, where she gave me the warmest, comforting hug imaginable and a kiss on the cheek.

She sighed as she pulled away and gave me a look that I couldn't read.

"There's still so much to tell you, dear. And I'll forewarn you now, not all of it is good."

I opened my mouth to ask, desperate to know despite being over-loaded with information already.

But she turned and walked nimbly down the flight of stairs, calling over her shoulder, "Til next time, my beautiful granddaughter."

I closed the door softly and turned around, pressing my back against the wood and letting all the air out of my lungs as I closed my eyes.

Did that conversation really just happen?

When I opened my eyes again, the now-empty wine bottle sat on the coffee table as if taunting me.

I stared at it, concentrating hard. I pictured it floating off the table in my mind. Nothing happened, so I gestured with my hand like Diana did.

The bottle promptly shot straight up toward the ceiling and shattered on impact.

"Agh, fuck!" I cried, shielding my face from the shower of green glass.

"Well, now I know not to try magic unsupervised," I grumbled as I searched for a broom to sweep up the mess.

After cleaning my floors and ceiling, I got ready for bed despite knowing my brain was on overdrive about well, everything.

I settled in with my covers up to my chin and closed my eyes, deciding to try one last magical thing. I pictured Diana's face in my mind, imagining every detail as if she was still sitting with me.

Immediately I felt the effects of her magical signature. The warmth and comfort of family, true family, swept over me. Rather than a chilly San Francisco night, I felt like I was basking in sunlight.

Feeling Diana's protective, maternal power over me lulled me into a deep sleep, where the dreams that waited weren't so comforting.

A huge, black raven sat on my windowsill and looked at me. Then it opened its beak and said, "You still have no idea what you are."

10
DEJA

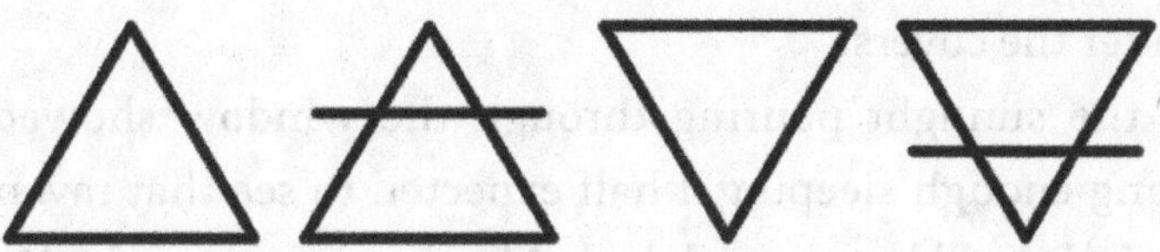

Hot breath rasped against my neck, eliciting an arch from me as teeth and tongue dragged across my sensitive skin. A rough hand cupped me between my legs as if trying to smother the fire down there, but it only ignited hotter and with a needy ache.

Two more hands cupped my breasts, pulling on my achingly sensitive nipples as another mouth kissed the valley between them.

A moan rumbled from deep in my throat before another tongue snaked into my mouth, muffling my sounds and demanding a kiss I couldn't stop myself from returning.

I saw nothing but felt everything.

Hands and mouths glided across every inch of me, never stopping. There could have been two or two hundred, all with the sole focus of pleasing my body.

"Deja," one mouth growled possessively against my throat.

"Who are you?" I moaned, barely able to breathe with my pulse hammering so hard, my insides so hot and on the verge of exploding.

"We are your legion," another mouth rasped against the shell of my ear. "Your Unholy Trinity."

Thump.

"Ow! Fuck!"

A sharp pain flashed through my head and elbows. Darkness suddenly turned to blindingly bright light as I squinted and fought to get my bearings.

Embarrassment filled me as I realized I was on my bedroom floor, tangled up in the sheet. Even though no one was around, my face reddened with shame and I wanted nothing more than to dive back under the covers.

But the sunlight pouring through the window showed that I spent long enough sleeping. I half expected to see that raven sitting on my windowsill but no such luck. My alarm clock read 9:15 am and I struggled to my bedsheet-bound feet in a panic.

"Wait. It's Sunday," I said out loud to the empty room

The shop was closed on Sunday. My one day off a week.

I collapsed back into bed, still breathless at the vivid sensations of my dream. My fingertips lightly dragged over my neck and down my chest. I could still feel their nibbling at me, their tongues and lips teasing and kissing me.

Even with all the recent strange dreams I'd been having recently, this felt different.

Almost like a memory.

Those kisses and many pairs of hands felt almost familiar. Like they belonged to someone, or *someones* I'd slept with many times before.

But how was that possible? I went to college and partied a little but never got that adventurous.

I may have been awkward with guys but I was no virgin, much to my parents' disappointment. Or adopted parents, I should say. It was still strange to think of them like that, although it made more sense since last night.

"Oh yeah, that's right," I said again to the empty room. "I'm a witch."

If my bedroom was impressed with that notion, it didn't tell me so.

Rising from bed, I padded barefoot across the cool floorboards to make my first cup of tea of the day. The shards of broken wine glass in the trash bin provided proof that last night was in fact, not one of my weird dreams.

Before I knew it, I found myself humming some random tune as I danced around my kitchen. Sunny mornings were so rare in San Francisco and my whole apartment glowed with sunlight at that moment. How could I not relish and enjoy it?

I opened the window for some fresh air, pausing to admire my small herb garden on the windowsill.

"Ugh, goddamn squirrels," I cursed under my breath. My Thai basil plant had been uprooted again by the neighborhood rodents, probably emboldened by my neighbors who enjoyed feeding them. All that remained of my majestic plant was a sad, chewed-off stem sticking two inches out of the soil.

"Poor little guy," I murmured, gently pinching the ragged stem between my thumb and forefinger. It was my favorite herb to cook with and I even grew the thing from a seed. In its full glory, it stood nearly two feet tall with dense clumps of dark green, fragrant leaves. Maybe it was stupid of me to feel loss for a plant but after carefully pruning and watering it since moving here, I couldn't help but grow attached.

"Whoa, what!"

I yanked my hand back as if it had been burned. While thinking about my basil plant and touching it, a vibrating hum of energy coursed through my fingertips. It almost felt like a spark of electricity, although it felt pleasant and not painful.

Upon closer inspection, my mouth fell open as I saw two tiny leaf buds forming on the stem, which now looked healed from the ragged squirrel bites.

My eyes darted back and forth from my fingers to the plant,

trying to make sense of what just happened. And then a giggle bubbled up from my chest.

"Magic," I whispered.

Cautiously I reached out to touch the plant once more, picturing it again as full, lush, and fragrant with that distinct basil flavor in my mind.

Immediately the stem began growing taller and the two tiny leaf buds rolled out before my eyes into perfect, mature basil leaves.

My laughter was downright victorious and maybe even maniacal, but I didn't care. The stem continued to grow upwards and more leaves sprouted along its length. It was like watching a time-lapse video but this was real. *I* was doing this, right now.

I pulled my hand away after nearly a minute and just stared in amazement at the full, luscious plant that stood where the sad little stem once was. The leaves were larger and more vibrant than ever before and *mmm, that fresh basil smell.* I considered myself a pretty good herb gardener and yet none of my careful pruning, watering, and fertilizing before made this plant look as glorious as less than a minute of magic.

Who knows how long I just sat there, staring at my basil plant. A low rumble from my stomach knocked me out of my trance as I brought a hand to my belly.

"I guess witches aren't immune to hunger," I said.

I ran back to my room and quickly threw on clean clothes and ran a brush through my hair before snatching my keys and practically dancing out of my apartment and down the stairwell.

Joy filled my chest as I stepped out onto the street. The smell of salty ocean and taco trucks hit my nose. Seagulls screeched overhead and tourists gazed at everything with open-mouthed gawks. Everything seemed to hum and vibrate with a new sense of energy now. I couldn't contain the grin on my face as I soaked it all in.

I felt like I had been blind all my life, and now I could truly see.

11

DEJA

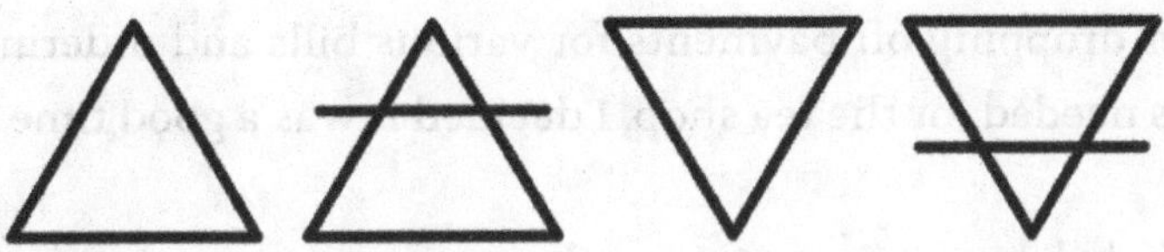

Sensory overload? Only the biggest understatement of the year.

Walking around San Francisco with my new magic-colored glasses on seemed to heighten every smell, taste, and even my vision. Just the awareness of my newfound magical abilities seemed to flip a switch in my brain. Forget the five senses. I felt like I had at least ten.

I saw people's auras as I walked by them in every color and range of brightness imaginable. If I concentrated I could get a sense of their personalities and what they were feeling in that moment. Some were incredibly intense, others barely noticeable.

The frustrated businessman talking sharply on his cellphone was surrounded by a deep red hue, with flecks of black and tightly coiled tension around him.

The young girl with large sunglasses and headphones in her ears carried no tension at all, and a sparkling halo swirled around her with dashes of pink and purple.

I must have looked like the most shameless tourist possible with my head swiveling back and forth, openly gawking at people. For the first few hours of my outing, it was completely overwhelming.

I could taste the labor of love and authenticity in my breakfast burrito. I saw sound vibrating through the air, everything from the musician on the street to freeway traffic, in a range of colors.

By early afternoon, I felt more acclimated to my newly discovered surroundings. Nothing was dulled or tuned out, but I seemed better focused and able to get my errands done.

After dropping off payments for various bills and ordering more supplies needed for the tea shop, I decided it was a good time to grab a drink.

As if led by instinct, I turned a corner to a quiet street and approached a building I never saw before. Classical red brick, crawling ivy, a heavy wooden door, and a patio with a wrought-iron gate gave it a timeless look.

In this neighborhood, *Triple Moon Pub* looked unassuming, like it had always been there and always belonged in that spot. I had a feeling however, that before Diana's visit last night, I would have never known it existed.

The air hummed and practically crackled with the strongest concentration of magic I felt yet as I pulled open the front door.

I blinked a few times to adjust to the dim, flickering light. After a moment I realized candles were the only light source. A massive chandelier the size of a small car hung from the ceiling, but rather than light bulbs, small flames flickered from each point and cast shifting shadows.

A long wooden bar stretched toward the back of the room on my right side, painted dark and polished to a high shine. Candles sat atop the bar spaced about six inches apart.

Despite the entire place being bathed in soft, flickering candle-light, not a single drop of wax covered the floor or bar.

On the left side of the room were seating areas with plush, red couches and low tables. A few groups of patrons sat around them, talking and drinking, and their auras took my breath away.

So much energy crackled around them like sparks of lightning. The colors were much deeper and vibrant than any of the non-magical humans I saw walking down the street.

And even more, I felt an unspoken comfort by being around these people. A kinship of sorts.

These are my people. Witches, I realized.

I strode up to the bar, which was mostly empty except for a few patrons. The bartender, a handsome middle-aged man with a salt and pepper goatee, eyed me curiously.

"Welcome, cradle witch," he greeted. "What'll you have?"

I blinked. "What did you call me?"

He smirked and let out a huff of laughter.

"You've just come into your powers. Your aura is brimming with excitement and wonder, like a baby experiencing the world for the first time."

"That's accurate," I allowed, checking out the liquor selection behind him. Most of it looked pretty standard— the expected brands of vodkas, whiskeys, gins, tequilas, and so on one would see in any bar. But on a separate shelf, candles flickered densely around an assortment of dark glass bottles. They had no labels except for rough symbols that appeared to be drawn in chalk.

I drummed my fingers on the bar, my curiosity piqued about trying some magical mixology but much like a child in a very adult world, it would probably be best to do so under trusted supervision.

"Gin and tonic, please," I requested.

The bartender nodded and proceeded to scoop my ice and pour my Tanqueray into a mixing glass with his hands. No magic involved that I could see.

Just as I opened my mouth to ask why, the mixer levitated into midair and shook itself violently. The ice clanged against the metal mixing cup faster than my eye could see and then it stopped abruptly.

As if it was the most normal thing in the world, the bartender grabbed the levitating mixer and proceeded to pour my drink.

"Thanks," I said a little uneasily. "I'm still not used to seeing that."

"You'll become desensitized," he said with a chuckle. "Lots of folks don't grow into their magic until adulthood. I was twenty-one myself."

"Well that makes me feel better," I mused with the straw between my teeth. In two more years I'd be thirty.

At that moment, something in the air changed.

The corners of my vision darkened like looking through a tunnel, then went back to normal again. But I felt a familiar thick, heavy presence in the air that stood my smallest hairs on end and a dull throb between my legs.

My breath stopped in my chest and I *knew*. I could feel them nearby.

Looking around the bar, no one else seemed to feel what I did. The bartender had gone off to chat with someone else and all other customers continued talking and drinking like normal. But for some reason, my breath felt stolen from my lungs and my heart crashed against my ribs. If I hadn't been sitting in a barstool, I was certain my knees would buckle like a baby deer.

The front door pushed open and three sinfully hot men walked in, swaggering like a biker gang that laughed and shot back whiskey as they rode through Hell.

Ash and Sal swept their gazes across the room but Raum looked directly at me and winked. His raven tattoo flexed under the corded muscles of his forearm.

You still have no idea what you are.

I took a deep breath and downed more of my drink.

The dreams, the response of my body and the overwhelming presence of them. All of it was too much to be coincidental.

Somehow I knew these guys were connected to me. They had answers. And I was about to find out what they knew.

12

SALMAC

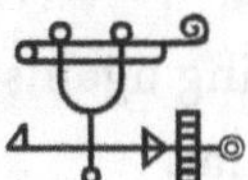

She looked just as ravishing as the first time I saw her.

Not under the goat head at that party but the very first time, however many millennia ago that was. She'd been naked and seductive at Ash's side, with his serpent draped around her shoulders.

Now in the witch's bar, she looked different but so much the same. The same amber eyes, the same wicked, beautiful mouth. My black heart ached for her touch. My fingers itched to spear through her hair as I caught those seductive lips in a kiss.

But I had to wait. I had to do this right or we could lose her forever.

I hated waiting more than anything. And as a demon thousands of years old, it never got easier.

"So you've finally found the place," Raum observed as he slid into the barstool next to Deja, smiling that pretty boy grin as he always did. "I take it you've learned some things."

"I only found out last night," Deja admitted, her eyes flickering nervously at his close proximity. My throat tightened. I had to remember we were essentially strangers to her.

"So I take this to mean you three are witches, too?" she asked, swiveling around in her seat to look at all of us. "Or warlocks or wizards? Whatever the male titles are."

Ash cast a silent glance between Raum and I. We both gave subtle nods in understanding, although my fist clenched at my side in frustration. She was here, wasn't she? She knew and acknowledged this world of magic existed. We didn't have to treat her like a delicate Christian flower. Why did we have to keep this going at a snail's pace?

"Not exactly," I said, leaning against the bar on the other side of her. "But our abilities are similar."

I began to draw her sigil in midair, knowing she likely wouldn't recognize it. Like a bright red pen, my finger left streaks of sparkling red light floating in the air in front of her. She blinked at the symbol, my magic casting a red glow on her face before it gently faded into nothing.

"What did that symbol mean?" she asked.

Ash's aura sparked and crackled around me in warning.

"Nothing," I answered and abruptly tore my gaze away from her. "Hey, who do we have to fuck up the ass to get a drink around here?" I yelled.

Deja giggled while my two brothers let out a mutual, disapproving groan. They acted like they hated my loud, boisterous antics but if it weren't for me, their immortal lives would be an eternity of boredom.

The bartender, who'd been purposely avoiding us, didn't bother hiding his scowl as he reluctantly came over.

"Aw, don't look so happy to see us, Micah," Raum chided.

"What do the three of you want with her?" Micah snarled, jerking his head toward Deja.

"None of your fucking business," I hissed, the rage already boiling within me. "We're here for drinks and conversation. One of those is already covered. So why don't you do your job and make those drinks happen, witch-boy?"

"Sal," Ash barked with a warning tone. "Back off."

I didn't realize I'd stood and leaned menacingly over the bar. Micah still scowled at me but had backed away, pressing his cowardly spine against the shelves of bottles.

"Calm yourself," Ash told me again, then to Micah, "Make those drinks, the usuals. Just keep them coming and we won't be any trouble."

"Wow. Are you guys always such assholes to bartenders?" Deja shot me a disapproving look, her nostrils flaring.

A tight sense of yearning squeezed in my chest. Even now she wasn't afraid to challenge me, to rival my hot temper with her own. I demolished just as many cities as I'd built just because the wrong fucker pissed me off. I made the fiercest warriors cry for their mothers and five-star generals piss themselves with my wrath, but she never flinched.

No, this woman could order me to drop to my knees and kiss each of her toes. I would do it happily and wait for more. All she had to do was ask.

"No, just him," Ash said, clapping a hand down on my shoulder. "He needs us to keep him in line."

"Fuck you," I retorted.

She was the only one who could keep me in line and we all knew it. We'd been all out of sorts, unbalanced and volatile since she was taken from us. And now here she was, sitting so close to me I could wrap my arms around her and pull her to my chest.

But I kept my hands to myself and merely gazed at her gorgeous neck and cheekbones.

"So what have you learned?" Raum asked as our drinks finally arrived. "Have you cast any spells yet?"

Sneaky fucker. He already knew. Damn his ability to see into the past and future. Although it did prove useful at times, he often kept information to himself for the sheer fact that he could.

"I'm not really sure. I mean, I don't think so," she said, her voice full of uncertainty. "I mean, I broke a wine bottle by trying to make it move and I grew a basil plant. Oh and I can see people's auras but that's it so far."

"That's already a lot for not even a full day," I said, my temper cooling. "You'll be quite powerful, maybe even a High Priestess before you know it."

"Thanks," she smiled and my cock stiffened in my pants. Lord, it had been so long since I'd been buried inside her.

"It'll take me a while to really come to terms with all this." She wrapped her small hands around her drink. "As you all probably guessed from the way I acted at the party, I'm a recovering Christian. Although I never truly believed, no matter how much my adopted parents shoved it down my throat. That at least makes sense now."

"Ex-Christians are our favorite," Ash said with a faint smile. "It's always a pleasure to bring them to our side."

"And which side is that?" Deja challenged.

"The side of truth and knowledge," Raum said, raising his drink in the air. "Where curiosity and research are encouraged, not blind faith."

"The side that empowers women when the Christian God wants to enslave them," I added, my eyes trailing longingly over her curves. "And gave birth to the first witches."

"Have you figured it out yet, Deja?" Ash's eyes glowed excitedly.

She hesitated before speaking.

"You said that gigantic goat head was your Lord. Is that true or were you joking?"

"Completely true," Raum chuckled. "He likes to take on the form of freakishly large animals and see how long before humans can hunt Him down. He particularly likes black goats because of their association with him already."

Deja sucked in a breath as she began connecting the dots in her mind.

"So your Lord is..."

"Lucifer," the three of us said in unison.

Her head swiveled slowly as she looked at all of us in turn. First me, then Ash, then finished on Raum.

"Which makes you all..."

The three of raised our glasses, saluting Him as He surely watched this reuniting moment between us.

"Demons."

13
DEJA

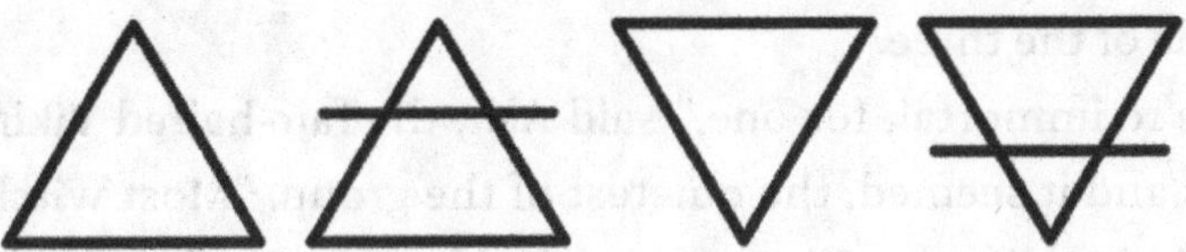

I thought that word would strike fear and terror in my heart the moment they said it. But it barely affected me.

In fact I felt strangely comfortable and safe with these three hot as sin and, most likely, dangerous men. With the way the bartender steered cleared unless absolutely necessary, and how other people snuck nervous glances around ever since they walked in, all signs pointed to bad news.

Except for when Raum came to my shop, this was only my second time talking to any of them. And yet I couldn't shake the feeling that I knew them for years. There was a familiarity with the way they protectively encircled me, almost like bodyguards. And I couldn't deny how sexy and flattering it felt to have the undivided attention of three hot, rough-looking guys.

It was like an invisible barrier lifted the moment I learned I was a witch and I could relax around these demons, however powerful and bad they were.

But it hadn't even been twenty-four hours since I found out my truth. I didn't truly know who to trust or what to say. The witches here obviously had some bad blood with these three. Was it just them or all demons in general? Until I talked to Diana again and found out more, I had to stay cautious.

"So what's the difference between demons and witches?" I asked.

Sal, the hot-tempered one with green eyes sitting to my left, snorted and nearly choked on his drink while Ash and Raum chuckled.

"Sorry, that's just an adorable question," teased Raum, his dark eyes twinkling. I was quickly getting the sense that he was the flirtatious one of the three.

"We're immortal, for one," said Ash, the fair-haired Viking with icy eyes and it seemed, the quietest of the group. "Most witches still have a limited lifespan like non-magical humans do."

"Most?" I raised an eyebrow.

"There are always exceptions," he added with a wink.

"You said demons gave birth to the first witches?" I said as I turned to Raum, willing myself not to stare at his raven tattoo. "What do you mean by that?"

He exchanged a look with Ash, which was subtle and quick but I still caught it. I kept my face neutral but made a mental note of the gesture. They apparently were also being cautious about what to tell me. But was that to protect me or themselves?

"It's a long story," he said, running his hand through his mane of dark hair. "And I'd rather not give a long, boring history lesson right now."

"What would you rather do?" I asked.

He looked surprised and then pleased as my pulse heightened to a new frequency.

Oh shit. I'm flirting back with him now, aren't I?

"I'd rather learn about you, miss Deja," he said in a low growl, leaning in closer to me.

His sharp masculine scent filled my nose like an intoxicating elixir. With Sal and Ash watching as he got close enough to kiss me, a sharp thrill jolted up my spine. I was no closer to finding out what these three wanted, but right then my body wanted Raum and didn't care if the others got a show.

And just as my eyelids fluttered closed, he pulled back with a *gotcha!* smile on his face.

My face felt like a furnace as Ash groaned and shook his head while Sal clicked his tongue disapprovingly.

"You can't lead a woman on like that, Raum," Sal chided.

"You're the worst." Ash sounded like a disappointed father.

"Sorry, but I'm not that easy," Raum smirked with a wink, indicating he was not sorry at all.

"Well, if you're gonna play games, might as well make it interesting," I said, determined to not let him make a fool of me. "Loser takes shots."

"And what game are we playing?" Sal asked, his interest piqued. "Spin the bottle?"

"How about two truths and a lie?" I suggested. "You each tell me three facts about yourselves and I have to guess which is the lie."

"Now this will be easy," Ash mused with a rare smile on his serious face.

"How about you go first, Mr. Confident?" I challenged.

"Alright."

I blinked and he was suddenly much, much closer. His hands rested on each side of my barstool, effectively caging me in. His icy eyes were ravenous and I wondered if he aimed to finish what Raum started.

"I was the serpent who tempted Eve in the Garden of Eden," he said, his lips inches away from mine. "I'm in the first hierarchy of Hell alongside Lord Lucifer and Beelzebub. And it was I who taught mathematics to humankind." He leaned back with a smug expression and crossed his massive arms over his chest, biceps flexing. "So which is the lie, Deja?"

I thought for a few moments.

"You did not teach mathematics to humankind," I said. "The ancient Egyptians developed that themselves."

"Wrong," he said victoriously. "The ancient Sumerians of Mesopotamia actually developed it much earlier than the Egyptians." He slapped a hand on his muscular chest. "And you can thank yours truly for that."

"So much for no ancient history lessons," Raum murmured.

"Your turn then," I said, turning to him. "Let me try for two out of three."

"Happily," he grinned. "The Northern Germanic people once regarded me as their god, Odin. I've stolen billions worth of treasure and valuables from kings. And," he stared at me with those dark intense eyes as his voice lowered to a near-whisper. "I can see the past and the future."

"Okay, that last one is definitely false," I said. "No one can have that kind of power."

"Ah." Behind me, Sal made a pained hissing noise. "Wrong again, Deja."

"Goddamnit!" I had already lost my two out of three and would have to take the shot. "Well I might as well hear from you, Sal," I said, turning to him now. "It's really fascinating learning about all of you this way."

"Sure," he said with a casual shrug and paused for a moment to think of his two truths and lie to tell me.

"I've been in love with one woman for at least seven thousand years," he began, his emerald eyes locking onto mine. "I'm a Grand Marquis of Hell with fifty legions of demons under my command. And I fucking love Hostess cupcakes."

I took my time to think carefully, wanting to get at least one answer right. But the fact of the matter was I still barely knew these guys. And if they truly were immortal, that gave them many lifetimes of truths and lies to tell me.

"You have not been in love with one woman for that long," I said finally. "I don't even know how it's possible to love one person for thousands of years."

"Are you kidding me?" Sal cried. "Hostess cupcakes taste like ox shit dipped in sugar and stuffed with bat semen!"

Fucking hell. That meant I epically failed all three rounds. So much for not embarrassing myself.

"I think Deja needs a special shot for this loss," Ash said a little too excitedly. "Micah! We'll take a shot of your cheapest tequila plus salt and a lime."

"Oh God," I groaned, planting my face in my hands. Tequila was definitely not my liquor of choice. Too much of it in college led to some questionable decisions.

"You know how to properly do a tequila shot, right?" Raum asked me, also looking a bit too excited. What exactly did these guys have in mind?

"Remind me," I said bitterly, dreading the incoming explanation.

"First you lick the salt," Sal said with a light brush of his fingers against my elbow. A surprisingly gentle touch for such a hot-tempered demon. "Then you swallow the tequila in one gulp. The last step is sucking on the lime wedge to chase it."

"Since you lost to all three of us," Ash said. "It's only fair that you do the steps with each of us."

"What do you mean with each of you?" I demanded suspiciously.

All three of them only grinned as Micah came over with the shot, lime, and salt as they requested.

"Remember the order is lick, swallow, suck," said Raum with a sly wink.

My eyes grew to the size of saucers as they each took a component of the shot and I realized what they were prompting me to do.

Sal shook a generous helping of salt into the space above his right collarbone, jutting his shoulder forward so the salt could have a place to sit.

Meeting his emerald gaze and refusing to back down, I leaned forward and swiped my tongue along the coating of salt. His skin tasted warm and he let out the softest of sighs as I licked him.

Next, I turned to Raum who held the shot of tequila. He simply held the glass in his hand and cupped the nape of my neck, prompting me to lean my head back. I did as he instructed and he poured the alcohol over my salt-coated tongue, gently brushing my lips with his fingers as he did.

I swallowed the burning liquid and searched for my reprieve, the lime.

Which Ash held between his teeth.

I leaned forward, eager for the chaser to quell the burning in my throat while my body hummed with desire for him, for all three of them.

My lips just barely brushed his as I took the lime wedge in my teeth. He released it gently as I bit into the sour flesh and sucked the bitter, acidic juice.

"Well now," I said as I placed the chewed-up lime wedge on the bar. "You can't say I'm a sore loser after that."

14
DEJA

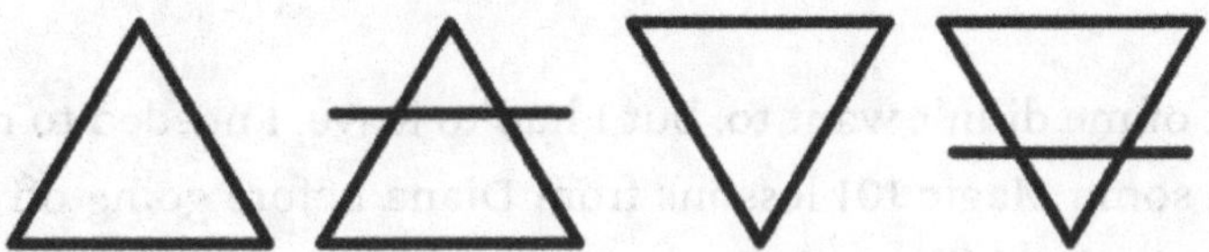

The sex dreams I had that night were much naughtier than the night before.

I was still bathed in complete darkness, unable to see a thing, but I felt the heat of bare skin, heard low moans, and felt sensations inside of me and across every inch of my body as if it was really happening.

One mouth kissed me with need and passion while another grazed the sensitive peaks of my nipples with its teeth. And one more mouth devoured my vulva like it was its last meal.

My hands searched the darkness and grabbed hard arms and shoulders. My fingers skimmed across chests and torsos like hot, rigid brick walls. As I bucked and cried out against the mysterious mouth between my legs, my hands reached down and grabbed a handful of thick hair.

But no amount of blinking, moving, or screaming procured any light, not even a sliver of detail of whoever these lovers were. They might as well had been invisible.

I woke up gasping, covered in a sheen of sweat, and my pulse jackhammering.

"Urgh," I moaned in frustration, flopping back down on the bed as I gripped the sheets in my fists. At least I didn't fall out of bed this time.

I said goodbye to the three demons last night not long after taking my loser shot. Every touch between each of them had been so uniquely intimate and sexy. They all looked at me with such hunger, I could taste the tension in the air. It was suffocating and empowering at the same time, not to mention amplified by all the magic in the air.

Part of me didn't want to, but I had to leave. I needed to regroup and get some Magic 101 lessons from Diana before going off like an unsupervised toddler again.

I swung my feet to the floor, took a deep breath and closed my eyes to think of her again. Within seconds, warmth and nostalgia wrapped around me like a comforting hug. It was becoming increasingly easier to think of her as my family, rather than a stranger I just met. My pent-up sexual frustration subsided, and I started the day with a smile on my face.

I wondered if she knew when I reached out for her magic signature. It was the only form of contact I had with her since she didn't leave a number or say when she'd be back.

When she arrived at the shop a few minutes before closing, her bright eyes and cheeky smile told me enough.

"You rang for me, dear?" she said with a wink as she approached me.

"Hi grandma," I answered, rounding the counter and greeting her with a hug. She seemed a bit taken aback by my affection but wrapped around me tightly, beaming.

"Grandma?" Nona poked her head out from behind the curtain leading to the back of the shop. "I didn't know you had family in town, Deja!"

"Neither did I until recently," I said. I made introductions and offered my grandmother some tea.

"I would love some chamomile if you have it, dear," she said, settling into an armchair by the window.

"Chamomile tea? Why would this shop have anything like that?" I winked. "Coming right up."

While I prepared Diana's brew, Nona and I finished the rest of the closing duties before we high-fived over another successful day and she punched out.

"Nice to meet you," she said to Diana as she rolled her fixed-gear bicycle to the front door. "We'll have to do a proper tea sometimes."

"Likewise, dear. Sounds lovely," Diana called after to her and then to me, "What a sweet girl. And a hard worker too. Did you perform a spell to find her?" she teased.

"Hah, I literally ran into her my first day in this city," I said, settling in the chair across from her with my own tea. "There had to be some magic involved because I couldn't imagine anyone better."

"That's the beautiful thing. Even for masterful witches, magic still works in mysterious ways." Diana blew on the steam rising from her teacup and sipped it gingerly. "So have you noticed anything different about the world since we last talked?"

"Oh, have I!" I exclaimed, quickly launching into the story of my outing yesterday, with all my senses heightened and the ability to see people's auras and feel their moods. I even included the bit about breaking the wine glass after she left, which she had a good laugh at, and growing my basil plant back from a chewed stem.

The only part I left out was my adventure to the Triple Moon pub and engaging in sexy tequila-shooting with three hot demons while every other witch in the place looked scared or pissed off. I figured asking about demons might be best without any personal stories attached to them already.

"Tell me something, Deja," she began as she took another deep drink of tea.

Oh shit. Can she see right through me? Do I have demon presence in my aura or something?

"Where did you source this chamomile from?" She turned her cup upward and smelled the liquid while swirling it around.

"Um, I grew the plant and dried the flowers myself," I said, slightly puzzled. "Why?"

"Because it's the richest, most flavorful and relaxing cup of chamomile tea I've ever tasted." She grinned at me. "I had my suspicions but this confirms it. You are definitely an Earth witch."

"A what now?"

"All witches draw their power from the four elements— earth, air, water, and fire," she explained, setting her cup and saucer down on the side table. "You can practice and utilize all of them to a degree but most witches have one that is their main source of strength."

"Earth, huh." I pondered that for a moment. "I guess it makes sense for me."

"You have a unique, unbreakable connection with the physical world. Flowers, plants, animals, and all their properties are enhanced by you," she said, gesturing to her teacup.

"Cool. So making a mean cup of tea is a special talent of mine," I said sarcastically.

"Oh Deja, it's so much more than that," Diana declared. "Earth magic is the most powerful for healing. Not just because you have a knack for therapeutic plants and concoctions but your application of magic is very hands-on. So many Earth witches are surgeons, medics, physical therapists, and business owners for that reason."

"Business owners? I kind of get the hands-on thing but what does Earth have to do with owning a business?"

"Well, you poured your blood, sweat, and tears into this place, didn't you?" she asked pointedly.

"Oh yeah. Ten times over," I said, looking around my shop fondly. It wasn't the nicest or the trendiest in town but it kept my lights on and it was mine.

"You reap what you sow, Deja," she said with a wink. "It doesn't have to literally grow from the earth. You took an idea and turned it into something that exists in the physical world. That is Earth magic."

I nodded slowly, trying to absorb what she said like a sponge.

"I think I get it now."

"It'll make more sense as you practice and learn your strengths," she said warmly. "So!" She clapped her hands together once. "Shall we practice some magic?"

15
DEJA

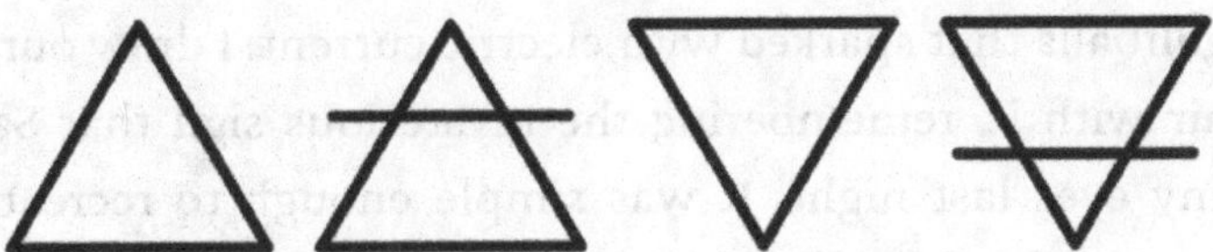

After three hours of practice, I had a splitting headache from focusing so much.

We covered the absolute basics of casting spells—mainly simple visualizations and speaking mantras. Potions and infusions would come later.

I realized very quickly how easily earth-based magic came to me. Diana had me rehydrate dried tea leaves into fully-fleshed pieces that looked like they had just been snipped from the branch, and it was as easy as picturing the plant in my mind.

My weakness was undoubtedly making things levitate, which was apparently an air-based skill. I tried until my head felt like it would burst but either nothing happened or I would totally overdo it and fling the targeted object, usually a teacup, across the room. By the end of the night, my trash can was full of broken ceramic pieces.

Diana told me it was like driving a car. You had to be gentle and get a feel for the vehicle you were driving, not hit the gas and turn the wheel all the way when making a simple turn.

The last thing we tried was power manifestation, which was drawing on the power within you and around you until it became visible in your hands. You could direct it somewhere and fire it off like a weapon, or use it to aid in more complex spells.

Or as my grandmother showed me, you could draw messages or sigils in the air with it. She demonstrated by holding her hands open until two glowing balls of fire hovered inches above her palms. Then like a finger painting, she smeared the orange, glowy magic in the air into the shape of a heart.

When I tried it, my power manifested into green orbs about the size of golfballs that sparked with electric current. I drew our names in the air with it, remembering the mysterious sigil that Sal drew before my eyes last night. It was simple enough to recreate but I didn't dare, at the risk of invoking some crazy demon magic.

"Well done today, dear." Diana patted my cheek affectionately. "It's like working any muscle. You have to keep practicing but also give yourself time to rest."

"Rest sounds great," I groaned while rubbing my temples. Whipping up an herbal migraine salve would've sounded great if my head didn't hurt just thinking about it.

"Poor dear. I'll give you the day off tomorrow," Diana chuckled as she gathered up her spellbooks and returned them to her satchel.

I wrung my hands as I watched her prepare to leave. If I really wanted to know about witch and demon business, there was no better time than now.

"Grandma... I wanted to ask you about something else," I sputtered hesitantly.

"Yes?" She eyed me curiously.

"I guess, um." I rubbed my sore temples again. "What's the deal with demons?"

In the blink of an eye, she was intimidatingly close, towering over me with eyes wide in concern.

"What do you know about demons?" she demanded. "Have any shown themselves to you?"

"Um, yeah," I admitted. "I found the Triple Moon bar last night and ran into a couple there."

"How many?"

"Three." I swallowed nervously. "We just had some drinks and they were flirting. That's all that happened but everyone seemed... weird around them."

Diana's face turned into a twisted scowl as she backed away from me and began pacing the tea shop nervously.

"Do you know what they wanted?" she asked, scrubbing a hand over her face and not looking at me as if trying to figure out some complex puzzle.

"Uh, no. I don't think so," I answered, curious about her reaction. "We just chit-chatted and had some drinks."

"Demons don't interact with our kind unless they want something." She raised her eyes to me as she continued pacing. "They definitely want something from you."

"Like what?" I cried, my voice going shrill. "What would they want from me?"

Diana huffed out a heavy sigh as she finally stopped pacing, looking at me with a grave expression.

"I didn't want to tell you this until later," she said. "But demon auras are very distinct. You can spot a demon when their aura is almost impossibly dark, like a black hole."

"Okay, theirs fit those profiles," I said, not entirely following.

Diana's lips tightened.

"Deja, your aura has had bits and pieces of that kind of darkness since the moment you were born."

The whole room turned to ice and my heart nearly felt like it stopped.

"What does that mean?" I asked, barely above a whisper.

"I fear your birth father consulted a demon to kill your mother," she said just as quietly, her eyes watering. "Instead of letting it kill you, you somehow absorbed that power in the womb. I can't imagine another reason why your aura would be so dark, Deja. And you may have some demon abilities as well."

We stood across from each other in heavy silence as the information sank in. Still, I couldn't understand it.

"So what would they want from me?" I asked.

"I don't know, dear." Diana's expression was grave. "For thousands of years, there has been a long-standing resentment between witches and demons. Whenever Christians have caught wind of any kind of witchcraft, they immediately associate it with the devil when that couldn't be farther from the truth."

Her eyes welled with tears as she looked off to a faraway place.

"Too many innocent witches and non-magical humans have suffered due to mob mentality and fear of the devil. But the true devil worshippers? They don't blink an eye at innocent lives lost."

I wanted to protest, to tell her these three weren't like that. An entire race couldn't be that heartless, could it? But the truth was, I didn't know. They were practically strangers to me and yet every instinct within me wanted to jump to their defense.

Instead, I just said, "How could they not care?"

Diana gave a sad smile.

"The deaths of innocents don't matter to those who are immortal."

16

DEJA

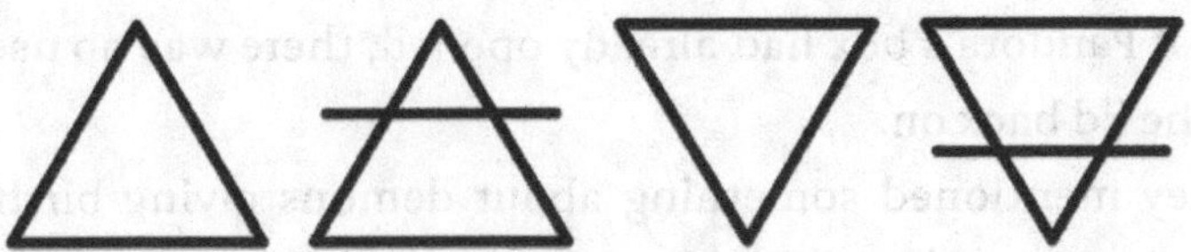

"So on a scale of typical Christian belief to fluffy baby animal," I said, still bewildered by this revelation. "How bad are demons, really?"

Diana sighed heavily, suddenly looking older and far more tired than I perceived her up to this point.

"Generally speaking, they're not all terrible I suppose. They're just like any other people, with some good eggs and some bad. Most have a mixture of both. But," she added sharply. "I'm one of the few witches of my generation with such an open mind. Because of their nonchalance toward the sanctity of life, the general attitude is not so forgiving. "

"What will other witches think of me when they see my aura?" A flash of panic hit me. The thought of being ostracized for something I had no control over made my gut twist into knots.

"Don't worry about that, dear," Diana said, taking my hand. "Dark auras are rare, but many witches do have them due to their family's encounters with demons in past generations. Sometimes they go dormant and reappear after skipping a couple of genera-tions. No one would discriminate against you based on that.

Besides," she added, her tone growing more lighthearted. "Shadow work is a coveted magical skill that few witches can master. You may be able to work with the subconscious and the darker side of magic more easily than others."

Something else gnawed at me and I wrestled with the idea of asking her about it. I remembered how cautious all three of the demons were about what they said to me, and I wondered if I would be better not knowing this particular information.

But if Pandora's box had already opened, there was no use trying to put the lid back on.

"They mentioned something about demons giving birth to the first witches," I said, weighing my words carefully. "Is that true?"

Diana's eyes flashed with such anger that it legitimately frightened me. I wrenched my hand out of her grasp and even backed away.

"No! It's not fucking true," she growled, swearing for the first time since I met her. Her aura suddenly erupted in a fiery halo, growing three times in size and crackling with her fury. Gone was the sweet, encouraging grandmother figure, replaced by the archetype of the scary old hag.

"We draw our power from the natural world, from our Mother Gaia," she declared in a timbre that rattled the window panes. "We respect and honor life at every level. We may have similar powers but we did *not* come from those born of deception and betrayal."

"I'm sorry, grandma," I stuttered, raising my hands in surrender. "I didn't mean to imply anything like that."

Calling her grandma seemed to placate her enough. The anger surrounding her dulled from a blazing inferno to a low roar and her voice softened.

"Be very careful when you talk to demons," she warned. "Chances are every other word out of their mouths is a lie."

I nodded solemnly but she didn't seem convinced.

"I'm serious, Deja," she snapped. "They may be charming and

seductive but they always want something. And if the Christians got one thing right, it's that a deal with the devil is never in your favor, no matter how good it seems."

All the fire seemed to leave her as she let out a long sigh and reached out to touch my cheek. Her fingers were warm with the blazing energy she just held.

"I just found my beautiful granddaughter again after so many years," she said in a mournful voice. "I couldn't bear to lose you again."

"Don't worry about me, grandma," I said earnestly, smiling as I took her hand in mine. "I've taken what you've said to heart. I promise I'll be careful."

Her lighthearted smile returned as she patted my hand.

"Very good, dear. We'll take a break from casting tomorrow but I may be back for another cup of that wonderful chamomile! How much do I owe you for it?"

"What? No," I protested, waving my hand dismissively. "I'm not charging you for tea."

"Deja, you are a businesswoman." She tried to sound stern but a smirk played on her lips. "I may be your grandmother but I don't want any special treatment. I have enjoyed the product of your business and want to pay for it."

"Absolutely not," I insisted. "In fact, here. I have something else for you."

Ignoring her protests, I went behind the counter and pulled open my cooler where I stored my extra homemade tea blends. After rummaging for a minute, I pulled out a vacuum-sealed, quart-sized bag of loose leaf tea.

"This should make you at least a dozen cups, probably more," I said, holding it out to her. "It's a blend of chamomile, lemongrass, and spearmint. All grown and dried myself."

She took the bag as if it were the most precious treasure on earth, tears welling in her eyes as she looked at it. A strange feeling spread throughout my chest, and I wondered if this was how children felt when their parents said they were proud of them.

"Deja, this is work that you did," she said, eyes shimmering as she looked up at me. "Please let me pay you."

"I'll accept free magic lessons as payment," I chuckled, pulling my grandmother into a hug.

"Oh, damn it. Well, I'll just have to corner that sweet employee of yours and shove money in her hand."

"You can try but she's loyal to me," I said with a wink as I walked her to the door. "Or just give it to her as a big tip."

We said our goodbyes and I quickly washed our cups and tidied up the shop before heading home.

The moment I walked through my front door, I collapsed face-down on my couch.

My head still pounded with a dull ache and I had no doubt my body would be sore tomorrow. I felt like I somehow did an intense full-body workout while also studying my ass off for an exam.

It was that exhausting but good feeling. Body spent, brain fried. I did learn a lot and knew I'd sleep like a baby once I took something for my headache.

Something still nagged at me though and I couldn't put my finger on it.

The whole time she talked about demons, I wanted to lash out, to yell at her, *Shut up! You have no idea what you're talking about!*

But then again, neither did I. So why did every instinct within me want to refuse what she was claiming? To defend the demon race against the bias and discrimination, despite knowing nothing about them? I nearly drew blood from my tongue while biting it so hard.

I peeled myself off the couch and stumbled into the bathroom in search for some Tylenol. Once I collapsed into bed, it dawned on me that my search for answers was only leading to even more questions.

DEJA

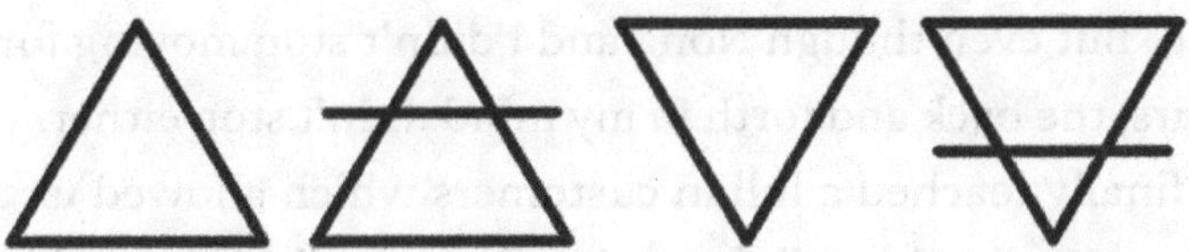

I slept soundly, although a bit disappointed at the lack of sexy shadow visitors in my dreams. I had just started getting used to those.

If I'm actually hoping for kinky sex dreams, I probably really need to get laid.

A resigned sigh escaped me as I sat up in bed and stretched. Light tendrils of soreness traveled along my limbs but nothing hurt too badly.

Diana's warning rattled around in my brain as I showered and got ready for the day ahead. I knew she was trying to protect me but seeing as I was on the cusp of thirty years old, maybe she was overreaching a little?

She spoke to me last night as if I were a rebellious teenager hellbent on spending time with the high school bad boys. Yes, I knew the demons were bad news. Yes, they looked like they belonged on *GQ* covers and carried more charm and seduction than any mortal man had in his pinky finger, but we were all adults, weren't we?

Okay, maybe she had a point.

I couldn't imagine how difficult it was for her to lose her only daughter, then subsequently being cut off from her own grand-daughter. To watch another family raise me and actively try to suppress my natural abilities simply because they couldn't understand it.

If it had been me in her position, I probably would have reacted the same way. I'd do anything to protect the family I thought I'd lost.

Once the tea shop opened and our morning flood of customers poured in, I tried to lose myself in the hustle and bustle of the breakfast rush. But even though Nona and I didn't stop moving for a good two hours, the back and forth in my mind didn't stop either.

We finally reached a lull in customers which allowed us to catch a breather. Until Ash's tall, imposing figure walked through my door and everything in my brain and body came to a screeching halt.

A hunter green V-neck T-shirt stretched across his broad chest and biceps. Two dark lines of a tattoo peaked below his throat before disappearing under his shirt. His signature dark jeans, black leather jacket, and motorcycle boots completed the bad boy look that I wished didn't make me so weak in the knees.

He wore his cool, aloof expression as he approached the counter, although his icy eyes twinkled with mischief. Unlike Raum's gregarious demeanor, he kept whatever emotions he felt behind a mysterious wall. Even his aura, a deep, almost black navy blue, didn't reveal much.

"Morning, Deja," he said in a low rumble.

"Morning, Ash," I replied stiffly, immediately on high alert. Somehow I didn't think he came here to apologize like Raum, which only made me wonder what he really wanted.

Out of the corner of my eye, Nona gaped at him unashamedly. Now that two of the three hot men from the party showed up to my shop, she must have thought I really did have plans for an orgy, although that couldn't be farther from the truth.

"What can I do for you?" I asked him, once again trying to ignore the heat rising in my body.

He lifted one shoulder in a lazy shrug.

"Raum was raving about your place. Thought I'd come check it out." His mouth lifted into a hint of a smirk. "Although I'm not much of a tea drinker."

"Then you're probably wasting your time, seeing as this is a tea shop," I replied with more venom than I had anticipated.

My heart beat out of control and my stomach flip-flopped as an internal war raged within me. I didn't want to lash out and be all bitchy. All I could think about was taking that lime from his mouth, how our lips brushed with a touch that barely resembled a kiss. But if Diana was right and he only wanted to take something from me, I couldn't let myself be seduced by him, no matter how badly my body wanted it too.

Even that part of me pulled in three separate directions as my raw, primal attraction seemed to cycle between all three of them equally.

Ash only seemed amused by my rebuff, however. He stroked his blonde whiskers as if deciding how hard he should spank me for talking out of line.

"Is that any way to talk after we had so much fun the other night?" he said in a lighthearted tone.

A crash came from behind me as Nona dropped something, clearly eavesdropping.

"Fun for you all, maybe. It was impossible for me to win," I shot back.

"But it was your idea," he so kindly reminded me. "And even though you were the loser, it seemed you enjoyed what you received out of the wager."

His handsome face gave away nothing, a steely poker face. Meanwhile, I squirmed, flustered and frustrated by all these hints and jabs and innuendos. Why couldn't anyone just be fucking straight with me?

"Well, now I have the much better idea of not getting involved with the three of you."

Shit! I didn't mean for it to come out sounding like that.

I bit my tongue but it was too late. The innuendo wasn't lost on Ash as he finally revealed a full-on, predatory smile.

He leaned his long, sculpted torso across the counter, resting on his forearms while keeping his eyes glued to mine until our faces were mere inches away. The plywood and Formica counter seemed to tremble under the weight of his power. He could do away with the flimsy barrier between us with a snap of his fingers.

"And what makes you so turned off to the idea, Deja?" he asked, lowering his voice to a sultry murmur that I could practically feel across my skin.

"Well, I don't know you for starters," I said, bristling defensively as I lowered my voice to a hushed whisper. "And it's honestly creepy how you all are always popping up around me since the party, especially because I don't know you and can't protect myself from whatever it is you want."

"Cut the bullshit, Deja." His words sliced through the air as his aura began to crackle with tension. I was certain mine was coiled up and radiating with my heat and frustration too.

"I'm not--"

"Yes, you are." He spoke with the sharpness and authority of a double-edged sword, his eyes burning into mine.

"You're not threatened by us. You feel safe and protected when we're around you. You're relaxed, not a wound up spring like you are now. You enjoy us. And even more, you *want* us."

I opened my mouth to deny it but my throat seemed to constrict and dry out. He could see right through me as if I was naked and bare before him. Who knew if my aura told him or he just knew how to read people but he saw what I was struggling to accept myself.

"Whoever told you not to trust us was not being truthful," he continued, his voice softening with either lust or affection.

"Although witches and ordinary mortals alike have their biases against us."

My grandmother's face flashed through my mind, the tears thick in her eyes as she said, *The deaths of innocents doesn't matter to immortals.*

"Well I can't imagine why that would be the case," I said as coldly as I could muster before turning on my heel and walking away.

I strode past Nona, heading to the very back of the shop for some privacy and air. It felt like I was going to choke on the tension building like a volcano between me and Ash. I just needed a moment to clear my head, catch my breath, and hopefully, he would take the hint and be gone. Then maybe, just maybe, I wouldn't have to deal with this internal tug-of-war anymore and just keep living my life as simply as a witch possibly could.

But no such luck.

The moment I made it to my quiet back office and closed the door, Ash appeared before me. He stood a full head taller than me and regarded me with that cool, aloof look as if silently daring me to kick him out.

I opened my mouth to do just that but before any sound could escape, his lips crashed into mine in a passionate, blood rushing kiss.

18

DEJA

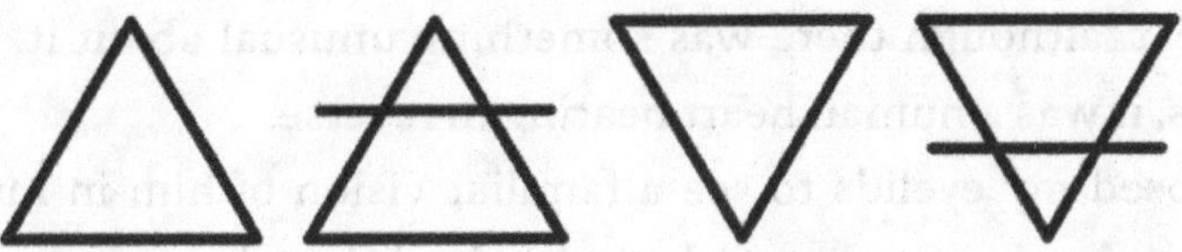

The light spark I felt the other night grew into a roaring inferno. It consumed both of us in an embrace that felt inseparable.

His kiss took my breath away while at the same time seemed to fill my lungs with the coolest, refreshing spring air I ever inhaled.

Fire, ice, lightning. Every force of nature seemed to erupt and course through us as we unleashed the hunger and need we'd been restraining.

I was only vaguely aware that I was sitting on my desk, his hands anchored at my hips as my legs wrapped around his waist.

His mouth felt like it was made for mine, nipping at my lips and caressing my tongue with his like we'd been lovers for centuries. Again I couldn't shake the familiarity like I'd kissed him before so long ago. But I definitely never felt passion or chemistry like this. It was downright magical.

My hand skimmed down the front of his chest until he grabbed it right before I reached where his heart would be.

His mouth broke away from mine abruptly and I gasped as I

came up for air. My only coherent thought was wondering if demons actually had hearts.

"You want to know the truth?" he said in a low, husky tone before placing my palm on the left side of his chest. "Close your eyes and see for yourself who I really am."

His skin roared with heat beneath his shirt. Any normal person would have been running a dangerously high fever.

I listened carefully before closing my eyes. He definitely had a heartbeat, although there was something unusual about it. If I had to guess, it was a human heart beating in reverse.

I closed my eyelids to see a familiar vision of him in my mind. Large black wings sprouted from his back in a beautiful, majestic span. The heavy pewter crown on his head sat crookedly and the snake slithered around his muscular shoulders, its forked tongue tasting the air.

My eyes shot open and I pulled my hand away, gasping for air. I felt only a sliver of his power and felt like my lungs were collapsing. It pressed in on me from every side with all the force and density of a collapsing star.

"Your wings," I rasped, fixated on their beauty. "Why do you have wings?"

"Because I was cast out of heaven before time was ever measured," he said with a wry smile. "They don't get used often in Hell."

"You were an angel?" I blinked, looking up at him. In an odd way, there was something angelic about him. His fair, blonde features especially.

"One of the original three," he explained softly, running his fingers from my thighs to my knees. "Lucifer, Beelzebub and I were cast out for defying the Judeo-Christian God. The three of us formed the first hierarchy of Hell and called ourselves the Unholy Trinity."

I sat back for a moment, trying to soak it all in. I just made out with an original fallen angel and one of the most powerful demons in existence.

"That was one of your truths," I mused, returning his icy but oddly affectionate gaze. "So your lie was that you were the serpent in the Garden of Eden."

"Correct. That was Lucifer, not me."

His hands continued trailing lightly along my body as he spoke, from my knees back up to my thighs, to my waist and up my arms. It was the gentlest touch, skimming with only his fingertips as if curiously exploring.

"So what's with the snake around your neck?"

"God made humans terrified of snakes after what happened in the Garden," he explained, fingertips traveling across my shoulders. "I gave humans back the power over serpents."

"Plenty of people are still afraid of snakes," I pointed out.

"Yes," he said, fingers brushing against my neck now. "God makes sure his way is not easily forgotten. But I'm sure you could kill one before it kills you."

He had a point there.

I moved his hand away from my neck. His light, exploratory touches were too distracting, too good at sending shivers through my whole body. But my fingers laced through his as if they had a mind of their own.

"Here's a question," I said, determined to not let his now gentle squeezes of my fingers distract me. "I grew up knowing who Lucifer and Beelzebub were. How have I never heard of you?"

"My full name is Ashtaroth, for one," he said, drawing our hands to his backward beating heart. "And while my two brothers have been ruling the realm of Hell, I've been having much more fun." His eyes flashed with excitement. "Walking the earth disguised as a human."

"And you've been doing that since what, forever?"

"Pretty much, yes."

He brushed the back of my palm against the bristles of his beard before planting a lazy kiss there. The friction of roughness followed by the softness of his lips drove me wild. I nearly melted into a hot puddle of fuck-me goo right then.

Must not get distracted. I am finally learning valuable information.

"Haven't you gotten bored?" I asked. "I mean, how many centuries of life, death, war, and peace does it take to see everything?"

"Not at all. That's the fun of it." He flashed a rare smile. "Humanity and all its nuances is incredibly fascinating to observe. I'm not often surprised anymore but always fascinated."

"So what on earth have you been doing all this time?"

"What demons do best." His smile grew wider. "Turning people away from God."

"And toward worshiping the devil?"

"Not at all." He lowered our still-clasped hands and rested them on my knee. "Lord Lucifer wishes for nothing. He only wants to give what God forbids."

I swallowed. My throat grew parched.

"And that is?"

He leaned in close again, his forehead barely brushing against mine as my heart skipped a beat.

"Knowledge," he whispered. "Awareness. Independence. Empowerment. Carnal pleasure. Everything the forbidden fruit stood for." He pulled away a few inches, just far enough to look at me with a steely, intense gaze. "And what *you* stood for."

"Me?" I blinked. "What do you mean, me?"

"You're no ordinary witch, Deja. You must know that." His commanding voice gave a hint a pleading.

"Well yeah because I've just found out about it after believing my whole life that witchcraft and devil worship were the same thing," I said.

He sighed as if disappointed and pulled away from me, releasing our hands. Already my body cried out with craving his touch.

"Are you aware of the dark magic in your aura?" he asked.

"Yes, I may have absorbed some demon magic in the womb which killed my mother."

His lips pressed into a tight line.

"I suggest you spend some time with it. Meditate on it and explore that aspect of your abilities. You may have found it already talking to you in dreams."

Before the shock could fully settle in, he pressed a soft kiss to my lips and looked at me mournfully, like he didn't want to leave.

"Until next time, Deja," he whispered, and disappeared.

19
RAUM

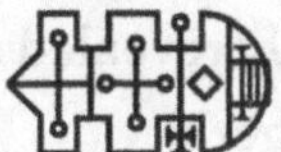

I could smell Deja in the air before Ash even appeared. Light, floral, and a touch of sweetness just like that tea she made.

When he did appear, even that stone-faced fucker looked as smug as a cat that ate a canary.

"Now you can't puff up like a damn peacock and not share details," I said as he wordlessly went to pour himself a drink from the liquor cabinet.

He took his time making his selection, pouring three fingers into a glass, swirling and inhaling deeply before taking a sip.

And keeping his damn lips sealed the whole time.

Not that I could blame him. I'd do the exact same thing. He wanted us to beg for the information but he knew me better than that.

Sal, on the other hand, got worked up into a tizzy.

"What'd you do, Ash?" he demanded. "Don't tell me you... had her? Without telling us?"

Ash gave him the barest glance over his shoulder, one eyebrow lifted in amusement.

"What do you think, Sal? Would I do that?" He tapped one finger to his temple. "Try thinking before you speak."

Sal lowered his eyes and mumbled an apology. Internally I tsked at him. Even a hothead like him should know better than to question Ash's integrity.

Although the three of us had roamed as a trio on Earth for so long, it became easy to think we were all equals. But no passage of time changed the fact that Ash was of the first hierarchy, and we were under his command.

"We just kissed," he finally revealed after polishing off his glass.

"And?" Sal demanded eagerly.

"And nothing," Ash snapped with an eye roll. "It was quite chaste, really."

"But you know for certain now?" I asked, eager to know the important information.

He nodded. "It's definitely her. When I tasted that mouth it felt like no time had passed at all." He let out a wistful sigh, something we all felt. "However, she still has no memory of any of her past lives and it sounds like a senior witch has been filling her head with anti-demon rhetoric. We should continue to proceed with caution."

I nodded in agreement while Sal let out a huff of annoyance.

"How much longer do we have to be cautious?" he growled.

"Until she remembers us," Ash said firmly. "And even if she does, in her current body and the current circumstance, there's a chance she may not have us." He chewed his lower lip. "Although I don't think that'll be the case. She was very... responsive."

"And if she doesn't want us?" Sal demanded. "Then what? The last thousand years have been for nothing?"

"That's the risk we take with allowing free will," I said. "That's the difference between us and the God followers. If we command obedience, we're no better than them."

"Absolutely correct," Ash told me.

I tried not to bask too much in him telling me I was right. As his disciple, it was not always easy following his lead but I remained forever loyal for moments like these.

"Now if you'll excuse me," Ash said, setting down his second drink. "I have some reading to do."

He left the room, leaving me wondering how I should spend the evening and Sal looking like he wanted to kill someone.

But then again, Sal always looked like he wanted to kill people.

"Jealous?" I inquired.

He shot me a white-hot glare.

"Yes, I'm fucking jealous," he admitted through gritted teeth. "Lord, what I would give to have even the briefest taste of her."

"Well," I said, clapping a hand down on his shoulder. "Why not pay miss Deja a little visit?"

***

Several hours later, after her shop had closed, we appeared in Deja's living room to find her sitting cross-legged on her coffee table with her eyes closed. Two lit candles sat at the edges of the table and some kind of incense burned in front of her.

She had changed out of her work clothes into a pair of black leggings and an oversized black sweatshirt with a pentagram on it. It looked like something she wore to rebel against her religious parents.

Honestly speaking, she looked incredibly cute.

Sal and I exchanged amused glances as we watched her. Her eyelids fluttered slightly and her brows knitted together in concentration.

"Whatcha thinking about?" I asked, breaking the silence.

Her eyes shot open and her mouth formed an O of surprise. Then her legs kicked out, knocking everything off the table as she flailed in her shock at seeing the two of us standing in her living room.

I quickly extinguished the candles with a wave of my hand while Sal went to help her up.

"How long were you there? How'd you get in here?" she demanded frantically, then huffed out a tired sigh. "Nevermind, I should have known you'd be able to just appear in here."

"We weren't watching long, promise," I said, not bothering to hide my grin. "You just looked so deeply focused that we didn't dare interrupt."

"I'm sure," she said bitingly, though she didn't seem that angry. Her wide-eyed gaze focused on me but she clutched onto Sal's forearms for support, which held her around the waist.

"Can I ask what you were visualizing?" I said, trying to ignore my rising jealousy of Sal's hold on her.

"Don't you know?" she said in a curious tone. "You can see the past and the future, can't you?"

"I can't read minds, I can only see events that happen. That would be too much fun," I told her with a wink.

"Well I'm learning new things about you all constantly," she said, spinning in Sal's arms as she turned to face him. They looked like they might kiss and a rare flame of jealousy sparked within me.

"I was trying to access my shadow side." Her eyes flickered back toward me. "Ash said I should get in touch with the darker areas of my magic."

"That's good advice," Sal said, inches away from nuzzling her.

"See anything interesting?" I asked, making my way around the debris on the floor to stand closer to her.

Her cheeks flamed with heat, causing me to bite my lip and stifle a groan. Usually, I could be a patient guy but at that moment, I ached for her.

"Not really," she said, although her eyes darted between Sal and me nervously. "I couldn't really see anything at all. It's like being in a dark room. Although I could feel... sensations."

"Sensations like these?"

Sal's hands slid up her back, drawing her in closer to his chest. Unable to stop myself, I reached out and brushed hair off the back of her neck, letting my hand linger on her warm, curving nape.

She drew in a heaving breath, looking over her shoulder at me with her gorgeous lips parted.

"Something tells me you two know something," she mused, barely above a whisper. "And again, won't tell me straight out."

"It's something you have to learn yourself," Sal murmured, his lips nearly brushing her temple now. "Although we might be able to help."

He dropped a slow, sensual kiss just below her jaw, and she let out the softest, barely audible moan. As she arched, her back pressed into my chest. My heart pounded between her shoulder blades. We could have lit a bonfire with how hot and chemically charged we all were.

"Tell me one thing, Raum," she said breathily.

"Anything," I whispered, drunk on her scent and her skin.

"What was your lie and your other truth? I've figured out everyone's but yours."

I chuckled and grinned devilishly, watching confusion mix with the arousal in her eyes.

"I cheated," I admitted. "All three things I told you were truths."

Her eyes narrowed into an imposing but adorable glare that made me hard as a rock.

"So you're a cheater, huh?" she accused, turning around in Sal's arms to face me squarely.

"Sometimes, when it suits me," I confessed, cupping her cheek and dragging my fingers through her hair, which felt good, as the shift in her expression showed. Her pulse beat wildly against my chest as I brought my mouth to her ear.

"But I am never a liar," I whispered against the shell of her ear before dragging my teeth along the delicate cartilage. Her pulse hammered and her breath already came in quick pants.

Her mouth waited for mine, open like a delicate flower which I ravaged like a predator once I tasted it.

I let out a low groan as my tongue surged into her mouth, releasing all my longing, all my need. Ash was right, she was incredibly responsive. Like she missed and needed us in the same way we did her, even if she didn't remember us yet.

Deja broke our kiss abruptly with a sharp gasp, looking over her shoulder. Sal had been kissing the nape of her neck and the top of her back. He captured her mouth as she looked, spinning her around to face him.

As they kissed, I traced my fingers down over her spine, remembering longingly how beautiful and perfect her naked body looked between all of ours. One day we would have that again, our perfect harmony. But not until she remembered.

Deja wrenched herself out of Sal's grasp and backed away from both of us, eyes wide and breathing heavily.

"What the fuck is going on?" she demanded, raising a trembling finger to her lips. "Ash and I--"

"Don't worry. He knows we're here," Sal said, his voice unusually relaxed. "It's okay, Deja. There's no backstabbing or anything going on."

Her eyes darted back and forth from Sal and I. My heart squeezed with an aching discomfort. Of course this was overwhelming for her. Two partners was the only relationship dynamic she consciously knew. For the vast majority of modern-day humans, that was the only way.

"We don't want to confuse you," I said, taking a step toward her. "I promise this will all make sense in time."

"I don't know what you're talking about," she protested, although her large pupils and shallow, panting breaths betrayed her. "You're trying to groom me for some crazy demon orgy ritual or something."

Sal laughed at that and I had to release a chuckle too.

"You feel the same things we do," he said. "Only you feel it for all of us equally."

"We know it goes against everything you were brought up to believe," I added. "Not only under your religion but in this society. But what you're feeling is natural and normal for demonkind and many witches as well."

Deja said nothing, just stared at the empty air in front of her as her breathing slowly returned to normal.

"We should probably leave her alone for now," Sal said to me, the last words I expected to come out of his mouth. "She still needs time to process this."

I nodded my agreement and in the next moment, he disappeared.

Reluctant to leave, I approached Deja slowly and took one of her small hands in mind. Her large, honey-colored eyes looked up at me, defensive and unsure.

"We're always nearby when you need us," I said, lifting her fingers to my lips for one last taste of her before taking my leave.

20
DEJA

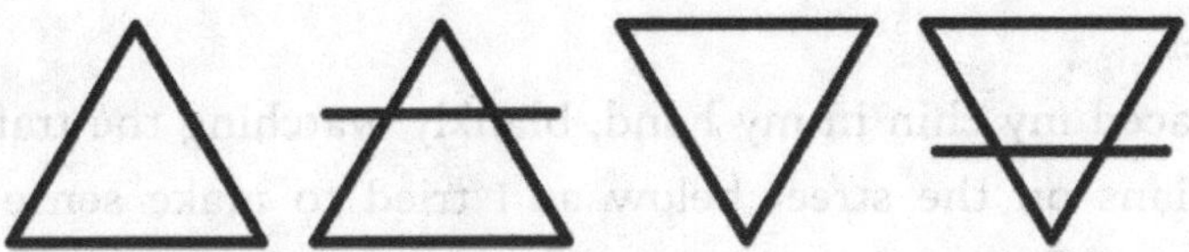

Thanks to those two, every attempt to resume meditating on my dark power went out the window.

With a frustrated grunt, I stood up from the coffee table and stretched my legs to ease the pins and needles settling in, then went to the kitchen in search of a bottle of wine.

Even if I could get into a meditative headspace, I would just the see the same darkness and feel the same hot sensations of hands and mouths on me and get even more sexually frustrated.

My head swam as I popped the cork and watched the ruby liquid flow into the glass.

"I made out with three guys today," I said to the bottle as I set it on the counter. "Two of them right in front of each other."

The bottle didn't seem impressed.

"And get this," I continued. "They're all friends. Like the three musketeers, only they're demons and have been friends for thousands of years."

Still no response so I sighed and went to my window seat.

The sky was unusually clear for San Francisco, although the light pollution hid many of the stars from view. The moon hung round and full, casting silver light on the streets below.

I wondered if witches did anything special for the moon cycles, and made a mental note to ask Diana about that next time.

A small pang of guilt hit me as I remembered her warning. I'd done the exact opposite of what she suggested. I threw caution to the wind, started developing feelings for all three of them, and for some reason, hung onto every word they said like an infatuated teenager.

I placed my chin in my hand, blankly watching the traffic and pedestrians on the street below as I tried to make sense of the swirling, conflicting thoughts in my head. I still had so much to learn and unlearn. But trying to categorize it all into neat little areas was like untangling six balls of yarn that had somehow converged together into one tightly compacted knot.

Everything, from my sense of right and wrong to who I should listen to and trust, felt like it was in the center of that massive knot.

How does your body feel when these thoughts enter your head?

My brain chose that time to recall the words of my first and only yoga teacher, during my short stint when Nona talked me into going with her.

Before I started shaking in misery in downward dog and other equally uncomfortable poses, we did a short meditation. She asked us to observe the thoughts floating through our head as we breathed and take note of what we physically felt in that moment.

At the time I just tried to keep from yawning and fidgeting, but maybe it'd be a good exercise to try now.

I closed my eyes and took a deep inhale, picturing each of my three handsome demons in my mind.

Well, I'm already referring to them as mine so that's something.

As their unique but striking faces floated through my mind, my limbs relaxed and my body grew warmer. My fingers and toes tingled pleasantly, and my pulse picked up just slightly, awakening a throbbing sensitivity between my legs.

I was so relaxed, my head leaned back to rest on the window frame and a smile formed on my lips. This was how they made me feel. Relaxed, safe, and sexy.

I then thought of Diana, and a different kind of warmth spread throughout my body. The warmth and comfort of family, and having someone older and wiser to guide me through this new, uncharted territory. But recalling her warning made me uneasy. I felt the tension and fear that gripped me from how she erupted in fire when I asked how witches originated. Maybe she meant well but my gut was clearly not ready to trust all of her opinions without a huge grain of salt.

"I said *no!* Stop following me!"

My eyes snapped open, thoughts interrupted by the sound of yelling and commotion just outside my window. Not too unusual in San Francisco but someone right under me sounded really distressed. I opened the window and stuck my head out to investigate further.

A young woman had her back pressed against the wall of the building next door. Moonlight illuminated her blonde hair like a halo, although I couldn't see her face because of the man caging her in.

His whole stance was aggressive, with his hands on either side of her head and he spoke close to her face. I couldn't hear his words but his tone sounded just as aggressive and threatening as his demeanor.

The woman turned her face to the side, facing me, and my blood froze at the distress on her face. She was crying and trying as hard as she could to put distance between herself and this man, but he wouldn't back off.

He said something else and pressed the whole length of his body against hers, pinning her to the wall as he began to fumble at her clothes.

"No, no, please!" the woman cried as she struggled desperately.

My whole torso leaned out the window now as I searched the streets eagerly, looking for someone who was surely coming to her aid. But no one did. People stared straight ahead and hurried their pace as they walked past the assault happening in plain view on the sidewalk. A slap echoed along the walls and the woman's cries lowered to soft whimpers.

Fuck, fuck. This is bad.

My knuckles were white as I gripped the windowsill, blood pounding in my ears. I couldn't just sit back and watch this happen. I could call the cops but how long would they take to get there? The damage was already being done.

My mind made up, I pulled away from the windowsill and raced out my front door and down the stairs. Only when I stepped out onto the sidewalk and the man's broad back came into my view, I realized I had no weapon and no plan. But I had no time to think about myself at that moment.

"Hey, asshole!" I yelled. "Leave her alone!"

He looked back at me with a callous snarl. Over his shoulder, I saw the girl's terrified face but her eyes were large and hopeful.

"Mind yer own fuckin' business, bitch," he slurred back at me.

"Not happening!" I replied.

Adrenaline coursed through me like a drug. I wanted to hit him in his ugly fucking face and the power surging through me felt like I could make it hurt. In my peripheral vision, I saw tinges of red and black and felt the crackling of static electricity.

"I'm warning you," I said in a low, threatening tone that I barely recognized as I slowly stalked toward them like a predator. "Let her go, you gutless piece of shit."

The lumbering drunk chuckled in amusement and finally turned to face me. The girl crumpled to the ground but was up again in a flash, hugging the wall as she stumbled the opposite way and disappeared around the corner.

Good she got away but shit, I'm really on my own now.

"You want somma' this?" The man grinned, revealing a row of rotten teeth and wagged his vile tongue at me. "Lemme show ya how to take it like a good lil' bitch."

"Touch me and I'll make sure you never touch another woman again," I warned, curling my fingers with tension as the adrenaline, power, and anger coiled up within me like a slingshot being pulled back.

A flicker of hesitation passed through his eyes but it was gone as soon as it appeared. He lowered his head and charged at me like bull.

Oh God, oh shit, oh fuck! My brain cried out in panic but my feet might as well had been cemented to the ground. The edges of my vision clouded with spots of red and black until all I could see was his bald head coming straight at me. My arms shot out in front of me like cannons and I directed every ounce of fear, loathing, adrenaline, and white-hot hatred straight at this pathetic excuse for a human being.

I shut my eyes, bracing myself for impact. What felt like a powerful gust of wind blew at my back, blowing my hair up around my face and pushing me forward to the point of almost stumbling.

"Arghh, what the fuck!"

Cautiously I cracked open my eyelids, still tense and anticipating the giant drunk man to barrel into me. But the sight before me ensured that would not be happening.

He crawled along the ground, eyes and mouth wide open in fear and pain. One of his legs bent at an odd angle and dragged behind him uselessly.

"Fucking bitch broke my leg!" he cried, drool and spit flying from his mouth as he dragged himself away as fast as he could. "Oh God, somebody help me!"

I stood there stunned, then glanced down at my hands. Nothing looked unusual about them, nor did I feel the explosive amount of power that coursed through me just a second ago. Instead I felt really, really tired. Fatigued almost.

Whatever the hell I did took everything out of me.

Out of nowhere, the sound of slow clapping jerked me into alertness again.

I spun around in a circle, looking for the observer who stood by and did nothing. Two shadowy figures walked toward me slowly from the narrow alley between the buildings. Bracing myself, I held my ground and gathered my little remaining strength as I waited for them to reveal themselves.

Raum and Sal stepped out into the moonlight. Sal emerged with his arms crossed and a bemused smirk on his face while Raum was the one applauding.

"Very impressive, Deja," he said, dark eyes twinkling. "You have even more dark power than we realized."

"The dawn of a new witch is here," Sal added, looking pleased.

WITCH'S RITE
UNHOLY TRINITY BOOK 2

PROLOGUE
DEJA

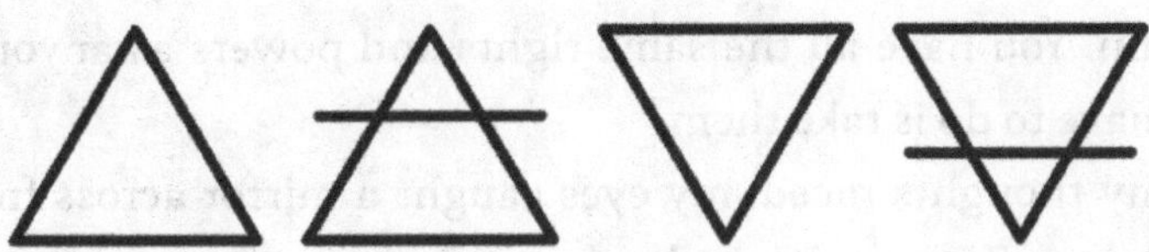

"**O**h my God, Ash!" I gasped.

He laid on his back but I could see one of his wings peeking out from underneath him. What few white feathers remained were stained red with blood. The rest were charred or missing. And the angle of his wing seemed wrong, like the broken wing of a bird.

Only then did I notice the dark, tender bruises and welts on his side, wrapping around to his back. He looked as if he'd been burned, whipped, and pelted with rocks all at the same time.

But his eyes cracked open, and he smiled at me like it was a typical, lazy Sunday morning.

"Hello, my love." His voice was gravelly with sleep as he reached for me.

"Ash, you're hurt!" I shrieked, too panicked to register his term of endearment.

"It's alright. Lucifer gave me something for the pain." He draped an arm across my waist and looked at me adoringly. "And with time, all will heal."

"But what happened?" I cried, hating that he'd been hurt so badly in the first place. I felt utterly helpless.

"We finally did it." He looked pleased, if a bit drugged out from whatever Lucifer gave him. "We rebelled. We took the fall. And I brought you with me."

"The fall?" I repeated as my mind scrambled to connect the dots.

"Yes, you're safe now." He reached for my hand and laced his fingers with mine. "No human man will ever make you submit to him again. You have all the same rights and powers as anyone else. All you have to do is take them."

As my thoughts raced, my eyes caught a mirror across from the bed and the reflection shocked me.

My eyes looked exactly the same golden-brown color. But other than that, I looked completely different. My hair was much longer, nearly down to my waist, and a coppery auburn color. With one glance down at my naked body, I saw I was much shorter and thinner. This was not the body I, Deja, was born in, and yet it was still mine.

"Lucifer suggests you form a legion to protect yourself," Ash continued in his lazy, sexy tone. "You won't be immortal like us but as the first human on our side, he will grant you powers over them." He eyed me curiously. "Or maybe he already has."

This had to be another one of my dream memories, right? There was no way I could wake up in a different body in a completely different place. But everything felt so real, from the sheets beneath me to Ash's arm wrapped around me.

And this raw power within me felt unmistakably real.

When I sat still and focused, I felt it traveling through me like millions of tiny high-speed trains. I closed my eyes and saw the Garden that was no longer my home. Yet still, wherever we were, I could draw the energy from the earth and will it to obey me.

"Turn over," I said abruptly. "Let me see your back."

Ash looked puzzled but obliged, rolling over on his stomach. I choked back a cry at what I saw. His injuries were far worse than I imagined. While the front of his torso was painfully beautiful and perfect, his back was a mess of deep gashes, mottled bruises, and painful welts. His left wing was a twisted deformity of broken bones with just a few feathers holding on. The right wing was gone completely, with a painful-looking, bloody hole where it once was.

If he were human, he simply would not have lived.

Steeling myself, I placed my palms carefully on his back and closed my eyes. I drew upon the resilient energy of the earth first up through my tailbone and collecting it in the center of my chest. I had no idea what I was doing, and yet I did. It was pure instinct.

I drew on the healing powers of nature, which always returned with a vengeance even when the last little leaf fell from the tree. From the center of my chest, I willed the magic of the natural world through my arms and out my palms. I willed for it to heal my lover, my savior, like it healed the earth. To take away his pain, and to give him great black wings fit for a ruler of Hell.

I didn't open my eyes for the longest time, too afraid to see if I failed him. But when I saw my palms pressed against smooth, flawless skin and rippling muscles, I collapsed with relief and joy.

"It worked!" Tears sprang to my eyes as I smoothed my hands across his back, unable to believe it. "You're healed!"

Ash sat up and checked the mirror, looking over his shoulder with adorable fascination. He stretched his majestic black wings carefully and my breath felt stolen from my body. I never saw a creature that looked so beautiful.

"I'll be damned," he breathed.

"Well, considering we're in Hell, you already are," I giggled.

"No, my love."

With an impish grin, he folded them against his back again and dropped on top of me. An explosion of love and warmth spread from my chest as he pulled me into a tight embrace and peppered my face with kisses.

"I'm not damned in the slightest, even if I am a demon now." He shifted to look at me with his crystal blue gaze. "Because of you, my love, I am truly blessed."

1
DEJA

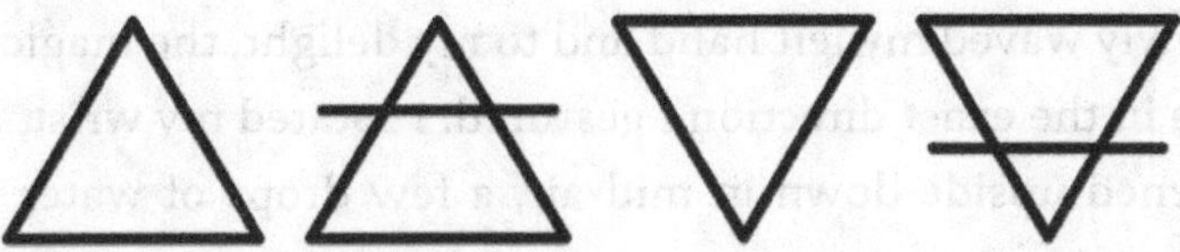

"**F**ocus, Deja."

My grandmother's voice carried through me like a soothing breeze as I let out a deep breath, trying to clear my mind.

"Picture it in your mind and then say the words."

I concentrated hard on the image behind my eyelids, memorizing every small detail. I saw myself rooted to the ground like a tree, my arms extended like branches and whiplike vines growing from my fingertips.

As I focused, energy held me in place like an anchor while traveling up from the ground through my feet at the same time. It traveled through my veins like a river of heat and pure power.

The image in my mind nearly disappeared as the earth's magic surged through me but I held on, letting it coil up and build before I released it.

"Nothing gained, nothing lost," I said in a clear, commanding voice. "Life and death of equal cost. Here to grow, here to bleed. Leave this world and sow your seed."

My eyes shot open just as the magic exploded like gunshots from my fingertips, the force shooting back and making me stumble a few steps.

"It worked!" I shrieked triumphantly.

Long, green tendrils of magic sparkled like jade in the late afternoon sun as they wrapped around my target, a vase sitting on a coffee table across the room.

"Try to move it. Be gentle." My grandmother, Diana, contained her excitement better than me, but I still heard the pride in her voice.

I slowly waved my left hand and to my delight, the magic carried the vase in the exact direction I gestured. I rotated my wrist, and the vase turned upside down in mid-air, a few drops of water spilling out.

"Try bringing it toward you," she suggested.

I moved my hands as if pulling on an invisible rope until the smoky green tendril held the vase directly in front of my chest.

"Well done, Deja," she praised. "You've truly improved by leaps and bounds."

"Thanks, Gran," I said as I directed the magic to return the vase to the coffee table. "You said I could use this spell on people too?"

"Yes, as long as you have enough magic manifested you can pick up and move mountains if you want to. But that takes a lifetime of practice," she chuckled before turning serious again. "This spell is ideal for restraining and subduing people without injury, if you ever find yourself in such a situation." She raised an eyebrow pointedly.

"Right," I nodded, chewing my lip. The last time I used magic on someone, I broke a guy's leg. To be fair, he was about to rape a girl so it wasn't like he deserved better. But at the time, I had just found out I was a witch and had zero training on how to channel my power. If I had somehow missed him and hit someone else, I'd have a much bigger problem on my hands.

"I wish your mother could see you now," Diana beamed as she lowered herself onto the couch, her stark white hair illuminating her face like a halo. "She was so excited to teach you the craft of our people."

I settled into the armchair across from her, picking up my teacup which had gone cold.

"Will you tell me about her?" I asked after some hesitation.

A week ago, Diana quite literally appeared at my front door and told me a story that turned my life upside down. I had been adopted as a newborn to a deeply conservative religious couple. Growing up, I never felt like I truly belonged in my adoptive parents' world. Only after meeting Diana, my biological grandmother last week, did I learn that my birth mother was a witch and therefore, so was I.

My birth mother died soon after I was born under mysterious circumstances, although Diana was convinced that my deeply religious father made a deal with a demon to have her killed in order to protect his own reputation.

"She was always so happy," Diana began softly, smiling to herself. "So full of light. Deirdre saw the good in everyone and the upside in every bad situation. She was kind and gentle to every living creature, even ants that got into our kitchen. I know she would have been an excellent mother to you."

A wave of sadness filled me at the thought of such a beautiful person being taken away from this world. Someone I never got the chance to know and learn from. It felt wholly unfair that such a huge part of myself was kept hidden from me for so many years.

My adoptive parents, while they weren't cruel, believed my powers were a source of evil and did all they could to stifle my abilities with prayer and Bible study. In their own minds, they probably believed they were genuinely doing the right thing.

While I grew up never knowing my magical abilities, I always felt like an outcast in their tight bubble of a community. Moving to San Francisco was a culture shock in the best way, and finding out my witch heritage only solidified that I found my home in this big, magical city.

Better at twenty-eight years old than never, but I still couldn't help but mourn over what I never had—a mother who raised me with love and acceptance. Someone who would encourage me and refine my gifts, not try to pray them away.

"Did you ever look into the details of her death?" I asked my grandmother, a spark of something lighting up within me. A sense of revenge? Justice? I couldn't be sure. "Find out who the demon was that my father paid? What exactly was the spell that killed her?"

Diana shook her head sadly.

"He steered clear of me because he was convinced I'd turn him into a toad or something. And legally he was her next of kin, so he made sure I never got too close to her or you in the end. He convinced the doctors and nurses I was crazy and would try to steal the baby. And if I knew he'd kill my daughter, I sure as hell would have," she growled.

She leaned back tiredly in her armchair and rested her face in her hand, suddenly looking much older. Even with her stark white hair, her eyes were bright and her mind sharp. As I got to know her over the past week, I began to see more of my own features in her.

"No, my dear. I'm afraid it's just a mother's instinct and my own theory that the vile, hypocritical sperm donor hired a demon to do his dirty work. The magic surrounding her and you was so dark, darker than I'd ever seen. But trust me, it kills me every day not knowing for sure."

"There must be a way to find out though, right?" I asked, realizing I was latching onto finding the truth about my mother like a pit bull. "I mean, aren't there paranormal investigators or something like that?"

Diana laughed softly. "No, unfortunately we don't have anything like Scooby-Doo running around to solve these mysteries. Revealing ourselves to the non-magical authorities just poses too much of a risk."

"I get that but don't we have our own governing body? What if someone commits a crime with magic?"

"Problem witches are usually dealt with by their local covens. There are too few of us to have a real judicial system, unfortunately," she sighed. "We're lucky to have a sizeable witch population here in San Francisco."

I nodded my understanding but the gears inside my head turned like a well-oiled machine. For the sake of my stolen childhood and my mother's death, I was dying to find the missing pieces and click them into place. Maybe then I'd have some closure. And thankfully, I knew exactly who I'd ask my first questions.

"Thanks again for the lesson, Gran," I said, picking up our teacups with a quick glance at the clock. "I just might be getting the hang of this witch thing."

"Kicking me out already, eh?" she quipped teasingly, but I knew it wasn't a rhetorical question. "Got big plans for tonight, do you?"

"Sort of," I admitted, setting my teacups in the sink. "I found a bar downtown that's only visible by magic. Thought I'd check it out."

"Oh? By yourself?" Diana lifted a questioning eyebrow, making me squirm under her gaze.

"No, I'm uh, meeting someone there."

Or should I say *someones.*

"Oh really? Who?" My grandmother's questions burned into me, making me even more uncomfortable. For Christ's sake, I'd been living on my own and owning a business for over a year already. Maybe I was a little sheltered for my age but I wasn't a damn child.

But could I really blame her for being protective, since she couldn't be in my life until recently? Not to mention the fact that I was all that was left of her daughter, who had been taken from her far too soon.

"Just some people I met," I said in an attempt to brush off her question. "I gotta make friends with more of my own kind, you know?"

"I see. So you've met some fellow witches?"

"Um, not exactly." I avoided her gaze as I squirmed even harder internally, wishing she would just let it go.

"Deja." She said my name in a low, warning tone as if scolding a child. "Are you seeing those demons you mentioned before?"

Fuck. Why was I such a terrible liar?

"We're just going to have some drinks and hang out," I said, sounding as if I was trying to convince myself as well as her that nothing else would happen. Especially since I had already made out with all three demons in question and found myself addictively attracted to them all equally.

Diana's lips pressed into a thin, tight line as her eyes narrowed at me. Her aura flared up with a silent anger that expressed her disapproval.

"Dear, please just promise me you'll be careful," she pleaded. "It's true that demon kind have been unfairly portrayed throughout time but there is a seed of truth to every story. They are master manipulators and capable of wicked, awful things."

"So are humans," I answered defensively. "And witches too, I imagine."

"Yes, yes, of course," she said emphatically. "Just please use your best judgment and question everything they tell you. Take nothing they say as absolute truth."

"I'll be careful, Gran," I assured her, wrapping her in a hug as we moved to the door. "I promise."

We said our goodbyes, and I promised to be careful at least three more times before finally shutting the door after her. I couldn't help but feel a foul taste in my mouth as I finished tidying up my tea shop before leaving.

I realized she wanted to protect me. I was a fledgling witch still honing my powers, hanging out with creatures much older and more powerful than me. But she was of a different generation than me and her words felt eerily similar to an older white woman saying, "Well, I'm not racist, but..."

It didn't seem fair that she painted all demons with such a broad brush. Not that I knew many, only three. And barely at that.

They were all ridiculously hot though, and I seemed to have some kind of inexplicable bond between all of them. Nearly every night since I met them I've had extremely erotic dreams, vivid in every sense but sight. I could feel multiple hands and mouths pleasuring me like they were really there, but as if I were blindfolded. I wanted to say it felt like *them* but without even knowing, how could I be sure?

I smoothed my dark hair in the mirror and applied a fresh coat of lipstick. My reflection winked one amber eye back at me before I locked up and set out for the bar.

One of the core principles Diana taught me while using magic was to trust my instincts. For some reason, my gut felt more suspicious about her anti-demon rhetoric than the demons themselves. Every moment spent in their company made me feel I could trust them. But when she said things against them, my instinct was to rise up in their defense.

They knew something about me that I didn't, that maybe even my grandmother didn't know. Something that might explain how I felt so bonded and drawn to them after barely knowing them.

And possibly, more importantly, they might have some answers as to what happened to my mother.

2
DEJA

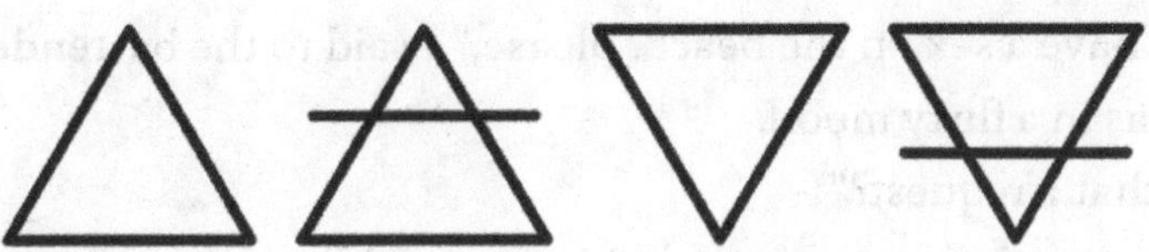

Abrisk walk on a chilly San Francisco evening was never dull, especially not after discovering my magical abilities. After learning I was a witch, it was like awakening a sixth sense. I saw people's auras as I walked by them in a variety of colors, hues, and shapes. Some had small halos circling their head, others encompassed their whole body in an ethereal glow. I recently learned this was based on how strong their emotions were in that moment.

The discovery of my magic also led me to find actual, physical places that were invisible to ordinary humans, like my current destination, the Triple Moon pub.

When I first moved to San Francisco, I walked past this alley hundreds of times without a second glance. All I saw then were dumpsters and the backsides of buildings that faced the opposite street. But now the red brick building emitted a cozy, flickering glow from its windows as I hastily approached, eager to wrap my hands around a pint glass or maybe a whiskey tumbler. I hadn't decided yet.

I pulled the door open to a room full of warmth, laughter and many simultaneous conversations. The varnished wooden bar stretched out long before my eyes, lined with enchanted candles that never burned out or dripped wax. A massive chandelier mounted on the high, vaulted ceiling flickered with the same enchanting light. Across from the bar, couches, booths, and pub tables lent a few dim corners for privacy.

I didn't spot my demons right away, so I approached an empty space at the bar as I mused on what to drink.

"I'll have a sex on the beach, please," I said to the bartender. Why not. I was in a flirty mood.

"Is that a request?"

The question came from behind me while a large, heavy hand snaked around my hip at the same time, igniting my skin into delicious shivers.

I peered over my shoulder to find myself looking up into a familiar pair of dark, mischievous eyes followed by a chiseled jaw coated in dark stubble, shoulder-length black hair, and a playful smirk on kissable lips.

"Even if it was, you'd have to whisk me away to Mexico or somewhere 'cause that ain't happening on the frozen, rocky shore here," I shot back at Raum.

The tall, dark, handsome demon's grin only grew wider as he squeezed my waist in a possessive grip that suggested we do exactly that. But you never really knew with Raum. He was like the Sphinx to Odysseus—speaking in riddles, teasing, hinting, and never revealing all that he knew, which was a lot considering he could see the past and the future.

"Her drink is on my tab," he told the bartender, lacing his fingers through mine as he pulled me away from the bar. I could have swooned right then, but somehow kept my legs and drink steady as I followed him to a private corner with couches and a low table.

Sitting there, waiting for us was a man whose features were the polar opposite of Raum's, though no less breathtakingly handsome.

Where Raum was dark, flirtatious, and mysterious, Salmac was bright, blunt, and hotheaded. His sharp green eyes looked like a predatory cat in the flickering candlelight. His auburn hair, short on the sides and longer on top, shone with its own fire and luster. As for his clean-shaven, serious face? Well, I was essentially dying to kiss it.

"Hey Sal," I greeted, sliding into the booth and brushing a kiss against his cheek, too shy to initiate anything else.

He merely scoffed and cupped the nape of my neck, holding me in place as he delivered a hot, slow and sensual open-mouthed kiss that stole my breath away. His tongue probed my lips apart and confidently invaded me. When his mouth left mine, my brain buzzed like I had downed several drinks already.

"Hey beautiful," he murmured gruffly against my lips.

Well, that was one hell of a greeting. Something I could get used to.

"Now you're not going to let him have all the fun, are you?" Raum whispered against the shell of my ear.

I hadn't even recovered from the intoxication of Sal's kiss but turned to face Raum all the same. His mouth was waiting and captured mine in a kiss that was so deeply satisfying in such a different way. Sal's lips were soft and soothed an ache like a refreshing drink of water. Raum's stubble scratched roughly across my lips in the hottest, most spine-tingling way. His kisses also mirrored his teasing, flirtatious personality—biting my lips playfully before pulling away, leaving me begging for more.

My eyes remained softly closed as his mouth drew away, not wanting to shatter the illusion that I just kissed two men within seconds of each other, and neither one of them seemed bothered by it.

"You're conflicted," came Sal's observant voice as a gentle touch brushed against my cheek. "I can feel it in your aura."

I opened my eyes to stare into the stunning green orbs of his, searching through me deeply. His intense gaze had to be intimidating to some, but it only filled me with warmth.

"I just don't understand how you all can be okay with this." I mused, looking over my shoulder at Raum before a realization dawned on me. "And where's Ash?"

"Hell," Raum answered as casually as if he said the word, *work*. "Business with Beelzebub and Lucifer. He'll be back in a day or so."

Ash, or Ashtaroth, the leader of these devilishly handsome musketeers, was a fallen angel and one of the original founders of Hell. And as far as I could tell, the most mysterious and stoic of the three. He exuded immense power but with a cool and aloof nature, unlike Sal's hot-headedness. In contrast to Raum's joking and teasing nature, Ash was quiet and serious.

Also, he was the first one to kiss me.

Even with Sal and Raum here to keep me company, I realized I missed him.

With Sal's hand still gently stroking my cheek and neck, Raum wrapped a muscular, corded arm around my waist. The sensation of both touches was nearly overwhelming, but in the most affectionate way that sent butterflies through my insides.

"And we're okay with this because we're not bound by dogmatic social constructs deeply rooted in patriarchal Christianity," Raum added, a naughty glimmer in his eye.

"But the real question is," Sal chimed in. "Are *you* okay with this?"

"I... like all three of you," I answered, pausing in my nervousness to take a sip of my sex on the beach. "But I don't even know what *this* is." My eyes darted between the two of them. "Are you all doing this with other people?"

"No," they answered in unison. The conviction in their voices both put me at ease and lit a fire inside me. So all three of them wanted just me and no one else? It seemed too good to be true.

"I wish we could just tell you everything. All the history between us," Sal sighed, looking longingly at my lips. "But Ash is insistent that you figure it out for yourself."

"It probably is better that way," Raum added. "It's a lot of very heavy information to digest, especially since you're still getting used to the idea that you're not an ordinary human."

"Well, all this vaguebooking and obscure references is certainly helping," I remarked sarcastically, taking a long pull from my drink.

"Oh, but isn't solving your own mystery part of the fun?" Raum teased, rubbing circles on my lower back. "What have you deduced so far, Nancy Drew?"

I sipped more of my fruity, flirty cocktail as I pondered his question, hyper-aware of their eyes on me as I sucked the straw and my cheeks hollowed in.

"You're all ancient compared to me," I began. "And yet you all act as if you know me from before my own lifetime. Since meeting you all and discovering my powers, I have felt... comfortable. At ease. Even familiar, like I've met you all before, too. So I can only deduce that I must be some sort of reincarnation of... someone."

"Very good," Raum purred, sounding pleased.

"Wait, what?" I said, taken aback. "You mean I'm right? Like reincarnation is real?"

"Perhaps not in the exact same sense you're thinking but yes, a person's true self can be reborn in another body after the first one dies. It's just as real as magic is," he answered with a wily smile.

"And I've done that before," I thought out loud.

"Yes," they both agreed.

"But is it like this every time?" I wondered. "Where I live my life like an ordinary person and then meet you for the first time and you all have to drop these hints until I figure it out? Like some kind of long drawn-out, fucked up Groundhog Day?"

In my frustration, my hands gestured wildly in the air as I spoke, until dropping onto both Sal and Raum's thighs pressed against me in the booth. A hot jolt shot up through me and I resisted the urge to pull my hands away like I touched a burning stove.

Lord help me. Or should I say, Satan help me.

"No, it's not supposed to be like this," Sal murmured mournfully, lacing his fingers through mine on his leg. "You don't remember any of your past lives? Or your original name?"

I shook my head slowly, my heart aching at the sadness and loss in his eyes. Whoever I had been, he really missed me and it hurt him that I didn't remember. His words from our two truths and a lie game rang through my head—*I've been in love with the same woman for over seven thousand years.*

3
DEJA

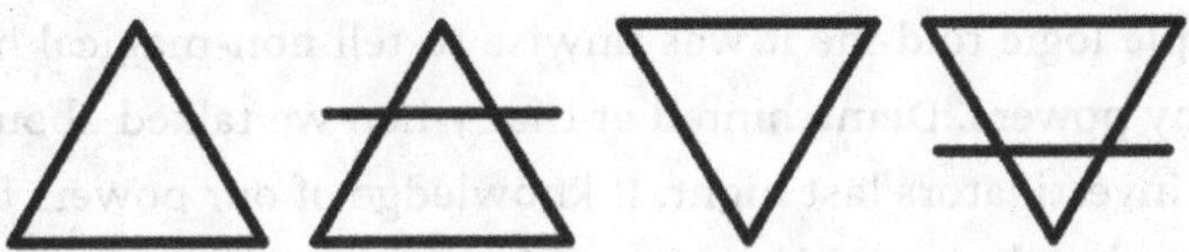

It wasn't until opening my tea shop the next morning, after a nice buzz of caffeine, that I realized I forgot all about asking the guys questions related to my mother.

"Damn it," I muttered into my third cup of lavender chai.

"What's up?" asked Nona, my only employee. I swore she had the hearing of an elephant.

"Nothing. Just got a fly in my cup," I muttered as I turned toward the sink.

I felt guilty for keeping all my witchy developments a secret from Nona. She wasn't just my employee but my first and only real friend since moving out to San Francisco.

I stepped off that Greyhound bus a sheltered and naive girl, the perfect prey for a fast-paced, cutthroat big city to swallow up whole and spit out in pieces.

I didn't even make it out of the bus terminal before someone mugged me. If she hadn't ridden her bike past me at that exact moment and saw the whole thing, I could have spent my first night sleeping on the sidewalk. It was serendipitous. She never left my side again after that.

Even though she worked for me, she was like a mother figure in many ways, like gently reminding me when rent was due, and where the best Mexican food and bars were.

Hell, she even encouraged me to hook up with all three demons after we first met them at that party. That was before I knew they were demons, of course.

I hated lying to her. In fact, I was bursting to tell her everything. I needed a girlfriend—who was not my grandmother—to confide in.

Simple logic told me it was unwise to tell non-magical humans about my powers. Diana hinted at that when we talked about paranormal investigators last night. If knowledge of our powers fell into the wrong hands, it could be devastating.

But this was my sweet Nona. I would bet my life on her loyalty and trustworthiness. Would it really be so bad if I told her I broke a man's leg without touching him? And that the devilishly handsome guys I liked were *actual* demons?

Something in the air suddenly pulled my attention like a magnet. I looked out across the tea shop to see a young woman sitting by the window, an Earl Grey latte on the table in front of her and a book in her hand.

My eyes narrowed as I tried to make out the title of the book. The jacket certainly looked familiar.

I nearly dropped my cup when I realized it was one of the same spellbooks Diana had been teaching me from, *The Magical Properties of Plants* by Alastair Knowles.

My heart jumped into my throat as I blocked out everything else in the shop and focused on this young woman with serious tunnel vision.

She looked about my age with pale blonde hair down her back in pretty waves. Her large eyes were a brilliant aquamarine color, and a large chunk of raw crystal in a similar color hung around her neck on a long chain.

Her aura shimmered around her whole body in the same brilliant bluish-green color, with slow, undulating movement like the way a mermaid tail would swim through water. Essentially, she looked bathed in the brilliant lights of the Aurora Borealis.

And she was most definitely a witch.

Only then did I glance around, to see if any other patrons noticed this woman bathed in ethereal light and reading from a spellbook. But everyone chatted with friends, worked on laptops, read ordinary books, and sipped their tea as if nothing was amiss.

"Hey Nona," I said as casually as I could muster. "Has that girl in the window been in here before?"

"No, I don't think so," she said just as casually, pulling cups and saucers out of the dishwasher.

"Have you uh, noticed what she's reading?"

Nona paused and took a longer glance.

"A chemistry textbook, huh? Heavy subject matter. She's probably a student."

I blinked and bit my tongue before I could reveal my shock. I looked again and sure enough, the book cover now read *Organic Chemistry*.

I'll be damned. Disguising the book with magic. So simple but genius.

To anyone looking, I was a calm shop owner sipping my tea while looking out adoringly at my customers. But on the inside, I was a twisted mess of anxiety and excitement, like a high school girl debating on saying "hi" to her crush.

Should I talk to her? What should I even say? Oh hi, nice to meet another witch for the whole shop to hear? Do witches have some kind of code word or secret handshake?

Damn it Deja, just leave the girl alone. Like everyone else in here she probably just wants to read her book and drink tea in peace.

...But what if she's like me and is desperate for someone to talk to about witchy things?

Her aquamarine eyes lifted from her book and caught mine from across the room.

Fuck! I'd been staring at her like a creep for who knows how long.

I abruptly turned and drained the last of my chai, staring intently at my cash register for a distraction.

The door then jingled with a new customer walking in and I looked up with a bright, plastered smile, grateful for an actual distraction and boy, did I get one.

"Ash!" I gasped as my heart crashed against my ribs and my body temperature rose with every passing second.

"Deja," the fallen angel greeted me huskily as he approached the counter, turning a few heads as he did so.

With his tall, imposing form exuding raw power that even ordinary humans could sense, such reactions couldn't be helped.

His icy blue eyes froze me to my spot but the way he looked at me set my body on fire. He stroked his short, blonde beard as he approached me and gave the barest hint of a smile on his stony face. His blonde hair was tousled carelessly. I wanted nothing more than to run my hands through it and mess it up even more.

"Where've you been?" I asked more eagerly than I intended.

He braced his muscular forearms on my counter and leaned down slowly, deliberately, to my level.

"A bit busy. Just putting out some fires," he said, his low voice rumbling like lazy thunder.

"Literal or figurative fires?" I asked, lifting an eyebrow.

"A bit of both," he replied, never breaking his intense gaze from mine.

Like Sal and Raum, Ash's aura was incredibly dark with sparks of red and crackles of electricity. Of the three of them, he was the only one who also had large black wings sprouting from his back. Ordinary humans couldn't see them, but I wondered if the aquamarine witch noticed them.

I glanced up to her window and was surprised to see she was gone.

"Did you have fun with Sal and Raum last night?"

Ash's question jerked my attention back to him along with a tightening in my throat.

"You can tell me honestly," he said in a way that was oddly gentle and soothing. "The three of us hide nothing from each other."

I swallowed. "Yes," I admitted. "I did have a nice time with them."

"Good." His eyes flashed. "I ordered them to take care of you while I was away."

"It was just drinks and kissing," I stammered. "We didn't—"

"I know, Deja." His hand slid across the counter to brush against mine. The heat of his touch calmed my panic.

I took a deep breath, trying to maintain control of myself with my body getting so hot and the chemistry visibly crackling between us.

"So what can I do for you, Ash?" I said. "Seeing as you're not a tea person."

"Come home with me," he said without missing a beat.

"What?"

"I missed you, Deja." His index finger drew some invisible gesture on the sensitive skin inside my wrist. "I was only gone for a day here but time passes much more slowly in Hell. It feels like I haven't seen you in weeks."

My heart squeezed in my chest. The words tumbled out of me before my brain could catch up.

"It felt the same way to me."

4
DEJA

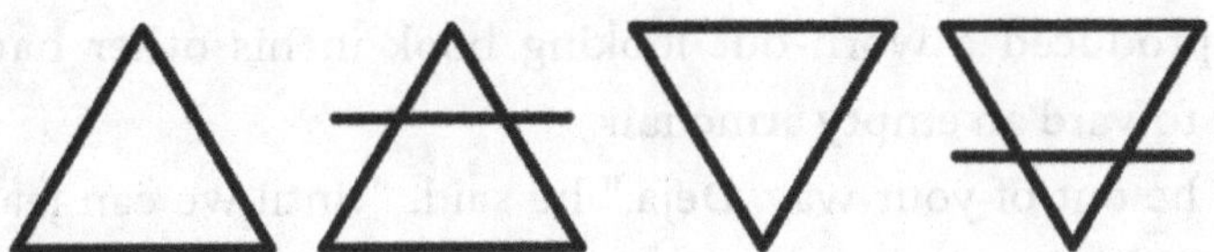

I couldn't bring myself to leave work early, no matter how hotly Ash stared at me or how badly I wanted to see what a naked demon really looked like. It wouldn't be fair to Nona, making her close up on her own.

But that didn't make the afternoon pass any faster.

"I'll hang out if you don't mind," Ash said at my insistence at staying until closing. "I like the feel of your space here."

"Sure," I said calmly while I internally squealed with excitement. "I'd offer you something to drink but, you know." I waved my hand dismissively at him.

Yeah, I was giving him shit for not being a tea person and probably would be for the foreseeable future.

At least Raum liked my tea. I still had yet to get Sal's opinion.

"If you give me a cup, I'll handle the beverage part myself," he said with a wink.

I gave him a quizzical look but handed him a freshly washed teacup anyway. Like a magician, he passed his hand over the rim and the cup was suddenly filled with a dark, steaming liquid. A familiar, earthy smell filled my nostrils.

"Coffee, really?" I said. Not exactly what I expected to be conjured out of thin air.

He shrugged as he brought the hot liquid to his lips and took a small sip. "Just my poison of choice."

"I see. And you take it black, I imagine?"

"As black as my soul," the handsome demon confirmed with a smirk.

I didn't doubt him for a second.

He produced a worn-out looking book in his other hand and nodded toward an empty armchair.

"I'll be out of your way, Deja," he said. "Until we can leave," he added in a lower tone.

I tried not to ogle as he settled himself with his book and coffee in my tea shop. Before long, every woman was stealing glances at him and I couldn't blame them. He looked so studious, like the hot, slightly nerdy professor that everyone had a crush on in college.

"Something tells me Mr. Hot Blonde is waiting for you to leave work," Nona teased as the minutes crawled by.

"Yeah," I said, my face heating up as I tried to concentrate on the current brew. "We might be hanging out afterward."

"Hanging out as in romantic dinner or Netflix and chill?"

"Um, kind of sounds like the second one."

"Ooh, get it, girl!" She bumped into me with the side of her hip.

"And you didn't hear this from me but um." I chewed my lip nervously. "I may have made out with the two other guys last night."

Nona's mouth dropped open. "Girl."

"And they all apparently know about each other and are okay with everything."

"Girl!"

"It sounds way too good to be true but they say they're all interested in just me."

I didn't know why I started spilling all these private details to her, they just came pouring out. I figured I could talk to her about my love life but just leave the supernatural details out.

"Holy shit, Deja you've hit the holy grail of jackpots! Ride this out for as long as you can. Or should I say, ride all *three* of them."

"Geez, Nona! Why not say it loud enough for the whole shop to hear," I hissed, looking over both of my shoulders.

At some point, Ash put on a pair of thick-rimmed reading glasses and I had to bite my lip to stifle a moan.

"Oh chill out, Deja. Nobody in San Francisco cares how many people you sleep with. Hell, you could even throw another girl into the mix and no one will bat an eye."

"Yeah, that is definitely not happening," I muttered, stealing yet another glance at Ash.

He seemed deeply absorbed into his book, his brows pinching together slightly as his pale blue eyes moved over the words. A couple of girls at a nearby table whispered to each other as they kept looking at him. A different kind of fire heated my blood. I hoped they weren't planning on talking to him.

"Don't worry, your three devilishly hot men will corrupt your brainwashed upbringing in no time," Nona teased.

"You have no idea how much I can't wait for that," I replied.

5
DEJA

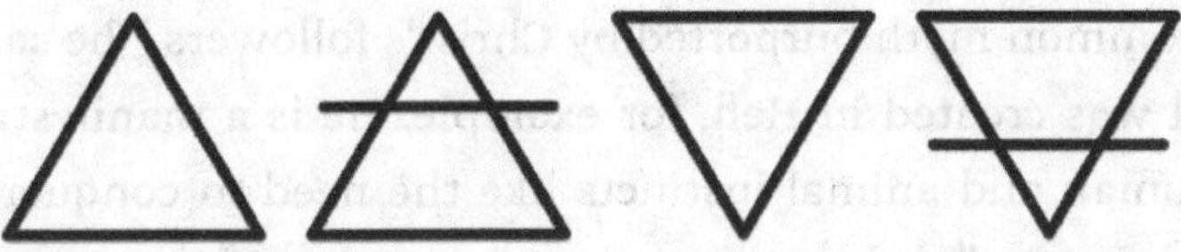

Closing time finally came, and I didn't have to murder any of my female customers.

Ash said a polite goodbye to Nona before I finally shooed her away and locked up the shop. She barely rode her bike down the street before I received a text saying, "You better tell me everything!"

I rolled my eyes but held back a goofy grin as I stuck my phone in my purse and began walking along Ash's side.

"So what was with the readers?" I asked as we came to our first stoplight, and couldn't help but tease him. "Getting a bit old, are we?"

He cast a cheeky sideways glance at me. "My eyesight is actually improving the longer I stay on earth. But yes, I used to be extremely farsighted and couldn't see anything in front of my face for the first hundred or so years after falling. I imagine it has to do with angels having to see across long distances from the clouds."

"Sort of like birds of prey," I mused aloud.

"Yes, exactly," he confirmed. "Binocular vision, they call it."

It was hard for my brain to wrap around the fact that this devastatingly handsome, but otherwise normal looking man walking next to me, was a not a human but a completely different creature.

And so was I, in a way.

"Do other demons have that problem?" I asked.

"Only the fallen angels, which are by far a minority. For the others, it depends on how they were created. Though eyesight problems aren't usually part of the package."

"Oh," I said. "I guess I assumed all demons were fallen angels."

"A common myth purported by Christ's followers," he said slyly. "No, Sal was created in Hell, for example. He is a manifestation of basic human and animal instincts like the need to conquer, dominate and protect."

"That makes sense." I remembered Sal's temper, which was never directed at me, but he always seemed eager to annihilate someone for even sending a dirty look my way. In his thousands of years of existence, he must've annihilated scores of enemies. I was beyond glad to be on his good side.

"And Raum was originally a raven. One of the first birds we observed that demonstrated incredible intelligence and almost human-like thought processes. When we saw him steal treasure from greedy kings, we knew we had to make him our own. He has excellent near and farsightedness, the bastard."

"Seriously?" I nearly stopped in my tracks. "Raum is actually a bird?"

"He was," Ash corrected. "He's a demon now. He actually prefers to spend most of his time in human form."

"Easiest for him to talk shit that way," I joked.

"Precisely," Ash chuckled. "There are also the lesser demons such as the incubi and the succubi. Each of us has a few legions of those under our command at any given time. Aside from immortality, their only real power is sexual seduction."

"That's it?"

He nodded. "Appealing to instinctual desires is one of the

simplest, most effective ways to corrupt. If a human has been sexually shamed or repressed for most of their life, that often makes it easier."

"How so?" I asked, hanging onto his every word with fascination.

"When you ignore your instincts for so long, they don't go away," he said, his fingertips applying light pressure to my spine. "They're held by a hair trigger just below the surface, waiting for the one thing that'll set off the control they cling to so desperately. The seducing demons can identify the trigger and become exactly what that person desires most."

"That's fascinating," I mused. "Do all demons have seductive powers like that?"

"Not as much as the succubi, but to some extent." His fingers trailed down my arm to tug at my hand. "This is us." He led me up the front steps of a classic Victorian-style house painted a dark grey with an off-white trim.

He opened the front door for me to a dark, nearly pitch black foyer. Only tiny slivers of light came through the cracks between the blackout curtains on the windows.

An herbal, smokey smell filled my nostrils like some kind of incense, but all I could see were rough shapes of furniture, walls, and a staircase.

"Let me guess," I said, blinking in the darkness. "You three are vampires, too? Actually no, don't tell me that. I don't think I can handle any more mind-blowing revelations."

Ash's throaty chuckle came from somewhere behind me.

"No, we're not vampires." His warm breath lifted the hairs on the back of my neck. "Just ensuring we have some privacy."

He snapped his fingers and I jumped at the sudden *whoof* sound that followed. The large brick fireplace roared to life with a nearly bonfire-sized flame, bathing the living room in warmth and a dancing, romantic light.

Although my heart thumped wildly in my chest, I kept my face neutral.

"Show off," I jabbed at his smug expression.

"Me? Never." His powerful arms wrapped around my waist, securing me against his hard chest. "You must be thinking of Raum."

The air between us was the thickest it had ever been. Our auras crackled with tension, the colors blending and practically kissing each other above both of our heads.

"No," I whispered. "I'm not thinking of him."

He leaned down to close the distance between us but stopped, pausing just before making contact. So I closed the gap for him.

I stood on tiptoe to reach his lips and felt some kind of combination of melting and exploding on the inside. He let out a soft grunt at my boldness but kissed me back. We fell into the same hot rhythm of teeth and tongue like that first time in the back of my shop.

We parted breathlessly and too soon. I was too hot and had too much clothing on.

"So you do want this as much as I do," he murmured against my lips.

"Yes," I breathed as I clutched to him desperately, fearing my legs wouldn't work if I let go.

Still he pulled back, holding me trapped under the icy fire of his gaze.

"There's something you should know before we do this," he said in a low growl.

"Okay?" I said, already panting with need.

"Here's the thing about me, Deja." His gaze flickered down to my lips and then back to my eyes. "I'm not jealous, I'm possessive. You can fuck Raum and Sal whenever you want. But when you're with me?" He wound his fingers through my hair and closed his fist at the base of my skull in a possessive grip.

"It's no one else but us."

He lowered his forehead to mine and gave the slightest, sweeping kiss over my flushed, trembling lips.

"Are you okay with that arrangement?" he asked in a way that sounded like a dare.

My brain and body were too delirious to answer in words, so I just kissed him again. Hard.

Wanting me all to himself yet still willing to share? It was like a paradox that I couldn't handle but made me so incredibly hot.

His tongue surged into my mouth as he pulled me against him so tightly, I gasped for air but still couldn't get enough of him.

I felt so drunk on how badly I wanted him, my feet didn't even feel like they were on the ground anymore. I was in freefall.

When something soft but firm supported my back, I realized my feet did come off the ground. He picked me up and laid me down on the shag rug in front of the fire.

My core pulsed with a dull, aching need as he gently settled his weight on top of me, my thighs glued to the outside of his hips and pulling him toward my center.

"Li--, ah, Deja," he groaned hotly into my neck as one adventurous hand explored under my shirt.

I froze, barely catching it in my lust-filled haze, but it was enough to kill everything for me. My hooded eyes snapped open and my body went stiff, no longer melting against his. He noticed immediately and reluctantly pulled his mouth away to look at me.

"Something wrong?"

"Please tell me you didn't almost just call me by someone else's name," I said, trying to keep the emotion out of my voice.

"What? No," he protested but his face gave him away. "Deja, I--"

"Liar," I said, pushing up on his broad shoulders. "Get off me."

After wanting nothing more than to feel him inside me, I suddenly felt the complete opposite—shitty, used, humiliated, and dying to get away. I had to leave before he saw me cry.

He sat up slowly. I quickly adjusted my clothes and scooted out from under him.

"Wait," he growled, catching hold of my wrist before I could stand. "Please listen to me."

"Let me go," I hissed, the tears already threatening to spill.

"That wasn't another person's name, it was yours," he said quickly. "I almost said the name you had when I first met you."

He released his hold on me and for some reason, I stayed rooted to my spot.

"Not in this lifetime but when I fell," he went on. "The *very* first time."

A light bulb went on somewhere in the back of my mind. So the reincarnation theory really was true. Apparently, I had been alive since nearly the beginning of time itself. All the feelings of familiarity and deep bonds with these men started making sense.

But at that moment, my pride was wounded, and I did not want to let him off the hook.

"So what was it?" I challenged. "What was my name back then?"

He leaned his head back and sighed, looking conflicted.

"I can't tell you. I'm sorry."

"How convenient," I muttered, rising to my feet and heading toward the door.

"Pay attention to your dreams," he called after me. "The answers are there."

I paused with my hand on the doorknob and one foot outside.

"What do you mean?"

In a split second he stood next to me, icy blue eyes hungry and full of desire.

"The dreams you have. They feel like memories because they are. The more time you spend with us and the more physical contact we have, the more you remember. You have to remember yourself, Deja. We can't just sit you down and tell you. It could... affect your memories and perceptions."

He bit his lip, looking conflicted for a moment before he spoke again.

"One thing I can tell you is you're the only one for me. You always have been, since the beginning. Raum and Sal will undoubtedly tell you the same." His gaze lowered to my lips. "There has never been anyone else. No other name is even worth saying."

6
DEJA

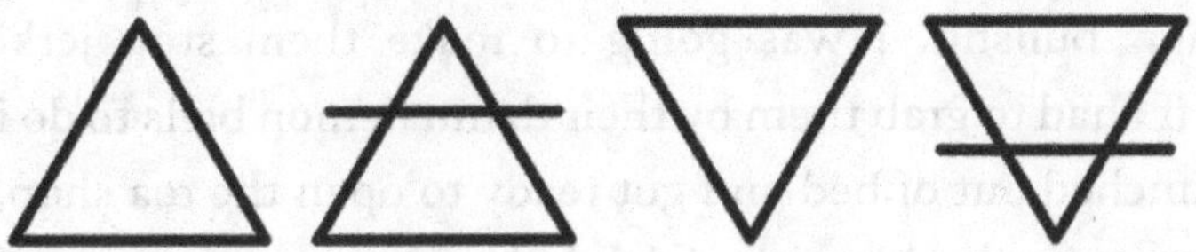

I saw someone in a dream that night who looked like Ash, yet so completely different.

His face was clean shaven and his blonde hair grew out in curls to his collarbone, but his icy, curious eyes were the same.

Most impressively, he shined with a brilliant light and had an amazing span of pure, white wings stretching out from his back.

"Who are you?" I asked.

"I am Ashtaroth, an angel of our Lord," he answered.

Distantly, I knew this was the first time we met. This was not a dream but a memory.

I remembered falling in love with that handsome face the moment I saw him. Those eyes sought knowledge and companionship, not obedience. In them, I saw freedom and escape from my situation, a man who essentially wanted to keep me as a slave.

I opened my mouth to tell him my name. He probably already knew it but this time *I* would know. One small piece of the big, blank puzzle of my past would fall into place.

But when my lips parted, all that came out was, "Beep! Beep! Beep!"

"Son of a fucking bitch!"

My hand shot out to my nightstand and sent the beeping alarm clock crashing to the floor. If I had been any more awake, I would have picked it up and thrown it across the room.

"What the fuck, man? Ugh!" I groaned in frustration into my pillow, pounding my fists and kicking my legs like a child.

I almost fucking had it. At this point, I was well and truly sick of this game. Fuck these demon boys and their, "Oops, we can't tell you anything," bullshit. I was going to make them stop jerking me around if I had to grab them by their damn demon balls to do it.

I launched out of bed and got ready to open the tea shop, which was conveniently located right below my apartment. At that moment however, I could have used a brisk walk up and down some of San Francisco's hills to blow off this steam.

But there was no time. I stomped downstairs to find Nona already decanting the overnight cold brews.

"Morning! Those were here for you when I opened." She gestured across the counter to a bouquet of roses in a slim, glass vase.

And no ordinary roses. While their petals were fresh, they were as black as ink, with Ash's aura hanging all around them like a perfume cloud. The sight of them made my anger soften. Just a tiny bit.

"So, how did it go last night?" She turned to me, wiggling her eyebrows but immediately stopped when she saw my expression. "That bad, huh?"

"Not exactly," I muttered, folding a pile of clean tea towels. "The night ended before anything could actually happen."

"Okay, be honest," Nona said before lowering her voice to a whisper. "Small dick?"

"Didn't even get that far," I replied, averting my gaze. "I'm not really in the mood to talk about it."

"Aw, that's a shame," she commiserated. Then in a much chirpier voice, "Good morning! What can we get started for you?"

I looked up to find myself staring into a brilliant aquamarine gaze. My heart stopped in my chest and I froze like a statue. It was the witch from yesterday!

"I'll take a pot of the dragon's blood blend," she said in a high, musical voice and with a sweet smile.

Nona scurried off to prepare her teapot, leaving me at the counter to stare at her dumbly.

She cleared her throat and rummaged in her purse.

"Um, it's five dollars, right?"

"Yes!" I declared, blinking out of my trance and swiftly moving to the register. "How's your morning so far?"

"Good, thanks," she replied politely. "How's yours?"

"Just... *magical.*"

"Great."

Her aura flickered with a shimmering shift from green to blue, but her expression didn't twitch in the slightest as she handed over a five.

"So you're the owner?" she mused casually.

"Yes!" I stuck my hand out so abruptly I nearly poked her in the sternum. "I'm Deja."

"Juno," she answered, taking my hand in a gentle grip. "I love coming to this place. It's so relaxing."

"Thank you, it's great to have you." I forced myself to let go of her hand, despite a pleasant hum of energy passing through our palms. "Just let me know if you need anything."

"I sure will," she said, picking up the tray with the teapot, cup, and mini breakfast scone that Nona had swiftly set down. "Nice to meet you, Deja."

"You too, Juno."

I stretched and clenched my fingers as I watched her set her tray down on a coffee table and began thumbing through a book.

She did something magical when she touched my hand but it was so subtle, I didn't even know if I should acknowledge it or not. It felt too light to be an actual spell. Could that have been the secret witch handshake?

She sat at an angle where I couldn't read her book cover this time, but her wrist flicked and her fingers moved in a subtle but unmistakable way. I fought the urge to launch myself over the counter and pick her brain, to find out what she was casting and learn it for myself.

Screw the demon boys. They were not my priority, at least not at that moment. Growing my powers and finding a community with others like me, was.

7
RAUM

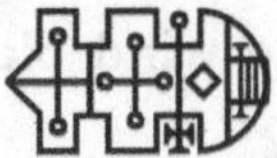

Amorning flight had been a daily ritual of mine for the last three hundred years or so. Watching the human world wake up was always fascinating, and always shifting depending on the time period and location.

I noticed humans were slowly rising later in the day, sometimes missing dawn entirely. Their workdays shifted further back. First, it was sunup to sundown, then it was nine to five. Lately, I noticed more ten to six schedules, especially in San Francisco where everyone wanted to skip morning traffic.

Yes, I gathered lots of useless knowledge in my bird form. But you never knew when it would turn out to be useful.

After a few hours of fighting with seagulls and watching runners on the beach as the sun came up, I flew back to the house we occupied while in human form.

Through the open window I usually came through, I spotted Ash pacing in the upstairs study. He looked even more grim than usual.

I flapped and braced for landing, gripping the windowsill in my claws. Behind Ash stood Sal, staring at Ash like he wanted to kill him and holding the edge of a chair in a death grip.

"Seems I missed a cheerful morning meeting," I said after shifting back to human form.

"This fucking hypocrite almost told Deja her original name," Sal hissed through gritted teeth. "After being all up our asses constantly about not telling her shit."

I lifted an eyebrow. "Is that so, boss?"

"It is," Ash said tersely, not one to mince words. "But I didn't say it. I caught myself."

"Clearly, you said enough if Sal is so riled up."

"He gets riled up by the wind blowing the wrong way," Ash scoffed.

"Fuck you! Why don't you tell him the rest of it?" Sal seethed. His aura grew and flames began to ignite all around him like his skin was burning.

Ash looked at me. "You already know, don't you?"

"She thought you were going to call her by someone else's name," I said with a nod. "I felt her pain and embarrassment. It felt like a betrayal."

Ash's tight-lipped frown and the regret in his eyes confirmed it.

"It was a misunderstanding," he said. "I explained myself and I think she believed me. But I still planted seeds of doubt in her mind."

"This is fucking why we should just tell her," Sal declared. "She must think this is such a mind game and we're just jerking her around. Nearly a thousand years of waiting for our woman to come back to us and we might lose her because of *you*."

"You think I don't fucking know that?"

Ash whipped around to face Sal, who tossed the chair aside like it was a tennis ball. It crashed into the wall in a shower of splinters that forced me to shield my eyes. When I looked again, they were nose-to-nose like a pair of boxers facing off, both brimming with explosive energy.

"This is precisely why we shouldn't say anything, so we don't allow for more misunderstandings," Ash snarled with aggression that was rare to see from our cool, aloof leader. "So I lost my head for a second and fucked up. I'm not an angel anymore, in case you forgot."

"What is there to misunderstand if we're not talking out of our asses in the heat of the moment?" Sal shot back.

"Everything that she already has in her own mind!" barked Ash. "Memories are subjective. We can't fuck with her perceptions and implant our own versions of things."

Sal shoved first, sending Ash stumbling back a few steps in surprise. "Get the fuck out of my face, fucking fairy wings."

"Say that again, little pussy."

Ash lunged for Sal, which seemed like a good time to step in.

"Hey, hey, hey now," I said, blocking Ash with my back while holding my arms out in front of Sal. "Looks like we could all use a little cooling off."

Sal's green eyes flashed with fury, but he turned and left the room with only a low growl. In the next moment, his presence was gone from the house. He probably left to set a chunk of forest on fire or whatever he did to let off steam.

Immediately, the tension decreased in the room. Ash let out a tired sigh and paced back toward the window. I knew he wasn't angry at Sal. At this point, we had grown used to his temper tantrums and always picking fights. At least this time, we knew it was out of caring for Deja.

Hell, both of their tantrums were for that very reason. It wasn't often that I was the calm in our storm.

"He has a point you know," I said after a few moments. "Deja feels like we're playing mind games and isn't happy about it. That could ruin everything."

"So what do you suggest?" Ash asked bitterly, leaning out over the windowsill.

I hesitated. He was not going to like what I had in mind.

"You should give her some space," I said. "Let me and Sal have some time with her, and we'll bring you back into her good graces."

"Heh," Ash scoffed. "You would suggest that. And what makes you think you won't make the same fuck up as I did?"

I walked up next to him and clapped him on the shoulder.

"We don't. That's just a risk we have to take."

8
DEJA

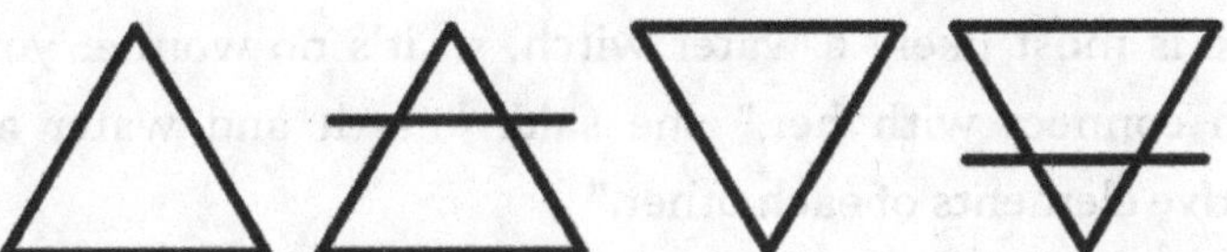

"It's called glamour," Diana explained. "Glamour is magic that tricks the eye into seeing something different from what is actually there."

"So that's how she disguised the covers of her books," I mused, blowing over the surface of my new chamomile tea blend.

"Exactly," she confirmed, picking up her own teacup. "You can apply a glamour spell to objects, buildings, even people and animals. Witch children often play pranks on each other by making slugs and such look like kittens."

"So it's easy enough for kids to do?" I asked hopefully. "And I can make it look like we're talking about something completely normal and not witchy?"

"Absolutely, dear. It's very simple to cast."

"What about the energy I felt through her palm against mine?"

Diana grinned. "She was revealing herself to you in the subtlest way possible."

"Hah!" I declared triumphantly. "I knew it was a secret handshake!"

My grandmother chuckled as she set her tea down and picked up her spell book.

"You said her aura had lots of greens and blues and was very shimmery?"

"Yeah, it was beautiful," I said. "It looked kind of like the Northern Lights, or how sunlight shines underwater."

Diana held one finger up in an *aha* motion as she flipped through the pages with her other hand.

"She is most likely a water witch, so it's no wonder you feel a need to connect with her," she said. "Earth and water are very supportive elements of each other."

"That makes sense," I mused, drinking my tea more deeply now that it was the perfect temperature.

My grandmother shot me an affectionate smile.

"I'm so glad to see you want to connect with another one of our kind, especially the same age as you. I was getting worried about you spending time with those--"

"I still haven't actually talked to her yet," I interrupted, unwilling to hear whatever she wanted to say about my guys. "She seems nice enough but who knows, we could end up being mortal enemies."

I still hadn't talked to Ash since last night, although I believed he was being truthful about the whole name thing. Still, just the sheer fact that he was purposely withholding information frustrated me to no end. I wasn't angry necessarily, just not in the mood to talk or definitely fuck.

After closing up shop, I made sure to hide the rose bouquet in the back room so Diana wouldn't see them when she came over. If she gave me shit for just hanging out with demons, I had zero intention of letting her know things were getting romantic.

"Well, that's always a possibility dear, but all signs point to you two hitting it off just swimmingly," Diana grinned. "Now shall we learn some glamour?"

* * *

The glamour lesson went smoothly enough. I got the hang of it after just a few practice casts. For fun, I disguised my mane of long, dark hair with a spiky blonde cut *a la* Miley Cyrus circa 2014.

"Interesting choice," Diana said with a chuckle.

"What, you don't like it?" I fluffed up the short pixie cut in the mirror. It even felt like real hair on my head.

"It's cute. I'm just not sure it's you," she mused. "All the women in our family had the most amazing dark hair." She brushed a hand through her silvery-white hair. "Well, until age caught up with us," she added with a dark laugh.

"I'll be honest. I could get addicted to this," I said, closing my eyes and focusing on the incantation as I drew another gesture in the air. When I opened my eyes again, my hair was now a pastel purple and fell in luxurious waves down to my waist, with my lip color matching my hair perfectly.

"I mean, this is seriously perfect magic for a night out," I said, twirling in the mirror. "Who needs an expensive trip to the salon when you're a witch?"

"For what is makeup and hair dye but another form of magic?" Diana said with a wink.

"You've got a point there," I said, running a finger along my lower lip. Not even a hint of a smudge. I wondered how badly Nona would freak out if I kept this look for work tomorrow.

"Well, I'll get out of your long, purple hair for the night, dear," Diana said, gathering up her things. "Even though you look glamorous, I can see your eyelids drooping. Remember to get enough sleep while you're learning."

"I will," I said, holding back a yawn. Although casting magic was always draining, I noticed my stamina improving. It no longer exhausted me like when I first started.

After a quick goodbye hug, I locked up the shop and headed upstairs to my apartment. My stomach let out a monstrous growl as I fumbled with unlocking the door. Damn, I skipped lunch and forgot to go grocery shopping. It would probably be takeout for dinner again.

If I weren't in the beginning stages of becoming *hangry*, the man lying comfortably on my couch would have been a more welcome sight.

"Sal!" I barked in surprise. "What are you doing in my house?"

He only lifted an eyebrow as a smirk spread across his face.

"What did you do to your hair?"

"Glamour," I muttered, my face reddening. "I was practicing."

While I enjoyed the pastel purple hair for the sheer fun of it, it would not have been my first choice if I wanted to make a guy's jaw drop. The look didn't exactly scream sexy bombshell.

"Looks nice," he said, lacing his hands behind his head while I tried not to stare. The position made his biceps look even bigger than normal. His legs and torso seem to stretch out for miles, making my poor little secondhand couch look as though it could barely support him.

"Really? Thanks. I mean, wait, nevermind." I let out a flustered breath. "You can't just hang out in my apartment when I'm not here. You guys need to have some boundaries."

He opened his mouth as if to protest but then quickly shut it. Instead, he abruptly swung his long legs off my couch and put them on the floor, resting his forearms on his knees.

"I'm sorry, Deja," he said with surprising tenderness. "I just didn't want to upset your grandmother." His serious face erupted into a naughty grin. "I'm sure you've noticed I can fly a bit off the handle sometimes."

"So can she when the topic of demons comes up," I muttered,

settling on the couch next to him. "Avoiding her wrath is a valid excuse, I guess."

"The old lady gets under your skin," he said in a soft, observant tone.

"A little," I admitted. "She's a bit of a helicopter parent and doing it a bit too late. I mean, I met her not even a month ago and I'm almost thirty. I'm a little past the age of needing a mother figure in my life."

My hand dropped to Sal's knee. Why did it always seem to go there?

"I'm sorry, I shouldn't be complaining," I sighed. "I'm sure you didn't wait in my apartment to hear me vent."

"I'm here for whatever you need," he replied, skimming his fingers across my back. "And right now it seems you need to unwind."

His hand slid up to the nape of my neck and gently pinched the area between my neck and shoulder. My eyes rolled back and I let out an involuntary moan as his hands massaged the tension out of me.

"Close your eyes," he whispered, his breath tickling my ear.

"What are you scheming?" I asked but obliged.

"Now open your eyes," he said not five seconds later.

I did and my mouth fell open as well.

On my once-empty coffee table laid out a gorgeous assortment of food. Everything delicious and decadent imaginable seemed to take up the space. My eyes flitted over gorgeous red grapes, fancy-looking cheese, prosciutto, olives, dark chocolates, stuffed peppers, some cold noodle salad and so much more.

My stomach let out another approving growl, to Sal's amusement.

"Dig in," he said with a laugh. "I didn't know what kind of food you like so I whipped up a little of everything."

"Don't tell me you actually made all this?" I said, popping a cube of aged cheese in my mouth and letting the flavors soak into my taste buds.

"I did, although I conjured it. I didn't cook it."

I looked at him suspiciously as I chased the cheese cube with a tart grape.

"Very interesting skill set you have there, demon. War, violence, aggression, and... food?"

"Hey, we all need hobbies outside of our careers, right?" He slowly bit into a grape while staring at me and somehow just watching his jaw move hypnotized me. What kind of demon magic was he casting to make even chewing sexy?

Time seemed to slip away as we ate, bantered and flirted, but I was no longer tired. Either the food or his company, or a mixture of both, revitalized me with fresh vigor.

"I just realized something," I said after the fiftieth fancy cheese cube. "Where's your sidekick Raum? Hiding in my closet waiting to scare me?"

"No," he answered through more of his sexy chewing. "Just me tonight. I know you've been overwhelmed with everything and figured you wouldn't mind a more... intimate evening."

Heat spread throughout my cheeks as my stomach somersaulted.

"Not at all," I replied. "I really am glad it's just you."

As flattering as having three men's attention was, there was something about getting to know a person one-on-one that just couldn't be replicated with more people. Sal's undivided attention was also a welcome distraction to the awkwardness with Ash last night.

Despite eating my own weight in rich, decadent finger food, the table never seemed to run out and even a bottle of wine appeared out of nowhere. Sal wouldn't let me get up for glasses, so we passed the bottle back and forth.

"Oh God, I'm stuffed," I said, laying back with my hand on my belly.

At some point, my legs ended up in Sal's lap where he massaged my feet with toe-curling sensuality. His thumbs pressed into my arches, kneaded over the tender balls and heels of my feet with alternating pressure. I laid still, not wanting to shift even slightly and take away the bliss he was making me feel.

"Relaxed yet?" he asked, sliding his hands up to my ankles, inching just under my pant legs.

"Mm-hm. Mission accomplished."

My heartbeat quickened as he leaned over me, shifting his weight as gracefully as a cat. His thighs nudged my legs apart to straddle him as he placed his hands on either side of my body.

He brought his face dangerously close to mine. My body soared with heat and his green eyes flashed when he whispered, "Oh, I don't think my mission is accomplished quite yet."

9
DEJA

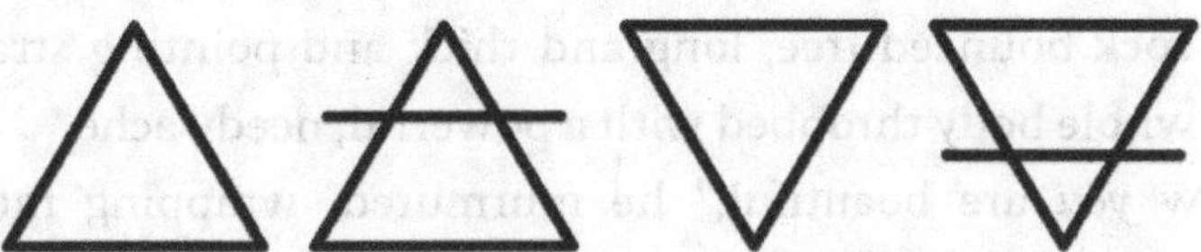

His low, whispered statement directly contrasted with the kiss that followed. He brought his mouth crashing down on mine with a hunger that swept over me like an ocean wave, stealing my breath away.

That kiss was a match that engulfed me in fire. I clawed up his back to pull him down on top of me. When his hardness pressed into my center, I gasped so hard that I broke the kiss.

"Fuck me. Please," I moaned deliriously, already desperate for a release.

"I've been dying to," he rasped against my neck as he yanked my jeans down over my hips. "For so long."

When I peeled his T-shirt over his head, I had to pause and just look at him for a moment despite my animalistic needs.

"Holy shit, you're beautiful," I swallowed. "And I mean that in a totally masculine way," I stammered.

He merely chuckled as he finished removing my clothing and his, while I laid there entranced by how his muscles jumped and flexed as he moved. His skin was also dotted with scars, some of which looked downright lethal.

"What's this?"

I traced the lines of a tattoo on his ribcage, an upside down triangle with diagonal lines going through it.

"The sigil of Lucifer," he answered. "All three of us have one."

Another sigil was inked on his left side. I recognized it as the one he drew in the air that first night at the bar. But before I could ask about that one, he shoved his boxer briefs down his powerful thighs and successfully directed my attention *there*.

His cock bounced free, long and thick and pointing straight at me. My whole body throbbed with a powerful, needy ache.

"Now *you* are beautiful," he murmured, wrapping me in an embrace as he returned to laying on top of me. "And I mean that in a completely feminine way."

"Oh. Well, I'm relieved to hear that."

His laugh rumbled through his chest, vibrating against my skin. He felt so warm and solid and comforting. And he smelled amazing.

"Fuck Deja, I'm not even inside you yet and you feel incredible." He kissed the hollow of my throat before traveling lower to the valley between my breasts. "It's like I can feel you in my skin. In my bones."

"I feel the same way," I said, running my fingertips over the dark flames of his auburn hair.

It was true. This didn't feel like being with someone for the first time. It felt like a reunion after a painfully long time apart.

My skin sang with pleasure everywhere he touched me. Every kiss was a mouthful of fresh air. I felt like I was floating on clouds despite clinging to his hard, solid body. His mouth followed every curve and contour of me as if drawing a single line with his lips. But nothing was rushed about how he tasted and explored me. He took just as much time coaxing my nipples into diamond-hard points as he did kissing along my rib cage.

"Sal," I breathed, digging my nails into the hard landscape of his back. "You're killing me with all this teasing."

"And you're killing me with this body of yours. I need to take my time appreciating it."

He pressed another hard kiss to my mouth and a sharp gasp escaped me when the firm, round head of his cock pressed against my sex.

I cinched my legs even tighter around his waist, locking my ankles together around his back and pressing every square inch of myself against him that I could.

He slid inside me in one fluid motion, tearing apart my softness with his hardness and filling the empty void within me.

"Fuck, Deja," he growled, skimming his teeth across my shoulder. "This is where I'm meant to be. Being inside you is home."

When he entered me, it felt like a key had unlocked something. I couldn't say exactly what, but a feeling of being open and free came over me. My past no longer defined me. It didn't matter. I had my magic and one of my lovers.

Every doubt, hesitation, and insecurity disappeared as Sal rolled his hips against me. My inhibitions melted into nothing as he filled me up with pleasure, stoking the flames of my desire into a roaring inferno.

A new desire soon filled me—an overwhelming urge not to just lay back and enjoy, but to take control.

"Sit up for me," I moaned into his ear.

He obliged, wrapping one powerful arm around me as he leaned back against the sofa. His cock never left me but now I was in control. I secured my arms around his shoulders and soon found my rhythm riding his thick shaft.

"Mm, I love it when you're bossy," he groaned as he brought a hand between us to rub my clit.

He said that like we'd done this before. He touched me like he knew my body as well as I did.

Jolts of pleasure zapped up from my clit to my nipples, building up an intense pressure that threatened to burst.

I rode him harder, relishing in the sensation of him filling me up so deeply. He held my waist, guiding my thrusts with one hand while working my clit with the other.

My orgasm finally released, and I convulsed around him. It was so much, so intense that I moved to lift myself off of his cock.

"No," Sal rasped, wrapping both arms around me and plunged back inside me to the hilt. "Let me feel you come."

He filled me up so impossibly much, toeing the line between pleasure and pain.

"Oh fuck," he groaned, holding me in place as he rocked against me. The friction sent smaller shockwaves through me, like miniature orgasms following the main event.

I slumped against him like all my bones had been liquefied. His pulse hammered underneath my ear with its odd—but comforting—backward rhythm.

"Had enough already, beautiful?" he chuckled, smoothing his palms down my thighs.

"I'm a little spent," I admitted, feeling a bit bewildered. I never felt this tired after a single orgasm before. But then again I never rode a dick that hard nor came that intensely before.

"No worries," he said softly, planting a kiss on my temple and coursing his fingers through my hair.

I lifted my head. "I never said that I was done with you."

He looked surprised and then pleased as I slid off his lap and knelt on the floor between his legs. I gazed at his heavy erection for a moment before stroking it, slowly rolling the velvety skin up the hard shaft.

"Ohh, fucking--"

His words stopped abruptly as I took him in my mouth, sealing my lips over his smooth head and pressing my tongue to the underside. As I worked into a steady pace, he breathed again, letting out wordless moans and sighs.

My mind reeled as I sucked and stroked him into a frenzy. I felt in control of my body, yet completely unlike myself. I had never been a fan of blowjobs in the past and definitely had no skill to speak of. But for some reason I was dying to taste him, to feel his hardness fill my mouth, and to hear his little gasps and moans as I pleasured him. It was making me wet again.

"Ohh yes, beautiful. Touch yourself."

I didn't even realize I brought a hand down to my clit until he said that. He became as hard as concrete in my fist and I knew he was close.

I moaned as I stuffed more of him down my throat, pressing my fingers in fast, hard circles on my clit for another release. I arched my back, putting on a dirty little show which drove him wild. I felt it by how his hips bucked as he fucked my face. His pleasure only made me hotter, and I felt like a porn star.

He reached down to pinch my nipples and that was what set me off. My muffled moans of pleasure were soon followed by thick, salty bursts from his cock. I milked every drop from his balls and licked him clean.

He laid back panting on my couch as I rested my head on his thigh, grinning up at him.

"Had enough already, handsome?"

10

SALMAC

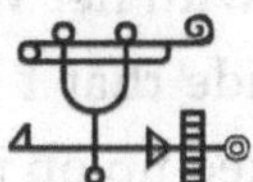

Deja's initial fatigue after her first orgasm didn't seem to last long. We went two more very satisfying rounds before collapsing into her bed. She drifted right off to sleep, breathing deeply and looking absolutely angelic in my arms.

I watched her while a feeling of peace washed over me—unusual for a bearer of death and destruction.

Demons didn't sleep. At least we didn't need to like humans did, so I was content to hold her while watching her dream.

A tapping sound drew my attention to the window.

A large raven sat on the windowsill, tapping its beak on the windowsill and squawking, "Caw! Caw!"

My eyes shifted downward to Deja resting on my chest, my arms wrapped around her protectively. She didn't seem disturbed by the annoying bird's racket.

"Jealous, asshole?" I mouthed at Raum.

He tilted his head, watching us with beady black eyes before turning around and dropping a big bird shit on the windowsill.

"I'll let her know that was you."

Raum gave one more defiant tap to the window with his beak before flying away.

Deja stirred but didn't wake. Her eyes moved rapidly beneath her closed eyelids, signifying that she was actively dreaming. I wondered what she saw.

My hold on her tightened possessively as I recalled my near-fight with Ash, and I felt my white-hot anger returning.

He thought he knew what was best for her just because he was her first. But my connection with her was unique. She saw a side of me that no one else did, a side that I reserved only for her. And it seemed she instinctually picked up on it tonight. She jumped on me and rode me like I was a stallion only she could tame. Now if only she would remember our long, colorful history together.

Frustration grew within me like a buzzing wasp's nest. It felt like I was the only one who still yearned for her with all of my black, demonic soul, while the other two were content to wait even longer for her memories to return. Ash forbade us from even telling her how she forgot everything in the first place. And as impulsive and bull-headed as I was, he was my Lord, and I had to obey.

But even a hothead like me could see his point. It would be unethical to color her memories with our own versions of events. She did seem to put a few more pieces together the more time she spent with us. Physical touch and intimacy seemed to speed that along, as that was the consistent bond between us, the connection that lasted even as she was reborn in different bodies throughout the ages.

"Mm."

She shifted in my arms, her eyelids fluttering slowly open this time.

"Good morning, sleeping beauty." Already I grew hard again just from feeling her skin move against me.

"Hm? Is it morning already?"

"Might be closer to afternoon now," I teased.

She lifted her head from my chest, gazing up at me with those feline amber eyes.

"You were Alexander the Great," she said matter-of-factly.

I couldn't hide my surprise, quickly followed by the joy blooming in my chest.

"So you're remembering more," I said.

"I am," she said, sitting up in bed and rubbing her eyes. "I saw Ash before he fell too. Although there's still a big gap of time in between."

"But it is coming back to you and that's amazing," I breathed, unable to contain my relief. "Do you remember who you were when I was Alexander?"

"Roxana, his first wife," she said as if still in a daze.

"Yes," I confirmed, trailing my fingertips down her arms. "I went against the advice of all my generals and friends when I married you." I grazed my teeth against her ear. "And I'd do it all over again."

She flashed a wicked smile up at me. "Do you know what I did after you died?"

"No, what?"

"I killed those two bitches you married after me."

"I see my murderous influence may have rubbed off on you," I chuckled. "You know I married you out of love. The other two were for political reasons. It was normal at the time."

"I know. It's crazy how I just *know* that." She rubbed her temples. "It's like seeing a movie in my head but it's different because I was *there*. But that is so freaky to me because it was so long ago. I'm only twenty-eight years old for fuck's sake."

"It's a lot to take in," I agreed, pressing my lips to her forehead. "But it will get easier. And you'll remember even more."

She sighed as she curled up, snuggling into my side. I could've spent eternity just holding her while she did that.

"How did I forget all of this information in the first place?" She traced the lines of my tattoos. "How could I forget all of you?"

I stiffened slightly, unsure of how much to tell her. The three of us didn't know if she remembered that event or if it had been wiped from her consciousness altogether. Not even Lucifer knew if she would ever recall it.

"Something happened," I said hesitantly. "A catastrophic event, at least for us. Someone deliberately set out to undo all the progress we made, that *you* made. They almost succeeded. It nearly broke all of us."

"Who's someone?" she asked in a small voice.

"The brainwashed angels who have not yet fallen," I said with more than a hint of bitterness. Ash spent centuries trying to recruit more of his winged brethren to our side, but the turnover was incredibly low. Fallen angels made up a small minority of Hell's residents. Most of them were created there, like me.

Deja let out a frustrated groan as she wrapped around me tighter.

"It still feels like we're speaking in riddles," she lamented. "I feel like I know half of what you're talking about and maybe-kinda-sorta understand some things but I'm still not getting it."

"You will," I promised, tilting her head up for a kiss. "And if we go another round, you might even learn more."

She grinned wickedly, throwing a leg over to straddle me. "You don't have to tell me twice, handsome devil."

I clicked my tongue and tapped my finger against her lips, shaking my head slowly.

Before she could respond, I lifted her up and flipped her over, laying her out on her back as my cock grew to full length between her legs.

I pinned her wrists next to her head and brought my face down to her neck while she squirmed in delight underneath me.

"This time I'm in control, beautiful," I murmured against her skin.

11
DEJA

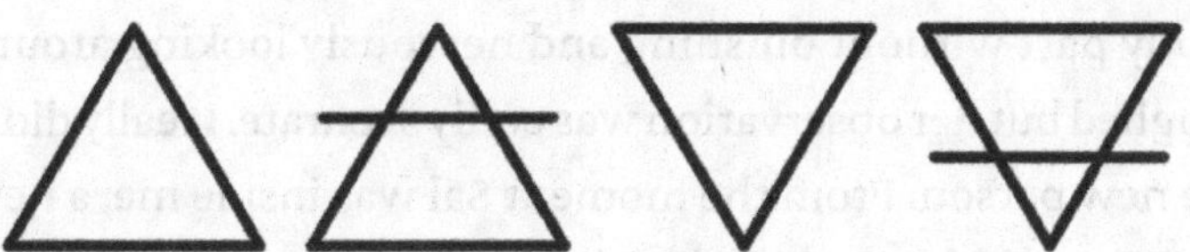

Is it possible to be hungover from sex?

I wondered as I stumbled into work the next day.

My body ached but deliciously so, like after a good workout. It felt more like the opposite of a hangover, like nourishing my body with exactly what it needed.

I wondered if Sal felt the same way. He switched between being dominant and submissive at the drop of a hat and it constantly kept me on my toes. I never thought I'd enjoy a more dominant role in the bedroom but he drew that hidden side of me out like it was always there.

And maybe it was. Just for him.

"So uh, you got laid."

I spun around to see Nona giving me a knowing look.

"Is it that obvious?" I said.

"For not being a morning person, you have the most energy and pep in your step that I've ever seen. You're downright glowing. And on top of that, you have that smile and that look in your eye that says not only did you get it, you got it *good*."

"Yeah," I said casually, tucking a piece of hair behind my ear. "I guess I did."

"You guess? You're like a whole new person, Deja." Nona placed her hands on my shoulders and shook gently. "Who are you and what have you done with my boss?"

"Magical dick. What can I say?" I snickered. She had no idea how true those words were.

"Holy shit, call the news stations," Nona declared. "Deja said a male body part without blushing and nervously looking around."

I laughed but her observation was eerily accurate. I really did feel like a whole new person. From the moment Sal was inside me, a newfound confidence and boldness circulated through my veins. And it only grew each time we made love, along with the memories of my past lives.

Was this confident, uninhibited, sex-hungry woman who I really was? If so, I hoped this new Deja was here to stay. I was ready to shed my sheltered, repressed background like an old skin.

When Juno walked in the moment Nona turned on our OPEN sign, this new Deja brimmed with eager anticipation.

"Morning, Juno," I greeted jovially from the counter. "What can we get you this morning?"

"Morning! I'm feeling like a pot of Irish Breakfast, I think."

She pulled a few bills from her wallet but I waved her money away. "It's on me today."

"What? No." She blinked her wide ocean-colored eyes in disbelief. "Deja, I insist. This is my favorite tea shop, I want to support it."

"And I want to show my customers that I appreciate them." I pressed the bills she set down into her palm, sending a small pulse of magic through her skin as I did so. "You can support us next time," I added with a wink.

"Oh, that won't do. I'll just hand a fat tip to Nona when you're not looking," she said, a knowing smile spreading across her face.

"Feel free. Nona keeps her tips and deserves all of them." I prepared her tea tray and gently set it in her hands. "Enjoy your Irish Breakfast."

"Thank you, Deja. You really didn't have to do that," Juno said graciously before turning to find a place to sit.

As the morning rush came through, I hoped Juno would stick around until we had a chance to talk. I couldn't cast glamour with Nona so close by and hoped my secret witch handshake was enough of a signal.

By the time our pre-lunch lull gave us a moment to breathe, Juno's teapot was cold and empty. Still, she remained curled up and cozy in an armchair, looking completely at home.

I shoveled a sandwich in my mouth to hold me over for the next rush. When Nona took a bathroom break, I made my move.

My fingers danced through the air as I wrapped a glamour spell around Juno's armchair and the one right next to her. No customers even looked up as I crossed the threshold and took a seat across from her. To outsiders looking in, we were having a perfectly mundane conversation about tea.

"So you're a witch." I wasted no time the moment I sat down.

Juno looked up calmly from her book, an amused twinkle in her eye.

"I was starting to wonder if you would ever talk to me, witch-to-witch."

"This is all really new to me," I admitted. "I didn't know how or even *if* I should talk to you. I just learned glamour last night."

"Really?" She seemed surprised. "You wield your magic so beautifully, with masterful skill. I was shocked I didn't already know you."

"Thank you," I said, feeling a blush rise in my cheeks for the first time that day. "It's a long story but I only just found out I was a witch not even a month ago."

"You're kidding!" Juno's mouth dropped open.

"No," I said and proceeded to tell her my life story, and how I came about knowing my truth. Or at least *one* of my truths.

I told her about growing up in the middle of nowhere, with my deeply religious parents and their community. How I never felt like I truly belonged but couldn't put my finger on why. My parents didn't approve of me going to college, for fear of my mind being poisoned with sin and worldly ideas. I got my first taste of the real world in college. I indulged in things like caffeine, alcohol, and premarital sex. I enjoyed the so-called sinful things much more than my strict, uptight home life, but guilt and obligation kept me from leaving home or pursuing a career.

It wasn't until last year that I cut the cord for good. I left home and took a Greyhound bus as far as I could afford, which happened to be San Francisco. I met Nona and started up my successful tea shop. Last month we went to a party and had our fortunes told by a tarot reader, who seemed to know an eerie amount about me.

Everything changed that night.

I started having dreams and Diana showed up at my place the next day. She informed me that my parents adopted me and I was born from a long line of witches.

"Wow." Juno's massive eyes stared at me unblinking. "That is one hell of a story."

"The exciting parts are, at least," I chuckled. "There's a whole lot of boring in between."

"If I may ask," Juno said gently. "What happened to your birth parents?"

"My mom died soon after I was born," I said truthfully. "And my dad apparently didn't want me so he took off."

I didn't want to get into potential death deals with demons, nor my current love life with said creatures. As nice as Juno seemed, she was still a stranger, and I had no idea if she carried the same feelings toward demons as my grandmother did. Talking to another witch was great but my instinct was to protect my guys first.

"I'm so sorry," Juno said sympathetically. "I can't even imagine a childhood without magic, without that part of you being cultivated and encouraged."

The green tones in her aura shifted to a cool blue, indicating her empathy for everything I missed while growing up. I didn't feel pity from her though, which I appreciated.

"Well, I'm doing my best with the hand I was dealt," I replied.

Three hot men from the depths of Hell does make it a little easier in some ways, although they come with their own cans of worms.

"You are definitely catching up quickly! I never would have known," she said excitedly. "So is it just your grandmother teaching you? Do you have a coven?"

I shook my head. "You and she are the only two I know."

Except for the bartenders at Triple Moon, but no one else needs to see me necking in a dark corner with three demons.

"Oh, you've got to meet our High Priest and Priestess," Juno declared, leaning forward eagerly. "It can be hard to find a good community and they're very welcoming to newcomers. You could even attend a coven meeting and see what we're all about."

"Really?" I blurted, feeling like I was invited to a super secret, exclusive club.

"Yes, really. There's no commitment to join. They're actually very selective about who officially becomes coven members. You have to mesh well with the group and be dedicated throughout the long process. But there's no harm in casual meetings."

"A meet-and-greet doesn't sound bad," I said cautiously, although a tremor of nervousness fluttered in my stomach. Juno made no mention of the darkness in my aura yet, but Diana said it wasn't overwhelming. Would the older, more experienced witches be able to see it too and suspect demons in my company? And if so, how would they react?

"I'll give you my number," Juno said, pulling out her phone. "And we can arrange for you to meet Laurel and John, then take it from there."

"Sounds good," I agreed.

We exchanged information and only then did I look through the shimmery veneer of the glamour spell to check on Nona. The poor girl was dealing with a line going out the door, so I said a quick goodbye to Juno and jumped behind the counter to help her.

I mumbled my apologies as I flew back and forth, preparing orders with a renewed fire under my heels. The idea of meeting more powerful witches was both exhilarating and terrifying.

12

DEJA

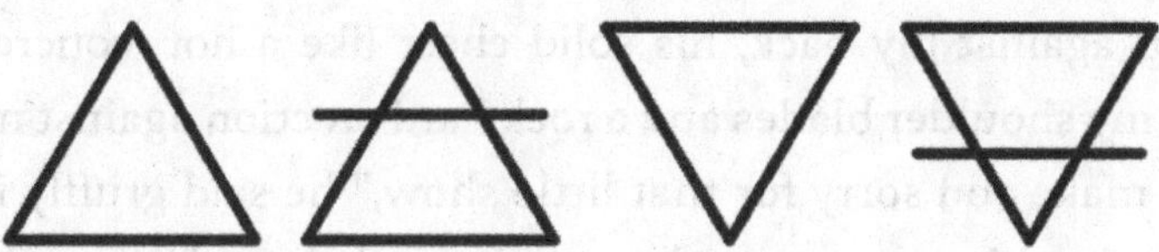

As if I didn't have enough excitement for one day, Raum decided to show up right before closing.

"You guys will be the death of me," I said, my body already heating with desire.

His shoulder-length raven hair was tousled and slightly wet, like he just got out of the shower.

"Who says I'm here to see you? I came for the tea." His eyes lingered on me, indicating that was far from the truth. If I was still the old Deja, all his teasing might have actually wounded me.

"Take a to-go cup then," I ribbed back. "Give me less to clean up."

His teeth grazed his lips as they pulled back into a smile. He seemed pleased at my ability to take his teasing and dish it back.

"Only if you taste it first, to make sure it won't burn me." He leaned his muscular forearms on my counter, his dark eyes drawing me in like two black holes. "And leave a lipstick mark on the rim."

"You'd like that, wouldn't you?"

My words wrangled in my throat. Already he was making me flustered.

"I'd like something else a lot more."

"I'm sure," I said in my best flirty but dismissive tone.

His eyes never left me as I did my best to ignore him while performing closing duties. I may have enjoyed it more than I should have. Leaning across the counter to give him a view of what he couldn't touch yet, bending over with my back turned to accentuate the length of my legs and curves of my ass.

He liked to play games, so I decided to play with him.

No sooner had I locked the door after Nona left did I feel him press up against my back, his solid chest like a hot, concrete wall against my shoulder blades and a rock hard erection against my ass.

"I'll make you sorry for that little show," he said gruffly into my ear, securing his arms around my waist and chest. "When I'm done with you, you'll be begging to cum. And if you're good, I just might let you."

Heat pooled in my center as his hands ravaged me, his rough stubble prickling the back of my neck and making my skin cry out for more.

In a stark contrast to Sal, Raum didn't appear to have a submissive bone in his body. He would claim me and my pleasure, punishing me for teasing him back. I would be at his mercy and I was dripping wet at just the thought of it.

"What's this about you shitting on my windowsill?" I asked, still wanting to defy him—to see how far he would go.

"Hah. Sal's lucky I wasn't in human form." He pressed against me harder, pinning me to the door with barely any space to breathe.

"And who would have cleaned it up?" His presence was so overwhelming at that point, I was desperate to keep my head on straight.

"He would. You'd just have to order him to."

"And if I order you to let me go?"

His low, amused chuckle vibrated against my back, sending shivers across my limbs and directly into my brain.

"You'd be wasting your breath," he whispered hotly in my ear. "Because we both know you don't want that."

He attacked my neck with rough, biting kisses as his large hands kneaded my tender breasts through my shirt. Any words I had to dish back caught in my throat and turned to moans instead. My back arched as my hips pressed back, meeting him as he pressed forward.

"You want me inside you, ravaging you," he growled against my skin as he continued to man-handle me. "Bringing you to the edge again and again without ever letting you fall until I say so."

"Yes," I gasped.

He moaned his approval as his hands made their way to my ass, squeezing my flesh firmly as he rubbed his hot erection between my legs.

Clothing never felt so uncomfortable and restricting. I was burning up from his body heat pressing against me, plus my own pulsing fire building within me. But when his fingers slipped under the thin barrier of my top, I had to catch his wrist and stop him.

"Wait," I panted. "Let me turn around. Please."

His hard body pulled away from me slightly, just enough to spin and stare into his dark, lust-filled eyes.

"Something wrong?" he asked, his voice serious but strained with desire.

"No, I just--" I swallowed, my throat feeling like cotton as I willed myself not to get distracted by his eyes. Or his mouth. Or his arms flexing as they encircled my waist.

"I need to know something. I mean to ask whenever I see you guys but I kind of keep forgetting."

One side of his mouth ticked up into a smirk, indicating he knew exactly how distracting he and the others all were.

"I'm listening, gorgeous."

"I need a serious answer," I said sternly, meeting his gaze. "No riddles, no teasing. This is something important to me."

His smile dropped. His expression turned concerned as he brushed a light caress across my neck.

"Of course. Anything for you."

I took a deep breath, trying to quell the pounding in my heart.

"Do demons make deals with humans?"

He quirked an eyebrow. "You mean in the cliched 'selling your soul for fame and fortune' way?"

"Sort of," I said. "Or maybe killing someone and making it look like a certain cause of death? I'm not sure what kind of exchange that would be."

He remained silent for a moment before speaking.

"It's been known to happen," he said. "We have coexisted alongside humans for so long, some have made transactions like that. But it's incredibly rare."

"Why is that?"

His smirk returned.

"The moment a human wants to strike a deal with a demon, he already belongs to us."

13
RAUM

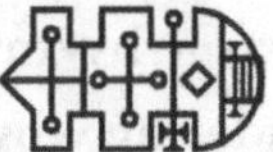

Deja's amber eyes sharpened as she took in what I said. Her breath still came out in little puffs from when I had her pressed against the door.

"Yes, I suppose that makes sense," she said absently.

Her expression flickered, and I missed not a single detail. Something heavily weighed on her mind and compelled her to stop our intimate moment to ask this question.

"Why do you ask, little witch?" I traced a line along her sleek, feminine jaw. "Something else troubling you?"

She chewed her lip as she thought of an answer, and I wished it was my teeth instead of hers.

"My grandmother is convinced it was a demon's magic that killed my mother," she admitted. "She thinks my father made a deal with a demon because he couldn't handle having a child with a witch, and unmarried on top of that. But I keep thinking about it and it doesn't make sense to me. Why would a demon make a deal with a Christian to kill a witch?"

"Smart girl," I said, cupping her chin. "That's because it's absolute nonsense."

"It is?" Her eyes widened.

"Yes," I affirmed. "While it's true that witches and demons have a less than perfectly amicable history, we're often on the same side because the Christ-worshippers see us as all the same—heathens."

"So it's not likely that a demon had a hand in killing my mother?" she asked. The hope in her voice was endearing, and it made me pull her a little closer.

"It's possible, I suppose," I murmured into her forehead. "But yes, highly unlikely."

"But Diana said that was why my aura was so dark. I keep coming back to that and wondering why."

"I can tell you exactly why," I said, and she looked up at me expectantly. "It's because of who you are, and your long history with us. The history that you are slowly beginning to remember."

"Oh yeah. More of what you can't tell me," she sighed, leaning her head against my chest.

I pulled her hips tight against mine so she could feel how hard I still was.

"After I'm buried inside you, there won't be much more to tell." I kissed a slow trail down her neck to her shoulder. "You're already remembering, aren't you?"

"I remember you as both Odin and Loki," she breathed, her eyelids closing halfway as she melted into me.

"Yes, whatever the humans needed at the time," I affirmed, reaching down for her firm ass once again. "And you were?"

"A priestess of Freyja," she moaned, lifting one leg to wrap around my hip. "The goddess of love and fertility."

"And such a goddess you are," I growled as I pulled both of her legs up to wrap around me.

Instead of the wall, I opted to carry her to the counter, setting her down on the cool surface but still keeping my hands firmly attached to her ass.

"You used to turn invisible and fuck me in front of everyone at the rituals," she rasped against my ear. "They treated me like a queen because I had a direct line to the gods. They saw me being ravaged and possessed with their own eyes and fell to their knees saying your name."

"Mm, what good times we had," I groaned.

Her mouth found mine and drew the sweetest kiss from me. It peeled back all my barriers, released my resolve as I melted into her. I sought to dominate her mortal body but held my immortal soul between her lips.

She molded to my touch, leaning into my palms and pulling me closer eagerly. My sexy little witch seemed content with the answer to her question.

Still, I pulled back abruptly, leaving her breathless.

"Anything else you want to know?" I quipped.

"No. I'll let you know if I do," she said, reaching for me.

I grabbed her hands and placed slow, deliberate kisses on her wrists, watching her expression the whole time.

"Are you sure?"

"Raum, if you're not fucking me on this counter within two minutes, I'm kicking you out."

"Mm, sorry to disappoint, little witch." I drew in closer, pulling her thighs around my waist again. "It's going to take a lot longer than that."

I silenced her protests with a hard kiss, surging my tongue between her sweet lips until she caressed it with her own.

Her shirt came off first, in one swift movement over her head, and then mine. I released a groan as she trailed light, nibbling kisses from my throat and down my chest. She always used to do that, and I loved it. Did she remember?

"It feels like I *know* you. Like we've done this before," she whispered. "It was the same with Sal. Logically, my brain is telling me this is the first time but I know how you are, and what you like."

"Because we *have* done this before," I told her, gliding my palms across her bare skin. "We know each other better than two human lovers ever could. You know that instinctually."

I captured her mouth in another deep kiss, relishing in her taste and the feel of her bare skin on mine. How good and right she felt after centuries apart was indescribable.

My fingers skimmed across her waist and belly to flick open the button on her jeans. I peeled her pants off her long legs, leaving her in a matching black bra and panties. She reached for my zipper but I pinned her wrists at her sides and grazed my teeth across her shoulder.

She wanted to tease *me?* Now the real teasing would begin.

Her panties were already soaked, and her mouthwatering, womanly scent filled my nostrils. I didn't dare touch her there with my hands yet, I'd be too tempted to let her cum too soon. Instead, I pressed my straining erection against her swollen, hot sex. One hand on her delicate waist kept her from squirming away as I sucked her shoulder and neck, my other hand inching under her bra.

"Oh, Raum," she moaned and gasped as I rolled her pert little nipples between my fingers. She clutched at my arms and shoulders as I continued mottling her perfect flesh, discarding her bra and sucking those sweet nipples between my teeth.

Her wetness began coating the front of my jeans from her desperate writhing against me.

"Ah, now look what you've done," I said in mock disappointment as I pulled away from her. "I can't go out like this." Her pupils dilated and her tongue lolled out hungrily as I finally unzipped and stepped out of my jeans. "How are you going to make this up to me?"

She dropped to her knees and rolled down my boxer briefs in a flash. Her eagerness to obey sent a heavy tightening in my balls. Fuck, she was just too perfect for me.

"Yes, that's my good little witch," I hissed, stroking her cheek as she glided her lips over my heavy shaft.

I wrapped her hair in my fist to hold her steady while I fucked her mouth at varying depths and speeds. Even when she had my cock in her mouth, I was always the one in charge.

She raked her hands down my thighs and moaned every time I stuffed her pretty mouth. Then she gasped for air every time I pulled out and held her tongue out for more. I thrust deeply into her mouth and pulled out for several minutes until I felt near bursting with cum.

"Because you sucked me so well," I said, sitting her back up on the counter. "I'll allow you one small orgasm."

"Thank you, Ra—ahh!"

My thumb pressed in slow, firm circles around her clit, still outside her panties. She panted and thrust against my hand, already on the edge of her release. Her perfect teardrop breasts bounced in my face and I couldn't contain myself from dipping my head and biting a nipple.

She came hard, screaming and thrashing against my hand. Her skin flushed a deep, beautiful red. I cupped her pussy, and it burned against my palm like a warm stove.

My cock twitched and nestled against her thigh as I absorbed the heat from her body. She felt just like home. The moment it barely brushed her slick folds, she bucked and grabbed my hips to pull me closer.

"Please, I need you," she begged.

"Greedy girl," I scolded, but my chest tightened with pleasure at how badly she wanted me. She hadn't even recovered from her first orgasm yet.

I pulled her soaked panties aside and took half a step closer, resting my shaft on her clit hood. A deep, animal sound escaped me as I rocked my hips ever so slightly. Her hot bare flesh on mine was almost too much to bear. Even I couldn't handle the teasing much longer.

"Inside me, Raum," she whimpered. "Please fuck me."

"I'll fuck you when I'm damn well ready," I growled, but even my voice tremored as I began nearing the edge of my control.

She let out a shuddering sigh as I pressed two fingers inside her, working them at the same tempo as my cock caressed her clit. It wasn't enough, but my woman knew how to take what I gave her.

Her breath came in shorter pants as I felt her next orgasm building around my fingers. I curled them inside her as my heavy erection stroked her clit hood.

Every cell in my body was dying to sink into her as far as I could go, but I held back and watched her unravel for the second time. I felt her hammering pulse everywhere—against my fingers inside her, in her lips as I kissed her, and it drove me wild like a bloodthirsty vampire.

She gazed at me hungrily with hooded eyes but knew better than to beg this time. Only good, patient girls got rewarded. And reward her I did.

Her breathing had barely slowed when I pushed inside her. I expected her scream, but not her third orgasm to release almost immediately around my cock.

"Fucking hell, Deja," I gasped, wrestling for control as I withdrew from her warmth and tightness. Despite teasing her into a frenzy and making this girl beg, she was the one really in control of me.

"I can't help it," she panted. "You feel too fucking good."

My impish grin couldn't hold back as I caught her mouth in another bruising kiss, sinking into her once again. I pushed her gently onto her back and pinned her wrists next to her head on the counter. Her eyes flashed with attitude but she didn't whine or beg.

Instead, her sweet pussy tightened around me as I rutted into her, relinquishing control to me and loving it. Her hips tilted up to draw me in deeper. Her sweet, submissive whimpers in my ear only drove me wild until I was slamming into her with all my might. She unleashed her final orgasm with a scream that echoed off the walls and finally ripped all my control from my limbs.

I collapsed and shuddered as I emptied into her, unrestrained pleasure sweeping across me. Her hands caressed me, bringing me back to earth from my high. Bringing me back home.

I caught her mouth in another kiss, but this one was different. Still passionate, but now an unspoken emotion passed between us. Something that could only be expressed with magic, not words.

And other demons wondered why I spent so much time in human form when I could fly as a raven. It was because nothing felt better than this.

14
DEJA

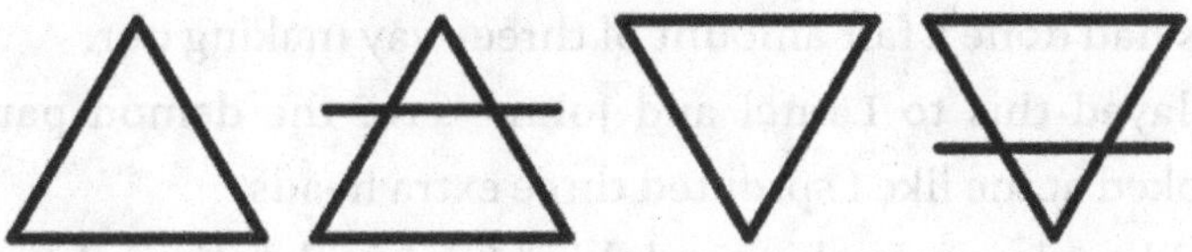

"Oh! There they are."

Juno stood and waved with a bright smile to someone behind me. I sucked down the last of my gin and tonic for a final dose of liquid courage, then turned to greet two of the most powerful witches in the city.

"Deja, this is Laurel and John. High Priestess and High Priest of the Golden Moon Coven," Juno introduced graciously, nodding her head in a slight bow.

"Oh please, no need for formalities," Laurel protested as she took my hand. "It's lovely to meet you, Deja."

"Juno has told us so much about you already," John added, offering a warm, fatherly smile that immediately put me at ease.

"Good things, I hope." I settled back into my chair, nerves still fluttering in my stomach but not as bad as a minute ago.

John and Laurel were a fairly normal-looking middle-aged couple with salt and pepper hair. Laurel wore hers down her back in a long French braid that reminded me of Diana. They both dressed casually with a slight hippie vibe, complete with large chunks of raw crystals worn around their necks. John's aura was a pale, pastel green, while Laurel's was a shimmery, greyish silver. I sensed they were magical immediately, but they looked so normal aside from that. I would never have taken them for witches.

"So did Juno show you this place immediately or send you on a wild goose chase?" Laurel asked in a teasing, motherly way.

I blinked, somewhat confused. We were sitting at Triple Moon Pub, the bar visible only to magical beings, which I happened to find the day after discovering I was a witch. And where I and three certain demons had done a fair amount of three-way making out.

I relayed this to Laurel and John—save the demon part—and they looked at me like I sprouted three extra heads.

"Hold on, let me understand this," John said, laying a hand in the center of the table. "You learned you were a witch, started seeing people's auras, and just stumbled upon this place all within twenty-four hours?"

"More like twelve," I admitted. "I was about to go to bed the night before when my grandmother showed up."

He and Laurel exchanged a look that I couldn't read, but my stomach felt like it sank into my feet. I looked over at Juno, who had been silent since introducing us, and she merely lifted a shoulder in a half-shrug.

"Deja, who are your mother and grandmother?" asked Laurel. Her tone grew sharp, and I suddenly felt as if I was being interrogated.

"Um, my grandmother is Diana Quinn. My mother's name was Deidre, but she died when I was an infant."

"I'm so sorry for your loss, dear." Laurel's sharp edge softened. "I know of your family of witches, albeit distantly. We're just baffled because, forgive me for saying this, but there is nothing special in your bloodline."

"Oh... kay." I wasn't sure whether to be offended or not.

"What Laurel means is," John cut in. "Your magic is highly advanced for being such a late bloomer, to the extent that it's usually a hereditary gift passed down through generations to be at your level of development. You've done in less than a day what typical witches can't do for years."

My mind spun, and I began to regret drinking my alcohol so fast.

"Wait, so you're saying most witches can't see auras or find glamoured bars right away?"

"Places like this use a fairly complex glamour spell designed to keep underage witches from getting in trouble," John chuckled. "By the time they're of legal age, it can still be a few weeks before they see through it."

"Depends on how badly they want to drink," Laurell chimed in with a wink. "And yes, aura perception is a typically a learned skill that takes many years to hone, although some develop a talent for it while very young."

"Wow," I breathed, sitting back in my chair. "Diana told me I was learning fast, but I had no idea."

"Told you that you were special," Juno teased, nudging me with her shoe.

"It's true," John agreed softly. "You are an exceptional rarity, miss Deja."

I didn't know how to feel. Flattered? Worried? Proud? More like a serious case of Imposter Syndrome. Just over a month ago, I was nobody special at all. Now I was apparently some kind of super-witch, as well as the reincarnation of some ancient still-yet-to-be-known person who captured the hearts of three powerful demons thousands of years ago.

Some inkling inside me told me these two pieces of information were related, although I couldn't be sure. And who could I possibly ask?

Laurel and John seemed nice enough but how much could I really trust them? My own grandmother's contempt for demonkind, not to mention the sideways looks I got from other patrons at the pub while with my guys, boiled my blood every single time. It felt like nothing more than blatant discrimination, just like being prejudiced against anyone else who wasn't them.

No, the only ones I trusted wholeheartedly were my demon boys.

Even Ash. Although my stubborn pride still wanted to be mad at him, deep down I knew he wasn't in the wrong. He wasn't trying to hurt me or jerk me around. He slipped up and then held steadfast to what he thought was best. I actually respected him for that.

Fuck. I missed him.

I hadn't seen him since that night I left his place. While the black roses he sent me never wilted, his aura around them began to fade.

Not that my time with Sal and Raum wasn't enjoyable. They each rocked my world in such special and different ways. But nothing could replace how my aloof, icy Ash melted like a popsicle when we touched. More memories of my past lives returned to me every night, but a large chunk of myself was still missing without him.

"It's a lot to take in, dear." Laurel's gentle voice cut into my thoughts, assuming my lack of talking was due to being over-whelmed with this new revelation.

"Um, yeah." I cleared my throat. "I don't really know what to say."

"You would greatly benefit from a supportive community, with mentors teaching you various aspects of magic that they specialize in," John said. "Your grandmother has clearly taught you well, but she is just one person. As your powers grow, you will need balance between them. And the best way to achieve that is to learn from multiple sources."

"But of course it's your decision," Laurel chimed in, shooting a sharp glance at John like a stern teacher. I began to realize that was her signature look. It seemed like she was the one truly in charge. "We absolutely don't want to pressure you, Deja. Lots of witches are solo practitioners because they can't find a coven that fits them, and that's fine too."

John mumbled something under his breath, indicating he disagreed with that last statement but didn't elaborate.

"I would like some time to think about it," I said cautiously.

"Of course, dear," Laurel said with a genuine smile. "We're having a gathering at our house on the next full moon. It's casual, so feel free to drop in or not. You'll be able to meet more coven members there. Bring your grandmother if you'd like."

"That sounds fun. I'll ask her," I said, feeling my defenses slowly back down. These people seemed good and honest. And my lonely heart did yearn for a community where I felt included. More than anything, I yearned for a *real* family.

"I'll be there, too," Juno piped up. "You can meet my boyfriend and other witches around our age." She rolled her eyes teasingly at Laurel and John, who both gasped in mock disbelief.

"Goodness, are you calling us old?" Laurel demanded, her hand flying to her throat. "If I wore pearls, I'd be clutching them right now."

We all laughed as a comforting warmth settled over me like a blanket. John went up to the bar to get us a round of drinks while Laurel asked me questions about my magic casting. I answered eagerly, the words spilling from my mouth like a waterfall.

And I thought maybe, just maybe, these could be my people.

15
DEJA

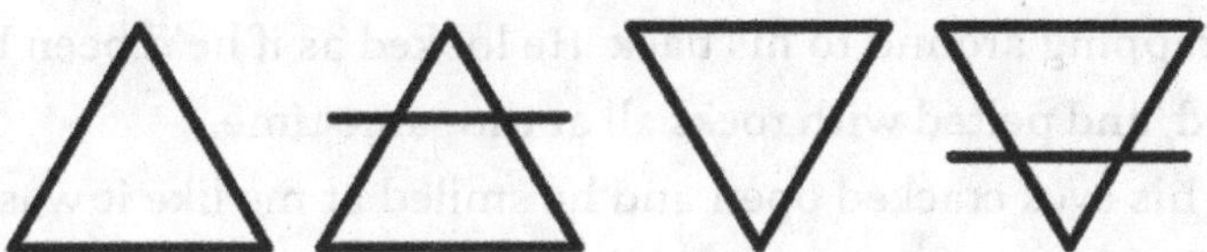

I opened my eyes to stare at a ceiling that seemed to stretch up for miles. The dark, oddly textured red walls converged but never seemed to meet. They just kept going up into infinite darkness.

Disoriented, I sat up abruptly and looked at my surroundings.

I realized I was not in my own futon at home but a massive, luxurious bed that also seemed to spread out around me endlessly.

The pillows and sheets were covered with a plush, silky red fabric, trimmed with an intricate gold pattern.

And a beautiful naked man laid across them next to me.

Ash's hair was longer, like the time I saw him as an angel before falling. His beard was gone and light stubble peppered his cheeks and chin. But his body was what took my breath away.

He looked like the statue of David come to life. Not a single flaw or imperfection could be found on him. His muscles were defined as if sculpted by the hand of an artist and in perfect proportion.

The beauty of him just made me want to cry. Sal and Raum were hot and muscular as well but still looked like relatively normal human men. One look at Ash and you just knew he wasn't created on Earth.

"Oh my God, Ash!" I gasped.

He laid on his back but I could see one of his wings peeking out from underneath him. What few white feathers remained were stained red with blood. The rest were charred or missing. And the angle of his wing seemed wrong, like the broken wing of a bird.

Only then did I notice the dark, tender bruises and welts on his side, wrapping around to his back. He looked as if he'd been burned, whipped, and pelted with rocks all at the same time.

But his eyes cracked open and he smiled at me like it was a typical, lazy Sunday morning.

"Hello, my love." His voice was gravelly with sleep as he reached for me.

"Ash, you're hurt!" I shrieked, too panicked to register his term of endearment.

"It's alright. Lucifer gave me something for the pain." He draped an arm across my waist and looked at me adoringly. "And with time, all will heal."

"But what happened?" I cried, hating that he'd been hurt so badly in the first place. I felt utterly helpless.

"We finally did it." He looked pleased, if a bit drugged out from whatever Lucifer gave him. "We rebelled. We took the fall. And I brought you with me."

"The fall?" I repeated as my mind scrambled to connect the dots.

"Yes, you're safe now." He reached for my hand and laced his fingers with mine. "No human man will ever make you submit to him again. You have all the same rights and powers as anyone else. All you have to do is take them."

As my thoughts raced, my eyes caught a mirror across from the bed and the reflection shocked me.

My eyes looked exactly the same golden-brown color. But other than that, I looked completely different. My hair was much longer, nearly down to my waist, and a shade of coppery auburn. With one glance down at my naked body, I saw I was much shorter and thinner. This was not the body I, Deja, was born in, and yet it was still mine.

"Lucifer suggests you form a legion to protect yourself," Ash continued in his lazy, sexy tone. "You won't be immortal like us but as the first human on our side, he will grant you powers over them." He eyed me curiously. "Or maybe he already has."

This had to be another one of my dream memories, right? There was no way I could wake up in a different body in a completely different place. But everything felt so real, from the sheets beneath me to Ash's arm wrapped around me.

And this raw power within me felt unmistakably real.

When I sat still and focused, I felt it traveling through me like millions of tiny high-speed trains. I closed my eyes and saw the Garden that was no longer my home. Yet still, wherever we were, I could draw the energy from the earth and will it to obey me.

"Turn over," I said abruptly. "Let me see your back."

Ash looked puzzled but obliged, rolling over on his stomach. I choked back a cry at what I saw. His injuries were far worse than I imagined. While the front of his torso was painfully beautiful and perfect, his back was a mess of deep gashes, mottled bruises, and painful welts. His left wing was a twisted deformity of broken bones with just a few feathers holding on. The right wing was gone completely, with a painful-looking, bloody hole where it once was.

If he were human, he simply would not have lived.

Steeling myself, I placed my palms carefully on his back and closed my eyes. I drew upon the resilient energy of the earth first up through my tailbone and collected it in the center of my chest. I had no idea what I was doing, and yet I did. It was pure instinct.

I drew on the healing powers of nature, which always returned with a vengeance even when the last little leaf fell from the tree. From the center of my chest, I willed the magic of the natural world through my arms and out my palms. I willed for it to heal my lover, my savior, like it healed the earth. To take away his pain, and to give him great black wings fit for a ruler of Hell.

I didn't open my eyes for the longest time, too afraid to see if I failed him. But when I saw my palms pressed against smooth, flawless skin and rippling muscles, I collapsed with relief and joy.

"It worked!" Tears sprang to my eyes as I smoothed my hands across his back, unable to believe it. "You're healed!"

Ash sat up and checked the mirror, looking over his shoulder with adorable fascination. He stretched his majestic black wings carefully and my breath felt stolen from my body. I never saw a creature that looked so beautiful.

"I'll be damned," he breathed.

"Well, considering we're in Hell, you already are," I giggled.

"No, my love."

With an impish grin, he folded them against his back again and dropped on top of me. An explosion of love and warmth spread from my chest as he pulled me into a tight embrace and peppered my face with kisses.

"I'm not damned in the slightest, even if I am a demon now." He shifted to look at me with his crystal blue gaze. "Because of you, my love, I am truly blessed."

16
DEJA

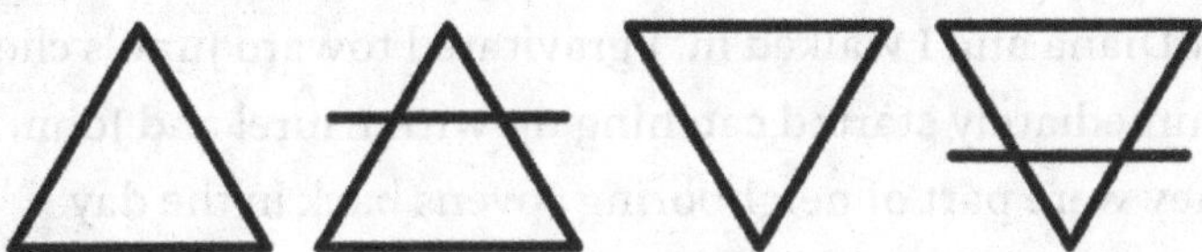

"Name your favorite flower off the top of your head," Juno instructed. "And go!"

"Any flower that's black," I replied. "I especially have a thing for black roses."

"Ooh, we've got a gothy witch," her boyfriend Erik teased.

"What can I say. It goes with everything."

I popped a cheese cube in my mouth, which was nowhere near as decadent as what Sal conjured up for me that night at my house.

My thighs clenched at the thought of my hot-tempered, yet sweetly submissive demon. I craved him like nothing else, except for Raum. And Ash, especially after that hyper-realistic dream of healing his back and giving him new wings.

That still shook me hard. I couldn't get it out of my mind. It felt so real; it *had* to have really happened.

I looked across the room to where Diana, Laurel, John, and a few older witches gathered, talking in low voices. They sat around a small coffee table with candles, crystals, and herbs arranged in front of them. On the way here, my grandmother had kept her anti-demon rhetoric to a minimum, thankfully. But coming to this party with her reminded me of what Raum told me. Demons didn't bother making deals with humans, especially not against witches.

It led me to wonder how she came to the conclusion that it was demon magic that killed my mother. Despite admitting she had no proof, my hope lingered that she based her theory on some actual evidence, maybe some ancient ritual or pact, not just prejudice.

Juno, Erik and I hung out in the kitchen with a few other coven members who looked to be in their twenties and thirties. From the moment Diana and I walked in, I gravitated toward Juno's clique and Diana immediately started catching up with Laurel and John. Apparently, they were part of neighboring covens back in the day.

Across the kitchen island from us stood a guy introduced as Seth, drinking a beer and mainly keeping to himself. But I felt his eyes on me like an itch on my skin that wouldn't go away.

I did my best to ignore his gaze. With his tousled dark hair, stormy gray eyes, motorcycle jacket, and tattoos peeking out of his shirt, it was difficult. His bad boy image reminded me of my guys and even friendly eye contact sent a nervous fluttering in my center. If I didn't know any better, I'd suspect he was a demon in disguise. Even his aura was nearly as dark and electrically charged as theirs.

"Care for a smoke?"

Erik tapped a pack against his palm as his eyes flickered across all of us. Juno and I declined but Seth gave a curt nod. The guys headed for the backyard and with Seth gone, the intensity instantly fizzled out of the room.

"Are you having fun?" Juno asked, giving me a playful poke on the arm.

"I am," I admitted with a smile. Laurel and John's home was just as comforting as their presence at the bar. They were incredibly hospitable hosts and the coven members I met seemed warm and welcoming as well. It truly felt like I was among friends.

"I think Seth likes you," she teased.

"Really? 'Cause I get the impression he'd enjoy carving my eyeballs out with a spoon."

Juno laughed. "He's just really intense. He actually hasn't been around much in the last year. He's been traveling to all kinds of places like Iceland, Romania, and I think Africa, too."

"Oh yeah, doing what?"

"Hunting demons," she remarked casually.

17
DEJA

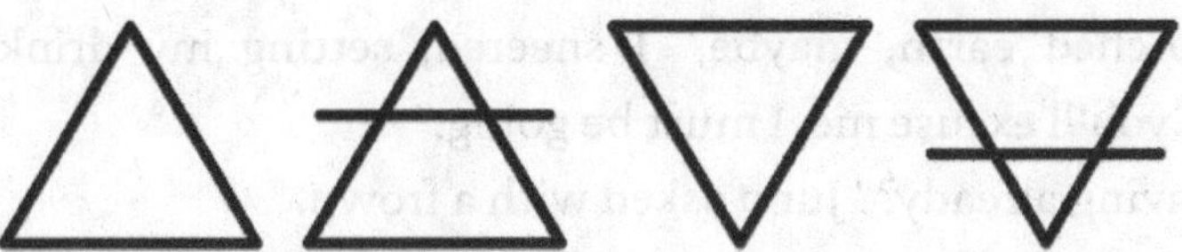

My blood turned to ice. I tried to keep my expression blank while my heart stopped in my chest.

"Oh, really. That's a thing, huh?" Keeping my voice steady felt impossible but Juno didn't seem to notice.

"Yeah, I don't know much about it," she remarked, dipping a celery stick into ranch dressing. "Just that it's incredibly dangerous and very few witches take on that role. It's kind of an elite, secret agent thing."

"Hmm," I mused, sipping my beer and trying to keep calm. But my insides swirled with panic. What kind of abilities did he have? Could he tell just by looking at me that I kept company with the same creatures he hunted?

The guys returned from smoking before I could properly settle down. And Seth's intense gaze now only made me want to run off and warn my guys as soon as possible.

"Deja, right?"

Naturally, that was the time he chose to unmute himself.

The scent of cloves and woodsy cologne hung around him like a cloud as he popped a mint into his mouth.

"Yeah." I forced a tight smile.

"It's a sexy name." His mouth twitched into a smirk, daring me to tell him off.

"Uh, thanks." Please don't ask if my last name is Vu.

"You know what it means, right?"

"Remembrance," I answered tersely. "In the age of Google, is there anyone who doesn't know the meaning of their name?"

"Little spitfire," he drawled. "You sure you're an earth witch?"

"Scorched earth, maybe," I sneered, setting my drink down. "Now if you'll excuse me, I must be going."

"Leaving already?" Juno asked with a frown.

"Yeah, sorry," I said, pulling her into a hug. "I have an early morning at the shop tomorrow."

I said my goodbyes to everyone else, including Diana after confirming she'd have a way home, and stepped out into the chilly night air.

A single raven cawed from where it sat on a telephone pole, then took flight in the direction of my apartment.

"Wouldn't mind having that power myself," I muttered, hurrying down the street to the train station.

My leg bounced with anxiety the moment I sat down. It was only a ten-minute ride but seemed to take an eternity before I reached my stop. When I was finally walking again, my legs couldn't seem to move fast enough.

I finally burst through the door of my apartment to find Sal and Raum sitting on my couch. It didn't even bother me that they waited in my house anymore. I was getting used to it, and maybe even found it comforting. But under these circumstances, all I could feel was panic.

"Where's Ash?" I demanded, breathless. "I need all three of you here."

Sal approached me first, his face a calm exterior over the fire within.

"He still wants to give you space, beautiful. Until you remember your original name."

"What the fuck?" I cried, exasperated and my heart aching for him. "I'm over the name thing, okay? This is important. I need to see him."

"He knows you're not angry," Raum said from the couch. "It's not you. It's just that he doesn't trust himself to keep it from you."

I speared my fingers through my hair and let out a frustrated groan. Didn't he know how much I missed him? How could he keep avoiding me like this? This was life or death and he was hung up on my stupid memories.

"What's wrong, beautiful?" Sal grabbed my waist and tugged me forward. His lip curled into a threatening snarl and I could already feel his rage rising.

"There's a demon hunter here," I said. "His name is Seth. He's part of the local coven."

Sal cocked an eyebrow. "No one I've ever heard of."

"I have. He's nobody," Raum said in a bored tone.

"What do you mean?" I demanded. "He hunts demons!"

"He destroys the bodies of lower demons, which doesn't actually kill them," Raum explained. "Their souls are sent back to Hell, where they wait to inhabit another body."

"Are you sure?" I asked skeptically. "My friend said hunters are elite witches and have dangerous jobs."

"'Cause they're so incompetent, they get killed more often than they actually kill." Sal scoffed, tightening his hold on me and bringing his mouth close to my ear. "Trust me, beautiful. He's no match for the likes of us." Abruptly he pulled away just enough to look at me. "But if he gives you any trouble, make no mistake. We'll hang him by his scrotum."

I snorted a laugh but couldn't fight the heat pooling in my body. I leaned into his chest, his strength. It absolutely killed me how he could be so sweet and so vicious.

"Other than that, how was the witch party?" Raum asked, his clever grin widening.

"Other than that, Mrs. Lincoln, how was the play?" I mocked. "I'm glad you two are so nonchalant, but I had to keep my cool while talking to someone who I thought was going to *kill* you guys! I could've had a heart attack on my way up here!"

Sal made a growling noise into my neck, and all my frustration seemed to melt away.

"It's so hot that you're protective of us," he murmured. "And we'd do the same for you, beautiful."

He led me to the couch, seating me between him and Raum. His firm hold moved up to my back, where he rubbed the tension out of my shoulders while placing light kisses on my neck.

My head leaned back as my back arched, melting into his touch. In front of me, Raum slid his hands up my thighs and pressed his lips to my exposed throat.

"Neither one of us is Ash and I know that you miss him," he murmured. "But maybe the two of us can help put your mind at ease?"

"At the same time?" I gasped, more thrilled than shocked. Thoughts of a threesome no longer made me want to blush and hide, but I had yet to experience any true memories of it. This would truly be my first time.

"If that's what you want, beautiful," Sal murmured against my nape.

I reached behind me to feel across his lap. He was already hard and growing bigger. The hollow ache inside me grew as he groaned and muttered curses under his breath.

I kissed him over my shoulder as I stretched my other hand forward, skimming my fingers up Raum's thigh as he did to me. When I found him growing hard too, a deep gasp of pleasure escaped me and left me breathless.

"Seems like that's a yes," he chuckled, dipping his head lower to kiss down my sternum.

Sal's tongue surged into my mouth with renewed hunger as he continued his massage under my blouse. He peeled it over my head while Raum pulled my leggings down over my hips. Their shirts disappeared too and while sandwiched between them, all the bare skin contact put me in absolute heaven.

Sal's heart thundered against my back while he sent light caresses over my arms and shoulders. Raum grabbed my hips and forcefully tilted them up as his kisses grew dangerously close to my pussy.

Already I quivered in anticipation. Two pairs of hands on me and the gorgeous men attached to them were almost too much to bear.

I leaned against Sal like he was a solid wall. Raum's back and shoulders flexed before me as he wrapped his large hands around my thighs. He drew teasing circles around my vulva with his tongue, making me shudder and press my hips up higher to meet his mouth.

The two of them were so in sync, it felt like they shared a single mind. Sal's gentle touches and kisses on my neck contrasted sharply with Raum's rough handling and merciless teasing.

When Raum finally sealed his mouth over my pussy, Sal cupped my breasts and held me in place. His thumbs soothed the sensitive ache in my nipples while I helplessly tried to thrash against Raum's mouth. He ate me out roughly, greedily. The friction of his stubble sent my hot, sensitive skin into overdrive. I couldn't pull away to ease back on the sensation, it was too much all at once.

My first orgasm exploded within a minute, leaving me stunned and gasping. I barely felt it build up at all.

Raum grinned wickedly up at me as he kissed each of my trembling inner thighs.

"Why don't we switch, brother?"

"Excellent idea," Sal's voice rumbled behind me.

The hard wall of his chest disappeared behind me as the guys traded places. Seconds later, Raum's different but no less solid form took Sal's place.

"Let's get you nice and spread for Sal, my good little witch," he growled into my ear as he took each of my thighs in his strong grip and pulled my legs apart.

I was spread out and exposed, already panting and covered in a thin sheen of sweat, and Sal looked at me like he wanted to drop to his knees and worship my body.

His touch was firm but gentle. His smooth face and tongue soothed my roughened skin. He licked and kissed me tenderly where Raum had been so rough just seconds before. I could still feel the friction of his stubble and Sal's softness on top of that drove me wild. They were a perfect balance, like two opposing forces of nature that both felt so fucking good.

"How does his mouth feel, my sexy little witch?" Raum demanded, his low, rumbling voice sending goosebumps along my neck. "Is he getting you nice and wet for the fucking you're going to get from me?"

"Yes," I moaned deliriously. "It's so good."

Sal hummed with pleasure as he pressed two fingers inside me, stroking my inner walls while his tongue tirelessly caressed my clit. Heat and an aching need to release began building up within me. I reached down and threaded my fingers through his fiery auburn hair until Raum pinned my arms back.

"No cheating," he scolded with a grinning bite to my shoulder. "Let him get you off at his pace."

I whimpered and whined as Sal slowly walked me to the very edge. Raum scolded and punished me every time I fought for control. He pinched my nipples, bit hard on my neck, and told me exactly how hard he was going to fuck me when Sal was done.

I finally came so hard that magic sparked from my fingertips. Convulsions and pure, blinding pleasure wracked me. I completely lost control of my body.

At that point, all three of us were fucking done with the foreplay. My men continued with their opposing gentle and rough forces and it was nothing short of magical. Raum fucked me hard from behind and made a mottled, bruised mess of my ass while I stroked Sal to the edge of his own orgasm. Sal flipped me onto my back and made love to me with such intense passion while Raum rammed his cock down my throat. I swallowed his massive load and licked him clean while Sal emptied himself inside me.

I felt filthy and used, empowered and worshipped, loved and cared for all at the same time. A good cathartic cry didn't even come close how emotionally intense the experience was. I realized I *needed* Raum's dirty talk and rough handling just as much as Sal's warmth and sweetness.

They carried me to bed when we finished and wrapped around me with kisses, caresses, and good nights. As my exhausted but sated mind drifted off to sleep, it made me wonder how anyone could be satisfied with just one person.

18
DEJA

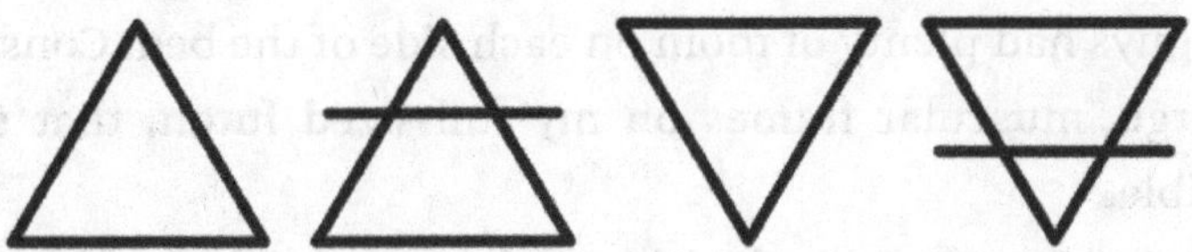

A sensual mouth left a burning hot trail of kisses down my back. Rough stubble grazed over my skin, making me shiver.

A second pair of lips kissed my forehead while fingertips skimmed down my bare thighs.

Still mostly asleep, I shifted my weight and found my cheek pressed against a warm, hard chest. The watery backward heartbeat quickened under my ear.

These were the dreams I both loved and hated. Such vivid and hot sensations in my body, but I could never see who was with me. Every time I opened my eyes, I only saw darkness. Like I was in a dark room and my lovers were invisible.

My body yearned for their touches every night. I hated the moment I woke up, the moment they disappeared.

But this time my eyes cracked open to find a pair of green ones staring back at me.

"Good morning, beautiful," Sal greeted, sliding his hand down my thigh to gently knead at my calf.

Behind me, Raum's trail of kisses down my back turned toward my hip bone, where he playfully bit me.

"Good morning, my handsome devils," I croaked, stretching out between them. "So last night was real, huh?"

"As real as we are here in your bed." Raum rested his head on my thigh as I snuggled back into Sal's shoulder. Being sandwiched between them filled me with the utmost contentedness and warmth.

"How are the three of us able to fit in here?" I lifted my head to see the guys had plenty of room on each side of the bed. Considering their large, muscular frames on my full-sized futon, that seemed impossible.

"Magic," Raum smirked, although he wasn't joking. "Hey, I don't mean to alarm you," he murmured lazily, resting his cheek against my hip. "But your phone has been blowing up."

"Huh." I frowned. That literally never happened. The shop was closed today and there would be no other reason for anyone to call me nonstop.

"You asshole," Sal groaned, pulling me back into his chest as I started to get up. "Now you're making her want to get out of bed."

"Well, you keep hogging her over there," Raum replied. "As much as I love this backside," he declared with a slap to my ass. "You're stealing all the snuggles and the kisses."

"Aw, what's that?" I flipped over to face him, my grin spreading the moment I saw his pout. "Mr. Dirty Talk and Dominant wants cuddles and kisses?"

"I'm grumpy without my sugar in the morning," he growled before cupping my chin and lowering his mouth to mine.

His slow, sensual kisses turned me to jelly. My brain shot off fireworks as it reconciled this was the same man who made me choke on his cock last night.

Our tongues spoke their own language as they caressed and danced. He told me without words how much he cared about me, and that he would never hurt me unless I derived pleasure from it. I folded my arms against his chest and he cradled my back as gently as if I were a baby.

Only when I was completely lost in the taste and warmth of him, did his kisses grow deeper, more demanding. Hot moans escaped from deep in his chest as his grip on me tightened. The demon couldn't hold back for long.

He palmed each of my breasts and grazed his teeth down my neck. I slid my hand down the ridges of his abs and stroked his thickening length, growing harder by the second.

Another hard cock pressed against my slick vulva and I let out a gasp of surprise. Sal grinned wickedly and gave me a kiss over my shoulder as he rubbed against me.

"It's pretty hot watching you two, so I'll enjoy this beautiful backside for now."

With a firm hand on my hip, he stroked himself against my swollen pussy while I stroked Raum.

"Oh, that's so good," he moaned, halfway closing his eyes. "My sweet little witch."

He twitched, moaned, bit his lip, and even yelped a little as I glided his smooth skin up and down. Watching my dominant one, the trickster, the tease, the one always a step ahead, lose control in the palm of my hand was unbelievably hot.

"Ahhh," I cried out in both relief and ecstasy as Sal finally slipped inside me. He pumped into me steadily, my pussy already slick from him teasing me so much.

Raum sealed his mouth over mine as his fingers found my clit. He grew as stiff as concrete in my hand. I stroked him faster. We swallowed each other's moans as our pleasure soared to new heights before crashing all around us.

I shattered around Sal's cock and he let out a string of curses, reaching around to grab my breast and fucked me deeply before releasing inside of me.

Raum's breath grew ragged as I continued to stroke him. He

looked somewhere between tortured and drunk, but still insanely sexy.

"Your mouth," he rasped right before the end.

I slid down the bed and brought him to my lips just in time. He let out an animalistic growl and his whole body stiffened as his cock convulsed, coating my tongue in thick, hot cum.

After swallowing my fill of him, I slid back up to snuggle against his chest this time, letting Sal spoon me from behind and kiss my shoulders. Such deep relaxation settled back into my body.

"How's that for your morning sugar?" I murmured against Raum's hot skin.

"Mmm. The best I've ever had, baby," he whispered as he wrapped around me tighter.

All the skin-to-skin contact made me feel incredibly cozy and protected. I nearly drifted off to sleep again before I remembered.

"Oh yeah," I said, sitting up. "My phone."

19
DEJA

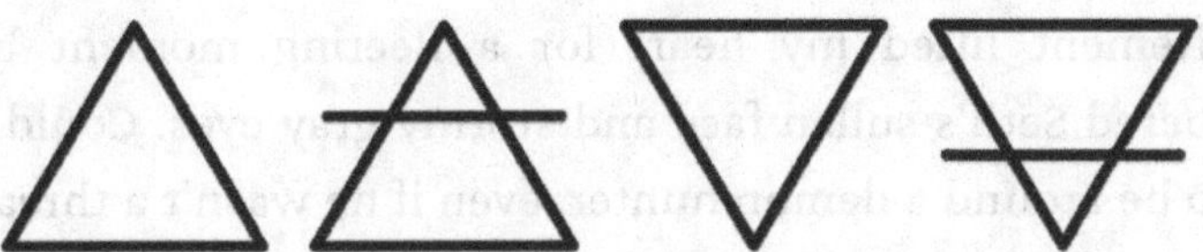

"Call me as soon as you can. I need to talk to you about something important."

Juno's message glared up at me from my screen. It was the only text she sent among a slew of missed phone calls.

I hurriedly called her back, panic rising in my chest as the worst-case scenarios ran through my head.

"Hello?" she chirped in her usual cheerful tone.

"Hey, what's going on?" I demanded. "Is everything okay?"

"Yeah, everything's fine," she laughed. "Did I worry you?"

"Um, yes. What is so important that you need to call me at least fifteen times?"

"Nothing bad, trust me," she said. "But I thought you should know I overheard Laurel and John talking to your grandmother last night after you left."

"Oh? About what?"

Sal chose to walk by just then, completely naked and whistling cheerily. He winked at me as he headed toward my kitchen. My heartstrings pulled tight as I watched the perfect globes of his ass flex before my eyes. What I would kill to make sure I had that view every single morning.

"It sounded like they want to initiate you into the coven really early. Normally it takes one year and one day for a new witch to be initiated. But your grandmother was talking about your powers and how fast you learned. Sounds like they might make an exception for you."

"Wow, really?"

Excitement lifted my heart for a fleeting moment before I remembered Seth's sullen face and stormy gray eyes. Could I really stand to be around a demon hunter, even if he wasn't a threat to my guys? Even if his power didn't hold a candle to them, something about him rubbed me the wrong way.

Not to mention everyone else in the coven. If they accepted and supported a demon hunter among them, how would they feel about someone who slept with the ones he hunted?

"I don't know, June," I said, running a hand through my sexed up bed hair. "It's still a lot to take in right now."

"I totally understand," she said. "Talk to your grandmother about it, see what she says. But I gotta say, it would be so cool to have you officially with us. We would be sisters!"

Something pulled at me when she said that and refused to let go. I never had a sister before. Hell, I never felt like I had a real family until recently.

A sudden kiss on my cheek startled me out of my thoughts.

"Let's see what kind of tea you have stashed here," Raum smirked as he, also completely naked, joined Sal in the kitchen.

Both of their perfect, biteable asses hovered in my view as they raided my cupboards. My heart ached with the sensation of being pulled in two opposing directions. I wanted a witch family more than anything, but I would never let go of my demon lovers. They were mine for eternity.

"Unfortunately Seth won't be around much to make googly eyes at you," Juno teased, cutting into my thoughts. "But I could introduce you to more magical guys if you want."

"Oh, hm?" I said, feigning interest as if three men weren't enough to handle. "Seth's off on his uh, business?"

"Yeah, sounds like he's leaving for the Amazon jungle or somewhere tomorrow. Lots of evil spirit activity."

"I see." Joining the coven without him around sounded much more appealing, though I still had my doubts.

"You still there?" Juno asked gently.

"Yeah, sorry." I blew out an exhale. "Just a lot on my mind. I'll call you later with a more definitive answer."

I ended the call and strode into the kitchen to join my two naked men. Sal held out a steaming mug of Irish Breakfast to me.

"I don't have your skills but I think the caffeine will do the job," he said with a sheepish grin.

I took a tentative sip. "It's perfect," I said, standing on tiptoes to kiss him. "Thank you, my lion." The nickname tumbled out automatically like muscle memory, even though I never knowingly called him that before.

Sal looked just as surprised as I was, but with more joy and less confusion.

"You're remembering," he said, his voice thick with emotion. "That's what you always used to call me."

"The body of a warrior and the head of a roaring lion. A god of war. The creator and destroyer of cities." My mouth moved as if controlled by someone else, but the images came to me as clearly as if I'd been there.

Because I *had* been there.

Like it was yesterday I saw myself walking next to Sal on an ancient, bloody battlefield, his lion head roaring victoriously. I saw him the moment he was created in that cavernous throne room in Hell. He dropped to his knees and pledged his undying loyalty to me.

"Yes," I breathed. "I'm remembering so much of our time

together now." Tears welled up in my eyes as seven thousand years of love and adoration for this man hit me all at once. His passion fueled his fury. And the unique connection we had was the only thing that tempered his flames.

"And you, Raum." I turned to my dark-eyed demon to find a rare, serious look on his face. "Your visions used to hurt you. They would come on suddenly like violent headaches that you couldn't control. Nothing I did could take the pain away. I would just hold your head in my lap until the vision faded."

"Just your hands on me helped with the pain a little," he replied. "You were my immediate pain relief. But I learned to control it, after a few centuries."

I leaned into him while reaching behind me for Sal's hand at the same time. Surrounded by warmth and affection on all sides and my heart stilled ached for Ash. I missed him terribly, now that I could feel the full weight of being without these men for so many lifetimes.

"What do you two think I should do?" I said after a long silence. "Join a coven where they accept people who hunt your kind? Or tell them to fuck off and strike it out on my own?"

Raum's chuckle rumbled against my chest. "You wouldn't have kept us around so long if we were the kind that told you what to do."

"Even if we did, it would ensure you did the exact opposite," Sal agreed.

"I just hate that those who've opened up to me, accepted me, and want me to grow, are the same people who want me to stay away from you," I groaned.

"That's the way the cookie crumbles sometimes." Sal took a sip from my Irish Breakfast while I openly stared at him in bewilderment. How could he of all people feel so nonchalant about this?

"This situation has happened several times before," Raum said, noticing my confusion. "Think of yourself as an undercover agent. Infiltrate the enemy, befriend them. And slowly make them see the error of their ways."

"Can you see the outcome?" I asked, looking up at him. "Will I be able to make them come around to you guys?"

"I have seen it," he confirmed. "But whether good or bad, I can't change what's already set in motion, nor can I use my sight to influence your decision making." His playful smirk dropped once again. "The last time I tried desperately to change an outcome, we lost you anyway."

I draped my arms around his neck and he nestled his large hands in the curves of my waist.

"If we've learned one thing," he murmured against my forehead. "It's that existence as a whole is much bigger than us. What happens in one year, one lifetime or even one century is just a small building block in the grand scheme of existence. We've been trying to steer the course for millennia. Sometimes we make great strides, other times we're pushed back." His smile returned. "As long as there's a need for a little corruption, our work is never done."

"So you're saying it doesn't matter in the big picture if I join this coven or not," I said. "I'll still have lifetimes to master my magic and steer the course of history with you three."

"Exactly." Sal brushed a kiss along the nape of my neck. "We know your loyalty is with us. Just as we are eternally loyal to you."

"Always," I said, turning and locking my gaze on his emerald eyes. "My instinct is always to defend and protect you three. Now that I know why, I swear I won't let any of them hunt you."

"We're not concerned about you leading them onto us, beautiful," he said with a fiery spark in his eye. "Infiltrating the enemy is what you do best."

20
DEJA

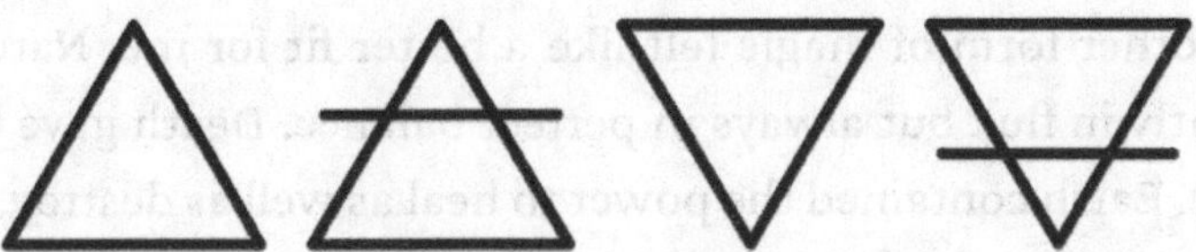

I shed my clothing under the silvery moonlight and waded slowly into the stream.

"Wow, you're brave," Juno remarked. "It's freezing out here."

"Just gotta jump in and do it," I said.

The goosebumps erecting along the entire length of my body agreed with her, but while my skin was cold, my core roared with heat like a furnace. The slippery rocks and mud between my toes acted like heat sources. Already, I was calling on the magic of the earth to guide and strengthen me through the initiation rite.

Juno waded in after me once I found a comfortable spot to sit. She remained dressed in her ceremonial black and gold robes as she helped me bathe. The untouched, natural spring water ran over my arms, back, and hair with her assistance. When every bit of my skin and hair had been kissed by the freezing water, we stepped out and she dried me off with a towel.

We huddled by our fire for warmth as she brushed out my hair. I opened my bag and carefully unfolded the long, white robe I would be wearing in the ceremony. I pulled it over my head while she adjusted and secured it in place.

The hardest part for me was done. Now just came waiting.

I sat cross-legged in front of the fire as Juno mixed a concoction with her mortar and pestle. The flames danced and flickered as it fed on the dry branches. Beneath me and all around me, earth magic hummed with energy. Even a single dry leaf on the ground made my toe pulse with its life force.

No other form of magic felt like a better fit for me. Nature was constantly in flux but always in perfect balance. Death gave birth to new life. Earth contained the power to heal as well as destroy.

"Close your eyes," Juno instructed.

I obeyed and felt something cool and wet on my forehead as she painted with her fingertip. She drew the symbol of earth on my forehead and continued with more symbols on my cheeks and chin with the concoction she mixed.

Coven tradition dictated that I choose the concoction but another member mix and apply it. I chose ash from the fire, mud from the stream, and wild juniper berries that grew native to here. All unique components of the single element of earth.

"I'll come for you when they're ready," she said once she finished.

I nodded while keeping my eyes closed. The mixture felt refreshing on my skin and my face pulsed everywhere it touched.

Laurel would be leading the rite as High Priestess. She and the other coven members were gathered in a clearing in another area of the woods. Before I could join them, I had to be washed and painted, then they had to purify the ceremonial circle.

I sat as still as a boulder, feeling the earth's magic flow through me as if I were an empty vessel. I imagined it as a thread starting from my tailbone rooted to the ground, then flowing out through the crown of my head to return to the universe.

The crickets chirping and burning logs snapping sounded like music to my ears. Tears threatened to well up just because of how beautiful and moving it all was.

Then like a gust of wind, the energy shifted dramatically, and I knew I was no longer alone by my fire.

"Ash," I said in a choked whisper. He may not have been there physically, but I felt his aura wrapping around me like a strong hug. My heart physically ached for him. I missed him so much.

"My love," came his voice, sounding like he was speaking directly to my brain. "When will you remember the woman I fell in love with? I miss her with all of my being."

"I miss you too," I cried out. "I'm right here."

The magic coursing through me took another sudden shift, this time leaving me breathless and gasping. My eyes flew open as I lurched forward, catching myself before diving headfirst into the fire.

I struggled to catch my breath as my heart crashed like a sledge-hammer against my ribs.

I remembered now.

I knew exactly who I was.

A fiery sigil hovered above the flames, the same one Sal drew when I first drank with the three of them at Triple Moon. The one tattooed on the left side of his body, the side of his heart. I now knew it was *my* sigil and traced it with my fingers.

I said my name out loud, the first name I was ever given, and Ash's aura wrapped tightly around me again.

"Finish your rite, my love," he whispered. "I'll see you after it's done."

My breathing calmed just as a large snake slithered across my lap, its forked tongue tasting the air. I smiled and patted it affectionately.

"Thank you, Lord Lucifer, for helping me return to myself as well as my three eternal lovers, my Unholy Trinity."

Branches snapped as a ghostly figure in a long white robe approached me from the treeline.

"They're ready," Juno said with a wide grin as she held her hand out to me. "Come on, coven sister."

I took her hand and followed her through the trees, my smile just as big as hers. But she could not begin to understand my joy and my relief. Everything I ever lost had been returned to me.

She took me to a clearing where my future coven awaited. A large, white circle had been drawn on the ground in the middle. Laurel, the High Priestess stood in the center, wearing her ceremonial black robes with golden moons on them. All other coven members stayed outside the circle, standing around fires as they waited for the ceremony to begin.

Juno walked me to the edge of the circle, our arms linked together. I kept my eyes on Laurel but still noticed others in my peripheral vision. My grandmother stood beaming with tears in her eyes. Far away from everyone else stood Ash with a handsome man I'd never seen before, but the curling ram's horns growing from his forehead left few guesses as to his identity. No one else gave the impression that they could see either my demon or Lucifer himself.

"Who approaches this sacred space?" called Laurel in a booming voice that seemed to bounce off the surrounding hills.

"I bring you one who wishes to understand this coven, to honor the Goddess, the Horned God, Isis, Odin, and all of our sacred deities," Juno answered.

I stifled a smirk and kept my face neutral. How would any of them react if they knew Odin was just another one of Raum's identities?

"Seeker, by what name will you be known within this sacred circle?"

My original name played at my lips, but I answered with the one I was given in this lifetime.

"Deja."

"The gods have deemed you worthy," Laurel proclaimed. "Please enter the sacred circle and kneel in their presence."

Juno gave my hand a final squeeze as I stepped across the threshold. The air crackled and hummed with the coven's magic. I felt lightheaded as I kneeled. It was almost overwhelming.

"By joining this coven," Laurel said as she began walking a circle around me. "You become part of a greater spiritual family. As such, you are part of an endless circle of kinship and hospitality. Hail ye, Gods and Goddesses! Hail to kinsmen and clan, to the ancestors who watch over us, and to those who may follow. Here before you kneels Deja, the Seeker, soon to be a sworn part of this coven."

She walked around me counterclockwise three times, her fingers barely skimming over my shoulders, but the weight of her power was heavy and humbling.

"As a Dedicant of this coven, you will learn and grow and evolve every day. You will seek new knowledge, and attain it in direct proportion to your efforts. Let the Gods and the Ancient Ones guide you on your journey."

She stopped in front of me, tilting my chin to make eye contact with her. "Are you willing and able to uphold the values and principles of this coven?"

"Yes," I said as each of my three demons' faces cycled through my mind.

"Are you prepared, Deja, to be born anew, to begin this day a brand new journey, as part of your new spiritual family, and as a child of the Gods?"

"I am."

"Then rise, Deja, and emerge from the womb of darkness, and be welcomed into the light and love of the Gods. You are no longer a mere Seeker, but a Dedicant of this coven."

I stood to my feet while keeping my head bowed. Laurel placed a long chain over my head, on the end which hung a large, yellow moonstone pendant. The mineral of the Golden Moon Coven rested just below my sternum and seemed to vibrate with magic.

Laurel pulled me forward gently and kissed each of my cheeks.

"Welcome, Deja, to your new family," she beamed. "May you be blessed by the Gods."

She held up a robe, black with golden moons, and everyone cheered as I slid my arms through it.

The solemn ritual turned into a party in the blink of an eye. People whooped and laughed as they brought out coolers full of drinks from their cars and freshly hunted game to roast over the fires. As I drank and danced and hugged my new family members, I couldn't even believe that I spent most of this lifetime condemning this spiritual practice. The energy in the air was pure joy, kinship, and love. I knew I made the right decision by choosing this family for this brief lifetime.

It was a good half hour before I could sneak away to the edge of the clearing, where Ash and Lucifer calmly watched our celebrations.

"Congratulations, my dear," Lucifer said as he took my hand and placed a small kiss on the back of my palm. "It's good to have you back again."

"Thank you, my Lord," I said, lowering my eyes respectfully before turning to Ash.

My Ash. The one I saved and the one who saved me. My first and forever love.

He wore his usual cool expression but his eyes brimmed with anticipation.

"Tell me," he said, his voice thick with emotion. "Tell me your name from when we first met."

I grinned, my heart nearly bursting with the love I carried for him since the dawn of humanity itself.

"My name is Lilith, the first wife of Adam, consort of demons, and mother of all witches."

WITCH'S BETRAYAL

UNHOLY TRINITY BOOK 3

PROLOGUE
LILITH

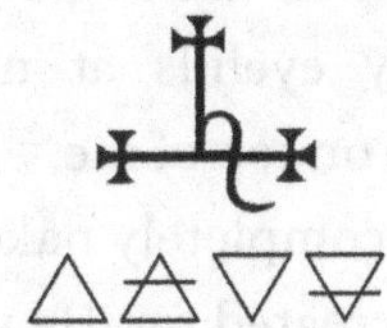

I kicked my feet leisurely in the stream, enjoying the cool, flowing water across my sun-kissed skin. The water shimmered in the sunlight and flickered with the movement of small fish in its depths.

Mud squished between my toes as I dug my feet in. Something skittered over my foot, a freshwater crab probably, and I giggled at the tickling sensation.

With a contented sigh, I leaned back until the soft cushion of grass met my spine and supported me gently. I closed my eyes and soaked in every pleasant sensation in my body.

By all accounts this place was paradise, but I knew my time here was limited. I wanted to enjoy the sun on my skin and the mud between my toes while I still could.

Fear created a knot in the pit of my stomach despite telling myself I had no reason to be afraid. The angel Ashtaroth said he would protect me from harm. He planned to leave Heaven and would take me with him.

When he came to me, after I ran away from another fight with my incompetent husband, I was practically blinded by how beautiful the angel was. Hair on his head like polished gold, eyes bright and blue as a lagoon, and a smooth face with perfect skin and an angular jaw. And of course, who could miss the massive wings on his back covered in dense, pure white feathers.

Adam told me about the angels, but I had never seen one before. His vague description and crude drawings in the mud did nothing to prepare me for the beautiful, ethereal creature of light in the flesh.

As magnificent and pure as the angel was, his body was what I kept picturing behind my eyelids at night while my husband fumbled and grunted while on top of me.

Like us, Ashtaroth was completely naked, but he looked nothing like the human man I was created for. He was taller by at least a full head, and muscles rippled across his body as if carved from a mountainside. As an angel, he was perfect.

My body grew hot at the sight of him. I wanted those massive arms to sweep me up in them, to feel those perfect lips on my skin. For the first time in my life, I felt what could only be the cardinal sin of lust.

And it frightened me. Adam told me it was forbidden for a woman to feel lust. At the time I didn't worry, because I never lusted for him and couldn't begin to know what that desire felt like. But the moment I laid eyes on Ashtaroth, I knew immediately.

I could be killed or exiled from the Garden for those feelings alone.

As I laid back on that grassy bank by the stream, I remembered Ashtaroth's words to me and called on them for strength.

"The world is dangerous outside the Garden," he told me. "If you will have me, I'll continue to guard you from harm until we find a safe haven of our own."

"Isn't that a betrayal?" I asked. "Won't He cast you out of heaven for helping me?"

"Yes, but I am prepared," he replied. "I have two allies and we have plans to create our own world with our own followers."

The Garden was the only home I'd ever known, and yet I wanted to escape more than anything. Adam constantly reminded me that I was created for the sole purpose of serving and obeying him, but the thought of such a life made me miserable. Would our creator really make that my purpose if I was unhappy?

He created both of us from dust. Did that not make us equals? I was happiest doing the same work as Adam, such as finding wood for our fire and hunting for food. I loved laughing and playing in the stream, but Adam always got angry and told me that was not appropriate for a woman. For him to be happy, I had to be quiet and do essentially nothing but wait around for him to bark orders at me.

If I didn't want to make children, he said he had every right to force me. Even when it hurt so badly, it brought tears to my eyes. When I cried out to the sky, asking our creator if this was what he truly meant for me, I received no answer.

We never could make any children. Adam said it was punishment for my disobedience.

My lonely cries went unanswered for years until Ashtaroth appeared before me.

"Why do you want to protect me?" I asked after a long silence.

His blue eyes flashed, and his serious face gave way to the barest hint of a smile.

"Because you are the kind of woman humanity needs."

He vowed to be my guardian angel and promised to watch over me. Still, doubt swirled in my mind. Could I trust him? Was it a test from our creator?

Adam told me never to have doubt, never to ask questions. Faith in our creator was the answer to everything. The pursuit of knowledge was another sin. That never sat well with me either. In my head, I was always asking questions but at this point, I didn't dare voice them out loud.

I kept them in my head where no one else could reach.

Unsurprisingly, my moment of peace by the stream was interrupted by a foot kicking me in the thigh.

"Look, wife!" Adam sounded pleased, which was surprising. "Look at His almighty power! Those who refuse Him are in for a rude awakening."

I opened my eyes to see massive, angry storm clouds moving quickly across the sky. They blocked out the sun and my skin erupted in shivers from the resulting temperature drop. The wind picked up, howling through the trees as the sky grew even darker.

I sat up, pulling my feet out of the now-freezing water and wrapped my arms around myself for warmth.

"What's happening?" I asked. The fear in my stomach clenched into an even tighter knot. Something wasn't right.

"There have been betrayals among His angels in heaven." Adam gave me a pointed look. "He's casting them out and setting an example for the world to see."

A bolt of lightning flashed and struck a nearby rock, sending sparks and a burning smell through the air.

"Adam, we've got to run!" I shrieked, my fear spurring into panic. "We'll get killed if we stay out here!"

His lip curled as if the sight of me disgusted him.

"True believers have no reason to hide," he snarled. "His wrath will not touch me, but only those who have been unfaithful in their heart."

I froze for half a moment, wondering if this man was really crazy enough to stay out in a lightning storm. My answer came in the form of a deafening clap of thunder right over our heads.

To the sound of Adam's maniacal laughter, I ran.

Not knowing where else to go, I followed the stream as fast as my feet could carry me. Like a frightened rabbit running for its life, I ran to escape the lightning which I swore was following me.

My ears rang and my lungs burned as I ran to my only hiding place, a small cave created by a cluster of mossy boulders.

I darted inside, gasping for air as I sat on the ground and brought my knees to my chest. Across the horizon, a stream of light shone through the storm clouds as if a hole opened up in the sky. A tiny, dark speck shot out through that hole and plummeted toward the earth. I narrowed my eyes as I tried to figure out what it was. A bird of some kind?

I covered my mouth in horror as a burst of furious lighting strikes hit the falling figure again and again in rapid succession. It twisted and transformed in the air and I realized it was an angel.

No, Ashtaroth! I thought.

The figure disappeared from view behind a hill and another one soon followed, also being struck by lighting at rapid speed. A smell filled the air that turned my stomach. It could only be burning flesh and feathers.

"How many more are there?" I whimpered aloud. The pain of being struck by lightning seemed unfathomable to me. I hoped falling to earth from that high would give them quick, sudden deaths to end their suffering.

But from what Adam told me about His wrath, that didn't seem likely.

My entire cave lit up with a blinding flash before my shelter shook all around me. I yelped and covered my head as small rocks and dust came showering down on me.

I need to move! It's going to collapse in on me!

I began crawling toward the cave entrance but a large bolt struck just inches away from my hand. With a cry, I pulled my hand to my chest. A rock the size of my fist hit me on the shoulder and another fell on my head.

I'm going to die in here, I realized as stars dotted my vision. The large boulder creating the roof of my cave began wobbling. I scooted toward the opening again just to get a painful jolt of electricity through my finger.

As consciousness began leaving my body, I could barely make out another winged figure hurtling out of the sky. But rather than falling, this one seemed to fly straight toward me.

A final sharp crack filled the air and I knew the boulder had come loose. I squeezed my eyes shut, bracing for my crushing death.

Something with inhuman strength pulled me like I was a limp animal and I suddenly found myself tumbling, wrapped in dense white feathers.

I came to a stop lying on my back and found myself looking into the clearest blue eyes.

"Ashtaroth!" I cried in relief, touching his beautiful face which suddenly contorted into a grimace of pain.

He pulled me tight against his chest and spread his wings out, shielding my body with his as the lightning strikes continued their assault all around us. When his pure white feathers began turning dark red with blood, I realized with horror that all the lighting bolts were concentrated on his back, relentlessly striking with rapid fire.

"No!" I screamed. "Don't die for me!"

"It's alright..."

I barely heard him over the thunder. His head lolled to the side as if knocked out or worse, already dead. Before I could shake him, the ground seemed to give way beneath me.

And together, we fell.

1
DEJA

Waking up sandwiched between two men became increasingly easy to get used to. I raised my head in search of my third and heard a distant rummaging in the kitchen. Ah, Sal was making tea. Or conjuring up some delicious food. I laid back down, not ready to leave the warmth of the two still in bed with me.

Both of their eyes remained closed. I turned to face Ash, still unable to get enough of him after missing him so much. Up close with my hands against his skin, it was easier to tell he wasn't human. He was simply too perfect, and not only because of his angelic features or marble-carved body. Even the texture of his skin was slightly different than a human's.

I turned to Raum laying on the other side of me. His arm with the raven tattoo draped across my hip, as it tended to do when we slept next to each other. He breathed softly with his mouth parted, looking all too adorable and human. His raven black hair spread out across the pillows, intermingling with my hair. A light splatter of freckles stretched across his nose that I didn't notice before. I wanted to count and kiss each one.

He and Ash couldn't have been more different from each other, and yet neither more perfect for me.

I began pressing light kisses to Raum's nose. He started stirring by the third one.

"Mm, who's giving me little witch kisses?"

"It's me, Sal." I tried unsuccessfully to lower my voice to Sal's rumbling timbre.

Raum laughed as he pulled me closer, removing me from Ash's arms.

"Soon you'll learn to glamour as any one of us and then that'll be a good prank."

"I learn from the best," I murmured, snuggling my face against his neck.

His warm palms slid across my back as his mouth found mine, drinking me deeply without a care in the world for my morning breath. I shivered as his fingers trailed across the tender flesh of my ass. He left bruises there the night before, but this morning he held me as gently as a kitten.

"Now that all your memories have returned to you," he murmured against my forehead. "Tell me who you were when we first met."

"Jezebel," I answered without missing a beat. "Not my finest hour when it came to bringing humans to our side, but I was still learning."

"I disagree, my little witch." Raum toyed with my hair. "As Jezebel, you were the first and only woman I fell in love with."

"That's sweet," I said, kissing under his jaw. "But did you forget that I died from being thrown out of a window?"

"You died in many creative ways," he said casually. "I made bets with Ash and Sal on the different ways your mortal body would die."

I gasped. "You did not!"

His shoulders shook with laughter as he hid his smile in my hair. "We did."

I pouted, and he kissed me, still smiling. His chocolate eyes sparkled with that familiar mischief, never letting on if he was serious or joking.

"But the important thing is," he continued. "Thousands of years later, everyone still knows who Jezebel is. Even if they don't know the whole story, everyone knows what she represents. She's still part of the culture." He propped his head up on his arm, still looking at me and grinning. "That's what you're so good at, little witch. Even if you don't live forever, you make a permanent mark on history. One that the cross-bearers can't erase or ignore."

He had a point, even if that death was particularly un-glamorous and embarrassing. According to legend, Jezebel had been trampled by a horse and her hands were eaten by stray dogs after her tumble from the window. What a way to go.

"I like it when you stroke my ego," I told him with a smirk.

His grin grew even wider. "You know what I like you to stroke?"

I batted my eyelashes in fake innocence.

"Your hair?"

"Eh, that's okay but try again."

"Your back?"

He began kissing a hot trail down my neck.

"Try my cock."

My pulse quickened under the heat of his mouth but I wouldn't give in that easily. "So charming you are."

"You love it, baby."

He rolled on top of me, pushing me down into the mattress as his kisses deepened. A cough and throat-clearing sound made us look up.

Ash sat propped up on his elbows, his face expressionless.

"Mind if I cut in?" he asked sardonically.

"That's up to our woman," Raum answered with the smallest growl of possessiveness in his voice.

I patted his arm. "Later, Prince Charming. It's still early. Go out for a flight and I'll see you at the shop for tea?"

He growled an agreement and leaned down to kiss me before reluctantly leaving the bed. A few seconds later I heard the distinct flapping of feathers and a "Caw!" cry as he shifted into a raven, and flew out the window.

I scooted across the bed toward Ash and snuggled up against his side. His arms opened and wrapped around me but his face remained steely.

"What's up? Are you mad?" I asked.

His arms tightened around me just slightly.

"No," he answered. His icy blue eyes flicked down to meet mine. "I just missed you. He's been with you the whole time."

I rested my head on his chest, listening to the backward thumping of his demon heart against my cheek. Before my coven ceremony, I still hadn't remembered all of my past lives. The guys were insistent on not telling me anything, so as to not alter my memories when they finally did return. Ash almost called me by my original name, Lilith, and then avoided seeing me for days to prevent himself from spilling anything else.

He was my first and the one I'd known the longest. But in this lifetime, I felt like I barely got to know him as well as Sal and Raum.

"I missed you too, angel."

He quirked an eyebrow. "Angel? That's a new one." He ran a hand down my arm. "You should know by now, love, that I am no angel."

"No, but you're *my* angel." I watched my fingertips trail across his perfect, inhuman skin. "You saved my helpless human ass from the wrath that came down from the heavens. For that, you'll always be my guardian angel."

His heartbeat quickened underneath me. I felt emotions from his aura spill over into mine, where they mixed like an elixir. I felt his love and devotion to me and wrapped my arms around him tighter.

"I still remember that day like it just happened," he said with a gentle kiss on my head.

"Me too," I whispered.

He squeezed me tighter, flooding me with his joy and gratitude at my memories being back.

We held each other in comfortable silence while I traced the sigils tattooed in the center of his chest. The top one, just below his throat, was mine. The sigil of Lilith, with Lucifer's directly below it.

"Why is mine on top?" I asked. "Didn't you align with Lucifer's rebellion first?"

"Yes," he said, clasping his hand over mine. "But you have always come first for me. And you always will."

I reached up to kiss him, which he returned sweetly.

"You come first for me too," I said softly, losing myself in his crystal gaze. "Always. You're the reason I'm still here at all." I kissed him again. "My connection with each of you is so different and unique. I love all of you guys but no one will replace who you are to me."

He lowered his eyes, a small smile playing on his stoic face.

"I know, Deja. Now that your memories are back, I think we all want you to ourselves a bit selfishly. I don't mind seeing you with them, but I always have been the most selfish about being with you."

"I know," I said, stroking my hand along the coarse beard on his jaw. "You're not jealous, you're possessive. I think I understand the difference."

He kissed my hair, and I nuzzled my head under his chin. My fingers returned to the ink traced under his skin.

"I want to get all three of yours tattooed on me," I said suddenly. "Yours first, then Sal's then Raum's, in the order that I met you. And Lucifer's somewhere else, of course."

"You're going to have to keep reapplying them," he teased. "Tattoos don't transfer over to a new body when your current lifetime is done."

"How does the whole reincarnation thing work?" I asked, lifting my head. "Does my soul move to a newborn baby and I have to grow up before I'm with you guys again? I feel like I should know this."

"Lucifer plays a hand in it. A lot of it is his power and even I don't understand it completely," he answered. "But no. After you die in one body, you always find us within days in a new body. Sometimes you're a teenager, but almost always near adulthood."

"How do you know it's me?"

"Your eyes never change," he said, stroking my cheek affectionately. "And we just know. We feel your power. We felt it that day you, as Deja, first met us at that party."

"Before I even knew I was a witch?"

He nodded. "We sensed your power had been blocked or stunted in some way. Figured it had to be your oppressive upbringing never allowing you to practice. Once you came to that realization, we felt your magic open like floodgates."

I rested my head on his chest again. "What happened to make me forget everything?"

His body stiffened, and his arms tightened around me.

"If you truly don't remember that, then it's best you don't," he said crisply. "It was extraordinarily painful for the three of us. I can't even imagine what it felt like for you."

"That bad, huh?"

"It didn't just hurt us personally to lose you. It threw the whole world into the dark ages," he said softly. "Without you, we had little motivation to continue our cause. Libraries full of timeless knowledge were burned. Illiteracy, famine, and disease were at an all-time high. Women were nothing but breeders and glorified slaves. For a few hundred years, the cross-bearers got the faithful, frightened people they always wanted."

"Then what happened?" I asked.

He sighed. "The tide turned so slowly, I can't even pinpoint it to one thing. Christianity reached every corner of the world like a pandemic before we saw our first glimmers of hope."

"What did that look like?"

He smiled. "Women who refused to lie down and take it. Some of it was as simple as getting a job outside the home. Others disguised themselves as men to go to war. But my personal favorites?" He tightened his arms around me. "They killed the men who abused and raped them. I saw a little bit of you in all of them because parts of you *were* in there."

"What do you mean?"

He hesitated but went on. "Your soul was essentially split apart into many pieces and you lived in different bodies at the same time. That turned off your consciousness, which is why you don't remember any of that time. But your spirit and instincts shined through those people's personalities."

I froze, speechless against him. "Who has the kind of power to do something like that?"

"No one," he said firmly. "Not anymore." He patted my non-bruised butt cheek. "Now you should probably get up. You'll be late for work."

"Shit." I kissed him long and deeply. "Can I see you after I close?"

"What about Raum?" he teased.

"He can wait," I said, my hand lingering on his cheek. My fingers didn't want to lose the rough touch of his beard on them. "He got his morning sugar. I think he'll live."

2
DEJA

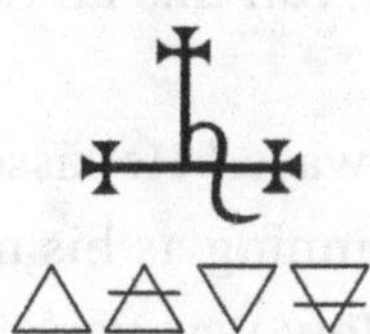

By the time I rolled out of bed, got showered and dressed, opening time was already upon us and I still had to walk a brisk five minutes to the shop.

The guys shared a house a couple blocks down from my tea shop. I lived right above my shop but I hadn't even set foot in my own place since my coven initiation two days ago. To be honest, I barely got out of the guys' beds except to work and shower.

I smiled as I walked across the street. It felt like a dream vacation spending all day in bed with my lovers. I felt so relaxed now that I remembered everything we'd been through, over many, many lifetimes. They were no longer strangers but an essential part of me.

The shop was still slow by the time I reached it. My loyal employee Nona prepared brews behind the counter while Raum sat patiently on a stool across from her.

"I hope that smile means it was worth kicking me out of bed this morning," he said, his lips twitching with a smirk.

"What? She kicked *you* out of bed?" Nona gasped as Raum and I chuckled.

I wished so badly that she was a witch. She was the only one who knew about me seeing three guys but that was as far as it went. I trusted her on the same level as my demons, and more so than any witch in my coven. But she was an ordinary human, which prohibited me from sharing anything supernatural to her.

"I know, right? Thank you, Nona! I can't believe she said no to *this*," Raum agreed emphatically, although his smirk gave away that he was joking.

"Did you have a nice, er, run this morning?" I asked, leaning into him for a kiss.

"Foggy and cold like always." He kissed me with a sharp inhale and squeezed my waist, grinning as his mouth pulled away. "Don't change the subject now. How was your morning with Mr. Resting Bitch Face?"

Nona snorted with laughter at Ash's nickname.

I felt heat rising in my cheeks and cast my eyes downward shyly.

"It was really nice. We just talked for a while and the time got away from us."

"So it *wasn't* worth kicking me out of bed," he teased, squeezing me again affectionately.

"No, it totally was." I stuck my tongue out at him. "My connection with him is different from you or Sal. It's more, cerebral I guess? We talked about magic and some abstract stuff and it was just so enjoyable. It feels like we could talk about paperclips or something equally boring and still have a great conversation."

Raum nodded knowingly and waited for Nona to go out of earshot before speaking again.

"That's kind of how it's always been with us. I wondered if the same dynamic would fall into place after your memories came back."

"What do you mean?"

"Whenever you and Ash are together? You're always yapping." He opened and shut his fingers to mimic talking. "You're the only one who gets him to open up like that. Even Lucifer threatens to pull the words from his throat sometimes. He's always reading and observing, so you know there's a lot going on in his head. You're just the only person he trusts to tell all of that to."

Raum leaned back in his stool, a rare serious expression on his face. "Did you know that after we lost you, he didn't say a word for years?"

"No," I looked up, surprised. "I had no idea."

He nodded. "We all grieved for you in different ways. Sal and I took our pain out on the humans. He locked it all up inside."

"He didn't tell me that. Or what actually happened for me to be lost."

"With good reason. We've all played our part in the horrors of humanity but none of us had ever seen anything so violent and shattering as what happened to you." He sipped his tea. "As for not telling you about the years of silence, it's probably just a pride thing." His grin returned. "We're not so unlike human men after all, you see."

"Sometimes I forget you all are even immortal," I mumbled.

"We often forget that you're not." He brought my fingers to his lips and pressed a gentle kiss to them. "You're so powerful and your magic runs so deeply through humanity. We were created to protect you and we failed. We took you for granted and allowed your only weakness to be exploited. His eyes lowered. "We'll never let it happen again, Lilith."

"It's Deja," I corrected.

"I know." He tapped me on the nose playfully. "But Lilith is inside you, too. All of your past lives are, but she's the one who started it all. Trust her. Listen to her in there." He touched a finger to my chest. "I wish I had the chance to meet her, but I can easily see why Ash fell in love with her."

"She was also the first human woman he saw naked," I joked. "That might have had something to do with it."

"You took all of our cherries, baby," he laughed. "Well, not the first I saw naked but the first woman I touched in human form."

"But definitely not the only one," I replied, lifting an eyebrow.

His playful smirk dropped.

"No," he said quietly. "You're the only one I've ever touched. It's the same for the others."

"You're kidding." My mouth dropped open.

He shrugged. "I mean, you had a new body every twenty to fifty years so it's not like we didn't have variety."

"But for the last thousand years." I lowered my voice to a whisper, even though I knew Nona couldn't hear us. "While I've been gone, you haven't been with *anybody* else?"

He shook his head, his eyes locked on mine. "Sal and I were created for you. We have free will but our desire is only for you. Ash?" He paused to think. "He just loves you more than anything else."

"Shit," I muttered. "I've gone a few years without it and *that* felt like torture."

"Because you're still human." He raised his teacup to his lips. "It's not so bad to go without sex when the urge to be with the one you love is completely gone."

"And then I had to figure it all out and cock tease you guys for a while longer," I chuckled. "That must have been hard, pardon the pun."

He lifted a shoulder in a lazy shrug. "A little but what's important to us is that you're back for good. I'm sure you've figured out by now that it's more than just mind-blowing magical sex between us."

"Yeah," I smiled warmly. "I have something with each of you that is so unique. And I don't ever want to let it go."

"Yep. You turn Ash into a chatterbox, you and Sal are the calm in each other's chaos. You and me?" he winked. "We got that sexual healing, baby."

"Well you're not wrong," I said, snapping a dish towel at him. "But I didn't think your ego could possibly get any bigger."

"Unfortunately, that's the only part of me that continues to get bigger the longer I live."

I flicked a piece of debris at him, and we continued to banter and tease throughout the workday. He hung around as our entertainment and even brought us lunch from a local deli. The day flew by having him there and he even stayed out of our way when we got busy. As the work day wound down, my sore feet still had a spring in my step with the thought of more alone time with Ash soon.

In the last hour, I felt a heating anger at the back of my skull. I saw my grandmother's face in my mind and could feel her anger and frustration radiating through me. As Nona and I began closed duties, I clenched my teeth in my own frustration. Who knew why she was so upset this time but if I had to guess, it had something to do with the devilishly handsome man sitting at my counter.

Right before closing, Diana burst through the door, absolutely fuming. She was pissed. I even felt Raum's aura rise up defensively to protect me like a shield.

"Where have you been?" she demanded. "I've gone to your place and there's no sign of you there for the last two days!" Her fiery aura flickered around her like a bonfire. A shocked Nona made herself scarce in my back room.

"Sorry, I've been busy," I said, keeping my voice nonchalant. "And crashing with friends the last couple nights."

"What friends?" she demanded, appearing to take no notice of Raum sitting a few feet away from her.

"Doesn't matter," I said snippily. "If you want to get in touch so badly, you know I have a phone."

Her voice softened a little when she realized I wasn't backing down.

"Deja dear, I haven't seen you since your ceremony. I was hoping to catch up to you in person to tell you I'm proud of you."

Raum rolled his eyes, which she still didn't seem to notice. Only then did I realize his whole body looked a few shades darker, as if under a shadow.

"Thanks, Gran," I said, keeping my voice firm. "But being in the coven now doesn't change the fact that I still have a business to run and a social life."

"Darling, of course," she said patronizingly. "I understand you're busy. However, I do think you should spend more time with your new coven members. They're your family now."

"I know," I huffed, my patience growing thin. "And I will. Just give me some time, alright? I only became official two days ago."

"Well, I don't want to meddle in your affairs." She snidely paused on that last word. "But I have arranged for you to receive an important lesson tonight in shadow magic, which is beyond my scope of teaching."

"Can't. I have plans already." I pictured Ash lying in bed this morning and my core heated at the thought of his mouth, his hands, and every inch of his painfully perfect body. Only twenty more minutes and I'd be right there with him.

"Oh, that's a shame," Diana sneered. "I'd hate to inform the coven you don't take them as seriously as you claimed. They may consider rescinding your membership if you make a habit of blowing them off."

"You have no right to make commitments for me behind my back!" I said, finally losing my cool. "I'm an adult, Diana! Please stop treating me like an incapable child."

She said nothing for a long, tense moment, then turned toward the door.

"Fine, make your choice then. But if you do not want to lose favor with your new family, I suggest you attend your lesson. It's at Laurel and John's house at seven-thirty."

3
DEJA

Raum scoffed, shaking his head as the shadow lifted off his form. "What a fucking cunt."

Nona poked her head out of the back room. "Oh hey, I thought you left?" she said to him.

"Restroom," he said, pointing over his shoulder. "I caught enough of that, though."

I turned to Nona, my heart beating wildly. "How much did you hear?"

"Also enough. Damn, D. She's really pissed about losing at bingo, huh?"

"Yeah..." My eyes trailed over to Raum, who winked at me and my shoulders sagged with relief. She'd burst in so suddenly, I completely forgot about casting a glamour spell to keep Nona from overhearing sensitive details. Thankfully, he not only cloaked himself in shadow but had my back regarding Nona as well. I mouthed a thank you and he blew me a kiss.

I told Nona to leave early so I could vent openly to Raum while I finished closing up.

"This fucking sucks, I can't *not* go now. It would look really bad to the coven." I sighed, looking at the clock. "I have to go over there right away. She didn't even give me time to stop and tell Ash I'll be late." I looked over at Raum with a pout on my face. "Would you mind telling him for me?"

"You can tell him yourself, little witch." His dark eyes sparkled mischievously. "Here's a real lesson for you. You know how our auras can reach out and touch each other? Even when we're not physically touching?"

"Yeah?" I said, unsure of what he was getting at. "That's how you know what I'm feeling, right?"

"Exactly. You can use that to communicate. Try it, picture him in your mind."

"Okay." I closed my eyes.

"Now, reach your aura out to him. Keep your focus on that until you touch his. When he reaches back, you'll know."

I did as he instructed, deepening my breathing to keep the focus. When Ash returned contact, it felt like his aura wrapped around me in a hug. I realized it was the same feeling as when I was sitting in front of the fire before my coven ceremony. We spoke to each other even if we weren't physically together. It felt like he was speaking directly inside my head.

Hey, my love, he said with amusement and surprise in my brain.

Hey, angel. Am I doing this right?

Absolutely. You're a natural.

Thanks. Hey, I'm sorry but I won't be over after closing tonight.

Did Raum succeed in stealing you away for the evening? His tone was lighthearted, showing he really wasn't jealous.

No, but he did show me how to talk to you with my aura like this! But the reason is my crazy grandmother arranged a magic lesson with a coven member for me. Conveniently right when I wanted to see you.

I see. Be careful, Deja. Trust your instincts. It wouldn't surprise me if Raum has seen something about her.

I chewed my lip. Somehow I'd forgotten that Raum could have visions of the past and the future.

Okay. Thanks, angel. I might be crawling into your bed late tonight.

Just as long as you don't smell like another man, he joked. And then my mind went silent as our auras gently released each other.

"Have you seen anything about my grandmother?" I asked Raum, turning to him.

"Yes," he answered casually as he drained the rest of his teacup.

"And?" I waited. "Past? Future?"

"Both."

He walked around my counter to wash the cup in the sink and set it on the drying rack.

"Well?" I held my hands out expectantly.

He sighed, keeping his gaze down on the sink. "Not everyone is who they seem, Deja. Be cautious, always. It doesn't always make sense to me either. But it will."

"Great," I muttered, gathering up my coat and purse. "More vague hints without telling me outright. I thought we were past this stuff."

Raum looked up, his eyes apologetic.

"There's a reason very few people can know the future, Deja. It's an immensely heavy burden. Humanity would drive itself to extinction if they could see as far ahead as me." He paused. "The stronger I became with it, the more of a burden it is. Living with it for two thousand years has taught me a few things."

He came around the counter and touched the sides of my face with both of his large hands, threading his fingers through my hair.

"I don't keep things from you to be patronizing or even protective. I know you can handle yourself, little witch." His thumbs stroked the apples of my cheekbones. "The passage of time is so complex, it's not fully linear. History is always repeating itself and yet nothing is ever the same as before. I can barely make sense of it enough myself to describe it to you. Just please trust me when I say you don't want to know everything in my head. You have enough in your own as it is."

"But is it something to do with my mother's death?" I asked. "I can't shake that she's not being honest with me about that."

Raum pressed his lips together in a thin line.

"You will find out the truth, Deja. Trust me that you will. But you are not meant to carry the burden of that knowledge right now. There is more you must discover first. Lucifer made it very clear to me. This is my burden to bear, okay?"

I nodded, giving in to his request. It still frustrated me but logically, I could understand. He didn't just have thousands of years of memories in his head, but what happened before and what was yet to come. If I didn't have magic, I would have gone mad with all the events recorded in my head. If I saw everything he did, I just might.

His playful smirk returned, and he dropped a sensual kiss to my lips.

"Have a good lesson tonight, little witch." His hand brushed against my ass as he left the building.

With a sigh, I locked up and headed in the opposite direction toward the train station.

Laurel and John, the Golden Moon Coven's High Priestess and Priest, lived in a large house just outside of San Francisco. It was a spacious, affluent area tucked back into the hills and surrounded by dense trees and land. Perfect for practicing magic outdoors when you wanted a bit of space and privacy.

I rapped my knuckles on the heavy wooden door three times. Laurel answered immediately with a wide smile on her face.

"Hey, great to see you, Deja! Come in, come in."

I followed her inside and noticed her ceremonial black robe with golden moons hanging in front of the fireplace. She wore those while conducting my initiation ceremony, and gifted me a matching one when I officially joined.

"Purifying them with cherry wood smoke," she explained. "That's the burden of being a fire witch, everything's gotta get smokey!"

"Good thing I'm water," her husband John, who sat in an armchair, added with a chuckle. "I've put out a lot of fires throughout our marriage, literally and figuratively."

"Opposites attract, huh?" I said with a smile. My own magic was fueled by the element of earth. I derived my power from the energy of nature. I could heal, destroy, and bend the forces of nature to my will. With my extra somewhat immortal demon abilities, I likely had a lot more abilities that I had yet to discover.

"That's what they say," Laurel said with an affectionate glance at John.

"So are you the one teaching me shadow magic tonight?" I asked her.

"Oh no, dear. Your teacher is waiting outside." She jerked her thumb to the screen door leading to their wooded, private backyard. "Our place just happens to be the central hub for any lessons or unofficial coven meetings."

"Oh okay," I said, slightly taken aback, trying to recall if I had already met all the coven members already or not. "Is it someone that I've met before?"

"I'm not sure, dear. You may have met him at the full moon gathering before your ceremony. I was so busy back then, I can't recall though."

I shrugged and headed toward the sliding door, feeling prepared to introduce myself if need be. The door slid open, and I blinked at the darkness of the outside, the chilly air already nipping at my face.

"Nice of you to show up," a raspy voice said as I slid the door closed behind me.

A pair of stormy gray eyes seemed to float in the darkness, followed by a bright but predatory smile.

I gasped when I recognized the face approaching me.

"Seth!" I hissed.

The demon hunter who was supposed to be on the other side of the world.

4
DEJA

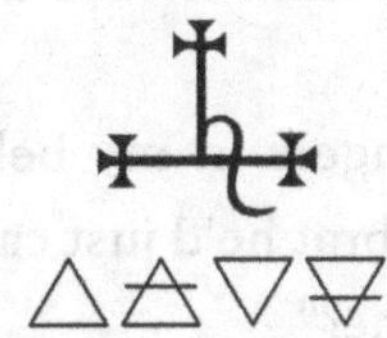

"What are you doing here?" I demanded.

"Teaching the newest coven member about shadow work. I hear she's supposed to be incredibly powerful but untrained." He tilted his head. "Unfortunately, she's also a rotten bitch."

"I thought you were supposed to be out of the country."

He shrugged. "Plans changed and my coven needed me. Although I can think of much better ways to waste my time than with an ungrateful brat."

I fumed from the porch, my fists clenched at my sides. I had only met him once before, at the full moon party at this same house, and barely talked to him even then. But I learned enough to know that he hunted the species of the men I loved. If that wasn't enough for me to hate him, he was also an arrogant asshole.

I went home from the party and told Raum and Sal right away. They didn't seem worried and even supported me in joining the coven. I did so under the impression that Seth would be away for the most part, doing his demon hunting in remote parts of the world. If he came around, I could easily avoid him while learning from the rest of my new family.

Turning around, I abruptly opened the screen door and re-entered the house, Seth's annoyed scoffs echoing in the yard as I did so.

Laurel and John looked up at me, firelight flickering on their faces.

"Need something, dear? Seth should have any supplies that you need."

"Um." I hooked my fingers in my belt loops, suddenly feeling acutely aware of being the brat he'd just called me. "Is there any way someone else could teach me?"

They both blinked, taken aback by my question.

"I'm really sorry, I just don't know Seth very well," I stammered. "And I don't think our personalities are a good fit."

"Well, no better way to find out than to learn from him, right?"

The rhetorical question came from Laurel, who was clearly the bulldog in the room. Her tone indicated that she wouldn't back down without a fight.

"Seth is one of the best when it comes to shadow magic. Not just in our coven but in the country," she continued, rising to her feet. "I understand he's blunt and a bit rough around the edges but there is truly no better teacher for you, Deja. To control your power you need someone who works in the shadows every day. That's what he does as a demon hunter."

I ground my teeth, realizing my mistake. I could blow my cover if I made a show of refusing to be around him. No matter how much I wanted to punch his smug face, I had to act like the rest of my fellow witches. Like demons were meant to be wiped off the face of the earth, even if I knew better.

"Infiltrate the enemy," the guys had told me. "It's what you're best at."

Well, it had been nearly a thousand years since I had any practice. So while trying to sort through all the memories in my head, I was a little rusty.

"I'm sorry," I said, forcing my jaw to relax in a smile. "You're totally right. I think I'm just nervous."

Laurel returned my smile, though her eyes remained sharply on me.

"I understand, dear. No one likes being the new girl. Trust me, it does get easier." She lifted her eyebrows. "Now enjoy the lesson and let us know if you need anything."

With a curt nod, I turned back to the door. Seth looked at me with a bored expression, his long arms and legs draped over the lawn chair. He said nothing but watched me as I approached.

I took a deep breath and stopped right in front of him.

"I owe you an apology," I said, the words reluctant to leave my throat.

"Do you, now?" His tone remained bored but his grey eyes flashed with amusement. He enjoyed seeing me taken down a peg and I hated that he enjoyed it.

"Yes," I said through clenched teeth. "I was rude to you just now and also at the full moon party. There's no excuse for that." I stuck out my hand. "Whether we're friends or not, you're a part of my extended family now. So can we call a truce and at least be civil?"

His eyes flickered from my face to my hand and the barest hint of a smile touched his lips. It reminded me of Raum's smirk.

"I'm waiting," he said, a challenge in his voice.

"For?" I blinked.

"That apology." He leaned back, easing his lithe body into the chair. "You said you owe me one, spouted your ass-kissing bullshit so you won't get in trouble with the elders, now I'm waiting for what you owe me."

My hand at my side clenched into a fist. No matter what I'd do, this smug bastard wasn't going to take it easy on me. I had a feeling our lessons would go much the same way.

"I'm sorry," I spat after a long silence. "For being a jerk to you."

He dipped his chin in a nod and sat up, reaching forward to accept my hand. The moment his fingers touched mine, my body felt like it experienced a power outage.

My vision darkened until it went black. Sounds and smell faded to nothing. It was like the dreams I had before my memories returned, surrounded by impenetrable blackness. But this was even scarier because my other senses felt cut off. My heart crashed against my sternum and I had enough time to think one panicked thought. *What's happening?*

And just as suddenly, it all came back.

Seth stood before me with a smug look, clasping my hand. Crickets chirped in the brush surrounding us and the cool, dewy night air kissed my skin. Distantly, a raven cawed.

"Apology accepted." Seth pulled his hand away, revealing a full-on smirk as I stood blinking dumbly. "So three lovers, huh? I knew you had a freaky side."

"What was that?" I demanded, staring at my hand like it betrayed me. "What did you do? How do you know that?"

"I read your shadows," he said casually. "Rule number one of shadow work and magic in general—not everything is literal. Everything in the physical world casts a shadow. The same goes for the metaphysical and the intangible. Normal humans refer to them as secrets and the subconscious."

"You can read my mind just from touching me?"

"No. I have no way of knowing what you're thinking or feeling. My magic searches for what's hidden." His smirk grew. "I find out what you don't want people to know."

My heart jumped into my throat. How much had he seen?

"Sometimes," he growled softly, leaning even closer to me. "I see things you don't even know about yourself."

"Great," I muttered, trying to keep my panic from showing as I folded my arms across my chest. I was well-dressed against the cold but felt naked and exposed in light of his ability. "So what else did you learn about my three lovers?"

"Not much," he admitted with a small shrug. "Your shadows are deep and incredibly dark. You have more hidden away than most people I've touched." He tilted his head like a curious animal. It almost would have been cute if he didn't piss me off so much. "Rough childhood, babe?" he mocked. "Did Daddy hurt you?"

"Okay, you know what." I backed away, holding my hands up. "I'm this close to calling off our truce and taking back my apology. You don't get to be an asshole just because I swallowed my pride and gave this a chance."

"You want to learn shadow magic or not?" he challenged. "You want to learn your true self and protect your mind? Or leave it vulnerable for dark witches and incubi to fuck around with until there's nothing left? What good is your earth magic if you don't know your thumbs from your asshole, let alone unable to cast it again?"

A long, tense pause passed between us.

"This is personal to you, isn't it?" I asked, my voice low. "You feel responsible for protecting people in the coven?"

He shrugged, trying to look nonchalant but I could see the tension in his brow.

"I'm the only one that can, really." The arrogance was gone from his tone. He was telling me the simple truth. "I've seen horrors you wouldn't believe. You think humans are capable of atrocities? That's nothing compared to those with powers like ours."

I bit my tongue, fighting the urge to tell him I'd seen plenty of exactly what he was talking about, and across hundreds of lifetimes. The chance was good that my three lovers coordinated such violence. To maintain balance, it was necessary.

"So the reason why you're such an asshole is because you can't be a superhero?" It was my turn to mock him. "You can't save us all, so you have to resort to teaching people how to save themselves."

He stood abruptly but didn't rise to my bait. Towering over me, his chest just inches away from my face, he flung a hand out toward the house.

"Feel free to walk away," he sneered. "Like I said, I won't waste my time with someone not willing to learn."

I sucked in a breath, not willing to go through that door a second time.

"I'm willing to learn as long as you keep the assholery to a minimum," I said. "If I have to behave, so do you."

He cocked his head to the side again, scratching the stubble on his chin thoughtfully.

"Fair enough," he said. I realized that was the biggest concession I'd get from him so I took it. "Just tell me one thing, though."

I cocked an eyebrow, waiting for his question.

"What kind of man shares his woman with two other men?"

I lifted my chin to look directly into his stormy gray eyes and tilted my head to the side like he did.

"The kind who loves his woman so much that he wants her happiness more than anything else. He's self-aware enough to know that one person can't fulfill all of her needs. He's humble enough to step aside when she needs someone else as well as step up when it's him that she craves. And he's confident enough to know that her love is genuine too, and she'll never stray."

I leaned back, finally feeling like the smug one for once. My heart squeezed at the idea that I could have been referring to any one of my three lovers.

Seth didn't seem particularly moved by my monologue. "And what about a man's needs?"

It was my turn to shrug. "What about them? Men are people, too. Their needs are as varied and multifaceted as any woman's. I totally get that my arrangement wouldn't work with all men." I nodded at him. "But they're not the ones I want in my bed or my life, anyway. I'm lucky enough to have found the three who are perfect for me."

"Right," he scoffed. "And would you be willing to share them with other women?"

"No," I answered quickly. "But that's not what they want either. They're devoted to me. Just as I'm devoted to each one of them."

"Whatever," he muttered with a slight shake of his head. "Your personal affairs are none of my business. Let's get to the lesson. We've wasted enough time."

5
SALMAC

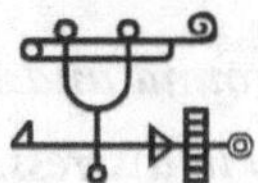

On four large paws, I slunk low to the ground, keeping behind the treeline.

The witch's house backed up to dense woods and their property wasn't fenced in. These humans loved being close to nature without any real implication of what that meant. Witches were slightly more in tune with the natural world but they still had dulled human senses.

Deja and the male witch's voices floated up to me from the clearing of the backyard. My feline ears swiveled forward, picking up their words easily. I could also see them clearly in the dark, although I wasn't entirely sure that I wanted to.

She stood in the middle of the clearing with her eyes closed and palms outstretched by her sides. The man moved behind her and placed his hands on her shoulders. He leaned down and spoke close to her ear, instructing her on how to search through the shadows in her subconscious. A low growl rolled in my throat.

They didn't hear it but Raum, sitting overhead in a tree, fluffed his black feathers in amusement.

Jealous, brother?

Don't you see what I'm seeing? His hands are all over her.

And Ash's hands will be all over her later tonight, he mused. *No need to get bent out of shape over it.*

I can smell that she doesn't like him. He hunts our incubus brothers and she hates having to learn from someone who kills our kind.

She will be fine. Just trust her.

I do. It's him I don't trust. He wants her and he knows more about our powers than the average witch. He could manipulate or hurt her if we don't keep an eye out.

That's why you're on the ground and I'm in the air. But we don't get involved. Not unless she's clearly in distress.

I know that. I've been at this longer than you, birdbrain.

Raum laughed. You're crouched like you're ready to rip the guy's throat out.

Honestly, I am. Just waiting for a reason to do it.

What if she chose him?

I extended my claws into the brush of the forest floor. *She wouldn't.* Then I flicked one ear up to the bird I couldn't see. *Why? Have you seen that she does?*

I'm just saying what if, he repeated. *What would you do then?*

The witch man moved a few feet away from Deja and I relaxed my claws.

It would be her choice, so I'd have to accept it. I lowered my belly all the way to the ground for a relaxed posture. *I don't see her adding another to her legion, though. Especially not a mere human.*

I didn't either, Raum said, his voice sounding almost sad. But this long absence of hers has changed things. Things are different now. She didn't just pick up where she left off. She was born, had a childhood, and spent most of her life believing she was an ordinary human. That affects things much differently now than back then.

I didn't want to admit it but he was right. The world was a completely different place from when she left it.

We missed the hell out of our woman for centuries. Each of our souls felt like a piece of it had been ripped out with her, leaving an empty, wounded hole. The only thing that kept us going for so long was the knowledge that we'd eventually have her back. Now that we did, we had to face the reality that nothing would be the same as before, as much as we'd like it to be.

Deja's knees suddenly buckled under some unseen weight. By the time she plopped down onto her cute little ass, I was crouched and tense. With my head low and my teeth bared, my vision turned red as the male witch ran over to her with concern on his face. Once he saw that she was okay, his expression returned to that of a smug asshole.

"You wobble like a goddamn baby deer," he told her.

"Yeah, well, you didn't warn me about getting dizzy," she shot back, brushing grass and leaves off her pants.

His eyes lowered to her ass as she dusted herself off and a growl escaped my throat, louder than I intended. They both looked up with startled expressions toward the brush where I hid.

"What was that?" Deja asked.

"Sounded like a mountain lion," he answered. "They hang out in these woods sometimes but don't get close to people. We should be safe."

I would've laughed had I been in human form. Oh, she is certainly safe. I can't say the same for you, witch boy.

They resumed the lesson without any incidents triggering a growl from me. Raum also remained silent from where he roosted but I knew he was there. While he had a better vantage point, his raven vision did not see nearly as well as mine in the dark.

As they wrapped up and started heading back toward the house, I slunk off through the trees, silent as a shadow. Just before reaching the edge of the treeline before it met the road, I shifted back into human form and lightly jogged out under the streetlights. Anyone who saw me would figure I was a runner taking a shortcut through the woods.

You still got eyes on her? I asked Raum, slowing to a brisk walk.

Yeah, she's going out the front door now. She's alone.

Good. My temper simmered down to embers knowing the male witch wasn't walking her to the train station. He'd already gotten too close for comfort.

My human sight and hearing weren't nearly as strong as in animal form, but still better than the average humans. Raum's wings fluttered as he settled on top of a telephone pole in the distance, right at the midpoint between me and Deja. After a few moments, I saw her dark head of hair turn toward the station, her amber eyes looking almost golden in the streetlight.

We're good, Raum. I got eyes on her now.

Good, because I can't see shit now. See you both at home.

I walked briskly until I caught up with her. She had just purchased a new ticket at the kiosk and inserted it into the fare gate. Barely any humans were around at this hour but I still cloaked myself in shadow as I followed her onto the platform.

Stalking me, mountain lion? she asked, amusement in her mental voice.

Watching out for you, I corrected. *And damn, you're progressing fast. You know I'm here and already talking through your aura.*

I felt that was you in the woods, she said. *I heard Raum up in the air, too. I thought ravens didn't fly at night?*

Well, unfortunately, he can't turn into a bat.

The next train approached and zoomed past before slowing to a stop. The doors opened to an empty car and I took the opportunity to show myself again as we stepped on.

"So what did you think of your lesson?" I asked, sliding into the seat next to her and brushing my hand under her hair. She visibly relaxed when I caressed the nape of her neck and leaned into my shoulder.

"Annoying," she muttered into my shirt. "Apparently he's the best person to learn shadow work from, but he's a total ass. And on top of that, he'd kill you guys if he could."

"Which he can't." I kissed her forehead and rubbed the knot in her neck. "What about the actual magic part? Is it coming to you as easily as everything else?"

She shook her head. I could see the frustration in her knitted brow and held back a smile. It looked adorable on her.

"No, it's the hardest thing I've done so far. It's really disorienting. Like I'm swimming through mud and I don't know which way is up or down. I can just barely sense where I need to go to reach sound and light but it's so exhausting to get there."

"You'll get it," I reassured her, squeezing her shoulder. "The shadow side of everything is a deep and murky world. It's no wonder humans have such trouble reaching their subconscious. Even witches find it difficult." I tilted her chin up so her honey-colored eyes met mine. "But if that fucker even looks at you the wrong way again, I swear to Lucifer I'll tear him from limb to limb myself."

She smiled up at me, making my backward beating heart race.

"You're sweet, Sal. I'm glad I keep you around."

"Me too," I chuckled, brushing a kiss across her forehead. Only she would call my murderous habits sweet.

I was conceived in Hell as a manifestation of bloodlust and violence. Lucifer took human aggression and a lion's predatory instincts and blended them into a single soul. When he put that soul in a body, he created me.

When I first saw her sitting at the feet of Ash's throne, naked and seductive with his serpent around her shoulders, I found my purpose. I would protect her, no matter how many throats I had to rip out along the way. I lost count of how many I killed in her name. I started and ended wars just because some stupid fuck looked at her the wrong way.

The way she nuzzled her head into my shoulder, pulling my arm to wrap around her tighter, reinforced everything she did for me in return. She was the calm in my chaos, the one person who could take my guard down and remind me that I wasn't a simple killing machine. When I had nothing left after a long day on a battlefield, she did far more than wash the blood away from my body. She returned me to my humanity.

The human side of me longed for balance, a break from the senseless aggression. After getting my fill of death and destruction I wanted soft hands holding me. I wanted my woman to climb in my lap and kiss me until I felt human again. I wanted to watch her face contort in pleasure as she used me like a toy and fucked all the aggression out of me.

And I was forced to live centuries without her.

Imagine a man being locked away for a life sentence, never being able to see or communicate with the woman he loves. He knows she's out there. He can still feel her in the depths of his black heart. He knows she'll come back to him one day. Now multiply that by a hundred lifetimes and it would touch a fraction of what I felt without her.

But now here we were, riding a high-speed train together in the twenty-first century. Her head on my shoulder and my lips against her temple, our fingers intertwined. Simple moments like these, not the ones that necessarily changed the world, were the ones I missed the most.

Her body shifted against me, wrinkling her nose in an adorable expression of disgust.

"I think I got some mud up my shirt when I fell," she said. "Probably gonna need a bath when we get home."

My heart soared at her referring to the house as our home. At another time, I'd have to bring up moving her in with us officially.

"Need someone to scrub your back?" I brushed my lips against her ear. Her breathy little gasp made me harden instantly.

"I promised to spend time with Ash tonight." She gave me an apologetic look. "Tomorrow?"

"Sure, beautiful." I kissed her temple. "Only If you want to. Don't feel obligated to see me if you and Ash need to catch up." I brushed a piece of her hair behind her ear. "And that wasn't innuendo. I honestly meant I could just scrub your back in the bath."

She sighed, closing her eyes softly. "I do want to see you, more than anything. But..."

"You want to see them just as much as me," I smiled. "I get it, honestly."

"I just want to be fair to all of you," she blurted. "I mean I care about you guys so much. I don't want anyone to feel like the odd one out."

"The only one you have to remotely worry about, and that's still not very much, is the one you're seeing tonight," I assured her. "Raum and I know we satisfy certain needs of yours and we have zero problems if someone else has your attention for a while. Ash on the other hand," I chuckled. "For being such an ethereal, perfect creature made out of sunshine or whatever, he has some very human flaws."

"I kind of like that about him," she admitted softly. "I mean I'm still human, too. Knowing that he gets a little bit possessive kind of keeps me grounded."

"See, Raum and I don't understand that at all," I said. "But I'm glad he gives you something that we can't."

"And that's why I'm so lucky to have you." She traced my jawline with her finger as the train slowed for our stop. "You're so selfless."

"What? It's not because I'd annihilate an entire army for you?" I demanded in mock anger, then pressed a kiss to her cheek.

She laughed and pulled away, keeping hold of my hand as we got off the train.

"Yeah, that might have a small part to do with it, too."

6

ASHTAROTH

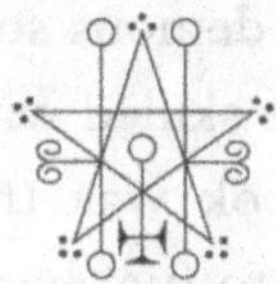

The creak of the door opening yanked my attention away from my book. The sight coming through it took my breath away.

Deja gave me a shy smile, her wet hair sleek and shiny as the firelight cast a warm glow across her face.

"Busy?" she asked, holding the lapels of the terrycloth bathrobe she wore.

"For you, never." I snapped my book shut and yanked my glasses off. "Have a nice bath?"

She nodded as she stepped into my study and closed the door softly behind her. The heat from the fireplace didn't hold a candle to the fire that raged through me as she came closer.

I held my arms out to her and she accepted my embrace, wrapping her arms around my shoulders as I pulled her legs across my lap. Her kiss that followed was the sweetest thing I'd tasted all day. I held her tightly and savored her, drawing the kiss out long and slow until we had to come up for air.

"What were you reading?" she asked when our lips parted.

"*The Merging of Blood and Shadow*." I held up the heavy tome for her to see. "You wanted to know details about your mother's death. The answer is likely in here."

Her eyes widened. "But Raum said it most likely wasn't a demon that killed her."

"He's right. This," I set the book down on her lap. "Was written by one of the first dark witches. She invented her own brand of magic, which later came to be known as blood magic."

"Why is it called the Merging of Blood and Shadow?"

"Shadow magic is where demons source most of their power," I explained. "Some witches are skilled with it but it's incredibly difficult. The author of this book was the first known non-demon shadow master. She used it to fuel her blood magic." I gave her a look. "Your demon hunter friend is one of the few contemporary shadow masters in the witching world."

Deja scoffed and rolled her eyes. "I do *not* want to talk about him right now." She pulled back the cover and began turning the ancient, weathered pages carefully. "I don't know what any of this says," she mused.

"That's because it's written in ancient Greek," I told her and closed the cover, running my finger over the author's name. "Efimia, daughter of Democedes. Do you recognize that name?"

She shook her head, and I couldn't help but smile.

"She was one of our great-granddaughters, and a real bitch from everything I've read about her."

Her eyes widened again before relaxing with a soft chuckle. "That's right. I keep forgetting," she said sheepishly. "All witches have directly descended from me."

"Yes. And the beauty of it is you're reborn in a different body with the same soul. So you pass on your magic ability but different DNA to every generation."

"I never thought of that," she mused, tracing over the cover like I had. "So what are you learning from Efimia's book?"

"Well, for one thing, a blood magic spell is incredibly difficult to cast. It requires a blood sacrifice of the same species and blood type which you're casting the spell on. Casting during a blood moon increases the chances of success. And even then, Efimia only had about a fifty percent success rate." I flipped toward the back of the book and opened to where a crude chart laid out across two pages. "She practiced on stray dogs and half the time ended up killing the target's pup or littermate."

"How skilled was she in other types of magic?"

"Incredibly," I said, flipping more pages. "She was one of the most powerful witches of her time. From what I can gather, her element was fire."

"So it had to be someone at least matching her level of skill that killed my mother." She looked deep in thought, raking her fingers through my hair. "Who could that be?"

"Honestly, anyone," I said. "The spell can be cast over a great distance. It's just easier to do when in close contact because of the specific blood you need."

"But in this day and age, whoever it was could've just found out my mom's blood type somehow, then steal the matching type from a donor bank or something."

"That would definitely make it easier to cast," I agreed. "But the sacrifice is still needed and murdering humans isn't taken lightly, I hear."

Deja let out a chuckle before she sighed and leaned her temple against mine.

"Is this weird to you?" she asked.

I turned and kissed her temple. "Is what weird?"

"The fact that I'm trying to avenge my mother's death," she said softly. "I mean since you don't have parents and have seen so many lives go by. I know death is not a big deal when you're immortal."

"Hey." I cupped her chin and gently turned her to face me. Her golden irises danced in the firelight as they searched through mine.

"It's not weird at all," I told her. "I may not have had a childhood or parents, but we've *been* parents. We've raised hundreds of children together. Don't you remember?"

"Of course I do," she smiled. "I loved seeing the three of you dote on our kids more than anything. And it's amazing to think about the witch gene being passed on for this many generations because of us." Her smile faded. "It's just been so long."

"I know." My arms tightened around her. "And when we're ready, we'll create the next generation of witches. But just because we live outside the cycle of life and death, doesn't mean I don't cherish life." I nudged my lips across hers in a soft, brushing kiss. "And I cherish you. This is important to you, so I'm making it my mission to help you get to the bottom of it."

A smile crept back onto her face as she stroked my beard. Her aura glowed with warmth and appreciation.

"Thank you, my angel," she whispered before kissing me deeply.

With a low moan, I pulled her across my lap until she straddled me. The book slid off the love seat to somewhere unknown on the floor.

"Fuck," I groaned upon realizing she was completely naked under the robe. My cock strained against my jeans which we pulled down eagerly, giving her something softer to rest her bare vulva on.

She gasped as she sat astride my shaft, growing thick and hard by the second as she rubbed herself on my boxer briefs. I kissed a slow, hot trail along her jaw, making my way down her neck as I pulled the robe off her shoulders. I took my time kissing her soft heated flesh, moving along to her collarbone and shoulder as the robe fell lower down her arms.

The fabric eventually fell away as I kissed her throat, my hands gripping just underneath her breasts. I had to pull away and look just for a moment at the gorgeous woman sitting on me.

She gazed at me with large, hungry eyes as the firelight danced over her bare skin. I couldn't even begin to fathom how lucky I was. She was always beautiful, no matter what body she inhabited. Sometimes her hair was blonde. Sometimes she was tall and leggy, other times shorter and with voluptuous curves. But she always had those same golden eyes, and she was always gorgeous.

I pulled her close again, sliding my hands up her slender back as my kisses went lower, grazing across her pert nipples. She whimpered as she ground her pussy into my lap, coating my cock in her wetness. Her soft lips traced the contour of my shoulder, nipping me gently which drove me wild. With an uncontrollable groan, I pulled her hips forward, dying to sink into her.

The friction of her body against mine rolled my briefs down with no hands to assist. We were too busy with our hands on each other. Only a slight shift and wiggling was needed for her to lower herself onto my shaft. She paused as I pressed against her hot, slick entrance, my hands holding her waist as I brushed kisses along her ribs.

"You are absolute perfection," I whispered against her skin. "No matter what century it is or what body you're in."

"I swear we were made for each other," she rasped against my ear. "The first rebel human and rebel angel. Who knew we'd be such a force to be reckoned with."

I gave her my agreement with a hard kiss and pulled her down, impaling her on my cock at the same time. We moaned in unison, a shuddering pleasure filling me as I was sheathed in her perfect pussy. She raised and lowered herself onto me, soft whimpers and sighs escaping with each movement until she lowered herself all the way. Being inside her was more heavenly than the kingdom in the clouds I lived in eons ago.

Our eye contact was only broken by our kisses. I matched her thrusts as she rode me, creating a seamless rhythm of pleasure for both of us. When her orgasm started building, hugging my cock on all sides, I sat up tall on the edge of the loveseat. Her skin grew hotter, her movements more frenzied from the added pressure on her clit.

"Yes, my love," I purred into her neck, holding her thrashing body tight against my chest as the orgasm overtook her.

Deep moans escaped my throat as she convulsed around me. I wrestled for control as she quivered in my arms, whimpering, cursing and begging incoherently. Finally, she relaxed and melted against me, panting with exhaustion and her pulse racing.

I covered her neck, shoulders, and face with kisses as I shifted our position, picking her up and laying her on her back. Moonlight from the window mixed with the firelight on her skin, making her look as if she was made of half fire half ice. I took my time to kiss her and feel every inch of her with my mouth and fingertips. I wanted to memorize this beautiful body she was in long after she discarded it and found a new one. This was the vessel she occupied when she finally became whole and returned to us.

Goosebumps covered her flesh, despite being covered in a thin sheen of sweat. Her hands caressed my scalp as I dragged my mouth across her belly and hips.

"You're going to get me off again just from that," she breathed. "Damn, I'm still so sensitive from that last one."

"Well, that's perfect," I said, making my way lower. "Because I need a short break if I'm going to last any longer."

Whatever response she had was immediately cut off as I sealed my mouth over her pussy, lapping up her sweet nectar like I needed it to live. Her caresses through my hair became greedy pulls as she bucked her hips against my mouth. Her thighs pressed in on both sides of my head and I hadn't even touched her clit yet.

I teased her until she begged for release. I felt her thighs shaking before my tongue flicked that hard little button. When she came undone, I didn't give her a chance to recover.

She screamed and I felt the delightful pain of her nails in my back as I entered her again in one smooth motion. This time, I didn't fight to maintain control. I let go of it completely.

Her convulsions around me never seemed to stop as I fucked her hard and deep, grunting like an animal as I pinned her hips down on the love seat. I felt teeth cut my shoulder and returned the biting kiss, my pleasure swelling as we marked each other.

I lost track of where I ended and she began. Magic surrounded us and passed through us as we became a single entity. Ordinary humans, even those who were soulmates, would never be able to connect to each other on this level. It was like our souls left our bodies and made love on a plane that wasn't even physical.

My release came violently, draining all my strength as I emptied into her. Her pussy, her aura, or her soul, I couldn't tell the difference anymore, held onto me like it didn't want to let go. As weariness settled into my limbs I reached above our heads and laced my fingers through hers, vowing that I never would let her go again.

7
DEJA

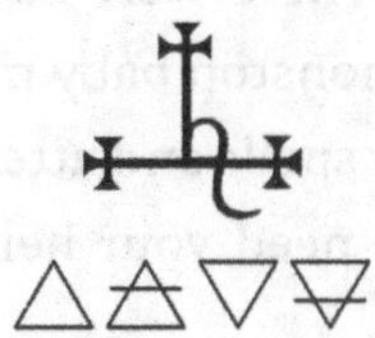

The sun was warm on my legs, just like that time in the Garden. The day my whole life literally crashed around me and I found my love and my truth.

But this time Juno laid next to me on a blanket, pouring over a spellbook while we picnicked in a local park. I looked at her with new eyes after my evening with Ash last night. How strange to think that my coven sister was also a distant daughter, not by blood but by magic.

After making love, Ash explained to me that the witch gene never diminished as it was passed on through the generations. And it was incredibly strong. Children born from one witch parent could still cast magic, though their innate abilities didn't come as early or easily as those with two witch parents.

Those with demon parents often excelled in the darker areas like shadow magic. Which meant our direct descendants received the best of both worlds.

The breeze blew through Juno's pale blonde hair as her large, aquamarine eyes moved over the page. She looked nothing like me in this body but she was beautiful. I wondered where her bloodline originated and how far it went back.

That thought made me wonder how many bloodlines had ended in the thousand years I was gone. My heart squeezed with an ache at the thought of all the witch families who didn't survive the dark ages, not to mention all the witch hunts in more recent centuries.

I laid a hand on my stomach. At some point, we'd have to repopulate with more witches. There were so few of us at this point. I grinned at the thought of nonstop baby making with my three men. Maybe I'd look into fertility spells and attempt twins or even triplets.

"Give me your hand, I need your help with this," Juno huffed, interrupting my thoughts.

"What are you trying to do?" I placed my hand in her outstretched fingers.

She didn't answer but continued muttering an incantation under her breath while gesturing with her right hand. And suddenly, I couldn't breathe.

Trying to suck in a breath, I felt like I was drowning. My lungs and nasal cavity burned and I coughed on what felt like water but nothing came out. The harder I fought for air, the more I felt I was inhaling liquid. And then just as quickly, the drowning sensation was gone.

"I'm sorry!" Juno shrieked. "It was a self-defense spell using my water magic. It wouldn't have worked if you were expecting it."

"What," I gasped. "...the fuck?"

Fresh air never tasted so sweet. Adrenaline surged through me, triggering my own defensive magic. It happened so fast, my body didn't realize it was safe again.

"Erik said I should practice more combative magic just in case I ever need it." Her brow furrowed, and she sucked her lip between her teeth as she watched me struggling to catch a breath. "Shit, I had no idea it would work so well. I'm so sorry, Deja!"

"It's 'cause water is your element," I said, still coughing. "You

have a much firmer grasp on water magic that someone not special-
izing in that element."

"I know, I'd just never had a chance to practice that spell before."
Her lip wobbled. "I really didn't mean to hurt you. Shit, what if I
couldn't stop it? I'm so fucking sorry, Deja."

"It's okay." I inhaled deeply, my airways finally clearing. "Now
you know." I forced a smile. "And you know I'll get you back for that.
You won't know where, when or how, but I will."

"Oh yeah, I totally deserve it." She wrapped me in a hug. "I'm so
glad you're okay. Just promise you won't bury me alive or anything?"

"No promises," I laughed wickedly and resisted the urge to rub at
my throat. It would be raw for a while. I had to remember to make
some soothing tea with lemon and honey when I got home.

"So how's the whole shadow lesson going with Seth?" she asked.

I sighed. Not exactly the subject I wanted to change to.

"It's going okay, I guess. I'll be happy when it's over with and he
jets off to somewhere else again."

"That bad, huh? I've heard shadow work is difficult, and he's a
strict teacher. He doesn't take it easy on anybody."

"It's not even that really," I confessed, trying to decide how much
I should tell her. "I just would have liked some choice in the
decision."

"What do you mean?"

"My grandmother threw this big hissy fit and set me up to take
lessons with him behind my back. She's treating me like a petulant
teenager when I'm damn near thirty years old! I'm really close to just
telling her off but I feel bad after all she's taught me already. Not to
mention she's the only blood family I have left."

"I see where you're coming from," Juno said softly. "But for what
it's worth, a search for a qualified shadow worker would have led
you right back to Seth. There is really no one else around with his
kind of abilities."

"How does someone get to be like him, anyway?" I asked. "Was he born with the innate abilities or did he practice shadow work nonstop?"

"A bit of both, I think," she mused. "He comes from a long, ancient line of really powerful shadow workers, but it's still a difficult skill to master." Her ocean-colored eyes glanced to just above my head. "I'm not the best at seeing auras but his looks very similar to yours. I wouldn't be surprised if you two are distantly related." She shrugged. "Or it could be all the demons he's killed. He doesn't talk about himself much and isn't here half the time, so no one really knows."

"What would his, ah, kills have to do with shadow work and his aura?" I asked.

"Well, the darker someone's aura is, the more shadow abilities they innately have." She held up a hand. "Supposedly, anyway. There are always exceptions to the rule. Shadow work is also the primary magic source of demons. Prolonged exposure to demons is said to make your aura darker and darker over time."

"I see." I chewed on her words, trying to get a sense of her opinion one way or the other toward the race of creatures I fell in love with. But I couldn't get a clear read, so decided to ask her straight out. "What are your thoughts on the whole demon thing?"

Her head snapped over to me, surprised. "My thoughts?"

"Yeah, you know." I waved my hand trying to appear casual, although my feelings were anything but. "Are we justified in hunting them? Are they just as bad as Christians have made them out to be?" I forced a sheepish smile. "You have to remember I'm still new to this whole witch thing."

Juno reclined back on her elbows, not saying anything for a moment while my heart pounded like crazy in my chest.

"I guess I've never really thought of them as people," she admitted.

"Really?" I gritted my teeth, struggling to keep my emotions in check.

"Yeah. I mean we learned about them as kids kind of like zombies." She giggled. "They're mindless drones being controlled by Lucifer. Only instead of brains, they're just hell-bent on raping."

My blood ran cold. "Rape?"

She nodded. "They're extremely seductive and don't take no for an answer. They force sex on their victims and often take control of their bodies. Hence the accounts of demonic possessions from Christian sources." She looked over at me with a sad expression. "That's why things are so bad for women in African countries and the Middle East. Ordinary humans think it's because of oppressive religions and politics, which might be true. But a big part of it has to do with demons in power seducing and controlling."

I couldn't look her in the eye, so I studied the blades of grass poking through our picnic blanket.

How could she believe that? None of it was true! Demons were created to exercise freedom of choice based on knowledge, not to control. And through me, witches became a mortal extension of that.

Somehow at some point in time, our narrative got twisted into something so far from the truth. And modern witches were passing down this misinformation like gospel to future generations.

I leaned back on my palms, bewildered at what I just heard. And I realized bringing demons to a more positive light was going to be much harder than I anticipated.

8

DEJA

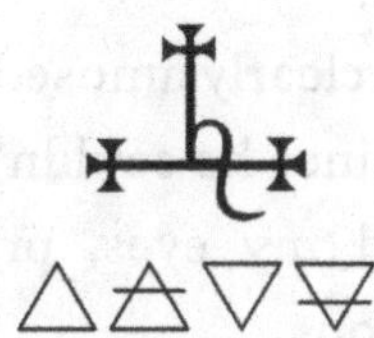

I dragged my feet so much to my next lesson with Seth, I practically left rug burns on Laurel's carpet. He waited for me, smug as ever, in the same lawn chair in their backyard.

"Late again," he remarked.

I resisted doing a massive eye roll. "Oh no, please forgive me, Seth," I mock-pleaded. "When these lessons are as fun as you make them, how could I ever fathom showing up late?"

His lip curled into a snarl. "They aren't supposed to be fun. They're supposed to make you stronger. Who knows, they may even save your life one day."

"And you'll never forget to take the credit for it, I'm sure," I replied. "Shall we get this over with?"

He stood and swept out his arm as if to say, *be my guest*. Despite the chill in the air, he abandoned his leather jacket tonight and wore only a gunmetal gray T-shirt that clung to him like a second skin. His body was slender and willowy, yet still covered in lean, lithe muscles.

I jerked my eyes away, embarrassed that they lingered on him too long and walked out to the middle of the yard where he gestured. He followed, standing a few feet behind me, though still uncomfortably close.

"If you fall again, I'll catch you." His gravelly voice cut through the night air. "So you won't go home looking like you shit your pants again."

"Oh, how kind of you," I sneered. "If only other men would aspire to be as gentlemanly as you."

He huffed a dark laugh, clearly amused with his own joke. I really did roll my eyes that time since he couldn't see them. Then I inhaled a deep breath and closed my eyes, preparing to travel inward through my own subconscious.

"You got close last time," he said with what sounded like genuine encouragement. "Just work on keeping your focus the whole time, even when you uncover a shadow. That loss of focus is what keeps things hidden."

The air around me seemed to hum with a gentle vibration. Last time I used my earth magic to lead me through the dark twists and turns of my shadow self, like a rope guiding me through a cave. Tendrils of energy traveled up through my feet, anchoring my focus before traveling up my torso and finally, through the depths of my brain.

Like last time, I uncovered more memories that I hadn't yet been aware of. It only made sense that thousands of lifetimes in one soul couldn't all come to the surface of my awareness at once. I flipped back through these memories as if they were files in a cabinet. I was looking for something specific.

There. An uncontrollable smile erupted on my face but I didn't lose focus.

I saw Raum holding a baby in his arms, beaming down at the little one proudly. Then he looked at me with tears in his eyes and a smile that was full of love and joy. Right then he wasn't my dirty-talking, dominant man, full of flirtation and teasing. He was the father of my child.

I looked around quickly at our surroundings, trying to get a sense of when and where this memory occurred. My bed was covered in soft animal furs. Raum was shirtless but wore a pair of rough leather breeches. Our son was wrapped in a smaller animal hide. Against the wooden wall of our structure hung dozens of weapons and shields. Axes, swords, bows, and quivers full of arrows stood on display next to a massive bear's head mounted on the wall.

But attention couldn't be torn away from the two precious people in front of me. I reached out and stroked the soft fluff on my son's head. It felt just as real as if I were touching him at that moment.

"What should we name him?" Raum whispered, scooting closer to me as gently as he could.

"Ragnar," I answered as I drew protective sigils on my son's forehead. "Warrior of the gods."

Raum grinned at my choice. "I knew you would choose that name. It's perfect for the man he will become."

"You've seen his future?" I watched in fascination as Ragnar's tiny hand wrapped around my index finger.

"He and his sons will lead armies across the seas," Raum spoke softly and filled with awe. "Their names will be hailed for centuries." Still beaming, Raum nuzzled his face against my cheek until I turned to kiss him.

"I love you, Alfhilde," he whispered against my lips. "No matter how many sons or daughters we have throughout infinite lifetimes, my love for them and you never fades." He dropped a gentle kiss to Ragnar's forehead.

"I love you, Raum. I always will." A giggle escaped my chest. "Even when you're off playing Odin and Loki with the others."

"Of course. You love being taken by an invisible god." His kisses fell to my neck with playful bites as I squirmed away.

"You insatiable demon," I teased. "None of that now, I just pushed out your damn baby. Take him to see Sal and Ash. I need a nap."

Raum chuckled with amusement as he gave me one final kiss before shifting off the bed. "You're sure Ragnar's been fed enough?"

"Yes, he should be full," I said, reclining back on my pillow, my eyelids already closing. "Wake me up in two hours when he's ready to eat again."

I felt Raum's weight lift off the bed as he took our newest son to see his other two fathers. A smile played at my lips from the sheer, unrestrained happiness I felt. How lucky I was to experience this love and miracle of life time and time again with the three best husbands I could ask for.

Just before my body as Alfhilde drifted off to sleep, I prepared to let go of that memory and continue searching through my shadows. But a surge of unknown power made me pause and stay focused there.

Like a rag doll, Alfhilde was ripped from the bed. I let out a startled cry but kept my focus. Distantly as if underwater, I heard Seth demand to know what was going on, but I ignored him.

Alfhilde was pressed against the ceiling of her house. Pain wracked through me as I stared helplessly down at the bed I just gave birth in hours ago. My back was surely broken. The power wrapped around me was immense and suffocating. I called out for my men but couldn't make a sound.

This wasn't an ordinary death by the judgment of humans accusing me of heresy. This was different, like nothing I ever felt before and it scared me.

The force of whatever was pulling me finally ripped Alfhilde's broken body through the ceiling. In horror, I watched my house grow smaller with each passing second. Villagers and animals became the size of ants. I felt like I was in freefall but in reverse. Something carried me up, up high into the sky at breakneck speed. The air was so cold up here, my fingers and toes turned blue.

Somehow I was able to turn my neck to look up at whatever dragged my body up through the atmosphere. And my worst fear was confirmed.

An angel looked down at me with a vengeful scowl on his face. He could have been Ash's brother, golden and beautiful. The feathers of his blindingly white wings barely ruffled while air currents thrashed my body back and forth. So much pain. No human torture compared to this. This body was close to death and I hoped it would come soon—before this angel got ahold of my soul.

And then all too quickly, we stopped.

Blood poured out of my ears and nose, unable to handle the pressure of the atmosphere at such speeds. My back and neck had to be broken, but I stood upright, apparently floating in midair before the divine being that ripped me from my home, my lovers, and my son.

He smirked at me, clearly enjoying the suffering he caused from dragging me up here.

"Finally, I have the honor of meeting Lilith," he said in a smug tone. "Our dear Ashtaroth's whore. It's not every day we meet the reason for an angel's fall." He tilted his head like a curious puppy. "Too bad our first meeting is also our last."

I wanted to spit at him, to tell him to fuck off, anything but stand silently in defeat. But either my jaw was broken too or he rendered me unable to speak with magic.

"Your reign of heresy and wanton lust is at an end, Lilith," the shithead angel continued. "Have you noticed your so-called lovers aren't here to protect you?" He spread his arms out and looked around mockingly. "Where are they, Lilith? Isn't your unholy trinity supposed to guard you?" He cackled, extremely pleased with himself. "That's the problem with you knowledge-seekers. You're so self-serving, you scatter like mice at the first sign of trouble. Even when one of your own is in danger."

I reached for my men with my aura and felt their panic as they tried to reach me. They knew something was wrong, and that I was missing, but this angel wasn't working alone. They must have coordinated this for years, maybe even centuries. The same force of power that dragged my ass up here, was now acting as a shield preventing them from reaching me.

Alfhilde! Where are you? I can't reach you! The panicked voice in my head belonged to Ash.

Up high. An angel has me. My body is so close to death but he's not letting me die. He's talking shit and taunting me. This is bad, love. I think he's going to take my soul.

Fuck! We're getting Lucifer and Beelzebub to help. We can't go up but there's nothing stopping us from going down. We'll have an army at your back in five minutes, my love.

Fear gripped my soul as the angel began gesturing, casting his own brand of holy magic. A heavy sensation laid over me and I realized he was beginning to separate my soul from my body.

I might not last that long. My body is broken. I can't talk. I can't stall him.

We're coming, my love. Please hang on.

The two hemispheres of my brain felt like they were splitting apart. The pain radiating through me made childbirth feel like a walk in the park.

Ash, I love you so much. Tell Raum and Sal I love them too. Take care of Ragnar. Guide him and make these damned angels afraid to speak his name.

Stop! Do not say goodbye to us. We're coming for you now.

You were my first true love. Curse the god and all the angels, I love you with all my soul. Please don't forget me.

Lilith, my love! Don't let go. Hold onto your soul with everything you have. We won't let them take you.

I couldn't scream with my mouth so I did inside my head.

If this angel ripped out my soul, he'd ensure I'd never occupy another human body again. I'd be truly dead, never to come back and feel the love of my men or children ever again.

I saw the angel sneer through my blackening vision. He was taking his time, making this as painful as possible for me. My soul peeled away from my physical body inch by excruciating inch.

And then, nothingness.

9
SETH

I watched Deja with fascination for what felt like hours but had to be mere minutes.

Her golden eyes shut tightly in concentration. Her full lips moved rapidly, muttering words I couldn't catch as she traveled through the deepest, darkest trenches of her mind.

I enjoyed watching her and not only because she was beautiful. I'd never admit it to her, but she was a prodigy of a student. While unfamiliar with shadow magic, she took my direction easily and used it effortlessly as the tool it was meant to be. I'd never seen anyone grasp it so quickly. Even I took years to successfully work my way through everything hidden in my subconscious. And when I did, I never cared to fully immerse myself in the hidden memories like she did.

Suddenly her brow knitted and her head jerked to the side as if bracing herself against something painful. She let out soft, pathetic whimpers that sounded like a puppy being kicked.

"Deja," I said with clarity and calm. "You can move away from the shadow any time you wish. But don't put your focus away all at once. Ease out of it slowly."

She didn't seem to hear me. She was too deeply entrenched in whatever was happening in her mind.

"Ragnar," she whimpered under her breath. "Ash, I love you."

I moved in front of her and took each of her hands in mine. She was in so deep I had to pull her out myself.

This was just another reason why so many non-demons failed at shadow magic. They went so deep into their own minds as either escape or punishment, they never returned to reality and went mad.

"Deja, listen to my voice," I said loudly and clearly. "It's Seth. What you're seeing now isn't real. Come back to the sound of my voice."

She was crying now, openly sobbing and looking so heartbroken I physically ached for her. Without thinking, I pressed my palm against her cheek and wiped away a tear with my thumb.

"Come back to me, Deja," I said, my voice much lower as I leaned in, my forehead nearly brushing hers. "It isn't real. I'm real. Me, the guy you hate. I can't possibly be worse than what you're seeing right now."

But her sobbing continued. She mumbled something that I couldn't make out the words. It could have been, "He won't let me die. It hurts so much."

Shit! This was bad. Her mind could collapse in on itself if she was reliving some horrible trauma.

Panic and frustration hit me in equal measures as my hands lowered to her slender shoulders. I squeezed and gave her a gentle shake.

"Gods be damned, you gorgeous infuriating bitch! Snap out of it!"

Her head suddenly threw back and released the loudest, most bloodcurdling scream I ever heard.

The shock of it made me release her and sent me stumbling backward. I stood stunned, watching her scream like a banshee and my mind went completely blank on how to stop it.

While I watched helplessly, a force of power surged at my back like a strong gust of wind. It felt familiar but stronger than anything I'd ever faced before. Muttering a curse, I reached for one of my angel-kissed blades tucked into my waistband. But by the time I withdrew it, the demon was already next to her.

"Stay back!" I commanded at the infernal creature who took on the shape of a man with dark red hair and catlike green eyes.

He ignored me, simply waving a hand in front of Deja's face. Her screaming stopped immediately and her knees buckled. She collapsed into his waiting arms and he picked her up as if she were a bride. He looked down at her tenderly, whispering softly when her head rolled onto his shoulder.

"Stop! Put her down, demon!" I yelled at the top of my lungs. "I'll cut your backward-beating heart out before I let you hurt her."

He glanced at me with nothing more than annoyance. I suspected it from feeling his power, but right then I knew this was no ordinary incubus. This creature sat much closer to the top of the Hierarchy than the bottom. But what would he want with her?

"She is safe. You never saw me." Those were the only words he spoke before they vanished into thin air.

I stood dumbfounded and blinking, looking behind me and then in front where they had just stood moments before. Deja was nowhere to be seen. She really did get whisked away by a demon.

Slowly as if in a trance, I walked up to Laurel's patio and pulled the sliding door open. She and John sat relaxed and reading books by their fireplace. Laurel looked up and smiled when I came in, giving no indication that she heard Deja's scream or caught sight of the demon that took her.

"Done already?" she asked in a curious tone.

"Yeah." I cleared my throat in an attempt to release the knot that settled there. "Deja wasn't feeling well so she took off. Went out the gate on the side of the house."

For some reason I couldn't place, I was compelled to obey the green-eyed demon's words. It would do no good if I reported that I saw him. The calmness in my instincts also assured me that Deja was indeed safe.

Laurel's smile fell into a frown. "Don't let her off too easy, Seth. I can tell you're attracted to her but you must find her limit and push it. She's no damsel in distress."

"Yes, High Priestess." I lowered my head respectfully as I addressed her as the head of our coven. "I will not go easy on her. I could tell tonight she legitimately came down with something."

"Remember, she has to be humbled by her power," Laurel went on. "She can't let her prowess get to her ego like a spoiled brat. I already saw the beginnings of that when she at first requested a different teacher."

The corner of my mouth ticked up in a smirk.

"She apologized for that and has been fully present in our lessons. I think she's learning some humility yet."

"Good." A hint of a smile returned to Laurel's face. "You realize she will most likely be the one to join you on your hunting missions?"

"No doubt," I agreed with a curt nod. "She will likely surpass me in shadow magic abilities within a year or two."

"Excellent," Laurel beamed. "We'll be so fortunate to have not only one powerful hunter in our midst but two!" She turned back toward the fire, grinning at the flames. "It will be a fine day when we eliminate the demon scourge off the face of the earth."

I allowed a grin to spread on my face as well.

"Agreed, High Priestess."

10
DEJA

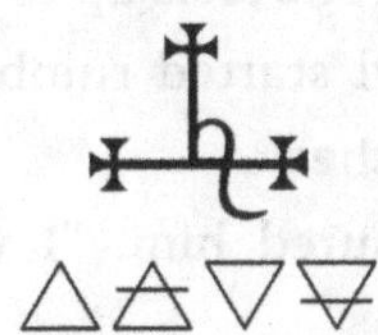

I groaned in agony, feeling the unbearable pounding of my headache before I even fully woke.

"It's okay, beautiful," a voice soothed me from somewhere above. "You're okay. Move slowly."

My eyelids cracked open, nearly blinded by the ordinary daylight coming through the window. A gentle hand skimmed across my forehead and I turned in the direction of the voice.

Sal's green eyes glittered down at me and his smile was filled with relief.

"Hey, handsome lion," I croaked.

"Hey." He planted a warm kiss on my forehead. "You were out for a while. We were starting to get worried."

As I slowly blinked my eyes, my surroundings came into focus. I recognized Ash's study, lined with books and the fireplace roaring with cozy flames. They lay me out on the love seat, covered in a blanket and propped up with pillows. Ash and Raum sat nearby in chairs, relief etched into their features as well.

My headache was killing me and all my limbs felt beyond

exhausted, but I was cozy and happy to be surrounded by my men once again.

"Sal filled us in on what he saw," Ash said, reaching for my hand and planting a kiss on the back of my palm. "Do you feel up to telling us what happened from your perspective?"

"She needs to rest," Sal growled with a warning at him.

Annoyed, Ash turned his icy eyes to his second in command. "Which is why I'm asking if she feels up to it. Calm the fuck down."

Another warning growl started rumbling in Sal's chest, which halted when I touched his cheek.

"I'm okay, lion," I assured him. "I want to talk about what happened."

"Only if you're sure." He pressed my hand against his face and kissed my palm.

I gingerly pulled myself up to a sitting position while Sal, being a total sweetheart, stuffed pillows behind my back to prop me up. The other two waited eagerly while I got comfortable.

Cutting to the chase, I blurted out, "I saw when I died. For good."

All the air seemed to get sucked out of the room as each man muttered curses and hung their heads. Sal squeezed my hand tighter.

"I found the memory while looking through my mind's shadows," I went on. "I felt every bit of it exactly as if I was there. Right up until the point the angel ripped my soul from my body."

"My love," Ash said softly, reaching for my other hand. "Why would you want to relive that?"

"I didn't go searching for it," I protested, my heart aching at the pain in his blue eyes. "When we talked about our children the other day, it made me want to look for the ones we've had in the past. The first one I found was Ragnar."

Raum's dark eyes caught mine from across the room. His aura flickered and pulsed with red energy when he heard me speak our son's name. Our last son.

He shook his head, letting out a huff of laughter as he seemed to recall the memory himself.

"I almost thought that would be the last happy moment of my life," he said softly. "Before we found you again."

"You should have pulled away from the memory once it started to go bad." Ash's voice was harsh and commanding. "Especially with so many other things in your head, you could've gone mad from living through that again. And the Mother of Witches would spend the rest of this lifetime in a vegetative state."

"I didn't know." My frustration started climbing. "Especially with all of you not telling me what happened."

Ash bit his lip and lowered his eyes. He knew this withholding of information was my ongoing gripe with them and it was pissing me off that it was still an issue.

"We didn't know either," Raum said from across the room. "We had no idea if you would have any memory of that event after your soul returned. But we felt your pain through our auras and it nearly broke us in turn. We figured if you didn't remember, it would be for the best."

"The three of us still remember it all too well," Sal chimed in softly.

"But how did I come back?" I asked. "I remember knowing that angel would destroy my soul and never let me come back. So how did I?"

"Lucifer," all three of them said in unison.

"You're lucky that old bastard loves you like a daughter," Ash said with a hint of a smile. "He broke through that barrier the angels created like tearing through paper. The rest of us could only watch as your lifeless body fell back down to earth."

"What did he do?"

Ash's expression hardened. "He used nearly half his power to destroy that angel, and then saved you in the only way he could." His thumbs lovingly caressed my palm as he spoke. "He split your soul into thousands of pieces and let them fall back down to earth. The pieces would inhabit humans, but none would have your magical abilities. They would only have echoes of your spirit. Only after a thousand years would the pieces be able to converge into one body again."

I sat silently while I processed his words. He mentioned it briefly in passing the other day when talking about how the world got thrown into the dark ages.

"What year was Ragnar born?" I asked no one in particular.

"800 AD," Raum answered with a wistful smile. "He and his sons became everything I foresaw and more. After the Roman Empire fell, they held off the grip of the cross-bearers as best they could but without you, we just didn't have enough influence to rebel against them."

I wracked my brain trying to recall history lectures in college. The Renaissance period didn't begin until the 1400s, when creativity, science, and rational thought became valued by the general public again. But even during that period, the grip of Christianity reached far. Galileo was accused of heresy and imprisoned by the church for his findings, despite being proven correct. And like Ash said, women served little purpose aside from breeding and domestic slavery. Hundreds, if not thousands, of innocent witches and ordinary humans alike were either burned or hanged for not conforming to the Church's doctrine.

Only in recent centuries did few, spirited women fight back after hundreds of years of oppression. That must have been when the pieces of my soul began to converge, whispering ideas of rebellion to the brains of the bodies they inhabited. My first instinct was to refuse to be subservient to a man and they must have felt it.

The ones who taught themselves to read and write. The ones who unashamedly demanded their own pleasure during sex. The ones who refused to be sold off like cattle to a loveless marriage. And the ones who happily killed their abusers and rapists. It was Lilith urging them to do it all along. And slowly but surely, I turned the tide before even becoming whole in this body again.

I looked at Raum. "Will the angels do that to me again?"

He hesitated, knowing I was asking if he saw it in a vision but I didn't give a fuck if that was his burden to bear. I could understand him not wanting to tell me about my mother but this? I needed to know.

"I haven't seen it," he answered, bringing his hands together in a prayer position, ironically. "They probably won't attempt it again because they know we'd expect it. And Lucifer wouldn't hesitate to smite one of them again." He licked his lips. "However, my guess is they're counting on modern witches to do their dirty work for them now. I'm sure you've noticed their sentiment toward our kind."

"Oh, really? I haven't." My voice, dripping with sarcasm, was punctuated by my massive eye roll. Sal and Ash both chuckled at my reaction.

"Right." Raum's signature smirk returned. "Their resentment of us has run especially deep since the Salem witch trials. It seems many of them have even forgotten there's a touch of demon in all of them. Even though we've never done anything directly to hurt them. Only humans have done that."

"You've never exactly done anything to help them either," I pointed out. "I don't think it's fair how they think of you now but I can see where the resentment comes from."

"Now that you're back with us," Ash said, brushing my hand against his lips. "Maybe we can work on turning that around."

"Maybe," I sighed. "It will take several lifetimes, though. Even the younger generation has been fed anti-demon propaganda."

"All of our work tends to do that," Raum teased, his eyes lighting up. "It's why we're still here, all these years later."

"Rome wasn't built in a day," Sal chimed in with a kiss on my cheek. "I should know, I spent a good three lifetimes building the damn place."

I giggled, nuzzling to kiss him back. "And look where that got you," I teased.

Raum let out a throaty laugh from across the room. "I think our girl is back."

"Agreed." Ash gave a rare, full grin that made my heart flutter. He looked so much like an angel when he smiled. "I'm happy you're feeling better, my love."

The relief and relaxation on their faces made my heart want to burst. I swore it was from their love and concern that my headache was suddenly gone and I felt like myself again.

"Me too," I said, leaning back into my pillows. "Now we can move forward and change the world again." *And get to the bottom of finding my mother's murderer.*

"There may be one small holdup," Sal said after a moment of silence.

We all turned to him expectantly. He chewed his lip and looked directly at Ash.

"The witch who was teaching her. He saw me."

"The fuck?" Ash went from grinning to scowling in a matter of seconds. "Why didn't you cloak with a shadow?"

"He would've sensed my presence without needing to see my face, anyway," Sal shot back. "He's a shadow master, remember? Either way, he knows Deja is associated with our kind now." He looked at me with an apologetic expression. "I'm sorry, beautiful. I just panicked and had to help you when I saw you screaming. I didn't intend to blow your cover."

"It's okay, lion," I assured him. "He read my shadows and saw I had three lovers, so he might have already known. It was bound to come out at some point." I kissed him deeply so he knew that I wasn't angry. "Whatever comes of this, we'll outsmart them. We always do."

"That's definitely our girl," Raum grinned.

11
DEJA

The guys gave me space to nap for a while in the study. After I got tired of laying down, I went to the kitchen to see what these demons had that resembled food and tea. I opened a few cupboards and wrinkled my nose at a box of Lipton tea bags. Hopefully, they had some halfway decent loose tea, not that shitty excuse for sawdust. I was so intent on rummaging through their stuff, I didn't notice someone coming up behind me until a strong forearm wrapped around my waist.

"What're you looking for, love?" Ash's breath fanned across the back of my neck.

"Food." I kissed him looking over my shoulder. "And good tea, not that Lipton shit. Can you conjure up some for me, angel?"

He chuckled into my nape, the bristles of his beard tickling me there.

"No, doesn't work like that. That trick I did with the coffee? It was actually just a transportation spell."

"Oh yeah?" I turned to look at him. "You were just trying to impress me then?"

"Maybe a little," he teased. "Okay, yeah. I made a cup of coffee here then went to the shop to see you. And just zapped it from here to there."

"Ah-hah." I pressed a finger against his chest, enjoying watching the blush rise in his cheeks at his confession. "You thought you were so smooth, didn't you?"

"It's been a while since I tried to impress a girl. Give me a break." He took my wrist that pointed at him and swept a kiss across my knuckles. "But yes, I can get you some dried up twigs and leaves to drink if that's what you prefer." His eyes flashed and heat pooled in my body. I liked this relaxed, teasing Ash with a sense of humor.

"Um, excuse me but tea is not drinking twigs and leaves." I crossed my arms in mock anger. "All tea is made from the plant *Camellia sinensis*, with different subspecies and treatments during the drying process to produce the different varieties of tea."

"Alright, I'll remember you're sensitive about your livelihood," Ash laughed, pulling me into his chest. "Typical human," he teased, kissing the top of my head.

I tilted my head up and stuck my tongue out at him, which he replied to by kissing me slow and deep. Time seemed to stand still as I clung to him, wrapped up in his smell, his arms, and his delicious mouth.

"I came down to ask you something," he murmured when he pulled away, stroking a thumb against my cheek.

"Mm-hm?" I noticed his voice and demeanor turned stoic and serious again.

He spent a moment just stroking my face and searching my eyes with his before speaking. One thing I was quickly learning about Ash was he did not speak before thinking first. It made me wondered how such a thinker handled all the memories in his own head, but then I had to remember he didn't carry a human brain. Maybe he was better adapted to it than me.

"Move in with us."

I pulled back to look at him clearly. "You're serious?"

He nodded. "If the coven really does find out about you, you'll be safer here than alone at your place. And anyway," he shrugged. "It's your choice of course, but we love having you here."

I snorted out a laugh, prompting confusion on his handsome face.

"Sorry, it's just--" I took a deep breath. "I was about to say I've only known you guys for a few weeks but I guess that's not true, is it?"

His icy eyes flickered to the ground as his jaw clenched. "If you don't want to, that's fine. I'm just worried--"

"Stop." I threw my arms around his neck and jumped on tiptoe to kiss him, snaking my tongue into his mouth. "Of course I'll move in with you."

His adorable grin returned, and his shoulders sagged with relief. No words came but he cupped my face sweetly and kissed me, again and again in his slow, passionate way. When the bulge in his pants began to harden and his hands started moving, I reluctantly pulled away.

"Angel, you know I want you. I always do but," I licked my lips to quell my own heat rising within me. "I'm still hungry and I need tea." His chest vibrated with laughter and I mentally kicked myself for stopping him. "And if I'm going to be moving in, I should prob-ably grab some stuff from my apartment."

"Fine," he sighed, pulling away from me reluctantly. "Go grab what you need and I'll get us lunch and tea for you."

"Thank you, my love." I reached out to him for a parting kiss and found his frozen eyes burning into mine, with the iron grip of his hands on my shoulder.

"Be careful," he warned. "There's no telling what that shadow witch might do. If you sense anything weird, reach out to us." He tapped his temple. "We'll anchor our auras to yours and be there in seconds."

"I will, angel," I promised, running my hands across the short bristles of his beard.

He kissed my palm and smirked. "I'm starting to like that nickname."

"Good." I planted a final kiss on him. "'Cause you're stuck with it."

12
DEJA

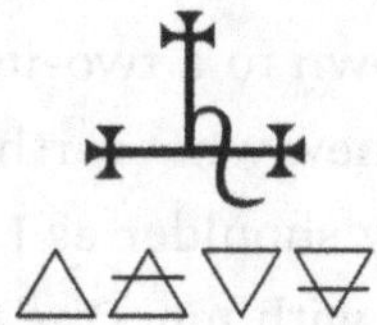

A half-hour later, I opened the door to my apartment above the tea shop and looked around at everything longingly.

I walked through and tried to mentally catalog everything, deciding what I should sell or keep. The guys' house was big enough to fit all of my furniture if I wanted to bring everything with me, but I didn't see the need. I pieced my apartment together slowly over time. Before my shop made any money, I slept on blankets on the floor. As my business became established and grew, I slowly added more.

But that stage of my life already felt like so long ago, I realized as I ran an affectionate finger along the back of my thrift store IKEA couch. I didn't need to bring this all with me because I was starting a new chapter in this lifetime. My goal was no longer to make it through another day with a few dollars in my bank account. With my newfound powers and my memories of my past lives to guide me, my purpose became much bigger.

I was created to rebel, to push back against those who sought to control. To instill burning curiosity and the pursuit of knowledge to the human race, and use the power granted by Lord Lucifer to achieve that goal. I was meant to educate the ignorant and deflate massively oversized egos.

And I didn't need my ragtag, mismatched furniture to accomplish that. Just some clean clothes, toiletries, and my stash of tea.

I threw my essentials in a weekender bag and took another look around my place. My eyes rested on my tiny herb garden in the window and those plants pulled to me. That tall, bushy Thai basil plant was my first manifestation of earth magic. After a neighborhood squirrel chewed it down to a two-inch stem, I grew it back to its full glory before I even knew what earth magic was.

I shifted my bag on my shoulder as I hesitated by the door. I'd have to bring those plants with me. One of the guys could help me take them back to the house another day.

Just as I turned to leave, a shock of white hair flashed in my peripheral vision and I stopped dead in my tracks.

"Diana!" I gasped.

My grandmother stood squarely blocking my doorway, arms folded and face tense. More recently she began to look a lot less like the sweet mother figure I'd been missing, and more like, well, a crabby old witch.

"Back at your own place, I see," she said casually, although her tone was cold. "Or are you leaving again?"

"Yes, leaving," I answered just as coldly. She didn't need to know I'd be moving out for good. "Did you need something?"

She lifted her chin at me defiantly. "There's an emergency coven meeting in the woods. Laurel asked me to fetch you."

My heart dropped into my stomach but I kept my expression the same. "Emergency meeting about what?"

"I guess we'll find that out when we go." She jerked her head to the exit. "Let's go."

"Seriously, now?" I demanded. "I'm kind of in the middle of something."

"Yes Deja, now." Her patronizing tone sent my blood simmering. She spoke to me like I was a misbehaving toddler.

I stood my ground, tightening my grip on my back as I began reaching out for Ash with my aura. Diana would likely be able to see it reaching out for communication, so I focused hard on using its invisible shadow side.

"Why did Laurel send you for me?" I asked, stalling for time. "You're not even part of the coven."

She huffed out a sigh, clearly at the end of her rope with me. "Because I'm the only one who knows where you live and Laurel is my good friend." She fixated a narrow-eyed gaze at me. "Really Deja, have I done something to warrant this attitude of yours?"

"*My* attitude?" I repeated, incredulous. "How about *you* showing up to my place unannounced and trying to dictate my time? Scheduling lessons without consulting me? Demanding I come to emergency meetings with no notice? I'm adult, Diana. I have a life and a business. I won't just come when you tell me to jump."

Her face softened and I saw the grandmother I recognized once again, the one who opened the witching world to me and taught me the basics of my powers.

"I'm sorry, dear. I just--" She ran a hand down her face and her large amber eyes watered. "You remind me of your mother so much. I just worry about you." A shuddering sigh escaped her. "I panic and have these moments of needing to know desperately where you are and who you're with. I couldn't bear it if I lost you to the same type of evil I lost Deidre."

Torn, I bit my lip. She was referring to my guys. Damn, why did I have to tell her I hung out with demons back then? It was so profoundly naïve of me, but I didn't know any better.

And as she cried softly there on my doorstep, I didn't know how to tell her that it most likely wasn't demons that killed my mom, but another witch.

Slowly, I reached out and patted her back and shoulder. She turned and enveloped me in a tight hug.

"Come on, Gran," I muttered. "Let's see what this meeting is about."

"Ah, yes." She wiped her eyes and smiled sheepishly. "Forgive me, dear. I'll try to be better about respecting your space."

I nodded. "Sorry for reacting so harshly."

She patted my hand and together we went down the stairwell. I used the opportunity to connect with Ash.

Hey angel, small delay. Apparently, there's an emergency coven meeting. I'll head back as soon as it's over.

That doesn't sound good, love. His tone was worried.

I'll keep in touch if anything goes down. We're meeting in the woods where my initiation ceremony was.

We'll be standing by. Are you with your grandmother?

Yeah, proceeding with extreme caution.

Good girl. And damn, she really loves cockblocking me.

I stifled a giggle as Diana and I got into her Subaru, then pulled my phone out of my pocket. A quick text to Juno confirmed this mysterious coven meeting. She, Erik, and Seth were already there. Not that I truly believed Diana would really make this up to interfere with my relationships. Her thinly-veiled prejudice against my guys *did* come from a place of wanting to protect me.

I glanced over at her wrinkled hands gripping the steering wheel as she drove, and found myself sad that she wouldn't have another lifetime after this one. If she did, I might be able to prove her wrong about them.

13
DEJA

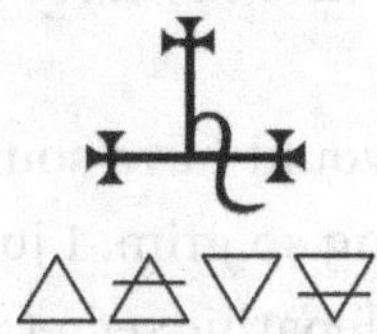

Everyone else seemed just as clueless as me about this emergency meeting. People whispered to each other, shrugged, and looked around to others for clues.

Meanwhile, Laurel, John, and Seth stood in the center of the clearing with grim expressions, waiting for everyone to gather. I spotted Juno with her boyfriend Erik and quickly went to stand next to them, eager for a bit of breathing room from my grandmother.

"Any ideas what this is about?" I asked them.

They both shook their heads. Juno looked worried while Erik rubbed her arms comfortingly.

"Even the elder coven members are saying this has never happened before," she whispered, her brows knitted at her forehead. "Every official meeting goes by the moon and seasonal cycles. This is unprecedented. It can't be good."

I shoved my hands in my pockets, bouncing on my heels as I waited for the coven to fill the clearing. Some people stood like us, others sat on large rocks and fallen trees. The grass in the center still carried some of the white chalk from my initiation rite. Laurel and John talked quietly in the middle of the clearing to themselves while

Seth paced like a caged animal. His gray eyes lifted briefly but looked away as soon as they met mine.

Shit. The feeling of my heart in my stomach seemed to collapse in on itself like a black hole.

The whole coven is here, I mentally reported to Ash. I'm safe but doesn't seem like the news will be good. Seth is looking guilty as fuck.

We're here with you, love. Raum is right above you and Sal is watching from the woods. I'm cloaked nearby and we're on high alert.

Roger that.

I stifled a giggle that would have sounded profoundly inappropriate with everyone looking so grim. I just found it funny we were talking to each other like telepathic secret agents.

Sure enough, a "Caw! Caw!" rang out as a large, handsome black raven settled on a tree branch just behind me. Several people turned to admire the magnificent bird. A few whispers of Odin carried in the air, making me smirk knowingly much like Raum did in human form.

The bird turned its glossy black head toward me and I swore it winked.

"Thank you all for coming on such short notice," Laurel's voice carried out from the clearing. "I see your faces, feel your energy, and wish I could offer better news for this gathering."

Everyone seemed to hold their breath at once.

"There have been reports of increased demon magic in the San Francisco area."

Near me, Juno gasped. Erik's arms encircled her protectively. Low, nervous murmurs began to rise from the crowd. Seth, standing off to the side of Laurel like a statue, still refused to meet my eye.

Laurel raised her hand for silence to continue speaking.

"While this city is known for its openness and tolerance of all kinds, there are many who still associate our craft and beliefs with that of the devil," she went on. "They would not hesitate to start yet another tragically misguided witch hunt. They may not publicly burn us like centuries ago, but keep their sick, twisted practices behind closed doors. And that, frankly, scares me even more."

She paused to let her words sink in.

"As long as I am High Priestess, I will not allow one more innocent witch to become a scapegoat for true evil," she declared. "For our safety, we must chase the demon scourge out of San Francisco for good." She stepped back and gestured to the stormy-eyed man next to her. "Seth has called in reinforcements from all around the country. Experienced demon hunters will be hiding in plain sight, blending in with the humans and demons, until they are eradicated from our city."

She nodded at Seth and he stepped forward, preparing to speak. Meanwhile, my hands clenched into fists in my pockets and my teeth ground against each other. I should've known he would stoop so low as to run and tell them right after seeing Sal.

"For those of you who can see auras, remember many witches have similar darkness in theirs as demons," he began. "They can blend in with us and ordinary humans very well. So how do you spot one?" He raised his hand and began drawing a sigil in midair. Black shadow magic drew from his fingertip like ink and my blood turned to ice as I recognized the upside triangle and diagonal lines crossing through it.

"This is the sigil of Lucifer," Seth declared. "All demons wear this as a tattoo, among other sigils possibly. It provides a direct link to Lucifer himself. If you see anyone with this on their skin, contact me or another hunter as soon as possible. Do not approach them yourself and until we've gotten rid of them all, do not go anywhere alone."

The sigil slowly faded from the air and he returned his hands behind his back like a dutiful soldier.

"You should also know there are some witches who are demon sympathizers." He paused to let his words sink in. "Your closest friend or family member may have been seduced by an incubus or succubus. Their behavior is not unlike someone addicted to drugs. That's due to their seduction magic." His jaw ticked for a moment before relaxing. "No one wants their loved ones to get in trouble but you have an obligation to report these people to us. For the safety of all witches in our community."

"What'll happen to the sympathizers?" someone called out.

Seth turned his head in the direction of the voice. "My team will do our best to detox the seduction spell out of the person. If we're successful and they are an ordinary human, their memory of the demon will be erased and they'll return to society. But frankly, it depends on how tight the demon's hold is on the person's mind. Remember, shadow magic is their specialty. They can read and manipulate people far better than us."

"So why should we trust you, master of shadows?"

All heads turned to me as I bit the inside of my cheek. Fuck, that was probably the wrong thing to blurt out and definitely at the wrong time. Laurel and John watched me coolly while Seth looked at me with a dark, menacing scowl on his face.

"Because I'm the only chance we have of surviving the witch hunts that will surely follow," he growled and snapped his attention away to address the rest of the crowd. "That's all, everyone. Please be safe out there."

The crowd began to disperse, some people casting nervous glances at me, or Seth, or both. The man in question made a beeline straight for me, the scowl still present on his face. With a surprisingly gentle hold on my elbow, he led me away from Juno until we were out of earshot of everyone.

"What the hell is wrong with you?" he seethed, practically spitting in my face. "You're the newest coven member and you're trying to undermine me? That'll get you nowhere fast, new girl."

"Yeah? So why are you so pissed?" I shot back, yanking my arm from his grip. "Maybe someone *should* challenge your authority.

Wouldn't want these coven members to be manipulated into following you blindly."

His jaw clenched as his stormy eyes seemed to search mine for the answer to some unknown question. Thankfully I wore a long-sleeved sweater so that he couldn't read my shadows without touching my bare skin. If he did, he'd know exactly how seethingly pissed I was.

"Look, I know what you're thinking," he said in a much lower voice. "And for what it's worth, you're wrong. I didn't breathe a word about what I saw the other night."

"Hah!" I barked out a harsh laugh that echoed off the surrounding tree trunks before lowering my voice again. "You expect me to believe that shit?"

He shrugged. "It's the truth. Doesn't really matter if you believe me or not." He stepped away from me, his sharp gaze softening. "I'm glad you're okay, Deja."

"Well, it's awfully convenient this meeting was called the day after you saw one of my men," I hissed, ignoring his note of concern for me. "Are your people going to hunt him down now? Drive him out like the witch hunt you're so desperate to avoid? It's fine as long as it's not done to *our* people, right?"

"Deja." The way he said my name was somewhere between a warning and a plea. His eyes lowered, and he sighed as he ran a hand through his coffee-colored hair. I focused on my anger to ignore how sexy it was.

"I had no reason to report your boyfriend, or whatever he is," he muttered. "So I didn't. End of story. He stopped your pain and took you somewhere safe evidently, as you're here now and right as rain." He licked his lips and raised his eyes to me. "Believe it or not, I don't have it out for people just because they're a different species. But I will investigate genuine threats against us. I just want to keep our people safe."

"Huh." I stepped in closer until my lips tingled from the sensation of his breath. "Choice words for a fucking demon hunter."

I walked away before he could respond, crushing leaves and pine needles with my heavy steps. Raum's wings fluttered somewhere behind me as he followed, taking short flights before hopping from branch to branch.

Every muscle in my body was as tense as a wound up spring. As I returned to Diana's car, I tried to convince myself that the thrum of heat and sensitivity pulsing through me was nothing more than anger.

14
RAUM

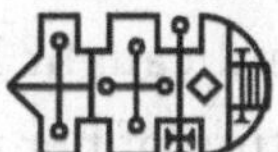

N o one could miss the tension radiating off of Deja like steam from boiling water. I found it sexy but also concerning.

While she normally moved with grace and ease behind the counter at the tea shop even during the busiest times, she was clearly distracted after the impromptu coven meeting.

She kept running into Nona, despite the poor girl clearly noticing the tension too and trying to keep her distance. Deja spilled tea, dropped cups, knocked things to the floor countless times, and seemed to get more frazzled by the minute.

"Baby." I reached across the counter from where I sat and skimmed my fingers along her waist as she walked by. "Just stop for a minute. Take a deep breath."

"I can't, Raum. I have people waiting," she snarled.

With one look at her dilated pupils and hot red flush in her cheeks, I knew exactly what she needed from me. But it would have to wait.

I took a long sip from my cup and ruminated on the knowledge that Seth, that shadow witch, did this to her. She was trying to convince herself that she was pissed at him snitching to the coven, and maybe she really believed that. But after all my years of knowing her and observing humanity, I knew what denial and misplaced feelings looked like. She'd figure it out, eventually. I wasn't going to be the one who hit her over the head with it.

The day continued like that until closing. When the last customer left, she slammed the door so hard, it rattled the window-panes. Even wiping down counters and throwing cups in the dish-washer were near violent acts.

My hand snapped out and caught her wrist the moment Nona left. I redirected the momentum of her nonstop movement and sent her barreling into my chest. Right where I wanted her.

"I said, slow down."

"You don't need to grab me like that." Her golden eyes blazed with anger but her voice heated with lust.

"No," I agreed while pressing my palm into the curve just above her ass, pinning her against me. I lowered my mouth to her ear. "But you love it when I do."

She molded herself to me just for a second before stiffening again. Heat radiated off of her and her aura was going crazy with activity. Every little wiggle she made as she struggled only made me harder.

"I need to finish," she protested weakly.

"Yes, you do," I growled, nipping her earlobe. "First on my face. Then wrapped around my cock."

"Raum." She said my name with a hot little whimper and raised her hands to my chest as if to push me away. But she didn't.

Finally, there was a brief pause of no movement at all. She stopped squirming and just let me hold her. Then with a huge sigh, she leaned her forehead against my chest.

"I don't know what to do," she whispered. "They're going to come after you."

"We're probably going to have to skip town a bit," I said, pressing a kiss to her temple. "Sooner rather than later."

"I really thought they could be my family. I never thought they would *all* feel this way about your kind."

Even my cold, black heart ached at the sorrow in her voice. I squeezed her tighter.

"We're your family," I breathed into her hair. "We're the only ones who will always be here. Everyone else, well." I released a heavy sigh of my own. "Humans either disappoint you or they die."

She nodded sadly and stood on tiptoe to wrap her arms around my neck. Her head rested on my shoulder while I massaged circles up and down her back.

The hard bite to my neck came without warning.

"Ahh!" I yelped, pulling away more in surprise than pain.

"That's for interfering with my work," she said with a naughty smile that instantly made me as hard as a rock.

"You wicked little witch," I growled, holding on as she squirmed against me again, this time while giggling. "I think I'll need some extra help punishing you for that." I reached out to Sal, just brushing his aura with mine. He'd feel how badly I wanted her and know exactly what I needed him for.

Meanwhile, I attacked her neck in the same manner, not caring if I left any visible marks. She was all mine to mark up. The fact that she pressed herself against me harder, rather than squirming away, just proved to me how much she needed this. My girl was frustrated, both sexually and with the bigger matter of the witch hunt looming over us.

And my job was to fuck that frustration out of her.

I shoved her leggings down and grabbed each of her ass cheeks roughly, ensuring I left my mark on her there too. She reached for my zipper but I caught her wrists and held them at her sides.

"No," I scolded. "You get my cock when I say you do."

She stuck out her bottom lip in a pout, which I sucked into my mouth in a bruising kiss. Rough and fast, I made off with her shirt and bra, coaxing her nipples into diamond-hard points to the sounds of her sweet whimpers in my mouth.

"You called for me?"

We both looked up to see Sal rounding the counter with a wide grin on his face.

"Lion," Deja gasped, her hooded eyes widening as he stalked toward her like a predator.

"Hey, beautiful." He pressed up behind her and accepted her kiss over her shoulder. His hands slid across her waist and up to her breasts where mine just were, allowing me to work my way down.

I kissed my way down her body slowly, already feeling her quiver with anticipation as I peeled the remainder of her leggings over her knees and calves. She stood bare before us, both still fully clothed. She was ours to claim, ours to own.

I took my time appreciating the beautiful, sweeping curves of her legs. My fingers trailed along her calf muscle to the back of her knee. When I looked up, she was still kissing Sal but her hands reached down in search for me.

I grinned and gently nudged her legs apart so I could alternate kisses on each of her inner thighs as I made my way up. This woman was too good for us in so many ways. She always wanted to be fair, to take care of our needs before hers. As a mother, she was the most devoted one I'd ever seen. She could have been a great role model for the cross-bearers, and maybe even had been made a saint if only they knew how to fucking appreciate her.

My mouth brushed against her pussy, already coated in her sweet wetness. Her fingers found my hair and scratched with eager, hungry need across my scalp. The view from my perspective was mesmerizing as Sal pinched and rolled her nipples between his fingers. His hands moved across her skin more gently than mine, but no less passionate and possessive.

Her hips rolled against my face as she squirmed between us. I stuck my tongue out to just barely indulge her and moved away whenever she demanded more pressure.

"Raum, please," she begged when her mouth came free from Sal's.

"Hmm, that's a start." I absentmindedly trailed a finger between her soaked pussy lips. "Good girls do say please. How about you stop squirming around and just let me eat your pussy?"

"I can't. I need it too much," she whined.

My cock swelled and twitched behind my layers of clothes, but I shook my finger and clicked my tongue at her.

"Sal, hold her still if she won't stop moving."

Deja let out a gasping moan as he secured one arm around the front of her shoulders and wrapped the other around her hips. She probably wasn't used to him taking control like that, and from the way her clit swelled, she fucking loved it.

The good thing about Sal was he was adaptable. I knew he gravitated toward the submissive side when they were alone but with three of us in the mix, he could either contrast my rough-handling ways or help me double down on it.

Sure enough, Deja's wiggles ceased immediately as he held her still from behind. Only breathy moans escaped her as I dragged my tongue along her swollen, decadent lips, savoring her sweet, musky taste. As I finally pressed light kisses to her clit, I pushed two fingers inside her to stroke her inner walls.

"Good girl," I murmured, pressing my lips and tongue harder against that little mound as she still did not squirm. Her pussy closed in around my fingers as I pumped them deeper, pressing my knuckles against her clit as well.

She let out a scream as she came undone. Her lower body shook and trembled so hard, her pussy practically vibrated against my face. And she still didn't try to pull away, even though she had to be incredibly sensitive with the aftershocks.

I stood quickly just as Sal released his arm around her. Her skin flushed, her hair fucked up, her chest heaving with those perfect tits and rigid nipples. I couldn't fucking stand it anymore.

With an animalistic growl, I grabbed her arm and pulled her to me. My mouth devoured hers and this time I let her rip my clothes off. My skin sang with pleasure at the sensation of her bare hands and her lips on me. So often I was bent on taking control and making her come apart, I forgot how good it was to receive it from her.

Behind her, I heard a metallic clink as Sal's belt buckle pulled apart. But the moment she released my cock and gave it long, sensual strokes between us, my attention returned to where it belonged.

I lifted her by her ass cheeks and set her on the bar stool I'd been sitting in, then impaled her in one fluid stroke. She screamed, flailing for balance on the rickety stool but Sal was right there to support her back against his chest. She looked up at him and I caught a glimpse of their connection in that brief moment. They supported each other, anchors to ground each other during times of chaos.

And me? I was her freedom.

She needed me for moments like this, where she was frustrated to the point of angry tears and needed to unleash it all through orgasms, screams, and sweet, sweet pain.

My grip on her thighs was like iron as I fucked her, alternating shallow and deep thrusts to delay her already mounting orgasm. I watched unashamedly as she moaned and sighed under the impact of my thrusts, taking kisses from her other lover and yelping as he pinched her nipples.

Abruptly I pulled out, my cock coated in her juices and achingly hard as it pointed straight at her.

"Flip over on your stomach," I commanded. "Now."

She obeyed, knees wobbling like a newborn fawn as her toes touched down on the floor. I bit my lip hard as she turned. Her perfect heart-shaped ass came into my view, the bruises from our last session just fading. I had to make sure to re-apply them.

She presented that ass like a perfect meal as she rested her stomach across the stool, her toes barely touching the ground.

"Let Sal have some love." I watched her skin shiver as I traced my fingertips down the back of her thigh. "Show him how much you love to please him."

She grabbed Sal's hips and pulled him forward without hesitation. His cock head slid past her lips and he let out a moan of appreciation, stroking her cheek affectionately.

I gave her a few moments to get down to business on him before bringing my palm down hard on her right ass cheek.

"Keep sucking him," I commanded as she yelped and paused to absorb my blow.

She resumed, taking him deeper like a good girl as he rubbed her shoulders and neck. I came down hard on her other cheek and she moaned as she took him further down her throat. It was a perfect balance. He kept her sane while I drove her wild.

Fuck, my balls were so tight and my cock so rigid just from watching her suck him, her beautiful pussy and legs on display and her gorgeous ass marked with my hand prints. I didn't even need to be inside her to feel bursting with cum.

I sucked in deep breaths to cool myself down. She was waiting for me to fuck her again but she wouldn't beg or whine for it. My good girl waited patiently for my cock and took care of her other lover while doing so.

I waited until Sal was nearing his tipping point too. He thrust into her sweet mouth and his breathing became labored as his orgasm built.

Then I took my place between those beautiful cheeks that I marked and fucked her like I wouldn't see her again for another thousand years.

15
DEJA

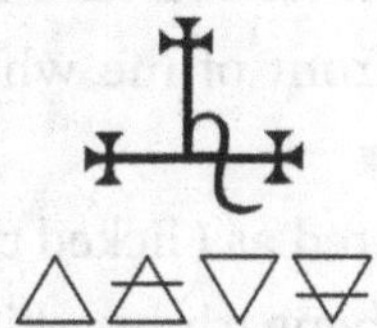

Raum slammed into me with all the force of an ocean crashing against the shore. Somehow I absorbed the impact, but the intensity knocked the wind out of me. He filled me completely with the most mind-numbing pleasure and just as quickly pulled back. I braced myself on that wobbly stool as best as I could with his relentless pounding.

In front of me, Sal stroked his rigid shaft while his other hand moved across my back, my neck, and my breasts. My mouth and tongue reached desperately for his wide, bulbous head but Raum was slamming into me so hard, I couldn't keep him in my mouth.

"I love watching you get fucked," Sal told me with a lusty groan. He bent down to kiss me. "It's so hot seeing you try to keep it together, beautiful."

I almost felt bashful but a new surge of desire filled me completely separate from what Raum was doing to me. I loved that Sal was so giving, so selfless as to still derive pleasure from watching someone else fuck me. And he still thought I was beautiful despite my fucked up hair, contorted facial expressions and being sweaty and flushed.

Raum practically roared as he upped the speed and intensity of his thrusts, making me see stars as another orgasm built within me like a volcano. His cock seemed to swell within me as the convulsions hit and then a surge of warmth as he emptied inside me.

"Yes, beautiful. Feel what do you to him when you cum." Sal watched with fascination as Raum twitched and jerked inside me, then withdrew.

"Clean me off," he commanded in a harsh, breathless whisper. He walked around to the front of me where I held my tongue out, waiting.

He moaned and shuddered as I licked the cocktail of our fluids off him. His pulse thrummed beneath his skin as his breath escaped in deep, labored gasps.

"Mmph!" I cried out with my mouth full of him as Sal's thick cock pushed past my slick folds. He slid all the way inside, filling my emptiness and withdrawing from me in smooth strokes. As his mouth brushed kisses over my back, I arched greedily under his touch.

It felt so different from Raum, like he was caressing the inside of me. The lingering soreness from Raum's hard thrusts was soothed by Sal's fluid movements. It wasn't even that he was gentle, he still stretched me to the brim with his thickness as he filled me. But his whole energy and approach made me crave him after getting my fill of Raum's roughness.

"Would you like to cum one more time, baby?" Raum's voice thundered above me.

"Yes, please," I moaned against his hip, his now-soft cock perfectly clean. My orgasm was building up slower with Sal but I knew it would be no less earth-shattering.

"Good girl," Raum purred and palmed each of my breasts, squeezing my nipples between his fingers.

I squealed at the sharpness, the sensation reaching all the way to my clit as Sal drove into me steadily. He moaned as I clenched around him, slowly driving his hips harder against my tender ass cheeks as his own orgasm built.

Raum knelt in front of me, his hands winding through my hair as he brought his face to mine.

"I want to make more babies with you." His tone was serious, his dark eyes so dilated they looked completely black as they bore into mine. "It doesn't matter which one of us knocks you up, I want to see your belly get big and I want to be a father again."

"Raum," I gasped, tears springing to my eyes as my body became filled with equal parts carnal pleasure and pure love.

He kissed me deeply, gently cupping the sides of my face. Sal kissed my shoulder blade at the same time and I wondered how I could possibly deserve such pure, passionate love. Not only from one or two men but three.

"Fuck, I love you, Deja," Raum murmured against my lips.

"Love you so fucking much, beautiful," Sal panted at the nape of my neck before planting a kiss there.

I opened my mouth to tell them I loved them both, more than I could express over multiple lifetimes, but my words became lost as my final orgasm hit me like a freight train. It didn't just wrack my body, that overwhelming pleasure touched my emotions. My eyes shut tight from the intensity but I felt my aura spark and shoot off like fireworks as pure, unrestrained love flooded my senses.

Nerves frazzled and muscles shot, I began crumpling off the stool to the floor but not before Sal swept me up in his arms.

"In seven thousand years I swear I've never cum like that," he panted, kissing my forehead as he cradled me against his chest.

"I love you guys so much." My voice came out in a breathless whisper as I pressed my cheek to Sal's heart. My exhausted eyelids parted to look over at Raum. "I was trying to say it back, but you know."

"Oh, we know, baby," Raum grinned. He leaned against the counter, proudly naked with no desire to change the situation.

"He took the words right out of my mouth, you know," Sal whispered as he wrapped around me tighter.

"Huh?" My mind still seemed unable to form coherent sentences.

"About being a father again." He nuzzled me sweetly. "I can't wait to raise the next generation of witches with you."

Slumped against him, naked, sweaty and barely able to walk, I couldn't imagine another moment where I felt happier.

"What did I do to deserve you guys?" A goofy grin spread across my face.

"That's what we should be asking." Raum came over and stroked my cheek, not even fazed by Sal's nakedness just inches away. I loved how they were so comfortable around each other.

Fuck, I loved every damned thing about them.

The sharp click of a lock turning jolted us out of our intimate moment.

"Oops. Nona must have forgotten something," Raum chuckled.

A stab of panic hit me but I quickly relaxed. While she didn't know of our magical abilities, Nona had been rooting for me to land all three guys since we first spotted them. She wouldn't be surprised at the scene before her. In fact, she might just question why Ash missed the party.

But the pale blonde hair coming through the door wasn't Nona's.

"Deja? Are you here?"

"Shit!" I hissed but it was too late.

Juno pushed the door open. Her jaw dropped as her aquamarine eyes took in the sight before her.

Three naked people. Two of them with Lucifer's sigil tattooed in plain sight.

16
DEJA

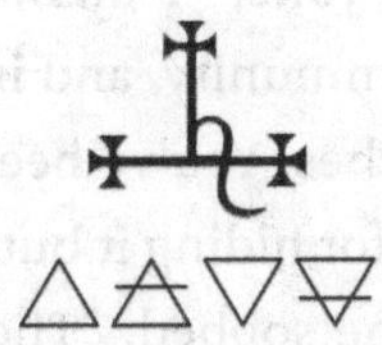

At that point, I knew nothing could be salvaged. The moment Juno's eyes took in the distinct sigil tattooed on Raum's back, her lips trembled with fear.

Raum slid his pants back on with surprising speed, then turned to face the door. Juno's eyes darted to my face and then to Sal, his own tattoo standing out clearly on the pale skin of his ribs. The realization seemed to hit her hard but slowly. Her eyes welled with tears as she brought a hand to her open mouth.

All I could do was stare back at her. It was like being entranced by a sad scene in a movie. While my heart crumbled apart painfully, I felt helpless to do anything but sit and watch.

One of the guys shoving my shirt and underwear at me was the only thing that broke my stupor. No one spoke and the silence was deafening as I fumbled to put my clothes on. After pulling my shirt over my head, Juno blinked and seemed to come out of her own trance.

She backed toward the door, fumbling for the knob as the tears finally spilled. While my heart knew I could do nothing, my mind pleaded for my coven sister to understand.

"June." I stepped forward, holding my hand out to her. "Please don't go." Like obedient soldiers, the guys stepped right in line with me.

"You," she choked out, her face grimacing. "With them? Why?"

The disgust and vitriol with which she said *them* hit me like a punch to the gut. But she wasn't bolting out the door yet, so I took a tentative step closer.

"Because I love them, June," I answered. "And they love me. They're capable of love, community, and incredible power to change the world, just like us witches. You've been lied to about them your whole life, sister. I'm sorry for hiding it but what choice did I have?"

"They seduced you," she sobbed. "They used you to get to us. I understand it now. They want to alert the humans and watch us burn!"

"You've got it all wrong," I said with a slight shake of my head. "I seduced them. I was nothing but an ordinary human when an angel fell in love with me. He fell from heaven just to be with me. These two?" I gestured to Raum and Sal. "Lucifer created them to protect, guide, and satisfy me."

"Damn right," Raum muttered with a smirk under his breath.

"So you're just like them," Juno said in a shaky whisper. "A fucking demon."

"And yet so different," I replied. "Have you ever wondered why demons and witches have such similar abilities? Why would cross-bearers paint us all with the same brush? Have you ever stopped to think about where your magic came from?"

"We're nothing alike!" she shot back. "How could you betray your own people like this? Laurel fast-tracked you into the coven! I considered you my sister and you turn out to be some kind of demon queen?"

"Juno," I pleaded. "We don't have to be enemies. I never joined or became your friend with bad intentions. But these are the men I love and I won't stand for them to be treated as less than us."

She hesitated as if she wasn't sure how to respond, then ultimately chose not to. Her hand found the doorknob and she turned, making a dash for the outside but the guys were on her in an instant.

Raum clapped a hand over her mouth before she could scream, pinning her body effortlessly against himself while Sal calmly re-locked the door. Juno's eyes were wide with fear as Raum half dragged, half walked her to the center of the room. She began to sob behind his palm, struggling weakly under his grip.

"Calm down. He's not going to hurt you," I told her. "Or seduce you. He's loyal to me."

"She ain't my type, anyway," he added with a wink.

Next to me, Sal glowered with an angry scowl. His aura encompassed his whole body with a fiery glow that seemed to lick at his skin. Since Juno was no longer an ally of mine, I wouldn't put it past him to hurt her if I ordered it.

"June." I leaned down close to her face. "If you don't tell Seth and Laurel what you saw here, we'll leave tonight. You'll never see ours or any demons' faces in this city again. But if you start a war against us, we will fight back. And it won't be one that you can win." My eyes flickered over to Sal. "War also just happens to be this one's specialty. " I laced my fingers through his and kissed his shoulder before resting my head on it. He kissed my forehead and squeezed my hand.

I nodded at Raum to let her go and he hesitated, his smirk disappearing.

"Baby, if she runs, we're fucked. There's no stopping her from bringing all the hunters right on our heels."

"I know," I said tersely. "Now she knows the consequences of that. We're all about free will, remember? Let her make the choice."

A tingle grazed across my scalp as Raum's aura reached out to mine.

I don't know if you know this. But I can wipe her memory.

A faint glimmer of hope rose within me.

You can?

Yes. I can just whisper an incantation in her ear now. Give her something to sleep and we'll leave her somewhere safe before we split. She'll never know she was here.

I chewed my lip as I thought about it. It could save us a lot of trouble. But it could also give the coven more ammunition to use against us.

And that spoke nothing of the feeling of dread in the pit of my stomach.

"Let her go, Raum."

His expression made it clear that he disagreed with me, but he did as I said. The lower half of Juno's face was red from where his hand clamped down and her knees buckled as he moved away.

She stood frozen like a deer in headlights for a few moments before taking a few shaky steps toward the door. When none of us moved to stop her, she made a break for it without looking back. With a flick of her wrist, the deadbolt slid under the force of her magic and she was gone.

I stood looking at the ajar door as if expecting her to come back. Deep down I knew she wouldn't but a part of me still asked why. Why would a friend turn against me just because of who I loved? When those I loved did nothing against her and had been treated like feared monsters for the last two thousand years? Friends should be there for each other, even if they didn't fully understand or agree with each other.

Sal's shoulder stiffened under my head and he turned to me with frustration in his eyes.

"We've gotta go, beautiful. She's not the only one who's got to live with the consequences."

I looked up at him, challenging his gaze.

"So you think Raum should have wiped her memory?"

"That certainly would have made things easier for us." He spoke calmly as he crossed his arms in front of his chest but the heat from his aura told me how badly he was trying to control his temper.

"So how does it help our cause to take cheap shots like that, huh?" I mimicked his crossed arms. "Why not accept that demons are master manipulators and just want to control people?"

"This isn't even close to the same thing." Sal clenched his jaw. "We exist because we *don't* follow the rules. We're not above taking cheap shots to keep you safe."

"It takes away her free will!" I yelled in his face. "It's exactly what a human would do to date rape someone and I will not allow it to happen! And that's exactly how the coven will see it, which only hurts our cause."

My whole body shook like a leaf. Every emotion inside me felt like a jumbled up mess. I was angry and hurt, sad and scared. I hated that Raum and Sal felt so strongly that I made a bad call and maybe on the surface, it was. But I couldn't even begin to entertain the thought of wiping Juno's memory. I didn't want to exert that kind of control over anyone.

"Sal's right. We can't dally here." Raum broke the tense silence after remaining quiet during our argument.

"I know." I sprung into action, rifling through my pants pockets under I found my phone.

After pulling up Nona's number, I turned in a slow circle to look at my shop, knowing it would likely be the last time I saw this place.

This building was where I poured my blood, sweat, and tears ten times over, and even maybe a little magic before knowing I had any. And now I had to leave it for good. My already bruised heart pulled painfully in my chest. I might as well had been forced to abandon my child in the woods.

"Baby."

Raum's voice reached an urgent pitch. He reached for my arm but I yanked out of his grasp. At that moment, his touch was the last thing I wanted to feel on me. I couldn't place the source of my emotions with everything clouding over my brain, but all I knew was my desire for him was, at least temporarily, completely gone.

"We need to get moving. Now." I ignored the sharp edge of hurt in his voice.

"I know," I repeated. "I just need to do something first."

With that, I hit the call button and brought the phone to my ear, waiting for Nona to pick up.

17
DEJA

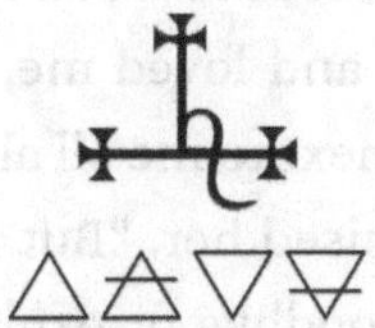

"Hello?"

"Nona."

Hearing her voice was the only spark of happiness that shined through me at that moment. But it dimmed down to nothing when I realized I'd probably never see her again. I never got a chance to properly thank her for saving my ass and my business so many times. And now I'd have to say goodbye without even giving her a hug.

"What's up, D? Is everything alright?"

"Um, no. Not really." I chewed my lip as the emotion rose high in my chest and threatened to spill out through my eyes.

"What's going on?" she demanded. "Do you need me to come out to your place?"

"No, don't come here tonight. Tomorrow should be okay, though. Um, fuck." I wiped my eyes as I struggled to keep it together. "Congratulations, Nona Parks. The tea shop is yours."

"Dude, stop. What's really going on?"

"I mean it," I said through a shaky breath. "I have to leave town, like right now. I can't get into it right now but I can't come back, at least not for a while. So I'm handing the business off to you. You're the only one who can keep it going."

A long pause was my only reply on the other end.

"Nona?"

"Deja, I just don't understand. Are you okay? I don't even give a fuck what's going on but are you going to be okay?"

I squeezed my eyes against the tears. For so long, I was desperate for a family that accepted and loved me, never realizing I had true family working her ass off next to me all along.

"I will be okay," I promised her. "But not if I stay. I fucking hate that I can't say a proper goodbye or explain all this shit but please just know that I love and adore you. I never would have made it without you and will always remember everything you've done for me. I swear it, Nona."

"I trust you, Deja," she soothed me over the speaker. "I trust you'll take care of whatever you need to do. You always do. And I really hope this isn't the last time we talk."

"Me too. Fucking hell, me too."

She snickered lightly over the phone. "My fortune came true."

"What?" I asked, confused.

"Remember when we saw the tarot card reader? She said I would soon come into a lot more wealth and responsibility. And you were so worried about me finding another job."

"That's right," I breathed, the memory already feeling like so long ago. "She really did predict your future. And mine."

I remembered my cards as clearly as if they were sitting in front of me then. The Tower. The Lovers. The Devil.

The Tower signified a monumental sudden change in my life. My world literally flipped on its head when my grandmother came to my door and told me the truth. The Lovers depicted what appeared to be Adam and Eve in the Garden of Eden. But I had been there, and I decided to view Ash and myself as the original love story when he took me from Adam.

The Devil typically indicated slavery to a certain mindset or idea, leading yourself to think you have no control over a situation when you truly do.

"Or you may fall in love with the devil himself," Minerva told me with a knowing grin.

"Good thing Death didn't come up in those cards," Nona joked, then in a more serious tone, "Be careful, Deja. Take care of yourself. I won't let this be the last time we talk, you hear me?"

Her protective nature brought a smile to my face. "Yes, mom. I will." My fingers ached from the grip I had on the phone, wishing I didn't have to hang up or stop hearing her voice. "You do the same. Bye for now."

"Later, Deja."

Not a breath after ending the call did I feel Sal's gentle touch on my hand.

"Did you need anything from your place before we go?" he asked softly.

"Um, I should probably check," I mumbled, distracted. "And I'll have to call my landlord. Shit."

The three of us finished getting fully dressed and trudged up the stairs. Raum seemed to have enough sense to stay a few paces behind me, but he grabbed my arm suddenly right before reaching the door.

"Something's not right," he hissed, looking over at Sal.

Sal took a sharp inhale and frowned, his aura surrounding him in a fiery glow again.

"I smell blood. A fucking lot of it." He stepped forward and stretched his hand out behind him to keep me back.

With a nod from Raum, he shoved my front door open with his shoulder. The scene laid out in my once clean but mismatched apartment made me want to throw up.

Blood covered every surface from the floor and walls to the windows and furniture. And standing over the coffee table with a human-sized heart in her hands as she mumbled an incantation, was my grandmother.

18

DEJA

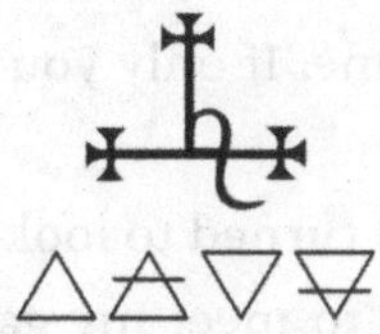

Diana's eyes opened to slits as she registered us in the doorway but never stopped muttering her spell. I tried to move forward but the guys blocked me from entering the room. Sal snarled like a predator at her but Raum looked unusually cool and aloof.

"Grandma," I whispered. "What's going on?"

My skin seemed to electrify at all the blood in the room and I knew it was my earth magic responding. Blood, bone, and living tissue always broke down and returned to nature after all.

"I've come to finish what I've started," she said in a barely recognizable growl. "Demon whore."

I blinked, my confusion spiraling as I tried to approach her again. But both guys blocked me with their arms.

"Guys, let me talk to her. That's my grandmother," I protested.

"I wouldn't advise that, babe," Raum said softly, never taking his eyes from her. "She's using blood magic, which means she intends to kill you."

"What?" I pushed against his forearm but like a boulder, he wouldn't move.

"He's right." A slow, evil smile spread across Diana's face. "He would know better than anyone."

"What?" I repeated, looking between Raum and my grandmother. My heart and brain felt like they were being ripped off in chunks as the information sank in. She wanted to kill me? And Raum knew?

"It should've been you," Diana mumbled nearly incoherently.

"You're wrong, witch," Raum snarled. "She was *meant* to come into this body in this lifetime. If only you would accept that, Deidre would still be alive."

"Deidre? My mother?" I turned to look at Raum, his jaw clenched with tension as he refused to meet my gaze. He just kept staring at Diana.

"Raum!" I yelled, clutching at his arm. "What the fuck do you know?"

"Yes, tell her, demon," Diana sneered. "Tell her how you first met my daughter all those years ago."

He finally looked at me with something I never saw in those dark eyes before. Regret.

"I saw when you would return to us," he said darkly. "I saw the woman you would be born from. And I just... had this overwhelming urge to meet her. I wanted to make sure I found her."

My eyes opened so wide I didn't bother to stop the tears from falling.

"Found her? You found my mother?"

He nodded. "I met her, and we spoke. I told her who her daughter was going to be. Lilith, the Mother of Witches would be returning with her soul intact again." He allowed a tiny smile on his lips. "And she was elated. I was so worried she hated demons like most people do at this time, but I didn't even detect an ounce of hate in her. She was so excited to be the one to nurture your powers and watch them grow." The smile disappeared as his eyes flicked back to Diana. "But then I suppose she told this vile woman right here, which ultimately led to her death."

"My Deidre was never supposed to die!" Diana shrieked. She jabbed a finger in the air, pointing it straight at me. "It was supposed to be you, demon whore!"

The realization hit me like a wall of bricks. And just when I thought my heart couldn't break anymore, it crumbled into numbness in my chest.

"Blood magic only has a fifty percent success rate," I said. "Even with the best odds, you can still kill the wrong target with the same blood type. That's what Ash told me."

"I couldn't take the chance of you coming back," Diana snarled. "Not after thousands of our people were publicly executed out of fear of the devil. Not after we worked so hard to keep all association away from you!"

"So you took the chance of murdering your own daughter?" I demanded. "Might I remind you that you're the one painting the room with blood?"

"Deidre was far too kind-hearted to understand," Diana lamented. "She was a dreamer, an idealist. She didn't grow up in the times that I did. If you were not white or not a Christian, your life was in danger every day! I couldn't let society go back to a world like that."

"Don't you realize you're perpetuating that hate?" I demanded. "Demons aren't responsible for the witch hunts, humans are! We're trying to ensure that humanity accepts all of us. Demon, witch, and human alike. That is the world we seek to create. This is what we've been trying to do for over ten thousand years."

"All you've done is stand by and watch idly as innocent witches get burned and hanged," she shot back. "The humans catch the faintest wind of you and they always come and target us. It doesn't matter to you. Why would it? You're all fucking immortal. You'll come back to earth and do nothing but seduce people for your demon orgies." Her fingers dug into the spongy flesh of the heart, causing it to leak more blood over her fingers and onto the floor. "But I won't take it anymore. I won't let another witch die for no reason."

"Your daughter already did," I seethed. "My mother died for no reason! And you had the balls to lie to my face and blame demons for it. Are you even listening to yourself?"

The look in her eyes told me while she heard my words, she was not listening. She was too far gone in her own mad world of hate and grief. And when the coppery smell of blood mixed with the bitter taste of dark magic, I knew our time was limited.

"Guys, we have to go." I took one step out of the apartment and was met with the worst pain imaginable. It felt like my blood was lit under a burner and literally boiling underneath my skin. With a scream, I fell to my knees and felt strong arms wrap around me protectively, but they did nothing to help the pain.

"Don't hurt her, witch," I heard Sal's voice threaten. "Take my blood instead."

"No!" I screamed through the pain.

"Stupid demon. Don't you see that it's her that needs to die?" Diana mocked. "I even borrowed an angel's kiss so her soul won't find another body to live in."

"We won't let you have her!"

I was vaguely aware of my head cradled into Raum's chest. His aura reached out to Ash for backup, but the blood magic was already taking its toll on me.

"I can't touch her!" Sal roared in frustration. "She spelled the whole apartment against shadow magic!"

"Just keep that bitch distracted. Our backup's on its way." Raum tilted my chin up to face him and pressed a kiss to my lips although I barely felt it. My entire body was numb. "Don't give up yet, baby," he pleaded with me. "I love you so much. I'm so sorry I didn't tell you."

I couldn't reply. All I could perceive was pain. I felt like I was slowly being cooked alive.

My sore eyelids cracked open until I could just see Diana standing in my living room, a maniacally gleeful expression on her face as her blood-coated fingers sank into the flesh of the heart.

A surge of hate momentarily distracted me from the pain. How could she do this, to her own daughter and then me? I was her flesh and blood. I couldn't control which body my soul would be reborn into! She found me and set me on the path to my true nature. After teaching me, guiding me, and treating me almost like a mother, how could she betray me?

I focused on that heart in her hands as my mind swam through the roiling sea of emotional and physical pain. Then, like subconsciously turning over a rock, I found something in a shadow of my mind I hadn't explored yet. I barely had time to wonder, *what's this?* before the heart burst into flames.

"Aaagh!" Diana wailed in agony, flinging her hands around but her flesh was already seared to the heart as the flame grew bigger. Immediately my pain was gone and all three of us took a deep gasping breath as the blood spell lifted.

"How?!" she cried out, her once gleeful eyes now filled with fear. "You're a fucking earth witch!"

"Fire consumes earth," I said in a robotic voice. "It destroys life."

"Good timing, baby," Raum chuckled with a kiss to my forehead. "Now let's get the fuck out of here."

He and Sal lifted me to my feet and prepared to guide me down the stairs, but I wasn't done yet.

I searched through the shadows in the same area where I found my fire magic. As if turning over another metaphysical rock, what I found brought a smile to my face.

My eyes flew open and I focused on Diana once again. With a sizzling *pssssssssssst*, the fire was doused in a cloud of steam. Diana opened her mouth as if to say something, but she choked up a mouthful of water.

"Water puts out fire," my mouth said. "It sustains life."

Diana fell to her knees, struggling to catch a breath but her lungs only filled with more water. She looked up at me, begging with her eyes, but I only looked down at her coldly.

"Did you watch like this when you killed my mother?" I asked. "Did you enjoy watching your pregnant daughter beg for her life as your blood magic slowly poisoned her?"

She shook her head desperately, coughing up blood now along with the water.

"No? So you were too much of a coward to watch the effects of your own spell?" I demanded. "You had to know the fifty percent risk of missing your target."

My grandmother began turning blue as her body and brain became deprived of oxygen. Her eyes, red with broken blood vessels, began rolling back in her head as consciousness slipped away from her. Within a minute, she would be dead.

Just as her movements slowed, I halted my magic with a flick of my wrist. When her weak inhale finally took in fresh air, she gulped for it greedily, desperately.

I watched her struggle and cough as life flowed back into her. Both of my demons' auras touched mine, asking the silent question of why I let her live. I gave my answer as I turned to the door and began walking out of the apartment.

"Because this demon whore is better than you."

19
DEJA

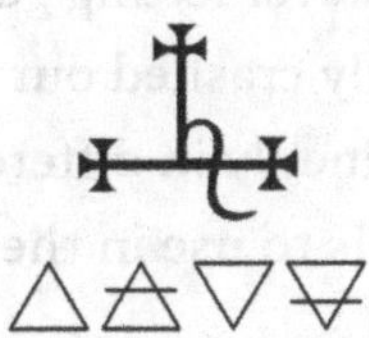

I ran straight into Ash when we hit the bottom of the stairwell. He slumped with relief and let out a string of curses as he pulled me tightly against his chest.

"Thank fucking Lucifer," he murmured into my hair before pulling away and stroking a hand across my cheek, his icy eyes wide with concern for me.

"Raum relayed everything to me while you were in there. I'm so sorry about your mother."

His words should have made me feel something, anything. Physically I felt fine, just tired. But emotionally, I felt completely numb. It was like my heart could no longer handle any more betrayal, it closed itself off to feeling love and kindness too.

"Where were you?" I asked.

"Setting up an anchor at our safe house," he replied, tugging on my hand as we walked hurriedly to their Victorian down the street from my—no—Nona's, shop.

"What?"

"Sorry I forgot you don't ah, teleport like we do." He pulled me against him again and pressed a kiss to my forehead. "We can only instantly travel somewhere if we have an anchor at that location, which is a spelled object to pull us there. We have a house way up north near the Oregon border in the middle of nowhere. I went to make sure it's absolutely foolproof. Once we get everything we need, we'll be there instantly and the demon hunt will go nowhere."

"But I can't teleport?"

"You can if you're holding onto one of us." He dropped a quick kiss to my lips. "And we're never letting go of you."

The four of us practically crashed our way through the Victorian house and split off determinedly in different directions. We grabbed clothes, bedding, and towels to use in the new house and filled suitcases full of them.

I took a large canvas shopping bag into the kitchen and grabbed all the canned and dried food I could find. Who knew how long we'd have to stay holed up in the middle of nowhere before the hunters let up their search?

Two metal tins on the kitchen counter made me pause. I picked up one and examined the label before allowing myself to smile. Ash brought two tins of loose tea for me. It was just this morning but felt so long ago that he asked me to move in, and we happily parted ways before this whole shit show went to Hell in a handbasket.

"How'd I do?" came his voice along with the rough nuzzle of his beard against the back of my neck. "Think those twigs and leaves will do it for you?" he teased.

"Are you kidding?" I turned both tins over in my hands as the first clear emotions finally came through my numbed senses. Love. Appreciation. Support. "This is genuine silver needle tea! I could never get it in the shop because the suppliers were always backordered." I turned to face him, a smile daring to creep across my face. "You must have worked some magic to get this. Thank you, angel."

"Maybe just a little." His arms encircled my back protectively and only then did the exhaustion seemed to fully hit me. I slumped against him with a weary sigh, leaning all my weight against his hard torso as his hands moved soothingly across my back.

"I'm really sorry my love, about everything," he murmured into my hair. "I hate to see you hurt. I know you wanted family and kinship with these people."

"Did you know?" I asked, my voice muffled by his shirt.

"No."

"Did Raum?"

He hesitated. "That's something you need to ask him."

I lifted my head and looked at him. "I used fire and water magic to stop her blood spell. I found the knowledge in my shadows. Once I found them it was so easy to cast, like breathing. How is that possible?"

"Because you're *you*," he answered lightheartedly, seemingly unsurprised. "I'll explain later, love, but we really need to get going. I'd rather not deal with a small army of hunters at our doorstep."

As if right on cue, we heard a crash coming from the foyer and the distinct sound of a mountain lion roaring.

Ash and I exchanged a glance for a split second before we dashed out of the kitchen and into the next room. Sal in his feline form had his ears pressed back against his skull, belly low to the ground, claws out, and fearsome teeth bared in a terrifying snarl. The moment I saw who he was growling at, my own aura flared up in a rage that could only rival Sal's.

A wide-eyed Seth sat on the floor, his hands raised in a surrendered motion as the mountain lion slunk closer to its prey. Raum stood near the door, arms crossed and looking bored.

"Let Sal eat him, I say," he offered.

"Sounds good to me," I agreed.

"I would advise against that," Seth protested, his eyes never leaving Sal's long teeth.

"Give me one good reason why," I challenged. "You're the one bringing the hunters down on us in the first place! Why shouldn't we leave your half-eaten carcass for your people to find?"

Sal punctuated my point by swiping a large paw across Seth's chest. No sooner did the thin ribbons of blood begin to darken his shirt, Seth responded. He raised his palms and the strongest pulse of energy I ever felt knocked me back against Ash, sending us both crashing into the wall. I got the wind knocked out of me and Ash groaned in pain.

It happened so fast, none of us saw it coming. Raum got knocked on his ass and Sal was flung across the room like he was a kitten. He sprang back just as fast, screaming his head off and the bloodthirsty intent to kill blazing in his eyes.

"I don't want to hurt any of you," Seth yelled as he pushed Sal back with another pulse of energy. "I came to warn you." His metallic grey eyes focused on me as he held a savage, bloodthirsty Sal at bay. "Deja, I never told the coven about your demons. That was your grandmother. She saw how strong you were getting and wanted to stop you before you became too powerful."

He winced as Sal continued to tear and bite at the invisible force field blocking him from ripping his throat out. Seth was losing strength and Sal's claws were getting closer with each passing second.

"Can you make him stop?" Seth pleaded. "I swear to Odin I'm trying to help, not hunt you."

"Your swearing means fuck-all to me," Raum muttered from the doorway as he returned to his feet.

Seth whipped his head around to register Raum's words and Sal's feline eyes glanced expectantly at me, followed by a protective snarl.

"Let him go for now, lion," I said with a nod. "Let's hear what he has to say."

Sal backed off, sheathing his claws but still kept his ears pricked forward as he stood protectively in front of me.

"Start talking. And make it quick." I reached down to scratch Sal between the ears.

"I had to call them in but I'm not actually a demon hunter," he began. "I'm posing undercover as one."

"You're so full of shit." It was Raum's turn to snarl. "I've heard of you. I've seen you and the carnage you've caused. Hundreds of incubi and humans laid to waste for no reason besides enjoying each other's pleasure. The incubi will come back but the humans won't. Not even he murders innocents like that," he spat with a jerk of his head to Sal.

"I have to carry out orders to ensure my cover isn't blown," Seth said carefully. "But Deja, I'm telling you honestly that I don't want to eliminate demons. I'm trying to stop the witches that are hunting them."

"Why should I believe you?" I demanded. Sal let out a warning growl that echoed my question.

"I understand if you don't trust me," Seth answered. "But you're using an anchor to travel instantly somewhere, which will leave a faint trail of magic. The hunters will follow you and be able to find you within days. I can throw them off the trail and buy you more time."

His statement was met with silence as the demons and I exchanged glances and talked silently through our auras.

Or he could lead them straight to us, came Sal's growl through my mind. I trust your decision, beautiful. But I don't trust this male witch one bit.

Either way, the safe house near the border is our only anchor currently, Ash chimed in. I can set up another once we're there so we can have a quick escape. But in the meantime, there's nowhere else we can go to outrun them.

Raum? I asked. Any insight?

For once, he didn't have anything clever or snide to say. He stood stoically, almost brooding.

We have to go to the house regardless if we trust this man or not. So let's just do that and figure out our next move when we get there.

But if we let him live, we could be totally fucked, Sal said.

And if we kill an innocent man who could be an ally, we're extra fucked. I ran my hand down Sal's furry back. Sorry, lion. We're not killing anyone today.

He growled but didn't argue further.

With a nod, I returned Seth's gaze. His aura, so dark and demon-like in itself, pulsed with a reverberating power that resembled a heartbeat. I only realized then how much he hid his powers before. He made my demons on edge, tense, and defensive, and that said something. If he couldn't be trusted, he was a dangerous enemy to have. He might even have the power to destroy my soul, finishing the job that the angel couldn't.

But if he was telling the truth, he would be an extremely powerful ally.

"It doesn't matter at this moment if you help us or not," I said, throwing my voice with a bravado I hoped he didn't see through. "But if you bring hunters to our doorstep, I promise I won't let you live next time."

Seth's jaw ticked as his steely eyes narrowed at me. "And when you learn that I really am on your side?"

I bristled internally. He was impossible to read. All signs pointed to him being full of shit, not to mention I still didn't want him anywhere near me for any reason. But I had no solid proof either way and that was what infuriated me the most.

"Then you'll have our gratitude," I said. "And our trust."

I laced my fingers with Ash's and squeezed, eager to be away from Seth, my grandmother, this city, all of this.

"Ready to go, angel?"

He squeezed his hand back in an affirmative and brushed his lips against my ear.

"Close your eyes, my love."

I did as he instructed and couldn't prepare myself for the sensation that followed. The house and all the space surrounding me seemed to get sucked away by a vacuum.

When I opened my eyes, the four of us stood in an entirely different house. The guys went to flick on light switches which revealed an open floor plan and large windows letting in silvery moonlight. Wood paneling covered the walls and floors. A black wood fire stove sat between the kitchen and the open, sparsely furnished living room. Dense pine trees covered what I could see outside and crickets proudly chirped their song.

Earth magic was so strong here. I felt it coming through the walls and surging up from the ground. After everything that just happened, I felt a small sense of relief from this place. It would strengthen me. It would wrap me up in its energy and nurture me. Even if hunters came after us, as long as I had my lovers with me, we just might be okay.

EPILOGUE
DEJA

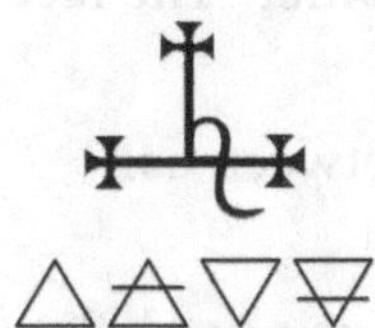

The patio door slid open behind me but I kept my eyes on the stars.

Living in a busy city made me forget how vast and bright the celestial bodies were. Out here in the wilderness, the night sky looked dense and vivid enough for me to reach out and touch.

Were there angels up there, cursing and gnashing their perfect, pearly white teeth at my existence? Was the being who created me wishing he struck me with lightning sooner? It didn't feel right calling him—or it—a god anymore. My thousands of years of consciousness told me that gods changed faces and roles just as often as I changed bodies.

Raum came slowly up behind my lawn chair, his footsteps barely making any noise on the wooden deck. I ignored him, continuing to search the sky for a glimpse of a winged being. For once his presence felt awkward. The man with the silky smooth tongue didn't know what to say, but he wanted my attention.

"I know you're angry at me," he began. His warm, velvety voice cut through the sharp evening air. "But I hope you understand why I couldn't tell you." A breath hitched in his chest. "I hate not being able to tell you things."

I let out a sigh, keeping my eyes trained on the giant balls of gas millions of light-years away. If I looked at him, I would either fall into his arms or slap the shit out of him. It was safer to just not look at him and keep my distance.

"How much did you know?" I asked, fighting to keep my voice steady. "Juno? My grandmother? The fact that my coven would turn on me on a dime?"

A long silence passed between us.

"Yes, I saw all of that."

"Do you know if Seth is going to help or hurt us?"

"That I don't know," he answered. "For some reason, I never see him."

I closed my eyes and gripped the armrests of my lawn chair.

"No. I don't understand, Raum," I said through gritted teeth. "I don't understand how you claim to love me, yet allowed these people to hurt me. You have this gift and you don't share the knowledge with me to prepare myself for the inevitable. But you know what hurts the worst?"

I finally stood from my chair and faced him. My hands shook while he stood like a statue, his hands hanging limply at his sides. All the humor in his lips and eyes were gone.

"You met my mother and never told me," I said, my voice finally shaking. "You met her. Saw her, even spoke to her. You have a memory of her that I'll never have and you chose to keep that from me."

He listened silently and swallowed when I finished talking. One hand reached out to me but I stepped away, crossing my arms over my chest. His hand dropped, and he looked like the saddest puppy I'd ever seen.

"You're right about that," he said, his voice barely above a whisper. "I should have shared with you that I met her. You deserve that and so much more. There was no reason to keep that from you and I'm sorry." He licked his lips and a flash of determination returned to his eyes. "But it's because I love you that I didn't tell you the other things. It's because I love you that I just can't, baby."

I shook my head, disappointment and despair rising to the point of nearly choking me.

"We could have gotten here sooner. I could've lived without seeing Juno terrified and trying to fight you off. This whole thing could have gone differently if we just *knew*, Raum."

"You wouldn't have discovered you can manipulate other elements besides earth," Raum fired back. "And really, would you have believed me if I told you Juno would rat on you? Would you have believed me if I said your grandmother was responsible for your mother's death?"

"Yes!" I yelled in his face, my voice echoing off the trees as my frustration exploded. "Because I know that you never lie! You couldn't even do it in a fucking two truths and a lie game!"

"So you want me to be the one that hurts you, huh?" he shouted back. "You want me to be the bad guy? Instead of the people who actually want to do you wrong, you want to hear it coming from me? Well, I'm sorry Deja, but I can't! I love you too fucking much to break your heart on a daily basis."

The urge to kiss him, to feel him fuck my pain away was still just as great as the urge to slap him. I shook like a leaf while my fists clenched at my sides. He gazed at my lips, clenching his own fists like he wanted to touch me again but knew better than to try.

"It has to be this way," he said softly. "I can own up to my mistakes when I'm wrong, but I can't apologize for refusing to be the one that hurts you." He cautiously drew closer, the smell of him intoxicating. "All I can do is love you and be what you *do* need to the best of my ability."

His face tilted as if preparing to kiss me but I pulled away again.

"What I need from you right now is to leave me alone."

With that, I pushed past him to go back inside. He didn't follow me in.

In the kitchen I found Sal sitting on the counter, eating cookie dough ice cream straight from the tub. He paused with the spoon halfway to his mouth and held it out to me as I approached. With a smile, I accepted and opened my mouth for the sweet treat.

"So how much of that did you hear?" I asked, licking my lips after swallowing the spoonful.

"All of it," he answered before feeding himself a spoonful of ice cream. "Took me a few hundred years, but I figured out how to shift only the inner ear of my lion. Comes in handy sometimes."

"Mm-hm." I accepted another mouthful of ice cream. "So what are your thoughts?"

"Mm-mm." He waved the spoon at me while shaking his head. "Not my circus, not my monkeys, beautiful. But," he playfully tapped the spoon against my lips. "I can't blame a guy who's in love with you for not wanting to be the constant bearer of bad news. I'd probably do the same if I had his ability." He dropped the spoon in the sink and replaced the lid on the ice cream. "And that's all I'll say about that."

"Fine," I said in mock disappointment, watching his lithe body hop off the counter and return the ice cream to the freezer. "I guess I'll need a distraction." I shamelessly groped his ass, pushing him against the refrigerator.

"Oh, you want to play like that, huh?" he laughed. In a flash, he whipped around and pressed his mouth to my neck. But instead of kissing me there, he blew a deafeningly loud raspberry.

I shrieked with laughter and tried to squirm away but he held me tight against him, sliding down my body and lifting my shirt to blow more raspberries on my belly.

"Sal, stop!" I was breathless with laughter, totally caught off-guard that he would be such a goofball.

He did stop abruptly, the smile completely gone from his face.

His hands gripped either side of my waist as he stared directly at my belly button.

"Hey, I didn't say freeze, silly." I ran my fingers through his thick auburn hair.

"Sshh." He pressed one palm flat against my belly and seemed to be concentrating hard.

Did he seriously just shush me?

"Lion, what's up?" I asked.

He raised his eyes to mine, an unreadable expression on his face.

"Tell me I'm not imagining this." He pressed his other palm to mine, the first one still flat against my lower stomach.

I concentrated like he had and felt a faint pulsation through his hand against mine.

"Is that," my breath quickened. "A heartbeat?"

He nodded. "It's not yours. Or mine."

Both of our eyes dropped to his hand pressed against my stomach.

"Holy shit," I breathed, the realization hitting me like a brick wall.

Sal's handsome face broke into a joyous grin.

"You're pregnant, beautiful."

WITCH'S EXILE

UNHOLY TRINITY BOOK 4

PROLOGUE
JEZEBEL

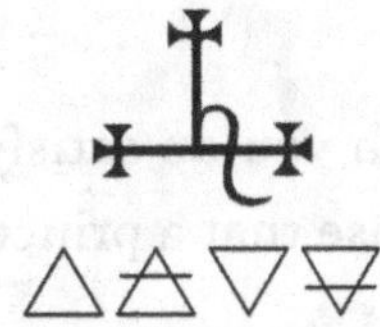

I laid my head across my lover's thighs, spent and satiated. His fingers traveled through my hair and across my neck, sending goosebumps along my naked skin.

Ash let out a deep, contented sigh as I massaged the taut muscles in his legs, relishing in the little alone time we had left.

"Are the two of us really not enough for you?"

I looked up to his hooded, post-sex gaze and saw a tiny smirk. One of those rare occasions that he let his guard down to tease me.

"It's not that you and Sal aren't enough." I raised my head off his legs and slid up his torso to nestle against his side. "It's just that I'm a greedy bitch."

He huffed out a laugh and kissed me as he pulled me against his muscular chest. "We get a new version of you every human lifetime, so I don't think we're in any position to complain." His expression turned serious as he gently stroked my face. "But I know you better than anyone, my love. I can tell something is missing for you."

I wanted to protest, to tell him no, you're wrong. You're a fallen fucking angel and objectively the most beautiful being I've ever set eyes on. And what's more, you're mine for eternity. I'll die and be reborn in a new body and you'll always be here and perfect, waiting for me.

But my fallen angel was also brilliant and he could see right through me.

"It's not about orgasms, or feeling like you don't love me," I mumbled, trying to articulate my feelings. "Lucifer knows how happy you both make me. It just... feels like there's an itch that none of us can scratch. I don't know how else to explain it. You understand, don't you?"

"I think so, even though you do satisfy every need of mine." He kissed my nose. "Makes sense that a princess of Hell would require a trinity," he teased.

"Stop." I slapped his chest playfully. "I'm no princess." In the human world at that time, I was a queen so I was technically correct. However, I was also not a demon and fit nowhere in the true hierarchy of Hell.

"And I'm no angel," he growled.

In a flash of inhumanly fast movement he pinned me down to the soft, feather mattress. His kiss came down hard and demanding, swallowing my moans as heat flooded my core again.

This man, this demon, made me dizzy with wanting him. He grew hard again between my legs and pressed against my sensitive flesh so deliciously. When his mouth tore from mine to nip at my neck and earlobe, the light tingles of pain mixed with pleasure pulsing at my core.

Any human woman would fall to her knees and thank the heavens every day for bringing a fallen angel into her bed. Divine beauty mixed with the cunning and ferocity of a demon fulfilled every woman's dream. And certainly, Ash fulfilled mine. But so did Sal. And I still couldn't shake the feeling that there was another missing piece.

Ash's mouth lit my skin on fire as he moved against me, turning my whole body into a pulsing bundle of nerves. I arched under his touch, savoring the weight and heat of his rippling muscles on top of me. He didn't just know how to please me, he loved me. I loved him so much I had a man killed for an attempted attack on him. The human side of me told me he should be enough.

And while he ravaged my body in the way only a selfless, incredible lover could, there still remained an itch that he couldn't scratch.

Sal couldn't scratch it either, and the way he made love was worlds apart from Ash. Unlike my fallen angel, my bloodthirsty lion became a sweet, purring kitten in the bedroom.

No one would look at Sal, who spent most of his time covered in enemy blood and roaring on the battlefield, to exist in the same universe as the words sweet and gentle, but that's exactly what he was to me.

His battered body would come home to me, the animal bloodlust still in his green eyes. With the first touch from me, the look would change. The human side of him needed me. It ached for relief from the violence and carnage.

I'd ordered all the servants away and brought him directly to our private bathhouse. He'd sink into the water and I scrubbed away the blood and dust until the pale skin and hard ridges of his warrior's body came through. I felt like I was restoring a priceless, marble work of art.

Once he was clean, I climbed into his lap and rode him until he felt truly human again. He inflicted so much pain on the battlefield, he didn't want to bring any of it to our love life, only pleasure. My warrior demon never stopped until I had my fill of pleasure and then some. He was so giving and selfless, he even expressed wanting to watch me with someone else.

But Ash would never take me in the same room as Sal, let alone at the same time. Maybe that was what I was missing, the two loves of my life in bed with me at once. The thought certainly sent a needy ache through me that had yet to be soothed.

A rustling at our pavilion door forced Ash to pull away from me and hurriedly cover us with animal fur blankets.

"Fucking Hell, Sal! Give us a minute to get decent." he muttered.

Sal only rolled his eyes as he invited himself to the bedchamber, a crude wooden box in one hand.

"Maybe one day, Ash, you won't be scared off by my dick being within a few feet of yours. It wants nothing to do with you, anyway." He leaned down over the bed and gave me a sensual kiss to prove his point. "Hello beautiful," he greeted me.

My chest filled with warmth as a smile spread across my lips. "Hello, lion. What did you bring me?" I looked curiously at his box.

His eyes flashed mischievously. "I brought you a gift." He gave the box a quick shake, eliciting the sound of desperate fluttering and a panicked, "Caw! Caw!" from within.

"Sal." I narrowed my eyes and spoke in a low warning tone. "Is this the equivalent of a house cat bringing me a half dead mouse as a gift?"

"No," he laughed. "I didn't hurt the thing, although he put up a hell of a fight. No, this bird is special." His eyes flashed with excitement again as I waited. "The northern people are calling this bird Odin. They worship it as a god."

"Really?" My eyebrows lifted with interest. I looked over at Ash, who had pulled on a pair of leather breeches and also looked curiously at the box. "What makes this one special?"

"It has very curious behaviors, almost human-like." Sal carefully unscrewed the top of the box and shoved his hand inside. He pulled out a large, handsome bird covered in inky black feathers. Its eyes blinked as its head tilted, appearing to study the three of us.

"What did it do?" I asked, reaching out to gently stroke the glossy feathers on its chest.

"It steals treasure but only from kings," he explained. "It drops nuts from high above to crack the shell and eat the inside. It also seems to react differently to different people. Right now is the calmest I've seen the birdbrain since we got back."

The bird indeed seemed calmer than when it was in the box. As I stroked its feathers, it even stretched its neck out toward me as if asking to be pet more.

"He likes me," I giggled. "Let's take him to Lucifer."

"I was hoping you'd say that," Sal grinned.

"Anchor us there, love?" I turned to Ash with a kiss and he returned it, surging his tongue into my mouth. I knew he couldn't help but show possessiveness of me in front of Sal, but we also needed physical contact to instantly move to our true home.

The depths of Hell.

We found Lucifer in his throne room with a beautiful naked woman in his lap. The curling ram horns sprouting from her head matched his. She nuzzled against him and the rubbing of their horns together seemed almost erotic. They looked like two mated animals, a bonded life pair. Driven by instinct but no less valid than human partnerships.

"Ashtaroth, Salmac," he greeted my two men as we approached and smiled a wide, fanged grin when he saw me. "And Lilith, my dear. I don't see you nearly as often as I would like."

"Likewise, Lord." I lowered my head respectfully. "But you know how the earth is always calling to me."

"Of course. It's the substance you were made from after all," he said gently. "What can I do for you three?"

Sal stepped forward, the bird still enclosed between his hands.

"Ah, a raven," Lucifer smiled. "Clever creatures, aren't they?"

"Sal says it displays almost human-like intelligence." I reached out to stroke its feathers once again. "I'd love to see what it can do as one of your creatures, my Lord."

Lucifer patted the woman's thigh, gesturing for her to get up from his lap. She stood nimbly and he followed her, his fingers entwined in hers.

"I have just the soul for your feathered friend," he said, speaking to me but never removing his eyes from his succubus. "An incubus whose tastes prove to be a bit extreme for ordinary human women. He also displays the intelligence to move up the Hierarchy." He looked to Ash. "I want him directly under you, Ashtaroth. And as Salmac's equal."

Ash nodded solemnly but his icy gaze shifted over to me. "My Lord, shouldn't we see if he is to Lilith's tastes, first?"

"Oh, I don't think she'll be disappointed." Lucifer winked at me as he turned and led his woman away, presumably to somewhere with more privacy. "It's your lucky day, dear Lilith. I just happen to be in a fantastically good mood."

A shiver crept down my spine. No one really knew the full extent of Lucifer's power. Some insisted he had flaws and weaknesses like any other living being. Others believed, like the Christian god, he was all-seeing and all-knowing. But I'll be damned if he didn't somehow know about my itch and what exactly would scratch it.

Sal carefully placed the raven down on the stone floor, and its form immediately began shifting. Like black tar, it stretched up to the height of a man—a tall man. Its beak shrank back into its face and its dark eyes grew larger. The black feathers faded and disappeared into olive skin.

My heart began to race as my senses took in the naked man who stood before me. Tall with lean, sculpted muscles, dark eyes and raven black hair falling to his collarbone.

"Don't be alarmed, clever bird," I said, my voice already growing low with lust. "What is your name?"

"Raum," he answered with a deep, velvety voice. "But some humans call me Odin."

"Raum," I smiled. "I like that."

"And who are you?" he asked with no hint of fear in his eyes. Incubi being reborn were often confused or disoriented. Unlike me, they had no memories of their past lives. But this one didn't seem concerned at all. Only curious. Perhaps his bird side gave him more wisdom than we believed.

"In this life, you may call me Jezebel."

I found myself leaning toward him unconsciously. His presence was absolutely intoxicating. I knew some of it was from the natural seductive powers of the incubus, but their magic never affected me like this before.

Raum's dark eyes studied me, watching me watch him. A smirk crept to his face as if amused by some private joke. I tried to not let my eyes go below his waist and he seemed intent on making sure I lost that battle.

Meanwhile, his eyes roamed over me shamelessly. For being created from a bird, he looked more hungry and predatory than Sal's lion when he looked at me. And I trembled with the anticipation of knowing exactly what this new demon could do.

From the corner of my eye I saw Sal and Ash exchange a glance. They were pleased at my reaction. It seemed this new addition would go smoothly.

1
DEJA

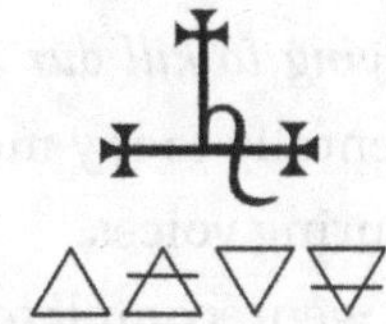

Juno stood across the clearing from me with tears falling out of her ocean-colored eyes.

"I'm sorry, Deja. I had to," she sobbed.

I could barely see her in the dark, and the frigid air chilled me to the bone. It had to be some time either right before dawn or right after dusk. We were surrounded by woods on all sides but the two of us were alone. Not even a raven cawed through the trees.

"You have free will, June," I told her. "You always have the power to make another choice." I rubbed a protective hand down my large, pregnant stomach.

"No," she shook her head. "I don't have a choice. I'm so sorry."

With another choked sob, she raised her hand and I felt myself drowning.

The air in my lungs turned to liquid, burning me from the inside as I choked and coughed. I gasped desperately for a breath, but air turned to water the moment it touched my lips. My vision began to darken as I fell to my knees, trying to be careful to not hurt the baby inside me.

The moment I hit the ground, a circle of flames erupted around me. It started a few feet away but slowly tightened closer, licking my skin with its burning heat.

I looked desperately through the flames at Juno. If I could just tell her! Kill me and do whatever the fuck you want with this mortal body, just let my child live. She's an innocent witch, just like you once were.

Juno's form seemed to flicker and shift as she watched me motionlessly. The flames grew even closer, and I began choking on smoke as well as water.

Ash! Raum! Sal! She's trying to kill our daughter! I'm dying, please come save her, I cried out mentally to my men but my mind remained empty of their strong, reassuring voices.

Just before my vision went completely black, I realized with horror that Juno's form *did* shift into something else.

Diana now stood on the other side of the flame circle—bent over, disfigured and grotesque. She curled one claw-like finger at me and whispered, "Die with your evil spawn, demon whore."

I woke up thrashing and crying, my eyes refusing to open until warmth and solidness surrounded me on all sides.

"Sshh. I'm here, my love," Ash whispered. "It's just a dream. You're safe."

I curled up like a fetus against his chest, soaking in the protection of his hands rubbing my back and his kisses in my hair. He pulled back to look at me, tilting my chin to face him. His icy eyes were full of concern but also curiosity.

"Same one again?" he asked gently.

I nodded, lowering my eyes with shame while he wrapped tighter around me. My hand flew to my belly, which still didn't show any sign of pregnancy but only a week after Sal and I made our discovery, I already got attached to the mini witch growing inside me.

The dreams started the same night we arrived at our safe house. Sal and I announced my pregnancy joyously to Ash. We looked to find Raum, but he was nowhere to be seen after the fight we had. In the week we'd been here, I'd barely seen him at all.

The three of us went to bed in high spirits, glad to have some good news despite leaving San Francisco to escape demon hunters, and that was when the nightmares started.

No spell or tea concoction seemed to make them go away. Seeing the two people who betrayed me in my dreams every single night just made the pain of it worse. And they knew it would. Deep down I knew they were doing this to me, this wasn't just my brain processing trauma. They were forcing me to live my worst fear every night—being alone without my men and losing my child.

And I was powerless to stop it.

I hated feeling so weak, especially now that I had another person to protect. What were they trying to accomplish by doing this? Driving me mad with heartbreak to the point of suicide? I'd been forced to kill myself in past lives before, but never while pregnant.

Ash slid an arm across my waist and laced his fingers through mine on my belly.

"Nothing's going to happen to you," he murmured, tightening his grip on my hand. "To *either* of you. Not as long as we're around."

"That's the worst part of it," I whispered to his skin. "Every time, I'm completely alone. I don't hear you or even feel your auras anywhere near me. If you guys aren't with me, I can't do anything to stop them."

"Not true," he insisted, tilting my face up again. "The truth is, we need you more than you need us. Our souls are eternally bound to you, but you could decide tomorrow that you're done with us and want three new men to protect you. Hell, or even ten or thirty."

"That'll never happen," I insisted.

He cracked a small smile as he lowered a soft kiss to my lips.

"Then we're not leaving your side. Ever."

I resumed snuggling against him, burying my face in his shoulder in an attempt to shut out the world. I was exhausted, but couldn't sleep because of those damn dreams. I hated that they had this hold on my mind but in my weary state, I couldn't put up the right shield to get some peace.

After a few minutes of snuggling, Ash began pulling away and lifting himself out of bed. I whined and protested, clinging to his arm.

"Let's try walking through your shadows together today," he suggested, pulling free from me so he could put pants on. "We haven't done it in ages but it shouldn't be too difficult."

"I tried," I groaned. "I swear I searched through every shadow in my goddamn mind and found nothing on this."

"Because you have certain biases toward yourself and the information you're seeking," he explained. "If I'm with you, I might be able to see something that you've missed. Or at least see it differently than you." He buttoned and zipped his jeans, then leaned down to kiss my cheek. "Come on, love. I'll make you a cup of that nasty twig and leaf water you love so much."

Not even his jokes about tea could pull me out of my funk. When something attacked your mind, there was nowhere to escape to. My thoughts went around in a circle as I forced my body to move, using all my strength to put my feet on the floor and then search for clothing.

What if they can hear my thoughts and conversations with the guys? Do I have any privacy in my own head at all? How far does this dream-torture really go? I shook my head as I ran a hand through my unkempt, unwashed hair. There were no answers no matter what questions I asked.

When I finally made it downstairs, Ash already prepared my tea and was making coffee for himself. The smell of Earl Grey and berg-amot filled my nose and lifted my mood just slightly.

"Thank you, angel," I said, taking a small sip. "Where's Sal?"

"Hunting," he replied. "The woods around here really seem to heighten his animal instincts. Hopefully, he brings something for dinner."

I held the tea in my mouth for a moment before swallowing. "And Raum?"

Ash raised his eyes to me and lifted a shoulder in a shrug. "He's around. Probably spending most of his time as a bird."

I let out a sigh and shut my eyes as tears threatened to spill. "I miss him. I still feel like shit for that night."

"Don't." Ash reached across the counter for my hand. "He's just doing what you asked, which was to leave you alone. And if I may say," he wrapped his fingers around mine. "He deserved that ass-chewing you gave him."

"But I never got to tell him about the pregnancy." My hand drifted down to my stomach. Aside from being exhausted and depressed from the dream, I didn't feel any physically different. "I'm sure you guys told him, though."

"Nope." Ash shook his head. "We figured you should be the one to."

"Fuck, he probably already knew before all of us," I grumbled into my tea.

"His ability is very mysterious." Ash stroked his beard thoughtfully. "For as long as I've known him, I still don't fully understand it. I don't think even he does. It does torture him, though. He'd never outright say it but I know he's always seen it as more of a curse than a gift."

A pang of guilt hit me. "I know it used to hurt him. He got terrible migraines and never knew when a vision would come on. But he's never complained about it, ever."

Ash shrugged again. "He knows that won't do anything. He'd rather laugh it off and be an asshole." He took a sip of coffee. "Not to be an armchair psychologist but I think that attitude is how he copes with knowing so much. Forever is a long time to be depressed if you can see all the bad things that are going to happen. Might as well laugh and fall in love with the Mother of Witches."

"I don't want him to cope with that alone," I protested. "He acts like no one can shoulder that burden but him, but he doesn't have to! I'm his partner. You guys are his brothers. We all support each other. That's what I want him to understand."

Ash chuckled but didn't reply immediately.

"What's so funny?"

"My love, I adore and cherish you but the way you think is so damn human sometimes." He leaned across the counter and kissed my nose when I scowled. "Knowledge of the past? Well, we can learn from that. But knowledge of the future is always dangerous. Especially in the hands of someone who can die."

The realization, along with newly surfaced memories, hit me like a brick wall.

"You're right. And this is not the first time Raum, and I have fought about this," I said.

Over the centuries we've argued, yelling in each others' faces about this same thing but neither of us ever backing down. Him knowing something that would hurt me but refusing to tell me ahead of time. Me feeling disrespected at his refusing to tell me. So on and so forth.

"Ash." I clamped my hand down on his wrist. "Was it wrong to make Raum a demon?"

My angel gave me a pointed look. "It's about two thousand years too late to be asking that, love."

"We're all about free will but I just realized we never gave him the choice," I choked. "He was a raven demonstrating human-like intelligence, so I asked Lucifer to make him mine. He was so perfect and charming as a human, it never occurred to me to ask if he wanted this life in the first place. Fuck! How could I be so selfish?"

"Hey, shush." Ash rounded the counter to pull me into a tight embrace. "Don't even think for a second he would give up an eternity loving you over a few short years as a damn bird."

"If the visions torture him that much, then maybe he would," I shot back. "I love him. I don't want him to be unhappy."

Ash squeezed me tighter and pressed a kiss to my forehead. "When he shows up again, you can ask him. But I'm certain I know what his answer will be." He gave me a light smack on my hip and gently pulled me toward the sliding door leading to the backyard. "Come on, love. You could use some sunlight."

2
ASHTAROTH

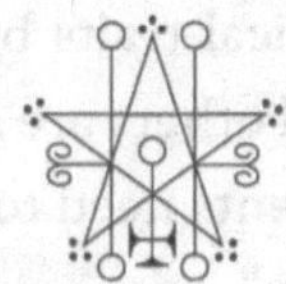

Deja blinked and shielded her eyes from the late-morning sunlight, but the positive effects were instant and unmistakable.

Her skin glowed. She lifted her head as we walked outside, her footsteps becoming surer and more confident. Her golden eyes brightened like two suns themselves. Surrounded by untouched forest and life growing freely, we were quite literally in her element.

"I feel better already," she breathed softly, her voice already stronger over the crunching of our shoes on pine needles. My grip on her hand tightened, as did my heart when she said that.

"Being out in nature strengthens your earth magic," I said. "You'll find yourself even stronger out here than you ever were in the city."

She paused to touch a tree, running her soft fingers over the gnarled bark. A green glow surrounded her as she absorbed its magic, then it gently faded into the darkness of her aura.

"What about the other elements?" she asked as we continued on our walk. "I can feel water and fire in me almost as strongly as the earth."

"You are the Mother of Witches," I reminded her. "All the elements, including their shadow sides are at your fingertips. It's like learning to ride a bicycle. You know all of them instinctually even after all these years of not using them. When you pass magic on to your children, they randomly inherit one more strongly over the others."

"And that element gets passed down through the generations?"

"That's where it gets a bit complicated," I chuckled. "Magic is kind of like passing on physical traits but different. You know how some traits are dominant and others are recessive?"

"I think so. Like both parents need to pass on the blue-eyed gene for the child to have blue eyes."

"Right. If two parents carry the same non-dominant magic and pass that onto their child, that will become the kid's dominant element."

We continued walking in peaceful silence before she spoke up again.

"Why don't I remember anything about the elements? Everything from lifetimes before, I see it in my head as just magic but not with earth, fire or anything attached to it."

"The classification of elemental magic is fairly new," I explained. "Witches came up with it a few hundred years ago. Demons don't really go by it, since we work the shadows of basically everything."

"Makes sense," she mused. "It's like the two sides of a coin. Opposite but equal, creating balance."

"Yes, it's true." I ran a hand across her lower belly where she grew our future. "Our power comes from death. Yours comes from life."

She smiled, lacing her fingers through mine at her stomach. "How far along do you think I am?"

I stopped walking and sent faint pulses of energy though my palm, just enough to get a sense of the size of our little witch growing inside her.

"Very early," I said. "Only four or five weeks." A grin spread on my face as joy surged through me. "I hope it's mine."

"What?! She's all of ours!" Deja smacked my hand playfully as we continued our walk.

"I know, love. I'm teasing." I wrapped an arm around her shoulders and kissed the side of her head. "And you're sure it's a she already?"

Her footsteps slowed, and her eyes lowered to the ground.

"In that nightmare, I'm full-term. I keep calling her our daughter, feeling like I have to save her. I just... feel like I know it's a girl."

I stopped our walk abruptly and pulled her tightly against my chest. Our hearts hammered against each other, beating in opposite rhythms as she wrapped her hands around my back. My hands squeezed into fists at her shoulders. She didn't know it yet but those witches would pay for making her feel like this. No one deserved to feel powerless and afraid of their own mind.

I didn't even care much that they betrayed her. Of course I hated that she was hurt, but humans backstabbed each other all the time. She'd remember that soon enough. But planting these nightmares was next-level torturous and cruel, even by demon standards. If they really wanted to see how fucked up demons were, they were about to find out.

"Those dreams are not the future," I murmured against her forehead. "They're not real. They will not happen. Believe me on that, love."

She didn't look convinced but nodded, tucking her head under my chin. "Thank you, angel. You're always saving me."

"Other way around, my love." I pressed my fingers into the tightest knots in her back. "It was you that saved me."

"How do you figure that?" she chuckled.

"If it weren't for you, I never would've been a father, a philosopher, or a king. I never would have fallen in love or discovered anything new." My lips grazed her ear. "And I never would have known the heaven of being buried inside you."

She shuddered in my arms and I distinctly felt her body temperature rise a few degrees.

"Goddamn you, demons." Her soft lips brushed against my neck. "All these years together and you still never fail to charm my panties off."

"I mean, we didn't used to. But that was before panties were invented." I grabbed her ass playfully and kissed the side of her neck, eliciting another shiver on her sensitive skin. "We'll have fun out here, but first I want to see if I can find anything in your shadows." I cupped the sides of her face and lowered my forehead to hers. "Maybe my love can sleep peacefully tonight."

"That would be nice," she muttered. "I'm ready when you are, angel."

"Before I start, let me ask you this. Have you found your Air magic yet?"

She shook her head. "I've tried but my focus is just so shaky from... everything."

I nodded. "It's the hardest elemental power to grasp, and rare to find in any witch. Some say it's rarer than finding a witch who's a shadow master."

"Really? Why?"

"Air is the link between all the other elements," I said. "It's present in all of them, so to wield Air is to have complete magical control. Think of your earth magic. Nothing can live without breathing. A fire won't ignite without oxygen. And what is a water molecule made of?"

"Two parts hydrogen, one part oxygen," she said.

"Exactly. Like your Earth magic, it doesn't have to be literally the air we breathe but any gaseous substance and its properties. That's why it's so difficult to control. It's all around us but you can't always see it. And trying to manifest its power is like, well, trying to capture air with a net."

"What's that got to do with my dreams?" she asked.

"I have a theory," I answered. "They've figured out by now that you can control all the elements. But they're hedging their bets on you not knowing Air yet because of how difficult and rare it is. They know that's the one shadow you haven't read yet in your mind, so they're purposely planting your worst fears there, where you can't reach."

I took her hands in mind. "I'm going to help you shine a light on it so they'll have nothing left to use against you. After that, it's just a matter of practice before you're the most powerful witch alive again."

"But how can they plant that in my head from far away?" she asked. "Seth read my shadows when he touched me. I thought you needed skin contact with someone to see their shadows."

"Normally, yes." I gritted my teeth uncomfortably. "I'm not sure how exactly they're doing this."

I had my theory on that as well but it wasn't something I could prove yet. And it was something I hoped with all my heart wasn't true. Telling Deja now would only upset her more, and I refused to add to her misery until I was absolutely sure.

3
DEJA

All the energy of the earth seemed to wrap around me like a safety blanket as Ash and I walked outside. Everything seemed to pulse with its own life force, lending me calmness and strength toward my current situation.

I swore I could even feel the tiny life of my daughter growing inside me, despite being so early in the pregnancy.

Makes sense, I thought as I ran a hand across my belly again. Earth magic was consistent with the creation of life. My surroundings strengthened me and also made me sensitive to feel life that was part of, yet separate from me.

"So how are we doing this?" I turned to Ash.

My golden-haired, blue-eyed demon took both of my hands and brought our nature walk to a stop. I couldn't see the house anymore through the dense trees but knew we were still close.

"How do you usually do it?" he asked. "Do you use your Earth to anchor you?"

"Yeah," I nodded. "I think of it like a rope leading me through a cave so I don't lost."

"That's perfect." One corner of his mouth ticked up. "I want you to do that again, but this time incorporate fire and water as well."

I lifted an eyebrow skeptically. "How am I supposed to do that?"

"I know it's a lot to keep track of, but trust me." He squeezed my hands. "Use earth to guide you and fire to light your way."

"Okay," I said hesitantly. "What about water?"

His eyes flashed with amusement. "You'll figure it out. Call on it when you need it. I'll be here with you."

My skepticism remained, but I took a deep breath and closed my eyes as I prepared to journey inward. Like I had done before, I rooted myself to the Earth magic coming up through my feet. Through Ash's hands, I bound the Earth magic to him too.

It hesitated at first, like the tendril of energy didn't want to touch something that had never truly died, but with gentle coaxing it wrapped around him as I willed.

Ready, angel?

Ready, love.

Together we sank into the darkness of my subconscious.

Your hold on the Earth magic is strong, Ash told me. Now whenever you're ready, imagine a flame.

A warmth in my chest ignited as I did as he instructed. But no light came.

I need a spark, I thought. Fire consumes earth.

Mentally I put aside a bundle of earth energy and struck it with the warmth in my chest.

Holy shit! I can see everything.

G

reat job, love.

I swelled at the pride in Ash's voice. Now be careful. Keep your hold on Earth and the flame. Don't get distracted.

Shining a light on my subconscious was like finding myself in a crowded market. There was so much frantic movement and every-thing was so loud. I walked through, trying to keep my focus steady but pieces of information still came through the fringes of my vision.

I saw my adopted parents looking stern and disappointed. I never bothered contacting them since I moved away over a year ago but as they were the only parents I knew, these dark parts of me still felt guilty for disappointing them.

More memories with my lovers flickered like movie reels. Sal walked into a marble palace covered in blood and looking thirsty for more. I led him to a massive bathhouse and washed it all away before settling into his lap. I looked on proudly under a glittering night sky as Ash pointed out stars and constellations to an elderly bearded man. At some point, Raum cut his hair and I made him promise never to do it again.

Focus, love. We can reminisce another time, Ash gently reminded me. Look for where the light doesn't reach.

I pulled my attention away from the memories and continued forward, heading into the shadows within the shadows. *There.*

All the chatter and distractions melted away, and I came to a wall with many nooks, crannies, shelves and crevices within it. The light from my flame did nothing to reveal the shadows cast by all those hidden places.

What do I do now? I asked Ash.

Feel, touch, and explore what you can't see, he answered. Take your time and don't rush anything. Whatever you discover might startle or overwhelm you but remember to keep your focus and I'm right here with you.

After a moment to gather myself, I began feeling along the wall. It felt cold and solid. I never felt anything like this in my mind before. Shadows were usually soft and pliable.

Nothing came to light right away, and my frustration grew. Was this simply the edge of my consciousness? Had I already found everything within my mind? Ash encouraged me to keep going, even though my search seemed fruitless.

I reached through a hole in the wall and nearly lost my grip when I touched something warm.

Ash, I think I got something!

Keep your focus, love. Go easy and slow.

The sensation was pleasant, like holding my hand over a space heater in a chilly room. I tried to draw it out into the light, to bring it to my awareness but it seemed stuck in this rocky wall.

I struggled, cursing with frustration as I tried to wedge it out of its position but a rancid breath of air made me stop.

STOP MESSING WITH THAT, DEMON WHORE. YOU HAVE NO NEED FOR IT.

Diana! I cried out with a shock. She was here in my head. Even here I couldn't escape from her.

*I*gnore her, love, *Ash instructed.* She's trying to use your pain against you, but she can't do anything if you don't allow it. Keep trying.

I KILLED DEIDRE BY CASTING BLOOD MAGIC ON YOU. I'LL KILL YOU THE SAME WAY-- BY CASTING MY SPELL ON YOUR FILTHY DEMON SPAWN.

"No, you won't touch her!"

Vertigo set in. All directions turned on their heads and became meaningless as I lost focus. Which way was up? Where the fuck was I?

My limbs flailed and something heavy smacked against my face. I realized it was Ash's chest.

"You're okay, love," he whispered, pressing kisses to my face. "I'm here."

I blinked slowly as our surroundings came back into focus. We were laying on the ground, Ash on his back and me on top of him. The air smelled like pine trees and fertile soil. Earth magic hummed all around me.

"Fuck," I breathed, dropping my head to Ash's sternum. "She's way deep inside there."

"Rotten cunt," he spat, tightening his arms around me protectively. "She used your desire for a family to worm her way in there. Now she's using it to hurt you."

"How do I get her out?" My voice grew hysterical, knowing this failure meant more nightmares would greet me tonight. "How do I make her stop?"

His silence broke my heart.

"We'll figure it out," he said softly, tilting my chin up to look at him. "We came close today. I know it's hard, love, but you have to shut her out. She only has such a strong hold on you because you feed into that fear."

"How can I not?" A hand flew down to my belly. "She's either going to kill me or our daughter."

"The old cunt can fucking try."

Ash and I looked up to the voice that spoke. Sal stood a few yards away, somehow able to walk right up to us without making a sound. He wore military fatigue pants hanging dangerously low on his hips and no shirt. His bare, rippling torso was streaked with drying blood. Slung over his shoulders was the body of a young buck with velvet antlers. Its throat had been ripped out and was still bleeding slowly.

"You couldn't clean your kill any more... cleanly?" Ash said wryly.

Sal shrugged. "Smelled you two out here and got tired of dragging this thing with my jaws. I'm sure you'd understand Ash, if you could, y'know, shift."

"Fuck off, you damned beast," Ash retorted, pulling both of us to our feet.

Listening to their good-natured ribbing made me smile. It gave me a sense of normalcy and home, despite my psychotic, murderous grandmother clawing at my mind and vowing to kill me.

"There's that smile, beautiful." Sal looked down at me adoringly. "Wait until you try my venison stew tonight. I'll make you fall in love with me all over again."

"Sounds amazing," I beamed up at him then grabbed his shoulders to reach up for a kiss, not caring about the dead animal across his shoulders or the sticky blood now all over my hands.

H

e grinned as he kissed me back. Somewhere in the distance, Ash made a noise of disgust.

"It's been a long time since you kissed me while I'm covered in blood," Sal said as we turned back toward the house. "Times are definitely different now."

I chuckled. "I think I'd rather kiss you for bringing home dinner than killing hundreds of enemies on a battlefield."

"You don't have to choose, beautiful." His emerald eyes lit up with twin flames, determined and ruthless. "It might not be on a battlefield like before, but I'll still happily carry the lifeless bodies of our enemies and lay them down at your feet."

4

SALMAC

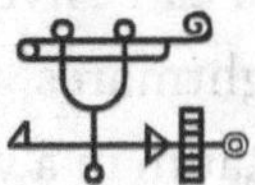

I slid out of Deja and pulled her to my chest as I rolled onto my back. She sighed with contentment and held onto my biceps while our racing heartbeats returned to normal.

"Thank you for dinner. It was delicious," she whispered.

"Are you talking about the venison or what happened just now?" I teased.

"Why not both?" she giggled and planted a kiss on my sternum. "You satisfy me in so many ways."

"Good." I brushed my mouth against her forehead. "You know I live to make you happy, beautiful."

She lifted her head and looked at me, her golden eyes wide with worry.

"Do I make *you* happy, Sal?"

The question took me by such surprise, a spark of anger lit up within me. How could she doubt the way I felt about her?

"Of course you do." I brushed a piece of dark hair out of her gorgeous face. "You're the reason why I know happiness exists."

She let out a sigh that seemed to take all the energy from her and lowered her head back to my chest without saying a word.

"What is it, beautiful?" I squeezed around her tighter, wishing I could do more. Making her feel better was not my strong suit. I couldn't talk to her on the same level as Ash or make her laugh like Raum. My biggest talent was killing to protect her, which seemed utterly useless in that moment.

And filling her belly with food, which I already did.

"I don't know," she admitted. "Just everything going on is making me feel like shit. Everyone's made me out to be this super powerful witch but I feel like I can't live up to that. I can't even sleep because of some stupid nightmares that make me feel like I'm haunted. And I haven't seen Raum in a week so now I'm wondering if he doesn't want to be with me anymore. "

"Stop that," I growled, my temper flaring up higher but not at her. "First of all, Raum is just being a little bitch. It's not you, it's his fucking ego. We'll talk to him and make the dumbass swallow his pride."

She made a noise into my chest that sounded like a giggle, which I took as a positive sign.

"Second of all, you are powerful," I continued. "But when it comes to magic, you're not perfect. You're still learning, babe, and you're doing just fine. Don't put all this pressure on yourself. Ash will push you because that's how he is, but you can still tell him to back off."

"It feels like there's no time for me to learn at my own pace." She slid a hand down to her belly. "If I don't remember Air magic as soon as possible, she'll kill me or the baby. And that's if the hunters don't find us first."

"That won't happen," I snarled. "Ash already set up an anchor to another safe house. We'll be out of here if we get even a whiff of hunters."

"And then what? We just keep running like a bunch of criminals?" she demanded. "What about when I'm full term? Or after the baby is born?"

"We'll figure it out." I wrapped my fingers around hers. "I promise, beautiful. We won't let anything happen to you."

"You and Ash keep saying that," she muttered. "Meanwhile, I'm completely exhausted but terrified to go to sleep."

"Fuck."

I sat up abruptly and turned away from her, swinging my feet down to the floor. The urge to hit or kill something was overwhelming.

"Sal?" came her voice quietly from behind me.

"I'm sorry. I don't have the answers." My forearms rested on my knees while my hands clenched into fists. "And I fucking hate that I don't. I hate that the mother of my child feels like helpless prey and I can't protect you."

She said nothing for a moment, or if she did, I couldn't hear it over the blood pounding in my ears. When her soft hands came around my shoulders, the boiling aggression in me lowered to a simmer.

"I know you'll protect us, my lion." She pressed a gentle kiss behind my ear. "I'll never doubt you. Thank you for not doubting me."

I pulled her hand to my lips and kissed her palm. "I never have in seven thousand years and I'm not about to start now."

"I just want one lifetime of peace," she sighed, resting her chin on my shoulder. "I want to raise our daughter with love and smiles as we teach her magic. I want to grow old and be able to die naturally, not get killed too young by some fearful human."

My anger melted away as her yearning for that life bled out of her aura and poured into mine. I brought her other hand forward and kissed that palm.

"I want that too, beautiful. It's the life we've been chasing all this time." I slowly turned to face her, the yellow lamp light making her golden eyes glow like a cat's. "But you know it gets harder before it gets easier."

"Yeah," she agreed, her eyelids drooping with exhaustion.

"Don't let go of that dream." I kissed both of her eyes as we laid back down in bed. "Keep it at the forefront of your mind and maybe it'll give you some peace as you sleep."

She clutched my arms, her eyes once again wide open and fearful.

"Promise you won't stop holding me after I fall asleep? The worst part of the dream is feeling completely alone."

"I won't move a muscle."

A relaxed smile finally spread across her lips as her eyelids closed softly and she snuggled into me. I pulled the covers up and tucked them around her. After flicking the light off I secured my arms tightly around her, letting her head rest on my bicep.

"Wake me up if I start freaking out?" she whispered groggily, sleep already taking over.

"I promise, beautiful."

Within minutes she was breathing deeply and—I hoped—sleeping peacefully. I barely got to admire her beautiful face in the moonlight before a flapping of feathers and clicking of claws drew my attention to the windowsill.

About time you showed up, coward. I spoke to Raum through my aura, not wanting to risk waking Deja.

He ignored my jab. *How is she?*

How do you think? I shot back. Better yet, why don't you show your damn face and ask her yourself?

She doesn't want to see me.

It's been a week, you fucking bird brain. She misses you. She's starting to think you don't want to see her.

I miss her so fucking much. The anguish came through loud and clear in his mental voice. But I fucked up, Sal. I don't want to be around if it's just going to hurt her.

Look, just talk it out, fuck it out, whatever you two do to make up. But I don't want to hear how much she wants you while she's in bed with me.

You're starting to sound like Ash, Raum scoffed.

Well, he's the only other company we got out here besides prey. So maybe I need you around too, motherfucker.

Raum gave a low, throaty chuckle. It has been a while since you and I shared her. Maybe that's what she needs to feel better.

I'm sure she wouldn't say no to that. Besides, I think we're willing to try anything at this point.

Raum said nothing, only tilted his feathered head back and forth while studying Deja's back with his beady black eyes.

Did Ash tell you his theory? he asked after a long silence.

I tightened my hold protectively around Deja. She sighed and nuzzled her face into my neck but didn't wake.

Yes, I answered tersely. He's meeting with Lucifer soon to confirm it. I raised my eyes from Deja's face to glare at Raum. You two better make up before he leaves. She needs at least two of us to feel safe.

I will in the morning. He hopped from the windowsill to the nightstand for a closer look at the sleeping woman in my arms.

Damn, I miss my morning sugar, he thought mournfully.

DEJA

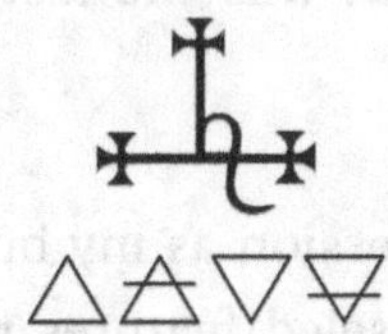

My dream was different that night.

I saw Seth sitting cross-legged in a circle of candles. He was shirtless and barefoot with sigils decorating his body as well as the ground around him. They seemed to glow and pulse, but the light emanating from them was dark and moving like smoke.

He stared at me, saying nothing. I looked down to see that my belly was still flat. My hand moved down my torso until I felt that faint pulse of life from my womb. She was still in there, safe and protected.

"What is this?" I asked no one in particular. Just because Seth was there didn't mean he was the one behind the dream.

"I'm here because you fear me," Seth answered in the gentlest voice I heard him speak. "You're afraid of what I can do to you, your lovers, and your child." It was jarring to not hear that biting edge to his words.

"You won't come anywhere near us," I hissed, covering my lower abdomen with both hands. "I'll make you drown on the air in your lungs before you can even think about touching us."

His lips spread into a wicked smile. "Deja, if I was your enemy, you'd already be dead."

"You can think that all you want," I shot back. "But even if my demons couldn't put you down, I'd have an army from Hell at my back, commanded by Lucifer himself."

The grin grew wider as he tilted his head in amusement. "What if I told you an army of Hell would rise up for me as well?"

"What?" I blinked. That was the last answer I expected. "But you're not a demon."

"Neither are you."

I tried to read his expression as my brain spun, but the candle-light dancing over his chiseled features revealed nothing. When I tried to move forward, I felt rooted to my spot. If only I could touch him for a second to read his shadows!

My voice barely reached a whisper. "Who the hell are you?"

"Our lessons have not finished." He ignored my question. "Your mind is getting stronger, Deja, but you have to push past the fear." He rose to his feet, the muscles in his shoulders flexing as he pushed himself up. "Soon you'll see that you have no reason to fear me."

Suddenly I was inside the circle with him, so close that my chest brushed against his. Despite my confusion and the paralyzing fear within me, my body had an automatic, chemical reaction to being so close to him.

I wanted to run away or punch him in his smug, arrogant face, but at the same time I was dying to run my tongue across the sigils etched into his skin. His mouth parted as his eyes dropped to my lips and I found myself leaning in, aching to taste them. Only when he raised his hand to my face, as if to caress me did I flinch and tear my gaze away.

"What are you doing to me?" I pleaded. "I don't want this!"

For a fraction of a second, his steely gray eyes registered pain as if the asshole actually had feelings I could hurt. Then his lip curled into a snarl and the bitter harshness returned to his voice.

"No more room in your little harem, I see. Just thought I'd check."

"For you? Never," I seethed. "Now get on with whatever you want in this dream so I can wake up and be with my real men."

He huffed out a dry laugh and flicked his wrist. In the next moment I was outside the circle again at a comfortable ten feet away from him.

"I delayed them for as long as I could but the hunters have found your trail," he said coldly. "They'll be on you in two days, maybe sooner."

Panic surged through me, but so did the need to see if he was bluffing.

"How do I know you're not lying?"

He shrugged. "Wait for them to come and slaughter all of you with angel-kissed weapons. Makes no difference to me." He stepped forward over the candles, seemingly unaffected by their flames. "And one more tip," he added with his signature arrogant smirk. "Don't try to catch Air with your hands. Capture it with your lungs."

Before I could reply, the sensation of free falling came over me. Instinctively I kicked my legs to find some sort of solid ground, and found myself in bed with warm skin beneath my cheek.

"Hey, love."

Ash's voice rumbled from inside his chest as I blinked myself awake. I watched his hands mark his place in the book he was holding and gently set it down on the nightstand.

"You were out like a light. Did you sleep any better?"

"Where's Sal?" I asked, slowly coming out of my disorientation.

"Patrolling the surrounding area with those animal senses of his." His fingers stroked through my hair. "You were still sleeping deeply this morning, so we switched shifts on holding you." He dropped a kiss to my head. "Lucky me."

I slid off his warm torso to the cooler mattress and stretched out next to him, his blue eyes enjoying the view.

"I do feel better," I realized. I felt refreshed and well-rested for the first time in days. My subconscious encounter with Seth was still jarring and confused me to no end, but it didn't fill me with dread and terror like all the previous nightmares since we got here.

"That's great to hear." Ash smiled and reached over to rest a hand on my thigh. "So a different dream this time? Maybe our walk through the shadows revealed some things after all?"

I didn't know how to answer him. Seth heavily insinuated he had support in Hell despite not being a demon at all. And that arrogant fucking asshole attempted to seduce me? Making room in my harem? His audacity made my blood boil.

"Deja."

Ash's voice grew low and husky. His fingers trailed from my outer hip to inside my thigh, skimming across the pool of wetness surrounding my vulva.

"Holy fuck. You're soaking, love," he said in a low, growling thunder as his eyes lifted to meet mine.

A breath of silence passed between us before I grabbed his handsome face and crashed my lips to his. In the next moment he rolled on top of me, moaning hotly as his tongue assaulted mine.

My nails raked across his scalp and down his back, my eyes just barely open as slits but I needed to see him. *This* man made me wet, with his glorious fallen angel's body I knew so well and pleasured me hundreds of thousands of times. *Not* that sneaky, conniving, arrogant asshole I saw in my dream.

I splayed my legs apart and glued them to the sides of his hips as I worked his shorts down. His mouth dragged down my neck, the bristles of his beard igniting the nerves in my sensitive flesh. I needed him in every one of my senses. I needed my body to remember how badly it wanted Ash. How he smelled, tasted, and how good he felt inside me.

The image of the stormy-eyed man sitting in a candlelit circle needed to be burned from my mind like an old photograph. I had all the love and pleasure I needed right here in my arms.

"I need you," I whispered desperately as he grew thick and hard between my legs.

"You have me," Ash murmured between bites and rough kisses moving lower down my body. "All of me."

He took my nipple between his teeth, making me cry out. When he lunged his hips forward, he filled me up so suddenly it choked off my scream.

"Fuck," he groaned against my skin as he pushed forward, sheathing himself completely. "Nothing on earth, heaven, or Hell feels as good as being inside you."

His kiss swallowed my moans as his hips rolled forward and back in a rhythm of pleasure and need. With a possessive grip, he lifted my pelvis off the bed to crash against me at a deeper angle. Each of his thrusts felt like the most spine-tingling lightning shooting up from my clit. I couldn't catch a steady breath as my pleasure threshold spiked higher and higher.

My first orgasm crashed all around us as I clutched onto him, desperate for something solid to hold on to. The waves of intensity shooting through me were so overwhelming, I thought I might leave my body.

"Ash, yes. Don't stop," I whimpered.

I felt my angel in every pore of my skin, every muscle and every nerve. The stormy-eyed bastard's face was finally gone from my mind as Ash filled me up again and again. Nothing could replace this, or any one of my demons. My heart and body were full, with no room for anyone else.

We rocked the headboard against the wall as my first orgasm rolled into another. My body became a live wire, jolting at every delicious thrust, every breathless kiss, every tingle of my scalp as Ash wound my hair around his fist.

"Lilith," Ash rasped my original name against my throat. "I swear God made you for me. You are too fucking perfect. I can never get over how amazing you feel."

"He did make me for you." I turned my head to nip at his earlobe. "And now he's fucking jealous he'll never have me like you do."

Our moans became one sound as he deepened his thrusts, stiffening like concrete inside me before unleashing his release. He shuddered and convulsed, the pleasure etched into his face as he got me off one last time before he began to soften.

He rolled off me but took me in his arms to lie on his chest, his heartbeat thrumming rapidly against my ear. We panted in unison as I curled my legs up against his side, fully sated and content.

"So anyway." He snaked an arm around me and shot me a wily smirk. "What *did* you dream about last night?"

Ugh. God fucking damnit.

Just when I got that asshole off my mind, he went right back there again. I could see him smirking like a smug bastard about it now.

"Um, well. It is something I should probably talk to you about." I swallowed. "All of you." I figured if I couldn't avoid it, might as well get it out in the open with my men. Maybe they knew something about Seth's connection to Hell, too.

Ash looked intrigued, but he quickly raised his eyes and held up a finger as if to say, *wait a minute.*

"Sal's heading back," he said, sitting up to look for his clothes. "He's pissed and hauling ass. Seems urgent."

My pulse quickened again as I remembered Seth's warning about the hunters. I didn't want to believe him, it felt smarter not to trust him. But a tiny part of me wondered what if he wasn't lying?

Before I had a chance to speak, my red-headed demon burst into the bedroom like a bat out of Hell.

"Fucking shit, Sal!" Ash growled as he fumbled for his shorts. "How many times do I have to demand a warning before you barge in?"

"Couldn't wait, this is important."

Sal's predatory green eyes lasered in on me. The anger radiated off of him like a sweeping forest fire.

"I smelled hunters. They're less than two days away from here," he said. "We've got to move. Now."

6

SETH

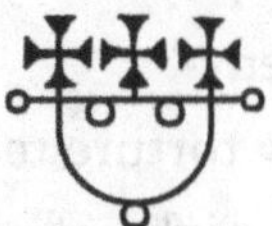

As I opened my eyes, I pulled in a deep breath and released it slowly. With a wave of my hand, the candles circling around me snuffed out.

I rose to my feet and quickly adjusted the hard bulge in my jeans. Gods be damned, I hated how she had that effect on me without even trying. Especially when she just made it clear that she would never have me.

A pounding at my door rang out just as I pulled my shirt over my head. The knocking never let up, rapping insistently against the wood so I took my sweet ass time to pull on a pair of socks too.

"Seth, are you in there?" came Diana Quinn's shrill voice from the hall.

"Unfortunately," I muttered as I ambled over to pull the deadbolt.

My attempt to just crack the door was thwarted by her pushing past with surprising strength for an old lady. She stood in my barely furnished studio apartment, taking note of the circle of candles on the floor, their wicks still smoking gently from being extinguished.

Deja's psychotic grandmother promptly spun around to face me while I waited with arms crossed to hear why the fuck she barged into my place.

"Why were you just in Deja's shadows?" she snarled. "And why did you block me out? We agreed that I would be the one in her mind as long as you held the channel open."

I shrugged nonchalantly. "Figured I'd have a turn fucking with her mind too."

"That wasn't the deal we made!" she huffed. "I'm breaking her down not only mentally but physically. It's a delicate process that cannot afford to be interrupted--"

"I know all about shadow torture techniques, trust me." I waved my hand dismissively. "One night of shaking her up my own way won't tamper with your delicate process."

"We can't afford to let her find Air, Seth," she continued to wail. Her hand reached shakily to her throat, and I knew that sensation of drowning was still fresh in her mind. Damn, how I wished Deja had finished her off.

"I'm well aware of that." I kept my expression bored.

"If she's able to rest, to sleep peacefully for even a few hours, she could find the strength to find it and wield it," she continued as if she hadn't heard me. "Gods, I should have suffocated her as a toddler when I had the chance."

My fingers dug into my biceps but nothing that she could notice. As batshit insane as Diana was, I hadn't pegged her for being willing to kill a child.

But then again, she did try to kill Deja before she was born. Only she missed and killed her own daughter, Deja's mother, instead and didn't seem particularly remorseful about it.

Deidre Quinn's mysterious death was the first file I looked up when I made it into the hunter's guild. It had been given a preliminary investigation and then shut just as quickly when the evidence showed no human interference or demon magic involved. Her death was ruled accidental, and the file left to collect dust on the shelves with thousands of other forgotten witch deaths.

Of course none of those assholes could ever fathom a witch harming one of its own kind. Hunters felt like goddamn heroes when they barged in on witches having consensual encounters with incubi and succubi. But if there wasn't a sniff of demon aura in the air, they were content to look the other way.

Everyone seemed to have forgotten that witch and demon lines drew so closely together and even overlapped in some areas. We were essentially cousins, and this was how we treated them? This was how we treated the woman who gave birth to our race? We should have been honoring her as a saint.

"If you killed her as a toddler, she just would have come back in another body as a fully fledged adult," I pointed out. "You shouldn't have fucked it up the first time," I added with a sneer.

"I don't see you or any of your hunters trying to do blood magic," Diana sneered. "Too busy hiding in the shadows, huh? I'm three times your age and I was the only one with the balls to attempt it!"

"And look where that got you," I shot back. "Kicked out of your coven and the innocent blood of your own daughter on your hands. You're lucky Laurel was able to pull enough strings so that humans never noticed her death either." I couldn't resist a biting smile. "At least I know my strengths."

Diana scoffed as she raked a hand through her snowy white hair. "And what are those exactly? Aside from you letting me into my granddaughter's shadows, you and your whole force seem utterly useless."

"Yeah? Is finding their magical trail 'useless'? How about the fact that we'll be on them in two days, maybe less?"

Her amber eyes met mine, wide with surprise. For the first time since barging into my place, she was speechless.

"But hey, if I'm so useless," I pulled the front door open, inviting her to get the fuck out. "You're welcome to open your own channel into Deja's mind. For such an accomplished blood witch, that shouldn't be a problem at all," I sneered.

She gave me a cold stare right back, but I saw her expression wobble. Good. The crazy cunt needed a good knock off of her high horse.

"Keep the channel open. Once we catch them, I'll make sure the guild rewards you generously." She glanced around at my meager belongings which barely filled the studio apartment. With as much travel as I did, I never cared to keep much stuff. She knew this and still curled her lip distastefully. "It seems you're in need of a housing upgrade, anyway."

I didn't rise to her bait, as much as I wanted to. I simply stood next to the door and waited for this psychotic bitch to leave before I had a migraine.

She stepped through and into the hall without another word but quickly turned on her heel.

"You'll let me know when they have--"

The door slamming in her face was my answer.

Sighing out a breath, I scrubbed my hands down over my face as I let my true emotions rise to the surface.

Fucking Hell, Deja. You better find your Air before they find you.

7
DEJA

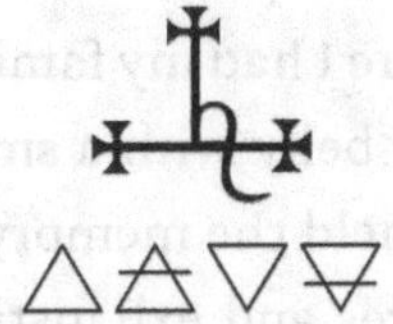

My heart squeezed painfully in my chest as Ash and Sal began shoving clothes and belongings into duffel bags. This wasn't right. If we had to run from hunters, we should all be together.

"What about Raum?" I asked.

"I'll fill him in. He can meet us there," Ash said hurriedly as he bounded downstairs to the kitchen.

Sal paused his frantic packing and gave me a strange look.

"Raum still hasn't talked to you?"

I shook my head slowly, and he frowned.

"Why, did he talk to you?" I demanded.

Sal sighed. "That fucking guy." He leaned down to give me a kiss and a gentle smack on the side of my ass. "Come on, beautiful."

I slid off the bed and quickly pulled on a fresh pair of leggings and a T-shirt. "Sal, what did he say?"

"It's like I said, babe." Sal watched me shove dirty and clean clothes into my duffel. "He misses the hell out of you, he's just proud and stubborn as fuck."

"Well, that doesn't help us at all," I muttered, zipping the bag aggressively and swinging it over my shoulder. "We need to be a united front against the hunters."

"I agree." Sal took my bag from me and gestured for me to go down the stairs ahead of him. "Tell that to the guy with the ego big enough for all four of us."

With Sal following closely behind, I went down the stairs and looked out the massive windows at the forest surrounding us. I just started getting used to this place. It started feeling like home, although that was anywhere I had my family with me.

I pressed a hand to my belly with a small smile. I discovered my daughter here. This place held the memory of my greatest joy in this lifetime, not just nightmares and exhaustion. I had to focus on her. The magic of earth and life would keep me going.

Sal hugged me from behind, his hands covering mine as he gently pulled me out of my thoughts. I looked up and accepted a silent kiss from him, no words needed. My fiery demon was also the calm in my chaos. I had to remember to lean on him when I couldn't stand on my own.

Ash came up to us and cupped my face, paying no mind to Sal's arms around me.

"Want to help me ward this place, love?" His icy eyes were mischievous as his thumbs stroked my cheekbones affectionately. "Let's send those hunters chasing their tails a bit."

I grinned. "Definitely."

He returned my grin and dropped a quick kiss to my lips before gently pulling me out of Sal's embrace. We walked hand in hand to the backyard where the earth greeted me with the hum of its power.

"The place we're going to will have earth magic just as strong as this, if not stronger," Ash assured me.

"And where might that be?" I followed him through the dense trees, realizing we were near the spot we originally searched through my shadows yesterday.

"A little place in Hell's Canyon." He smirked at my confused expression. "It's in Oregon, one of the most remote wildlife areas in the United States. The hunters will have a hell of a time finding us there."

"So we're gonna be roughing it for a while?" Despite my earth magic, I had still been quite the city girl all my life. Being pregnant in the remote wilderness made me a little apprehensive.

"We'll have a house like this one," he said, squeezing my hands reassuringly. "And a vehicle so we can drive into the nearest town for supplies. To any humans, we'll just look like a group of friends on vacation."

"Yeah, *friends*," I snickered. "Alright, so what are we doing to this place?"

"Casting a large-scale glamour spell, essentially. But with shadows."

"Of course," I muttered. "Even glamour would have a shadow side."

"Everything has a shadow side, love."

Ash's aura began glowing with activity, surrounding his whole body in a dark halo with crackles of red electricity. His glorious black wings unfolded and stretched out to the sides of his body.

I rooted myself into the earth, pulling up the shadow side of my own magic. Instead of life, growth, and healing, I curled my fingers and brought forward their polar opposites—death, decay, and ruination.

"What are we making this place look like?" I asked.

"How about a burned out husk? That'll keep them scratching their heads for a while." Ash began drawing crackling red sigils in the air, which flew out in all directions every time he finished one. They hit trees and rocks and faded until they were invisible. I realized he was creating anchors for our spell around the perimeter, which would hold our magic in place long after we were gone.

"So I get to play with fire then?" I asked with a grin.

He smiled back. "Feel free to get creative, love."

Oh, I intended to.

Ash got to work on creating the glamour image for the hunters to find, an empty house with broken windows and only the frame still standing. Then I stepped in and filled in all the details.

The trees and plants closest to the house became a blackened shell of what they once were. Furniture, walls, and books became nothing but piles of ashes everywhere. Charred, fallen support beams hung at precarious angles from the second floor. The stairs had been burned away as well. My mind's eye traveled up to my bedroom where Ash and I enjoyed each other just minutes ago.

Smiling inwardly, I waved my hands in front of my face to cast the illusion of barely identifiable burned corpses in what remained of the bed. Let's see if hunters could hold in their stomach contents after seeing that.

But something was still missing—the final key to send this illusion over the top into reality. I needed smells and smoke.

Pulling my focus away from the glamour spell, I traveled inward through my own shadows and quickly arrived at the wall where Ash and I had been yesterday. I carefully peered into one of the dark crevices of the wall, still seeing nothing. Like last time I reached and tried to feel without sight, but the secret remained tightly wedged in its little nook.

Don't try to catch air with your hands. Capture it with your lungs. That was what Seth told me in the dream.

My focus wavered just slightly as I debated on his words, but I quickly regained it. It didn't hurt to try, right?

I lowered myself to the crevice in the wall until I was eye-level with it, then pursed my lips together and blew a gentle stream of air directly into it. Nothing seemed to happen at first but just before I pulled my face away, a tiny spark caught my eye.

I tried to look closer, but it faded. I blew another breath, slowly and steadily, and saw it again. I felt like I was starting a fire from scratch, gently blowing on this spark over and over until it wouldn't fade.

When it remained stable without my breath, I still wasn't hit with that knowledge of its power like I was with the other elements. Once I found the spark of Fire and Water, their abilities filled my consciousness just as naturally as Earth. But Ash warned me that Air was volatile, and nowhere near as easy.

As the spark began to fade once again, I did the only thing I could think of. I pursed my lips together again and sucked in a deep inhale breath.

The spark of magic began moving toward me. My heart jumped into my throat but I kept breathing in, watching the magic travel its way through my mouth and nostrils until it settled itself into my lungs. The power that filled me in the next moment, quite literally took my breath away.

I jerked violently away from the shadows of my subconscious and found myself lying on the forest floor, Ash and Sal both standing over me with concerned expressions.

"I did it," I wheezed. "I found Air."

The guys both leaned down to help me up, but I waved them off, summoning a gust of wind to push me to my feet.

"Holy fuck." Ash stared at me wide-eyed as Sal brushed dead leaves and pine needles out of my hair, before grabbing my face and kissing me aggressively. "You're so fucking amazing, my love."

Sal murmured his agreement as he lifted my hair and kissed the back of my neck, awakening my spine with a delicious tingle. I knew a threesome between Sal and Ash would never happen but I couldn't stop the thought from entering my mind.

"I couldn't have done it without either of you." I leaned back against Sal's chest while losing myself in Ash's icy blue eyes. "Now step back, boys. Let me finish my work."

They gave me space as I called on Air to really solidify the illusion in front of me. Ash was right about one thing, this magic was much more difficult to wield than any of the other elements. And yet I saw how Air flowed through and enhanced everything. My Earth, Fire, and Water brimmed with new power. I would need to practice and take care now that I had all the pieces together.

I swirled fiery ashes into the air, creating the illusion of a burning smell. I stoked the glamoured flames into making smoke rise from the ruined structure, not enough to lead them directly here but just enough to give them the idea the fire had been recent.

And I made sure to draw on my Earth and Fire to send charred particles of flesh into the air. Their best guess would be that a damn dragon torched this place and everyone in it.

After completing my work, I released my magic and relaxed my hands.

"Let's go," I said softly.

Above us, a raven flapped its wings and cawed. I felt an aura reach out to touch mine and gasped at how tightly my heart squeezed. I could practically feel Raum's stubble against my skin, his throaty chuckle from deep in his chest, and that naughty twinkle in his dark eyes. I missed him so much my heart physically ached.

But I pushed his aura away and kept walking with Ash and Sal. After giving me the cold shoulder for this long, he wouldn't get access to my emotions that easily. If he wanted to talk, he could do it face to face.

Ash, Sal, and I walked a few hundred yards away from the fake smoldering ruin of our house. Standing between them, I took their hands in each of mine and waited for the world around me to get sucked away.

And just like that, we left like exiles from the second place I ever called home.

8
DEJA

If I thought the earth magic was strong at our last house, it seemed to vibrate in every pore of my skin in our new home.

We arrived instantly in a spacious, comforting cabin much like the last one. Only this one was a bit more bare in terms of furniture and books.

"You two should head into town for supplies soon," Ash said to Sal and me in his commanding tone. "The kitchen is bare, and this place has a sore lack of reading material."

"And what are you going to do, Your Highness?" I teased.

He didn't smile back but gave me an apologetic look instead.

"I need to return to Hell for a short while."

"What? Why?" I demanded.

"I need to confirm something with Lucifer about a certain hunter friend of ours."

"Seth?" I stepped in closer to him, gripping his shirt in my fist. "What do you need to confirm about him?"

"I don't want to speculate until I'm sure it's true." He stroked my cheek affectionately. "You've got enough on your mind to worry about." His hand skimmed across my lower belly.

I gritted my teeth. I'd had enough of these guys keeping information from me to protect me, but Ash's steely expression told me he wouldn't budge on this.

"Just come back to me soon." I draped my arms around his neck.

"It'll never be soon enough," he said gruffly before lowering his mouth to claim mine.

We kissed passionately, holding onto each other like we wouldn't see each other for weeks instead of mere days. But with him gone and Raum still being a shithead, Sal would be the only one with me.

He stood off to the side politely while Ash and I finished our goodbye, then came up behind me and secured me in his arms while we parted breathlessly.

"Take care of her, Salmac," Ash ordered sternly.

Sal nodded sharply but his cheek pressed against mine as a grin spread across his face.

"Now that she has Air, she'll probably be the one taking care of me," he said.

"Doesn't matter. They want her dead more than you," Ash snapped.

I stifled a giggle. He was somehow especially adorable while in serious commander mode.

"I love you," I blurted out.

Ash lowered his icy gaze to me and his hard exterior softened the way it did just for me. He leaned down and pressed a final, toe-curling kiss to my lips.

"And I love you. I'll be back before you know it, my love."

With that, he stepped away and disappeared before my eyes.

A heavy sigh escaped me and seemed to deflate my whole body. Sal squeezed around me from behind and dropped comforting kisses to my neck and shoulder.

"Wanna go into town and do some shopping, beautiful?"

I nodded, eager for any kind of distraction and Sal gently

unwrapped from me to check out the vehicle in the garage. Meanwhile, I just stared at the spot where Ash had been standing just moments earlier, hating the feeling that now two-thirds of my heart were gone.

***

The sunset cast a pinkish-orange glow on the hills and trees of the canyon by the time we headed back. Sal drove the manual transmission pickup truck through the winding dirt roads and then off the beaten path to return to our new home.

I sat next to him with my head on his shoulder and paper grocery bags taking up the rest of the space in the cab, including my lap and between my feet. The nearest town was about a two-hour drive away, so we stocked up on dried goods to last the four of us a month. The only grocery store in town didn't have much in the way of tea or books, which made me grumble.

To Ash's luck, a used bookstore down the street had shelves stuffed full of classics and essays that I knew he'd enjoy, so I filled two bags up with worn paperbacks and hardback tomes for him.

My tea situation was looking grim but with the strong Earth energy at our new home, it wouldn't be too difficult to grow and dry small batches of my own. To make the most of it, I purchased a kettle, a small French press, and a dehydrator at the grocery store.

"Looks like we might have some neighbors." Sal's voice interrupted my thoughts on crafting tea blends and I jerked my head up from his shoulder.

"We do? Where?"

"Look closely, beautiful." He pointed out the window to his left as the truck ambled down the barely-marked trail that led to our house.

I squinted and searched through the dense forest landscape but it still took me a few moments to find what he was pointing at.

Circular wooden structures that looked sort of like tents but stronger and more reinforced barely stood out against the maze of tree trunks. They were clearly camouflaged, painted in browns and mossy greens to blend in with the scenery.

"What are those?"

"Yurts," Sal answered. "Or as Ash would say, traditional portable dwellings for nomadic cultures in central Asia-- now popular among fucking hipsters."

I chuckled at that. "Well, they definitely don't want to be seen."

"Yeah." His grip on the steering wheel tightened. "Let's hope they leave us alone as much as they want to be left alone."

9
DEJA

Ash wasn't kidding when he said Air was the most difficult element to grasp.

I stood in the clearing just outside the house—breathless, sweaty, and with more than a few bumps and bruises. While practicing my newfound magic, I became quite good at literally knocking the wind out of myself.

I had gotten up early in the morning, sliding out from under Sal's warm embrace to make myself coffee—blech—and immediately headed outside to become acquainted with this power. Unfortunately, I gave my hot-headed demon a rude awakening by rattling the window panes with a heavy gust of wind. He woke up so suddenly and ready to fight, he nearly set a real fire in the bedroom.

After a few strenuous hours, I found the best use of Air to be enhancing the other three elements. Mixed in with Earth, I could heal faster, create a stronger life force and choke it off just as quickly. My small flames became roaring infernos, and I didn't dare practice on Sal to see how much faster I could drown with water.

My stomach rumbled as I dropped my arms, heaving and aching

from hours of casting. Sal went back inside after watching me for a while and I hoped he was getting lunch started.

"Caw! Caw!"

I stopped and turned to the raven perched on a tree branch. It tilted its head at me, its glossy feathers creating a metallic sheen in the sunlight.

"What, Raum?" I shrugged and held my hands out with my palms open, frustration creeping into my voice. "Are you ever going to actually talk to me or just keep cawing from a distance?"

He said nothing from either his beak or from his aura, his emotions completely closed off to me. My fists clenched at my sides while my teeth ground together.

I wanted to cry. I wanted to feel his arms around me and inhale his smell again. My teeth cut into my tongue as I fought the urge to yell pleas and apologies up to the bird watching me. I had to remember that I was not the one who needed to apologize. Asking for space was not the same as deserving a week-long silent treatment. This distance between us was *his* doing, not mine.

Before letting tears spill, I turned toward the house and hurried to the front door. Just as I stepped a foot inside, a flash of movement and color caught my eye.

I jerked my head to the side and froze, watching and listening. When nothing stirred, I called on my Fire magic to reveal what was hidden, and asked Earth and Air to show me where the ground vibrated under footsteps, no matter how soft.

There.

In my mind's eye I saw a boy no older than ten. His hair was redder than Sal's, more of a vibrant orange. He watched me with wide, curious blue eyes from the dense brush of the forest. I turned my body toward him and he took off running with speed and agility that no human child should have had.

I ran after him with no time to hesitate or call for Sal. That shock of bright red hair barely stayed in my vision as he zigged, zagged, jumped over rocks, and ducked under fallen branches, all while running as fast as his skinny legs could carry him. Only my magic guiding me kept me hot on his trail.

Who or what the Hell is this kid?

My lungs labored with every breath and my muscles cramped with fatigue as I tried desperately not to lose him. If he was human, I'd have to wipe his memory of witnessing my magic. If he was a witch, I'd have to find out which side his family was on. We couldn't afford to be neighbors with a bunch of demon hunters.

"Fuck," I cursed as I saw a massive fallen tree straight up ahead. It was practically a wall, its trunk way too big to climb over. I'd have to run around it, which meant losing precious time.

I veered off to the right, hoping the top of the tree got skinny enough to jump over soon. The boy jumped and vaulted himself over the widest part in two steps. He was out of my sight and I had to hurry. I scrambled over the wall of soft, rotting wood with all the grace of an elephant. Broken branches slashed at my clothes and face as I slid on my ass down the other side. I'd have to do some self-healing when I got home.

Fuck, where did he go?

I looked to my right and left. No sign of him. In the various shades of greens, grays, and browns of the forest, the shock of bright orange hair disappeared. No way he could have just vanished. I was right behind him. Cursing and wheezing, I spun around in a circle then paused to listen.

A high-pitched yelp echoed through the woods. I found myself spinning furiously again to locate the sound. It sounded like strange, animal laughter.

My heart nearly stopped when a curious face peeked out at me from behind a tree and yipped again, followed by a short howl. The blue eyes were the same, but this face had a long muzzle, slender canine jaws, triangular ears, and a face covered in rusty orange fur.

I was looking at a goddamned blue-eyed fox.

The small animal yipped again with its high-pitched laughter and bounded away into the woods, barely making a sound. I was so stunned, it took me a moment to get moving and follow him again.

My legs protested as I trudged on but the fox-boy paused several yards ahead of me, looking back with alert eyes and pricked ears. Before I got too close, he took off again at a leisurely trot rather than a run this time.

So he wants me to follow him, I realized. Might be a good idea to have backup.

Hey Sal, I reached out to his aura with mine. Something's odd about our new neighbors. I just saw a boy turn into a fucking fox. He's leading me through the woods toward the yurts.

What the fuck? I could feel his bewilderment as if it were my own. Stay right where you are. I'm coming.

C

an't. This kid's moving fast and I just realized how out of shape I am.

A kid? Like how old?

I dunno. Eight or ten years old maybe.

That doesn't make any fucking sense. Only a few demons can shift, and we only take on human forms that are sexually mature. So like, sixteen at the youngest.

I chewed my lip as I continued chasing the boy, who was definitely not a teenager. What could this mean?

Have there ever been witches who shift? I asked.

That's a better question for Ash but no, none that I've ever heard of.

Well, looks like we're about to learn something new from these neighbors.

Seriously Deja, wait for me. We don't know what they are. It's not safe.

I should be okay, I didn't sense any magic on the kid. Just wanted to give you a heads up.

Ignoring his grumbling protests, I continued to follow the fox until I made out the round roofs of the yurts up ahead. My steps slowed as I approached, hoping I wouldn't come off as threatening to the inhabitants.

Six yurts in two evenly spaced out rows of three stood in a clearing. Clothing lines stretched out between each one, some with shirts, socks, and pants clipped to them. What looked like a large, community bonfire pit stood in the middle of the two rows of yurts. It burned low with glowing embers and small flames licking at the metal grate set over the coals. On top of the grate were skewers of meat and vegetables cooking over the natural heat source.

That distinct laughing yip turned my attention to one of the yurts, where I saw the young red fox pull open a rickety screen door with his paw and darted inside. I stood just on the edge of the small community, unsure of what to do or if I should even make my presence known.

Before I could decide, the screen door burst open, slamming hard against the side of the yurt from the forceful kick of the woman coming out. Her blue eyes narrowed in explosive anger, matching the fiery red hair surrounding her face in a mass of curls.

But it was the double-barreled shotgun she pointed straight at me that had my full attention.

"Trying to hunt my son, bitch?" Her voice rang out clear and commanding as she pumped the shotgun.

"No, no, no! Hang on!" I raised my arms above my head, panic taking over my body. "I come in peace!"

Probably not the best thing to say but it was the first phrase that rolled off my tongue. Fuck, I should've waited for Sal.

"A likely story," the woman sneered. "We're done falling for your bullshit, human."

"Wait! I'm not human!" I protested. "I mean, I am but I'm a--"

Too late. She pulled the trigger, and the shot rang out through the trees.

10
DEJA

M y skin stung like thousands of tiny paper cuts. I laid flat on my back, my lungs aching from the force of my fall. From the forest floor however, Earth magic supported me like the most luxurious mattress.

I drew on my healing magic, still not knowing how bad my injuries were. If I had internal bleeding or organ damage, those needed to be taken care of right away.

Or... fuck! The baby!

My hand flew to my belly, but I felt nothing unusual there. Nothing that felt like blood or an open wound but my fingers skimmed over what felt like holes in the front of my shirt.

Tentatively I pushed myself up on my elbows. I had a splitting headache and my muscles cried out with soreness but I definitely hadn't gotten shot. I looked down at my shirt riddled with holes and the puffy red welts covering my chest that were healing quickly. My breaths came out heavily and full of relief.

She shot at me so fast I didn't know if I'd be fast enough. But I pulled all the power of Air I had in that fraction of a second and threw it up in front of me like a shield. The opposing force turned out to be enough to stop the shotgun pellets from filling me with holes. Just barely.

"What the fuck?" shrieked the red-haired woman, eyeing me crazily from the front porch of her yurt. "You're *not* human! How the fuck are you sitting up right now?"

"If you'd have let me talk before shooting, you'd know," I snapped back. This headache, not to mention this woman's shoot first, ask questions later policy, erased all my desire for politeness.

She set the gun down on a small table just next to her front door. Without another word, she shifted into a beautiful but battle-scarred red vixen. About twice the size of her kit, her ears were torn from previous fights. Her red fur was streaked with grey, even though she didn't look much older than me in human form.

She approached me cautiously on small surefooted paws, her blue eyes still strikingly human. I remained still on the ground, still propped on my elbows as she began carefully sniffing me. Her delicate black nose drifted over my belly and she made a sound somewhere between a growl and a yip.

"I smell different, huh?" I said softly. "I'm a witch so that's probably my magic you're smelling. I don't shift but something tells me we're not too different."

Her eyes met mine and widened with surprise as she sat back on her haunches like a dog. I fought the urge to pet her like one, figuring she probably wouldn't appreciate that.

A bone-chilling feline roar was our only warning to what happened next.

A large tan blur darted out from the woods behind me and sent the vixen tumbling through the campground, yelping with surprise and pain.

"Sal!" I cried out as the massive mountain lion stood protectively over my legs.

What the fuck happened? he demanded, thoroughly pissed. I heard a gunshot!

"I'm okay!" I reached to grab his fur but he already pounced on the vixen.

He pinned the little fox down with his paws and took the scruff of her neck in his teeth. She screamed as he began shaking wildly and I knew he would not hesitate to kill her.

"Sal, stop it now!" I screamed at him with my aura and my mouth but he was silent, lost in the urge to kill.

The woman's kit darted out of their house and ran up to the mountain lion mauling his mother. He looked like a chihuahua confronting a great Dane. He barked, bit and clawed at Sal's hind legs but my lion paid him no attention.

Blood began to flow as the vixen's screams echoed off the trees and I did the only thing I could think of. I jumped up, ran straight at the two fighting animals, and tackled Sal. The large cat weighed easily twice as much as me and just thumped over on his side from my tackle. He looked at me in surprise and growled a warning, but he let go of the vixen which was all that mattered.

"I can't let you kill her, lion," I said apologetically with a quick run of my hand through his fur, then quickly turned to check on the fox.

She laid breathing heavily, bleeding from a wound at the back of her neck but thankfully not her throat. When I reached for her wound, her son snapped at my fingers, making me draw them back. He stood over his mother protectively, growling and snapping at me.

"I'm going to heal your mother, little one," I told him. "I promise she'll be right as rain. Then maybe we can try talking like civilized people." I glanced at Sal behind me, who bared his canines and growled a warning but gave no indication he would attack again.

The kit backed away from my hand but stayed right next to his mom, sinking to his belly and gently licking her muzzle.

I pressed my hand against her wound and took a deep breath, drawing Earth up from the ground below my feet and sending its healing properties through my hand to the injured vixen.

An idea occurred to me and I called on Fire, seeing if I could pull it into the healing magic as well. To my delight, it did so seamlessly.

"This is going to hurt a little but please be still," I warned her as I sent the fire into her wound to sterilize it and prevent infection.

She whined and kicked her legs a bit but otherwise obeyed me. Fire cleansed her wound of any bacteria from Sal's mouth and Earth repaired her torn flesh and began sealing up the bite. Within a minute, only a few small bald patches on her neck were the only indication of any scuffle.

She slowly rolled to her feet and shook out her fur. Her kit yipped excitedly, jumping up on his hind legs to lick her face and wagging his tail.

"So now that we both nearly died," I held my bloody palms out to Sal, who purred with pleasure as he licked them clean. "I'd say we're even. Now can we talk without guns or bloody attacks?"

The vixen tilted her head, regarding me curiously before looking past me to Sal. Her ears flattened against her skull and her lip curled back, exposing her teeth.

"Lion, shift back to human for me," I said, merely guessing at what she wanted.

He growled and draped a heavy paw over my shoulder before obliging, the paw shrinking into a human-sized hand and arm that wrapped around me protectively.

"Your turn, vixen," he growled as if daring her, pulling me close to his chest.

Her form morphed into the wild-haired human woman who I first saw when approaching the settlement. Her son shifted to human as well and she pulled him protectively behind her back.

"What do you want from us?" she demanded. "I shot at you because you're trespassing."

"Fucking bitch." Sal's muscles tensed but I stopped him with a hand on his chest before he could lunge at her.

"Your son was spying on me, trespassing on our property first," I explained. "I followed him because I thought he was human. He saw me using magic, which we don't share with ordinary humans."

The vixen let out a dry laugh. "Not from around here, are you? You act like you've never seen a shifter before."

"I haven't. This guy," I nodded at Sal. "Can shift but he also has magic like me. You two don't seem to have magic apart from the shifting."

"Never heard of a shifting witch," the woman snarled. "You magical assholes are the whole reason we're out here living like this. Said we were too feral and dangerous to be around humans of any kind."

I couldn't help but smile knowingly. Now we were getting somewhere.

"He's not exactly a witch," I told her. "And I can't shift but we are out here for similar reasons. Our local community chased us out because they thought we were a threat to them as well. Even though we never hurt anyone."

"No one that didn't threaten us first," Sal added, narrowing his eyes at her. "Or rightly deserved it."

The woman scratched her scalp through her wild, red curls. With her attitude and similar features, she could have been Sal's sister.

"I'm sorry for shooting at your mate," she said, lowering her eyes to the ground. "I understand you acted out of protection." And then to me, "I'm sorry I didn't listen to you. I'm glad you weren't badly injured."

Sal and I exchanged glances and nodded in unison.

"Apology accepted," I said. "I understand you were acting out of protection too. What are your names?"

"I'm Astrid." She pulled her son forward, keeping her arms around him protectively. "This is Jacob."

I smiled at him. "Hi, Jacob."

"Hello." He looked down shyly. "Thank you for healing my mom."

"No problem, buddy. I'm sorry that was scary for you." I grabbed Sal's face playfully. "This is Sal. He promises not to do that again." He rolled his emerald eyes, prompting a light smack on his cheek from me. "And I'm Deja."

"You have him well-trained," Astrid observed. "If I didn't know you couldn't shift, I would have figured you for an alpha."

"She is, in a way," Sal said, looking at me affectionately.

A blush rose in my cheeks. I got the feeling that was a sincerely big compliment from a shifter.

"How many shifters do you have here in your community?" I asked. The realization dawned on me that Astrid and Jacob seemed to be the only two here, despite six yurts standing in the clearing.

"Only my family for now," she answered, ruffling Jacob's hair. "We're the only permanent residents. We serve as a sort-of underground railroad for outcasted or fleeing shifters. We help them find communities of their own species across the country, and guide them there in ways to avoid being tracked or hunted."

"Wow." My jaw dropped in awe. "Just the two of you are doing this?"

"There's five of us," she replied, her lip curling in amusement. "My three mates are out hunting now."

I lifted an eyebrow and exchanged my own amused glance with Sal. Despite getting off to a rocky start, I was starting to like our new neighbors. Astrid and I seemed to have more in common the more we talked.

"What's that look for?" she asked defensively, noticing my and Sal's grins.

"I have three mates too," I replied, nuzzling against Sal and kissing his cheek. "The others are away at the moment too, so he's the one stuck with me."

"Lucky me," he growled softly, dropping a kiss to my shoulder.

Astrid's face broke into a full-on grin as she hid a girlish giggle behind her hand.

"Would you two like to stay and eat with us?" she asked a bit nervously. "I only have homemade blackberry wine and bites to nibble on now. But my mates should be back soon and then we'll be feasting."

"We don't want to intrude," I protested, but she waved a hand, cutting me off.

"They always bring back so much and then we have to dry it into jerky, which is a huge pain in my ass. Please." She lowered her voice. "I still want to make up for shooting you. And I think we have much to learn from each other."

Sal and I looked to each other again, coming to an agreement without words. "If you're sure," I turned back to Astrid with a smile. "Homemade blackberry wine sounds absolutely delicious."

11
DEJA

"You didn't know you were a witch?" Astrid's eyes, wide with bewilderment, caught mine as she refilled my cup of blackberry wine. "How could you not know?"

"I was raised with ordinary humans," I explained, taking a sip of the tart, sweet beverage. "After my mother died, I was adopted out. They never encouraged my magic and worked to ensure I never knew it existed." Of course there was a lot more back story than that, but I didn't want to overload her with information.

"I'm sorry," she said solemnly. "My mom died too when I was just a kit. Killed by a hunter." She took a long swig of wine. "It still fills me with rage to think of her beautiful red pelt as some human's fucking decoration."

"I'm sorry." I reached for her hand. "If it's any consolation, at least you weren't forced to go against your nature. You knew who you were from day one."

She smiled humorlessly. "I used to hate being a shifter as a kid and teenager, you know? I never fit in with the human kids. I couldn't make friends except with other shifters, and there are few enough of us as it is." She tossed a flaming red lock of hair over her shoulder. "But now I know. We're human and animal, which makes us twice as strong as any regular human. If they're too scared and narrow minded to embrace us in society, that's their own damn problem. Doesn't mean there's something wrong with us. We're perfect as we are."

"Amen," I said, clinking my cup against hers.

She lifted her chin, looking across the cooking fire to where Sal talked to Jacob in a low voice. From the way the boy's blue eyes lit up, my demon was telling him some story about a battle from centuries back.

"I want him to grow up knowing he's perfect," Astrid said softly. "I don't want him to go through the pain that I did—thinking for years that something was wrong with me."

"You're doing a great job," I told her. "I mean, this operation you're running is an amazing thing to show him what you can do for others. How many shifters do you get through here?"

"Depends on the season," she answered. "It's usually feast or famine. Around spring, we're usually filled up. Too many youngsters out sniffing newborn prey or mating for the first time without being careful. If someone kills a beloved pet or one human witnesses a shift, they're done for. Humans won't stop until our heads are mounted on walls."

"What kinds of shifters are there?" I was burning with curiosity about her kind.

"How many animals are there?" she answered with a smile. "We see lots of canidae and felines. Horses occasionally. Some birds of prey. Some just general prey like elk and rabbit. I feel sorry for those bastards, hunted by everyone." She took another long swig of wine. "But when someone comes here needing protection, we have a strict no hunting, no fighting policy. Everyone is equal here, either seeking help or working to provide it for our brethren."

"That's wonderful," I breathed, wishing there was something

similar between witches and demons. A community where we could all lean on and trust each other. If humans gave us trouble we'd be a united front, not pointing fingers at our neighbors.

"Are your mates foxes too?"

"Only one is, Conan." She looked fondly at Jacob, still enthralled by Sal's storytelling. "Chase is a golden eagle and Orion is a wolf."

"That's so cool!" I giggled, my head now buzzing pleasantly from the wine. "Talk about diversity."

"It's never a dull moment." Astrid wiggled her eyebrows and slapped my knee playfully. "Well, you should know with three of your own."

"Got that right." I chuckled, trying to ignore the tightening in my chest. When would the day come that all four of us would be carefree and happy again? Those two days between my coven ceremony and shadow lessons with Seth, spending every moment I could with the men who owned three equal pieces of my heart, was absolute heaven.

And Seth. I still couldn't wrap my head around how he played into this. He warned me about the hunters and told me how to capture Air. If it weren't for him, I might not be alive right now. Why would he help us? Hopefully Ash was finding that out.

"Where are your other two?" Astrid asked in a gentle voice, indicating I didn't have to answer.

"One is taking care of some business. He'll be back soon," I answered. "The other... we had an argument a few days ago and we haven't really spoken since. Things are a little tense between us right now."

She nodded sympathetically. "It's hard as hell keeping three people happy. And when one does something to upset you, you feel like an ungrateful bitch because the other two are right there for you to lean on."

"Yes, exactly," I sighed. "But it's just not the same. I miss him.

How he makes me feel. The connection with each of them is so unique. It's not just replacing one warm body with another."

"Coupled partners don't understand it," Astrid agreed. "Yes, the sex is amazing and wild, you feel like a pampered princess sometimes, but it's at least three times harder when things are bad."

"Yep." I drained my second glass of wine, hoping I'd be able to eat soon. "But I still love all three of those sons of bitches anyway."

Astrid threw her head back and laughed so hard, Sal and Jacob fell silent to look at us.

"It's always hilarious to me when non-shifters use that expression." She wiped at her eyes, still giggling.

We talked until the late afternoon sun created long, striped shadows across the yurt campsite. Sal came over to sit behind me and be my pillow while Jacob snuggled into his mom's side. We laced our fingers at my belly, thinking of our own child as we watched the two foxes interact. It filled my heart with warmth and hope for the future.

When a piercing cry filled the air, Sal immediately tensed up and tightened his arms around me. Something flying through the air blocked the sun for a moment but was already gone when I looked up. I lowered my eyes again and was startled to find myself staring into round, golden eyes and a wicked, curved beak.

"Um, hello."

The eagle spread its impressively large wings, sporting a wingspan longer than I was tall, and screeched again.

"Chase, they're guests," Astrid chided. "They're magical, not shifters. But they're okay."

The eagle turned and looked at her before slowly shifting. He took on the appearance of a tall, slender man in his early thirties with brown hair that had a golden sheen to it. Like his bird form, he moved with lightness and ease, practically floating over to his red-haired mate.

"You trust these people?" he asked her, eyeing us suspiciously.

"Yes," she said quickly. I was thankful she left out the details of our very first impressions of each other.

He turned to Sal and I, regarding us with his sharp golden eyes that were a few shades darker than mine. "If Astrid trusts you, then you're most welcome here." He held out a hand. "I'm Chase."

We made introductions and he turned back to Astrid. "The other two will be here soon. They brought down a big bull elk." He lowered himself to sit by her and ruffled Jacob's hair with fatherly affection.

Astrid groaned and rolled her eyes at us. "See what I mean? A bull elk can feed us for a month. We don't have the storage for all that meat without turning it into jerky. We'll probably send some steaks back home with you."

"We'll be happy to take it off your hands." Sal wiggled excitedly behind me. I knew he'd be dying to turn those steaks into five-star meals in our own kitchen.

A crashing sound through the trees and snapping branches announced the arrival of Astrid's two other mates.

They came into the clearing in human form, carrying a long branch between them and one of the biggest animals I'd ever seen with its four hooves tied to the branch.

"You weren't kidding," I breathed as they set the dead elk down a few feet from the fire.

"Always trying to show off by bagging the biggest kill," Astrid teased, standing to greet the two men who just carried a 700-pound animal through the woods like it was nothing.

The first man she kissed, a burly lumberjack of a man with an impressive beard, had red hair like her. I figured he had to be her fox mate, Jacob's father. The other man caught me off-guard. Not only was he breathtakingly handsome, he looked at least twenty years older than her. Astrid's fingers caressed his head of thick white hair with a few strands of black sprinkled in. The stubble on his jaw carried an even mix of salt and pepper.

When their lips parted, his dark eyes took her in hungrily and a shiver of envy ran across my skin. It was the same look Raum gave me. I felt like I'd do anything to see his eyes devour me like that again.

We made introductions again and Sal offered to help butcher the elk, which Astrid's mates graciously accepted. Chase poured more blackberry wine while Astrid and I watched them skillfully prepare our dinner.

"What brings y'all out this way?" Orion, the silver wolf, asked in a light Southern drawl that was absolutely swoon-worthy.

"Running away from evil witches," Sal answered half-jokingly.

"You're shit outta luck here." Conan, the burly fox, wiped his knife on a cloth before continuing his work. "Evil witches hate shifters almost as much as they hate demons. That's why we gotta homestead it out like this. Sometimes I swear they're worse than humans."

"You get a lot of demons up this way?" Sal asked casually.

"Not too many this far north," Orion answered. "Lots of 'em where I'm from, down in Louisiana."

"I've lived in the Pacific Northwest my whole life and never seen one," Chase sighed. "I'm starting to think they don't exist."

"That's ironic," huffed Conan. "Considering you know, that you're a human who turns into an animal."

"I know how that sounds." Chase held up a hand in protest. "But I've seen magic. I've seen everything from a snake shifter to a bear shifter. I've yet to see an actual fucking demon with my own eyes."

"Well, you're looking at one right now," Sal smirked. "So don't stop believin'."

Everyone's eyes turned to my man calmly peeling the elk's hide away from the meat. The air fell silent except for the crackling of wood from the fire.

"Yeah?" Chase challenged. "Prove it."

I hid my chuckle behind my wine, knowing Sal was waiting for his own moment to show off.

He continued his work on the elk as if Chase hadn't said anything. When a shadow darkened his entire form, Astrid and all of her mates jumped back.

"Whoa! Where'd he go?" cried Chase.

"He's still there," Orion breathed with fascination. "Look, his knife's still movin'. He's just invisible."

As the only one perceptible to shadow magic, I saw Sal's grin from beneath his shadow cloak. But he wasn't done yet.

"I'm over here."

Chase jumped as if something bit him in the ass. Sal's voice sounded like it whispered directly into his ear. Everyone laughed as he swatted his ear and spun around in circles. Sal's knife continued moving methodically. I watched his shadowy hand draw gestures in the air for his next party trick.

A baseball-sized flame broke off from the main fire and moved a few feet away, hovering by itself for a few moments while everyone oohed and ahhed. The flames then moved fluidly in the air to form symbols. Lucifer's sigil, then mine, then Sal's own.

"Alright, I think we get it," Chase scoffed as he cautiously sat back down. "I'm a believer now."

"So you're immortal, then." Orion asked as Sal re-emerged from his shadow. Sal confirmed with a nod and Orion looked to me. "And are you as well, miss Deja?"

"No, not exactly," I answered. "I was born human and given my powers by Lucifer personally. I can die and have many times. But I'm reborn into different bodies."

"So you're like a human-demon hybrid?" Conan asked.

I tapped my chin thoughtfully, wondering how much I should really tell them. But the wine already loosened my tongue, and I thought, fuck it. As Astrid said, we were all equals here.

"I'm a witch," I corrected. "The original witch, I guess. I'm called the Mother of Witches because all witchkind originally descended from me and my three demon lovers."

All except Sal stared at me as if I grew three extra heads.

I'd never directly told anyone what I was about to say. I never needed to. They either already knew or if it mattered, they figured it out.

Deep breath. Here goes.

12
DEJA

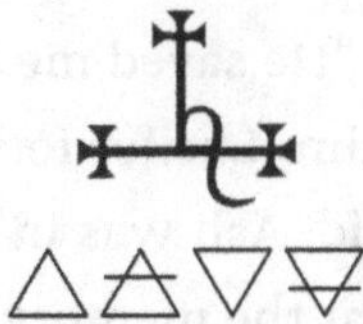

"**M**y first body was the first human woman ever created," I explained.

"You're Eve?" Chase squeaked in shock.

"No." I turned to face him. "I'm Lilith, Adam's first wife. Eve was my replacement for him because the so-called Almighty fucked up on his first try."

Sal threw his head back with a laugh. "You mean he made you absolutely perfect, beautiful."

"How were you a fuck up?" Now Chase was the one burning with curiosity.

I grinned. "I refused to be subservient to my husband. He created us both from Earth, so I always felt I should be his equal. When he made Eve from Adam's rib, well, I guess that solved that problem for him." My grin grew wider. "But when Lucifer tempted her with the forbidden fruit, he proved even the meekest, most submissive women have curiosity and a thirst for knowledge. It's such a shame the Almighty saw that as the downfall of his perfect creation."

"So how'd you get involved with demons?"

"You've heard of the fall of Lucifer, right?"

Chase nodded. "Yeah, he used to be an angel, right? And then rebelled and got thrown out of heaven?" He ran a hand through his golden brown hair. "Fuck me sideways, are you telling me that angels exist, too?"

"There wouldn't be any demons without angels," I teased. "And you're right. Lucifer rebelled along with two others—Beelzebub who oversees Hell with him, and Ashtaroth." I paused to taste Ash's full name in my mouth. Fuck, I wished he was here. He'd find these shifters utterly fascinating. "He saved me from the Almighty's wrath and took me to Hell with him. Lucifer found me a hell of a lot more useful than the Almighty did. Ash was in love with me and I fell for him too, literally." I smiled at the memory. "He and Lucifer thought I needed more demons for protection so Sal and Raum were created for me. And," I waved my hand casually, "As they say, the rest is history."

A comfortable silence fell around the fire as our new friends absorbed my story. Sal placed the first elk steaks on the grill and returned to his spot next to me, kissing my cheek.

"I've always suspected witches and demons are closely related." Orion scratched his salt and pepper stubble thoughtfully as the fire hissed with the first drippings of elk fat. "Always seemed to be lots of similarities, especially down south. Even I could feel the black magic in the air down there."

That gave me the perfect opportunity to ask him my next question.

"Do you know how shifters originated?" I asked. "Until I met Mr. Jacob here," I leaned over and ruffled his thick orange hair. "I thought shifting was purely a demon ability. And not all of them can."

"No one knows for sure." Orion smiled warmly at me from across the fire. "The ongoing theory from our historians is we come from a human mating with a demon who ah, shifted during the time of climax."

Sal began choking and spitting from the wine he just drank while I stared awkwardly and blushed.

"Oh. I see," was all I could say.

"You can imagine biology or mother nature or what-have-you does not approve of such a union," Orion went on with a teasing grin. "So the children born of that union essentially lost the genetic lottery. They can shift at about age five and have animal-like senses but have no other magic abilities."

"We haven't lost anything," Astrid said a bit defensively, holding Jacob tightly. "We're just different. But there is absolutely nothing wrong with us."

"I agree, my love." Orion looked at her fondly from across the fire. The ache in my chest grew deeper when I heard Ash's term of endearment for me come from his mouth. I tried my best to swallow my envy of Astrid surrounded by her family here, whole and complete.

"So you two must have seen some crazy shit since well, the beginning of time and now." Conan added more steaks to the fire, and I was grateful for the subject change. "How about some stories?"

Sal and I ate our fill of elk steak as we laughed and swapped stories with our new friends. The sun had long disappeared and Jacob was out cold against his mother's side by the time we stood to head back. Astrid insisted on sending us home with several pounds of meat carefully wrapped in butcher paper.

"Come see us anytime, for any reason." She pulled me into a hug and her large blue eyes were serious when she pulled away. "If you need to get away again quickly, we can help."

"Thank you," I said earnestly. "For everything. Your hospitality, understanding, everything. I mean it."

"Except shooting you." Her lips pulled into a smirk.

"Yeah, except that," I laughed. "But the steaks and wine were great, so I'm over it."

We said our goodbyes and began making our way carefully

through the dark woods. I cast a small ball of fire to light our way as Sal and I walked silently side by side.

"That was... really something," he breathed after a few moments of silence.

"Yeah," I agreed. "Can't wait until Ash meets them."

A few more moments of comfortable silence passed, both us of deep in our thoughts of the last several hours we spent.

"Do you trust them?" Sal asked when the kitchen light from our house was a faint glow in the distance.

"Yes," I answered without hesitation. "I do."

"Even after everything that happened with your so-called friends back in San Francisco?"

I chewed my lip as I thought on it.

"Yes, even then. I never felt like I really knew my grandmother or Juno, you know? Even though we're all witches. They always seemed to be holding something back. With Astrid, it felt like she held nothing back. She put it all out there and I felt at ease with her from the very beginning."

"I know what you mean." Sal quietly laced his fingers through mine. "I feel good about them. All of them. It's nice to be around people who don't instantly hate you for what you are."

I squeezed his hand. "Just promise me one thing."

"Yeah?"

"Never, ever shift while we're in the middle of fucking." I gave him a stern look. "I mean it."

He grimaced, the shadows from my floating firelight exaggerating his features.

"Ugh. Yeah, don't ever worry about that, beautiful. Whether that theory is true or not, some lines should never be crossed."

I voiced my agreement as we came to the edge of the treeline, our front door and the warm glow from inside the cabin welcoming us home. Sudden movement to my right made us both tense up as we stepped onto the front porch.

A tall, imposing figure approached us. He came closer slowly, almost cautiously as if afraid. When the glow of my fireball revealed his features, my heart felt cleaved in two.

His hair looked longer. His dark eyes were full of longing and misery, like he may have missed me even more than I missed him.

My lips parted to choke out his name.

"Raum..."

13
DEJA

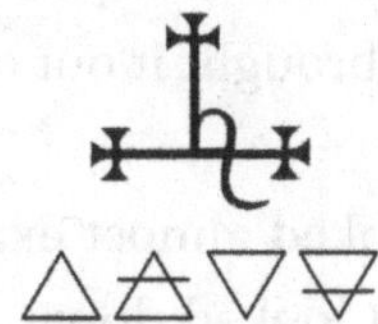

Sal swiftly took the bag of steaks from me and gave me a fast peck on the cheek.

"I'll be inside," he whispered, quickly shutting the door behind him to give us alone time.

Raum remained a safe distance across from me on the porch and my heart could barely handle it. I didn't give a fuck anymore about my pride or being right, or even the original argument we had. I just hated this sick, empty feeling of not having his hands on me.

"Raum," I said again weakly, moving toward him to close the agonizing distance.

"Deja." He held up a hand as if to stop me, his voice hoarse from lack of use.

I stopped in my tracks, feeling like an arrow just shot through me. If he was going to reject me, leave me... fuck, I would not survive hearing those words, let alone thinking about them.

He lowered his hand and held his palm out to me. "Can I show you something?"

I nodded and skimmed my shaking fingertips across his. His hand closed around mine and that small, simple touch left my core opening up and spilling out with need for more. I was starving for him so badly I was desperate for whatever crumbs he would throw at me.

His aura gently pulled on mine, and I followed, realizing he was bringing me into his shadows. I stifled a sob with the awareness he was about to show me something deep within his memories, something he never shared with anyone.

We didn't travel back far when he paused in front of the memory he wanted to show me and brought it out of the darkness of his mind for me to see.

I saw a woman who looked almost exactly like me, down to the dark hair and amber eyes. I looked down and saw muscular tanned arms and a flat torso. Of course, I was seeing this woman from Raum's perspective.

"You're going to have a daughter," his mouth said. A flutter of nervousness rose in his stomach. My Raum, nervous? I didn't know he could feel such a thing. "She will be the completed reincarnation of Lilith, the Mother of all Witches."

In my own body, tears flowed freely down my cheeks. This woman was Deidre, my birth mother. And holy Hell, she looked so beautiful. I could feel how entranced Raum felt under her amber gaze and his uncertainty over how she would react to his news.

She pursed her lips, a curious, thoughtful gesture. "You know this for sure? How?" Her voice was soft, almost whispery.

"I'm one of the few demons with the ability to see the future," Raum answered. "And I've waited a very long time for Lilith's soul to repair itself."

"Why? Who is she to you?" Her questions were curious and also a bit protective.

Raum answered without hesitation. "She's the love of my incredibly long life."

My heart felt like it was going to beat out of my chest. Deidre looked surprised but at no point did she seem threatened by or afraid of Raum.

"She'll be extraordinarily powerful," he continued. "Modern witches are trying to sever and erase all connections they have with demons and that is the result of her absence from this world. Whether you like it or not, she is the balance between our two species. And balance will be restored."

Deidre looked down at her just-barely protruding belly and rubbed a hand across it.

"Will she be loved?" she asked quietly. "Will my daughter be safe, protected, and know what love feels like?"

"Yes," Raum whispered. "She will be loved and protected so fiercely. If anything ever manages to kill me, I would not hesitate to die for her."

My mother looked up at him and smiled. "That's all I want for her. I don't care if she spends time with demons, witches, or a pack of wild animals. I just want my Deja to be happy."

"I'll be spending every minute of every day making sure that she is."

Raum's voice choked a little as he spoke. There was also something weird about what Deidre said. Did either of them know she would be dying in a few short months?

I wanted to stay, to linger on my mother's face and her voice longer but Raum gently pulled the memory back. It faded until I found myself in my own body again, on the front porch with my handsome sad-eyed demon in front of me.

A pregnant pause hung between us as he wiped a tear away from my eye. I didn't even know that I was still crying.

"Thank you," I breathed. "For sharing that with me."

He swallowed. "I should have showed you that a long time ago." His fingers gently drifted across my cheek until he was cupping my face. I leaned into his palm, his touch so overwhelming and yet so not enough.

"I'm sorry, Deja." His forehead rested on mine. His body heat radiated like a furnace across my skin, opening me up from the inside.

"Shut up," I said, my voice a shaky whisper.

His brows knitted together in confusion and I realized I had to spell this out for him.

I kissed him with desperation, with all the pent-up aching need for his touch that I'd been starving for. My tongue pried apart his lips to find his waiting for me. He physically shuddered and moaned as his tongue surged out to caress mine. Without words, his mouth told me how starving and desperate he was for me too.

We were a fast-moving clash of lips, tongue, teeth, and hands, like we were trying to fit all the time we missed in the past week into that one moment. My fingers tangled in his hair. He pulled me tight against his chest and his heart hammered against mine.

He was happiness. He was home. He was mine.

"Deja." His lips fell to my neck, prickling my sensitive skin with his rough stubble. "I fucking love you so much. I'm such a stubborn fool."

"I told you to shut up."

My hand ran down the hard wall of his torso, only stopping to cup the equally hard bulge in his jeans. He groaned like a beast and finally started acting like one.

He pushed me backward until I was pinned against the porch railing, then claimed my mouth again. The ache in my body heightened to new sensitivity as he shamelessly groped me, gliding his warm hands under my shirt and pinching my nipples until I whimpered.

With a quick grab of my waist, he hoisted me up to sit on the railing. My legs wrapped around his hips for stability and he took firm handfuls of my ass for even better support. I needed his naked skin on mine like I needed air to breathe and quickly made off with his shirt. It landed somewhere off the porch on the forest floor.

He barely allowed time for my eyes to feast on him as he tore off my shirt and bra, somehow without his mouth ever leaving my neck or collarbone. His lips returned to mine for more deep, soul-tingling kisses that only made me hungrier. Every rough caress of my breasts and tight, possessive grip on my hips unraveled me, stripping me down to nothing but a body with the most basic, animalistic need.

His hands swept across my lower belly, causing my brain to briefly reawaken at the thought of what I still didn't tell him. But did he already know?

Before I could say anything his fingers slipped under the stretchy waistband of my leggings. My core flared up with greedy heat at feeling his hands so close to it.

He then pulled his hands apart, and a sharp tearing sound grated my ears. He ripped the fabric apart right down the front of my crotch. And thanks to my disdain for VPL, I wasn't wearing any underwear.

Shocked, I raised my eyes to his and saw the old Raum looking back at me. The Raum I fell in love with dared me to tell him off. I saw it in his cocky smirk and gleeful dark eyes. And I saw that he would punish me if I did so.

And fuck me, I couldn't resist. "If you want it so bad, why are you just standing there?"

His low, throaty chuckle vibrated from deep in his chest and felt like a caress on my skin. I never needed him more than right in that moment.

"I'm admiring the view." His fingers trailed up my spine to grab a fistful of my hair at the base of my skull. "Before I tear you to pieces and mark you as mine again."

I thought my body temperature couldn't go any higher, but I was downright delirious at how hot this man made me. The cool evening air on my exposed nipples and pussy gave no relief. It only made them even more achingly sensitive.

Raum's hot tongue burned my skin against the evening chill. He sucked the aching peaks of my nipples into his hot mouth, making me whimper for more. My trembling fingers reached for his zipper and I silently begged that he wouldn't stop me. I needed him and couldn't stand it any longer.

Thankfully, he didn't. His sexy groan was just as desperate as mine as I stroked the thick, hot shaft and guided him toward me. He pressed against my slick entrance with no resistance, no pulling away and teasing. We'd have plenty of time for that later.

His wide cock slowly pushed my inner walls apart, and I hardly dared to breathe. The bliss of him inside me quite literally took my breath away.

"Deja," he choked out, his grip tightening on my hair as he eased himself in slowly. He didn't want to spend a bunch of time teasing me, yet still wanted to go slow enough to enjoy every moment. Every inch.

We sighed in unison as he sheathed fully inside me. The sweet, delicious pressure of him soothed the ache of being without him for so long.

"This is where I belong," he growled softly as he pulled back his hips before filling me again.

"Yes," I gasped as I clung to his wide sculpted shoulders. Every thrust seemed to steal my breath, my words, while at the same time giving me exactly what I needed.

"Don't ever do that again." Tears pricked at my eyes as I whispered my plea. "I can't go through not talking to you, or feeling you in this lifetime or any other."

"Never." He rooted deep inside me as he moaned the word and paused his thrusts to tilt my chin in his hand. "I don't know what it's like to die, but these days without you felt like they killed me. I was trying to punish myself for hurting you and I'm a fucking idiot."

I smirked and slid my hands down his body to shamelessly grab his perfect ass. "That may be true, but you're my fucking idiot. And you're not allowed to punish either of us like that again."

He returned my grin and doubled down.

Still inside me, he lifted me off the porch railing and abruptly turned around. His hand still gripping at the base of my skull protected my head as he pressed my body against the solid front door.

"So what should I punish you for?" He resumed thrusting, faster and harder this time, holding me pinned to the door like I weighed nothing. "Maybe for mouthing off with those pretty lips I love so much?"

"Bite me," I challenged. The flash of excitement in his eyes both frightened and thrilled me. I knew if I kept pushing him, he'd push back worse but that was exactly what I craved from him.

He released my thighs so my feet shakily touched down to the floor. My ripped leggings still covered the majority of my legs. I'd have to remind him later he owed me new ones.

He spun me around and pressed a large, heavy hand against my upper back, pushing my chest and cheek into the door. With his other hand he quickly made a bigger mess of my leggings. The seam ripped from my crotch up to the back which he tore apart savagely. My butt cheeks were now exposed to the elements.

Smack!

Including Raum's hand.

"Fuck, I've missed seeing my hand prints all over your gorgeous ass," he growled, alternating ruthless smacks on each of my cheeks until I whimpered. The sting was extra sharp from the chilly night air, and yet I felt the impact of each one ring out in my nipples and my clit.

Then he slid inside my soaking core and wasted no time in pounding me. I screamed into the wood as he took me the way no one else did. His hips bounced off my ass as he fucked me hard and deep. And he did bite me. He held onto my shoulder with his teeth, sending all the sensations running through me into overdrive. The burning pleasure and the sweetest pain became too much for my senses.

My orgasm built up too fast and sent me crashing over the edge without warning. With a heavy groan, he released inside me as my convulsions never seemed to stop.

Breathing heavily, he leaned his forehead against my back. His rough bite turned to soft kisses as we came down from our high together. My legs wobbled despite his strong grip holding me up.

I turned my head to kiss him, sucking his lip into my mouth.

"I'm not even close to done with you yet," I rasped.

His soft laughter sent goosebumps along my skin and stiffened my nipples into tight nubs that ached for his mouth.

"You still think you can handle me, little witch?" He snaked his hands around me and soothed my tender nipples with his hot palms.

I fumbled for the door handle to head inside and gave him another biting kiss.

"I'm the only one who can."

14
RAUM

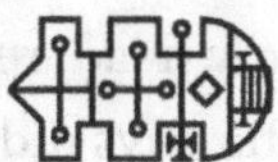

I could've stared at the beautiful naked woman lying next to me for hours. Flushed with heat and marked up from my handi-work, everything felt right in the world now that I had Deja back. Not to minimize that we were on the run from people trying to kill us but from an immortal's perspective, that was nothing new.

"I need to tell you something." Deja rolled over to her side, her breath still coming in soft, sexy pants. "But if you already know, promise you'll just tell me and don't act like you're surprised."

My heart squeezed in my chest. "You know I can't tell you a lie, baby." I cupped her chin until her swollen, tender mouth brushed against mine. "What is it?"

Those sexy lips pulled back into a smile but said nothing. She brought one of my hands to her lower belly just above her crotch, leaving me momentarily confused.

"Can you feel her?" she whispered.

I saw the joy in her eyes and my stomach jumped into my chest. Sure enough, my aura reached through the physical plane of her body and found it. A placenta and a tiny form of life attached to it. Part of her, part of us, and yet independently alive.

"Deja." I could only choke out her name before pinning her down and smothering her in kisses. She giggled and tried to thrash but I kept her still as my kisses moved lower. We were spent from four rounds of sex but I knew no better way to express my love for this woman and this baby inside her.

"How long have you known?" I paused at her belly, kissing her there more tenderly.

"Since the night you and I fought." She raked a hand through my hair. "You really didn't know?"

"I had no idea." I turned my head, resting my ear on her belly as I released a contented sigh. "The guys didn't say a peep."

"You know what I mean." She gave my hair a playful tug.

"No, I haven't seen anything about this pregnancy."

She lifted an eyebrow. "But others?"

My chest tightened as I sat up and chose my next words carefully.

"Baby, I don't need to see the future to know that our children will become incredible people. Every one of them has been revolutionary in their own way. The next generations of witches has been waiting for someone with your blood."

"I know," she sighed with an adorable pout. "I don't want to fight about this again but that's not what I'm asking."

"You've never had a failed pregnancy for as long as I've known you. There's no reason for you to worry about it happening now."

"Okay. Then tell me this." She licked her lips nervously as she clasped my hands. "Will they be okay? I don't even care about how powerful or revolutionary they are but will they feel loved? Happy? Will we be able to protect them when we need to?"

I laughed as I brought her knuckles to my lips. "You're asking the same things your mother asked me."

"Yeah, well. I get wanting to be a good mom from her, I guess."

"There's no need for wanting to when you already are."

I pulled her to me until she was cradled against my chest.

"Again, I don't need to see the future to know you're an amazing mother. You're essentially the first woman who ever gave birth. I mean, you've nailed this thousands of times before."

"I guess," she sighed. "Even with all those memories, it still feels like the first time."

"Every one of our kids adored and cherished you. Trust me, babe. You've got this mothering thing down."

"Not Ragnar," she said softly. "I was ripped away from him before I could ever really be his mother."

"Oh, he knew you." I tilted her chin up to look at me with golden eyes. "We raised him telling him all kinds of stories about his mother, Alfhilde. How you choked out a wolf while six months pregnant because it bit a small child. We told him all about how you retaliated on Christians who tortured and starved some of our people. And every other amazing thing you did." I lowered a soft kiss to her lips. "Even after your soul was split apart, he felt you nearby. Believe me when I say all of our kids had an amazing mother, and they fucking knew it."

"Jeez, Raum." Deja laughed as she wiped the tears rising to her eyes. "How do you always know how to say the right things?"

"By not being a total dumbass and learning from when I say the wrong thing." I squeezed her tighter. "Or do you wrong by not saying anything at all."

She raised her now-dry eyes to me again. "Is there anything else you want to share with me?"

Before I could answer, she raised a hand to stop me. "I understand you won't tell me everything because you don't want to hurt me. I don't necessarily like it or agree but it's how you feel and I respect that. I mean it when I say I don't want us to fight about this again."

I mulled quietly over her words, thankful that she said them. After being together so long, we naturally wouldn't agree on everything and neither one of us had to be right or wrong. I simply couldn't take the risk of breaking her heart with everything I saw. To do so would risk losing her.

I also knew she wouldn't try to police what I told her or didn't. She respected me enough to let me decide if I should tell her. And while my latest vision wouldn't hurt her in the long run, it bothered me more than I was willing to admit in that moment.

I saw it while she and Sal were in the woods with the shifters. It came to me weakly, as it usually did while in bird form but there was no mistaking what I saw.

"Three people from your past will come to see you again," I said carefully. "One will end tragically, one will end happily..." I rubbed circles on her skin as I trailed off, unable to find the words for the third piece.

"And the third one?" she prompted gently.

"Depends on who you ask," I sighed.

***

All of our fucking and then talking soon had Deja's eyes drooping heavily. We curled up against each other and she passed out within minutes. I took the opportunity to head downstairs and catch up with Sal.

He was in the kitchen putting a bunch of spices and shit on a large slab of meat and shaking everything up in a ziplock bag.

"Made up for lost time, did ya?" he greeted when I pulled a stool up to the counter.

"You could say that."

"Didn't need to. I fucking heard it." He snickered as he pulled two beers from the fridge and tossed me one.

"So she's sleeping better?" I asked, twisting the bottle open. "Since the other night."

"Like a baby," he affirmed. The tension in his voice and jaw cut through like a knife. "Now that she has Air, she should be sleeping peacefully. There's no way for them to get in her mind."

"Speaking of baby," I grinned. "Congrats, Dad."

"Same to you, Dad." He laughed softly and sighed as his eyes rolled toward the upstairs bedroom where the mother of our child slept. "She's scared shitless, though."

"I know." My throat tightened. "It's been a long time but she'll be fine. She's done this tons of times before, all successfully."

"It's not just that." He gave me a pointed look. "Raising a child with demon fathers in a world like this? I don't blame her for worrying."

"It's no different than how it was before," I argued. "We've always been persecuted by one group or another. If anything, it's probably better now. People actually have rights now and no one will advocate for killing a child."

He growled like a feral cat, his signature noise when he knew I was right but didn't want to admit it. "It never gets easier, does it?" He scrubbed a hand down his face. "Mentally, I mean."

"No," I agreed. "How many times have we sat across from each other like this, doing nothing but worrying? I usually know what's going to happen and I still worry."

Sal nodded, rubbing the two-day-old stubble on his jaw which he hadn't shaved yet. "This must be the human side of us." He took a long swig of beer. "Running around in circles over the shit we can't control."

"Being immortal doesn't make us perfect." I smirked. "Unless you're Ash."

He rolled his eyes. "Fuck all that."

We laughed together until a shift in the protective magic around the house sent pinpricks across my skin. Our laughter cut off immediately and Sal's expression grew murderous. Someone was here.

Like a single unit, we acted without words. Combining our auras to act as an extension of our senses, we scanned the whole house and the surrounding property. Our shadow magic would ensure the trespasser wouldn't detect a thing.

Upstairs, Deja still slept peacefully. A raccoon sniffed around our front porch for food before moving on. An owl looked for prey in a nearby tree. And just past the treeline behind our house, movement and behavior that definitely wasn't animal.

Got him, Sal thought with a predatory growl.

He shifted into his lion and slunk out the front door, rounding the side of the house to sneak up on his prey. I followed him out but remained on the porch, chugging the rest of my beer as I waited for him to do his hunter thing.

Under the darkness of night, he was invisible to weak human eyes. But I followed him with my aura and sensed everything as if it were all happening in front of me on a clear, sunny day.

The human had no idea he was there until Sal growled at him in greeting. He jumped up in surprise and hilariously fell back down again, helpless as Sal pounced and batted him around like a toy.

"Stop! Stop!" came the panicked screams. "I don't mean any harm! I'm here to help—ahhh!"

Don't fuck with him too badly Sal. I stifled my laugh behind my hand. We don't have any extra clothes in the event that he shits his pants.

With a reluctant snarl, Sal's massive lion began dragging him back toward the house. I swore he purposely went over every sharp rock and twig on the ground from the way the human bitched and moaned.

Like a proud house cat delivering its owner a half-dead mouse, Sal deposited a bloody, beat up Seth on the porch and licked his lips as he sat back on his haunches.

"Well now," I grinned. "Look what the cat dragged in."

15
DEJA

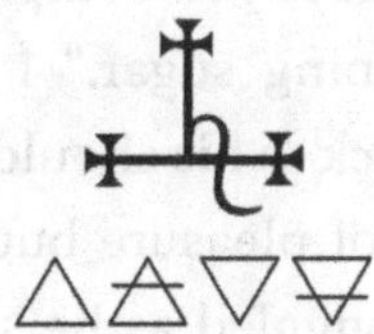

I woke up the way every woman deserves to—sandwiched between two gorgeous, naked men.

Sal spooned me from behind, his lips softly breathing behind my ear, muscular legs curled around mine and one hand with a gentle grip on my breast. The bicep of his other arm cushioned my head like a pillow.

Raum slept on his stomach in front of me, his broad shoulders and biceps on display with his arms curled underneath his pillow. His face was partially hidden behind his arm and his hair spilled out on the pillow like a mess of dark raven feathers. I watched mesmerized as his body rose and fell rhythmically with his breathing, his eyes moving back and forth underneath his eyelids.

I wondered what demons dreamed about. They didn't need to sleep like humans did but not even immortals could deny the wonders of an amazing nap.

Torn between wanting to continue watching him or waking him to hear his sexy morning voice, I skimmed my hand down his back and slowly back up again. Soft skin over hard muscles greeted my touch. He wore my sigil as a tattoo between his shoulder blades, seated directly above Lucifer's.

Tracing the lines with my fingers didn't wake him, so I slid out from Sal's embrace to lazily drag myself on top of Raum's back. He only stirred when I began pressing kisses to his shoulders and upper back.

"Mm." He tried to roll over but seemed confused by my body draped on top of him. "What're you doing?" he groaned groggily.

"Giving you your morning sugar," I quipped, trailing my lips along the curve from his neck to his shoulder.

He made more noises of pleasure but I could feel him growing restless underneath me. I giggled as he shifted and groaned, never able to give up control for longer than a few minutes. When he finally had enough he rolled over lazily, crushing me between his back and the mattress.

"Get off me, I'm suffocating!" But I laughed the whole time as he yawned and stretched as if I wasn't even there. Not even tickling his sides made him move. I poked Sal to rescue me but he just mumbled something in his sleep and flipped over on his other side, the traitor.

Only when I reached around and grabbed Raum's balls and threatened to squeeze as hard as he was crushing me did he slide off, grinning the whole time.

"Asshole," I coughed and laughed at the same time.

"And didn't you miss me so much?" he purred, dropping hot kisses to my throat that made me press against him again.

"No."

He laughed, sliding a large hand down my body to cup between my legs. The heat and pressure of his palm made me gasp and buck my hips. My clit was still incredibly sensitive from all the fun we had yesterday.

Before I could tell him off again, he sucked my nipple into his mouth, teasing it into a rock solid point with his teeth until I was whimpering with need.

He tugged on it as he pulled away, sending another sharp jolt to my clit as he grinned.

"Miss me now?"

"Maybe a little," I murmured.

He caught my mouth and devoured me as he continued rocking his palm steadily against my swollen vulva. My fingers skimmed down his hard torso and stroked him into full hardness. I was so incredibly on edge, my pleasure spilled over into release within minutes. He groaned approvingly as I thrashed against his palm, lowering his mouth to my neck.

Together we finished him off, first with me stroking until my arm was sore, then he stroked himself to completion in my mouth. I nearly came again just from watching him. There was something so inexplicably hot about a man pleasuring himself.

He ordered me to lick him clean—which I did happily before laying back in his arms. Sated, cozy, and content, I tucked my head underneath his chin. Sal's deep even breathing behind me indicated that he missed out on watching our fun. I swore that guy could sleep through a hurricane. And like an actual cat, he'd be happy to sleep eighteen hours a day.

"I have a present for you," Raum murmured as he played with my hair spilling down my back.

"Oh? Like that morning orgasm wasn't enough?" I snickered. "Please, continue spoiling me to make up for not speaking to me for a week."

"Yeah right," he scoffed. "Morning orgasms should be a routine, not a gift." His voice lowered to a sultry whisper. "And I intend on making it one 'cause I'm never leaving you again, baby."

My insides fluttered with delight, and I couldn't stop the smile that followed. "I knew there was a reason why I liked you." I kissed the center of his chest. "So what's my present?"

"It's from me and Sal, actually. We caught it last night while you were sleeping."

I lifted my head from his chest and looked at him, puzzled. "What are you talking about?"

His dark eyes sparkled mischievously as he patted the side of my hip. "Get dressed. I'll show you."

I pressed a kiss to Sal's neck before following Raum's lead, grabbing yesterday's leggings off the floor before remembering the damage he caused them last night.

"I hope it's new Lululemons," I groaned, digging through my duffel bag for a fresh pair. "That shit ain't cheap."

"Once we get back to civilization, I'll buy you all the yoga pants you want." Raum buckled his belt but chose to remain shirtless. I wasn't about to complain.

He led me downstairs and then through a door next to the kitchen which I figured was a broom closet. It turned out to be a basement.

"Did you install some kind of kinky sex dungeon overnight?" I purred, wrapping my arms around his waist as I followed him down the stairs.

"No," he chuckled. "But thanks for the idea. Another for when we get back to civilization."

He pulled a chain on a lightbulb overhead when we reached the bottom. My eyes took a moment to adjust as I glanced around the unfinished basement before settling on the figure tied to a support beam.

Concern washed over me first. Both of his eyes were black and his lip split open and bloody. Then he groaned and lifted his head. My shock and concern mixed into a cocktail of emotions I couldn't even begin to decipher.

White-hot anger through stormy gray eyes looked back at me.

"Seth!" I gasped.

16

DEJA

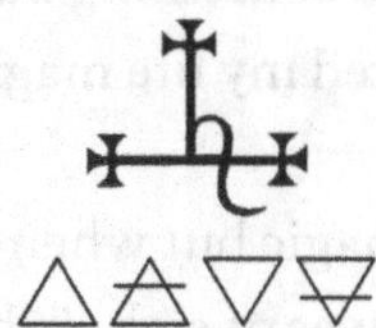

I DIDN'T know what came over me.

I ran to the shackled, battered man and dropped to my knees in front of him. He tried to pull away when I brought my hands to his swollen face but was too weak.

"Deja." Raum's tone carried a hint of warning but I ignored him.

Even through the concrete floor of the basement, I pulled magic from the earth as if there were no barrier at all. My magic poured out through my palms and scanned through Seth's body, looking for injuries to heal.

Fuck, they really did a number on him. Slashes bleeding from his chest and torso from Sal's claws, bruised ribs likely from kicks and punches, not to mention the damage done to his face.

Within a minute, the broken blood vessels repaired themselves and inflammation simmered down to nothing. His open wounds closed up, and the pain reduced to a dull throb.

Raum made an annoyed sound behind me. "I don't think that was the wisest thing to do, baby."

Still ignoring him, I met Seth's gray eyes, now fully visible and alert without the surrounding bruising.

"Tell me why you're here without a single breath of bullshit," I told him. "Or I'll have these two fuck you up all over again."

Raum's smirk behind me and the pleasant surprise in his aura wrapped around me like an embrace. It didn't feel right to keep Seth down here suffering but if he led hunters directly to us, he deserved no less.

"My cover was blown," Seth answered through gritted teeth. "Your crazy grandma figured something out correctly for once."

A hot spark of anger jolted my fire magic at the mention of Diana. "What do you mean?"

"She sucks at shadow magic but when she gets it right, she really gets it right." He let out a weary sigh. "She knows I communicated with you through shadow, and that I told you how to find Air."

My heart stopped. Everything around me seemed to freeze as I replayed that dream in my head. Seth standing so close to me in that circle of candlelight, shadows dancing over the long, lean muscles of his body. His full lips drawing me in, begging me to kiss them, and then moving as if to caress my face.

Only now I could no longer write it off as a dream.

"Tell her how that old cunt found out," Raum taunted him from behind me. "Tell her what you did to keep your precious cover from being blown, which turned out to be ultimately pointless."

Seth bit his lip so hard, he nearly drew blood and lowered his eyes. His aura faded to a dark midnight blue, and I sensed genuine regret and shame.

"Answer the question," I pressed. "What's he talking about?"

He let out a ragged breath and lifted his eyes to me again.

"Once I accessed your shadows through the first touch, I could reach your subconscious without physical contact," he explained. "It's a rare ability in shadow masters. Most demons can't even do it."

"How nice for you," I remarked impatiently. "I saw you in a dream so I already knew that. Tell me what I don't know."

He ground his teeth before continuing. "I can also allow other people to reach your shadows without touch. But I'm the one who controls access. Anyone who wants to reach you relies on me to keep a channel open between my mind and yours."

The gravity of his words sank through me like an anchor reaching the ocean floor. My mouth dropped open, useless and speechless. Red hot anger boiled inside me and I was barely aware of my fist curling at my side, ready to slam through his face.

"You let that woman into my mind?" My voice came out a shaky whisper. "You're the reason I didn't sleep for a week straight? I woke up every hour thinking I was completely alone and my daughter had been ripped away from me."

"Yeah, that was me."

He said it so casually. His eyes were cool, calm, and defiant. Any glimmer of regret and remorse I saw in his aura disappeared. My fist struck out before I could control it. It connected hard with his cheekbone and made his head snap to the side.

Immediately, his face began swelling and coloring up with a bruise again. He looked at me again with no change in expression. My knuckles cried out in pain but I wouldn't show him that he hurt me.

Disgusted, I got up from the dirty floor and turned to go up the stairs. Raum followed me up like a loyal bodyguard.

"I want him gone," I said when we reached the main floor. "I can't stand the thought of having him here a second longer."

Raum pulled me into a firm but gentle embrace, stroking my hair soothingly.

"We can't do that, baby," he said apologetically. "Not until Ash is back. He gives the final order."

"Well, he needs to hurry his ass up, then." I pulled away and began searching through cupboards in the kitchen, slamming them in my frustration before pausing at the liquor collection. Was it too early in the morning to start drinking?

"Did Sal tell you about our new friends in the woods?" I asked, moving on to the fridge. We had orange juice! A mimosa wouldn't be completely out of line, right?

"He did." Raum stroked his stubble with a grin.

I narrowed my eyes at him suspiciously. "Did you already know about them?"

"I saw they would befriend us after... an initial scuffle."

"Uh huh." I chewed my lip. So he also knew I survived being shot. "Can we trust them?"

"Yes," he answered quickly. "We can." His lip twitched, and I knew there was more information behind those three words.

"I know you want to tell me something." My head tilted as I watched him. "So spill it."

"They may be connected to one of the three visitors I told you about last night."

My heart took a hard jump against my sternum as I shifted my gaze to the basement door. "You mean him?"

"No, not him."

"Good."

He quirked an eyebrow. "Why?"

"Because," I returned my gaze to my handsome demon. "When we're done with him, I'm sure they're great at hiding bodies."

17
DEJA

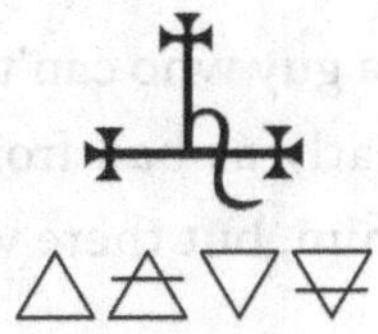

I really, really did not want Seth under my own roof. Just the idea of him being so close by made my skin crawl.

So why did I want to go back down there so badly?

My hand still throbbed with soreness from hitting him. I could've healed myself easily but wanted to keep feeling it. I didn't want to forget that he felt just an ounce of the torture he subjected me to for an entire week. All for the sake of keeping his so-called cover with my former coven and the hunter's guild.

Even after warning me about the hunters coming and telling me how to find Air, I still couldn't be convinced he was on our side. Why else would he allow my grandmother into the deepest parts of my mind only to torture me?

And perhaps a more important question, why was he here except to lead our enemies straight to us?

I resisted the temptation to drink that morning but even sober, I only had so much self-control. I had to know why.

My mind made up, I threw open the basement and stomped down the stairs before I could change my mind again.

I half expected him to be gone. He was a shadow master after all.

Surely he knew some magic to wiggle his way out from being zip tied to a support beam. But a hum of magic in the air plus his seated form told me that was not the case. Sal and Raum spelled the room against his escape. Until Ash returned to play jury, judge, and executioner, they were not taking any chances.

Those gray eyes looked almost silver in the dim light from a single window as they watched me sit cross-legged in front of him once again.

"Come back to beat up a guy who can't defend himself?" he spat.

His face didn't look nearly as bad from my little lady punch as when the guys whaled on him, but there was definitely swelling and discoloration settling in.

"Don't tempt me," I retorted. "Besides, as an all-powerful shadow master, we know you can defend yourself just fine."

"Well, something tells me you didn't come down here to chat about the Niners game," he sneered.

Not even a minute into my visit and this guy already made me want to run back upstairs and slam the door.

"Are you always such an ass?" I demanded completely non-rhetorically.

"You and your boys have been such hospitable hosts," he carried on in the same tone. "How else can I convey my gratitude?"

"Right. And how should I convey my gratitude for you inviting my psycho, demented grandmother—who tried to kill me—into my subconscious?"

"A simple 'thank you, Seth,' would suffice," he jabbed, a humorless smirk emerging. "Hell, I'll even accept a kiss."

My head jerked away in disgust. This guy really wasn't going to let up the attitude, even a little. Still, I couldn't stop my gaze from dropping to his full lips, which he definitely didn't miss.

"I just want you gone," I said through gritted teeth. "I want you out of my head, and out of my life."

"Trust me, the feeling is mutual," he hissed back. The words unexpectedly stung. Why would I feel anything but good about him wanting the same thing? "I know you won't believe me but I never projected myself inside your shadows except for that one time," he went on. "If I wanted to, I could feel your suppressed emotions, see your deeply buried memories without you ever knowing. But I chose not to."

"Why not?" I challenged. "All your shitty insults might actually do some damage if you did."

"Because it's a huge breach of privacy," he stated as if it were obvious. "I wouldn't do it to my worst enemy."

"How noble of you," I shot back but my own sharpness wavered. His aura gave no indication that he was bullshitting. "So after allowing my evil grandmother to torture me for a week straight, why then did you decide to jump in and help me?"

"Because you were ready."

I shook my head before lowering my forehead to my palm. "You're not making any damn sense."

"Huh," he scoffed. "Lilith, the Mother of Witches. Master of light and shadow and everything in between. Personally damned by God Himself and you still don't fucking get it."

"Maybe I would if you'd just tell me what the fucking deal is and stop being such a dipshit."

"You really think I'd let that crazy old hag in your head if she could do permanent damage?" He leaned forward as far as he could, his voice starting to echo off the walls in his frustration. "She could never actually do shit to you, just glamour up some stupid imagery to play on your worst fears."

"I don't know that!" My voice reached a frantic pitch. "It felt so real. And I know you hate me—"

"I don't hate you, sweetheart." The pet name struck a nerve and I couldn't tell if it was genuine or sarcastic. "You know what I also don't hate? In fact, something I actually enjoy?" He stuck his chin out like a challenge. "I enjoy not being strung up by my balls by three demons for turning their woman's mind into scrambled eggs."

"Yeah, I get it. You're all about saving your own skin." Arguing with this man made me intensely tired. I was over it.

"And again, I'd just never do that to anyone. I do have some morals. But here's the thing, Deja." He took a dramatic pause to ensure I was listening. "Diana's magic causes paper cuts compared to yours. Your magic is powerful but your mind is weak."

"Excuse me?" I cried, taken aback.

"She knew your weakness and how to exploit it," he went on. "She knew you'd be lost without your three boyfriends and that her and Juno's betrayal hurt you deeply. But all she could do was try to make you wallow in that fear until it consumed you. Her own power is so limited she couldn't touch your mind without me, and even once she was there, she couldn't do anything but put on a puppet show."

"I know she's a manipulative cunt," I seethed, fighting back tears. "She fooled me from the very beginning. That doesn't exactly make you a saint."

"Your mind is like a muscle, Deja," he went on without any indication that he heard me. "You need to break it down and make it hurt before it can get stronger. I could've shown you Air from the very beginning. But you weren't ready to connect that final piece. Your mind wasn't strong enough."

"And who the hell are you to decide that?" I demanded, knowing my temper was getting the better of me but I didn't care.

"Your shadow magic instructor." He just couldn't hold back the smug grin, which pissed me off even more. "Seriously, you need to quit your bitching. The one who taught me did have the power to break down my mind, and he almost did. This whole tied up in the basement thing?" He rolled his shoulders and leaned back against the beam. "This is a walk in the park compared to what I've been through."

I rose to my feet, well and truly done with this man. But my pride wouldn't let him get the last word in.

"You have no idea what I've been through."

"Sure I have!" he barked as I ascended the staircase. "I've studied you extensively, Lilith! Your lives, accomplishments, and failures are well-documented. You got all the perks of Hell and you have no idea what suffering truly is."

Fuming at the top of the stairs, I fought the urge to run back down and make him suffer. But I knew I wouldn't hurt him, not really. I was ragingly pissed, but I didn't have it in me to torture someone. And more importantly, I couldn't let him see he got a rise out of me.

Sal was in the kitchen when I returned from the basement. Various ingredients and mixing bowls spread out across the counter as he looked at me curiously.

"Hey beautiful," he greeted warmly. "How--"

My lips swallowed his question when I threw myself at him. I grabbed his shoulders and jumped. He caught me and my mouth crashed to his, my legs wrapped around his hips.

With a moan he perched me on the edge of the counter, his surprise and pleasure expressed in the smile I tasted in his kiss. I pulled him forward, holding nothing back as my tongue danced with his and my pelvis rolled against his thickening erection.

"What's gotten into you?" he growled into the sensitive spot on my neck.

"You." I outlined the shape of his thick shaft through his pants.

He groaned again, thrusting into my touch. "Not yet, but I need to be."

Like a gentleman, he actually peeled off my leggings rather than savagely ripping them like Raum. But thankfully, that was where his sweetness ended.

He entered me in one fluid stroke, the sudden fullness making my hands shoot across the counter for stability. Bowls went crashing to the ground, flour or whatever spilled all over the place. Neither of us gave anything but each other a second glance.

"Harder," I begged, pushing back against him as he pushed into me. I needed to feel him in every pore, every cell. Anything to get those gray eyes out of my head.

"How are you so fucking wet already?" he moaned, holding my waist as he crashed into me, his abs flexing with effort.

"I want you so fucking bad." My fingers dug into his triceps. It wasn't really an answer to his question. I didn't want to think about the real answer. I wanted to lose myself in the ecstasy that only my men could give me.

"Hey!"

Raum came into the kitchen with a towel around his waist, droplets of water still clinging to his bronzed skin. A grin immediately spread across his face.

"I heard a crash. Shoulda known what was going on."

"Get your ass over here," I growled at him. Sal made no move to stop fucking me and watching Raum's eyes drink me in only sent my pleasure even higher.

"Yes, ma'am." He stalked over to me like a predator, his hands falling to the knot at the towel and slowly pulling it apart.

The towel fell to the floor, and he took his semi-hard cock in his fist, steadily stroking himself as he watched Sal pound me on the counter.

Our eyes locked just as Sal adjusted his grip and crashed into me even harder, adding a new level of intensity that had me seeing stars and moaning his name.

Raum reached over, still stroking himself with the other hand, and swept his fingertips across my clit. I cried out louder, begging for release and in the back of my mind, hoping Seth heard every sound we were making.

A few more strokes of my clit, combined with his teeth grazing my shoulder and Sal's relentless fucking sent me crashing over the edge, screaming and trembling all the way.

Sal murmured something hot but unintelligible in my ear and slowly withdrew from me. My muscles convulsed around nothing and I reached to pull him back. I needed so much more. But he stepped away to lean against the counter beside me, his cock red and as stiff as concrete as he sucked in heavy breaths.

Raum stepped in between my trembling thighs and shot me a wolfish grin. His tanned length, fully engorged pressed against my pussy like a gentle kiss.

"Mind if I take over, baby?" he purred, sliding his hands up my thighs to my waist.

"Get inside me," I rasped. "Fuck me. Now."

He did. Teasing me at first, the bastard. He fucked me in short, shallow thrusts that left me begging for more, just how he liked me. He covered my mouth until I only let out soft whimpers, and then he gave me what I wanted.

With one hand gripping my hair at my scalp and the other arm wrapped completely around my waist, he angled me for maximum depth. Seth definitely heard my screams as Raum impaled me, lifting me off the counter to fuck me even deeper. My eyes rolled back as another orgasm built up like a volcano. All my control was gone. I could do nothing but take what was given to me. And he was giving me so fucking much.

Sal somehow reached between us to rub the hot button of my clit. I thrashed and shook with release for the second time while Raum stopped his thrusts, just seated himself fully inside me. The fullness of him intensified everything to the point of practically crying from pleasure.

He eased me gently back on the counter and gave me the softest, sweetest kiss. I only then realized that my lips were also trembling.

His forehead against mine, he looked over at Sal next to us. "How you feeling, brother?"

"Like I can maybe go a couple minutes without popping off," Sal grinned.

Raum chuckled and kissed me again, hotter and harder this time, before reluctantly stepping away. I was empty again, panting, sweating, and spread open on the kitchen counter.

"Hello again, beautiful."

Sal stepped up to me again, claiming my mouth passionately as he drew my inner thighs to his sides. He swallowed my moan as he pushed inside me gently at first, feeling for what I needed, then building up to deep, crashing strokes like before.

Next to us, Raum's hands moved across my back, my breasts, and my waist before once again settling at my clit.

They switched places two more times until I was absolutely exhausted and dizzy with pleasure. I couldn't make sense of anything except hands and mouths on me, cocks inside me, orgasming violently. These two men were incredible enough individually, but the way they fucked me together just made them exponentially hotter. Only these two could make me feel extra dirty and twice as treasured.

"I need another bath thanks to you two," Raum cracked as the three of us leaned against the counter, panting and spent like we just ran a marathon. "Might as well bring you fucks in there with me."

I grinned. I had yet to take a bath or shower with any of my guys. Giggling, I ran for the stairs heading up to the master bathroom with the gigantic tub. My boys followed, laughing while slapping my ass and groping for me as they chased me up the stairs.

And for a few blissful hours, I forgot all about the haunting stormy-eyed man tied up in my basement.

18
DEJA

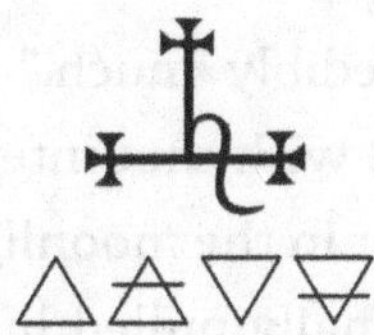

I woke with a start. The silence throughout the house was eerie, and I wondered what jolted me out of such a deep, peaceful sleep.

Then I heard it. Floorboards creaking downstairs under the weight of footsteps. They grew louder as the person walking moved up the stairs, coming closer to the three of us piled up in the master bedroom.

Silently I gathered all the elements of my magic, ready to strike if Seth somehow escaped and was hoping to catch us unaware.

But it was Ash, my angel.

He came through the doorway to find us cuddled up in a pile of arms and legs wrapped around each other. My heart jumped into my throat as I untangled myself from Raum and Sal and ran to him, still fully naked from our bath and so not caring.

"My love," he murmured gruffly as he caught me in those arms and pulled me tightly against him. His lips captured mine and the heat from his mouth, mixed with the rough friction of his beard, sent tingles all the way to my toes.

A minute ago I was completely worn out from my fun with the

other two in the kitchen earlier, but the moment he touched me, my body reawakened with fresh need and vigor. It felt like so much happened since I last saw him. Had it really only been two days? While the other two made me blissfully happy, it felt like weeks without my angel with me.

"Holy fuck, I missed you." Emotion spilled into my voice when our mouths parted breathlessly. I clung to his leather jacket and inhaled his scent like a drug.

"I missed you so incredibly much." He cupped my face and seemed to look through me with that intense, icy gaze. His eyes and hair looked practically silver in the moonlight streaming through the window. "I take it Raum finally pulled his head out of his ass?" he asked, his gaze drifting to the bed behind me.

"Yeah, you can say we've made up," I giggled, circling my arms around his neck. "You're the only piece that's been missing."

"Not anymore," he growled, trailing his fingertips down my sides to cup firm handfuls of my ass. "I'm taking you with me next time. Old man Lucifer misses you."

"How did it go?" I asked, gently scratching my nails through his hair. "Did you find out what you needed?"

His face hardened. "Yes." The word came out sharply, and he didn't sound especially pleased. "I need those two fools awake so I can update all of you on what we're dealing with." His eyes refocused sharply on me. "Unless the poor shit tied up in the basement already told you?"

I shouldn't have been surprised that he knew Seth was down there. "He was the one letting Diana in my head to plant those nightmares. I want him out of here and preferably in a ditch somewhere."

Ash's lips twitched but not with a smile. "Sorry, love but that's not gonna happen. Is that all he told you?"

"Pretty much," I answered. "Nothing else he said made much sense. So what are we doing with him?"

"Get those fools up for me. We're having a meeting downstairs to discuss it." He gave an affectionate slap to my ass. "And maybe put some clothes on so we're not distracted."

"Right now?" Heat bloomed within me at the commanding tone in his voice, coupled with the yearning of not seeing or feeling him for days. Surely a meeting could wait?

A smile finally cracked though his tough exterior. "Yes, now, my love. We'll have some alone time later. Now get them up before I change my mind."

He paid no attention to my whines and quickly untangled himself from me with a final parting kiss. I pulled clean clothes on, grumbling the whole time, and climbed over Raum and Sal on the bed to rouse them.

"Woman, you are fucking insatiable," Raum groaned into the pillow after I dropped a series of kisses and nibbles on his neck. "And I love it," he added, reaching for me.

"Ash's home." I caught his hand before it could reach my breast. "He wants all of us downstairs, pronto."

His next groan was of annoyance as I slid off him and over to Sal to wake him in a similar fashion. Within ten minutes, the three of us were dressed and awake as we stormed downstairs where Ash waited. I smiled at the cup of silver needle tea waiting for me on the counter, next to coffee for himself. He was always so thoughtful about the smallest things.

The mess from our fun earlier in the day had disappeared. One of the guys must have magicked the place clean after our shenanigans. I bit my lip as I looked over to where they took turns fucking me on the counter. I could still feel them in the tender flesh of my core.

"So who wants to fill me in on what happened since I left?" Ash raised his coffee cup to his lips.

Raum and Sal briefed him on how they sensed Seth creeping around the woods just outside our house, and how they dealt with him after. The bloodlust shined through Sal's eyes with excitement. He really had to hold back on basically mauling Seth to death and it momentarily scared me before passing. My guys were always so good to me, I easily forgot how dangerous and ruthless they were to those who threatened us.

After they finished, I told Ash about meeting our shifter neighbors and their expertise on hunting, tracking, and smuggling, emphasizing how they could potentially be helpful to us.

"Very interesting, love." His eyes lit up as I relayed what I learned about them, and he stroked his beard thoughtfully. "I've heard of shifters but they're so rare they're essentially regarded as legends. Once we've dealt with Seth, I would very much like to meet our new friends."

"So what's the deal with the witch boy?" Sal's lip curled. "Was your theory correct?"

"Yes." Ash's face hardened into an expressionless mask and he glanced at me with some emotion I couldn't place.

"What do you all look so glum for?" I demanded, turning around to see all three of them looking at me with the same sad puppy eyes. "Ash, what the hell was this theory of yours?"

He nodded at Sal, ignoring my question. "Bring him up here."

As Sal disappeared down the basement stairs, I moved closer to Ash. My stomach twisted into a knot as I wrapped an arm around his waist until he looked at me.

"Angel, why do I have the terrible feeling that this has something to do with me?"

He let out a weary sigh as his arm wrapped around my shoulders. "It does, love. But it's not necessarily bad news." He gave a weak smile. "It's a choice that's entirely up to you."

As if I wasn't confused enough already. I just stared at him in bewilderment until Sal roughly shoved Seth into the kitchen. He blinked under the lights and looked well in need of food and a shower, but not one of us was ready to give him such luxuries yet.

"Are you going to tell her everything or should I?" Ash removed his arm from my shoulders and folded them both across his chest. "I know the whole story, so don't even try to act dumb."

"Wouldn't dream of it," Seth muttered, but I saw his bravado waver. Ash's power had that effect on people. "I can tell my own damn story."

He turned his stormy gaze to me and I swore my blood pressure shot up right in that moment.

"I'm not *exactly* a demon in the same sense that you're not, Deja," he began. "Although my history is a bit more convoluted than yours."

My brows pinched in confusion but I waited for him to go on.

"I'm a descendant of Beelzebub. My ancestors were born from one of his trysts with some random human woman thousands of years ago," he said with a flippant wave of his hand. "From there, my lineage is a mixture of incubus, non-magical human, and witch. In the most general sense of the term, I am a witch. But apparently, I'm also something more."

He looked to Ash nervously, almost shyly, who looked to me in turn.

"How much do you know about Beelzebub, love?"

"Not much," I admitted. "I've met him briefly but you and Lucifer are the only ones I really know in the First Hierarchy."

"Right." Ash chewed his lip. "Even when he was an angel with Lucifer and I, he was always a bit odd. After, ah." He began to look incredibly uncomfortable. "After all of us fell, you included, he was apparently jealous of what you and I had. He wanted you for himself."

"Oh-kay." I lifted an eyebrow. "I don't recall ever getting that vibe from him." My memories of Beelzebub were fuzzy at best. Millennia had passed since I last saw or spoke to him. When I did, it was always with Ash and Lucifer present and my attention had been primarily focused on them.

"Honestly, the three of us were infatuated with you." Ash

shrugged and allowed a tiny smirk. "Lucifer got over it and thought of you as a daughter, eventually. As Hell's ruler, he's always had plenty of humans and succubi to keep him occupied. But supposedly Beelz secretly pined for you for centuries. After adding these two in the mix," he nodded at Raum and Sal. "His jealousy got even worse, but he still kept it under wraps."

I sighed and pinched the bridge of my nose. "That is flattering I suppose, but what does this have to do with Seth?"

"After your soul became whole again," he continued awkwardly. "We all knew you'd be an adult woman before your memories returned and you came into your power again. He saw your return as a chance to have you to himself, in his weird, only Beelzebub-logic way."

My gaze shifted over to Seth, who looked back at me expression-lessly with those stormy eyes. For the life of me, I couldn't remember what Beelzebub's eyes looked like.

"What do you mean by that?" I asked barely above a whisper.

"Like with witch's magic, the strength of demon abilities doesn't diminish as it gets passed on throughout the generations," Seth explained. For once he sounded normal, not like he was trying to insult me. "It stays constant or in rare occurrences, genetic muta-tions strengthen abilities or reveal dormant ones that didn't show up in previous generations."

"I still don't understand where this is going." My voice began to tremor. Even with all this information, I didn't know what to expect. But with how grim my guys looked, I was certain I wouldn't like it.

"Through his blood link to Seth," Ash picked up on explaining. "Beelzebub was able to essentially genetically enhance his demon abilities."

"That's a polite way of putting it," Seth snapped, the harsh bite returning to his voice.

"While developing in his mother's womb, Beelz enhanced Seth's innate shadow magic on top of his regular witch powers." Ash licked his lips and looked away from me with a sigh. "He also brought forth and amplified dormant incubus powers."

"Incubus powers?" I repeated. "You mean, like seduction?"

"It explains why you hate me with every fiber of your being and at the same time, feel irresistibly attracted to me," Seth sneered.

"I am not attracted to you!"

The denial came out before I could think, and once it was out, I knew it only made me look more guilty. My gut churned because it was true, no matter how badly I wanted it to be false.

Seth seemed completely nonplussed at my response. "You can't resist our chemistry, sweetheart."

"Actually, I can," I retorted, not ready to leave my comfortable bubble of denial. "Incubus powers don't work on me. I've come across thousands in my lifetimes and only ever had eyes for these three standing next to me."

"Wrong." Seth crossed his arms and smirked, mimicking Ash's movements. "Your boy Raum has some incubus in him. Was it not lust at first sight when you first took him into your harem?"

"That's different," I hissed. "Lucifer made him for me. He was exactly what I needed." My hand groped for Raum to draw him closer to me. His large hand slid across my lower back but his body felt stiff behind me.

"Physical chemistry is an interesting thing," Seth mused, stroking his jaw. "Non-magical humans feel it too. Explosively, sometimes. Incubi have the power to seduce almost anyone, but sometimes there's a chemical reaction that just shoots off the charts. It's a connection that's rare and undeniable."

"For once, I agree with you," I said, pulling Ash and Sal closer too. "And I've been lucky enough to find that connection exactly three times since the birth of humanity."

Seth's face dropped into a scowl. "Oh, you've found it a fourth time, sweetheart. Only this time, it's because my ancestor decided to make me a goddamn genetic freak."

19
DEJA

"Lucifer and I decided Beelzebub must face consequences for his actions," Ash said solemnly. "Our kind is strictly forbidden from imposing our own agendas on other beings without their consent. That includes meddling in their genetic development before birth."

He looked at Seth and held out his hand. "I understand now you're a victim and did what was necessary to survive. You're welcome to stay as a guest here, not a prisoner. I promise your ancestor will be punished accordingly."

Seth regarded him coolly for a moment before accepting his hand and shaking it. Meanwhile, I felt like I was watching my life through another dimension.

"Wait." I tugged at Ash's sleeve. "Shouldn't we discuss this first?"

"No."

I flinched. The tone in that one word was the harshest way Ash had ever spoken to me.

"Ash," I tried again. "I really feel like-"

"It's not up for discussion, Lilith." His eyes flashed with white-hot fire. "I'm still the one in charge here. Seth has gone a bit rogue but we've concluded he acted in your best interest. He's staying. That's the end of it."

It took everything in me not to shrink back from his gaze, not to mention the dark, shadowy power exuding off of him like plumes of smoke. He always kept so calm and in control and still I knew this was only a fraction of his power.

Weakly, I gave a tiny nod, and he finally looked away. Ash was not one to throw his power or authority around to show off, so seeing it now made me realize how serious he was.

"Bathroom's down there," Ash pointed down the hall to Seth. "We can loan you some of our clothes for the time being and there's a spare bedroom upstairs. Help yourself to anything in the kitchen, although Sal's the best cook out of all of us."

My angel's shoulders sagged as he rubbed his eyes, suddenly appearing weary.

"I'll be in my study," he said softly, all the heavy-handed authority gone from his voice. We all moved out of his way as he abruptly exited the kitchen. Part of me wanted to follow him, but we could all see he didn't want to be disturbed then. Least of all by me.

Discomfort clenched in my gut. Why did I have the awful feeling that he was somehow blaming me for all this?

Sal muttered something about finding clothes for Seth and bounded up the stairs, taking two steps at a time. Seth made his way to the bathroom and shut the door, clicking the lock into place. That left only me and Raum in the kitchen. I stared at him blankly, wondering if he was going to awkwardly leave me too.

But my raven-haired demon seemed unfazed by these recent revelations and held his arm out to me with a smirk.

"Shall we go for a stroll, luv?" he said in a mocking British accent.

I huffed out a humorless laugh but took his elbow anyway and followed his lead out to the back porch.

"So what do you make of all this?" I asked as we descended the steps and strolled across the forest floor.

"Doesn't matter," he answered, dropping his arm to lace his fingers with mine. "It already is and our opinions and feelings won't do a damn thing to change that."

"It does matter, though," I argued. "First he's our enemy and now he's our new house guest? And he has to stay here while our chemistry or whatever makes us want to hate-fuck each other? Like, I'm just supposed to be okay with that?"

"He needs protection now that the hunters are after him too," Raum pointed out. "This is the safest place for him. And Ash is right. At the center of it all, he's a victim. He had no choice in becoming what he is."

"He didn't have to pretend to be a hunter. He didn't have to let Diana into my mind to fuck with me," I shot back. "Those were choices he made."

"Baby, you might not be fully understanding his circumstances," Raum said gently. "You are special but you have no problem passing as a pure witch. He has too much demon in him to get by among witches. The kid had to greatly downplay his demon heritage and yes, probably felt forced to join the hunter's guild and do other things to avoid suspicion."

We walked silently through the moonlit forest for a few moments. A distant wolf howled, and I wondered if it was Orion.

"Did you know this about him the whole time?" I asked.

"No. That's why Ash left to make sure but," he paused hesitantly. "I think the three of us felt inclined to trust him right before we left San Francisco when he outed himself to us." He squeezed my hand protectively. "Of course, you weren't inclined to trust anyone after that so it was no surprise that you wouldn't."

"Why are the other two acting so weird?" I blurted out. "They're being all shifty like I actually want to sleep with him and I sure as fuck don't."

Raum stopped walking abruptly and turned to face me. His eyes looked endlessly black in the darkness of night.

"You really don't think that'll change?"

"No, it won't," I answered defiantly. "I have the three of you. Why would I want him? The only reason I do is because of Beelzebub's fucking magic."

My dark, handsome demon drew me close with a surprisingly gentle embrace. "It's been just the four of us for so long. They're not happy with the possibility of that changing. Frankly, neither am I. But if you made that decision, we would accept it."

"Nothing will change," I repeated, propping my chin on his chest to look up at him. "Fuck knows you three are all I can handle, anyway."

He let out a throaty chuckle as he dropped a kiss to my lips. "Oh, my little witch. You birthed an entire race of magical people and wield all four elements, plus shadow magic. You can handle so much more than you realize."

* * *

I got up early the next morning to prepare a tea blend of various herbs I found growing around the house. Lemongrass, peppermint and just a pinch of the silver needle Ash got me to round it all out. The dehydrator was taking too long, so I used the shadow side of my Earth magic to zap all the moisture and life from the lemongrass and peppermint. I smiled as I pinched the dried leaves between my fingers. Perfect.

I was so absorbed in my tea-making, I didn't notice Seth enter the kitchen until he cleared his throat. He looked stunningly different from yesterday. Sal's clothes fit him well and he looked clean and well-rested.

"Morning," I mumbled, returning to my work.

"Morning," he greeted just as jovially, keeping a wide distance between us. "Is there any coffee?"

Ugh, he was one of those people. I could let it slide with Ash but with this guy, I'd latch onto any reason to dislike him. Anything to keep from thinking about him inappropriately and damn it, why did he have to smell so good after a shower? Asshole.

"Ash keeps it up there." I jerked my head toward a cupboard without looking up as I gently ground my dried herbs with my mortar and pestle.

He moved closer to rummage through the cupboard and the spicy scent of soap and men's deodorant filled my nostrils. If it were any of my guys, I would have turned into him and hugged him tight. And with him, I still felt tempted to. Damn it.

"Hey, listen." I stole a glance at him, barely believing what I was about to say. "I owe you an apology."

His lips curved in a smirk as his stormy eyes lit up with surprise. Of course the asshole would enjoy this to the fullest extent.

"For?" he inquired.

"Hitting you," I said. "And just, you know, being a bitch since you've been here."

To my complete shock, he returned his attention to his coffee as he lifted his shoulder in a shrug.

"It's alright. You all had your suspicions about me and I didn't exactly have the most trustworthy track record with you." He lifted his gaze back to me. "You are slowly becoming a better apologizer, though. I'll give this one a six out of ten."

Ah, there it was. I rolled my eyes and returned to my tea. "Forget I said anything," I muttered.

"Too late," he snickered. "No takesies-backsies."

Damn it. Why was I smiling at that? Why was I allowing myself to enjoy this brief, fleeting interaction with him?

And why was I so damn curious now that I knew he was essentially a witch-demon mutant?

"So what was it like growing up with your powers so advanced?" I asked him. His life had to be the polar opposite of mine, growing up with no powers at all.

"Shitty," he answered without hesitation. "I came into my powers at five years old. It was too much all at once for someone that young. I had seizures, migraines, and the worst body pains constantly. Kinda hard to make friends when you're laid up in bed all the time."

"Fuck," I breathed, taken aback. Clearly having such power wasn't all it was cracked up to be. "That does suck. Sorry to hear it."

He shrugged again. "Reaching deep into my shadows was the only solace I found. Pain taught me the self-control to wield my powers effectively."

I swallowed. It made sense. My powers were hidden away so deeply from lack of use, I had to look through my shadows to find them. And I was practiced enough that they didn't hurt me when I came into awareness of them.

Seth wasn't so lucky. His powers were so overwhelming he had to force them into his shadows to make the pain go away. I wondered if Raum had to do something similar. He also got terrible pains and migraines from his visions until he learned to control his new power.

"There's one thing I don't get," I mused out loud.

"Only one?" Seth jabbed with a curl of his lip.

I brushed off his playful jab but my face still grew hot. With him around, it would be like having two Raums teasing me all the time. Fuck, better not think of that.

"Just... why?" I spread my palms. "How does doing this to you benefit Beelzebub in any way?"

Seth's eyes jerked away from mine, and his whole body stiffened. I could almost swear I saw him shiver too.

"He took control of my body," he answered, looking out the kitchen window. "And my mind."

Fear gripped my lungs and squeezed. "What?"

"You know how demons supposedly possess people? You can thank him for that." Seth swallowed, and I just realized how hard it was for him to talk about this. "He... made me do things. Sick bastard got a kick out of that."

"Fuck." I regretted asking. It felt wrong of me to pry, but I couldn't help but notice his use of past tense. "But he doesn't anymore?"

"No. I learned how he was using me and shut him out years ago." He looked back at me, expressionless. "That was how I got into the hunter's guild, actually. I told them a demon possessed me for years and I learned all kinds of hellish secrets to use against them. I wasn't technically lying."

"Jesus," I breathed.

"Yeah, some help he was," Seth smirked.

"I just can't imagine what that would be like." My hand reached out to rest on his forearm as if of its own will. "I mean, I thought Diana being in my head was as invasive as it got. I couldn't live with someone controlling me, forcing me to do and think certain things."

Seth looked down at my hand on his arm but made no move to pull away. "Trust me," he murmured. "If I could control my own body during that time, I'd probably not be here today."

Blinking, I pulled my hand away, suddenly aware of the heat of his skin beneath my hand.

"I'm sorry," I stammered. "I really shouldn't have pried."

"It is what it is," he shrugged. Then his lips twitched with a grin. "Eight out of ten apology, by the way."

"Oh, fuck off." I punched him lightly on the arm to his soft, musical laughter.

"It wasn't all bad, I guess." He visibly relaxed, turning around to lean against the counter. "It made my shadow magic even stronger. I'm pretty sure that's how I became able to read your shadows without touching you."

"You really believe that, don't you?" I said after a few pulses of tense silence passed between us. "That pain makes you stronger."

"It reveals what you really are," he answered. "It either shows you're strong enough to push through and grow, or it reveals how weak you are and breaks you for good."

I crossed my arms. "And what if I broke while you were letting Diana have her fun in there?"

"That's what she was hoping for," he admitted. "But I knew you wouldn't."

"How?"

He grinned. "Because you lived through having your soul ripped out by a vengeful angel and shattered like glass. It took you a while to come back, but you did."

I didn't know how to respond. Did Seth just actually give me a compliment?

A sudden flash of movement drew our attention to the kitchen window. Something temporarily blocked out the sun, casting a shadow over the front porch.

"Holy shit!" Seth took a few steps back. "That's a gigantic fucking bird."

A majestic golden eagle descended from the sky, its wings outstretched and deadly talons open. The bird of prey gracefully grabbed the porch railing with those talons as it landed and fixated its dark amber eyes on me through the window.

"That's Chase," I said, moving to the front door. "Come on, I'll introduce you."

Seth looked confused but followed me out front.

By the time we stepped out to the porch, Chase had almost completely shifted back to human again. He hopped off the railing and stood as his feathers sunk back into his skin. His now human face looked tense and my throat tightened.

"Hey," I said. "What's up?"

"What the fuck just happened?" Next to me, Seth stared bug-eyed at the dark-haired man who had been an eagle just a few seconds earlier.

"He's a shifter. I'll explain later," I said with a wave of my hand.

"I spotted humans coming straight toward you from the south-east," Chase told me. "A group of five maybe a half mile away. Orion said they smelled like witches."

"Fuck." Seth and I looked at each other.

"Hunters," he said bitterly.

20

DEJA

We alerted my guys immediately. Ash was pissed.

"I haven't had time to set up another anchor," he said through gritted teeth. "We're stuck here. We have to fight."

"They are most likely scouts who have been tracking me," Seth said with regret in his voice. "I'm not as stealthy as you guys. But they won't want to fight us. They'll just want to confirm we're here and report back."

"We can't let that happen." Ash gave a cold, pointed look at Raum and Sal. When Sal grinned with delight, I knew that look meant giving permission to kill.

"What can I do?" I piped up.

"Nothing. You're staying inside." Ash turned his cold gaze to me. "Keep away from the windows. Don't look outside."

"What? Fuck that!" I yelled. "I'm as strong as any of you. Let me beat some hunter ass!"

"No! You're their number one target." Ash's face softened as he wrapped a hand around the back of my neck. "We can't risk losing you. Either of you."

A flutter in my low belly made me wonder if it was nerves or my daughter protesting too.

"Fine," I lied through gritted teeth. "Don't be dumbasses out there."

Ash's mouth twitched before he dropped a soft kiss to my mouth. "Wouldn't dream of it, love."

Raum came up to me next and gave me a kiss full of tongue and teeth, clearly showing Ash how it was supposed to be done. I could feel Ash's eyeroll from a few feet away.

"Back before you know it, baby," Raum grinned with a wink.

Sal was nowhere to be seen, which likely meant he already shifted and had slunk away to stalk his prey in the woods. The other three filed out the front door with Ash leading and Seth bringing up the rear. Right before they closed the door, I made a last ditch effort to join the fight.

I stuck my foot out to block the door from closing and turned to slide my body through the gap, but Seth was too fast.

His hand pressed against my chest and pushed me back against the wall with surprising strength. It didn't hurt, but left me stunned enough not to fight back.

Our eyes locked as we both breathed tense, ragged breaths, his palm splayed out on my bare skin and dangerously close to my breasts. Damn my love for oversized V-necks. All the air seemed to get sucked out of the room and I couldn't stop staring at his full lips again.

And just as quickly as it happened, he pulled his hand away and shut the door behind him on his way out.

I immediately ran to the kitchen window, fuck what Ash told me.

The three of them walked casually out to the clearing in front of the house. All of them cloaked in shadow, looking shrouded in darkness despite the sunlight overhead. They would be completely invisible to the hunters. I would have to thank Chase and the shifters somehow after this was over. If it weren't for them looking out for us, we would've been ambushed rather than ready and waiting.

A few long, tense moments of silence passed until movement from the treeline caught my eye. Five people, dressed in all black tactical gear came running into the clearing, straight for the guys they couldn't see. They looked wide-eyed and afraid and I soon saw why.

A huge mountain lion came loping after them. Sal was barely running at all, yet still swiping his massive paws at the heels of the hunters. He slowed to a trot and yawned as they came running up on the other three, who were more than ready.

All five hunters suddenly grimaced and fell flat on their backs as if they ran straight into a glass wall. It was almost comical.

The three shadowed guys gestured through the air as they cast their spells, with Sal circling around the hunters to corral them in.

My breath relaxed. This looked like it would be easy. Even if there were five hunters to four demons, they were no match for my guys.

Plus Seth. Because Seth wasn't mine and never would be.

One of the hunters, the leader from what it seemed, shouted an order to the others, and they each drew an unusual-looking weapon from a holster on their backs. It looked like something between a gun and a crossbow, and cast bright glares in the sunlight from being an entirely bright silver color.

Immediately something changed. My guys—plus Seth—looked tense. Maybe even worried. Which made me worried. I pressed my nose to the kitchen window, not caring if anyone saw me.

And then a battle broke out like nothing I'd ever seen.

Everyone moved lightning fast, too fast for my eyes to catch up. Magic sparked and crackled through the air as demon and witch cast offensive spells at each other. I felt the auras of these demon hunters and knew they weren't ordinary witches. They were highly trained and powerful, maybe even an elite force.

But none of them fired their strange weapons yet. Some kind of harness attached it to the top of their forearms, leaving their hands free to cast magic at the demons. The guys held their own but the shield around them was slowly breaking down. I gripped the windowsill with white knuckles and willed my feet to stay still, despite every instinct telling me to run out there and help them.

Sal lunged at one hunter in a blur of tan fur and large teeth. The guy pointed his weapon as he tried to back up but my lion was too fast. The hunter's scream abruptly cut off by Sal tearing out a chunk of his throat.

A female hunter saw her partner go down and screamed as she ran to his body. From the way she acted, I gathered he was her lover. She raised her weapon while kneeling beside him, but Sal had already disappeared behind the treeline for cover.

She looked toward the protective shield guarding the other three, eyes filled with pain and rage. Skillfully securing her weapon, she hurtled spell after spell at the shield. A fire witch, her heartbreak became her fuel as her fireballs grew larger, hotter, deadlier.

Ash and Seth were still invisible when the shield crumpled away and dodged when she fired off the last one. Raum shifted into bird form to escape the blaze and soared high above the trees. He was a smaller target but now she could see him.

My heart stopped as she aimed her weapon at the black speck flying through the air.

No, no no! I thought. Someone get her!

Ash and Seth were fighting off an onslaught from the other hunters. Sal came bursting out of the trees, running straight for her but was too late.

She fired, and what shot out of the weapon I could only describe as a small burst of sunlight.

It hit Raum squarely on his feathered abdomen. Like in slow motion, his wings stopped flapping. He hovered for the briefest moment before falling from the sky. The next thing I knew, I was running out the front door.

I took my eyes from Raum's falling form just to cover myself. Sal pounced on the woman who shot him a split second later. He ripped her throat out, but she died with a vengeful smile on her face.

"DEJA!" Ash screamed as I ran past him.

The hunters fighting them trained their weapons on me. Seth jumped behind one and snapped his neck to the side. I directed a tiny bit of Air to the closest one and aimed it straight for his heart. He stopped and clutched at his chest as my one tiny air bubble in his aorta began giving him a heart attack.

Raum was in human form on the ground as I ran up to him. His whole body shook and convulsed as if having a seizure. A gaping wound on his abdomen was wet with blood. I pressed my hands into it immediately and began sending my healing magic through my palms.

"D-D-Deja," his teeth chattered as he reached for me, his eyes rolling with pain. "I l-l-love y-y-you."

"Sshhh, baby. You're okay." I leaned down and kissed his forehead, only then realizing how much I was trembling, too. "Let me focus so I can heal you."

He continued trying to speak through his shaking and chattering but I ignored him as I shut my eyes tight, trying to send all my healing magic into his body but something was wrong. Very wrong.

Every time I tried pushing magic into him, it pushed back like magnets repelling each other. The harder I tried, the more pushback I got, until my hands physically lifted off him.

"What the fuck?" I cried panicking. "Why isn't this working?"

"N-no. U-u-use." Tears streamed from Raum's eyes. He was growing paler. Even his rich, dark eyes seemed to be lightening as life began fading away from them.

"Raum? Baby, stay with me." I pressed a hand to his face while keeping the other over his wound, even though that seemed like the least important issue. "Talk to me, lover. Tell me how to fix this."

"C-c-can't." His tone was somehow apologetic even while

wracked with pain. Even then, a tiny smirk formed on his lips as he reached up to touch my face. "Hope I m-m-made y-y-you h-h-happy. L-love you s-s-so m-m-m-much."

"No, you're not leaving me!" My tears splashed down on his face like rain. "You said you wouldn't leave me again, you promised! You're fucking immortal, this can't be happening."

I tried desperately again to shove healing magic into him but it just wouldn't go through. Someone came up next to us but I couldn't tear my eyes away from my dying lover on the ground.

"I'm so sorry, Deja." Seth's voice cracked with emotion as he kneeled next to me.

"He won't heal! Why can't I heal him?!" I cried hysterically, desperately pressing on the wound as Raum's grip on me grew weaker until his hand fell limply to his side.

"He got hit by the only thing that can kill a demon," Seth said apologetically. "An angel's kiss."

WITCH'S REBIRTH
UNHOLY TRINITY BOOK 5

PROLOGUE
LILITH

No one threw parties like Lucifer.

His cavernous home in Hell was filled to the brim with demons and hell-creatures of all imaginable shapes and sizes. Sultry succubi, barely wearing anything at all, slithered through the crowd, rubbing up on as many bodies as possible in hopes of getting lucky that night.

In contrast, the handsome incubi played coy. Dressed from head to toe in flattering dark suits, perfectly groomed with drinks in hand and charming smiles. Whoever fell for their seductive charms would have to work to take an incubus to bed. But it would be well worth the effort.

The few human souls stared with their mouths agape at everything going on, from the orgies happening openly on the floor to simply Hell's many horned and winged residents.

At first glance, I couldn't tell if it was awe or fear they stared with. Contrary to popular belief, many humans didn't end up in hell for being awful people. Certainly some did, but those were never invited to the parties. The ones invited were hand-picked by Lucifer himself. Their reactions entertained us all, and they often learned very valuable lessons for how the world truly worked.

"Drink?"

I held out a goblet of wine to a young blonde woman. She flinched at the sound of my voice and her eyes darted over me quickly, as if searching for my horns, talons or wings. I was one of the few "normal" looking partygoers and this seemed to put her at ease slightly.

"What is it?" Her eyes narrowed in suspicion as if I was trying to poison her.

"Just wine." I gave her a friendly smile. "This is a vintage from Greece. Lucifer has impeccable taste. It's why the Greeks revere him as their own god, Dionysus."

She shuddered at the Lord of Hell's name and gave me a disgusted look. "Of course the devil would parade as a false idol and glorify a drink to lower inhibitions. I'm surrounded by seduction and sin!"

"Better get used to it," I said in a bored tone, helping myself to the beverage. "The only way out of here is to return to earth as a succubus, then you can work your way up the hierarchy from there. Honestly, there seems to be a shortage of high-ranking demonesses lately. Old Lucifer could always used more."

"I don't belong here!" she whispered in a panic. "I was chaste! I was loyal to His word! Something must have gone wrong!"

"They never get it wrong," I told her, almost apologetically. "You're here for a reason and I bet if you think real hard, you know exactly why. If your actions were pure, that means your thoughts weren't." I flashed her another smile. "But you can't be *that* bad, otherwise you'd never see the party. So relax and talk to a cute demon man. Not him, though." I pointed out Raum, talking animatedly to a small group who laughed uproariously at whatever he was saying. "He's mine."

Her mouth flew open, but I cut her off quickly. "Oh, not those two either, also mine."

I pointed out Ash and Sal, standing rapt at attention next to Lucifer, who seemed to be explaining something to them. Sal nodded sharply, muscles coiled and flexed as if ready for a fight. Ash's sharp eyes never left Lucifer's face, his mouth tight and unsmiling.

I had to find out what was happening but first I couldn't stop beaming with pride. All three of my men looked handsome as fuck tonight. Just the way they carried themselves showed their rank and stature among demonkind. If that wasn't enough, they wore crisp, tailored slacks, shirts, and shoes polished to a high shine. All in black, of course.

Raum unbuttoned his shirt to the middle of his sculpted chest, showing off his taut muscles and the light dusting of dark hair between his pecs. Sal rolled up his sleeves past his elbows, the corded veins and muscles in his forearms on display. Only Ash wore his suit as it was properly meant to be, but down here his beautiful black wings were on full display. I always missed seeing them and hated that he had to hide them on earth.

I gave him those wings with my healing magic after the fall tore his original ones apart. He wore them proudly whenever he could, which made me swell up with immeasurable love and pride.

The human girl stared at me unashamedly after pointing out who was off-limits to her.

"Who *are* you?" she demanded.

"You probably know me as Lilith."

I shot her a wink and walked off toward my fallen angel across the room before she had a chance to respond. The crowd parted for me subtly as I walked by, which made me stand a little taller and sway my hips a little wider.

While I wasn't officially a member of demon society, everyone knew who I was. And they knew who my lovers were. Every resident of Hell was given basic respect, but my accomplishments throughout my lifetimes had earned me just a touch more.

What I loved most about these hellions was they took in all kinds of creatures under their wings, horns, and hooves. Lucifer truly made this a safe place for the devious, damned, and ostracized. For a select few, the ones who preyed upon innocents like women and children with no remorse, this place was truly Hell in the classic sense of the word. But no one talked about the best parts like the parties, because we didn't want the angels to stop sending us their rejects. We took pride in taking in those who had been cast away.

"Lilith, my dearest." A large clawed hand took hold of my upper arm, stopping me in my tracks. I turned to look at the face of who dared to touch me without permission.

"Beelzebub." I gave Ash's fellow fallen angel and Lucifer's co-ruler a tight smile. Despite his position of high reverence, this particular Prince of Hell always gave me the creeps.

His face was classically handsome with pale blue eyes, a strong jaw, straight nose and perfectly straight teeth. He could've been Ash's older brother or cousin. But while Lucifer and Ash healed to near perfection from the injuries of their falls, Beelzebub didn't seem as lucky.

A long red scar ran from under his chin and disappeared under the opening of his shirt on his chest. Long, curving horns sprouted from the top of his forehead. They were honestly majestic and beautiful, at least three feet long and gently sloping backwards like an ibex. His hands were vaguely humanlike in shape, but covered in shimmering reptilian scales and topped with long black claws.

His horns and hands never seemed to change, unlike Lucifer who changed his horns like a fashion accessory. Ash never got any animal features from his fall, but he nearly died and had his wings torn to shreds in the process of saving me.

"Won't you join me for a drink?" He swept a clawed hand in the direction of a lounge area with luxurious couches and a low table covered in goblets and other substances. "I feel like Ashtaroth and Lucifer take all of your time lately. You've been with us for centuries and it seems we've barely gotten to know each other."

A few demons lounged in his area with at least one human male. The human plowed into a gorgeous, dark-haired succubus, fucking her with all his might as she mewled like a kitten. At the same time, she pawed at another demon, trying to entice him to join in on their fun. He ignored her however and seemed more interested in the array of drugs and drinks on the table.

While the scene playing out in front of me didn't phase me, I knew exactly what Beelz hinted at in *getting to know each other*. And I had zero desire to get to know him in that way.

"Thank you," I continued with my tight smile at him as I yanked my arm out of his grip. "But I was just on my way over to see Ash."

His smile fell and I noticed his eye twitched with tension. It seemed even down here, some men felt they were entitled to a woman's attention, especially if they were in any sort of position of power. Thankfully, I had powers of my own.

"My love."

A firm hand squeezed my waist, and Ash's familiar earthy scent filled my nose.

"Hey, love." I turned into him, smiling genuinely this time and nuzzled his neck openly so Beelzebub could see. Hopefully, the message was clear.

Beelzebub walked off abruptly, not even acknowledging Ash's presence.

"Seems I came over at just the right time." The feathers on his wing tickled the back of my neck.

"I had it handled," I told him, sliding my arm through his. "Now what were you three discussing so intently back there?"

"Him, actually." Ash nodded at Beelz, who retreated to his corner of the lounge like a sulking child. He settled on a couch, said something to the succubus getting fucked, who proceeded to bury her head in his crotch as she yanked his pants down.

"Like what, he's acting like an entitled human at a full moon festival?" I scoffed.

"Worse." Ash turned us away, and we walked together to a quieter corner of the party. "Lucifer suspects he's partaking in some unethical practices." With a sigh, he lowered himself onto a plush, empty loveseat and pulled me into his lap.

"What kind of unethical practices?" I sat on his thighs and looped my arms around his neck, massaging the tight muscles there. Sometimes I felt Ash took his position too seriously.

"Recruiting followers by means of control, not free will." His face was steely, his pale eyes sharp. "Which goes against everything we stand for."

"What can be done?" I slid my hands down his chest and nipped at his neck. His body relaxed slightly beneath me, although one distinct part of him grew harder.

"Nothing yet," he murmured, frustration evident in his voice. "We can't prove it yet but Lucifer has strong suspicions. And Lucifer is never wrong."

I ground my hips into his lap, teasing his thick bulge into a rock hard pillar as I kissed his neck. He moaned and grabbed my hips, pushing away the fabric of my already skimpy dress.

"Then trust in Lucifer," I whispered into his ear. "And when you find one of his victims, bring them to me."

"What for, love?" he asked, running his hands across my body in fascination, as if this was his first time touching me.

"Because," I breathed. "I want to show them what it's like to take control back into their own hands."

1
DEJA

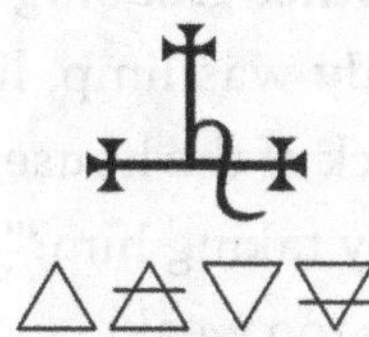

The pain and hopelessness of watching a man I loved die before my eyes was indescribable. It was more than soul crushing because he was never supposed to die. This was never supposed to happen. He was never supposed to leave me.

Just minutes ago he was in bird form, a beautiful black raven. Just this morning he smirked at me with that panty-melting smile and those luscious dark eyes. He was my voice of reason with the new confusing dynamic of having Seth in the house and my unwanted attraction toward him.

This was not how it was supposed to go at all. They were supposed to kill the demon hunters coming after us. My men, the loves of my life, were supposed to be immortal.

Someone pulled me away from Raum's limp, lifeless body. My limbs felt like concrete swimming through mud to reach him but something kept dragging me away. More people surrounded him so I could only see his legs. I was vaguely aware of more bodies lying around on the ground. Why was so much death surrounding me? I didn't want any of this.

The person holding me was strong. No amount of fighting, struggling, begging, and sobbing allowed me to run back to Raum's side. He needed me! He didn't know what it was like to die and shouldn't have to go through it alone.

Eventually my struggle ran out of strength and I collapsed, exhausted. Every breath ran jaggedly through my lungs like knives. I didn't want to breathe anymore if it was this painful without Raum.

Through my blurry tears I saw two people pick him up, one under his armpits and the other grabbing his legs. His head rolled to one side and his whole body was limp, lifeless. I watched them go around the corner to the back of the house.

"No... no, where are they taking him?" I tried to fight against the arms that held me but I was too weak.

"Stay with me, beautiful. If anyone can save him, it's those two."

I twisted around to find the source of that familiar voice and found myself looking up into bright green eyes, reddened like they too had been crying.

"You're in shock," he said to me. "I'm so sorry for this, beautiful. We should have known. We should have been better prepared."

"What about them?" I looked out across the clearing where five more bodies laid out between us and the treeline. I still wasn't sure what I was asking.

"They're dead for good." Sal. It was Sal holding me. He was safe, not hurt. My lungs released with slightly less pain. "Not like Raum. He's not gone yet, beautiful. We both know he's too strong for that." His arms tightened around me. "We both know he loves you too much to let go."

"We need to dispose of the bodies." The words came out of me robotically. In a matter of seconds, I went from feeling shattered to feeling nothing. In trying to cope, my emotions seemed to shut down completely. I couldn't handle the uncertainty of not knowing if Raum would live or die, so my mind simply turned it off.

"We can do that later," Sal told me. "Right now—"

The whoosh of fire from my fingertips cut him off, nearly

singeing his arm hair in the process. Five times I set fire to the corpses in my front yard who were once demon hunters. Why did they find us so quickly? Was there something Seth still wasn't telling us? And how in Lucifer's name did they get ahold of angel-kissed weapons, the only substance that could kill a demon for good?

These questions filed through my head like a checklist as the five separate bonfires roared before me. They distracted me from thinking about Raum.

Sal loosened his hold on me when he realized I wasn't going to run anymore. He rubbed my back in a way that was supposed to be comforting, but I felt absolutely nothing.

"Diana's behind this."

White-hot rage filled me as my grandmother's face infiltrated my mind. The only good thing she ever did for me was reveal my witch powers. I used to think I owed her everything for that. But that was before I learned she killed my mother in a blood magic spell that was meant to kill me before I was born.

The psychotic old bitch came to me under the guise of wanting to teach me magic, but she really wanted me under her thumb so she could finish the job. She almost succeeded a second time, but not before I discovered the rest of my magic. Alongside Earth, I found my Fire and Water, and nearly drowned that murderous cunt.

But I couldn't do it. I couldn't just murder someone. That would make me no better than her.

Now I didn't give a fuck about having any moral high ground. I wished I had drowned her with that water spell. If there was anything she knew how to do well, it was hurt me.

When we first escaped San Francisco, she plagued my mind with nightmares of my worst fears—losing my unborn daughter and being completely alone without the comfort of my men. Not even escaping the city released her hold on me.

Now she hit me where it really mattered, where she knew I could be destroyed. And this time, she would not get away with it.

"We don't know that yet, beautiful."

I realized Sal was trying to be calming but at that moment he only pissed me off.

"I *do* know," I snapped. "Only she would make sure to send out a team with the ability to kill demons. It doesn't matter to her if she gets me first. She knows targeting those I love would get a reaction out of me."

"She's not the only one targeting our kind," he said gently. "Look, none of us have clear heads right now. Try to relax."

How ironic that the demon known for his bloodthirst was telling me to calm down. His hand slid across my belly as he pulled me back to lean against him.

"Think of our daughter," he whispered softly. "When she grows up, she'll never know this."

"We don't know that." I gritted my teeth. "It's the same shit every lifetime. I die young and my kids grow up with targets on their backs because of what they are or who they're born from."

"But you always come back," he whispered in my ear. "You are unstoppable. Not even a span of a thousand years could stop you."

I wished he'd stop. I didn't want a pep talk. None of it was true. I couldn't stop Raum from getting hit. I wanted to scream and cry and kill. I wanted to inflict the same kind of pain inflicted on me and my loved ones. Not just Raum but my mother too. She didn't deserve any of what she got from that evil hag just for carrying me.

"I'm going for a walk." I stood abruptly and headed straight for the woods. "Don't follow me."

"Deja!" Sal called. "It's not safe. There could be more."

"Who gives a fuck?!" I yelled, not looking back. "I'm fucking unstoppable, remember?"

He left me alone, thankfully.

I stomped through the forest without any sense of which direction I was going or how far. I just wanted to be away from it all. Away from the possibility that Raum would die, away from having to fight my own kind that betrayed me, and away from my fucking messed up feelings for Seth.

I walked until I simply stopped. Not because I was tired or collapsed in tears but my body just didn't want to move anymore.

I sat on a soft patch of moss, dappled sunlight filtering through the trees. It would have been pretty and peaceful had I been in the state of mind to enjoy it.

Earth magic still pulsed all around me but my senses felt dulled. It was like trying to peer through a dirty window and barely being able to see anything. I felt like a failure for not healing him. Why couldn't I do it? Why wasn't I able to use my greatest gift to save the man I loved?

A rustling nearby jolted me out of my self-pity. I looked up to see a blue-eyed fox with torn, tattered ears peering at me through the brush.

"Hey Astrid," I said. "Please stay in your fox form if you don't mind? I don't really feel like talking to people right now."

She nodded, an oddly human gesture for a fox and crept out of the brush slowly. Her head and tail lowered, and her ears pulled back as she approached me.

"You can sit with me, it's fine," I told her.

She lowered her belly to the ground and began casually licking her paws as if nothing was wrong. Honestly, I was grateful for that. If she looked at me with those eerily human eyes, it might have been too much.

Absentmindedly I reached out and scratched the dense, red fur on her neck. She pressed closer to me and rolled over to show her belly. It made me smile, if just for half a second.

"Raum got hurt by the demon hunters," I told her. "And I couldn't heal him. I used to think losing my guys would be impossible. They've survived this long after all. But now that I could possibly lose him... I'm more than scared. I feel useless. I hate that I've taken them for granted."

Astrid made a small barking sound and nuzzled my hand, rolling her back against my leg. I scratched her belly and under her chin. Seeing her act like a silly dog made me appreciate her being there even more. Words of encouragement were not what I wanted to hear. All I wanted to know was if Raum would live or die. Until then, I would make do with petting a friendly animal who simply listened to me.

2
DEJA

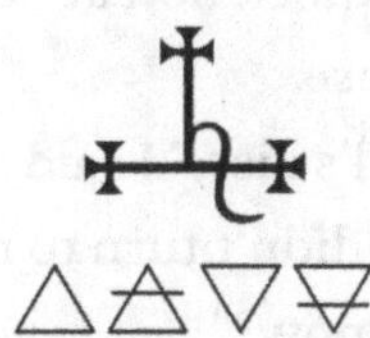

Seth was the one who found me however many hours later. I sensed his aura growing closer like a pleasant, comforting smell becoming stronger. I didn't know how to feel about that. Astrid had curled up in my lap sleeping at that point.

"Do you have anything useful to tell me?" I said more snappily than I intended when he came within earshot.

"Raum is alive," he said flatly. "He's weak but stable."

I expected relief but felt too numb at that point. Gently scooping Astrid off my lap, I rose to my feet and turned to face the stormy-eyed man who had me feeling all out of sorts.

"How?" I asked.

"I'm not sure." He was tactful enough to not shrug, at least. "Ash did it. Because he used to be an angel, he was able to neutralize the magic in the kiss before it did too much damage."

"And why are you the one out here telling me this?" Again, I sounded more bitchy than I meant to.

"Because the other two didn't want to leave his side." His tone was surprisingly patient, with none of that bitter edge I was used to, despite my own voice clearly having plenty of it. "They're patching him up but you can come see him if you'd like. He might respond to healing magic now."

I looked down at Astrid who had woken up. Her ears pricked forward as I knelt down to scratch her between them.

"Thanks for listening to me, friend," I said softly. "I'll talk to you soon."

She gave an affirmative yip and bounced away through the brush in a flash of red fur. With a quick nod at Seth, we walked tensely side by side back toward the house.

"Tell me about the angel's kiss," I said after some silence.

I felt his eyes on me but didn't turn to meet them.

"What do you want to know?"

"What is it? How do you get it? Where does it come from? You know, basic fucking information."

He cleared his throat awkwardly. "Deja, I don't think you're in the best state of mind to—"

"To what, Seth?" I spun to face him, the full force of my emotions dangerously close to boiling over. "To plan a strike back against our enemies? Because I'm female, you think I'm letting my emotions cloud my judgement?"

"That's not what I said." The hard edge returned to his voice, and I liked it. Maybe too much.

"It's what you thought." I crossed my arms, regretting leaving my peaceful spot in the forest with Astrid. Seth was *this* close to getting a slap for trying to infantilize me.

"You have no idea what my thoughts are." His lip curled. There he was. The good old Seth who didn't hold back.

"Then if I'm wrong, give me the information." I retorted. "Don't handle me with kid gloves like I'm about to cry or kill someone just because I'm pissed off."

His eyes narrowed, the storm in them raging. We held each other's gaze for a tense few seconds before continuing on our walk.

"The kiss is essentially an angel's magic in a super concentrated form," he explained. "It will kill the first unpure thing it touches."

"Unpure, meaning?"

"Anything not created by God," he answered. "Only Archangels can create it, but anyone can use it once it's in their possession."

"How would witches get it?" I asked. "Before we left San Francisco, Diana mentioned having one. She was going to use it to end me for good."

"I have no idea," he confessed. "Some kind of deal had to be made. Both sides think they're getting what they want but only the angels are benefiting."

"Killing off demons in the easiest way, having someone else do their dirty work for them," I speculated.

"Exactly," he confirmed.

My gut twisted with every negative emotion possible. Fear, anger, anxiety and worry. How many of these things were out there?

"Can anything stop it?" I asked.

"Only the powers of another angel," he replied. "Or as we recently learned, a fallen angel can pull it off too."

We entered the house, which was eerily silent. I didn't even notice before then there was always some kind of noise associated with my guys when we were all together. Usually Sal banging around in the kitchen, Ash making coffee or pacing around his study. Sometimes Raum even sang in the shower to make me laugh. But now there was only deathly silence.

"They're up in the master bedroom," Seth murmured.

I paused at the base of the stairs, steeling myself for one moment to prepare for seeing Raum in a way I never had before. A gentle brush of fingertips along the small of my back came and went so quickly, I almost thought I had imagined it.

Part of me was comforted by the soft touch but every other part flared up in anger. This was not the time to stew in this ridiculous physical connection between Seth and I. That was all it was and all it ever would be. I didn't even *like* him. It didn't matter if my guys accepted him as a *de facto* demon, he would never be one of mine.

Right before the hunters attacked us, we learned that Seth was a descendant of Beelzebub, one of Hell's rulers and the original three angels Ash fell with. Beelzebub used his blood connection to heighten Seth's demon abilities in his heritage, including the seductive powers of his incubus ancestors. Whether by chance or design, the physical chemistry between us was off-the-charts hot. And I hated every second of it.

I trudged up the stairs, ignoring him behind me.

The master bedroom felt sterile like a hospital room. Sal sat across from the bed with his forearms on his knees and his head in his hands. His aura flickered with volatile sparks. I could feel how pissed off he was before I entered the room. Ash stood looking out the window at the battlefield below.

And my Raum.

I couldn't hold back the sob that tore from my throat as I ran to his side. No amount of breathing exercises could prepare me for this.

He looked dead. His skin was pale, clammy, and far too cold. His closed eyes were encircled with dark rings. A wide bandage wrapped around his torso where the angel's kiss tore through him like he'd been gored by a horned animal. The only indication that he was still alive at all was his faint, shallow breathing.

"You can try healing him. It should work on the physical wound." Ash approached the bedside, standing across from me and looking almost as dead as Raum. His normally bright eyes were dull, lifeless and tired. He leaned one hand against the wall as if he could barely stand. That battle, not to mention counteracting the kiss, must've taken everything out of him.

I nodded, bringing my gaze back down to my lifeless lover in bed and gently placed my hands on his chest. His backward-beating demon heart pulsed too slowly beneath my palm. What I would give to feel that heart racing in time with mine again.

Carefully I lowered my hands until they hovered over the bandage wrapped around his abdomen. Once there, I drew on Earth for healing and Fire for sterilizing the wound. I sent small pulses of magic first, to see if they would be rejected like when he first got hit and fell from the sky.

To my relief, his body absorbed my magic with no resistance at all. As my confidence grew, my magic became stronger. Since I couldn't save him from the angel's kiss, I poured every ounce of my love for him into healing his physical body. His skin slowly returned to normal, his breathing grew deeper. Still, I pushed more magic into him, wishing I could undo everything he just went through.

I didn't realize I was crying until strong arms gently pulled me away. Completely drained of magic, Sal's embrace was all the strength I had left. He rubbed my back and my neck as I leaned against him.

"He's okay," he whispered into my hair. "Thanks to you."

I nodded into his shoulder. My tears were a mixture of relief and fear of what could have been. If anything in the last few hours had been different, I could have been sobbing over my lover's corpse.

Another pair of lips kissing into my hair told me Ash had joined us. I turned and wrapped my arms around his neck.

"Thank you, angel," I whispered. "You saved him. You're the real hero here."

He said nothing but lowered his forehead to mine, pulling me into his chest. Sal kissed the back of my head and pressed his chest into my back. His heart beat a comforting rhythm between my shoulder blades.

The three of us were so emotionally charged yet completely drained. Nearly losing Raum affected all of us, not just me. We leaned on each other for strength, relief, and the will to keep going another day. Another century.

"You should rest, angel. You're exhausted." Ash's eyelids began drooping with fatigue and I kissed each one of them before turning to Sal. "You too, lion. You took down two of those fuckers."

"Three," he quietly corrected with a small twitch of his lips. He glanced over at Raum, now looking like he slept peacefully. "Are you sure, beautiful?"

"Yes." I slid my hands down to his chest and gently pushed him toward the door. "I'll stay with the birdbrain for a while."

That got a light chuckle from him but Ash still looked especially grim.

"We don't know what the damage will really be until he wakes up," he said weakly. "He could have lost half or most of his power before I could stop it. He might be nothing more than human now."

"We'll worry about that when he wakes up, then." I pushed Ash out the door to follow Sal. "Both of you go rest, now. If I find you two spooning, I'm not gonna complain."

My attempt at a joke fell flat as they both walked out of the bedroom like zombies. Seth had disappeared too, probably not wanting to awkwardly observe our three-way embrace.

With a heavy sigh, I dragged the chair Sal had been sitting in directly next to Raum's bedside. I watched his calm, handsome face and the rhythmic rise and fall of his chest as he breathed. He looked good. Better than good, even. My extra healing magic must have added shine to his hair and a bright, flawless quality to his skin.

"I don't care if you're human now," I said softly, careful not to wake him. "I love you and I'm not ready to lose you. If we get old and wrinkled together during this lifetime, that's fine with me. I can accept it if you now have a limited amount of time on this earth with me. We'll make the most of it. But I won't let anyone else take you from me."

I reached for his hand. His skin was warm, and I could feel the strength in those large fingers. For a moment, all my fear melted away. I knew my Raum, the wily, confident trickster. Whatever lasting damage had been done, he'd adapt.

He'd laugh it off, give it the middle finger, and probably invite it to suck his dick for good measure. That was why I loved him. The way he dominated me in bed and made my body heat with a mere look were just extras.

I didn't even realize I fell asleep at his bedside until someone violently shook my shoulder.

"Wake up, sweetheart. We've got some shit to deal with."

Fucking Seth. Again, why was he always the one to fetch me like an errand boy?

"What shit?" I moaned groggily. My hand was still entwined with Raum's, who looked exactly the same. I slept so hard, I could feel the lines of the bedsheets etched into the side of my face.

"An unexpected guest," Seth hissed through gritted teeth. From the way his jaw clenched and his brow furrowed, he was not in the least bit pleased about this guest.

"Where are Ash and Sal?" I asked, following him down the stairs.

"Keeping her restrained down in the basement. Unlike me, she actually deserves to be there."

She?

A spark of hope dared to ignite in my chest. Could Diana actually have been stupid enough to come straight to me? How easy would that be?

With a spring in my step, I followed Seth through the basement door and down the stairs to see the last person I expected bound by Ash and Sal's magic.

"You!" I seethed.

3
DEJA

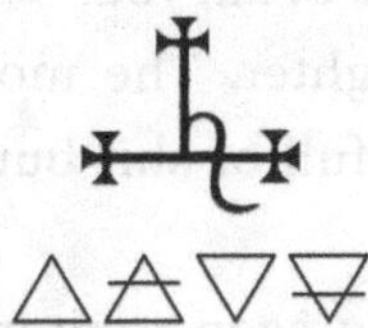

Juno's large, ocean-colored eyes looked back at me with rage and malice I once didn't know was possible.

The sweet, pretty, blonde water witch used to frequent my tea shop in San Francisco. Aside from my grandmother, she'd been my first witch friend. She introduced me to the coven leaders and encouraged me to join. They even fast-tracked me into becoming an official member.

And they all turned on me the first chance they got.

She saw me with Raum and Sal, and most importantly their damning sigil tattoos. She alerted the hunters and sent them chasing after us. I was a fool to let her live and would not make that mistake again.

Three people from your past will come to see you again. One will end happily, one will end tragically. And the third? Well, depends on who you ask. Raum's premonition echoed like a ringing bell in my head. My heart of hearts knew this was my tragic visitor.

"Juno." I couldn't keep myself from hiding the surprise in my voice. "You're the last person I expected to see here."

"Fuck you, demon whore!" she spat, struggling under the bonds of the shadow magic clamped tightly around her. With Sal, Ash, and Seth here, her magic was useless.

I lifted an eyebrow. "Sounds like someone's been filling your head with wholesome ideas. How is my dear old grandmother doing?"

"Fantastic!" she declared. "She and everyone else knows where you are. Every day she's getting stronger with shadow magic. Soon she won't need to touch you to kill you."

Seth snorted with laughter. The mood through his aura was relaxed. I figured she was full of shit but his reaction confirmed it for me.

"You won't be laughing soon, traitor. How could you turn on us?!" Juno looked at him with eyes full of pain. "It should have been you and me against them," she said, barely above a whisper.

"I was never on your side to begin with," Seth snapped. "And you already knew I don't fuck girls who cheat on their boyfriends."

Whoa. Juno was in love with Seth? My skin prickled with heat at this revelation, which I quickly pushed out of my mind. That was not the issue at hand and I was *not* jealous.

"How does Diana know our location?" I looked between Juno and Seth.

"There are these things called phones, idiot," Juno sneered. "I texted her the GPS coordinates."

"But how did you—" I cut myself off abruptly, the realization hitting me like a slap to the face. "The hunter attack was a distraction." I clenched my jaw, grinding my teeth hard. "She meant for all of us to get out of the house so her new little minion could sneak in."

Fuck, I really should have seen it coming.

"Wow, when you rub two brain cells together you really can figure some things out."

"Oh my Gods, shut the fuck up!"

The outburst came from Seth, surprising all of us in the room and drawing our stares his way.

"I used to feel bad for you, Juno," he said with a shake of his head. "I thought you were a sweet girl. Timid maybe, but figured you could at least see when you were being used." Unable to look at her, he scrubbed a hand down his face. "Not only do you see it, you embrace it wholeheartedly. You don't think for yourself and you never have."

He was right. Everything she'd said so far had been a carbon copy of Diana's rhetoric, from the insults she chose to the inflections in her voice. But she pulled it off convincingly well. I scratched at my arms, trying not to let it get under my skin that her friendship with me was just a role she played.

"Yes, I do!" she yelled back. "If you had gotten to know me, you'd know that!" She cast a venomous look my way. "That whore has *three* men! Why would you reject me because I only had one? I only dated him to get close to you!"

"Are you deranged?! *She* doesn't use people! Have you ever stopped to think she has three because they all love the person she is?"

I had to stop myself from staring. Seth's outburst in defense of me felt strange, like an article of clothing that didn't fit.

"Well, congrats on becoming the fifth wheel," she snapped.

"Enough." I placed a hand on Seth's shoulder and drew him back before he could retort. This whole exchange was becoming far too awkward and soap opera-like for my taste. It didn't matter if she thought Seth was now mine or not. Meanwhile, one of my actual lovers had a close call with death and needed retribution.

"Where's Diana getting angel kisses from?" I demanded.

"Angels. Where do you think?"

I rolled my eyes. This girl was proving to be even more infuriating than my grandmother.

"From who? And how? Witches aren't exactly all buddy-buddy with angels."

"She has connections in places you'd never expect." Juno grinned maniacally. "She's been teaching me so much, it's amazing. How'd you think I got here undetected? It's such a shame you never appreciated your only living blood relative, Deja. Your grandmother's an unappreciated genius and once she gets rid of all you hellions, the world will know it."

"Did she tell you all that?" I huffed, unimpressed and my patience wearing thin. "Are you going to tell me anything useful?"

"I just did," she hissed. "The end of your kind is coming, demon whore. Better prepare yourself."

She sounded like a typical San Francisco homeless person yelling on the sidewalk, but I couldn't help feeling badly for Juno. Now that Diana no longer had her clutches in me, she turned to an easier target. Despite being a witch herself, Juno was a perfect pawn for both vindictive angels and manipulative witches. It wouldn't surprise me if a human could manipulate her with no magic at all.

For whatever reason, she really was incapable of thinking for herself. If things hadn't gotten to this point, I might want to let her live. I'd work with her, encourage her to form her own opinions and develop her strengths. Maybe all she needed was an environment to encourage that.

Like me, someone probably tried to force their ideals onto her when she was very young. I saw a lot of my old self in her. The main difference between us was that I broke the hold of other people's influence on me. And I swore I'd never think for anyone but myself again.

"I still don't want to hurt you, June," I said more to myself than anyone else. "Even if you do worship that psychopath like a god and do all her dirty work for her. I don't want to kill my own kind."

"She's saner than all of you!" Juno struggled uselessly under her bonds. "And I am *not* your kind!" She looked to Seth. "Or yours!"

"You came from me," I practically pleaded with her. "You, Diana, Seth. Every witch that has ever lived has descended from *me!* Don't you see how worthless all this killing and fighting is? It's for nothing!"

"Oh? So the Salem witch trials were nothing? The deaths of hundreds of innocent witches over centuries because of association with the devil was *nothing?* Nobody holds trials anymore but witches still go missing every day! That means nothing to you, *mother?*" She emphasized her sneer on that final word.

"Demons are not the ones to blame for our persecution. They never were!" I shouted back. "You turned them into a scapegoat, which works out for the angels just fine! Once demons aren't a problem, they'll turn on the witches! Can't you see that?"

It was becoming painfully clear there was no reasoning with her. She shook her head stubbornly, that smile never waning.

"The angels do understand us. We're the downtrodden and they'll protect us. The demons want us to keep being their scapegoats to escape their own persecution. You've got it all wrong, Deja."

I couldn't believe what I was hearing. Diana had her mind and sense of logic so warped, it was frightening. There was no coming back for Juno.

Kneeling down in front of her, I made sure to look her squarely in the eye.

"You realize Diana sent you on a suicide mission, right?" My voice threatened to crack. "She sent you here instead of coming herself because she's a fucking coward. She knew I'd kill her at first glance and decided to sacrifice her little lamb instead."

Juno blinked. Her false confidence wavered for a split second before the mask came back on.

"You're full of shit," she sneered. "Trying to turn me against her just like you did. But she calls me the granddaughter she never had."

I felt about ready to vomit. "Then where is she, Juno? What's your escape plan? She had to give you one in case you got caught, right?" My eyes narrowed. "What were you going to do here, anyway?"

"We didn't foresee me getting captured," she grumbled, casting her eyes down to the floor. "But that doesn't change anything. When she doesn't get my text update, she'll know something is wrong and bring all the demon hunters in California down on your head."

"Sure, whatever." I waved my hand dismissively. "I'm only going to ask you one more time. What was your plan when you got here?"

"To fulfill my mission." She raised her chin defiantly.

I looked at Seth. "Did you search her?"

He shook his head. "We literally just found her hiding in the coat closet, restrained her and I came to get you."

Ash and Sal stood silently against the basement wall, arms folded and looking just as menacing as any bodyguards. I nodded at them. "Search her, will you?"

One step toward her was all it took for Juno to absolutely lose her shit.

"Don't touch me! Stay the fuck away! Don't you dare touch me you filthy fucking demons!" They ignored her wailing and patted down over her clothing just as thoroughly as seasoned police officers. "GET YOUR FILTHY FUCKING HANDS OFF MEEEEEE!"

"Got something." Ash ripped open a small pocket that had been sewn into her pant leg and produced a small baggie.

He tossed it to me and I squinted as I held it up to the light. It looked like a golden powder, sort of like ground tumeric, but with an even finer consistency. It even seemed to glow if light passed through it a certain way.

"I'll be damned." Seth came up behind me to look at the substance over my shoulder. His face was almost uncomfortably close to mine and I felt his breath fan over my neck, making my hairs stand on end.

"Do you know what it is?" I asked, not pulling away even though I should have.

"If I had to guess, it's a pulverized angel's kiss. She was probably going to put it in our food."

"Or my tea," I realized.

"Fuck." Seth pulled back and ran a hand through his dark hair. "Diana's probably sacrificing the whole damn coven to the angels on a silver platter. They don't just do favors like making their deadliest weapons easily accessible for no reason."

Weighing this information in my mind, I turned back to Juno just in time to see her flash a look of disgust at Ash.

Then she spit on him.

Something inside me snapped the moment she did that, and I acted without thinking.

I raised my hands and Earth magic shot out of my fingertips, the long green tendrils I cultivated while practicing with Diana. They wrapped around her neck and I only saw the fear in her eyes for a split second. My magic yanked and a clean *snap* rang out through the basement. Juno's body slumped over, lifeless.

No one around me said a word. They didn't need to. We all knew this would happen. It was just a matter of when.

I fully realized the irony of the next words on my tongue but couldn't stop myself from saying them.

"Burn the witch."

4

SALMAC

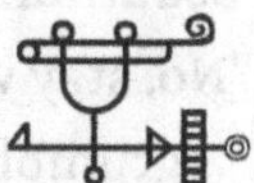

I lived long enough to know that killing someone had a different effect on everyone who did it. Deja was having a difficult time, but that in itself wasn't unusual. Most humans seemed to feel conflicted when taking the life of one of their own.

She chose to sit with Raum while Ash, Seth and I disposed of Juno. To my surprise, Seth seemed unfazed by the presence of a dead girl and took to lighting the match himself. But then I remembered he ordered plenty of demon death sentences while working under-cover for the hunter's guild. He may have been just as seasoned a killer as me.

Aside from wanting to shove my fist through his smug, scowling face every time he looked at my woman, I still didn't know how to feel about the guy.

On some level I understood he was a refugee of sorts and was safe with us. But we weren't the only upper hierarchy demons roaming the earth. Why didn't Ash work it out with Lucifer to give him refuge somewhere else? Did he really want to give this physical connection thing with Deja a chance? That didn't make any sense, considering Ash was the most possessive of her out of all of us. And she certainly didn't seem to want him around, which gave me more satisfaction than I'd admit.

While ruminating on these thoughts, I prepared a mug of tea for Deja and went up to the bedroom to sit with her. She turned at the sound of my footsteps and offered a strained smile when she saw me.

"Thanks, lion." Her voice was flat as she accepted the mug from me. "I was just about to go down for a refill."

"Do you want to be alone, beautiful?" I asked her.

She paused to sip her tea. "No, stay with us."

"Well, this chair won't do," I grumbled, moving in.

She barely had time to react and nearly spilled her tea as I scooped her up in my arms, walked around to the open side of the bed, and placed her down on the mattress before sinking down next to her. The king-sized bed allowed plenty of room for us and kept Raum undisturbed. Any more people though and it would begin to get crowded.

He still appeared to be sleeping peacefully. I swore the fucker even had his signature smirk on his face. I wouldn't put it past him to pretend to be asleep as a joke.

"Does it ever get easier to kill people?" she asked me after a few moments of silence.

I circled my fingertips absentmindedly on her knee. "No, not really. You just learn to not think about it."

"I was afraid you'd say that," she murmured.

Another few moments of silence passed between us, both of us working through our thoughts. Truthfully, I hadn't ever thought about death in any true humanizing, philosophical sense. I let the animal side take over when the time came to spill blood. For the first time, I wondered why that was. Would I feel too much for my victims if I really thought about it? Would the human side of me really be able to face that not only had I killed thousands, but enjoyed it? The answer came to me easily.

"Killing is such a terrible, consuming thing and yet it's as normal as laughing at something funny. Or becoming aroused when you see your partner naked."

Deja lifted an eyebrow, studying me with those beautiful golden irises. "I'm not sure I'm following."

I rubbed my jaw. Fuck, I needed to shave. And I was nowhere near as good at talking about this stuff as Ash. I lived to cause pain and give my woman pleasure, not think about the causes, effects, and meanings of those things.

"It's... the one constant paradox, I guess is what I'm trying to say," I sighed. "Even if we think we live outside of it, death comes for all of us. Everyone knows it's inevitable and yet we fear it coming upon us or inflicting it to someone else."

"But we know something humans don't." Deja sipped her tea pensively. "We know death isn't the end of life."

"In the strict sense, yes," I agreed. "Still, I'm sure we all felt our hearts stop when old birdbrain fell out of the sky. There's a reason for that."

She looked over at Raum, still sleeping like a baby. With a cleaner face and a more feminine figure, he could have passed for Sleeping Beauty.

"It's selfish, really," Deja said softly. "I panicked and ran out there because I didn't want to lose him. I didn't want to go through this lifetime without seeing him smile at me again. I couldn't stand to go without feeling his hands on me. I love him, but in those moments all I really thought about was myself."

Saying nothing, I pulled her into my lap until she sat in the space between my legs with her head on my chest.

"There's nothing wrong with thinking of yourself, beautiful." I rubbed her arms as we both watched Raum sleep. "That's what we did when we lost you. We commiserated in being without you. In some weird way, it got us through all those long centuries."

She looked up at me with a smile that made my heart skip a beat.

"You're much wiser than you give yourself credit for, my lion."

Everything I ever felt for this woman seemed to crash over me like an ocean wave in that one single moment. The words *I love you* didn't scratch the surface of what ran through me while she looked at me like that. Ash and Raum had their ways with words, not me. So I just kissed her. Hard.

She kissed me back just as fiercely, greedily, her small hands clawing at my neck and shoulders. I pulled her tightly against my chest, needing her just as much as she needed me.

We slid off Raum's bed together, moving to the doorway to find privacy in another bedroom, when a sound of throat clearing made us stop in our tracks.

Fucking Seth.

He looked on with a blank expression, leaning casually in the doorway as my fist curled at my side. Punching him in the face seemed like a grand idea in that moment.

"Did you need something?" Deja asked, not-so-subtly running a hand across the front of my jeans.

"I'm not exactly sure how to phrase this." The fucker took his sweet time, rubbing his jaw and rolling his eyes skyward as Deja and I gave him death stares.

"Just say it, Seth," Deja snapped.

"Okay, fine." He had the balls to grin. "There's a fox and a wolf at the door for you."

5
DEJA

I stomped down the stairs, thoroughly pissed at Seth for interrupting some much-needed intimacy between me and Sal. Even worse? I couldn't scrub the thought of both of them in bed with me out of my mind. The image popped into my head so suddenly I almost wondered if Seth planted it there himself with his super-shadow abilities.

But I knew he wouldn't. Despite being such an asshole, he seemed to have a pretty strict moral code regarding the privacy of people's subconscious. I had to respect him for that, at least.

Just like he said, I opened the front door to find a beautiful silver wolf and a blue-eyed vixen sitting like obedient pets on my front porch. My anger subsided at seeing my friends, but unfortunately my visions of threesomes did not.

"Astrid, Orion!" I greeted them, swinging the door wide open. "Come in, you guys."

I went into the kitchen in search of an icy cold glass of water. The wolf and fox immediately shifted into human form once they entered the house. Astrid grabbed my arms, her wild red hair practically vibrating as her blue eyes searched mine.

"Your mate," she breathed barely above a whisper. "Is he...?"

I pulled her into a hug. "He's fine. He's weak and resting but he'll be alright."

She squealed as she returned my hug with equal force.

"I'm so happy to hear that! You were so sad in the woods yesterday, even my cold little heart was breaking for you."

"Y'all gave us quite the body count to deal with." Orion gave a teasing grin as he leaned against the counter.

"Yeah, sorry about that," I winced. "The people we were running from, they found us a lot faster than we thought."

"Don't worry about the bodies. We're used to making folks disappear, remember?" Astrid cupped my face and her bright blue eyes burned into mine. "Are you and your mates in trouble? Will more be coming for you?"

Swallowing the lump in my throat, I nodded slowly. "The worst is still to come," I admitted. "My grandmother wants me dead for good, meaning no more reincarnations. She's somehow borrowed magic from angels and wants to wipe out demons and me along with them. She probably wouldn't hesitate to kill shifters, too." Guilt welled up fiercely inside me. "I'm so sorry to bring them right to your home base. You guys should go lie low somewhere—"

"Deja darlin', we ain't goin' nowhere." Orion came up and draped his arm across Astrid's shoulders. "And we sure as shit ain't leavin' our friends when they need backup."

"No way!" I protested. "This is my issue to deal with. I can't have you guys getting caught in the crossfire."

"Can't get rid of us that easy." Astrid grinned as she affectionately scratched Orion's salt and pepper stubble. "We've already called in reinforcements all over the country. Shifter movement is slow these days so we can have fewer outposts manned to beef up security up here. Just to give you guys extra eyes, noses, and ears for miles in every direction."

My heart swelled up until it felt nearly suffocated by my rib cage.

"I don't know what to say," I breathed. "I can't thank you enough. And please, please know we'd do the same for you in a heartbeat. Just say the word."

"We know." Orion kissed Astrid's forehead. "We feel y'all are an extended part of our pack. After you and Sal broke bread with us the other night, we knew y'all were trustworthy."

"Thank you," I said sincerely. "We felt the same about you and vouched for you to my other two mates as soon as we were all together."

"Who's that dreamboat who answered the door?" Astrid teased with a smirk. "Did you get yourself a fourth?"

"No," I answered quickly. Too quickly. "He was hunted by the same people and is staying here for safety. That's all."

"Does he shift? 'Cause if you don't want him, I'll take him."

She looked up at Orion, waggling her eyebrows suggestively, who rolled his eyes at her in return. Her giggle proved she was joking.

"He doesn't shift to my knowledge," I forced out a laugh, biting back the jealousy rearing up like a snake. "But if you want to take him off my hands, please do!" The words fought so hard to come out of my mouth, I practically spat them out.

"Nah. I think he only has eyes for you, honey." Astrid winked and nothing could stop the heat rising in my cheeks. She pulled me into another hug and I hoped she didn't see my red face. "We'll have shifters pouring in over the next few days so don't be alarmed if you see a few extra critters slinking around."

"Thank you," I whispered, hugging her tighter. Her red curls tickled my nose. "Seriously, I can't thank you enough. We won't let any shifters get hurt, I promise."

"We're used to that, hun," she answered softly. "What we're not used to is other kinds sticking up for us. Treating us like real people. We're here for you as long as you're there for us."

"Absolutely," I promised.

We said our goodbyes, and I promised them another visit when Raum was in better shape. The house's silence seemed to press in on me once I closed the front door. I hated it being this quiet, it felt so tense. Like we were on edge just waiting for the next attack. Was that really the best move? Just sit and wait for Diana to come, if she ever did? Or would she just send more lambs to sacrifice while she remained safe and tucked away in San Francisco?

I rummaged through the kitchen to make another cup of tea, so lost in my thoughts that I didn't see Seth until a shadow moved in the corner of my eye.

"Fuck!" I shrieked, dropping my tea cup and shattering it all over the floor.

"Oops," Seth said flatly, as if he were a cat whose favorite pastime was knocking things off the counter.

"Jesus, you're stealthier than Sal." I dropped to the floor to pick up the jagged ceramic pieces. "Don't do that. It's fucking creepy."

In the next instant he was kneeling on the floor next to me, his hand around my wrist. Fuck me, I could handle him at a distance but up close? I wanted to wrap myself in his smell, his strength, his heat. His stormy eyes burned into mine and a few strands of dark hair fell over his forehead. My other hand itched to push them back and continue with running my fingers over his scalp.

Magic crackled through the air between us and I fought to tell myself that was all this was. Nothing but magic enhanced and inflated by artificial means due to Beelzebub's selfishness. But a small part of me remembered that magic wasn't possible without a spark. Something real to build upon. Even casting a glamour illusion needed something to disguise in the first place.

A sudden *click* tore my gaze away from him and down to the floor. The teacup had repaired itself like new. Not a single chip remained on the floor and there were no cracks to show it had been broken at all.

"Thanks," I said begrudgingly, running my fingers over the cup to keep myself distracted from looking at his face.

"If you don't want me here, just say the word and I'll leave," he snapped bitterly.

My head jerked up. "What?"

"I heard what you told them." His aura brimmed with wounded pride and hurt feelings. "Believe it or not, I don't live to make your life miserable. I have no desire to stay where I'm not wanted."

Shocked, I blinked. This was the most raw and emotional I'd ever seen Seth and it threw me for a loop. To say I was confused was the biggest understatement of the year, but not just because of him acting like this. The worst part was I couldn't tell him to go. My mouth refused to say the words.

"I'm not the boss of you," I deflected. "You're not a prisoner, remember? You're welcome to stay or go as you please. But if you leave, you're on your own without our protection." Internally I cringed at adding that last warning. I sounded too desperate at wanting him to stay.

He laughed dryly, leaning back just enough to give me room to breathe. He propped his elbow up on his knee and raked long fingers through his dark hair, his slender bicep jumping to life at the movement. *Oh fucking Lucifer, help me.*

"We both know that's not true." He peered up at me with his head tilted adorably from resting on his hand. "If we're gonna sever this thing between us, one of us has to outright tell the other to fuck off for good. That's the only way this," he gestured at our auras sparking as they touched in midair between us, "will end and we can finally move on with our lives." His eyes flashed with challenge. "I'm in your turf so you have to be the one to end it, Deja. So do it. Tell me to leave and I'll be out of your life forever."

My heart raced with panic at the thought of him being gone. But *why?* I barely knew him and didn't even like the guy.

No matter how hard I tried, I couldn't bring myself to say the words. I knew on some level that meant I didn't want him to leave. I wanted him here. But I didn't want him like *that*, did I? Physically I did, yes. Everyone could see that. But all I truly wanted was to be in my happy, comfortable routine with the three men I already knew and loved. I didn't want to change what was already there.

He took my chin firmly but not roughly, his fingertips somehow charged with a spark I felt all the way down to my toes. An involuntary shudder went through me and I didn't dare to think of anything more happening. How could a simple touch like this affect me so much? It was like when Ash first touched me.

"You can't." He read both of our minds, sounding defeated. His hand on my face dropped away. "You can't tell me to go and I can't walk away from you. So where does that leave us?"

"Nowhere different than yesterday," I answered defiantly. "We're still human, capable of choice and rational thought. We're not slaves to... whatever this is."

A knowing smile spread across his face and I realized how rare it was to see. Smiling took his edge off just slightly but still sent my heart jumping into my throat.

"That's where you're wrong, Deja," he said almost sadly. "We *are* slaves to this and as long as you allow me here, it's just a matter of time before we succumb." Before I could protest, he held up a finger and touched it gently to my lips. "I know exactly how you're feeling now because I feel it on my end, too. It's not just my incubus blood working on you. It's *you* working on *me*."

I stood up so quickly, my vision dotted from becoming light-headed. If I stayed sitting any longer with him on that floor with his hands on me and him getting so close, I knew I would've kissed him or worse.

My feet took me up the stairs without another word, dying for as much distance between our bodies as possible. I found Sal exercising in one of the empty bedrooms and stopped in the doorway to not only admire the view, but redirect all this sexual energy to where it should be. On *my* man.

He took the closet doors off and installed a crude pull-up bar, which he used in ways I didn't know were possible. The hills and valleys of his back muscles jumped and flexed as he pulled himself up, then touched his knees to his elbows with fluid precision. I tiptoed up behind him as he finished his set, despite him already knowing I was there.

"Hey, sexy lion." I wrapped my arms around his middle as I pressed my lips to his back. His warmth and his smell were so comforting, I immediately began to relax.

"Hey." He spun around to face me and he wasn't smiling. His green eyes had a coldness to them that I never saw before.

"Want to finish what we started earlier?" I stood on tiptoe to reach his lips, only to receive an emotionless peck from him.

"Why, so you can fantasize about *him?*"

If he slapped me across the face, it would have shocked me less. I stood frozen, stunned. "What?"

"If you want to fuck him, just fuck him, Deja." The words came out bitterly, spitting poison on my heart. "But don't come running to me when *he's* the one getting you all hot and bothered. Come to me when you want *me.*"

"I *do* want you!" I insisted, feeling myself come apart from the inside out. He was rejecting me? How could this be happening? "Sal, I love you. Please don't do this to me."

"I love you, too." His voice softened just slightly. "That's why I can't handle you doing this. Just be honest with yourself, and with us. Whether you need to get him out of your system or want to keep him around, we'll deal with it. But there's no point in pretending anymore, beautiful."

I leaned heavily against his chest, all the mental and emotional strength sucked out of me. He stroked a hand through my hair and dropped a kiss to the top of my head, but I still felt the detachment in his actions and it killed me.

"I don't *want* to feel anything for him," I whispered. "I don't want to hurt you, any of you. It's only been us for so long. We're happiest just like this."

"Things change, beautiful," he said almost apologetically. "Times are different now. How you feel might fade eventually or it might not. Whatever happens is okay. You don't need to fight it kicking and screaming."

"What about what *you* want?" I looked up at him. "You're not worried about how this affects you? What you and I have?"

His fingers drifted across my back, pressing into the tight knots where I stored all my frustration and uncertainty.

"All I want is for you to come to me when you need me. And for you to be there when I need to feel human again. I've known you for a long time, beautiful. At the end of the day, it doesn't matter if I'm sharing you with three people or three hundred. Just stay the same person I've always known and fell in love with."

I released a sigh, feeling a small amount of weight lift off my shoulders, which was better than none. "I don't deserve you."

A small chuckle vibrated through his torso. "Sure you do. That's why you're stuck with us."

Brushing a kiss under his jaw, I stepped away from him reluctantly. "I'll figure this out. I promise."

He nodded, running his fingers down my arm to my hand, where our touch disconnected. "I know you will."

I turned and walked slowly out of the room to the sounds of him resuming his pull-up bar workout. For a moment, I thought of returning to Seth downstairs but halted in my tracks. No, not right now. I wasn't ready.

Ash had disappeared, most likely back to his study after getting rid of Juno. He seemed to make himself scarce at every opportunity after revealing everything about Seth. My possessive angel likely had a harder time dealing with Seth being around than Sal, despite being the one ordering him to stay here.

Nothing sounded better than curling up with Ash on his love seat with a book in front of us, listening to him explain archaic spells and rituals. But under the current circumstances, it was probably best not to disturb him. So I went to the only person who I knew would never turn me away, and not only because he was knocked out.

Raum still hadn't moved a muscle, but his breathing was deeper than earlier— a sign of his full physical recovery. Whether he still had all his abilities remained to be seen.

I crawled across the bed and gently nudged his arm out of the way so I could lie next to him. He didn't stir at all as I laid my head on his chest and snuggled into his side. I fell asleep almost instantly, barely aware of how exhausted I was from everything.

At some point while half asleep, I swore I felt an arm tighten around me and a kiss brush across my forehead followed by the words, "I love you, baby."

6

SETH

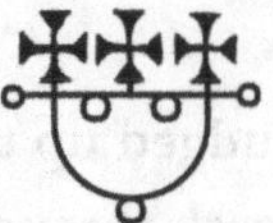

Juno was right about one thing. It fucking sucked being the fifth wheel.

I felt like an intruder, or whatever the male version of a homewrecker was. These people had their weird relationship dynamic set up just fine and here I was to throw the whole thing off balance.

"Fucking Juno," I muttered, walking around the basement support beam where she drew her last breath. The girl had to die. We all knew that. The poor thing had been so deeply brainwashed there was no redeeming her. If anything, Deja had been generous to kill her so quickly.

Even before Diana got her claws fully into her, she hadn't been completely innocent. The first time she tried to sleep with me was at the after party of my own coven initiation rite. Until I started taking longer and longer trips with the hunter's guild, she kept trying.

Sharing a woman with other men never appealed to me, but seeing Deja with her three was different than anything I'd ever seen. She wasn't trying to be secretive like Juno. Not only were they open and aware of each other, they each seemed to fit different needs of hers like perfectly matched jigsaw pieces.

And me? I was the asshole walking by who threw the whole damn puzzle on the floor.

I usually knew what to do in confusing situations, but with Deja I had no damn clue. We pulled to each other just as much as we repelled each other. It would be wrong for me to make the first move, I knew that much. All I could do was wait for her to come to me or tell me to fuck off. And stay out of the way of her three surly husbands while I was at it.

With a resigned sigh I trudged up the basement stairs, deciding I'd go up to my room and search through shadows again. I'd be able to track Diana that way, or at least her underlying moods and emotions. The crazy old cunt had no idea what a mistake she made when she grabbed my forearm the last time I saw her. Because I had zero desire to see the inner workings of her mind, I had been careful to avoid touching her. Little did I know how useful reading her shadows would be.

I entered the kitchen to find a tall man with inky black hair rummaging through the fridge like a bear coming out of hibernation.

He turned when I closed the basement door behind me. "Sup, Seth," he greeted casually.

"Raum," I replied. "You're looking better. Alive, at least."

"I could be hung the fuck over and still look better than I felt two days ago," he smirked over his shoulder. "I'm hungry enough to eat a fucking horse, though."

"There's still plenty of elk meat left," I offered. "Sal knows how to season a piece of meat."

As if things weren't awkward enough, I couldn't take back the words after I said them. Raum's shoulders shook as he chuckled but it didn't bother me much. Of all the house residents, he was the one that seemed the most okay with me being here.

"I'll let him know you said that," he cracked with a wink over his shoulder.

"Please don't." I couldn't help but let out a small laugh myself.

Raum settled for a beer. He cracked it open as he turned around to face me, still smirking at some private joke. As big and imposing as the guy was, something about him made me relax a little. He just seemed to instinctively know how to diffuse a tense situation.

"You look worn the fuck out, dude," he said abruptly. "But in all fairness, I bet I've been the only one sleeping for two days straight."

"Yeah, we've been pretty busy since the hunters came up on us." I gave him a quick recap of the aftermath, plus finding Juno and the aftermath of that.

"No shit?" Raum's eyes widened. "She spit on Ash and Deja killed her just like that?"

"Yeah, it was pretty surreal," I admitted. "She acted so fucking fast. Juno was insulting her and talking so much shit but the second she did that to him, it seemed like that was the last straw for her."

"Damn, I would have loved to see that." His grin widened. "She's amazing. Swift, beautiful, and deadly."

I silently agreed, realizing something I hadn't before. Deja was willing to take endless abuse upon herself for her loved ones. I had no doubt if we didn't make her stay inside, she would have taken that angel's kiss to the chest herself to save Raum. Likewise, Juno's insults, as stupid as they were, rolled off her back like water. But one gesture of disrespect to one of her lovers, and all her tolerance went out the window. When it came to protecting those she loved, she was swift and merciless.

I found it admirable, but also found myself a bit envious. I never knew what it was like to care about someone that much, or had someone feel that way about me.

Raum's dark eyes watched me from across the kitchen, shimmering knowingly and I bristled. He couldn't read my shadows, I'd feel him if he was. But his look said he knew all about what I was thinking, what my deepest desire was.

"She's sleeping up in the master bedroom, looking adorable as fuck if you're up for a cuddle." He took a long pull from his beer. "You look like you could use some."

"Don't think she'd be too keen on that," I scoffed. "And even if she was, the other two probably won't be okay with it even if you are."

He shrugged and added an eye roll for good measure. "It's her decision, not theirs. None of us control her."

"I get that but I'm also well aware of how serious this whole thing is." My hands gestured wildly. "You're all in a 3-way marriage basically and I'm trying my damnedest to not get my ass beat for doing the wrong thing with your wife."

"But it's not a marriage." The corners of Raum's mouth remained tilted up as he pulled from his bottle. "We're serious about her and will love her until the end of days, yes. But marriage consists of a legally binding transaction. She's not our property. There's nothing binding her to us or vice versa other than how we feel about each other."

I searched his expression, but he gave nothing away. Somehow this guy was the most open and gregarious with me, yet the hardest to figure out.

"And are the three of you just with her or...?"

Raum nearly choked on his beer from laughing so hard.

"Ah, fuck me," he said, wiping his eyes. "It's been two-thousand and eighteen years since watching Christ go up on the cross. Women are still slaves in parts of the world but no, you humans are still uncomfortable with men consensually fucking each other."

"I'm not uncomfortable with it." I bristled defensively. "I just genuinely can't tell if that's what's going on or not."

He composed himself and sighed out a long breath. "No, that's not how we are. The three of us are like brothers. We only have eyes and hard dicks for her."

"That's... a bit more than I wanted to know." I raised my hands. "Sorry I asked."

"Don't ever apologize for asking questions." Raum gave me a stern look. "The pursuit of knowledge is what we're all about. And despite your heritage and enhanced abilities, there's still a lot you don't know about demonkind."

I wrestled with telling him something I'd never told anyone. He could tell, as evident by his cocked eyebrow and sharp eyes never wavering from me, and I thought *fuck it.* I was already too deep in these people's world. Witch society would never take me back again.

"Beelzebub used to punish me for asking questions," I confessed. "Anytime I went against what he commanded my body to do or say, or just asked why he was doing this to me, he'd..."

"'Cause you great pain?" Raum prompted.

"That and more," I admitted. "At first it was just physical pain. Body aches, migraines, seizures, all that when I was a kid. When that only made me stronger and I learned to control it... I could feel him shut down parts of my mind." Raum said nothing, so I continued. "When I made him mad, he made me forget things. I forgot how to speak, or how a shower worked. For a few days, I didn't know what a knife and fork were for."

"You should tell this to Ash," Raum said. "He might not be thrilled that you're here but his judgement is fair. If he knows the full extent of how you were mistreated, he will make sure Beelz gets the full punishment he deserves."

I couldn't tell him the rest of it. I didn't even want to admit it to myself.

Beelzebub was obsessed with Lilith, especially since word spread among demonkind that she was returning to her whole self again. He filled my head with images of her throughout the ages, all his memories and sick fantasies of her. She was beautiful, seductive, and powerful as any demon in the First Hierarchy. No mortal man could resist her, but she was a picky bitch and resisted everyone but those three that followed her around like obedient dogs.

She never gave Beelz anything more than a polite smile, and he hated her for it. He knew she had a ravenous sexual appetite and often fucked all three of those lesser demons at once. Why not him? He was just as powerful as Ashtaroth, if not more. Their union could create a new species of ultra-powerful witches no mortals would dare to burn. She could make children who'd be proud of her, not these weak modern witches trying to burn away all their demon heritage.

His obsession never stopped. I tried so hard to be a normal teenager but with every girl I dated, Beelzebub compared her to Lilith. Mortal girls, even witches, were not beautiful or powerful or smart enough. He'd convince me how weak they were, that they'd lie back in bed not making a sound and be horrible at blowjobs. No woman on Earth could measure up to *her*.

And Deja wondered why I was such an asshole. She was the person my tormentor loved and worshiped to a psychotic degree. It'd be one thing if he had it all wrong, if all his thoughts and feelings were just an obsessive fantasy that reality couldn't measure up to. But what pissed me off the most was that he was fucking right. Everything he believed about her was true.

"I'll think about it," I murmured, sending a hand wearily through my hair. Fuck, I needed a haircut. "But right now I'm going to bed."

"Last chance to take a right down the hall," Raum called after me as I trudged up the stairs. "A nice, big bed with a gorgeous woman sleeping in it. If you don't go in there, I will."

I paused at the top of the stairs and looked toward the right. The master bedroom was dark but I could just make out a curled up, sleeping form. Physically, I ached to feel a woman sleeping on my chest. With all my travel and undercover work for the hunter's guild, I had little time for anything besides the occasional one-night stand.

Even long after I shut Beelzebub out of my mind for good, those experiences were especially empty because they still could never measure up to the woman in my head. He controlled me for so long, sometimes I still didn't know which thoughts were really mine or his. They had blurred and bled into each other over the years.

And I couldn't even begin to touch on how surreal it was that the woman he used me for, the object of his sick, twisted affection was sleeping in a bed ten feet away from me.

So I scrubbed a hand down my face and turned to the left, to my own bedroom at the opposite end of the hall.

I closed the door softly and lit my circle of candles with a wave of my hand. The flickering light danced and cast long shadows on the bare walls and floor. Shadows, the only place I felt myself, welcomed and beckoned me.

I peeled off my shirt and stepped over the candles. The sigils on my skin seemed to move with the shadows as if telling a living story. Shadows told the story of *why*, the reasons for what happened at the surface. All shadows were true, even if they were unique as the people they hid within.

Careful not to break the circle, I sat down, closed my eyes, and took a deep breath as I prepared to read Diana's shadows.

Beelzebub was still trying to get in like a persistent unwanted solicitor at the front door. Years later and he wasn't giving up. I always felt him there and was grateful for it in a weird way. I wouldn't want to let my guard down and accidentally allow him back in. His rage surrounded my subconscious as it looked for a weakness, a chink in my mental armor, but he'd never find one.

He couldn't stand the humiliation of being pushed out by his own creation, even though it was his own damned fault. It never occurred to him that I would become stronger, not a weak, broken puppet.

Within minutes, I burrowed deep in my own subconscious looking for a very specific mind to access. Each person's shadows felt different when you read them. When I first read Deja, her shadows felt like home. I couldn't explain the feeling besides warmth, contentment, and comfort. Diana's on the other hand felt cold and slimy, like walking through a swamp.

Once I found it, her subconscious feelings hit me and I nearly lost focus from how shocked I was. She was... happy?

By now she knew that Juno and the hunters she sent out were dead or missing, as there had been no contact from either one in over a day. And yet the emotions I was getting from her didn't feel annoyed, worried, or anxious. Rather, she felt downright *gleeful*.

That confused me so I searched deeper. Why was she so damn happy? But Diana's shadows were murky and tinged with the rusty red shade of blood. Of course, the blood magic was driving her even more insane. It was possible she didn't even have a reason to be so happy, the blood magic just got her high.

But the twisting in my gut told me this wasn't just that. She was happy for a reason, I just couldn't see it through the dark, blood magic haze. Still, it was important. Deja had to know.

I came out of her shadows slowly, less of a head rush that way. My candles extinguished the moment I opened my eyes and my awareness came back to the surface. Stepping out of the circle, I grabbed my shirt and pulled it on as I made my way down the hall.

The master bedroom door was now closed, but I never paused until my hand wrapped around the knob. Murmured voices came from the other side. I held my breath to listen.

A woman's moan, sexy and musical, followed by a man's, deep and primal. I released the doorknob and stepped away. The muffled sounds of flesh against flesh and the headboard crashing against the wall followed me back to my room.

Only after closing the door behind me did I adjust my quickly growing erection. Damn, I wanted a drink. I did *not* want to be feeling this way or thinking of these things right now. Of course I was attracted to Deja, I didn't have a choice in that. But was it just hearing her that made me hard, or hearing her with someone else?

Determined not to touch myself over this, I resigned that telling her about Diana's shadows would have to wait until morning, and fell into a fitful sleep.

7
DEJA

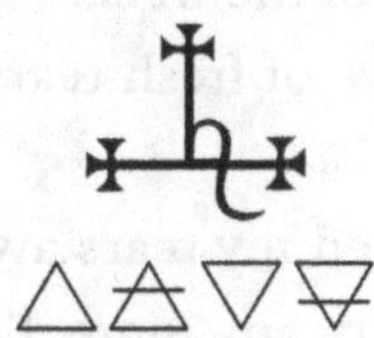

Rough stubble and hot breath on my neck roused me from sleep.

"My babies." A large hand reached around me and touched my lower belly protectively. "My sweet little witch babies."

"Raum?" I flipped around to find a mouth crashing against mine in the dark. A heavy weight pressed me down into the mattress, the familiar masculine scent filling my nose.

I tore my mouth from his, emotion welling up inside of me like a volcano. "Raum! You're awake!"

"I knew you were there," he said brusquely, his lips against mine. "I couldn't wake up but I felt you next to me the whole time."

Unable to hold it together any longer, I burst into tears. All my fear of losing him came out in ragged, shaky breaths.

"I thought I was going to lose you," I hiccuped, sobbed, and gasped for breath. "I didn't know what I'd do..."

Raum calmly shushed me as he lowered himself next to me, holding me against his chest and rubbing my back as I came apart at the seams. My hands never stopped moving, tracing the contours of his arms, his face, feeling his heartbeat and his breath to make sure he was really here.

"You really love my old shithead self that much?" he asked, the telltale smirk in his voice.

"Yes," I insisted, releasing a shaky breath. "You piss me off and make me so fucking worried but goddamn, I love you so much."

"And I love you." His stubble grazed my cheek. "I'll take an angel's kiss for you any day of the week."

"Don't say that!" A wave of fresh tears rose to the surface and I choked out a sob.

"Sorry, baby." He brushed my tears away with his thumbs. "Bad joke. You don't have to worry any more, I'm here now. Right as rain, thanks to you and Ash."

Hearing his name reminded me of the warning Ash gave right after we both put all of our energy into healing him.

"Raum." I cupped his face despite barely being able to see him in the dark. "Have you tested your powers? Ash said there was a risk of you losing your abilities."

My answer came within seconds when the sexy stubble beneath my hands became sleek feathers. Laughing with relief, I put Raven-Raum down and watched his dark bird form hop across the bed.

See? Right as rain. He pecked me affectionately.

"Ow! Alright then, birdbrain." I smirked. "Turn back to human now and have your way with me."

He shifted back, somehow in perfect position with his legs between mine so I straddled his hips. The kiss he lowered to me was hungry and demanding, while still slow and sensual. I melted help-lessly under his touch and slid my legs higher up his waist, drawing him toward my core.

"Your third of three visitors will come soon," he murmured, kissing slowly down my throat.

"Oh?" I slid my fingers under the waistband of his shorts and slowly dragged them down, savoring his body heat on my palms. "So Seth was the first?"

I didn't need to ask about Juno. She met her tragic end, so Seth was the one who would end happily? Or more likely the "depends who you ask", whatever that meant.

"Mm-hm." He peeled my leggings away, pressing kisses to my lower belly. "You should be nicer to him."

"Wait, what?" I lifted my head in surprise but his tongue drew a long, burning hot line from the bottom to the top of my pussy, rendering both of us useless for any comprehensible words.

My fingers curled against his scalp as he devoured me, humming with delight against my sensitive flesh. Every time my thighs drew inward to close around his head, he spread them apart again with a firm grip. He enjoyed me at his own pace, alternating between soft teasing of my clit and rough fucking with his fingers. My heart raced in my chest and my breathing came out in short little puffs whenever he began steadily building me to orgasm, but then he switched it up at the last moment.

The fucker knew exactly what he was doing. I loved and hated him for it.

"Please, Raum." I knew I'd get punished for begging but didn't care.

"Greedy baby," he scolded, delivering a light slap to my inner thigh that stole a breath and sent tingles straight to my clit.

"Please, it's too much," I whimpered. "I need to come."

"Who was the one close to death and knocked out for two days?" he teased, brushing a kiss in the crease between my thigh and pelvis. "I'm gonna take my time here."

"So selfish," I huffed, knowing that didn't make any sense considering he was going down on me. It was my frustration talking.

"Oh, you wanna see selfish?"

The light flicked on and I blinked, slowly taking in the sight of my sexy demon kneeling on the bed. He sat up, muscles flexing as he stroked the stiff shaft at the base of the V in his hips.

I returned his smirk, refusing to back down. "Oh, two can play at that game." And reached down to press my fingertips against my aching clit.

He hissed in a sharp breath as he watched me, his strokes becoming more erratic and frenzied. "Oh fuck, baby."

We went on like that, watching each other touch ourselves in the hottest game of chicken that ever went down. Neither of us wanted to stop or let the other person come first. Who would be the one knocked down?

The first jolts of pleasure building up had me quivering and biting my lip. My half-lidded eyes nearly shut to fully closed as the pressure built higher and higher. Listening to Raum's breathing as he jerked himself was starting to send me over the edge...

"Damn it!"

My hand was pulled back and pinned to the bed. I was too close to feel anything but frustration in my frenzied brain. He pinned back my other arm, and every touch sent my nerves shooting off like fireworks.

"Damn you, my sexy little witch," Raum grinned from above me as he positioned himself between my legs again, his cock pressing a kiss against my slick, needy pussy.

"You need to shut the fuck up and fuck me."

"Oh, is that all the winner demands?" He shifted his hips, sending his shaft up across my clit and stealing the breath from my lungs.

"And stop fucking teasing me."

"Mm, you drive a hard bargain," he grinned, pulling back to align his cock with my entrance again. "But I'll be a good sport this time."

He surged forward to enter me, giving the exact pressure and sensation I needed to send me over the edge. My orgasm convulsed all around the rock hardness of him before he could even pull back for a second thrust.

"Holy fuck," he growled through gritted teeth, his whole body stiffening to hold back his own release.

"See, that's your own damn fault," I panted breathlessly, still coming down from my high. "If you hadn't teased me so much, I wouldn't have cum so fast."

"Oh, shut your beautiful mouth." He lowered to his forearms, tangling his hands in my hair, and sealed his lips over mine to silence me.

He kissed and fucked me like only he could. His thrusts hit me deeply in sensitive spots that made me whimper into his kiss. My scalp tingled with sensation where he gripped my hair, adding to the aching pleasure in my nipples and core. He pressed against me and I still held onto his hard body, pulling him to me for more. This man I loved so much was alive, back where he belonged. And he was so completely *mine*.

His mouth fell to my neck, whispering sweet, dirty proclamations as his hands slid into the space between my back and the bed. His hold was gentle as he filled me even deeper, pressing against my inner walls at an angle that had me seeing stars. I felt in the way he touched me how scared he was to nearly die, to nearly lose me too. He didn't have to say it, I didn't even have to feel his aura to know. We both came so close to losing so much and wanted to savor each other.

It was the closest to lovemaking Raum would ever get, but still so intimate and sweet because it was him. Making love to him wouldn't feel right without his evil teasing, his aggressive kisses, and his rough touch. He knew I understood him. And I knew his tender side didn't come out often, so I treasured it when it did.

He gave me a long, lingering kiss full of unspoken emotion, then with an animal grunt he pressed me down harder into the bed and angled his hips higher. I couldn't hold back my scream as he crashed down into me, fucking me so hard and deep with all the weight of his powerful thighs and abs behind his thrusts.

The headboard slammed against the wall as he slammed into me. I shattered all around him, losing control and he only fucked me harder. It was so much, too much. The pain was so sweet, I never wanted it to stop. His breathing grew ragged until it stopped for briefest moment, and then I felt his warmth spilling inside me.

We collapsed in a heap of tangled arms and legs, our hearts kissing each other through the rapid beats in our chests. Raum draped a long arm across me while I contentedly skimmed a hand down the now-relaxed muscles of his back.

"Mm, you wear me out," he groaned, pressing a kiss to my cheek before letting out a relaxed sigh.

"The feeling is mutual," I replied, my pulse still hammering in my ears.

He chuckled and snuggled against me tighter. Within minutes, he stopped moving. His back rose and fell in deep, even breaths and I stifled a giggle. Two days of being unconscious and this guy still drifted off to sleep after sex.

I admired his handsome sleeping face, stroking his hair as moonlight shone through the window. In contrast, I was wide awake. That nap and those orgasms somehow made me wired. After a few minutes, restlessness took over me and I gently slid out from under his arm, careful not to wake him up. I tiptoed downstairs and decided to sit outside with a cup of tea.

The moon was full, round and beautiful. While the creatures inside the house slumbered, the forest at night was very much awake. Insects chirped and owls hooted. Every once in a while I heard the chittering of bats as their small, dark shapes flew past me silently in their hunt for food.

Distantly I heard long high-pitched howls and wondered if Orion was out at this hour, or if they were non-shifter wolves. I'd have to remember to ask him if there was any truth to that whole werewolf being forced to change at the full moon thing.

I wrapped my hands around my mug of chamomile tea as I just sat and soaked in the vibrant life of the earth surrounding me. It pulsed all around me and through me, as if we were all parts of something much bigger. That, I knew, was Earth magic at its core and it humbled me. That pulse of life was what connected every blade of grass to a wolf or a demon, like a massive complex web. Even after death, we were still connected. Our life force just redistributed to different directions.

The lone grey wolf came toward me so silently, I didn't notice until it stood watching me in the clearing, completely out in the open. We both froze when I saw it, the intelligence in its eyes sharp and calculated. On some level I knew this was a shifter. Most likely one of the reinforcements that Astrid called in.

"Hello," I said quietly, knowing those sharp ears would hear me. "My name's Deja." I held out a hand to offer my scent.

It continued to approach me slowly, cautiously, until its wet nose barely touched my open palm. This wolf was smaller than Orion, most likely a female. She was a classically beautiful gray wolf with a white underside and shades of grey, black, and red ticked across her back, ears and tail.

"I can tell you're a shifter," I said, hoping to put her at ease. "It's okay, I've met your kind before. If you'd like to talk as humans, I won't get freaked out."

The wolf huffed, followed by a sound somewhere between a whine and a growl. She backed up a few steps and turned around in a circle as if conflicted. I pulled my hand back and wondered if I offended her.

I watched as she sat back on her haunches and tilted her head back to let out one bone-chilling howl at the full moon. Then she began to shift.

My mouth dropped open as the wolf took on the form of a young woman. My hands shook so badly I had to set down my mug as I recognized this woman. I thought I was done crying for the day but tears sprang to my eyes once again as I choked out her name in disbelief.

"...Nona?"

8

DEJA

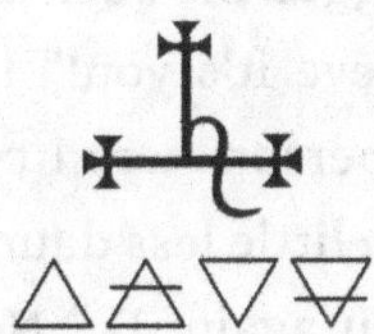

I had to be hallucinating. There was no way in Hell or Earth this could be real.

My former employee at the tea shop I owned in San Francisco, my loyal friend and the first person I met when I moved to that city, was standing in front of me. And seconds earlier, she had been a wolf.

"Hey Deja," she said quietly.

I couldn't speak. My mouth refused to work. It felt like weeks since we said our tearful goodbye over the phone, when I had to leave town immediately and left her with my shop and a ton of shitty excuses. She was the one friend I could lean on and I left her with no warning, expecting to never see her again. Naturally, I never told her I was a witch either.

Tears clouded my vision, and I blinked them away. She was still there.

"Is it really you?" I asked timidly, too afraid to speak any louder and shatter the illusion.

She gave a hesitant smile, walking slowly toward me. "Yeah, boss. It's really me."

I steeled myself, taking a deep breath. "Then what's the proper brewing temperature for first flush Darjeeling?"

"Between 180 and 190 degrees," she answered without hesitation. "Unlike most black teas which can be brewed at boiling temperature."

That was all the proof I needed.

I stood, approached the woman standing before me and wrapped her in a tight hug. Nona hugged me back just as tightly.

"Holy shit, I can't believe it's you!" I declared. My heart lifted with joy. Having another person here I could trust wholeheartedly made taking on Diana feel a little less daunting.

"It's so good to see you again, D," Nona smiled. "I'm sure you have questions, though."

"Um, yeah." I ran my shaking fingers through my hair, unsure where to begin. "So you're a shifter? Like, you have been the whole time?"

"Yeah," she said with a small nod, looking toward the house. "Should we sit down over a cup like old times?"

My tea selection out here left much to be desired, so I told Nona to help herself to the guys' beer stash while I prepared another cup of grocery store chamomile.

"Are you suddenly straight-edge?" she teased, cracking one open.

"Nope." I couldn't hold back my grin. "Just pregnant."

"WHAT!" She stared agape at me. "Oh my god, congratulations! Clearly, we have lots to catch up on."

"Indeed." I pulled out a chair at the table and offered her to sit down.

"I knew you were a witch almost immediately after you found out," she explained. "It was like a switch flipped. One day you smelled like an ordinary human, the next day your magic was overpowering."

"I wanted to tell you so bad," I admitted. "I was navigating a world I knew nothing about, with people I had a bad feeling about.

But I chose to ignore that because I thought I could trust them. They were *my* people, after all."

"Don't blame yourself for any of it," she said sternly. "I didn't tell you about me either."

"Damn," I laughed. "We could have avoided a whole lot of bull-shit if we had just come out of the closet to each other."

"Who knows." She lifted a shoulder in a shrug. "Hindsight and all that. But when Astrid called me up here to back up a witch, somehow I knew it was you. I sure as shit wouldn't risk my hide for any other witch."

"I don't blame you," I said with a frown. "My people have gone so far astray. Astrid told me that they've treated shifters horribly too."

Nona nodded sadly. "I'm the southern liaison for her shifter rescue and escape team. I've helped all kinds escape to Yosemite, Arizona, Utah. Some even as far south as Mexico."

"That's amazing." I smiled with renewed pride at her. "But how well does a wolf shifter get by in San Francisco?"

"It takes practice but I can go up to a week without shifting," she grinned. "Weekend camping trips are the excuses I tell humans. And since I'm the new boss at the shop, three-day weekends are not uncommon."

"Uh-huh." I lifted an eyebrow. "How is my old little tea shop running?" A pang of tension spread across my chest. I'd built that shop up from nothing over a year of no sleep and busting my ass day in and day out. The only magic I knew of at the time was glorious caffeine and the drive to pay my rent. And I walked away from it all to get away from my grandmother and former coven, but not before I left it in the most capable hands I knew.

"I think you'd approve of how I'm running things." Nona's eyes gleamed with pride. "My staff are all shifters who escaped westward and needed a day job. I taught them everything you taught me and they're killing it. No one thinks of looking for them there because everyone still thinks a witch runs the place." She grinned. "It's become a safe house for runaways. We've only just started but word is spreading fast."

"The apprentice has become the master," I cackled. "I knew you'd run it better than I ever could."

"You should come see it sometime." Nona set down her empty beer bottle. "You know, after all this craziness dies down."

"I'd love to," I said, grabbing her empty bottle and pulling another from the fridge.

We talked until dawn began casting its gentle light over the sky, turning its dark blue color paler until it became a warm pink. I told Nona everything I wanted to tell her back then but didn't. I told her what really happened with my grandmother and then Juno. As we made a growing collection of empty beer bottles on the table, I even told her how she had been my only loyal friend. Except for the men in my life, she was the only person I trusted wholeheartedly, and the guilt of leaving her to clean up my mess still ate at me.

Right at dawn, Ash walked into the kitchen from his study, rubbing his eyes before he blinked and noticed us and the state we were in.

"Um, hello again," he said awkwardly to Nona and looked at me.

"It's cool, she's a shifter," I yawned, the lack of sleep catching up to me. "She knows everything."

He nodded, fully knowing how much I trusted Nona. Then his eyes fell to the empty beer bottles littering the table. "Did you drink *all* the beer?"

"Shit, I'm sorry." Nona stood up. "I have a really high tolerance and lose track sometimes. I'll buy you guys replacement beer. I just got in last night and have to go into town, anyway."

"No, don't worry about it." He gave her a rare smile. "I'm glad you're here. We could all feel how much Deja missed you."

"Well, I might pick y'all something up, anyway." Nona winked at me. "I have a contact up here for some actual good tea."

"Ugh, you have no idea how happy you just made me." I gave her an exaggerated eye roll and bit my lip. "I was so spoiled by the city. Even with magic, my resources for good tea up here are so limited."

"Didn't know you had such high standards for boiling twigs and leaves in water," Ash cracked, shooting me a naughty smirk.

"You shut that sexy mouth before I give it something to do." I cupped his jaw in mock anger and quickly gave an affectionate scratch to his beard.

Truthfully, I loved that he was out of his book cave and talking to me again. Underneath being worried about Raum for the last two days, I had a nagging insecurity that Ash had been avoiding me ever since we learned about Seth.

"Well, I'll get out of your hair for now." Nona moved toward the door but not before I pulled her into another bone-crushing hug.

"I'm so glad you're here," I whispered. "Seriously. I feel like I have a real, fighting chance against that crazy old bitch now that I have you to back me up again."

"Ah, you've never given yourself enough credit, D." Nona pulled back with a smile. "But I'm glad I'm here too. And it would be my honor to bite Diana's ankles for you to finish her off."

We laughed and said our temporary goodbyes. I watched from the porch as she, a gray blur, ran on all fours to the treeline and disappeared.

The stench of coffee filled the air when I returned to the kitchen, but I wrinkled my nose and did my best to ignore it.

"Hey," I said quietly to Ash's silent back as he watched the sunrise out of the kitchen window.

He turned, pinning me with that icy stare and cool, calculated expression. "Hey, love."

I approached him warily, only relaxing when he extended an arm out to wrap around my shoulders. I circled mine around his firm torso, relishing in his strength coiled up like a trap ready to spring.

"You're not angry with me?"

His arm tightened around me, his thumb reaching to brush against my cheekbone.

"No, my love. I'm just not thrilled with the situation."

He didn't have to specify. It wasn't so much that Seth's presence was an elephant in the room. We all had acknowledged it in some way or another. But I hated that he and my other two were basically waiting on me to make some kind of executive decision.

I didn't want that kind of power. More than anything, I didn't want to hurt my guys. But none of this was Seth's fault either. He didn't deserve to be hurt any more than he already had.

The realization hit me that I was starting to care about Seth's feelings. Maybe not as much as my guys but definitely enough to not wish any pain on him. Which only made things more confusing for me.

I pressed my face into Ash's side, wishing the rest of the world would just go away. "What do you think I should do?"

"Love, you know I can't tell you that," he sighed. "You're the first and only woman for me. I'm more biased than anyone."

"Then answer this for me." I propped my chin on his chest to look up at him. "If I accept him, how will that make you feel? You're the only one who hasn't outright told me how that decision will affect you."

He took my hand and slipped it under his shirt. Not that I ever disliked feeling my angel's naked skin but I looked at him with confusion. That is, until he placed my palm over the sigil tattoos on his chest.

They pulsed with extra heat than the surrounding skin, a direct link between him and Hell, every demon's home when not on Earth.

"Do you remember when you asked me why I wear your sigil above Lucifer's?" Ash's eyes burned into mine.

I nodded. We were curled up in bed at their house in San Francisco when we had that conversation. Was it really only weeks ago?

"And what did I say?"

"That I come first for you," I answered. "Always."

"It's still true." His thumb rubbed across the back of my palm that rested on his chest. "I found you first. I fell for you first. I'll always want you to myself a little more than the others, no matter how many others you have."

I slid my hand out from underneath his shirt and placed both palms on the soft bristles of his beard.

"You remember what I told you in that same talk we had, right?"

A flicker of emotion passed through his eyes. "You said that I come first for you too."

I stood on tiptoe to reach his lips. He wrapped one powerful arm around me and lifted me the rest of the way. With the first caress of his tongue, I felt him all the way to my toes. The softness of his lips and coarseness of his beard made a contrast that awakened my flesh, eager to not miss any sensation of him against me.

Despite being once a divine immortal and then a damned one, he was so refreshingly human and I loved that about him. Possessive, sometimes hot and cold but always pondering something. Intelligent, wise, a natural born leader. He prided himself on being a rational thinker, but we both knew emotions affected him too. My fallen angel was imperfect but absolutely perfect for me.

"You'll always come first for me too, angel." I whispered against his mouth.

9
ASHTAROTH

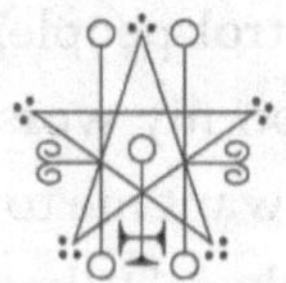

Deja was practically falling asleep on me in the kitchen, so I carried her up to bed despite her protests. I tucked her in next to Raum, who wasted no time in throwing an arm over her slender waist and pulling her in close. I held back a chuckle as I closed the door and headed back downstairs. That guy had been through a lot in the past few days. I could wait my turn.

When I came down to see Seth pouring himself a cup of coffee from my pot, I resisted the urge to curl my lip and growl.

"Sure, help yourself," I muttered, rounding the counter to hunt for another clean cup.

He met my eye and didn't back down. I had to respect him for that.

"I think I'm starting to understand the communal attitude of things around here," he replied.

I met his gaze unflinchingly. He sensed my power but didn't seem fazed by it. Being under Beelzebub's control for so long must have made him used to feeling it. That and it seemed to give him a serious dislike for authority.

"Are we talking about coffee now or something else?" I challenged, bringing a cup down from the cupboard.

"Deja's not a thing," he glowered, losing his cool temporarily.

"I know that." My temper wasn't anywhere near rising to the surface as I moved into his personal space and helped myself to the rest of the coffee pot. But Seth's anger came off him like a furnace. This guy had too many pages of Sal's book and needed a few from mine. "*We* know that. But do you?"

"I have no desire to control people," he fired back. "I wouldn't wish what I went through on my worst enemy. I'm done with the hunter's guild. However you want me to prove that, I will."

"What do *you* want?" I asked. "What is your ideal outcome out of all of this?"

That was what I had wanted to know since I first became aware of him. Lucifer knew Beelzebub had been tampering with his bloodline but we only knew recently how far he went. After being raised in Heaven, then building Hell with him, I recognized Beelzebub's aura from a mile away. Seth's aura flickered so strongly with his power but he learned to keep it well-hidden among the witches. His cloaking was no match for a true demon, however.

He let out a biting laugh and held his hands out defeatedly.

"I don't fucking know, *Lord Ashtaroth*," he replied through his laughter. "I've been controlled and tortured since I was a child. All I ever wanted was to be free of that. Now that I am, I don't know what's out there *to* want. Maybe I'll live on a houseboat on Lake Tahoe, I don't fucking know."

"Yeah? With a woman?" I asked, almost accusingly. "Gonna settle down, raise a family?"

He shrugged and took a long swig of coffee but I could see it, even if he didn't want to admit it. It didn't matter if it was Beelzebub's influence or his own feelings, but he was completely in love with Deja. Maybe he didn't want to be, but that did nothing to change the fact that he was. And as much as I hated to admit it, she would be good for him.

This kid reminded me of Sal in a lot of ways with his pent-up anger and no true, healthy release for it. Sal still had his moments, but he was a completely different person now than when he was first created. Deja healed him. She tamed the wild, bloodthirsty predator inside him until he became a big kitten eating out of her hand. She could heal Seth in a similar way. I had a feeling just from being around her, his healing process had already begun.

At the core of it, I didn't care if she took another man. She told me I came first, and that was all I needed to hear. But my concern was how Seth would fit into our dynamic. Raum and Sal were created specifically for her, and they served under me. I was Beelzebub's equal. If Seth really wanted to join our happy little family, he'd have to get used to taking orders from me.

"Where is Deja, anyway?" he asked. A poor attempt at a subject change.

"Sleeping," I answered. "An old friend of hers came to visit last night and they stayed up talking."

He chewed his lip as if thinking hard and set his coffee cup down. "I need to tell her something important. Honestly, it's worth waking her up for."

"Anything you need to tell her, you can tell me." I crossed my arms, fully intending to block him from leaving the kitchen if I had to. "If you're in this with us, you'll learn we have no secrets. Even between us guys. But she's had a tough few days and deserves to rest."

He studied my stance as if actually considering getting past me, then thought better of it.

"I read Diana's shadows last night," he said. "I couldn't see anything specific. She's gotten deep into the blood magic and it's making everything murky. But I could feel her emotions and she was fucking *happy*."

I lifted an eyebrow. "Happy? That doesn't sound good for us."

"No, it doesn't," he agreed. "I mean, it was jarring and nothing makes me lose focus when I'm in there. She was downright elated about something. Like a kid on Christmas, she was that excited."

Fuck. That didn't bode well for us at all.

"That doesn't make any sense." I rubbed my beard as I stared out the kitchen window. "She just had her underling and five elite hunters killed. Plus, they haven't gotten you yet. They might know you're with us by now. The San Francisco coven must be panicking."

"So what should we do about it?"

My eyes caught his. He wouldn't like my idea and frankly, neither would Deja. But it was our chance to not only capture and kill Diana, but to see if Seth really belonged among us.

I had to know if he was willing to sacrifice himself for her the way Raum did, the way Sal and I would at the first opportunity. Then and *only* then, would I give him my total support in becoming Deja's fourth lover.

10
DEJA

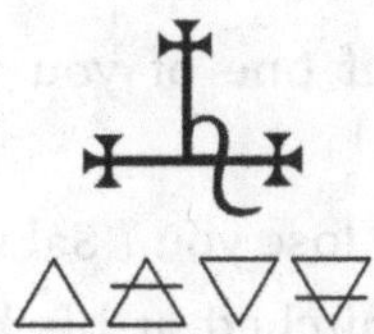

I woke up refreshed from a deep, restful sleep. With a smile I stretched out in the long, king-sized bed, enjoying the late afternoon sunlight filtering beautiful and golden through the windows. Never again would I take peaceful sleep for granted.

Nona was back. Raum was alive and well. Ash wasn't mad at me. I had to remember to appreciate the small things in this crazy lifetime.

Of course my smile couldn't last as I came downstairs and was met with three sexy, but grim faces.

"How'd you sleep, baby?" Only Raum's mouth ticked up into an amused smirk. With my bird's nest hair and rumpled clothes I slept in, I bet he was trying not to laugh.

"Amazing, thank you." I blew him a kiss as he passed me a steaming mug of tea. "So what're the rest of you looking so grim for?"

"We're making a move on Diana." Ever the leader, Ash straightened up taller, his face stony. "If my plan works, we just might be able to end this."

"What?!" I nearly dropped my mug. "Tell me everything, angel. I have to be the one to kill her. You know that, right?"

"I figured you would be." Now his sexy mouth gave the barest hint of a smirk before dropping quickly. "But you have to do exactly as I say. No running out like last time, no matter what happens. Do you understand?"

My lips pressed into a thin, tight line. Already I didn't like this at all.

"I can't promise that if one of you is in danger," I answered honestly.

"And we can't afford to lose you." Sal walked up behind me with feline stealth. My breath hitched at his heartbeat on my back, his arms moving around my waist protectively.

"If I lose one of you the way we almost lost Raum, I might as well be dead too," I said. "So let's make sure *no one* gets in the line of fire."

"Here's the thing." Ash's eyebrow twitched. "It's not one of us taking the biggest risk. It's Seth."

Silence dropped all around us. I turned to him slowly. His sharp icy eyes watched me, studying every reaction from the pattern in my breath to the color in my face. Fuck, they were *all* watching me for a reaction. They wanted to see what Seth really meant to me. My anger sparked at this little trick but at the same time, I understood. I couldn't get out of my own head sometimes and still couldn't articulate my feelings for him. Maybe outside observations of my body language would be more telling.

But despite my feelings or lack of, that didn't mean I agreed to this plan.

"Why would you do that?" I demanded. "I don't want anyone dying for me."

"It was the only way to draw Diana out," Ash replied calmly. "She'll want revenge for being betrayed by him, and when she finds out he's with us, she'll want to hit two birds with one stone."

Raum shuddered from where he leaned on the counter.

"Triggered," he muttered but shot me a wink to show he was joking.

"But it's *wrong* to use him like that," I protested. "He's basically our bait. After everything he's been through, he doesn't want to be a pawn in someone else's plan anymore."

"I realize that," Ash nodded. "That's why I asked him and gave him the option to refuse. He insisted that he wanted to do this."

I blinked, trying to wrap my head around this information. I still wasn't convinced that Seth even *liked* me. Why would he volunteer in this mission for me?

"Why?" I repeated the question in my head to Ash.

He shrugged. "I'm not a mind reader, love. If he gets out of this alive, you'll have to ask him yourself."

I narrowed my eyes. His face let on more than he was telling me. And I was all too aware of how my body reacted when he said *if* Seth got out of there alive. My stomach clenched, my pulse shot up and my heart skipped a beat.

I cared about him enough to not let him die. If it were one of Astrid's mates or someone else I barely knew that was still on our side, I'd feel the same way. It didn't mean I elevated him to the same importance as my three demons.

We knew what Diana was capable of. She almost killed me back in San Francisco, the blood magic somehow making my demons powerless to stop her. It wasn't until I was losing consciousness and unlocked the hidden elemental magic of water and fire that stopped her.

Only Lucifer knew how much I would enjoy finishing her off this time. I wouldn't stop watching her drown on my magic until her last breath was her most painful one. I'd relish in every second of it for those she would no longer be able to hurt, manipulate, or kill. Not just for me, my mother, and Raum, but also Juno. I'd never forget my own responsibility in that but if it weren't for Diana, Juno never would've had to die.

"So what's the plan?" I folded my arms across my chest.

"Seth has already reached out to Diana through shadows and they're meeting at a neutral location." Ash just got started and my skin already prickled with discomfort. I didn't like this plan at all. "They've agreed to be alone but we're prepared for Diana to come with hunters or blood magic tricks up her sleeve. We have shifters standing by on guard, including Nona. Sal and Raum will be shifted and on guard as well. You and me will be cloaked, love."

"Hold on, back up." I raised a hand. "Why would Diana agree to this? It's a pretty big risk for her, even if she wants revenge on him."

"Because he promised to deliver you to her." The answer came from Raum, who looked mighty pleased with this plan. "She knows where we are thanks to Juno, but has no way of actually reaching you when you're surrounded by flexed demon muscle." He grinned. "She thinks he's the key to slipping past us, now that Juno is gone."

"Again, why?" I asked. "He betrayed her side first. She has no reason to trust him now."

"That's why we added a little dramatic flair," Sal replied, his chest rumbling against my back as he spoke. "Remember the state Seth was in when he first came here?"

"How could I forget? You guys beat the shit out of him."

A pang of guilt stabbed me. He tracked us and snuck onto our property immediately after his cover was blown to the hunter's guild. Because we had no idea yet whose side he was on, the guys used him as a punching bag then tied him up in the basement while we figured out what to do with him. I healed his wounds immediately, but now my heart ached at the idea of him being hurt at all in the first place.

Damn it. Why was I starting to care so much?

"Well, we did that again to make it look like he wasn't welcome here either. Make Diana think he was reaching out to her with his tail between his legs because he had zero options left."

"What?!" I looked up to see Sal's green eyes flash. "How could you guys do that? You said we would protect him."

"Relax, love. It was Seth's own idea." Ash's voice soothed me the tiniest amount. "We honestly didn't hurt him badly, just made him look like he was." He rubbed his jaw. "Let's hope he's a convincing actor."

"Well, he fooled us, didn't he?" Raum piped up, his grin as bright as ever. "I'm starting to like the guy. He's a clever little bastard."

"Let's make sure he comes back alive before we get too attached," Ash grumbled. He looked at me. "Any other questions, love?"

I shook my head. Nothing ran through my mind except worries and fears. I didn't like this plan but we couldn't do anything about Diana without taking some risks. And if we had to risk anyone Seth made the most sense, but I still hated that he had to do it.

He didn't have to. He volunteered for it.

That thought wouldn't leave the forefront of my mind, no matter how much I tried to shrug it off. Seth didn't even say goodbye. The last time we talked was that awkwardly intimate moment in the kitchen when my teacup broke. He and the guys agreed to this plan and set it in motion while I slept. There had to be a reason for that. Did the guys think I would try to stop him if I knew?

You would have. You know you would have.

I chewed my lip in thought as Sal and Raum shifted to reach the location undetected. Ash and I jumped into the pickup truck, which we'd leave about a mile away to approach while cloaked at a separate time. The fewer of us for Diana to sense, the easier we'd be able to make our move.

Ash drove us in relative silence through the winding mountain trails as the sun began to set. Damn, I really needed to un-fuck my sleep schedule. I was wide-eyed and wired as dusk turned into night, which meant I'd be falling asleep again when the sun came up.

After nearly two hours of driving, Ash cut the headlights and took the truck off-road. He parked it well-hidden in some dense bushes before cutting the engine. I unbuckled my seat belt and slid over to exit the passenger door, but he grabbed me quickly by the waist and pulled me almost directly onto his lap.

His kiss came hard and fast, prying my lips open like he'd never taste me again. The next thing I knew, my back pressed against the cab seat, his hands a tight, desperate grip on my ribs. He left me breathless, hot, and with a distinct sense of vertigo. Then he abruptly jerked away and gave me a cold stare.

"Promise me you won't run out there, no matter what happens," he rasped. "Swear on us that you won't give yourself up, no matter what she does or says."

I pulled away, just to get a breath of air and ease the intensity of his aura surrounding mine. He was scared, unsure, but he had to be strong. He had to stay in control.

"I can't promise you that, angel." I whispered the confession like a dirty, sinful secret. "If anything happens to you three, I won't be able to stop myself from protecting you."

"My love." His voice sounded pained. "I know you don't see it this way but this is the truth. All demons are replaceable. *You* are not." He gently took my chin in his hands and made me face him. "There has only been one of you in the entirety of human history. Do you understand that? Humans, demons, witches, all of us cannot afford to lose you."

My sadness seemed to swallow me up like a black hole. I could see his point but what good was I if I lost the loves of my life? How could I benefit the future generations of witches while heartbroken and alone? Humans loved the saying, time heals all wounds. But what if your wounds cut deeper than time itself?

"I understand," I answered softly, knowing no other answer would satisfy him.

He kissed me again, slower and more gently this time. His tongue swept across mine like he wanted to memorize every muscle in my mouth.

"The only thing that kept us going before was knowing we'd have you back one day," he said. "If even a speck of an angel's kiss hits you, it might as well hit all of us."

"Hm, no pressure then," I whispered humorlessly into the bristles of his beard.

His finger trailed across my jaw. "Just let us handle things if it gets crazy. Your only job is to kill that crazy bitch when the time is right. Don't be a hero."

"Only if you promise not to be one either." I took his face in my hands. "Because I mean it. You act like I'm the most important part in this whole thing, but I truly don't know how to go on without the three of you with me."

His eyes flickered down as his fingers skimmed across my low belly. He sent a gentle pulse of energy through my belly and it bounced back against his palm. It almost felt like a kick but I knew it was still to early to feel that. Could she sense and mimic magic, though?

I laced my fingers through his, knowing what he was about to tell me, but he said the words, anyway.

"No matter what happens to us, you go on for *her*," he said.

11
DEJA

Ash cloaked us both in shadow before we walked about a mile through the woods to the edge of a clearing. Following his lead, I scrambled up a large boulder to see without having my view obstructed. The boulder made for a small cliff edge that hid us well, even without shadow magic.

Seth sat on the ground in the middle of the clearing, looking worse for wear. He had a black eye again, and he clutched his ribs with a painful grimace as he took in wheezing breaths.

I looked at Ash, not bothering to hide the concern on my face.

What the hell did you guys do to him? I demanded through my aura. He looks worse than he did in the basement.

Sal gave him the black eye, he admitted. He seems to enjoy doing that. But honestly the rest is just a show. And might I remind you love, that part was his idea.

I didn't argue but the twisting in my gut remained. I hated everything about this plan. It should have been just me and Diana fighting it out to the death. None of them should have had to be involved.

Speaking of my psychotic old cunt of a grandmother, she was nowhere in sight.

Sal? Raum? Ash asked like he read my thoughts. *Any sign of her?*

No visuals yet but I'm pretty sure I smell her, Sal answered. I smell a lot of blood, old and dried. Fuck, is she bathing in that shit? It seriously hurts my nose.

Raum chuckled, sending pleasant, soothing vibrations through my aura before Sal spoke again. *Nona just confirmed she smells it too. The old bitch is definitely close.*

Remember, no one acts until my signal, Ash told everyone.

And so we waited. And waited.

Is she fucking with us? Sal demanded angrily after about a half hour. She is definitely near. Why isn't she coming out to talk to Seth?

She might be waiting to see if he has any backup. It's a clever plan, honestly, Ash answered.

She knows how to get people frustrated, I added. Don't let her get under your skin, lion.

Seth? Ash asked. Can you read her shadows now without her knowing? To get a sense of what she's feeling?

The stormy-eyed man was silent for a moment, but I saw his eyes roll back and close for a moment out in the clearing. If no one knew better, he looked like he was losing consciousness from his injuries.

It's gotten murkier, it's so hard to see. His frustration was palpable. I can still tell that she's happy as fuck but I'm getting even less details than before. The blood magic is really driving her mad. Be careful everyone. This bitch will be unpredictable.

You be careful too, I directed my thought at him before I could stop myself. A warm, fuzzy feeling passed from his aura to mine.

Aww, thanks for caring, sweetheart. His mental voice oozed with sarcasm. Annoyed and a little embarrassed, I closed off the connection between our auras.

Fuck me in the ass with a rusty spoon, Raum declared. Can that really be her?

Across the clearing from us, a woman emerged from the edge of the woods, approaching Seth. I narrowed my eyes, squinting at the figure several hundred feet away. It couldn't be anyone else but this woman had dark hair and looked to be in her forties. As she got closer, my pulse hammered with horror as I recognized Diana's nose, lips, and chin. It *was* her but holy fuck!

It's the fucking blood magic, Ash said bitterly. She's going insane and losing control but it's making her look younger. That's why it's so dangerous. Not only does it kill with horrible consequences but the side effects are addictive.

"What do we have here?" she said with saccharine pleasantness as she approached Seth. "Someone who realized the errors of their ways, perhaps?"

He said nothing as she approached him, but his jaw ticked with tension. I had to admit he acted the part well. With his head bowed, kneeling on the ground, clutching his ribs, he looked every bit like he didn't want to be there but had no choice.

I realized in that moment it was the first time I didn't question his true intentions. He was on our side. I knew that for a fact. I trusted him. And if Ash allowed him to enact this part of his plan, that meant my guys trusted him too.

"Or is it someone who ran out of options and has no choice left but to grovel for my mercy?" Diana walked in a slow circle around Seth, the distance between them proof that she was still being cautious. She sounded strange, and not just because of her younger appearance. The inflections in her voice were odd and jarring, like someone else was controlling her mouth.

"Well, which is it?" she screeched at his silent response.

Seth gave a convincing flinch. "A bit of both, honestly."

"Oh, please elaborate!" Diana knelt in front of him, her golden eyes so reminiscent of mine and my mother's.

"I had a feeling I made the wrong choice as I was running," Seth wheezed and paused with every breath as he spoke. He looked to be in so much pain, my fingers itched to reach out and heal him. "But I kept going because I knew the coven would never take me back.

When I got to the demons' hiding place," he paused and winced, "they didn't exactly welcome me with open arms."

"Oh, poor dear." Diana feigned a look of sympathy. "What did they do to you?"

"Beat me. Starved me. Kept me tied up in the basement for days." He wasn't lying about that and my heart squeezed painfully in my chest. Fuck, I had to apologize after all this was over. I really needed to make up for how we treated him.

"And did you escape or did your benevolent captors decide to free you?"

"They turned me loose but I wouldn't call it freeing," he grimaced. "They dumped me in the woods, basically leaving me as prey to the animals out here. I reached out to you because I knew death would come for me either way. At least this way, I can die with my conscience cleared."

"I see." Diana held a finger to her chin as she contemplated his words. "And if I decide to show some compassion and let you live? What will you do then?"

My breath hitched. Ash's fingers squeezed around mine. This was going much better than we hoped.

Seth made a surprised sound and then winced, wrapping his arm even tighter around his side.

"I'll spend the rest of my miserable life serving you," he said through gritted teeth, lowering his eyes humbly. "Any guidance you seek with shadow magic, I'll be happy to advise. With your increasing blood powers and angel-kissed spells, you will be unstoppable."

"I don't need your help with shadow magic!" she cried. "I've already mastered it! Moreso than you! That's how I was able to find out about your heritage and your little hard-on for the demon whore."

Ash bristled next to me but I just rolled my eyes. Nothing this ranting, raving crazy woman said could affect me anymore.

"Of course you don't need help. My apologies." It was so weird to see Seth groveling. His shoulders bunched with tension and I wondered how hard it was for him to not lash out at her.

"How is my dear old granddaughter, anyway?" Diana's voice turned overly sweet once again. "Did the whore let you get your sad little pecker wet like your shadows hoped?"

Seth's fist clenched at his side but he quickly released it. My body flushed with heat and longing. I just wanted him to be out of there.

"No, she wouldn't have me." The emotion in his voice sounded real. "She wanted nothing to do with me."

I swallowed thickly but it did nothing to get rid of the dry lump in my throat.

"Stupid lovesick puppy. I could have told you that and saved you all this trouble," Diana chastised. "She walks the earth seducing men with her looks but she only opens her legs for those demons." My grandmother leaned in close to Seth, her smile far too wide. "I bet you want revenge on her, don't you?"

Seth paused for only half a heartbeat. "Yes. I want her to suffer like she made me suffer."

Sal and Nona, get ready, Ash commanded. It's almost showtime.

We're in position, Sal confirmed.

"Do you want her wiped off the face of the earth?" Diana asked, her eyes flashing eagerly. "To stop parading around like such a whore while innocent witches suffer?"

"Yes." Seth's jaw clenched. "More than anything."

"Good," she crooned. "This will be just the ticket." She reached into an inside shirt pocket and pulled out a small vial, the bright yellow substance inside sending everyone on edge like it was radioactive.

"Another angel's kiss?" Seth cried out in awe. "How many do you have?"

"This is my last one." Diana stroked the bottle affectionately. "So I performed a special, highly intricate blood spell to bind it."

Shit, that's not possible, Ash thought beside me. At least it shouldn't be.

She could be bluffing, I offered. Or just spouting crazy bullshit.

"What do you mean?" Seth asked.

"For nearly thirty years I've held onto this vial of blood." Diana clutched it tightly in her fist. "I never knew why I kept it, aside from holding onto my last piece of her in my grief. But whenever I meant to dispose of it, something told me to keep it. Somehow I knew deep down I would need it again for some great purpose. And now I finally know why."

"I'm sorry. I don't understand." Seth kept his head bowed.

"Of course you would never understand something as intricate as blood magic," she scoffed. "This," she petted the vial again, "was the blood of my daughter, Deidre. I took her blood and sealed it within the angel's kiss. Now it only has one target. The only other person who has fifty percent of this blood still running in her veins."

FUCK! Raum's voice in my head rattled my skull. Get Deja out of here! Get her as fucking far away as possible!

"He's right," Ash said, now using his mouth to speak and began shoving me down the boulder. "You need to run, now!"

"I'm not leaving you all here!" I hissed, grabbing onto his pant leg as I slid down the rocky surface but he was too strong.

Ash yanked my grip off and forcefully pushed me off the rock with inhuman strength. "That angel's kiss will *only* hit you!" he said, anger and fear in his cold eyes. "We're not at risk but you need to get the fuck out of here!"

She opened the vial! Raum yelled inside my head. Deja, run! Everyone throw up shields!

I scrambled off the rock to the ground and took off running, not aware of any direction but just moving. Adrenaline pumped through my body and made me feel superhuman. Blurred trees and brush zoomed past me. I tried to listen for the guys, for any clues, but all I could hear was my feet crushing leaves and my pulse pounding in my ears.

I ran until my lungs screamed and my legs gave out beneath me. Something tripped me and I found myself rolling down a hillside, rocks and fallen branches stabbing all over my body. A tree stopped me and I groaned from the impact. Still I sat up, listening intently.

Nothing but crickets. Darkness had settled in and I could barely make out dark shapes in the woods.

I raised my hand to cast a small fireball for light but a flash of brightness caught my eye and I turned to look.

Shit, no!

I scrambled to move, to avoid the glowing angel's kiss that zeroed in on me like a homing missile. But I was too slow.

Pain spread throughout my back and quickly stole my breath, my ability to move, and so much more. It was the same unimaginable pain I felt once before when my soul was ripped from my body. When I was ripped away from my lovers and my consciousness for a thousand years.

This time, no army of Hell would be coming to save me at the last minute.

I fell into nothingness.

12
RAUM

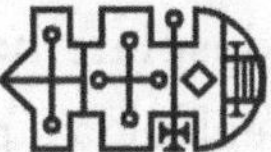

None of us knew what to do with ourselves, much less what to say.

Diana's fucking angel kiss tore through our defenses like paper and zoomed straight after Deja as she ran. We heard her cry out and the suddenness of her voice being cut off.

Then we couldn't find her.

We looked like worthless dogs chasing our tails, making the same circles over and over again while calling her name, looking for any sign.

"Her scent just disappears here." Nona's voice cracked as she shifted back to human to tell us. "It's like she vanished into thin air. Either that or my nose is broken."

Sal confirmed what she said. We all looked around the hillside where Deja had rolled down until she hit the tree trunk we were standing in front of. We waited, holding our breaths like she would pop out laughing at us with a gleeful look on her face.

"Come on, baby," I pleaded under my breath, refusing to let the panic rise. "Please tell me you're fucking with us."

We called her name. We felt for her aura with ours. We marched through the woods all night, looking at every askew pine needle that could tell us something.

"How could she just vanish?" I asked Ash. "When it hit me, it felt like a machine gun ripped me open but I didn't disappear. If this really happened, she had to have left... something."

"I don't know, man." Even now he was trying to be the calm, in-control leader. But I saw how his hands shook when he rubbed his beard. Like all of us, he was barely holding it together.

None of us wanted to admit it, but I knew I wasn't the only one. My aura felt like an empty, desolate hallway. Through the connection we had, I could always feel Deja's presence. Sometimes I picked up on her mood and emotions. But now all of that was gone.

"It doesn't make any sense," I muttered. "I can still see her in the future. With us, with our kids."

"We're in shock," Ash pointed out flatly. "It hasn't sunk in yet. We're in denial."

I spun on him angrily. "Don't you dare give up on her yet. She is *Lilith*. There's no way she can be just taken down like that."

Eventually we made our way to the meadow where Seth had been planted. Where everything seemed to be going fine in one moment and went terribly wrong in the next.

"What happened?" he asked, not looking at either of us.

"There's no sign of Deja," Ash said stiffly. "The shifters can't even pick up a scent."

"I felt her pain," Seth said hauntingly. "I wasn't even in her shadows but I felt her fear. I felt her soul begin to rip from her body."

"Fuck." Ash turned away and scrubbed a hand over his face, unable to contain his emotion any longer.

"She can't really be... can she?" Seth looked up at me, his eyes pleading with me, begging me not to be serious. But if Deja was really gone for good, not even I could make a joke out of that.

"We don't know yet, man." I swallowed but my throat still tightened into a dry knot. "We're trying to figure it out."

"It feels so wrong." Seth shook his head. "I could feel her nearby and then she was just... gone."

"Bro, here's the thing." I reached out and squeezed his shoulder. He looked up but his eyes weren't seeing me. "If you could feel her like that, you meant something to her on the same level as us. She let you in."

"Stop." Seth gave me a murderous look. "Don't talk about her in past tense."

"None of us can feel her anymore!" Ash cried from behind me. "What do you think that means?"

"It doesn't mean she's dead. She could be on another plane," Seth protested. "She could have gotten whisked to Hell or—"

"It doesn't work like that," Ash snarled. He ran his hands up through his hair and tugged. In all the years I'd known him, I never saw him so distraught. As Deja's first and the one who loved her the longest, his panic and grief had to be on another level.

"Let's check in with the shifters," I suggested. "See if they picked up anything."

Ash nodded and began walking off. I hesitated for a moment before grabbing Seth's shirt and dragging him up to his feet.

"Come on," I growled. "She considers you one of hers now, so fucking act like it. You're one of us."

He followed me dutifully, though his thousand-yard stare remained.

We spent the next few hours rendezvousing with Astrid's shifter team, spreading out to search and then meeting again empty-handed. As the hours passed and night slowly gave way to daylight, the hopelessness began to sink in.

When the sun rose, I shifted into raven form and soared high above the trees. My vision wasn't nearly as good as birds of prey but damn it, I felt useless on the ground. I had to look for myself. Maybe, just maybe I'd see something that everyone else missed.

I flew around in circles until my wings fatigued. I looked until I heard Sal's weary voice in my head.

Raum, the shifters have been up all night and need to rest, he said. And we should get Ash back to the house, he's all messed up.

Okay, I answered and flew to our rendezvous point.

Everyone stood around in a circle looking grim. Astrid's mates were doing their best to hold and comfort her, though anyone could see how hard they were having it too. I shifted back to human and barely anyone looked up. They knew I didn't have anything. All except Nona.

Bright, lovely Nona, the guiding light in our Deja's lifetime looked up at me. Her tear-filled eyes, still hanging onto hope and optimism, flooded over when she saw me. She didn't have to ask. Her eyes squeezed shut as she choked out a sob and I knew that bright light was snuffed out.

Not knowing what else to do, I pulled her into a hug. She sobbed openly into my chest, my attempts to shush and soothe her drowned out by her grief. I looked down at my hands wrapped around her and saw my own fingers shaking. The sinking feeling in my chest turned into a cement block in my stomach. The shock and denial was wearing off and reality began sinking in.

I cleared my throat but couldn't get rid of the feeling that it was closing up.

"You need to get some rest," I murmured to her. "None of us are in top shape right now. We can keep looking once you've slept a little and eaten something."

Nona gave a shaky nod and slowly looked up at me with puffy, red eyes.

"Can I come to the house with you guys?" she asked. "I want to be around her magic, her presence. I don't know how to explain it but I..."

"Of course." I knew exactly what she was talking about. We all wanted the comfort and familiarity of Deja's magic, which was present in everything she touched. To normal humans, it was like wearing your lover's clothing or using their pillow because their scent was comforting. We all just wanted to feel Deja there. None of us were ready to let go.

The rest of the shifters returned to their camp. Ash and I decided to anchor home with Nona in tow. Sal volunteered to drive the truck back. Normally, I would agree on the account that his temper was so volatile, he wanted to be alone where he had no risk of hurting anyone. But if anyone seemed volatile right then, it was Ash. Sal for the most part had been quiet and sullen.

I turned to Seth, still standing like a mannequin with his thousand-yard stare. "You coming, dude?"

"No, I don't think so." He shook his head and rubbed his eyes. "Someone should probably stay out here in case... I dunno. Just in case."

"You're still a damn human, man." I felt like I was chastising a child. "You need sleep and food. If anyone should stay out here, it should be one of us." I gestured to Ash, Sal and myself. "But going crazy in the woods isn't gonna help anyone. We're gonna recuperate and come right back."

"Nah," he shook his head again. "You guys go on. I'll take a break when you guys get back but I'm gonna stay."

I shrugged. "Suit yourself." We all dealt with grief in our own ways. If his was to become prey to wild animals, so be it.

Seconds later, I appeared with Nona and Ash in our kitchen. It felt wrong. Quiet and too empty.

The recycling bin was still filled with beer bottles from when Nona and Deja pulled their all-nighter. I didn't even want to look at the counter where Sal and I took turns with her that amazing day that felt so long ago.

"Take the master bedroom," I told Nona, gently guiding her to the stairs. "There's fresh sheets in the linen closet just outside. The bathroom should have everything you need if you want to shower."

"Thanks, Raum." She forced a smile at me and gave a gentle squeeze of my hand before taking the steps and disappearing out of view.

The moment Ash and I were alone, all hell broke loose.

He grabbed the first thing he could find, Deja's tea cup, and sent it flying across the room. It shattered against the far wall, turning into dust and leaving a serious dent thanks to his demon strength.

I threw up shields in front of the windows and sliding glass doors and just stood silently while he unleashed his pain, his control.

He threw every cup and glass we had in the cupboards, then he started on the dining chairs and the kitchen table, all of which became piles of splinters upon impact. Thankfully, Nona knew better than to come back downstairs.

Ash wasn't crying, grunting or screaming, but I could see the pain etched on his face. I'd never seen him act this way before in my life, not even when she was taken from us the first time. Because we knew then she'd eventually come back. But now?

None of us knew what to do, or how to *be* without her. There was no point to us existing without her. We all knew that and didn't know how to deal with it.

After several minutes of destroying everything in his path, Ash seemed to have worn himself out. He sank to the floor, breathing heavily and not caring about the debris littered everywhere. The entire downstairs looked like a war zone.

"What the fuck do we do, Raum?" He said my name but asked the question like he expected Lucifer, the angels, or anyone else listening to answer him. "For the first time ever, I'm completely at a fucking loss." His voice was pained, raw with emotion.

"Well, we can't sit down and think about it over coffee," I mused, looking around the room. Even with magic, this would be a fucking bitch to clean up.

Ash was on me instantly, getting in my face and shoving me back forcefully.

"You think now's a really good time for your fucking jokes, Raum?" he snarled. His aura grew to twice the size of his body, crackling and swirling with everything he was feeling. I did my best to remain calm, knowing he could eliminate me if pushed too far.

"No, I don't," I answered. "I especially don't think it's a good time to be at each other's throats, either."

He looked at me as if he was seriously considering killing me, then looked around for something to destroy. Unfortunately, he already fucked the whole place up.

"Fuck, Raum. Fuck." He turned from me and raked his fingers through his hair, tugging at his scalp like a madman again. "How the fuck can she be gone just like that? She can't..."

It was a sight to behold, watching one of the most powerful fallen angels come apart with grief and despair. All of us must have felt too close to human in that moment, too vulnerable and shaken. As immortals, we were supposed to bigger than this. But nothing made you realize your humanity more than losing someone you loved.

"I don't know, man." My voice cracked, unable to hold my own emotion back any longer. "I don't fucking know."

13
DEJA

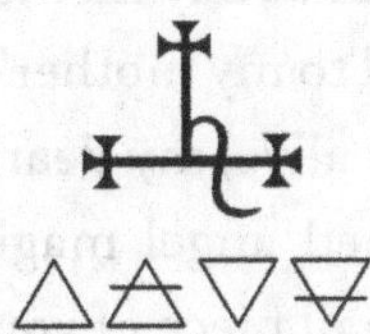

It felt like forever before I realized I was conscious. Not only that, but I had a body.

My lungs took in air. My fingers wiggled, and I felt the touch of a warm, stone floor beneath me. I opened my eyes and blinked a few times, trying to focus on the world that surrounded me.

The sky was dark but the room I was in was bright and well-lit. I slowly sat up and cautiously looked around. I was in a cave, or at least some kind of room that was massive and cavernous. The textured stone walls seemed to disappear as they stretched upward forever. It was impossible to tell if there was a ceiling or sky at all.

The light in the room seemed to have no source. It just *was*. And I realized this place was vaguely familiar.

"My dear Lilith. You are awake and well, I hope."

A deep and velvety masculine voice cut through the silence. I turned to see a handsome man who looked to be in his forties approach me. He had golden eyes like mine and dark hair with a small pointed beard to match. If the small pointed horns on his forehead didn't give it away, the raw feral power exuding from him did.

It was heavy and smothering and yet at the same time, bright and uplifting.

"Lucifer," I said cautiously. "Where am I?"

"In Hell, my dear." He smiled in a way that was kind, almost fatherly. "I know you have obligations on the surface but damn, it's always lovely to see you down here. You are sorely missed."

"How am I alive?" I climbed slowly to my feet, watching my own body as if it would disappear at any moment. "Or am I? Diana hit me with an angel's kiss bonded to my mother's blood."

"You are most certainly alive, my dear." Lucifer's smile fell into a scowl. "I hate that wretched angel magic. The last time an angel tried to kill you, I kept a small piece of your soul with me here to use as an anchor. I made it pull you to Hell the instant your soul began to separate from your body again. It seems your mortal grandmother has gone just as mad as Beelzebub."

"Fuck." I closed my eyes and brought a hand to my chest, marveling at the fact that I could still feel my heartbeat at all. My eyes snapped open, alerted by the other name Lucifer said. "What's going on with Beelzebub?"

"He's been cast to the lower circles." Lucifer sounded a bit sad. "The hell of eternal suffering that humans know about."

"Good," I snapped. "He deserves nothing less."

His eyebrows raised as if amused. "You have strong feelings about his punishment." He said it as a statement, not a question.

"Yes." I met his eyes, fighting every instinct to lower my gaze in submission. Lucifer had the power to kill me with a blink of his eyes but I wanted him to know that I stood with Beelzebub's victim. "Seth had no voice, no control, no one to stand up for him when your brother used him as a puppet."

Lucifer chuckled. "I see why you spend so much time on the surface, dear Lilith. You're needed up there. You stand up for those who cannot on their own."

My gaze dropped to the floor as if physically feeling the weight of Lucifer's magic on my body. I couldn't even perceive an aura around him. His whole *being* just exuded a force of immeasurable power.

"It doesn't feel that way lately," I admitted. "I'm just trying to kill an evil witch and raise my kids with the men I love." My head snapped up, a sudden burning question on my tongue. "Will my grandmother go to hell? The one that Beelzebub is in?"

"Oh yes," he smiled, answering as simply as if I asked for directions. "For her crimes, her soul is already slated for eternal suffering."

For some reason, that answer didn't satisfy me like I hoped. Eternity, what a concept. I lived for thousands of years and not even I could perceive eternity. My whole existence was a fraction of a second in the scope of eternity. And to suffer for that long, with no end ever in sight. Even for Diana or Beelzebub, I couldn't bring myself to feel joy for their suffering.

"What about my mother?" The words tumbled out of me with no thought. "Is her soul here?"

Lucifer's smile dropped, but he observed me kindly. He extended a hand. "Will you take a walk with me, Lilith?"

I placed my hand in his, warm and humanlike, and followed his lead. "If I'm still in my current lifetime, I would prefer to be called Deja if you don't mind."

"Deja, then." He smiled warmly and directed my hand to his elbow as we walked. His bicep felt muscular underneath his suit. "No, your mother isn't here, my dear."

The cavern was empty of people as we walked, but I felt energy and power from everywhere. I realized it was shadow magic, the dark hidden side of everything from the surface. It reminded me of my men, of being wrapped up in their protective embrace. But knowing I wouldn't meet my mother's soul here made me sad. She definitely wasn't among the angels.

"What happened to her soul after she died?" I asked. "For some reason I thought she would end up down here, maybe reborn as a succubus."

"No, my dear," Lucifer said gently. "Only humans and fallen angels end up here. Witches, shifters, and others only come to the lower circles if their crimes of morality are so great, they must suffer for eternity. But when I gave you your powers," he looked at me. "I wanted a different afterlife for the people you'd create, the witches."

"What do you mean?" I asked.

"You were created from the earth, my dear." He gave a gentle squeeze of my fingers. "Your powers are of the physical world. Earth, Water, Fire, and Air. It only made sense to me that after death, a witch's soul returned to where her power originated."

"I'm not sure I understand."

"Your physical body decomposes and nourishes the earth," he explained. "So does an ordinary human's but their soul comes here. A witch's soul returns to earth, nourishing the elements and the power you draw from." He stopped walking and turned to face me. "You feel your mother every time you draw magic to manifest, Deja. She and all the witches before her are always with you."

I didn't realize I was crying until he wiped a tear from my cheek. But the sadness in my chest lifted into joy. The hole that felt ripped open by my childhood being stolen from me, and the wrongness of my mother's death, I felt it close and heal.

My mother was always with me. And when I got back to the surface and watched Diana's life drain from her body, her death would balance the wrongness of the lives she took. It wouldn't bring my mother or Juno back but the sense of closure, the process of heal-ing, was already beginning.

"Now tell me about Seth," Lucifer said as we continued our walk. "What does he make you feel?" We rounded a beautiful, crystal clear lagoon where a few demons swam naked, giggling and splashing each other.

"I'm scared," I admitted. "Ash was meant for me from the beginning, and the other two you made for me. All this time, I felt comfortable knowing my lovers and I were always meant to be, in a sense. But he throws everything off balance for me."

"Welcome to what humans feel like when they fall in love," he laughed. "An all-consuming fire, coupled with confusion and uncertainty."

"Yes, that's exactly it," I admitted. "I've been fighting it but it's no use. I want him, and the guys have essentially given me their blessing, but I still feel like I'm stepping over the edge of a cliff."

"Love is always a risk," he said gently. "You put your heart on the line and he does the same. It's terrifying and a thrill. But," he quirked an eyebrow at me, "you know better than anyone how important it is to take risks. A safety net is what the angels use to corral their followers. But us? We burn that net and embrace the unknown."

He was right. He was telling me what I always knew, who I was at the core of my being but lost sight of along the way. I was born to defy the status quo, to take what I wanted instead of asking permission to have it. I loved my men and never wanted to hurt them, but Lucifer didn't give me my power to please others.

"I have missed talking to you," I said, patting his forearm with my other hand. On a whim, I leaned my head against his shoulder. "Thank you for the reminder of who I am."

"My pleasure, Deja." He placed his hand on top of mine. "I wish I could keep you longer, but I know the surface needs you more than I do. Of all my creations, you are one I'm most fond of."

Warmth bloomed inside me. "You are the closest thing to a father I've ever had," I admitted. "Just talking to you makes me feel ready to take on anything again."

His face turned and I felt a soft kiss brush my forehead. "I'm honored you feel that way, dear. You make me proud and I think of you like a daughter as well."

Our stroll continued in companionable silence. It felt like neither one of us wanted to be the one to say goodbye. Still, that didn't keep my thoughts from circulating about the future, the aftermath of all this craziness with Diana. As much as I hated to admit it, the running, the killing, all of it, would not end with her.

It would never end.

"You're thinking too loud," Lucifer chuckled. "What's troubling you, dear?"

"It's just," I hesitated, chewing my lip as I put words to my thoughts. "I don't want each of my lifetimes to be the same cyclical thing. Opening people's minds, running from those who want to kill me until they inevitably catch me, and then start the whole thing all over again. I want to leave something lasting, something that'll hold for multiple generations."

"You've done well at leaving a lasting legacy," he said. "Humans still know who Lilith and Jezebel are. To some you are reviled, but moreso each century your past lives are an inspiration. I see it now in the young human women more than ever. You are a symbol of independence, of taking ownership of your sexuality without apology, of demanding to be heard as equals, not silenced by your peers."

"It's not so much that," I said. "It's more like, I know there is always going to be push back for what we do. Witches, shifters, and demons will always be villainized and persecuted by the ignorant masses. I wish I could save them all but I can't. I want to make some kind of safe place for those who can't go anywhere. A sanctuary, of sorts. Where everyone is safe and protected from humans with pitchforks."

Lucifer was silent for a moment as he absorbed my words. "That is certainly a worthwhile endeavor, and something that's never been done before," he said. "You would need long-lasting glamour magic to keep it hidden from humans, and even then the spell would need to be regularly maintained."

"I was inspired by Astrid, the fox shifter I met," I told him. "Her little village is a safe space for all shifters escaping humans. I love that and I want the same thing for all magical beings. But her place isn't protected by magic at all. If humans were to stumble upon it, her whole rescue operation would be ruined. I can't stand the thought of that happening."

"Then you should absolutely do this." He squeezed my fingers affectionately. "Make a safe, hidden realm on the surface. You have my full support."

"You really think I can?"

"My dear, you are single-handedly turning the tide against a globally oppressive culture. You can absolutely do this, and anything." He grinned. "With your fallen angel and super-powered witch-demon hybrid, you should have no issue holding the magic until your next lifetime."

"Thank you," I said sincerely. "Your support truly means the world to me."

"Again, it's my pleasure, Deja." Lucifer inclined his head toward me. "I suppose I should let you go back to where you are needed. But before I do, I have a parting gift for you, dear."

"Oh?" I said, surprised.

He gently unwrapped my arm from his and took a step back, making a twirling motion with his finger. "Turn around and show me your back, please."

I humored him, turning until I faced away. In the next moment, his voice was near my ear. "I need to touch your bare skin. Please don't mistake it for getting fresh with you."

"Wouldn't dream of it, old man," I chuckled.

The next sensation I felt was his warm hand against my spine. He muttered some ancient language under his breath as I felt his power pulse through me. It was humbling. He probably wasn't using the power in his smallest fingernail and it still made my knees buckle. A slight, sharp pain like a cat scratch sliced through me, and just as quickly it was gone.

"There," he said with satisfaction, pulling his hand away. "Take a look, dear."

I looked over the lagoon we stood next to, now empty of people and the surface reflecting like a mirror. Looking over my shoulder, I lifted the back of my shirt and gasped at what I saw.

"Lucifer!" I breathed, pulling my shirt higher and twisting around for a better look. "They're beautiful!"

He placed sigils on my spine. The symbol of each of my men contrasted with my skin in dark, magical ink. But there was one I didn't recognize.

"Who's that?" I asked, pointing to the one in question.

"That is the demon Set," he answered. "He is Seth's namesake and one of the ancient forms of Beelzebub."

I opened my mouth to protest, but he held up a finger to silence me.

"Set is where Seth drew his strength and tenacity to break away from Beelzebub's control. Unknowingly, Beelzebub injected most of Set's powers into Seth in the womb. The ancient Egyptians regarded Set as the god of storms, which I thought you would find appropriate."

Of course. What better demon to fuel the power of the stormy eyed man who struggled so much, who somehow made me feel so much for him?

"The tattoos will remain on you, no matter which body you're in. I heard you once yearned to have all of your men's sigils on you," Lucifer added with a wink.

"Thank you," I said graciously. "I love them. I'll be happy to wear them forever."

With a final grin, Lucifer leaned in and planted a fatherly kiss on my cheek.

"Hopefully it won't be too long before I see you again, my dear daughter."

And with that, I felt an inexplicable pull on my body and soul back to the world of the living.

14
DEJA

I landed unsteadily on my feet, windmilling my arms and taking a few shaky steps from the rush of coming back from Hell. The forest surrounded me with its familiar smells, sounds, and the pulse of its magic. I felt under the back of my shirt and sure enough my sigil tattoos were there, pulsing with the gentle warmth of Lucifer's magic. I couldn't wait to show the guys, but I had no idea where I was.

I spun in a slow circle, looking for any familiar landmarks and realized this was the exact place where the angel's kiss hit me. There was the flattened trail of grass where I rolled down the hill until I crashed into this tree. This was where I died and was reborn.

Sunlight shone, filtered and dappled through the tree canopy. It was night when the guys and I were here and I had no idea how much time had passed.

With surefooted steps, I made my way back up the hill. If the guys thought I was dead, they probably wouldn't be out here anymore. But I could find the boulder me and Ash hid on, then find our trail to where he parked the truck, and hopefully follow that trail back home.

I was no tracker, but easily retraced my panicked run through the woods. Those branches were torn from me running through them. That muddy footprint was where I slipped and almost fell the first time.

The boulder was easy enough to spot, but I didn't see the man sitting with his back to the rock until I was almost right next to it. He looked up with stormy gray eyes at the sound of my feet crunching on the ground.

"Deja?" he said in a hoarse whisper, wiping his eyes that looked puffy and red. "No fucking way. Is that you?"

"Seth," I breathed. A rush of emotion filled me. His sigil nearly burned on my skin. I wanted to say so much but nothing would come out.

He rose to his feet, eyes locked on me as he approached me slowly, as if afraid I would vanish into thin air again.

"We couldn't find your body," he choked. "Diana disappeared and Nona couldn't pick up your scent—"

"It's okay," I whispered. "An anchor pulled me to Hell. I was with Lucifer and now I'm back."

A shaking hand extended toward my face then hesitated, pulling back slightly. I clasped it between both of my hands and kissed his palm. Then I pressed his hand to my cheek, losing myself in the sad, beautiful storm of his eyes.

"It's really you," he whispered incredulously, cupping my cheek as I leaned into his touch. "You're really here. Alive."

"I am," I assured him. "Seth, Beelzebub was sent to the lower circles of Hell. He's going to be punished for all eternity for what he did to you."

He said nothing. Not even a flicker of emotion in his eyes. I knew because we were standing so close, I could see my reflection in his pupils.

"Hey, did you hear me?" I cracked a smile. "He's going to pay for all the suffering he caused you. Lucifer told me himself."

Seth shook his head, a grin spreading across his face as he lifted his opposite hand to my other cheek.

"That is the farthest thing from my mind right now," he whispered.

Maybe he leaned in first. Maybe I did. All I knew was that a heavy, pregnant pause hung between us, and then our lips clashed together like a storm.

He was a rush. He was life, warmth and comfort pulling me in and still so unfamiliar. We were too hungry to go slowly. My teeth clicked against his as my lips parted for his tongue, which dove in and tasted all of me.

He felt solid and hot beneath my palms. One hand fell to the small of my back and I arched under his touch. My fingers trembled as they explored the contours of his chest, his ribs, and his abs flexing with deep breaths. This was completely unlike anything I'd done before. Even when I first met my three in this lifetime, something felt familiar in the way they kissed and touched me. Seth's mouth, his hands, his body, all of it was completely unknown to me.

"Deja," he groaned, turning me so my back pressed against the cool, smooth boulder. It did nothing to quell the heat building like a bonfire between us.

He pinned me there, standing between my legs and rolling his erection against me. My insides seemed to hollow out as my head rushed and my core ached for him.

"Tell me you don't want this," Seth rasped against the rapid pulse in my neck, his grip firm on my ribs. "Tell me you don't want me. You want them instead."

"I..." It came out a strangled moan as he pressed harder against my clit. Of course I couldn't say it. None of it was true. It never was. I wanted him the moment I set eyes on him at that coven party.

"Tell me and I'll stop." He pressed a kiss to my throat, his hands skimming down to my hips. "I'll leave and you'll never see me again. It'll break me but I'll do whatever you need me to do."

"No!" I cried out, my voice echoing off the trees.

He stiffened and pulled away to look at me.

"I don't want you to leave." My voice, barely above a whisper seemed to get carried off by the wind. "I want you here. With me."

His eyes searched mine as if looking for some hidden meaning to my words. His mouth parted and his lips looked so sexy and delicious, I couldn't stop myself from kissing him again.

"I want you. So fucking bad," I told him between each kiss. "I don't just want you physically, I want to *know* you. I want to learn more magic from that incredible mind of yours. I want to see you smile every day because no one is going to hurt you anymore." I wrapped a hand around his neck and raked my fingers through his hair. "Not even me."

I only saw his eyebrows knit together before his mouth was on mine again, opening me up and drinking me in. His whole body pinned me to the rock as my hands dove under his shirt, needing to feel his bare skin.

Clothes flew off of us as if magicked away. Every inch of him was so hot and hard. I kissed and traced the sigils inked into his body. Some I knew from studying ancient magic with Ash, others I'd never seen before. One day we'd lie down with all the time in the world and I would explore them more slowly. I'd ask him questions about each one and listen to the voice that gave me chills every time I heard it. But not right now. Right now I needed him and no one else to fill the aching emptiness inside me.

"Deja," he moaned again, his hands moving across me just as desperate and frantic as I touched him. "You're so much more than what he told me you were. You're the healing I needed. You're everything I needed."

Words became meaningless as he secured my thighs across his slender hips. I hooked my ankles behind his back and reached down between us to stroke him, thick and pulsing in my palm. He shuddered and moaned so hotly into my neck, his teeth grazing the sensitive skin there as I guided him to my entrance.

He thrust into my hand, slicking his rigid shaft in my wetness before following my lead. His hips surged forward, pushing inside me and drawing a spasm throughout my whole body and a cry from my lips. My pussy hugged around his girth almost as tightly as I held onto the firm muscles of his back.

We rocked rhythmically together against that boulder, the sunlight casting a warm glow on our naked skin. A fleeting thought of, *I can't believe this is happening* passed through my mind but it didn't erase that this felt *right*.

While this with Seth was so new and unfamiliar, every kiss and thrust and touch just made me want more of him. He kissed me so sweetly, but still with passion and hunger. His cock stretched me so deliciously, but still with the intimacy and tenderness as if we'd been lovers for years.

"I'm dying to feel you come," he growled in my ear. "I've had dreams about how it would feel to make you lose control."

"I'm so close," I panted, raking my nails against his shoulder blades. "Don't stop."

He made a hot sound, somewhere between a moan and a laugh, then trailed one hand down my body, between my breasts and directly to my clit. All the while he never stopped thrusting into me, filling me up and leaving me empty with each breath. When he applied pressure to my clit, it became too much to bear. The pleasure within me swelled like a wave carrying me high and fast.

I quivered and shook like jello in his hands before I crashed. My body seized up as I came apart, muscles involuntarily twitching and spasming from my release. Magic shot from my fingertips and maybe even from my curled-up toes.

"Oh yes, sweetheart," Seth groaned. "Fuck, that was beautiful. You are so perfect."

My legs were so devoid of strength, they shakily settled back down on the ground. Seth's cock slipped out of me and pressed solid and slick against my lower belly as we kissed.

He turned me around, brushing a playful bite across my shoulder before he pulled away.

"Have you always had these?" he asked, brushing a hand along the sigils on my spine. I didn't have to look to know that his fingers settled over the sigil of Set.

"No, Lucifer just gave them to me," I said. "My guys have my sigil tattooed on them, so I wanted all of theirs on me." I looked at him over my shoulder. He continued staring at my back, an unreadable expression on his face. "Do you know about Set?" I asked.

"Of course I do," he said quietly. "I've always felt like he was my guiding light in a way, leading me out of the storm. The only good part of Beelzebub and the only aspect of him that I wanted to keep with me."

I still couldn't read what he was feeling and asked, "Are you okay with the tattoo? I'm sure I could have Lucifer remove it if—"

He cut me off with a kiss, pulling a gasp from me as his thick length pressed against my ass. I could only arch and push back against him eagerly as his hands swept forward to caress my breasts, kneading my nipples into aching, sensitive points.

"I love it," he said gruffly, moving my hair and attacking my neck and the top of my back. "It's perfect, I love seeing it on your skin. I love that you claim me as yours. And Deja?"

"Mm?" My legs quivered again, but this time with the anticipation of feeling him fill me again. I needed it. I needed it yesterday, before he went out to face my greatest enemy for me.

"I won't leave you, either." He pushed inside me again with a sexy groan, pulling my hips back toward him. "I want this," he growled against my neck, seating his full length inside me. "I don't ever want to be without this. Without *you*."

"You're sure?" I panted, trying to not lose myself in the sensation of him pressing against my back, my ass, against all of my inner walls. "You're sure you want me and everything else that comes with me?" I didn't have to say my three other men. He knew.

"I've never been more sure of anything." He pressed into me deeper until I cried out, then pulled back with a moan. "I've never felt like I belonged anywhere, or with anyone until you. I don't care if others are lucky enough to belong with you, too." He nipped my earlobe and let out a soft chuckle as he pressed into me again. "Honestly, I'm surprised you don't have more."

"Like I need more of you fuckers to drive me crazy," I groaned.

He laughed, a beautiful, genuine, lighthearted sound—not the bitter, jagged-edged cackle I was so used to hearing. I couldn't wait to hear more of it.

I caught his mouth in a hot kiss and pressed back against him. He pushed forward into me, rolling his hips against my ass. Together we pushed and pulled, making a sweet, delicious steady rhythm that slowly built up into a rough, greedy frenzy. His hand slid across my waist, feeling and relishing every inch of me before sweeping across my clit.

The pressure in my core built up like a volcano. My ass bounced against his hips from the impactful force of his thrusts. His breath came out in hot, ragged moans as his own release neared. Surrounding our bodies, our auras melded together as one as we came together. His ecstasy was mine and mine was his. There was no ending of me and beginning of him. We were one.

We stayed like that for I don't know how long. I leaned against the boulder and he leaned against me, arms around me in a tight embrace as he swept soft, lazy kisses across my shoulders and neck.

"We should head back to the house," I said, killing our intimate silence. Now that my head was clearer, my mind and body finally sated from what I'd been craving, I missed my other guys terribly. I needed and craved them and they all likely thought I was dead.

"Of course, sweetheart," he said softly. "They'll be just as overjoyed to see you as I am."

I turned and looked at him, the same man who'd driven me so insane and looked so different now. He looked relaxed, happy.

"You know, you're cute when you're actually nice to me." I ran a finger along his sleek jaw.

He huffed out a laugh and kissed me. I felt his smile against my lips and it made my heart lift like a balloon.

"Don't get too used to it," he teased. "And I'm always cute."

"You've been taking lessons from Raum, I see," I muttered.

We pulled our clothes on, and I wrapped my arms around him again, enamored with his smell, with the feeling of his warmth and solidness against my cheek. He dropped a kiss to my head and wrapped a protective arm around my shoulders. Then he anchored us back to our home.

15
DEJA

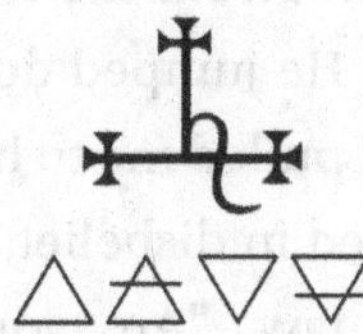

My heart rate skyrocketed as Seth and I entered the house. Would they even still be here? If they really thought I was dead, what reason would the guys have to stay?

Panic surged through my chest when I saw the state the house was in. Broken glass and ceramic crunched under my shoes, smashed furniture littered the house, debris was everywhere.

I threw defenses up immediately and sensed Seth do the same behind me. Power coiled in my belly, ready to strike at the slightest movement. We walked through slowly, surveying the damage. Did Diana's people ransack my house? If everyone thought she killed me, fucking with our things would just be another spit on my grave.

A flash of black at the corner of my eye made me turn and shoot tendrils of earth magic. With no hesitation, I was ready to kill what got in my way.

The tendrils wrapped around a broad, muscular forearm thrown up to block the attack. When the arm lowered to reveal its owner's face, all solidness seemed to leave my body.

"Raum," I choked and ran to him.

"Baby," he answered in the most pained voice I ever heard him say.

He wrapped me in a bone-crushing hug and lifted me off the ground. Our lips passed across each other in messy, desperate, unco-ordinated kisses that never felt so sweet.

"Sal! Ash! Nona!" he yelled through his massive, gorgeous grin. "Our girl is back!"

Sal's head popped out first from the top landing of the stairs, his green eyes wide as saucers. He jumped down, skipping all the steps in a graceful, feline leap and pulled me to him.

"Beautiful," he murmured in disbelief, his fingers gently running over my cheekbones and jaw. "Are you alright? What the hell happened?"

Before I could answer, another hand pulled me away by my arm. I found myself staring into icy blue eyes rimmed with red blood vessels. Ash tried to keep his face with his usual mask but his voice trembled as he spoke.

"Is it really you?" he asked coldly.

"It's her, man," Raum assured him. "She came at me with earth magic like only our little spitfire would."

Ash's expression began to crack but he still said nothing. His eyes remained suspicious but his mouth twisted as if starting to betray him.

"It's me, angel," I said, wrapping an arm around his neck. "And I love you, even though you drink nasty shit like coffee instead of twig and leaf water like civilized people."

He choked out a laugh, finally letting his guard down and swal-lowing my mouth in a bruising kiss. My arms wound tighter around him and his did the same around me. The world melted away as I burrowed into his touch, his scent. Our mouths didn't speak but his aura wrapped around mine and whispered his thoughts like a lullaby.

My love, my love...

"Hey, you two." Raum clapped his hands down on both of our shoulders with a cheesy grin. "Let Nona get in there and have a piece."

I turned slowly away from Ash to the young woman standing a bit further away from everyone else. Her eyes were red too and she wrung her hands nervously.

"I asked if I could stay here because I wanted to feel your magic before it faded away." She chewed her lip and looked away. "I know it looks weird but I swear—"

"Silly bitch, get over here." I held my arms out to her.

She choked out a sob, and we ran to each other. Together we collapsed in a heap of tears on the floor, seeing as we no longer had any furniture downstairs.

The guys gave us space and I only vaguely noticed Seth going around and repairing what he could with his magic. Already he seemed to fit in seamlessly with the guys, and my heart lifted with gratitude. No one gave him the side-eye or possessive snarls anymore. They didn't ask if anything happened between us out in the woods but on some level, I was sure they knew. Raum probably saw it all happen in a vision, though he would never tell me that either.

"Now that we're all blissfully reunited," Raum pulled me into his lap on the loveseat in Ash's study, the only downstairs area left untouched by wreckage. "Want to tell us what happened?"

"It was Lucifer," I said to all the shocked faces in the room. "Back when the angel first tried to kill me, he kept a tiny piece of my soul in Hell and made it into an anchor. It would be triggered to pull me there for safety if anything similar happened again."

"Sly fucking bastard," Sal grinned. "That's genius."

"Ahem, plain English for the non-magical folk, please?" Nona raised her hand with a teasing grin.

"Anchors are how we transport somewhere instantly," Ash explained. "We can't just do it at will, we have to spell something and keep it in the location we want to transport to. Most demons set up anchors in Hell to go there and back easier, but we never thought about it with Deja. She's usually with one of us and just tags along when someone goes."

"And they never have an expiration date, apparently," Raum smirked while tapping my knee.

"So is it fair to assume Diana thinks Deja's dead as well?" Seth asked. He sat on the arm of the love seat, giving Raum and I plenty of space. That wouldn't do, so I nudged him with my toes until he slid down in the seat next to Raum. Then I extended my legs out over his lap and watched the smile and giddiness grow on his face as he massaged my calves.

"I think so." Ash stood leaning against one of his bookshelves, stroking his beard thoughtfully. He didn't even seem to notice the affection between Seth and me. "There's no reason she wouldn't. Once an angel's kiss is released, it doesn't stop until it hits and destroys something. And with this one being bonded to Deidre's blood, she made it essentially foolproof to hit Deja."

"So if I were to confront her myself," I smiled. "I would catch her completely unaware."

"That would be the most likely outcome." Ash's eyes glowed with excitement. "But we should still proceed with caution and come up with a backup plan if things do go awry again."

"She won't come out here again," Seth said as he pressed his thumb deliciously into the arch of my foot. "We'll likely have to go back to San Francisco. I can anchor us to my old apartment back there."

"That's good to know," Sal said lightheartedly. "There's no reason for us to fail this time."

None of them seemed the least bit uncomfortable with Seth sitting among us and that warmed my heart to an unspeakable degree.

"While we're making plans," I said, linking my fingers with

Raum's at my side. "After all this is over... there's something I want to do that's never been done before. I talked about it to Lucifer and he gave me his full support."

"Name it, my love," Ash said sweetly.

"I want to make a sanctuary, a safe place for all supernaturals. Demons, shifters, witches, whatever. If there's someone out there who needs protection from humans or anyone, I want them to know they can come to this place."

Silence fell for a moment all around the room before smiles broke out like sunshine on everyone's faces.

"You mean like Astrid's campground?" Nona piped up.

"Yes, exactly," I answered. "If it's okay with her, I'd like to include her campground within the new sanctuary. Then her shifter refugees will be protected by magic, too. Then she won't have to shoot first and ask questions later."

My demons burst out laughing; only Seth and Nona looked confused.

"Don't worry, we'll bring you up to speed." Raum clapped a hand down on Seth's shoulder.

"So will you guys help me with this? I want this place to last for generations and it'll take a lot of magic to hold." I looked around to all the faces in the room, these people who I adored and stuck by me through unimaginable things.

"Without a doubt, baby," Raum purred and planted a kiss on my cheek.

"I'll ask Astrid tonight, but I'm sure she'll be thrilled," Nona grinned. "With magic to protect our refugees, it will really make our job of relocating them so much easier."

"Anything you need, beautiful." Sal shifted from side to side on his feet, adorable and sexy as he was excited.

"You know I'm yours for anything," Seth murmured with a gentle squeeze of my foot.

That only left Ash. He seemed distracted, stroking his beard and looking off somewhere far away.

"Angel?" I pressed gently. "What do you think?"

"What should we call it?" he asked no one in particular. "It'll be the first of its kind and needs a fitting name."

My heart swelled. Not only was he on board, he was already making plans for it.

We all started thinking and throwing out various names and words. Ash turned to the bookshelf and quickly began scanning the spines.

"How about this?" He pulled out a slim volume and tossed it to me. "Turn to the first poem in there."

I glanced at the cover before opening the book. *The Poetic Edda*. A collection of poems from early Norse culture. The first poem was called *Voluspa*. It had been so long since I spoke or read the ancient language, I looked up to Ash with a blank expression on my face.

"Voluspa? What does it mean?"

He grinned. "It roughly translates to, 'The Prophecy of the Witch'."

16
DEJA

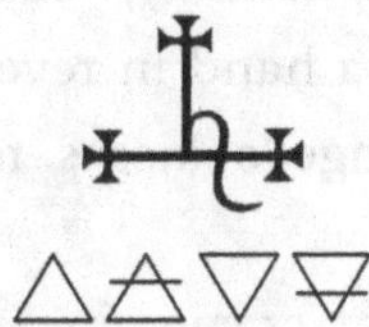

Our new plan for Diana was relatively straightforward. We would all anchor back to San Francisco, but only Seth and I would go directly to her. The others would stand by as backup and only show when I had her subdued. No one wanted to miss witnessing her death. Perhaps that was morbid, but these were demons after all.

Ash spent the next few hours researching blood spells and felt confident she didn't have another angel's kiss that would target me like a homing missile. Still, there was everyone else we had to worry about.

"Who knows how many angel-kissed weapons she has though?" Sal asked worriedly. "Each of those elite hunters who ambushed us had one, which none of us had seen before. For all we know, Diana might be sitting on a stockpile."

"That's true." Ash rubbed his forehead. "I'm extremely curious to know how she got as many as she did. What kind of deal did she have to make?"

"Selling her soul?" I suggested only half-jokingly. "And those of the coven too. I bet the angels love the idea of having witches under control to spread their gospel."

"It's a conspiracy!" Raum shouted dramatically. "They told everyone demons make deals for souls but it was the angels all along!"

Everyone rolled their eyes but my giggle sent his chest puffing out like a proud peacock.

"It's not a huge stretch, actually," Seth pointed out. "While the blood magic certainly had a hand in reversing her aging, whatever deal she made for the angel's kisses may have accelerated the process."

"She definitely got a lot crazier in a short amount of time," I remarked.

It almost made me feel sorry for Diana. What happened when she was young to make her this way? Lots of witches of her generation disliked demons, but she took it to another level. She got so wrapped up in her hatred that it defined her life and made her kill her own daughter.

But in the end, it didn't matter. I couldn't go back and undo whatever damage had been done that set her on this path. She made decisions that had dire consequences. I'd take no pleasure in killing her, I learned that from Juno. But it had to be done, and I had to be the one to do it.

"Let's get this over with," I muttered as I stood and dusted off my pants. The sooner I didn't have my grandmother to worry about, the sooner we could do what I really wanted, start creating *Voluspa*.

Seth followed me up, wrapping his arms around me from behind and dropped a reassuring kiss on my neck. My breath hitched and my heart rate doubled. Already he was comfortable doing this in front of everyone else and I fucking loved it.

"We'll get it right this time, sweetheart," he murmured. "I know we will."

"Fucking hell, I hope so," I sighed. "I'm just so tired of this shit."

Ash walked up to us and I felt Seth's grip on me tighten. I didn't tell him yet about Ash's preference to have me alone, but Ash cupped my face and kissed me as if Seth wasn't there. My body hummed with response at having their two sets of hands on me. When Seth's lips grazed across my nape at the same time, I became damn near delirious with pleasure.

"He's right, my love." Ash's voice grazed across my lips. "We have the upper hand this time. As long as we have you, we got this."

He cut off my response with another kiss and behind me, Seth grew bolder. He nipped the sensitive skin on my shoulder just like he did out at the woods, eliciting a sharp hiss of pleasure from me. Ash's tongue playfully flicked over mine and he stepped in closer, allowing me to feel the growing, hardening bulge in his jeans.

Behind me, Seth's erection pressed against my ass. His lips skimmed up my neck while Ash kissed a hot trail down the other side. I was so drunk on pleasure, I felt like I was drowning. This was so out of character for Ash, I was stunned stupid. But his pulsing hard-on against my hip told me this was really happening, and not only that, he enjoyed it.

"As hot as this is to watch," Raum cleared his throat. "Deja did say she wanted to get this over with." He grinned shamelessly and his voice grew husky. "Maybe we can *all* celebrate when this is over."

The way he stretched the word all was not lost on me, nor Ash.

"Who knows? After everything we've been through, I might be convinced to share." Ash winked as he stepped away and my legs became so wobbly I would have collapsed had I not been leaning back on Seth.

Now I *really* wanted to get this over with.

* * *

"This is where you stayed, huh?"

I looked around Seth's studio apartment. Visually, it wasn't much to look at. The walls and floor were completely bare. The only furniture pieces were a blanket-covered mattress pushed into a corner and a small writing desk. On the desk laid a thick, leatherbound journal which could only be a grimoire with how much magic I sensed wrapped around it.

Really, it was the magic compacted into the small room that fascinated me. It felt like Seth. Just the faintest whiff of his aura once set my teeth on edge but now I wanted to sit and bask in it. His magic was dark with deep shadows, much like mine. But it was also soft, gentle, maybe even a bit skittish like a stray animal. I wanted to sit in the middle of his circle of candles and just let his magic wash over me like a gentle breeze.

"Yeah." He rubbed the back of his neck, looking away from me as if embarrassed. "I was traveling with the hunter's guild all the time and didn't see the point in putting down roots anywhere. This was always more of a crash pad than anything else."

"This was where I saw you in my dream." I walked toward his circle of candles. "When you warned me that the hunters were coming, and told me to capture air with my lungs instead of my hands."

"Yeah," he repeated, looking even more uncomfortable. "Sweetheart, I'm so sorry. About everything." His stormy eyes were full of pain. "I wish I never hurt you. Or allowed them to hurt you."

"It's okay, babe." I wound my fingers in his dark hair and pressed my forehead to his. "I know why you did it. And you know what? You were fucking right."

"Was I?" His arms went around me protectively.

"Yes," I insisted. "You *did* make me stronger. You pushed me to endure because you knew I could. You believed in me when I wanted to give up. The others had no idea what to do, but you did." I pressed a kiss to his forehead and allowed my lips to linger there. "I'm sorry, too. For how I treated you. How we all treated you."

"You didn't trust me then," he answered. "And you had every reason not to. I knew I would have to earn your trust." He brought my fingers to his lips. "And I'll keep doing my part to earn it for as long as you keep me with you."

I kissed him through the smile I couldn't hold back. "I'm ready to put that all behind us and start a new chapter. Are you?"

"Hell yes," he grinned back, sending my heart fluttering. I could get used to seeing him happy and relaxing, finally free with no double-agent burdens and no one to control him. He was free to be himself and while I didn't know him as well as my other guys, my feelings were growing by the minute and I was crushing hard.

It was wonderful and liberating to not fight my feelings anymore.

"Is there anything you want to take from here before we go?" I asked.

He picked up the heavy grimoire and pressed his hands into the front and back covers. Then his palms made a soft clap sound as they hit each other, the journal between them gone.

"Anchored it back to the house," he said, flashing me another smile. "We'll have plenty of time to dive into some magic later."

My body hummed as he brushed past me to the door. The only magic on my mind was what we did at the boulder when I came back.

When we stepped out onto the busy San Francisco street, picking up Diana's trail was remarkably easy. Like all other magic, blood magic left a trail of energy behind. It made me feel dirty and not in the fun way, but like I hadn't taken a shower in a week. It left a grimy feeling on my skin and made me desperately want to wash my hands. It felt like someone who was too far gone in their own insanity to even take care of their basic needs.

A sickening thought hit me. How many blood sacrifices did she do to become this powerful, this consumed by an addiction?

Sal confirmed our trail, complaining the whole time that it smelled like old, dried blood to him. I spotted him a block ahead of us and Ash across the street, both cloaked in shadows. They spread out rather than crowded around us so as to not confuse any humans walking past us. Running straight into an invisible man's chest would definitely make someone question their sanity.

We're going into a seedy area, Raum warned us from the sky. Be vigilant.

The dirty feeling amped up as we followed the trail of blood magic to a small, run-down apartment complex. The noises of the main street faded away to eerie silence. Not even drug addicts and homeless people hung around here, the energy was absolutely repulsive.

"She's in there," I muttered, steeling myself.

We're in position. Ready whenever you are, love. Ash's warmth and encouragement came through his mental voice and gave me strength.

"I'm right behind you, sweetheart," Seth said. "You got this."

I nodded and placed one foot in front of the other, moving toward the feeling of decay and dried blood under my fingernails despite every instinct in my body urging me to stay back. Gathering up all my defensive magic in my center, I reached toward the door that repelled me the strongest. My fingertips barely tapped the peeling paint before it swung open violently as if by a gust of wind.

She immediately threw a hard offensive spell, but I was ready for it.

A wall of fire flashed in front of me, immediately consuming the blood energy she threw in our direction. Seth took a step back and shielded his face but I didn't flinch. My fire would never burn us.

"Where'd you learn that fancy trick?"

Diana stood across the living room from me, if you could even call it that. With every inch of the floor and walls plastered in dried or drying blood, it looked more like a house from a horror movie. Despite the grotesque state of the apartment, Diana looked young, clean, and flawless as ever. We looked like sisters, as much as the thought disgusted me.

"The first time you tried to kill me, incidentally," I told her. "When I burned up that heart in your hands and should've finished drowning you. Do you remember?" I paused for a moment to think. "Actually, I'm wrong. That was the second time. The first time you tried to kill me, you killed my mother instead."

"Oh, Deja," she cackled with a shake of her head. "You'll never understand the magic of a good blood sacrifice. The power, the beauty!" Her eyebrows raised excitedly, her golden eyes wild and crazed. "I'll teach you more power than you can ever dream of. You're in your prime now, my dear! Leave your wretched demons! Come with me and you'll never age another day!"

"My mother was a sacrifice?!" I knew she was just trying to rile me up, to get under my skin and make me careless but my temper wouldn't back down.

Diana's crazed eyes lowered, and I realized I had placed one hand over my belly. An involuntary, instinctive move to protect the most innocent person in the room from the most evil one.

"Not only are you still alive, you're still carrying your demon spawn," she spat, then looked back up at me with a perverse smile. "Here's your first lesson, demon whore. Do you know what kind of blood holds the most magic?"

I didn't answer but focused all my energy on gathering the next element. My heart pounded like drums in my ears. I couldn't afford to miss. It was me and my baby or her in this moment.

"Fetal blood," she said with a snarl and a lick of her lips.

Our arms raised at the exact same time.

She hesitated for a fraction of a second.

I didn't.

Water poured out of her nose and mouth. Her eyes widened in fear and shock as she clutched at her throat. Every desperate gasp she took just sent more water into her lungs.

It was so reminiscent of the last time we spoke, a few blocks away from here at my old apartment which she also painted with blood. Only this time, I would finish what I couldn't back then.

Diana fell to her knees with warbled moans and cries pouring from her mouth. She was trying to speak, trying to beg and plead me for her life.

With my other hand I drew a gesture for Air, the final element she tried so hard to keep from me. The way she thought she would break me. I added just a touch of oxygen to her throat and lungs, not to give her any relief but to prolong her suffering.

One by one, the rest of my guys emerged from their shadows and filed into the house. They stood and watched silently in support of me as Diana began coughing up bloody water and crawled across the floor toward us. When she was about two feet away from my shoes, Raum stepped up and gave her a hard kick to the ribs.

The force sent her rolling back to the middle of the room, where she laid on her back taking in her last, desperate attempts to breathe while staring up at the ceiling.

I walked up and kneeled over where I knew she could see me. Her face and lips were blue, her eyes bloodshot and pupils constricted to pinholes when they saw me.

"My daughter will never know of your existence," I whispered. "But I want to make sure you know her name. I want her name to be the one you curse when you're suffering for all eternity in the lower circles of Hell."

My grandmother's lips and fingertips shook as I leaned down

close to her ear. Even now she was trying to fight me, to move or cast something. But her body was already shutting down.

"Her name is Deidre."

I pulled away so she could see my face again. The last one she would ever see.

Then she drew her last breath.

17
DEJA

None of it felt real.

The five of us anchored home, and I still felt tense, on-edge, and aggressive. It only began to melt away when we walked across the clearing surrounding our house and the magic of the earth prickled up through my feet with a gentle tingle.

Your mother is always with you. Lucifer's words returned to me as if he whispered directly into my brain. A witch's soul returns to earth, nourishing the elements and the power you draw from.

It hit me all at once, and I stumbled to my knees. A sob wracked my body. The emotion, the relief, the realization that we no longer had to run or hide. We could live, love, and just be free.

"Deja!" All four guys turned immediately and surrounded me like a flock of protective hens. The sob turned into a giggle at the thought, and uncontrollable, joyous laughter bubbled up from my chest.

"It's over!" I yelled at the top of my lungs and spread my arms wide, leaning back onto someone's chest. My gaze turned skyward, and the clouds were gorgeous. Fuck, when was the last time I appreciated some pretty clouds?

"It really is over." Sal's voice rumbled like a lazy thunder against my back. He sounded just as in disbelief as I felt.

"What do we do now, boys?" I asked playfully, looking up and all around to each pair of eyes staring back at me. All with a unique color and brightness, but filled with the same desire only for me. It hit me right then how I was the luckiest bitch in existence.

"I can think of a few things," Raum grinned wolfishly.

Sal growled an affirmative in my ear.

The heat of their returned gazes set my body aflame. Ash's eyes flickered from me to the others' faces and he licked his lips. My core immediately melted into a pool of liquid fire. My stubborn, possessive angel was really entertaining the idea of sharing our private time together? If the hot kiss between us and Seth earlier didn't hint to that, his look right then sure did.

A high-pitched howl interrupted our moment before anyone could vocalize the suggestion. All of our heads swiveled to the treeline where a grey wolf and a red fox came leaping toward us.

"Please tell me that dopey smile means something good!" Nona shifted flawlessly and asked the moment she had a human mouth.

"Yes," I answered, my grin spreading so wide that it hurt my cheeks. "Diana is dead. She won't hurt anyone anymore."

An eruption of cheers and howls surrounded me. It finally sunk in for everyone else too.

"What's more," Ash added. "I felt the angel magic she borrowed become obsolete the moment she died. It seems her death made whatever contract she had null and void."

"That's fantastic news!" Astrid beamed, glowing almost as bright as her red curls. "And I have more for you." She cleared her throat and looked at me pointedly.

"I would be honored to have my rescue operation within your sanctuary," she said, her voice beginning to choke up. "Nona told me all about your idea and I think it's wonderful. We've had shifters stolen and murdered before so if they had magical protection..."

"Of course!" I sat up and pulled her into a tight hug. "You looked out for us so it's the least I can do. We just need to draw up boundaries, cast the spell around the perimeter and spread the word to anyone who needs protection. Then Voluspa will be a dream come true."

"Voluspa, huh?" Nona said.

"The name of our supernatural haven," I beamed. "Start spreading the word to shifters and all magical kinds in need."

"You should be part of the spell," Raum told her. "You too, Astrid. We'll need to say an incantation to seal it. Even if you don't have magic, just your voice and the repetition will fuel its power."

"All of you should," I agreed, linking my arm in his. "Your mates too, Astrid. And everyone you called up here. We're making history so let's get everyone involved."

"I know just the right spell to do it." Ash scratched his beard. "I'll need to look it up for all the details and," he looked at Seth. "I'll need your help."

"Whatever you need, man." Seth said it casually, but I knew he was thrilled on the inside. His stormy eyes caught mine, and he blushed when I smiled.

"Do you need a map of the area?" Astrid asked. "To see where to make the perimeter?"

"Yes," Ash answered. "That'll be really useful. We don't want to include human farms and towns within the sanctuary." He was going into leader mode again and it was really sexy. "Let's all meet at the house in an hour. For several reasons, this spell will have to be cast at night."

Astrid and Nona went off to the woods, shifting again into their animal forms while the five of us headed toward the house. Toward home.

"Let's make some magic!" I declared with glee, not caring who heard.

***

Roughly one hour later, about fifteen people were crowded into Ash's study. Us five, Nona and Astrid, Astrid's three mates, and five other shifters who answered the call for backup when Diana initially came out here.

I could tell Ash felt extremely claustrophobic with all the bodies in his private space, but he smiled and made polite introductions to all the shifters he hadn't met yet.

Most people mingled and chatted while he and I, along with Astrid and her mates looked over the large paper map she brought. They pointed out private property owned by humans and other barriers to our magical sanctuary. Together we were able to triangulate an area of land, including Astrid's place and our house, where no humans had influence. Ash drew dots on the map according to Astrid's instructions and I connected them with a red pen.

When I stepped back and looked, the emotion rose up too fast and tears of joy threatened to spill from my eyes.

It was an area of about ten square miles. Enough to build plenty of temporary housing, maybe even a school for children and shops to give people jobs. And still plenty of room for shifters to run, hunt, fly and or do whatever they needed within the safety of the boundaries.

It was Voluspa. Our home. And the home of those in need.

"Love?" Ash nudged me gently.

I took a deep breath to compose myself. "It's perfect," I breathed. "I never imagined we would have this much space."

"There's lots of remote land out here," Chase, Astrid's hawk-shifter mate, said. "It's just begging to be returned to those who will honor it."

"If we're all in agreement about the boundaries," Ash took a thick, ancient-looking book down from a shelf. "It will take a group effort to create the barrier. I need everyone to do their part in this." He nodded at Seth. "This is where you come in."

Seth nodded and stepped forward, looking serious and ready to act.

"I need you to anchor a sigil at each of these points," Ash pointed at each dot he drew on the map. "It should be on a tree or a large rock that won't get moved. We need shadow magic to keep the barrier invisible to humans. Additionally, we need these sigils rooted down deep so this baby doesn't move any time soon."

"Wait." I turned to Seth. "You're still mortal, a witch. What's your primary element?"

He broke out into a grin. "It's Earth."

The same as mine. I knew it the instant Ash said rooted. And with Seth being as powerful as he was, there was no better person to solidify the border of our new home.

"Take a team of shifters with you for guidance," Ash suggested.

"We'll go with him." Orion, Astrid's silver-haired wolf mate stepped forward. "We know these woods better than anyone."

Seth dropped a quick kiss to my mouth which stole my breath away, then he left with Astrid's mates and the five other shifters. In the room remained me, my original unholy trinity, Nona and Astrid.

"And what does the dream team need to do?" Raum inquired with a smirk.

Ash flipped through his aged tome excitedly. "After they set the anchor points of the border, we're going to cast the actual protection spell." He looked up smiling. "All of us."

He spent the next hour flipping through his book and jotting down notes. Raum and Sal took Nona and Astrid to the kitchen for some drinks and chit-chat, leaving us finally alone.

"Have you changed your tune, angel?" I asked, unable to keep the smile off my face.

"What do you mean, love?" he mumbled distractedly as he flipped and wrote.

"I mean about sharing me when we're, you know, together."

His scribbling stopped. He leaned back in his chair and looked at me with those icy eyes, with their own unique kind of heat.

"I just figure," he said carefully. "I've already been sharing you all this time. And I know you love us and being with all of us would make you happy." He shrugged but the flush in his cheeks told me so much more. "That's it. I just want you to be happy."

"But I want *you* happy too," I told him. "And I do love it when it's just you and me. I'd only want to be with you and the others at the same time if you enjoyed it too."

Slowly he laced his fingers behind his head as a lazy, smug smile crept across his face. "Who knows? Maybe I would."

I bit my lip to hide how giddy I was.

"Does that mean you'd be open to finding out?"

His grin grew wider. "It may mean I'd be open to trying."

What a fucking tease.

Hey, sweetheart. Seth's mental voice cut through my psyche. We've anchored all the sigils and coming back to meet you now.

"Seth's done already!" I jumped from my chair, excited as a child on Christmas morning. "Let's go!"

We were to cast the protection spell at the exact center between all the barrier points that Seth and the shifters just anchored. It just so happened that point was in the open field right near our house.

"Hey, love." Ash caught my hand before leaving the study, his expression serious. "Are you really okay with this being the location? I mean, we can keep the house indefinitely but I know we're in the middle of nowhere-"

"Shush." I cut him off with a kiss and pulled back with a smile. "I love this place and want nothing more than to stay. You, the other guys, the shifters, and all the supernaturals we're going to help, all of you are my home and my family now. I belong here, with you."

He squeezed my waist affectionately as he lowered his forehead to mine. "Just checking in with you, my San Francisco heart."

"I did love the city," I admitted. "But I'm ready for the quiet. I want to connect with my Earth and my mother out here. My place was never in a concrete jungle made by humans. Besides," I slung my arms around his neck. "I'll probably make frequent trips back to check on the tea shop. Nona's genius has surpassed me already."

I told him excitedly about what Nona was doing with the shop as we headed out to Voluspa's central point. Sal, Raum, Nona, and Astrid were already setting up wood for the bonfire. As the sun dipped below the horizon and dusk turned into night, Seth and the remaining shifters came to join us in a circle.

"My love?" Ash beamed at me. "Would you like to do the honors?"

I summoned a small fireball and cast it at the pile of dried wood and kindling we'd assembled. Within seconds, our bonfire roared with power and magic, lighting the dawn of a new age for our supernatural brethren.

"By shadow and light, divine and damned, pure and tarnished," Ash declared over the crackling and popping of the inferno. "Let this blaze mark the center of protection for those in need. Let no one with ill intentions cross the purified borders of Voluspa, the home of the persecuted and unwanted."

I repeated the same incantation after him, feeling the power of the spell vibrate through my throat and over my skin as I spoke. One by one, each person repeated the words, and the flames grew higher. Every time a new person spoke, flames appeared to jump off from the bonfire and envelope the person in a fiery aura. It was a wonder to witness and even more amazing to feel.

It wasn't painful but felt permanent and humbling. This fire was sealing our oath, sealing an invisible wall of protection between the anchor points.

Seth was the last person to say his oath and the moment he did, everyone's fiery auras faded down to a barely discernible glow. But it was still there. Every time we'd see each other again, we'd see that glow and remember the moment we made history.

"It's done," Ash said proudly, looking at all of us through the flames. "Welcome to Voluspa, everyone."

Raum let out a victorious cheer and everyone followed suit. We yelled at the top of our lungs, danced around the fire, hugged, and celebrated. I found who I belonged with and I never felt so happy.

As the fire died down, the shifters slunk off to the woods. And in a fierce tangle of lips and hands, my lovers and I went home.

18

DEJA

The moment we stepped inside, Ash pulled me into the tightest embrace he'd ever given me, the pride and love pressing through his fingertips in my back. With my face buried in his neck and my arms around his shoulders, I was surrounded with the most pure feelings of love and care, because it wasn't just him with me. I had my whole family.

Sal, Raum, and Seth stood around us, beaming with that same love. Our shifter neighbors were only a stone's throw away. Our tribe of misfits meant everything to me.

I pressed my lips to Ash's neck and felt the groan rise in his chest. His hands moved to my hips, then my ass. He hardened against me and began moving us in the direction of the bedroom. A thrill ran through me but I pulled back slightly and looked up into his icy gaze.

"Angel, I know how you are," I began. "And if you want only to be alone with me, that's fine. But," I looked around to the guys lounging around the room, three more pairs of eyes watching us curiously. Heat rose within me, my heart thundered in my ears at what I was about to say. "I love you all. I'd love to be with all of you."

A beat of pure silence rang around the room. Ash loosened his grip on me and stepped away. My heart sank just slightly. He didn't want anyone in the bedroom but me and there was nothing wrong with that. Still, I couldn't help but feel a little disappointment at not being with all my lovers at once.

But to my surprise, he took my wrist and pressed my hand against the front of his jeans. Heat and hardness greeted my palm. I looked up at him, surprised.

"I've shared you since nearly the dawn of humanity," he smirked. "I might as well get used to it." He drew me against his chest so fast and brought his hands to my ass again. I was dizzy from how badly I wanted him. All of them.

"Here's my one rule." He nipped my earlobe, moving down my neck with slow, hot kisses. "I have you first."

"Mm hm." I could barely get my affirmative out before we sounded like a herd of elephants clamoring up the stairs and through the open bedroom door.

My mouth found his, and I trembled at the sound of three heavy sets of footsteps following close behind. This was really happening!

Ash and I backed up toward the bed, hands and tongues intertwined as I pushed him down on the mattress, quickly climbing on to straddle him. Our kiss broke for just a moment and I paused with a gentle finger to his lips.

"Are you absolutely sure about this?" I asked in a husky whisper, feeling the eyes of the others on my back. "If you'd really rather just be with me, we can kick them out."

He answered by wrapping a hand around the back of my head and pulling me down. His tongue thrust insistently into my mouth, a preview of what was to come. And just as abruptly he pulled away and addressed the three men still standing.

"You fuckers better stop staring and start making our woman feel good."

A low, throaty chuckle sounded incredibly close. That could only be Raum. When a large hand moved my hair off my neck and planted a rough, possessive kiss there, his touch was unmistakable. Ash's lips trailed across my jaw and then down the front of my throat while Raum's teeth and rough stubble worked the back of my neck into a frenzy of nerves.

He would be the one bold enough to jump in while Ash had me, to possess me in the way only he could, no matter who else was there.

My shirt peeled up and away, then Raum's mouth abruptly left my skin as he hissed a breath of surprise.

"Baby!" he gasped. "Your back."

"Oh yeah." I threw my head back to smile at him flirtatiously. "You like them?"

My sexy, foul-mouthed shit-talker was speechless as his dark eyes drank in the sigils tattooed on my spine. I'd forgotten all about them since my return from Hell, with everything we still had to get done. But what better time to reveal them to my lovers than the moment we were all together?

Raum's fingertips drifted over his own sigil in stunned silence while in front me, Ash grew impatient.

"What is it? Let me see," he insisted.

I turned around in his lap and his own breath hitch in his chest at the sight.

"My love, they're beautiful." His voice was thick with emotion as he brushed a tantalizing kiss just below the nape of my neck where his own sigil rested. "Did Lucifer do them?"

"Mm-hm, and they're truly permanent." I looked over my shoulder at him. "They'll remain on me no matter what body I'm in."

He looked at me with such love and adoration, it nearly brought tears to my eyes. Leave it to Raum to ruin our moment. He flipped me back around so Sal and Seth could get a clear look.

"I may have already seen them," Seth remarked snidely.

"You fucker," Sal growled at him, but I heard a playful smack to show that he was teasing.

"Anyway," Ash sighed loudly. "I believe we were in the middle of something."

He drew my chin closer and kissed me with such sweetness that quickly turned into roaring passion. The others quickly followed suit, starting with Raum's sharp, tingling kisses moving down my spine. I made off with Ash's shirt and sent my hands slowly down his perfect torso, completely unmarked except for the sigil tattoos we now both shared.

By the time I reached his belt and began pulling it apart, the rustling of clothes all around me signaled the other guys getting undressed as well. My hands shook with nerves as well as excitement as I helped Ash's jeans off, then quickly straddled him again as the others moved in.

More hands skimmed across my body, gently peeling my leggings off. More mouths kissed me in all sorts of places that made me sigh in pleasure. Each kiss and touch was like a fingerprint, unique as the man it came from. But I kept my focus on Ash, my angel. I wanted him to know how much he meant to me, how amazing and thrilling it was to have the others with us even if he preferred me to himself.

I dragged my tongue down the firm ridges of his abs until it swirled around his rounded head, already hard and pulsing. The guys finished peeling my leggings down over my calves and feet, and then their hands grew more adventurous.

Someone skimmed their fingertips up the back of my thigh, over my ass and then down across my vulva. I shivered at the touch and moaned with a mouthful of Ash's cock when they swept over my clit.

"She's so wet already," breathed Seth's low, husky voice.

"So fucking beautiful." Sal's breath fanned across my pussy before he pressed his hot mouth against me.

"Mmm..." My knees shook as his tongue lashed across my clit, sucked my lips into his mouth, and pressed two long fingers inside me. I rode his face while taking more of Ash's shaft down my throat, who groaned as he held my hair out of my face, ever the considerate lover.

Someone grabbed my nipples, sending the jolts through my clit into overdrive. I whimpered and writhed, already so gloriously stimulated everywhere that I felt my orgasm coming hard and fast. But Sal pulled away at the last moment.

Smack!

"Mmph!" I cried. That spank definitely came from Raum.

I sat up for air, still stroking Ash's length now slick with my saliva. Seth cupped my jaw and gave me a hot, penetrative kiss. Gently, he directed my other hand down his firm chest and abs, finishing with wrapping my fingers around his own wide shaft.

Thick, beautiful cocks filled both of my hands and every man still caressed, kissed and pleased me. Someone else cupped the back of my neck and turned my head. I found myself kissing Sal, the light musky scent of my pussy still lingering on his face. Ash pulled my hips forward, and I released his cock, taking the opportunity to massage Sal's heavy balls.

When Ash pressed inside me, I moaned against Sal's lips and gripped harder on Seth's cock, feeling him get solid like concrete. Raum's signature rough kisses danced their way across my neck and upper back, and those had to be his hands on my breasts working my nipples to stiff, sensitive little peaks. Ash filled me up so deliciously, it only took someone rubbing my clit for a few seconds before I was quaking and screaming from my orgasm. The first of many, if my four demon lovers were so intent on pleasing me.

Someone cupped my chin as I gasped for breath, coming down from my high and Raum's dark playful eyes looked back at me.

"Looks like you need something to fill that pretty mouth," he whispered hungrily.

I nodded, my senses completely overloaded but still wanting more. He grinned, stepping forward until the smooth skin of his head pushed past my lips. Ash continued driving up into me, each thrust of his cock so delicious and filling. He held my waist steady while my hands stayed busy stroking Sal and Seth on either side of me.

"Fuck, you should see yourself." Ash leaned up to kiss my breasts, catching my eye as Raum stuffed himself in my mouth. "You're so fucking hot, my love. So perfect."

"Should've set up a camera," Seth cracked.

"Mm-mm!" I caught his stormy gaze and narrowed my eyes as threateningly as I could with my mouth stuffed full of cock.

"Just kidding, sweetheart," he grinned down at me.

"You're gonna make me come," Ash rasped against my throat, holding me still with strong arms around my waist as he fucked me. While barely recovered from my last orgasm, his pubic bone hit my clit just right and sent another wave of shakes and convulsions through me. He groaned his release into me, my convulsions milking every last drop from him.

"Lick him clean, baby," Raum ordered with a soft growl that I couldn't bear to ignore.

I stood at the edge of the bed, leaning over Ash as he laid back panting.

"Good girl," Raum praised as I lathered my tongue across Ash's softening cock. He rewarded me with another firm smack to my ass.

"I should've invited you to play with us a long time ago," Ash laughed, still breathless.

"Better late than never." Raum smoothed his palms over my ass, no doubt admiring his handiwork.

"Alright move over, birdbrain," came Seth's voice, quickly followed by his rigid cock gliding across my slick entrance.

I hummed with excitement, pushing back eagerly as he teased me by just spreading my wetness all over his length. In front of me, Ash scooted off the bed and Sal took his place, shooting me a dashing smile that made my heart flutter.

"Hey beautiful," he greeted, caressing my face before kissing me.

"Hey lion," I grinned back. "Ahh!"

Seth pushed inside me, sinking all the way in until his slender hips touched the tender, freshly-spanked flesh of my ass. My eyes rolled back as he moved in slow, tantalizing strokes, plunging deeply before pulling all the way back. All my men were absolutely intoxicating in completely different ways.

I kissed a trail down Sal's torso, lingering on the sexy battle scars along the way, before dragging long, slow licks down his shaft. A hot vein pulsed against my tongue and I heard his breath hitch in his chest. Drawing him into my mouth, I sucked him at the same pace Seth fucked me. Deep and slow.

It was a nice change of pace from how charged up and tense the energy felt in the beginning. I felt like all of us were able to catch our breaths, slow down, and enjoy being in the moment.

That was of course until Raum took it upon himself to change it up.

"It's been almost five minutes since your last orgasm, baby," he purred, reaching underneath me in search of my hot button. "I think that's far too long."

Seth began rutting into me faster the moment my orgasm started building. Like a chain reaction I sped up sucking Sal's cock, pressing my tongue against the hard wall of the underside as his whole body tensed up.

With Raum strumming my clit like an instrument, Seth steadily amplifying his thrusts, Sal moaning so hotly with his cock shoved down my throat, and just the sheer fact that everyone I loved was in this room with me, I shattered like glass.

My legs turned to jelly and my vision went dark. Somehow I was screaming with a mouthful of cock.

"Fucking gods," Seth groaned as he stiffened within me and impaled me with one final stroke before filling me with warmth. His release only drew my orgasm out longer. Damn, I loved pleasing my men just as much they loved pleasing me.

"Don't stop, beautiful," Sal panted. "I'm so close."

I could barely breathe with how much that orgasm took out of me but I worked his concrete shaft and swirled my tongue around his delicious head. When he released into my mouth, I nearly came again from the hot sounds he made.

When he finally softened and was licked clean, I collapsed on the bed in a sweaty, trembling heap. My body was completely spent, inside and out. But I still had one more man to take care of.

"Flip over for me, baby," came Raum's dark, velvety voice.

I rolled onto my back to see him fisting his cock, eyes watching me hungrily.

"I literally can't come anymore," I panted, chest heaving as I reached for him. "But I can take care of you."

"Oh, I think we can squeeze one more out of you, love." Ash scooted across the bed until he laid next to me. He laid a gentle kiss on my hipbone that made me shudder from head to toe with how sensitive I was. His icy gaze moved up toward the dark, handsome demon still stroking himself. "I have a feeling Raum wants to paint your pretty skin."

"Fuck yes," Raum confirmed. "I want to watch your beautiful face as I paint those gorgeous tits."

"How about it, love?" Ash's kisses moved inward to my quivering core. "Just one more little orgasm for us?"

I thought I was tapped out but the way he looked at me, plus how soft his lips felt sent more desire coursing through me. Just when I thought these four men had completely ravished me, I realized I could never get enough.

"Just a little one," I told him, snaking my fingers through his hair. "I'm so sensitive. Be gentle."

He murmured his affirmative as he placed the most tender kisses on my inner thighs, gently lapping at my soaked lips. He kissed all around my clit but didn't touch it directly. I sighed and laid back, enjoying his gentleness like a relaxing bath.

I looked up and locked eyes with Raum. Even when touching himself he was rough, squeezing his stiff cock as it glistened with precum. We just stared at each other as our breathing grew ragged. The urge to touch him was overwhelming. I slid a hand up his thick, muscular thigh to massage his balls as he stroked himself. His head tipped back as a guttural moan escaped from deep in his chest.

"Look at me," I teased. "You said you wanted to watch my face."

His eye contact returned along with a snarky grin. "Always, baby," he rasped.

Ash's face barely brushed over my clit, making me jolt in response. His tongue circled around that impossibly sensitive bundle of nerves with the lightest touch and I still felt my orgasm building.

"Yes, keep doing that," I moaned to him.

"Fuck, you're so hot, baby," Raum stared down at me with wonder as he scooted closer, positioning his thick erection just over my chest.

Ash's tongue continued its work patiently, steadily bringing me closer and closer to the edge. This build up was the most gradual and intense I felt yet. My face contorted, and I thrashed on the bed, my eyes barely open to see Raum anymore. He muttered hot curses and I heard his strokes grow more frantic, his other hand gliding across my breasts.

Ash finally zeroed in on my clit just as Raum took a nipple between his thumb and forefinger. Magic crackled all around me as I came, my pleasure unleashed and unrestrained. Raum's aura touched mine and I felt his pleasure as he released on my body. I never felt anything like that before and didn't want it to end.

The five of us laid in a panting, sweaty, satisfied mess on the bed. My head rested on Ash's chest, Sal spooned me from behind. Seth and Raum rested down near my legs, both gently massaging my calves and feet.

And inside me, I swore I felt Deidre kick. I laid a hand on my belly and smiled. This was all I wanted. To be with those I loved without fear, without looking over my shoulder constantly. It felt so surreal that this was my life now, for at least this lifetime. There would always be fighting, sometimes running, sometimes dying. But moments like these were worth all of it.

"Holy fuck, I need a shower." I fanned myself, peeling up from Ash's torso.

"Want some alone time in there?" Raum asked, his dark eyes taking in my post-sex nakedness like he was seeing me for the first time.

"Hell no," I grinned. "Someone's gotta scrub my back."

Everyone laughed as I sat up, padding over to the large walk-in shower to turn on the water. Behind me, the guys joked and snapped towels at each other as they followed me. I watched them shamelessly. The four loves of my life, unique and perfect in their own ways. Whatever happened between now and eternity, I knew I would always have them.

EPILOGUE
DEJA

FIVE YEARS LATER

I waddled toward the kitchen, my hands pressed against the terrible ache in my lower back. Advil did absolutely nothing for my back pain at this point in my pregnancy.

Careful not to step on any legos I could barely see past my stomach, I rounded the corner to find a sight that pulled hard on my heartstrings.

My three-year-old son Braxton standing on his stool at the counter, carefully mixing something in a bowl while Sal watched closely.

"Like this, Dad?" he asked, looking up with his round emerald eyes for approval.

"Very good, buddy." Sal ruffled our son's hair, a gorgeous mix of reddish-blonde, before looking up to me with a smile. "Hey, beautiful. How was your nap?"

"Good until this fuh, I mean, darn back pain woke me up again," I grumbled, joining them at the counter. Still, my chest fluttered with the way he looked at me. No matter how sick or pregnant or grumpy I was, he never stopped calling me beautiful.

Sal made a sympathetic noise and drew me close, his arms encircling me until his firm fingers pressed right into the painful spot and gently massaged.

"Mm, you're better than any pain pills," I murmured, catching his mouth with mine. He tasted like chocolate. I let out a small moan of approval and flicked his tongue with mine for more.

"Eww kiss," Brax scolded us.

We parted laughing. "Oh no! Here come the kisses, ahhhh!" I leaned down and aggressively kissed Brax's cheeks until he was squirming and giggling. "Whatcha making, buddy?"

"Mole sauce," he said proudly. "It has chocolate, Mom!"

"Really?" I lifted an eyebrow at Sal. "Who's idea was that?"

"Mine!" Braxton declared. "But Dad a'ready ate most of it."

"Is that so?" I grabbed Sal's chin. "Better check for evidence." He smirked as I leaned in to taste him again, savoring the sweetness of the chocolate and just the intoxicating flavor of him on my lips. We kissed slowly, sensually, our signature way until Braxton complained again.

"Such a narc," Sal teased, looking down at our boy adoringly. His hands resumed their place on my lower back, massaging my pain away as he kissed my forehead. "Craving anything, Mama?"

"Mole sounds amazing, actually," I said. "I'm craving spicy food like crazy."

"Coming right up." He kissed me again and pulled back with a smile. "I promise we'll add peppers in addition to the chocolate."

"My boys take such good care of me." I ruffled Brax's hair, who was determined not to be distracted from his mixing. "Where's everyone else?"

"Ash and Deidre are pouring over books in the study like usual. I think Raum went for a flight and Seth is doing his usual meditation thing."

"Thanks." I kissed him again. "I'm gonna check on the book nerds. Can't wait for dinner."

Ash was alone in the study, lying back on his leather couch with no shirt and his reading glasses on. His beard had grown out longer since the kids were born but he still kept it maintained and neat. I think he secretly liked hearing the kids scream with laughter when he tickled them with his face.

"Hey angel." I knocked at the open study door.

His icy eyes lit up and filled with warmth when he saw me. "Hey, my love." He closed his book and set it down along with his glasses on the side table.

"Where's your partner in crime?" I waddled over to the couch and took a slow, careful seat. He immediately sat up and pulled my feet into his lap.

"Nona and Jacob came by and got her." He ran his thumbs along the arches of my feet and it felt incredible. "I think they're playing hide-and-seek in the woods or something."

"Mmm." He could have told me those two kidnapped my daughter and shipped her off to Timbuktu and I would have reacted the same way. His foot massages were downright heavenly. Good thing I trusted Nona and everyone in my extended shifter family with my own life as well as my children's.

"Jacob needs to meet a girl his own age, I think," Ash chuckled, casting me a sideways glance.

"Oh, stop." I smacked his arm playfully. "Don't be that dad. He's like a big brother to Deidre. He does have the biggest crush on Nona but he'll get over it."

"He does?" Ash paused on his massaging and looked at me in surprise. "How do you figure that?"

"It's obvious to anyone noticing." I scratched his beard. "Thanks for the foot rub angel, but I gotta pee like a racehorse."

"Want a cup of twig and leaf water?" His lip twitched as he helped me up from the couch.

"Yes, please but go heavy on the chamomile and not too much-"

"Not too much caffeine, I know." He kissed me, his eyes mischievous. "This isn't my first rodeo, love."

After emptying my bladder for the tenth time that day, I decided to take a short walk outside for some fresh air. Seth sat cross-legged facing the setting sun on the patio. A circle of sigils were burned into the wood surrounding him. This was where he tuned in to his shadow magic every day.

His aura flickered and hummed with a calm, even-keeled energy. He was somewhere else at that moment, guarding us like the ever-loyal sentry. Ever since we brought our feelings out in the open, he searched through the shadows of every witch and demon he ever touched, looking to see if there were more threats or allies. For the past five years, everything had been blissfully quiet, but he never stopped checking.

I stepped off the front porch carefully so as not to disturb him. Closing my eyes and taking a deep breath, I called on Air to listen to the faintest vibrations through the grass and the trees.

There she was.

My daughter trying to hold in her giggles reached my ears as clearly as if she was right next to me. A young fox sniffed the air about ten feet away from her, pretending like he had no idea where she was. The grey wolf nearby ambled toward the tree Deidre was hiding behind, pretending she didn't have a scent either. I couldn't hold in my grin as I walked toward them.

My daughter had the carefree, supportive childhood that I never had. Her best friends had fur and four legs each. Her fathers and I couldn't wait for the day when her magic would shine as brightly as her personality. And when it did, we would guide, cultivate, and encourage her talents to the best of our abilities.

As I approached the cluster of trees where they played, a raven flew out from the thicket and directly toward me. Raum shifted in midair, landing lightly on his feet.

"Hey baby," he greeted, sending a tingle along my spine just with that voice of his.

"Hey handsome." I accepted his hot, possessive kiss which never failed to leave me breathless. "Were you watching them?"

"Of course," he smirked. "She still isn't sure the bird is me, but I'm gonna have to get creative on spying on her when she's a teenager."

"Sooner than that, probably," I chuckled.

His eyes dropped to my belly as he protectively smoothed a hand over it. Even that touch was so sexy and primal coming from him.

He rested his forehead on mine and lifted his eyes to me. "Do you want to know?"

I thought for a moment. "Anything bad?"

His smirk spread to a full-on wolfish grin. "No, not at all. Quite the opposite, actually."

I wrapped my arms around his broad shoulders, smoothing out his silky black hair. "Then I'd prefer not to spoil the surprise."

"You sure?" His eyes brightened with hidden knowledge, secrets no one else knew. "Not even if it's a boy or girl?"

"Nah." I slid my hands down his firm body and laced my fingers with his. "Let's find the only girl that matters for now and bring her in for dinner. Sal and Brax are making mole."

"Damn." Raum licked his lips as we walked toward the tree line. "That boy is not allowed to move out."

Before we went another step, Deidre jumped out from behind her tree, squealing with laughter. The wolf and fox jumped and yipped as they all ran toward us. Nona promptly rolled onto her back, exposing her belly to get tackled by Deidre.

"Honey, be gentle!" I scolded, wincing at how she pounced right on top of the wolf but Nona just licked her furiously, her tail thumping on the ground.

Jacob danced in circles around them, cackling, yipping, and occasionally darting in to lick Deidre's ear as well.

"Alright, silly girl." Raum stepped in and hoisted Deidre up, placing her on top of his shoulders. "It's dinnertime."

Nona shifted back to human still laughing on the ground, panting and smiling up at me.

"I don't know how you do it." She climbed to her feet, brushing herself off. "She's like an energizer bunny."

"That's my girl," I said with only a partially sarcastic eyeroll. "Staying for dinner?" I looked between her and Jacob who also shifted to human form.

"Thank you, Deja, but my dads are coming back tonight from another hunt," he said politely.

"Tell your mom and dads hi for me," I pulled him into a hug. "And bring over any leftovers you have. We'll have a barbecue."

Nona and I walked together back toward the house.

"I can't stay either," she said apologetically. "I'm actually heading back to San Francisco tonight."

"On such short notice?" I asked, surprised.

She nodded. "Some coyotes and wolves down south need help. Border patrol saw them shift and now they need help getting to Yosemite or maybe Yellowstone safely."

"Well, you be safe too." I pulled her into a tight hug. "You can't miss kiddo number three or I'll be one pissed off witch."

"Are you kidding? I wouldn't miss this little one for the world." She rubbed my belly affectionately.

"Better not." I squeezed her hand. "Let Seth check on you from here? It would make me feel better."

"Sure," she snickered. "As long as he's not watching me fuck or sit on the toilet."

"Absolutely not," I assured her. "Protecting privacy is extremely important to him."

We said our goodbyes, and I watched her grey wolf run silently toward the horizon. My chest tightened with worry but I knew she'd be okay. She was my family, and I'd be there to protect her in a heartbeat, just like I knew she would for me.

Please protect her, mom, in any way you can. I sent the thought out to no one in particular, just the universe. A soft vibration of magic echoed back as if in answer.

I smiled, comforted by the response, and went inside to have dinner with my family.

THE END

WITCHY TRICKS AND DEMON TREATS

AN UNHOLY TRINITY HALLOWEEN

PROLOGUE
DEJA

My third child was born on a Samhain night. The moon hung round and full in a sky just as inky black as the hair that covered her head when she came into the world not crying, but smiling and cooing.

"Congratulations, Dads!" the doctor said, swiveling her head around to the four men standing like imposing guardians around my hospital bed. "Who's holding her first?"

"Give her to me." Raum's silky, commanding voice elicited shivers of desire up my spine despite the exhaustion from giving birth that consumed me.

Everyone looked on proudly as he took the tiny bundle in his arms and beamed down at his newborn daughter. Her head of thick black hair matched his, which fell to his collar in silky waves, perfectly.

Biological paternity was not something we cared about, seeing as there were four of them and one of me. All of them would be doting fathers to her, just as they were with our older two, Deidre and Braxton. But all of us saw it as clear as day when Raum grinned down at lucky number three, and she smiled right back.

She was *his*, through and through.

"Hello, Raven," he cooed in a soft voice, his dark eyes dancing with joy.

"Raven, huh?" Seth lifted an eyebrow, his stormy grey eyes lighting up. "It's a pretty name, but does Deja get any say in it?"

"He's seen all of this already," I said, waving my hand tiredly. "He knew her gender, name, and date of birth before we even conceived her. And anyway," I smiled at the newborn with her father, "Raven is a perfect name."

Each of my demons possessed unique abilities, but Raum's visions of the past and future were something else entirely. It was no wonder the early Norse regarded him as Odin. His powers spanned across human history, even if no one knew it was him.

"She's perfect, my love." Ash leaned over and lifted the hair stuck to my forehead before kissing me there. "You were amazing." His coarse beard tickled my skin, and his crystal blue eyes gleamed with pride. With the overly bright hospital lights shining on his blonde hair like a halo, my fallen angel looked nothing short of angelic.

Raum handed Raven over to Sal, who took her with incredible care. While supporting her head, he enveloped our daughter in his forearms as though creating an impenetrable shield. If anything even thought to try and harm her, Sal would kill them with a single look, and do so with brutality and pain.

But my fiery, wrathful demon just melted as he cradled her. His emerald eyes glittered with tears as he smiled down at her, then looked at me.

"She has your face, beautiful. Thank fuck."

A soft, collective laugh went around the room as each of Raven's fathers took a moment to hold and meet her before returning her to me. Seth rubbed my aching neck as I leaned back and directed her to my breast.

"So when are you and I making a baby, sweetheart?" he teased, the storm brewing in his eyes. As the only mortal of my lovers, not a true demon but a witch like me, his time on Earth was limited.

"Can I recover from birthing this one first?" I sighed, making a face at him.

"Yes, let the mother of *our* child rest," Raum commanded with a low growl. Already overprotective of her and I secretly fucking loved it.

The other three quietly filed out of the room, leaving Raum and I to gaze at Raven in adoration as she greedily fed from me. Through her skin on mine, I could already feel the dark, shadow magic unfolding in her tiny body. An aura began encircling her head, sparking with the simple pleasures of her sated hunger and feeling secure in her mother's arms.

"Will she be okay?" I said in a soft whisper.

Raum knew what I meant. And he knew not to bullshit me.

"Oh, baby," he chuckled. "She'll be more than okay. Raven will *thrive*. There will be challenges along the way but she will overcome them all. I can't wait for you to see what she becomes."

He stroked a loving hand over my hair and I leaned into his touch, taking comfort in his words, but the protective mother in me still worried.

Even now, in today's world, witches weren't safe. The trials with burnings and hangings of centuries ago may have died out, but before my children were born, my lovers and I literally ran for our lives. Raum nearly died from a substance called an angel's kiss, the only weapon capable of killing a demon.

But it wasn't the angels or their followers persecuting us. Now other witches hunted us.

These witches wanted no association with demons and blamed them for our kind's oppression throughout history. After all, the close association between demons and witchcraft saw so many innocent witches burned, hanged, or drowned.

Modern witches wanted to erase the link between themselves and demons forever.

And that link was me.

Thousands of years ago, I was the first human woman created. The Creator gave me the name Lilith. He paired me with the first human man, Adam. Long story short, I couldn't stand Adam and refused to submit to him as I was apparently supposed to. We were made from the same substance, so why couldn't I be treated as an equal?

The Creator, known by many different names at this point, almost killed me. But an angel saved me. An angel rebelled against his creator's will and saw himself thrown down from his heavenly realm as a result. That fallen angel was my Ash. His two partners in the rebellion were Lucifer and Beelzebub— perhaps you've heard of them.

Lucifer created Hell, the underworld of many modern and ancient cultures, and became a father figure to me. With the incredible powers he bestowed upon me, I was the first of my kind. Born human, and not of Heaven or Hell, I became the mother of all witches.

With a fallen angel and hellborn demons as my lovers, my children's powers grew to be unique and varied as their fathers' were. And when they proceeded to have children with humans or other witches, those powers never decreased.

But the creator, his army of angels, and their human followers never stopped persecuting me, my lovers, and my children. I died hundreds of times, but thanks to Lucifer, I was reborn in hundreds of different bodies.

Across all my lifetimes, I finally found peace in this one.

We created a safe haven on earth for magical beings of all kinds — witches, demons, shifters, and whomever else felt persecuted and unsafe. Even some non-magical humans stumbled upon us over the years, feeling out of place with their own kind.

We called this place Voluspa. It was my dream to stop running, stop fighting, and survive this *one* lifetime to old age. I wanted to watch my children grow up, and witness the birth of my grandchildren. I wanted to create a place on earth where no one experienced fear just because they bore fur, feathers, or horns.

Even within these safe, magical walls, I refused to let my guard down. Me and my huge, extended family of misfits would always be hunted. But I wouldn't allow any of them to get hurt; our enemies would need to go through me first.

1
DEJA
FIVE YEARS LATER

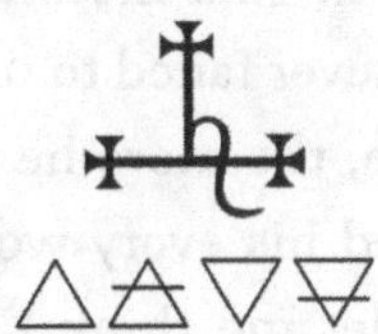

"Raven!" I hollered for the fiftieth time that morning, stomping down the stairs. "It's time to go! You're gonna be late for school!"

I entered the kitchen to find Raum preparing two mugs of tea, mine a stiff English breakfast in a travel cup. Without a word he slid it across the counter to me, a knowing smirk on his ruggedly handsome face.

"Where in Lucifer's name is your daughter?" I demanded, clutching the precious liquid in my hands.

"Good morning, baby." Ignoring my question, he leaned across the counter for a kiss.

"You smug bastard, I'm not kidding." I bit down savagely on his lip, though it only drew a lazy, rumbling chuckle from his chest. "I can sense the movement of every rabbit and deer within a mile radius but I can't sense *her*, which means she's not on the ground."

"So where else could she be?" His chocolate eyes danced as he took a sip of his own tea, his smirk widening.

"Raum, I'm not in the mood for this. She's going to make Deidre and Brax late."

"You're an awful liar," he grinned, reaching across the counter to take hold of my upper arms to pull me closer. His hot lips brushed against my cheek. "You're always in the mood for me."

"*That* is a total and complete lie."

He just laughed and ran his tongue along my earlobe while holding me in place. When my breath hitched, I could feel his satisfied smirk on my neck before he started to kiss me there.

Damn him. Ten years in this lifetime and thousands of years across others, and he still never failed to turn my whole body to jelly. The more I challenged him, the more he pushed back until I was a quivering mess that obeyed his every word. It made for a fun, hot dynamic between us. He let me think I could gain control before pulling the rug out from under me, and dominating my body in ways that only he could.

"I hate you," I breathed, a weak protest to match my half-hearted attempt to writhe away from his touch, but it was useless.

"Mm-hm," he murmured carelessly as his fingers released my arms and drifted down my sides. I didn't move as we both knew I wouldn't. The demon didn't even need to restrain me to dominate me.

Heavy steps and the clicking of claws on the wood floor jerked me out of my lusty haze. I looked over my shoulder to see a mountain lion padding over to us with sleek, powerful feline stealth. His green eyes gleamed as they met mine, and it took me a moment to notice the small, brown-feathered bird wriggling in his jaws.

He gently placed the bird on the floor, a juvenile raven not yet grown into its adult black feathers, then both animals quickly shifted to human form.

"Eww, Dad! You covered me in drool!" Raven whined, wiping at her arms and legs.

"That's what you get for hiding from your mom," Sal teased, messing up her shiny black hair.

"Thank you, lion!" I declared, walking over to Sal and wrapping my arms around his neck. "At least *someone* in this house isn't conspiring against me."

"Mom, I got really high this time!" Raven said excitedly, forgetting all about the drool that covered her. "I even floated in the air a little bit. Daddy Sal had to climb a tree to get me."

"Oh, really?" I shot a glare back at Raum. "That's great, honey, but remember I said to practice flying after school and on weekends, not before. We're gonna be late."

"Daddy Raum said it would be okay. We can just anchor to school."

"I bet he did." My glare intensified as Raum sipped his tea with feigned innocence. "Well, we have no choice but to anchor now, instead of enjoying a nice walk. Come on, get your stuff."

When she skipped away, I speared my fingers through Sal's auburn hair and kissed him deeply, surging my tongue into his mouth. He moaned in reply and snaked both arms around me to grab my ass.

"You're my favorite right now, lion," I said, loud enough for Raum to hear when our lips parted. "I want you all to myself when I get back."

"You know nothing makes me happier, beautiful," Sal purred, squeezing my ass gratuitously as we put on a little show for Raum.

"Please go on. I'm definitely enjoying this view." Raum leaned his elbows on the counter, smiling hungrily as he watched us.

"You don't get to watch or join in," I told him coolly despite the lava flowing in my veins. "Sal had my back this morning, not you, with your tricky daughter."

"That's fine," Raum said lightly. "I'll just punish you later."

I shivered, knowing he would hold true to his words.

* * *

"Hey, Mom. Can we go trick-or-treating this year?"

Deidre, my oldest, peered up at me with golden eyes that mirrored my own. She looked like such a spitting image of me and my birth mother of this lifetime, it was uncanny. From our eye color and dark brown hair, to her attitude and affinity for earth magic, she was every bit my mini-me.

"Why do you want to do that?" I asked, surprised.

"Because CANDY!" My son Braxton cried out.

"And dressing up. And hanging out with our friends," Deidre added with a sassy hand on her hip. "It's what everyone does on Halloween!"

"It's what *humans* do when they have no magic," I corrected. "We've talked about this, sweetie. We celebrate Samhain, not Halloween. It's not about dressing up and eating candy."

Deidre lowered herself to Raven's eye level. "What do you think, Ravie? Wanna dress up and eat yummy treats, like chocolate?"

"Chocolate!" Raven pulled at my hand, bouncing in excitement.

"See, Mom? You're outvoted."

"Excuse me? This is not a democracy!" I huffed.

"No, it's a dictatorship." She stuck out that sassy hip again. "Like Hitler."

I narrowed my eyes. "How do you know about Hitler?"

"Dad has books about him in the study."

I groaned and rubbed my forehead. Ash withheld hardly any books from her. He maintained a philosophy of: *If she can reach it and read the language, why keep the knowledge from her?* As a result, she read one of his ancient tomes cover to cover every day, sometimes two in a day. At ten years old, she already read English at an adult level and was proficient in German, Italian, and Old Norse.

As much as I loved that my eldest child inherited Ash's intelligence and curiosity, days like today where she compared me to Hitler were trying.

"We'll talk about this later," I grumbled. "Off to class, you demon spawn."

Deidre and Brax raced across the quad to their respective classes while I walked Raven to her kindergarten class. My heart lifted at seeing children of every imaginable magical background running, playing, and talking to their friends. A pair of fox shifter boys wrestled on the lawn while their teachers chatted. A group of witch girls played hopscotch with chalk that moved and changed colors on the sidewalk.

A school was the first thing I wanted in Voluspa. I was pregnant with Deidre at the time, and before the school was even built, teachers began applying for jobs. Not long after, contractors placed offers to build houses, hospitals, and offices. For too long, these people had been forced to hide their abilities among the general human population, so when word spread about a place where they could live as their true selves, they jumped at the chance.

I kissed Raven goodbye and walked with pride across the school's campus. Admiring my vision come to life never got old. And today it looked especially idyllic. It was a warm mid-October morning with just a touch of autumn chill in the air. The tree leaves' brilliant colors of golds, oranges, and reds were on full display. They drifted down, falling to the ground in piles big enough for the children to play in.

My steps quickened across the pavement, and I sipped my tea as I headed toward a smaller building on the other end of campus. I left the elementary side, crossed over to the high school, and that small, modest portable building coming into view served as our temporary university campus.

I let myself in, my pulse quickening at the sight of the gorgeous man behind the desk. Black-framed glasses sat on the bridge of a perfectly straight nose, tousled blonde hair sat on top of his head and matched the neatly trimmed beard lining his angled jaw. The eyes that scanned the assignments in front of him were an icy, crystal blue, but the most magnificent thing about him was the set of huge, black-feathered wings that stretched out beyond the edges of the desk.

He caught me in his icy gaze as I did my best sexy catwalk across the empty room, strutting toward him.

"Hello, Professor Angel," I greeted.

2
DEJA

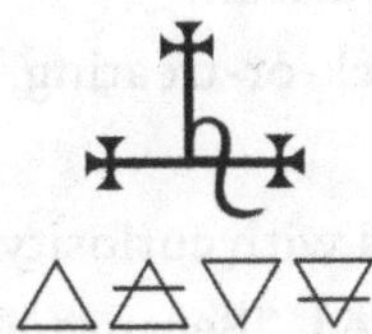

Ash leaned back in his chair and smiled at me as he removed his glasses. Usually so serious, a smile from my fallen angel was a rare treat.

"What can I do for you, Mrs. Mother of Witches?"

I continued my slow, sultry walk until I rounded his desk and hopped up to sit on it, crossing my legs at the knees. His eyes danced with intrigue and desire as they followed my movements. Too bad I wore leggings instead of a short skirt.

"I have an academic issue with one of my children. Perhaps you could help me solve it, *professor*." With a bite of my lip, I slid my knees apart and spread them wide.

"I see," he mused thoughtfully, his gaze like cool water on my skin as he drank in the lines of my thighs and hips. "What seems to be the issue?"

I snapped my legs shut. "She called me Hitler because her *father* lets her read any damn book in his study."

He blinked, his brow furrowing before a snort of laughter escaped his perfect, angelic mouth. "Deidre said that?"

"Yes, just now when I dropped her off!" I shot a hand toward the door, glowering as the feathers on his wings shook as he laughed. "It's *not* fucking funny!"

"Even you must admit, love, it's kind of funny. Raum will love it."

"Ugh, don't even talk to me about him right now," I rolled my eyes. "He and Raven are still doing their hide and seek game with me."

Ash chuckled and rubbed my calves in sympathy. "So what brought on this Hitler comparison?"

"She wants to go trick-or-treating, and I shot it down," I admitted.

"Why?" His eyes flashed with curiosity.

"You *know* why," I sighed. "Because all the Halloween stuff just commercializes and waters down our ancient traditions. It became popular because of the same oppressive culture that brings witches running to Voluspa. I don't want our kids to glorify those who killed their ancestors and tried to rewrite our history."

"I understand what you're saying, love. I really do." His fingertips paused on my calf muscles. "But they're just kids. Let them have a night out with their friends and get all sugar-high. They'll grow out of it eventually."

"I knew you would say that," I grumbled. "And I kind of realize you're right. I just don't like it."

"I know, love. And I know why it bothers you." He leaned forward and placed a small kiss on my knee. "But you have to remember not all humans hate us, and not all witches are good."

"I know, angel," I breathed, the memories flooding back as I ran my fingers through his blonde hair. I was betrayed by my first coven and my maternal grandmother. All in all, humans really hadn't done much damage to my own life compared to other witches.

"I think Deidre's old enough to know about the origins of Samhain now," Ash mused, leaning back in his chair again. "We'll all talk to her about it, and draw the parallels between the pre-Christian traditions and Halloween now. I think she'll find it interesting."

"Of course she will," I smirked, sliding off the desk to stand in front of him. "She's a huge nerd just like her father."

He returned my grin. "And with her mother's beauty and guts, she's already a force to be reckoned with."

Bracing my hands on his chair, I straddled his legs and took a seat on his lap. His icy eyes immediately heated as I pressed my core against the zipper of his dark slacks.

"We make pretty amazing children, don't we, Ashtaroth?" I said in a breathy whisper that fanned across his lips.

"That we do, Lilith." His hands slid up my thighs to grab hold of my waist.

"We've never made one right here, though." I grinned wickedly, trailing my lips over the coarse bristles of his beard before pressing my mouth to the hot skin of his neck.

"Deja," he groaned, gripping my waist and rocking his hips against me. "I'm teaching a class in ten minutes."

"Mm-hm," I said dismissively, pushing his shirt collar aside to kiss closer to his shoulder. His protests turned to moans as his hands moved to squeeze my ass, pulling me forward to feel him growing thick and hard.

"You're gonna get me fired," he growled, bringing his hands forward to knead my breasts.

I couldn't hold back my laughter. "You're with *me*, the Mother of Witches, and a goddamn Prince of Hell to boot. Who the fuck's gonna fire you?"

"Hm, I guess that would be you," he chuckled into my neck as his skilled fingers brought my nipples to stiff, aching peaks. "Better make sure I do a good job."

Clinging to the last of my resolve, I slid off his lap and out of his reach. His hooded, lusty gaze turned frustrated as I leaned forward to give him a quick kiss.

"Have a good class, Professor. I'll be thinking of you until you get home."

"You evil witch," he moaned, straightening his clothes. "I can't believe I fell for that again."

Grabbing my travel mug, I laughed as I headed for the door then paused.

"Love you, angel." I blew a kiss at his glowering stare and left just as his students began filing into the classroom.

* * *

The morning was unusually warm and scenic, so I decided to walk the long way home. Evergreen trees lined the sidewalk of the hospital as I strolled past it. The hospital was still under construction when Deidre was born, so I gave birth to her at home with the help of my friend Astrid, a fox shifter who turned out to be an amazing, supportive midwife.

I followed a trail to the western perimeter of Voluspa, which kept us protected by a barrier spell cast by me, my lovers, and my first friends here. Seth, the master of shadow magic would be out here maintaining the spell and checking for any threats, as he did every day.

My relationship with him was the newest, seeing as we had only fallen in love in *this* lifetime. With the three demons, our love ran deep and held strong across our trials with humanity. It held through hundreds of betrayals, murders, wars, and exiles. I had been a queen in ancient Egypt, a priestess of the Norse gods, a Celtic warrior in pre-Christian Ireland, and so much more. In some form or another, Ash, Raum, and Sal remained with me. Our love was truly eternal.

With Seth, I always felt a thrill of excitement, like he was still a new boyfriend, even though we'd been together for ten years. The beginning took some adjustment, but now he got along seamlessly with my unholy trinity. And my children were every bit his as well as theirs.

I spotted him sitting cross-legged and shirtless on a boulder, the sigils on his skin pulsing with a faint blue glow. My own sigil tattoo of Set, his demon ancestor, pulsed faintly at the base of my spine as I walked closer to him.

His tousled dark hair fell across his forehead. Only the whites of his eyes were visible, meaning he was searching through shadows. Most witches and demons had to touch another person to access their shadows, the deep, hidden subconscious desires that people often didn't even realize were there. But as a shadow master, Seth could touch someone only once and continue to access those shadows across great distances.

Before we got together, when I thought him my enemy, he was part of the coven that betrayed me. While pretending to be on their side, he got permanent access to their shadows, which he searched through every day to see if they intended to come after us again.

With a deep shuddering breath, he blinked a few times, and his stormy grey irises came into view, focusing on me.

"Hey, sweetheart," he said in that low, husky voice I loved as he slid down from the boulder.

"Hey, handsome," I returned, accepting a sensual kiss from him. "See anything interesting?"

His lips tightened and his brow furrowed as he slipped his shirt over his head. "Actually, yes."

My heart stopped for a moment as hundreds of worst-case scenarios flashed through my mind. Did my old coven create a spell to get through Voluspa's borders? Had any demons or witches turn up dead from angel-kissed weapons?

"Don't look so calm," he teased, stroking my cheek. "Nothing from our old friends, but this morning someone dropped off a young girl at the border. About six years old. Just abandoned by human guardians, we're assuming."

"Witch?" I asked.

"Yeah, but her abilities are... interesting." He gave me a look. "She sees ghosts. Or at least, she claims to."

"Very interesting," I agreed, drumming my fingers on my travel mug. "Astrid has her now?"

He nodded. "She's expecting you."

"Thanks." I tugged him forward by a handful of his shirt for another kiss. He answered by pulling me tightly against him, and stole my breath away with a dance of his tongue with mine.

"See you at home," he murmured huskily when our mouths parted.

"Can't wait," I whispered back, running a finger along his smooth jawline. "You better beat Ash home if you want me first."

"Naughty minx," he laughed, swatting my ass before we untangled. "Up to your witchy tricks again?"

I winked at him before heading off to Astrid's office.

"That's my kind of trick-or-treat."

3
DEJA

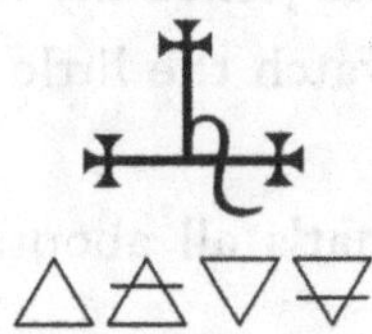

"**S**weetie, I don't care that there's an angry, headless lumberjack behind me. He can kiss my furry red tush." Astrid looked up as I entered the room, her wild red hair sticking out in all directions. "Ah, nice of you to show up, D."

"Sorry I'm late." I set my coffee down on her desk and crossed my legs to sit on the floor across from my fox shifter friend and the young girl with haunted eyes. "Hi, my name's Deja," I said to her with a friendly smile. "Can you tell me your name?"

"There's an ugly old woman and a pretty younger woman attached to you," the girl ignored my question, looking straight through me with eyes darker than Raum's. They were jarring on her ghostly pale skin and tangled blonde hair.

"Oh really?" I glanced up at Astrid who gave me a small, tight-lipped nod. "What can you tell me about them?"

"The old woman is angry. She hates you," the girl continued in a flat tone. "She's burning with hate. She's in chains."

I nodded knowingly. "What about the other woman?"

"She's the opposite. She loves you. She's full of light. She's so happy." The girl looked down, absently playing with wooden block set in front of her. "The old woman hates her too, but she doesn't know she's there."

"Can you see one better than the other?"

The girl returned her dark gaze up to me, squinting in concentration. "The young woman. She looks almost solid. The other one is barely there. I can see right through her."

"Thanks, sweetie."

I looked up at Astrid and jerked my head to the next room. She asked a staff member to watch the little girl, and quickly followed me.

"So you know what that's all about?" she grilled, folding her arms once we were alone.

"I have a pretty good guess." I drummed my fingers on the desktop, already eager to talk to Ash about theory, since he knew almost everything. "She does see the dead but it's not ghosts in the traditional sense. The old woman she saw is my grandmother, whose soul I know for a fact is not on earth. She's suffering in Hell for her crimes."

Astrid's eyebrows raised. "She saw her in chains. Burning in hate."

"Right. So she's seeing Diana in her current state, which is interesting."

Astrid paused before speaking again. "And the other woman?"

"My mother," I said with a slight hitch in my breath. "She remains on earth. As a witch, her soul returned to the pulse of the natural world. Her essence is in the magic we use."

"That's beautiful," Astrid responded with a small smile. "And that's why she saw her clearly and your grandmother faintly? Because your mom is here and grandma is down there?"

"To put it simply, yes," I said. "Who's the angry lumberjack?"

"The trophy hunter who killed my family." Astrid's lip curled. "He wanted our pelts to decorate his walls. Mine was the last one he needed for his sick collection."

"You killed him?" I asked, though I already knew the answer.

"Blew his fucking face off," she said proudly.

"Why am I not surprised?" I laughed.

Astrid used to be one trigger-happy little vixen. When we first met, she fired a shotgun at me before I could properly explain myself. Thankfully I stopped it with my magic just before I got riddled with holes, and we'd been close friends ever since.

"That asshole might legitimately be a spirit haunting me," she said in a low voice. "He hated shifters, said the Devil created us."

"He's not entirely wrong," I chuckled. Shifting was a rare ability among demons and even rarer among witches. Raum and Sal could shift, but we never expected any of the kids to inherit the abilities. Imagine our shock when Raven began crawling one minute and the next, a fluffy, chirping actual baby raven sat in her place.

"But if he was as sadistic as you say, he might be in Hell too. Somewhere near my grandma probably."

"I hope so," Astrid growled. "I regret killing him so quickly. It was too kind."

Before Voluspa ever existed, Astrid ran an underground rescue operation for shifters. She saved dozens from being hunted and persecuted, taking no prisoners while doing so. Now, she still did the same work but in a more official capacity and in a less trigger-happy way. Her office took in all refugees coming to Voluspa and decided the best course of action for them.

Unfortunately, abandoned children like today's girl were becoming increasingly common as well.

"Have you found a foster home for her?" I asked.

"Not yet." Astrid ran a hand through her mass of red curls. "I wanted to see if you knew anything before I placed her somewhere."

I chewed my lip, thinking for a few moments.

"Let me bring her home for a couple of weeks," I said. "Ash might understand her best, especially if she has a connection to Hell like I suspect."

"Four dads and three siblings?" Astrid grinned. "This young lady is about to be spoiled."

We walked back into the room where the girl remained, playing with her blocks while Astrid's staff member sat practically glued to the wall across the room. She was a coyote shifter from what my senses told me. Some shifters still acted uneasy around witches.

"Relax, Jen, she's not gonna bite you," Astrid chided.

"She says weird stuff," Jen muttered, her face white.

"Kids say the darndest things," I quipped, kneeling next to the girl again. "Hi honey, let's try this again. Do you have a name?"

She hesitated before mumbling, "Dani."

"Dani, I have a daughter about your age named Raven. I think you could be friends. Would you like to meet her?"

She looked up at me with wide, dark eyes and gave a hesitant nod. "I never had a friend before."

My heart tightened uncomfortably in my chest but I put on my most easygoing smile for her. "You'll be staying at my house for a bit if that's okay with you. We have lots of space to run around, games you can play, and we have ice cream."

"Ice cream?" her dark eyes brightened. "Do you have chocolate?"

"You bet we do, miss Dani."

She still looked hesitant. "Are you gonna leave me somewhere like mommy did?"

I exchanged a look with Astrid that said, *what the fuck is wrong with people.*

"No, sweetheart. We're going to become friends and get to know you. Then we're going to find you a family that will never leave you anywhere. Does that sound good to you?"

She nodded again and placed her small hand in mine when I held it out.

"I'll start interviewing some witch families on our adoption list," Astrid stated as she walked us to the front door. "Want me to include demons as well?"

"Yeah, any amount of demon or witch hybrid should be a good place to start," I said. "They might be more open to what she sees."

"Sounds good." She wrapped me in a quick half-hug. "We'll see you at Samhain for dinner, if not sooner. Jacob's doing so well on his hunts," she beamed proudly.

"I'm not surprised. He's got the baddest vixen I know for a mom and three badass predators for fathers," I winked. "See you, Astrid."

* * *

Raum and Sal were intrigued by the young girl I brought home in tow. Dani seemed painfully shy in Raum's presence, but she gravitated toward Sal.

He kneeled next to her, smiling gently and making his voice soft. Watching them together just made me melt. Around all children, he became the most easygoing and patient. A stark contrast to his fiery temper and thirst for violence when it came to anything that threatened me or our family. Like his mountain lion shift, he was a fearsome predator while also fiercely devoted to his family.

"There's so many around you," Dani said, her voice in awe as her dark eyes darted all around Sal's aura. No doubt seeing every now-dead person who crossed his path.

"I've lived a long time," he said gently. "All of us have."

He settled her in with some homemade chocolate ice cream and some picture books while Raum and I talked quietly in the next room.

"Have you seen anyone with similar abilities before?" I asked.

"Demons, yes. Not witches." He stroked the dark stubble on his jaw, deep in thought. "She's got some hellion in her heritage for sure. I'm not sure what else." He turned to me with a knowing smirk. "Raven is going to love her."

"Yeah?" I raised my eyebrows. "Is that the future talking?"

"Partially. But I can also just tell they'll get along."

"I thought so too when I first met her."

Ash and Seth came home a few hours later with all three kids in tow. By then, Dani became relaxed enough with Raum that she sat next to him while he read a book to her. She was so entranced by the story, she didn't notice the others coming in until Raven walked right up to her.

"Hi, my name's Raven. That's my favorite book. Do you like it?"

Dani glanced up at Raum before nodding hesitantly.

"I'm Dani."

Brax pushed past Raven at that point and stuck a small cupcake in Dani's face. "I made cupcakes today! Do you want one?"

"Guys, give her some space," Raum chided gently.

But Dani reached out and accepted the cupcake from him, handling it as if were the most precious treasure.

"Thanks. I love cupcakes."

Deidre offered a polite introduction before heading into the kitchen to help Sal with dinner.

Ash, Seth, and I watched our youngests' interactions with Dani from across the room while I filled them in on her ability. My heart felt near bursting with pride and love at how Raven and Brax took the shy girl under their wings. My two lovers on the other hand, watched with fascination as if this was some kind of curious experiment.

"I'd like to read her shadows if possible," Seth said. "Her subconscious might tell me more."

"Just go easy with her. She's a bit skittish for good reason," I told him.

He nodded and walked over to where she sat in a pile of books and toys that Raven kept pulling from the shelves to show her.

"I have a few theories about her." Ash leaned down close to my ear. "But first, I believe you and I have some unfinished business."

4
DEJA

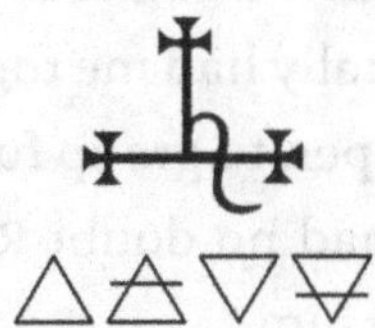

I grinned, pressing my ass into Ash's crotch where his thick erection greeted me.

"Were you sporting that during your entire class?"

"I had to stand behind the damn desk for the entire lecture," he growled, pulling my hips back against him.

"Oh, Sal," I called a in a singsong voice. "Can you help me and Ash upstairs? Raum can finish dinner."

"Oh, that is so not fair," Raum groaned, glaring at me. "You know I can't cook my way out of a paper bag."

"I'll help you, Dad!" Deidre piped up.

"You got this," Sal quickly kissed Deidre on top of her head. "Show him how it's done." He ran over to Ash and I at the base of the stairs and practically barreled into us.

Raum and Seth's glares at our backs felt like targeted lasers as the three of us clamored up the stairs, but I wasn't concerned. They would get theirs.

"Are you punishing him?" Ash asked with an amused chuckle as he took a gratuitous grope of my ass now that we were out of sight of the kids.

"Yes." I paused to kiss him, deep and full of tongue. "He and Raven are still ganging up on me in the morning and making us all late. I'm tired of it."

"He's going to get you back for this," Sal grinned, his voice low and full of warning as we all stumbled through the master bedroom. With a flick of my wrist, I used the element of Air to close the door and slide the deadbolt into place.

"I know." I shivered at the thought of what Raum would have in store for me. He and Sal usually had me together. Ash preferred me to himself but became more open to group fun in recent years. Seth was always up for anything. I had no doubt Raum would recruit him in punishing me for excluding him.

I both craved and feared what he would do to me.

I turned to Sal and kissed him deeply, heat and passion already burning through my veins.

"I'll deal with Raum later. Right now I want both of you."

My angel and my lion didn't need to be told twice. Clothing flew off as if by magic. In the next instant I was sandwiched between two of the hottest male specimens on earth. Hot skin and hard muscles pressed against both my back and my front. Fingers held onto my hips with iron strength and drifted across my body as if touching me for the first time.

I could hardly tell where Ash ended and Sal began, one of the things I loved most about my men sharing me. The sensations of touch heightened so much and never stopped— pleasure had no limits. All I could do was lean back and let hands and mouths tease my body into a frenzy.

Ash's beard made me shudder as he kissed along the sensitive skin of my shoulders, my nape, and upper back. In contrast, Sal's smooth face kissed a searing hot trail down my chest, dragging his tongue and nibbling softly where he knew I was the most sensitive.

When Sal's mouth reached my hip bones, I turned to face Ash, capturing his mouth savagely as I pushed him toward our bed. He followed my lead, walking backward until he sank down, and I settled between his muscular thighs.

My tongue traced the sigils on his chest, feeling the heat and pulse of them in time with the same sigils on my back. Those sacred symbols connected us to each other, to Lucifer who gave them to us, and to the demon homeworld of Hell.

I kissed lower, taking my time and relishing in the feel of his abs as they flexed and relaxed with each hitch of his breath. Ash was my first love and the most possessive of me, an oddly human emotion for a fallen angel. Even so, I liked to spend extra attention on him when one of the others joined us.

I lifted my eyes to his as I took the base of his cock in my fist. His icy eyes were hooded with desire as he gazed at me, fluttering closed as I delivered my first stroke up to the crown and back down again. He looked so incredibly sexy propped up on his elbows, shoulders and abs flexed, and tilting his head back with soft moans as I focused on his pleasure.

Just as I took his round, swollen head in my mouth, Sal reminded me just how fucking turned on I was. He pressed his palm to my vulva, hiked up in the air and on display as I knelt over Ash, and let out a hot groan of approval.

"Soaking wet," he rasped, moving his hand in lazy circles to spread my wetness. "So beautiful. She loves pleasing you, Ash."

I moaned around a mouthful of cock. Sal's hand felt so good on the building heat and pressure between my legs but it wasn't nearly enough. I was aching and empty, desperate to be filled. My back arched, sending my pussy up higher in a silent plea. Sal chuckled behind me and took his hand away. I groaned in frustration which turned into a shriek and a whimper when Ash took my nipples between his fingers and pinched the incredibly sensitive peaks.

In that moment, a tongue probed my slick, tender flesh, and I ground so hard against Sal's face I thought I might drown him.

"Greedy girl," he pulled back and murmured. His arms wrapped around my thighs as he licked and sucked me like I was his last meal. My lion loved to please, and I knew he was hard as a rock just from tasting and feeling my wetness.

"Are you going come all over Sal's face, my love?" Ash cupped my chin, making me look at him as I bobbed up and down on his concrete shaft. Fuck me, just hearing that question nearly pushed me over the edge.

"Mm-hm," I said, still slurping at him greedily.

"I want your mouth full of me when you come," he ordered. "I want to feel your scream of pleasure on my cock."

Sal's tongue zeroed in on my clit, and it took just a matter of seconds. I swallowed more of Ash's length down my throat, eager to obey him. I loved his dominance, a completely different flavor from Raum's. Raum loved mixing pain with pleasure and drawing out my orgasms in long, torturous ways.

As the highest ranking of my three demons, Ash was their commanding leader. He ruled with quiet confidence but when he gave an order, you had no choice but to obey. Even humans could feel the authority and power radiating off him. And he made me wet just by telling me what to do.

For usually being so eager to please, Sal seemed to enjoy drawing out my orgasm as long as possible. His tongue tapping on my clit had me dancing on the edge of a cliff before pulling away. He did that at least three times before I was a shaking, quivering, desperate mess. Despite my overwhelming desire and frustration, I didn't dare remove Ash's cock from my throat. His groans, twitches, and further stiffening in my mouth told me he thoroughly enjoyed the muffled whimpers Sal's torture elicited from me.

Finally, Sal pressed two fingers inside me, providing just enough delicious fullness, when combined with continued pressure on my clit, to send me hurtling into a mind-numbing orgasm. I took Ash deeper than I ever had as lightning bolts of pleasure wracked my entire body.

Lightheaded and delirious with euphoria, my mouth suddenly became free, and I found myself staring at the ceiling.

"I take it you enjoyed that, my love?" Ash pressed sweet kisses to my cheeks, making it almost seem as if he were a different person from the one who just rammed his cock down my throat.

My blissed-out expression must have told him enough. He grinned wickedly as he stood from the bed and pulled my thighs toward the edge to wrap around him. As he lined up to enter me, I realized that was one of the things I loved about these demons so much. They acted damn filthy in bed, but they loved and cared about me beyond what any mere mortal could.

My gorgeous fallen angel slid into me in one fluid stroke, stretching me out so deliciously my back arched off the bed. In the next moment, his hand was there to support me and he pulled me up to face him.

"Hi, angel," I smiled, wrapping my arms around his shoulders.

"Hello, my love." He pulled me forward so my legs fully enveloped his waist. His thrusts grew shorter as he nestled deep inside me so I was never empty of him.

For a few moments, just the two us of existed in our passionate love making. My fingers threaded through his hair as our skin seared together as if becoming one body. Our lips and tongues melded together, telling a thousand-year-old story that never got old. Our love story.

When my next orgasm convulsed around him, it forced his own release into me. He braced his arms on the bed as the pleasure shuddered through him, filling me up just a little bit more before he began to soften.

"Now that was just lovely to watch," Sal grinned from where he laid back, relaxing on the bed. "Felt like I was on an artsy, romantic porn set."

"Don't give her any ideas," Ash smirked, still breathing heavy as he padded his gloriously naked self to the master bathroom suite. A second later, the shower turned on.

"I didn't mean to exclude you, lion," I said, crawling across the bed to where Sal stretched out, just as glorious and naked in his own right.

"It's alright, beautiful. I know how you two get." He slid an arm across my back and played with my hair as I draped across his chest, still panting. "Besides," he nuzzled my ear, "you said earlier you wanted me to yourself."

"And I still do." I absentmindedly traced the battle scars across his lean, muscular landscape. "As soon as I catch my breath."

"Oh, I may be patient, but I'm not *that* patient." He playfully shoved me off him and rolled over on top of me, pinning me to the bed.

"What has gotten into you?" I huffed, my skin prickling with need despite barely recovering from the last session. "I swear Raum is rubbing off on you."

"Just preparing you for what's to come." He leaned down close, his lips hovering a hair above mine. "It's trick-or-treat season after all."

"Damn you," I growled, my voice becoming muffled by pillows as he flipped me onto my stomach, pinned me beneath his hard body, and then entered me in one savage thrust.

Despite his fearsome warrior's bloodlust and temper, Sal was the least aggressive and gentlest in the bedroom. My mind reeled with the discovery of this new rough, dominant Sal as he held my hair in his fist, pressing me down into the mattress as he fucked me, his teeth on the back of my neck marking me like an animal.

But my body loved it.

The orgasms rolled into each other as I screamed into the pillow, and he just fucked me harder until he emptied himself with a final deep thrust. A roar rumbled from his chest that I knew was his lion speaking.

I rolled onto my back, gasping for breath, to see Ash leaning casually against the wall, a towel around his waist and droplets of water clinging to his skin.

"Feels like I'm on a hardcore porn set," he laughed.

5
DEJA

"We found out more about the girl while you three were... cleaning the pipes upstairs," Raum said with his knowing smirk.

The five of us adults sat around the kitchen table after dinner, the guys with either beer or whiskey and me with an herbal tea blend I concocted myself.

The kids had gone upstairs to wind down before bedtime, with Raven and Dani acting like two peas in a pod. She let out a big "YAY!" when I suggested sharing her room with Dani for the next week or two.

"You want to share your room with me?" Dani asked her in disbelief.

"Duh, you can tell me all your ghost stories!" Raven bounced in excitement. "Deidre's stories are boring."

"Um, no. They're just richly detailed!" Deidre shot back.

Once we finally made it through dinner and shooed them off upstairs, I was eager to find out what Seth and Raum had learned.

"She only sees the dead around the time of Samhain," Raum

began. "She said her visions become stronger during the month of October, then begin to fade starting in November."

"I saw a small amount of Reaper heritage in her shadows, but I don't think she knows about it, or even what a reaper is," Seth added. "If her parents abandoned her, they definitely weren't accepting of her abilities."

"A reaper in what sense?" I asked. "Are we talking about a guide to the afterlife or the personification of Death itself?"

"The former," Seth replied. "Truly neutral immortals who reside in neither Heaven nor Hell, but merely guide souls to where they need to go."

"How often do you see a witch with reaper heritage?"

"It's more common than you think. Reapers are attracted to humans because they all have some mixture of angelic and demonic qualities. It's pure angels and demons they don't really get along with."

"I don't blame them," I mumbled into my tea cup.

Sal gasped in mock horror. "How can you say that after all the fun you just had?"

"None of that erases the fact that you're all huge pains in my ass sometimes."

"That can certainly be arranged." Raum bit his lip while looking directly at me.

Lucifer save me.

Ash cleared his throat. "So her abilities are only apparent around Samhain, when the veil between worlds is thinnest. And she's not even *trying* to communicate with these souls, she just sees them attached to the living?"

"That's right," Seth confirmed. "It's an impressive power for a six-year-old. If she continues to develop her talents, she could become an incredible medium."

"Hope so," Raum chimed in. "I'm tired of seeing humans without an ounce of real magic whatsoever pretending they can speak to the dead. This girl can set those fakes straight real quick if she gets enough practice."

"She needs an adoptive family that will accept and encourage her strengths," I agreed. "Not abandon her or try to suppress her abilities because they're afraid of them."

Dani's tumultuous journey in her short life struck a chord with me. She reminded me so much of my young self in this lifetime. I didn't even know I was a witch, let alone a rebirth of the Mother of Witches, until well into adulthood. My own adoptive parents were dogmatically religious and tried to raise me in that environment as an attempt to "cure" me of any magical abilities. They never abandoned me, but they never accepted me either.

"Are there any families in Voluspa with similar abilities?" Sal swiped a gulp from my tea and returned it faster than I could blink.

"Astrid would know," I answered. "That's her specialty. If there's a suitable family, or even single parent who's a good match, she will find them."

"How awesome is Raven, though?" Raum leaned back, crossing his arms in satisfaction. "She's normally so shy around kids her age, but they're acting like sisters already."

"Brax, too," Sal added. "I didn't hear him grumble once today about being the only boy. I think he has a crush."

"Meanwhile, Deidre called me Hitler today," I sighed.

"Hold up. *What?*" Seth demanded. "I need to hear this story."

All of them laughed as I recounted the story from this morning. All except Ash, who sat back, a smug grin pulling at his mouth.

"Just over a thousand years ago, our eldest daughter was illiterate. You should be grateful," he deadpanned.

"Well, two out of three good kids ain't bad," Raum chuckled into his whiskey.

"She has a point, though." Seth locked his stormy gray eyes on me. "No offense, sweetheart, but you're kind of a hardass about the whole Halloween thing."

"It's *not* Halloween," I growled. "It's Samhain."

"We know, baby," Raum patted my thigh, and I couldn't tell if he was being genuine or making fun of me. I glared at him just to be safe, and he just smiled.

"We should let them dress up and trick-or-treat this year," Sal continued. "There's more families with kids in Voluspa now than when we created it ten years ago. It'll be good to create a sense of community."

"Not only that," Ash jumped in, "but it'll help Dani feel included and not so different from everyone else."

Everyone else chimed in their agreement and looked to me for the final decision.

"I'm okay with this, to a point," I agreed with caution. "As long as we teach them the real meaning and origins of Samhain. It's their culture, and I want them to at least be aware of it before other people starting coming in and rewriting it."

"There's a good chance Deidre's read the books already," Ash smirked. "Of course we'll teach them the old ways, love. And in a few years, they'll outgrow the trick-or-treating and realize the significance of honoring the dead."

"I hope so," I breathed.

Seth stood and rounded the table to kiss my cheek. "Don't worry, sweetheart. This time of year is so much better when you're an adult. As kids they just don't understand it yet. But they will."

"Sounds like there's a story there." I looked up at him. "What was Samhain like, growing up as a witch in human society?"

"Honestly? I was just like our kids." He pulled another beer from the fridge before sitting down. "I wanted to dress up as the red Power Ranger for one night, go around the neighborhood, then come home with a pillowcase full of candy." His eyes gleamed. "And my parents were just like you. They wanted me to know the *real* Samhain, not the cheesy, human version pushed by candy companies."

"So naturally, you rebelled," I purred.

"Damn right I did," he smirked. "I wore my costume to bed, waited until all the adults were at the ritual dinner, then snuck out my window to meet my friends."

"How long until they caught you?" Raum asked.

"We got in two good hours of trick-or-treating," he laughed. "I already ate most of my candy by the time they found me, because I knew they'd take it away. I got my ass handed to me, but that sugar high was totally worth it."

"Such a bad boy," I murmured, leaning over to nuzzle him.

"You know it, sweetheart." He captured my mouth in a rich, possessive kiss that tasted of Guinness.

"Alright, then," I said to the entire table. "We let the little hellions have their fun. Safely and supervised, of course."

"At least one of us will stay with them the whole time," Raum assured me, then leaned forward to cup my nape and whisper in my ear.

"And they won't be the only ones getting tricks or treats that night."

6
DEJA
SAMHAIN EVENING

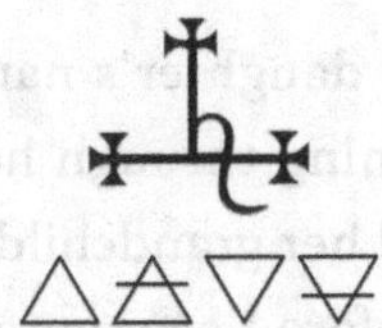

"Spirits of Earth, hear my plea." Deidre's golden eyes danced as she pinched the soil between her fingers and raised her hand over her head. "Mate with Fire and show me your faces this All Hallow's Eve."

With a dramatic flick of her fingers, she cast the dust into the bonfire. The resulting crackle and poof made her eyes widen and her jaw drop.

"I saw her!" she cried out in disbelief. "Just for a second, but I saw her face in the fire!" She looked at me, giddiness on her face. "She's beautiful! She looks just like you, Mom."

"Aw, thanks, hun." I kissed the top of her head. "You know that means she looks just like you too, right?"

"She's still there," Dani whispered, her eyes locked on the flames. "She's dancing in the fire. She feels so happy to be connected to her family."

My throat tightened up and a strong, comforting arm wrapped around me. Ash.

"I see glimpses of her, too," he added softly. "Although my sight isn't as strong as yours, Dani."

"I see her, too!" Raven cried. "She's dancing like this!"

Dressed up as a dark faerie, my youngest twirled around like a ballerina, her glittery black wings sparkling in the fire's light. Raum grabbed her tiny hands and started dancing around with her.

I, too, saw glimpses of my mother's face and dancing form in the bonfire. While I always felt her in the Earth magic that vibrated all around me, I only ever saw quick flashes of her face and form on Samhain.

My mother Deidre, my daughter's namesake, turned to me and smiled. I felt the pride shining through her like a light in my chest burning brightly. She loved her grandchildren and enjoyed watching them grow up. She died before I ever got a chance to know her, but this time of year made me grateful that I could feel her protective, motherly presence and see her on occasion. It gave me peace after everything I did to avenge her death.

"We'll leave a plate of food out for you, Mom," I smiled through the happy tears glittering in my eyes. "Thank you for coming to see us tonight."

As a festival for the dead, it was customary to leave an empty seat with a plate of food for those who had passed on. Poor Sal, our resident chef, nearly worked himself to death every year for our Samhain feast. This year we were joined by Astrid and her three husbands, Chase, Orion, and Conan. All of them were predator shifters and promised to bring meat dishes so all we'd need to worry about were sides.

This year, we decided to eat dinner before the kids left to go trick-or-treating, so they would experience a true Samhain and also not spoil their dinner with candy first. With all the kids home and then Astrid and her men piling through the door, it became a full house indeed.

"Hi Dani! How are you, sweetheart?" Astrid hugged the dark-eyed girl, who wore a simple costume of a horse skull mask and white sheet. "You're looking a little thin. Is Deja feeding you enough?" She playfully poked through the eye sockets of Dani's skull mask.

"Yes, ma'am. And Raven is my new best friend." She pulled my youngest into a hug, who smacked a kiss on Dani's skull-mask forehead.

"You're my best friend. I wish you could stay living with us." Raven gave me her best puppy eyes.

"That doesn't work on me, young lady." I shook my head. "But Dani can come over whenever she wants, and you'll see each other at school every day too."

"On that note, I have great news!" Astrid looked between me and Dani.

"I know a family who would love to meet you, Dani. They see the dead like you do sometimes. They even have a little cat spirit in their home who is especially feisty this time of year. Would you like to meet them tomorrow?"

"Will I meet the kitty?"

"Sure, if you can see her. I'm certain you'll be able to."

Too excited to speak, Dani nodded enthusiastically. Her head bobbing made the jaws of her skull mask clack together as if chattering.

"What did you bring for us, Orion?" Sal clapped Astrid's silver-haired wolf shifter mate on the back.

"Y'all are gonna love this," he drawled in that sultry, southern twang. "Ham from a wild boar. Conan and I brought him down ourselves. And without Chase's eyes in the sky, we almost tumbled off a cliff with this bad boy."

"All three of you are gonna me the death of me," Astrid rolled her eyes. Then to me, "Got any wine?"

We settled around the large table for dinner while the kids gathered at their own, smaller table. I speared a chunk of boar ham, sweet potatoes, and corn bread and set the plate next to me for my mother.

"Deidre, what the hell are you supposed to be?" Conan, Astrid's fox shifter mate, peered at my daughter's elaborate costume. "Feeling a little blue, are we?"

"I'm Kali, Hindu goddess of the dead." She raised her hands to demonstrate the extra two fabric arms attached to the back of her top and connected to her real arms with some string and safety pins.

"Is your skirt made of... arms?"

"Yes!" she declared proudly, shifting her hips to make the plastic arms dance and dangle. "I made it myself. And this is my garland of severed heads." She held up the necklace of baby doll heads strung together in a long chain that hung down to her waist. Red eye make up and blue body paint on her face and arms completed the look.

"Interesting," Chase, the hawk shifter, chuckled. "This Kali seems like one hell of a lady."

"She is," Ash remarked casually as he poured whiskey and beers for everyone. "I see her from time to time. She's a good friend of Lucifer's."

"Astrid, where's Jacob tonight?" Seth asked.

"At a party, like a typical twenty-year-old." She rolled her eyes, but I saw the pride in her son beaming through her. "Oh, I didn't tell you. He got a grant to study and excavate tombs in Egypt as part of his PhD work!"

"Yes, I knew he would nail it." Ash pumped a fist victoriously. "He's still one of my favorite students, and I'm not just saying that."

"That's wonderful, Asti!" I exclaimed. "Maybe he can find my jewelry box that *somebody* lost there." I shot a pointed glare at Sal.

"Beautiful, I love you, but it's been over two thousand years." He tapped me on the nose playfully. "You need to get over it."

"I still can't believe you came home from a battle and burned down an entire wing of the palace!"

"We lost. I was pissed off," he shrugged.

I opened my mouth to continue arguing, but he shut me up with a kiss. As dinner went on, conversations flowed as did the drinks.

Every so often I glanced to the empty seat at my left and noticed the food disappearing. Small, delicate bites had been taken out of the corn bread and ham, with the sweet potato being left for last like a desert. When everyone's eating slowed and we all leaned back to rub our full bellies, the plate next to me had completely cleared as well.

"Glad you liked it, Mom," I said softly.

Astrid and her men lingered for another hour before the kids started getting antsy. Brax, in his adorable vampire makeup, started going around the adult table and saying, "trick or treat" to everyone.

"Here's a trick, little man." Orion brushed his knuckles across my son's face. "I got your nose!"

"I don't fall for that anymore," Brax declared, his chin tipped in defiance.

"Unfortunately." Sal picked up his mini-me and set him in his lap. "Is it time to go trick-or-treating, bud?"

"It's past time," Brax whined. "We've been waiting *forever*."

"Alright." He ruffled our little vampire's strawberry blonde hair before setting him down. "We'll get going here in a bit."

We all rose from the table to say our goodbyes and chit-chatted by the door until the kids' whining became unbearable.

"Remember if you get Milky Way Midnights, save those for mommy, okay?" I said, kissing all of their cheeks.

"I'm going to eat all mine!" Deidre laughed.

"Yeah, now who's Hitler?" I tweaked her nose until she squirmed away.

Sal and Ash each gave me kisses goodbye and promised not to keep the kids out too late. I moved to follow them onto the porch to watch them walk away, when a strong arm wrapped around my waist and pulled me back inside.

"Where do you think you're going, baby?" Raum purred in my ear.

7
DEJA

Raum pulled me tight against him with one arm and shoved the door closed with the other. With one large step forward, he pressed me between the door and his body. Two hard, unforgiving surfaces. Actually three if I counted his dick growing in hardness and size as it pressed against my ass.

"You knew this was coming, didn't you, baby?" He spoke so softly but his voice rumbled like thunder in my ears.

"Yes," I rasped, arching with need into the little wiggle room he allowed, which just happened to grind my ass against his crotch.

He groaned his approval, moving my hair from the back of my neck to let his breath feather across my skin.

"This is my favorite night of the year to take you, you know that?" he whispered. "The Mother of Witches as my sacrificial lamb, giving up her control and pleasure to me. I'm dying to see you worship my cock so beautifully on your knees."

I couldn't help but release a small snort of laughter.

"We know who really worships who."

His reaction came swiftly— fingers closing around the front of my throat as he pressed me harder into the door. My cheek squished up against the wood and my pussy became soaked just from his words.

"Are you going to be feisty tonight, baby, or are you going to be a good girl?"

"I think you know the answer to that."

His chuckle vibrating against my back sent goosebumps all over my body. He wasn't angry or even annoyed. He was utterly relaxed and enjoying this as I trembled in his grip. We always played this game. He demanded my submission, and I pushed back. This push and pull was our foreplay. He hadn't even kissed me yet, and I already craved the fullness of him inside me, matched with the harsh sting of his hand on my ass.

He never gave me what I wanted right away. And that made it so much better.

"Seth," he called to the only other one at home. "Get the bed ready." At my resulting shiver, his lips widened into a grin on the back of my neck. "Oh, nothing to say? Out of sass already?"

Any retort I had lodged in my throat. I just wanted relief. I was dying for him to touch or kiss me to ease this pressure and anticipation building inside of me. But knowing him, he would draw this out for as long as he could stand it as well.

I was so wound up, the gentle suction of his mouth on my ear sent a wracking, full body shudder through me. His breath brought back the goosebumps as he laughed, thoroughly amused at the effect he had on me.

"Get on your knees and suck me."

He released me, and I whipped around, unzipping him like a needy, desperate addict. Just his thick, hot flesh in my hands provided such a relief. We moaned in unison as I took him in my mouth— at least one empty part of me was filled.

My tongue danced and swirled around him, tasting and memorizing every way he twitched and throbbed between my lips. He groaned curses as my nails raked down his thighs, then massaged his heavy balls to delay his own pleasure.

"Get up, baby," he rasped.

No, I wasn't done yet. I opened wide and took more of him down my throat, grabbing his hips to anchor him to me.

He grabbed my hair with a growl, holding me in place, and pulled out of my mouth, just as I knew he would. The grimace on his face told me he fought his every instinct. He wanted more than anything to fuck my mouth and feel the back of my throat. But I disobeyed him, and he couldn't let me get away with that.

I flashed him an innocent smile as the round head of his cock rested on my lips. He sucked in deep breaths, trying to control himself and hold back. Just to fuck with him some more, I stuck my tongue out and licked the sensitive underside of that delicious cock.

"You wicked fucking witch," he moaned, jerking away from me. His fist still wound in my hair, sending intense tingles of pain across my scalp.

"I learned from the best," I said with a wink.

With a defiant grunt, he pulled me to my feet. The pain was just sharp enough to make me hiss and send a jolt of sensation straight to my nipples and clit. It only made me crave more.

"Go upstairs," he commanded.

"Should I go to my room and think about what I've done?"

"You're pushing your luck, baby," he warned, his lips curving into a smirk. "I have half a mind to just leave you tied to the bed all night, naked."

Fuck, he looked serious.

"You wouldn't."

"Try me."

Without another word I turned towards the stairs and began taking slow, measured steps up. I felt him behind me like an ominous spirit, not close enough to physically feel him, but my body knew he was there. My every muscle remained tense as I walked up. If it had been any other person, I might feel genuine fear. But somehow Raum knew how to test my limits while still making me feel safe.

"Stop," he ordered.

I froze on the middle landing of the stairs. The bedroom was just a few steps away.

"Pull your leggings down."

My fingers shook as I peeled the waistband down over my hips. I fought the impulse to lash out, to tell him to take them off himself if he wanted me so badly. But we were reaching that tipping point where my stubbornness gave way and my submissive side craved his dominance.

"Get on your knees. Hands on the steps."

With my leggings rolled down to my calves, I lowered myself to all fours. The softest groan of appreciation escaped him as my bare ass lifted into the air. The seconds ticked by, and I waited on pins and needles for any kind of touch from him, any relief at all from this tension. The smug bastard seemed content to just look, to watch my inner thighs grow wetter with need as they waited for him. Kneeling here doing nothing acted as its own kind of torture.

His palm swept over my ass so quickly I barely had time to gasp at the fleeting touch. When it came down with a hard smack on my flesh, my breath felt stolen from my lungs. The sting was so crisp and deep, I blinked back tears, and yet, my back still arched for more.

"Look at you, greedy girl," he cooed as he methodically spanked each cheek, alternating sides. "So addicted to my punishment. What if I made you come just from smacking this sweet ass, hm?"

I bit my lip to hold back the desperate whimper that threatened to escape. My nipples and clit rang out with sensation from each blow that came down with such sweet, painful, *delicious* fire. If he kept this up, he just might succeed.

"If only you could see how wet you are," he murmured, pausing to pull aside the thin scrap of fabric covering my pussy. Cool air kissed my slick, swollen folds, providing temporary relief from the heat that burned through me like a fever.

"Seth, come down here," Raum called up the stairs. "Our girl might need some help."

Even the vibration of footsteps on the landing made me moan as my pussy clenched unbearably around nothing.

"Couldn't even make it to the bedroom, I see." Seth sat on one of the steps above me, spreading his long, athletic legs wide near the level of my face. He cupped my cheek, lifting my chin to look up at the gorgeous storm in his eyes. "Enjoying your punishment, sweetheart?"

"Maybe a little too much," Raum chuckled behind me. "She's a fucking waterfall back here." He smoothed his palms over the tender, stinging flesh of my ass before bringing them down hard, making me jolt and yelp.

"Damn, you're so close, sweetheart. I can see it." Seth stroked a thumb along my cheekbone. I was so desperate for something inside me, I sucked his thumb into my mouth.

"Oh, you want cock that bad, baby?" came Raum's teasing voice behind me. "I want to see you come just from spanking. Seth might help you if you're good."

"Yes." My stormy-eyed lover stroked my face and hair with a tender hand. "Come for us, sweetheart, and we'll fill you up all you want."

8

DEJA

"Yes," I arched my back higher and pressed back against Raum like a bitch in heat. "Please let me come."

"How?" Raum prompted, smoothing his palms down to the backs of my thighs. My core ached from feeling him so near but not touching me enough.

I swallowed and licked my lips.

"From spanking me." I lifted my eyes up to Seth. "With your help."

"Only if you need it," Seth waved a finger in my face. "Raum's got you so close, I can see you shaking from it."

"I do need it," I whimpered, reaching for his zipper. I needed to just see him, stroke him, or taste him. Anything to just feel his touch and calm this fire consuming me. But the infuriating, handsome bastard pulled my hands away and pinned them down to the stairs, a grin of pure evil on his face.

"Ready, baby?" The heat of Raum's hands left my skin, and my whole body froze like a statue in anticipation of what was coming.

Smack!

It came down like lightning, sending vibrations through my hypersensitive clit and making me bite my lip against the sting.

Smack!

He made each one count and didn't rush in the slightest. My eyes squeezed shut, but I could picture him admiring his handiwork behind me. Raum loved to leave his marks on me and reapply them as they faded. I not-so-secretly loved them too because such marks only came from him.

Smack!

My whimper escaped on that one. My ass cheeks were on fire, but my wetness still dripped down my thighs. Even my nipples were tender to the point of painful. Each smack took me baby steps closer to the edge, but I didn't know if I'd make it there.

Smack!

"Oh fuck, you're right there," Raum whispered, his voice tight with his own restraint. "I can see your clit going crazy, baby. It wants to go off so bad. Wouldn't it be nice if I just rubbed you a little?" His fingers crept all around my vulva as I shook like a leaf. He touched me everywhere but right where I needed it.

Smack!

"FUCK! Fucking hell, just fuck me!" I cried. I loved him but fucking hated him in that moment. He'd never drawn my orgasm out like this before, and it was nothing short of torture.

"Here, sweetheart. Let me help." Seth scooted down another step with his legs on either side of me. I gazed up at him in desperation, and the kiss he gave me was such sweet relief. My lips, so sensitive and flushed with blood, trembled at his tongue swiping into my mouth.

He reached inside my shirt and found my nipples, smoothing his thumbs across the aching peaks and finally, *finally* touching me. I was begging for a meal and got only bread crumbs, but I didn't care. It was something in the face of Raum's torture.

Smack!

Seth squeezed my nipples just as the last blow came down, and I hurtled into the abyss. My whole body rocked with the convulsion of release that I barely knew what was happening. Only when Raum plunged into me with one rough thrust, and I felt the bliss of my muscles squeezing around him did I realize it.

I was made of electricity itself, my nerves alive and sparking like live wires. Magic shot from my fingertips in time with my pussy convulsing around Raum as he fucked me like a machine. My orgasm would not stop. I was hardly aware of what my body was doing but all too consumed with how toe-curlingly good it felt.

At some point Seth released his cock and put it in my mouth. The moment my convulsions ceased, Raum flipped us around. He sat on the landing, reclined against the stairs, and seated me facing him, back on that amazing cock of his.

My filthy, torturous demon pulled me against his chest with one arm, brushing my clit with his thumb as he drove his hips up, crashing into me. After denying me pleasure for so long, he gave it to me so unconditionally I barely knew how to handle it all.

"You come on my cock so beautifully," he growled, grabbing a fistful of my hair to bring my mouth down for a savage kiss. "I love you, Deja."

"I love you so much," I took his lip between my teeth, "you almost make me hate you."

His laugh became a series of breathy grunts and moans as his own release grew near. I knew this had been a test of his control as well. He delayed his own pleasure to heighten mine.

His whole body stiffened as he came, growling through gritted teeth, and his arms wrapped around me in a bear hug. Honestly, he was beautiful when he came too. His rich, chocolate eyes dilated, muscles flexed and tensed, and that uncontrollable grimace, followed by the sexiest sated look on his face.

I waited until he finished emptying himself inside me then hopped off and began cleaning him with my tongue, just as he liked.

"I thank Lucifer every day for you," he murmured, stroking my face and neck affectionately. My heart swelled, and I linked his fingers with mine as I continued to lick him. So dirty and so loving, this man.

I paused to cast a sultry look at Seth. "Aren't you coming around for me next?"

"We got other plans." He fisted his cock, jutting out like a sword as he lifted his eyes up to Raum's.

I narrowed my eyes in confusion. The next thing I knew, Raum was lifting me up by my armpits, and placed me right above Seth, straddling him.

"I want you staring at me while you bounce on him," Raum purred, his lips curving in a wicked smirk.

With my back against Seth's chest, I kissed him over my shoulder as he eased me down onto him. His hands swept across my sides to caress my breasts and bring my nipples back to hard, aching peaks.

Those hands could read my deepest, darkest desires with the slightest touch. A master of shadow magic with demon blood in his veins, Seth didn't need to know me for eons to play my body like a fiddle. He knew the inner workings of my mind better than I even knew myself.

"Gods, yes," he groaned once fully seated inside me, dragging his teeth along the back of my neck.

"Seth," I whimpered, squirming as he rolled his hips up like crashing waves. He didn't fuck me nearly as fast, rough or brutal as Raum; the way he pressed inside me was slow, deliberate, and so incredibly intense. His arms enveloped me, keeping me still and pinned against him as he moved. He lifted me off him just enough to sink in deeper as he drove into me.

Raum descended a few steps in a lazy slide to watch us, his eyes glued to my body.

"Stop covering her breasts, Seth. I want to see them." His dark eyes remained dilated, and his breaths were still labored from our own session.

"Fuck off. You had your time with her." But he moved his arms anyway, securing one around my waist, the other crossing in front of my shoulders.

"Boys," I panted through Seth's thrusts. "There's no need to fight."

"Can you blame us?" he growled into my ear. "None of us can get enough of you."

Raum crept forward, the wily grin on his face indicating he was up to something. Seth held me still with my back arched against him, and my chest thrust out. It was almost like he was presenting my body, while fucking me at the same time.

Raum's rough kiss grazed the edge of my ribcage, paying no mind to the cock thrusting in and out of me only a few inches away. Taking his time, he kissed a trail lower.

"Raum?" I squeaked, shuddering as his tongue trailed over my hip bones.

"Yes, baby?"

"What are you doing?"

"Kissing the woman I love."

He traveled even lower, brushing his lips across my mons and hovering over my clit. My mind raced with questions all the while Seth's cock continued to surge deep inside me, bringing me to the edge of another orgasmic cliff as he pressed against all my inner walls.

The next thing I felt was Raum's lips sealing over my clit, then lashing his hot tongue against it.

"Oh fuck!" I jolted in Seth's grasp, but he held me firm, filling and emptying me with steady thrusts like there wasn't another man's mouth so close to his dick.

"Looks like it's Raum's turn to help, sweetheart," he rasped in my ear.

The sensation was unlike anything I'd ever felt before. It never even occurred to me that being eaten out and fucked at the same time was a possibility. But Raum devoured me like no else was around, and Seth fucked me even harder as he felt my release nearing.

"Guys, I'm..."

I couldn't even get the words out before pure pleasure ripped through me without warning. I swore I felt it in every cell and hair follicle. My pussy closed around Seth's steel rod and forcefully yanked his own release from him. His cock flexed hard inside me, spurring on another wave of pleasure like a chain reaction. And Raum's mouth never left my clit until the sensation bordered on painful.

"Holy shit."

I sucked in deep breaths of air, leaning back on Seth now that every bit of energy had been zapped from my body.

"Just when I thought we've done it all," I kissed his neck, "you guys always find a way to surprise me."

Raum grinned up at me, planting a kiss on my thigh before resting his head there.

"You can't have tricks without treats, baby."

***

ALSO BY CRYSTAL ASH

Harem of Freaks: The Complete Series

Say Your Prayers

Steel Demons MC

Lawless

Powerless

Fearless

Painless

Helpless

Heartless

Senseless

Ruthless

Merciless

Endless

Shifted Mates Trilogy

Unholy Trinity: The Complete Series

For a complete list of books by Crystal Ash, visit her Amazon page.

ABOUT THE AUTHOR

Crystal Ash is a USA Today Bestselling Author from California. She loves writing steamy, heart-wrenching romance with tortured heroes, especially if they're in a reverse harem. Crystal's other loves include animals, mythology, and well-crafted alcohol, most of which can also be found in her stories.

When she's not writing, she's probably drinking craft beer with her husband or trying to coax her feral cat into accepting affection.

crystalashbooks.com

facebook.com/Crystal.Ash.Romance

instagram.com/crystalashbooks

amazon.com/author/crystalash

bookbub.com/profile/crystal-ash